Lee had never known such violent need existed within him.

Suddenly he had an unrestrained, powerful desire to wrap himself in Meredith's softness, to drown himself in it.

He was like a man starved for warmth, and sunlight now flooded his soul. Meredith had given life to a part of him he'd thought dead. Renewed him. Opened his heart to the throbbing rhythm of the universe.

He needed her. All of her. And the temptation was too strong to withstand.

But with the agonizing need to possess Meredith came the bone-chilling certainty that, once he did, he would be bound to her forever.

And *that* thought sent an icy knife of fear into Lee Stratton's soul.

He broke free of Meredith's sweet embrace, gazing into the blue eyes of heaven…yet haunted by visions of his own private hell...

Dear Reader,

May celebrates the coming of summer with a refreshing Special Edition™ line-up! Leading the way this month is *The Secret Wife* by bestselling author Susan Mallery, it's the second book in her TRIPLE TROUBLE mini-series and the final story will be out next month. They can all be read alone but together they're terrific!

Travel to Wyoming with *Pale Rider* from Myrna Temte and meet a stubborn man, who thinks a glamour girl won't be tough enough to be his wife. But this woman has no intention of walking away from her man and she's just as stubborn as him! Terri Sommers is another beauty who finds the man she wants and has to convince him that he and his children are a dream come true for her; that's the latest POWER OF LOVE story from Carole Halston, *Mrs Right*.

Courtney Tamberlaine needs a temporary husband and John Gabriel seems perfect but, as Marie Ferrarella shows us in *Wanted: Husband, Will Train*, he's too perfect—Courtney wants to keep him!

Beauty and the Groom is a passionate reunion story by Lorraine Carroll, while *Lone Star Lover* from relative newcomer Gail Link is the tale of two lovers who move on from a whirlwind affair to a more long-lasting passion.

Enjoy them all.

The Editors

Beauty and the Groom

LORRAINE CARROLL

*All the characters in this book have no existence outside the imagination
of the author, and have no relation whatsoever to anyone bearing the same
name or names. They are not even distantly inspired by any individual
known or unknown to the author, and all the incidents are pure invention.*

*First published in Great Britain 1998
Silhouette Books, Eton House, 18-24 Paradise Road,
Richmond, Surrey TW9 1SR*

© Lorraine Beatty 1997

ISBN 0 373 24128 3

23-9805

*Printed and bound in Great Britain
by Mackays of Chatham PLC, Chatham*

To Carolyn Pohl,

for showing me the Friendship Oak

LORRAINE CARROLL

says, 'There's something about the South that brings out the romantic in everyone.' Born and raised in Columbus, Ohio, Ms Carroll was first inspired to write by one of her teachers. But her talent lay dormant until 1978, when her husband was transferred to Baton Rouge. Being surrounded by the romance and the history of that region set her on the path to writing romance. She has also published several articles on television history, and has worked as a staff writer for a community newspaper.

Ms Carroll has been married to her husband, Joe, for twenty-seven years. They have two sons, Matthew and Daniel. Her hobbies include sewing, reading, gardening and playing piano. But her favourite pastime is curling up in a chair with pen and paper and her dog, Pixie Dust, and writing a love story. 'It just doesn't get any better than that.'

Other novels by Lorraine Carroll

Silhouette Special Edition®

Lead with Your Heart
The Ice Princess
Playing Daddy

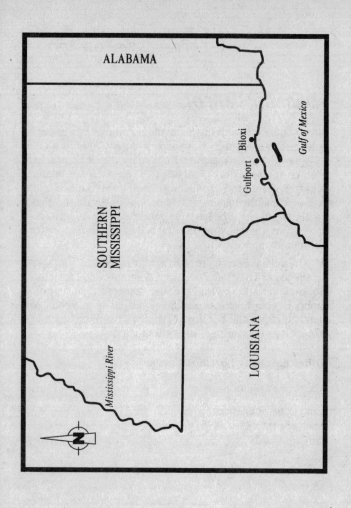

Chapter One

Lee Stratton tapped the steering wheel impatiently as he inched his gray sedan forward in the bumper-to-bumper traffic on the Gulf Coast Highway. Through the dusty windshield he could see the Victorian turrets on his father's home not a quarter mile up the road, but at this rate he wouldn't get there in under twenty minutes.

Not that it mattered what time he arrived. No one knew he was coming. No one would care. He wasn't sure why he hadn't told his father he was coming home. In fact, he wasn't entirely sure why he'd decided to return in the first place.

Lee let up on the brake, moving the car forward another few feet.

Staying in Houston after Doreen dumped him two days before their wedding seemed awkward. Too many explanations. Too damned many sympathetic friends. Too many snickering acquaintances eager to say they knew it would never work out.

His car rolled forward three more feet and he silently cursed the traffic. The casinos were probably to blame for this mess. Riverboat gambling had turned the once sleepy coastal town into the Vegas of the Gulf, robbing the shore of its heart.

You don't have a heart. The only passion you have is for your work, not me. I can't live that way, Lee. I want someone who's able to love me completely and I'm not sure you're capable of any real feelings at all.

Doreen's parting words still reverberated inside his head.

But it wasn't losing her that still gnawed at him, it was the fact that she'd been right. He didn't care. The woman he'd chosen for his wife had rejected him and he felt nothing.

He'd been like this for as long as he could remember. He could walk away from anyone without a regret or a qualm. Why? What was wrong with him?

He glanced again at the imposing rooftop of his childhood home. He had a month off; a canceled honeymoon and nowhere to go. For some inexplicable reason he'd wanted to come back here to Sand Castle.

Finally reaching the turn lane on Beach Boulevard, Lee stomped on the accelerator and roared into Sand Castle's driveway. His eyes eagerly scanned the familiar Victorian home, the house built by his great-grandfather.

Something about the old place was different. It wasn't the slightly shabby white elephant he remembered from five years ago. The one-hundred-and-thirty-year-old house had been completely restored from the top of the slate-tile roof down to the foundation landscaping.

He hardly recognized the old girl. He swallowed a lump of bitter sadness, then realized that he had just proved Doreen wrong. He wasn't a complete emotional wasteland.

He could dredge up a twinge of sadness, at least for a house.

Pulling his car around to the back, he parked it near the old carriage house. Even it had been restored, its muted tones echoing those of the main house. He climbed out of the car and removed his sunglasses, a growing uneasiness forming inside him. As he started up the brick walkway he wondered what other surprises awaited him.

He didn't have to wonder long. The moment he stepped into the kitchen three unfamiliar faces turned sharply to look at him in surprise. Standing at the sink was an elderly woman who looked like a refugee from the pages of a storybook. Sweet-faced, slightly plump, and wrapped in a flowered apron, she was the image of the perfect grandmother.

Huddled over the kitchen table were two young girls about eleven years old staring at him with wide-eyed curiosity.

He stared back, searching his memory. As far as he could recall he'd never seen these people before. His uneasiness escalated to apprehension. Where was Walt?

"Excuse me, young man, but do you usually walk into other people's homes without knocking?" the grandma demanded in a deep, husky voice that was at odds with her storybook image.

Her proprietary tone did little to calm Lee's growing concern. *Other people's homes?* "Who are you?" he asked, a little more sharply than he'd intended.

"Not that it's any of your business, but I live here," she said, planting one fist on her hip and glaring back at him.

Lee didn't like her answer nor the surge of alarm and concern for his father it brought with it. But as an attorney he knew better than to jump to conclusions without hard evidence to back it up.

The two little girls were still staring at him with un-
abashed interest. He wondered briefly if he had dirt on his
face or perhaps an arrow coming out of the top of his head.
It unnerved him to be stared at like an unusually interesting
specimen.

He focused on the dark-haired girl, who appeared awe-
struck. "I suppose you live here, too?" he asked.

The girl ducked her head shyly. The other girl, a carrot-
topped, gangly child with a mass of freckles and a mouthful of braces answered for her friend. "She lives at her
own house over on Twenty-fourth Street. I live over there,
in the tower," she said, shoving her glasses upward on the
bridge of her nose and wiggling a finger in her ear.

Lee frowned, feeling more and more like he'd walked
into an episode of "The Twilight Zone." He had a bad
feeling about this whole situation. Walt would never take
in boarders.

He made another swift survey of the people in the room.
These people looked innocent enough. A cheery-faced
grandma and two gawky adolescent girls, both of whom
were still gazing at him with wide-eyed amazement.

"Can someone tell me what is going on?" he practically
shouted, hoping to break the spell.

"Young man," Grandma said, pointing a finger at Lee.
"I don't know who you are or why you've barged into my
kitchen but—"

"Your kitchen?" Lee ran his fingers through his air as
a strange dread filled him. "Where's Walt?"

"He's in New Orleans on business."

Lee turned in the direction of this new voice.

For one insane instant he thought an angel had descended from heaven and landed in the kitchen. Sunlight
from the west window bathed the womanly form standing
on the threshold. The fan circling overhead gently stirred

her reddish gold hair. Dust motes danced around her like excited fireflies drawn by her magic.

A sensual curiosity coursed through him, warming his blood and making his heart beat faster. He squinted and turned his head slightly to get a better look. As the woman stepped forward he could see it was no heavenly body that stood in his father's kitchen but a flesh and blood woman. A very soft and appealing woman. She was pretty. Not beautiful, but pretty like a fresh spring bouquet is pretty or a field of daffodils is pretty. A naturally lovely woman.

Her proud forehead and heart-shaped face were framed in shoulder-length red hair. The heavy strands of burnished copper softness curved under at the ends as if caressing her neck.

Where he'd expected green eyes, hers were a shocking clear blue, the color of a high summer sky.

She gave the illusion of height though he doubted her slender frame and gently curved legs stood her more than five foot four or so.

Dressed in faded jeans and a loose-fitting chambray shirt, the tails of which were tied at her narrow waist, she had an air of softness and a sensuality that was impossible to ignore.

Lee managed to withstand the sensual assault by reminding himself of the situation at hand. "All right, so Walt is out of town." He took a step toward the woman. "That doesn't explain what y'all are doing here."

The redhead took a step toward him, crossing her arms over her chest and frowning like a disapproving parent. "We live here. In fact, we've all lived here for a very long time."

Her defiant, challenging manner brought him a step closer. "No one told me."

She took a step closer to him. "Perhaps if you came

home now and then these little changes wouldn't be such a shock to you.''

Lee studied the woman more closely. Did he know her? Had they met somewhere? Something about her teased his memory, but when he tried to chase it down, he found he was strangely reluctant to pursue it.

No. He would remember a woman as soft and sensuous as this one. "Who are you?"

The woman's eyes widened before she lifted her chin in a manner that said, "Hit me with your best shot."

"My name is Meredith. Meredith Cole."

There was a tension in the air, an expectancy, as if she was waiting for his reaction. She stared at him with anticipation in her soft eyes. He shrugged and shook his head slightly. "Is that supposed to mean something to me?"

With a suddenness he could barely grasp, the color drained from her face. Her shock-filled blue eyes were in stark contrast to her deathly pale cheeks. Stunned, Lee searched for an explanation only to see a flush of scarlet stain her neck and rise into her face with the same speed it had left.

Not only was her color back but the softness had been replaced with steel. Her eyes were now gray and those soft lips stretched into a hard, thin line. The word *mercurial* sprang into his mind. She had changed moods like the flick of a switch.

His patience evaporated. "All right. I don't know what's going on here but I want some answers right now. Walt would never turn Sand Castle into a boarding house. That's not his style."

Meredith cocked her head at a challenging angle. "And what would you know about Walt's style?"

The anger in her blue eyes stunned him. It was directed at him personally. But why? They'd never met. He was sure of that. He wasn't likely to forget someone like her.

But she seemed to know a great deal about him. Like the fact that he'd not been home in a while.

Lee didn't like being on the witness stand. He was more comfortable when he was asking the questions. He also resented being thrust into a confrontation without all the facts.

He met her fiery gaze with his best courtroom glare but had trouble maintaining his defensive stance against the sight of this stunning woman vibrating with anger. There was lightning in her eyes, under her skin. Her anger was more of a challenge than a deterrent. The contrast of her soft appearance and the fire in her eyes was a temptation Lee found hard to resist.

"Look, Ms. Cole, I'm not interested in your personal opinions. I just want an explanation for your presence here."

He took another step toward her but found his way blocked by Grandma, who was making the time-out sign with her hands.

"Why don't we all just drop back ten and punt. Let's call a huddle and sort out the plays. Now, I'm Florence Merritt and this is Meredith, but of course she told you that. This dear child is Meredith's daughter Julianna." She placed a hand upon carrottop's shoulder. "And this is her little friend, Robin. Now, what might your name be?"

Lee opened his mouth to speak but the woman named Meredith beat him to it.

"His name is Leland Stratton. He's Walt's son."

Lee stared at the redhead more closely still, puzzled as to how she knew his name but more stunned by the accusation in her eyes. What was she accusing him of? He was the one with the mounting pile of questions.

"Walt's son," Grandma said in surprise. "Well, I knew you existed but I didn't expect to ever meet you. You sure keep yourself scarce, fella."

Lee let Grandma's chatter swirl around him, his gaze fixed upon Meredith Cole and the icy daggers being hurled in his direction from her blue eyes.

Abruptly, Meredith turned on her heel and walked away, leaving him facing a sweet-faced grandma and two frankly curious adolescent girls. So when had he lost control here?

Meredith strode quickly and angrily through the main section of Sand Castle, out the front door, across the wide breezeway and into the tower she and Julie called home.

She went immediately to her desk. Pulling open the top drawer, she started rummaging through the contents.

Her hand trembled as she lifted out the red folder marked Important Papers. She forced a deep breath into her lungs, furious with her lack of self-control.

She'd practiced this moment in her mind a million times over the past thirteen years. She'd visualized how she would act and what she would say when she saw Lee Stratton again. She'd even rehearsed how Lee would probably respond. So why had she forgotten it all when she finally stood face-to-face with her past?

She should have expected this. Lee had to come home eventually. Even though he'd never called and hadn't been home in nearly five years. But she'd blindly convinced herself it would never happen.

She shivered. Her knees wobbled and threatened to fold on her. She'd lost control because she'd never been good at confrontations. They defeated her every time. She should have told him exactly who she was, but her courage had been buried under humiliation.

Stepping into the kitchen and finding Lee Stratton there had been a tremendous shock. All of her senses had gone momentarily numb.

He'd shown up out of the blue demanding explanations he had no right to. Well, she'd prove to him that she had a right to be here. He wasn't going to run her out of her home. She'd also show him that what happened between them all those years ago was wiped from her memory. To her it was as if it had never occurred.

Summoning all her courage and determination, Meredith stomped back outside, over to the main house and into the kitchen. She was fully aware that she was skirting the real issue here, ignoring the huge knot of tension that was growing in the center of her chest. There would be time to deal with her own feelings later. First things first.

Marching into the kitchen, Meredith shoved a copy of her lease under Lee's nose. "I'm sure you'll find everything in order. It's all legal and binding."

Lee held her gaze but she refused to show any sign of weakness. She had to see this through, despite her rapidly beating heart, her shaky knees and the blood rushing willy-nilly into her head.

He took an inordinate amount of time looking over the document. Meredith strove for a confident, unflappable attitude but after the silence had stretched on and on, she exhaled audibly in irritation.

He glanced at her, holding her in place with the power of his icy green eyes. His eyes had always been his most intriguing feature. It was as if they held some hypnotic power, some mystical force that could lock onto her and read her innermost thoughts like a palmist would read the lines in a hand.

She stared defiantly back at him, daring him to say a word, determined to withstand the penetrating gaze of those still-too-sexy eyes. He arched one eyebrow slightly then looked back at the lease.

The arrogance reflected in his stare and the tilt of his head drove Meredith's thoughts back into the past and the inevitable comparison between the boy he had been and the man he'd become.

Lee Stratton had fulfilled and surpassed all the promise of his youth. His lean hardness, the hint of muscle and strength that lay beneath his well-tailored clothes exceeded her expectations. He was as virile, as earthy, as sensual as she'd always envisioned him. Everything about him was elegantly, strikingly male.

The clean facial lines now held a depth of character that had been missing before. His emerald eyes were bracketed by tiny lines at each corner. His mouth was likewise etched at each corner, signs that perhaps the intervening years hadn't been all that kind to him. Nevertheless, Lee Stratton was a very attractive man.

But in her opinion, his attractive features were marred by the arrogant tilt to his shoulders, the cynical turn to his lip and the jaded cast to his eyes. There was a cold, detached quality to him now, as if he cared about nothing and no one.

Apparently he'd changed little from the spoiled, thoughtless boy who had broken her heart so completely that no man since had been able to lay claim to it.

"Well," Lee said, straightening and handing back the paper. "Everything appears perfectly legal."

Meredith took the paper, careful not to brush his hand in the exchange. She wanted to keep as far away as possible. She knew his tricks too well. She remembered the false sincerity he could conjure up, the pretty words and the sympathetic timbre of his voice. She'd never fall for his charm a second time.

"I told you from the beginning we had a right to be here."

Lee sighed irritably and looked down his nose at her. "I said, everything *appears* legal. But I find it hard to believe that Walt would rent the tower to anyone."

Meredith refused to look away from his probing gaze. "Then you don't know your father very well. I'm sure

Walt will be able to answer all your questions when he gets home tomorrow.''

''Forgive me for being cautious but it's disturbing to come home and find a family of strangers living in the house.''

Meredith bit her tongue to keep from screaming at him. *I'm not a stranger. Don't you recognize me?* How could he have forgotten? He was responsible for the most devastating event of her life. He'd deliberately broken her heart and he didn't even remember!

Anger and humiliation warred inside her. ''You haven't been home in five years. Why would you care who lived here?'' she snapped. Why didn't he just go away? But she could see by the glint in his eye that Lee was primed for battle. He wasn't going to back down. His jaw flexed and he pointed a finger at her.

''May I point out, Ms. Cole, that my life is none of your business—''

Florence whistled shrilly and stepped in front of Lee, holding out her hands like a referee in a boxing ring. ''Round one. To your corners.'' She smiled up at Lee. ''Mr. Stratton, why don't you get your luggage and bring it in and I'll run upstairs and freshen your room for you.''

Florence pointed past Lee to Julie and Robin. ''Girls, you run along now and find something else to gawk at.''

Meredith clenched her teeth and gave Lee one last glare, grateful for Florence's well-timed interference. ''I have work to do.'' She walked past Lee and out the back door, heading for the tower.

Her hands were still trembling from her encounter with Lee as she returned to her office and rammed the file back into its place.

Shoving the drawer shut, she allowed her emotions to spill over at last. How could he have forgotten her! How could he have forgotten that summer, what he had done, what his friends had urged him to do?

Meredith ran her fingers along her scalp. No. It wasn't Lee she should be angry with, it was herself. A teenage prank from tenth grade shouldn't still have the power to call up all the old pains and make her feel rejected and unlovable.

But it did. The hurt had never left her. It was still as fresh as the night it happened. Why couldn't she get over it? Why hadn't she grown immune to the memory, desensitized to the pain?

Meredith took a deep breath and tried to gather her tangled emotions. Maybe Lee's coming here was a good thing. It was time for her to confront the past and put the betrayal behind her. Perhaps his presence would give her a better perspective on the whole issue. Over the years she'd probably distorted the whole thing anyway. She was remembering it as more painful than it actually was.

A wave of humiliation washed through her. She couldn't fool herself. Having Lee around, seeing him every day, would be like sandpaper constantly rubbing against her overly sensitive heart.

Meredith cursed softly and shoved her hair back behind her ears. Why did he have to show up now? When everything in her life was finally perfect? When she'd finally found a place where she belonged?

She had a wonderful daughter, a good job, and a family of people who loved her and cared for her and for whom she cared deeply. They might not be related by blood but they were bound by love, and as far as she was concerned, love, not blood, was what made a family.

Walt might be Lee's father, but Lee didn't love him the way she did. Walt Stratton was the closest thing to a father she'd ever known. Living at Sand Castle these last three years had given her a sense of permanence and tradition she'd always craved.

Orphaned at age two, she'd never experienced the love and security of a real family. Only two people in her life had given her a sense of belonging and Walt was one of them. He'd taken her under his wing from the moment they'd met, encouraging her in her struggle to start her own business and freely advising her on the finer points of being self-employed.

Their friendship had grown when they discovered a mutual passion for restoration. And now they were as close as any true family could be. She was happy, fulfilled, and there was nothing she needed or wanted to complete her life.

She certainly didn't need old memories resurrected that would dredge up her insecurities and stir feelings of isolation that had no place in her life today.

Lee's presence would only complicate things. He would disrupt all their lives, including Walt's. Guilt settled heavily upon her shoulders. For the first time she wondered how Lee's unexpected return would affect his father.

Walt rarely spoke of his son and she knew little about their relationship outside of what Lee had told her that summer long ago. She was, however, keenly aware of the constant sadness in Walt's eyes whenever he saw her and Julie together. It didn't take a giant leap in logic to figure out that Lee's indifference had wounded his father deeply.

Walt didn't know about the incident between her and Lee all those years ago. She'd known Walt was Lee's father, of course, but she'd never seen a need to tell him about something that had no bearing on their friendship.

Now, though, the thought that Lee might cause further heartbreak for Walt infuriated her. How dare he come home without warning and throw their lives into turmoil!

Glancing down at the number scribbled on her calendar,

Meredith wondered whether she should call Walt at his hotel in New Orleans to warn him that Lee had come home.

Walt's health hadn't been the best these past six months. His doctor had discovered a heart problem. While it was not a critical condition, it was enough to slow him down and to make her nervous and protective of his well-being.

Would his son's unexpected return be a terrible shock or a welcome surprise? Should she warn Walt that Lee was here? Or would that be interfering? She wasn't really family, even if she felt like she was. Would it be better to let Walt find Lee here when he came home?

Damn.

Lee was already complicating their lives. She uttered her favorite expletive several times in frustration.

"What you so hacked about, Mom?" Julie asked as she draped herself over the back of Meredith's chair.

Meredith leaned forward, gathering up a few folders and some pens and putting them in her briefcase. "I'm not hacked. I'm insulted."

"'Cause of that hunk?"

"Yes. I mean, no." She turned and looked at her daughter. "What hunk?"

"Mr. Walt's son."

So even Julianna wasn't immune to Lee's good looks and charm. Great. Another person to guard.

"What are you insulted about?" Julianna insisted.

"What? Oh." Meredith brushed her hair behind her ears, searching for a suitable explanation for her daughter. The truth was always best. But this was going to be awkward. The less old dust she disturbed, the better. "I used to know him."

Julie's eyes lit up. "Cool. When?"

"When we were young. Back in high school."

"Were you high school sweethearts?"

"No! We just...." How could she make Julie understand what happened without getting into all the painful details? How did she explain about the friendship that developed between an unattractive fifteen-year-old girl and the seventeen-year-old heartthrob of the beach? How could she reveal she was once so naive that she honestly believed she'd found in Lee a kindred spirit, a soul mate? How did she explain that his attention had been nothing more than a dare, a bet by the local boys that Lee couldn't steal a kiss from her?

Most of all, how could she tell her daughter about the night Lee betrayed her and brought the world crashing down upon her, changing her outlook on life and people forever? She looked over at her daughter's curious face and knew Julie wasn't ready for any of this. "We hung out one summer, that's all."

"Did you date? I mean, like, were you a hot item?"

Meredith stood and walked across the room, wrapping her arms around herself protectively. Good grief, this was getting harder with each moment. "No, we didn't exactly date."

Julie shoved her glasses up on her nose and fiddled with her hearing aid. Her curious daughter wasn't about to miss any of the juicy details.

"But he didn't act like he knew you."

"That's why I'm insulted. He didn't even recognize me!"

Julie nodded thoughtfully. "Oh. Wow. Bummer. I'd be hacked, too."

Meredith gave her daughter a sour frown. "It's no big deal. I shouldn't have let it bother me."

"Well, hell's bells, Mere, why didn't you just come right out and tell the guy who you were?"

Meredith and Julie turned to look at Florence as she

walked into the room. She had obviously overheard the last of their conversation.

"I did," Meredith reminded her. "He didn't even recognize my name."

"Men are pigs," Florence groused. "But as pigs go, he's a good-looking SOB."

Meredith frowned at Florence and the older woman promptly grimaced in regret.

"Sorry. Julie, you didn't hear what I just said."

Julie nodded wearily.

"So, was he as easy on the eyes when you knew him?" Florence asked.

Meredith walked back toward her desk, shrugging. "I guess so."

"Mom, maybe he didn't recognize you cause you look so different."

"He didn't recognize me because I didn't make a very big impression on him back then, that's why." Julie's comment did start her to thinking, however.

"I don't know, Mom, you were pretty geeky-looking back when you were in school. Those pictures you showed me were awful. You had those barfy glasses and your hair was all frizzy and you were kinda...fat."

Meredith frowned at her daughter again. "Thanks for reminding me." But Julie had a point. Her appearance was the very root of the entire episode with Lee.

At fifteen she'd been forty pounds overweight, burdened with a plague of freckles, and had carrot-red hair that had been permed into a fright wig. She'd had a bad complexion and glasses so thick they could double as telescope lenses. Her self-esteem had been low, her social skills even lower.

At thirty, she was a completely different person. She was an inch taller and a good deal slimmer. Maturity had darkened the carrot-red hair to a burnished copper. Her complexion had cleared and contacts replaced the glasses.

Most important of all, her confidence and self-esteem were firmly in place.

"I guess I have changed a good deal." She'd also changed her name since then. She went by her given name now, before she'd gone by the nickname of Penny. A name she'd been burdened with because of her copper-colored hair.

Her name. Maybe Lee hadn't recognized her name, either. She'd introduced herself as Meredith but he'd only known her as Penny back then. But surely she'd told Lee her real name during that summer they'd spent together.

Not that it made any difference. She was the one who remembered that time as if it were yesterday. She was the one who remembered every word he'd ever spoken to her. She was the one who couldn't seem to get over the whole childish thing. Not him.

"I'll bet if you told him who you were he'd sure act different," Julie commented with heartfelt enthusiasm.

The suggestion opened up other more disturbing possibilities. She wouldn't humiliate herself by reminding him.

Yes, I'm Meredith the girl you used to win a bet, the girl you befriended, who trusted you. The girl whose heart you trampled and betrayed so you could be a big man with the guys.

No. It was best for all concerned if she dropped the whole thing. Ignore it and pretend they were total strangers. She wished now she'd never brought the subject up. "No. And I don't want either of you to refresh his memory."

"Why not?" Florence demanded.

"Because..." She started to explain the repercussions and then thought better of it. "Never mind. Just please let it be."

But thoughts of Lee and the past they'd shared plagued

her through the evening meal and into the late-night hours as she poured over her business papers.

Every moment of that summer was laser cut into her memory, every detail finely etched, every word recorded. But to him it had been a minor incident. So unimportant that he didn't even recall her face.

She could never forget. They said you always remember the thrill of your first love and the pain of your first heartbreak. That was true for her. Her first heartbreak had colored every relationship that came afterward.

Meredith stood up from her desk in the corner of her upstairs bedroom. She wasn't about to jump into the pity pool. That incident was over and done with. She had too many wonderful things going on in her life now to worry about something that happened so long ago.

Maybe it was best that Lee didn't recall their past encounter. This way it could be buried once and for all, laid to rest and never resurrected. She actually should be grateful to Lee and his practical joke. It had made her stronger; it had given her an ability to read people, to see their true motives and to maintain just enough wariness to keep her from making foolish mistakes in her relationships and in her business dealings. She might never have gotten that critical edge without his help.

She had to look toward the current problem. She had to learn from the past and apply it to today. All that mattered now was that Lee's presence didn't aggravate Walt's condition.

But she wished to God she knew why Lee had come home after all this time. What did he want here? How long was he staying? Why did he still have the power to shake up her emotions and rattle her cage?

Wrapping her robe around her, she walked out onto the balcony and rested her elbows on the railing. There were too many questions without answers.

All she knew for certain was that Lee was the intruder here and he would remain so until he proved otherwise. She hadn't been able to trust him before and she sure wasn't about to trust him now.

Chapter Two

Lee Stratton couldn't sleep. Memories of his unorthodox homecoming and the woman named Meredith kept chasing around in his mind. He ran her name through his memory banks once more but came up empty. Neither could he find an explanation for her hostility toward him.

Despite her legal documents he was eager to verify the situation with Walt when he returned tomorrow. Thoughts of facing his father brought additional concerns to his mind. It had been a long time since his last visit with Walt. As usual, they had parted in anger, neither one able to see the other's point of view, neither one willing to compromise. He had no reason to think this meeting would be any different.

So why *had* he come back here? He still wasn't certain. But after Doreen had left he'd been filled with an almost primal need for security and acceptance. A need for home.

Now it seemed the joke was on him. All he'd found

were more surprises and more changes. Changes that made him uncomfortable.

Even the old house, the one thing he'd always depended on to remain the same, had become a stranger to him. Sand Castle looked like an advertisement for a well-heeled bed-and-breakfast. Gone was the slightly careworn old home, its unimaginative white facade and black trim replaced with pastel colors that reflected the soft hues of the seashore from blue to pink to mauve.

The overgrown camellias and oleanders that had served as "forts" and "hideouts," and provided shady respite from the scalding coastal sun, had become a manicured lawn with artfully designed Victorian flower beds. The grounds were a landscape architect's dream.

Even inside the old gal had changed. Gone were the homey welcoming smells he remembered so vividly, that combination of dry musty air, furniture polish and roses.

Now the house smelled like potpourri and fresh paint, newly stained kitchen cabinets and synthetic carpet. It was bright, airy, fresh and new.

He hated it!

To make matters worse, he found his father's house filled with strangers. Strangers who were more at home here than he'd ever been.

Lee let his gaze travel around his old room. It looked exactly the way it had when he was ten. At least nothing here had been changed. He couldn't help but wonder why. Hadn't the restorations reached this far yet or was there some other explanation? Whatever the reason, he found a small measure of comfort in the fact that this room had been left untouched.

A lonesome, endless moan penetrated the quiet darkness, magnifying the emptiness in his heart.

He'd forgotten about the trains in Gulfport. The tracks intersected the city streets at every block, cutting a diagonal swath through the populated downtown. The whistle had to be sounded at each crossing, resulting in a virtual nonstop wail as the train passed through town.

Lee rolled onto his back and stared at the ceiling. He'd known it wouldn't be a comfortable homecoming, but he hadn't been prepared for the tidal wave of memories that had assaulted him at every turn.

Memories of his happy childhood and the closeness he'd once shared with Walt. Memories of the peace and contentment he'd known here at Sand Castle. Memories he had blocked out years ago and had no desire to disturb.

The mournful whistle echoed endlessly in the night air.

How the hell was he supposed to sleep when every five minutes the blast of a train whistle sliced through him?

Draping an arm across his eyes, Lee tried to block out the old memories bombarding him, but they refused to stop.

The summer he was seventeen loomed in his mind. He'd told his father he wouldn't be going into the family business, that he intended to study law instead. Walt had been furious and the breach between them had become too wide to ever bridge.

Lee had rarely come home after that. The few times he had was to see his grandma Stratton; the only stable relationship he'd ever known. After she died five years ago, Lee'd had no reason to return to Gulfport.

Until now.

The whistle sounded again.

Trains! How did people sleep with the damned trains!

Lee muttered a curse and yanked back the covers. He rose from the bed, tugged on his khaki slacks and shoved his arms into a shirt, leaving it unbuttoned.

Running a hand through his hair, he glanced at the window. It was April and a cool breeze gently ruffled the lace curtain. Hoping that a little fresh air would help him unwind, he pushed open the French doors and went out onto the broad upper gallery that surrounded the old house.

He stopped at the railing and inhaled deeply. The breeze was heavy with the mingled scents of wisteria and salt from the sea. The sound of the surf caressed his ears like an old lullaby. It didn't make him sleepy but it did help to clear his thoughts.

Movement from the far end of the long balcony drew his attention. He looked toward the tower and saw a lone figure hunched over the railing. Meredith. Apparently he wasn't the only one who was restless tonight.

He watched her for a moment, captivated by the ethereal image. She was bathed in the soft glow of the porch lamp and the moonlight. A soft, fragrant breeze gently lifted her hair about her face.

In her long white robe and with her arms crossed over her waist, she looked like a sad angel who'd wrapped her wings around herself for protection. She seemed fragile, soft and delicate. A waif of the night.

Lee rubbed his chin thoughtfully. What was behind her thorny attitude? The lawyer in him was damned curious. The man in him was strangely reluctant to probe too deeply.

Still, something about Meredith beckoned him, lured him to her side. He told himself it was nothing more than the basic awareness of a disturbingly sensuous woman.

He strolled across the wide gallery, speaking to her softly as he neared her side. "Haven't we met before?"

She gasped, whirling around to face him, her eyes wide and filled with fear.

"Sorry," he apologized quickly. "I didn't mean to frighten you. I thought you heard me walk up."

She took a deep breath and stepped back, clutching the railing with one hand, the other toying with the collar on her thick terry robe.

"I was thinking about something. I guess I didn't hear you."

Lee leaned against the rail, resisting the overpowering urge to reach out and touch her hair and her cheeks, just to make sure she was real and not a vision created out of his fatigued mind. "You couldn't sleep, either?"

Meredith glanced at him briefly, then shook her head.

"It's been a…difficult day for both of us," he offered.

"Having one's integrity questioned usually is," she replied, staring straight ahead.

"So is coming home to a houseful of strangers."

Her eyes never wavered when she finally turned to look at him. "Strangers to you. Not to your father."

"Point taken," he acknowledged with a nod. Lee didn't want to be angry with her but it seemed no matter what he said she bristled. Maybe he was coming at this the wrong way. Perhaps a more congenial approach would be better than badgering the witness. "We obviously got off on the wrong foot today. Why don't we start over." He held out his hand. "I'm Lee Stratton."

She stared at it a moment and he fully expected her to ignore the gesture. But then she slowly reached out, hesitantly, as if reluctant to make contact with him.

"I'm…Meredith."

The moment they touched all coherent thought fled from his mind. He looked at their hands, her small ivory one nearly obscured in his large tanned one. Nothing unusual about either of them. But her touch set off a series of tiny explosions along his nerve endings, pinpoints of sensation and awareness that spread throughout his veins, into his chest and down into the pit of his stomach.

He looked into her eyes and saw she was feeling something unusual, as well. There was something vaguely familiar about the emotions reflected in her expressive eyes. An old image peeked out from the shadows of his memory, then ducked away. Déjà vu. Had he held her hand this way before? He had a memory of standing in the moonlight, high above the ground with the sound of the surf in the background. He remembered holding the hand of someone with sad blue eyes. He grasped at the shadowy memory but it eluded him.

Meredith tugged at her hand and he released it, resisting the urge to stare at his palm to see if she'd left some sort of indelible imprint there.

"It's late," Meredith said quietly. She backed up, then turned and started to walk away.

"Don't go." He'd called out to her before he'd even realized his intentions.

She stopped. Her back to him.

"Why not?"

"I'd like to talk."

Slowly she turned to face him, her eyes shooting daggers again.

"You and I have nothing to talk about."

Her reaction irritated the hell out of him. She acted as if he were the intruder here. "I don't know what you're so angry about but you can hardly blame me for being concerned about Walt's well-being."

Meredith's chin lifted defensively. "No. I'm concerned, too. I'm worried about someone I love being hit with an unwelcome surprise."

A sourness pooled in the pit of Lee's stomach like an old familiar ailment. He didn't need a stranger reminding him of how he wasn't wanted. "You think my being here will upset Walt?"

"Yes," she said, meeting his gaze. "If he's not prepared."

Lee shook his head, smiling wryly. "It won't matter one way or the other to him."

Meredith pursed her lips, crossing her arms over her

chest. "I can't believe you. You drop in here without warning after five long years and don't even stop to consider how it might affect your father. I should have predicted this. It's so typical."

Her assessment of him rankled, even if there was some truth to what she said. "I might have known you'd take Walt's side. But did it ever occur to you that the problem might originate with Walt and not me?"

"No." Her lips tightened into a thin line. "I know all about you—" She stopped abruptly. "Your relationships."

Lee shifted uncomfortably. Something in her tone made him feel like he was on the witness stand again, but he was fully capable of turning the tables. "And what about your relationship with Walt? Why don't you tell me how that came about?"

Meredith tucked her hands inside the pockets of her robe and lifted her chin. "A mutual friend, Ann Conner, introduced us. She thought I could help Walt with a problem."

"What kind of problem?"

"The faux *marbre* on one of the mantels had deteriorated and the wood beneath was exposed. Ann recommended me for the job."

"The what?"

"Faux painting," she explained. "It's what I do. It's a special painting technique that makes ordinary pine resemble marble or a more expensive wood, like mahogany. I'm a stencil artist and restorationist. My studio is in the old carriage house. I was just starting my business when I met Walt, and couldn't afford much advertising. He was so pleased with my work he recommended me to his friends. Thanks to him, business doubled."

"How fortunate for you." He didn't try to keep the sarcasm from his tone.

Meredith's eyes flashed—Lee could almost see fire shooting from them.

"What do you mean by that?"

"Nothing. I'm just curious how you came to be living in my father's house."

"I thought lawyers liked to deal in facts," Meredith challenged.

Lee shook his head, enjoying goading the passionate redhead. "Judges like facts. Lawyers ask questions."

"Fine, then here are your answers. Walt Stratton is like a father to me. He helped me at a time in my life when I needed a friend. When the casinos came, housing around here was scarce and expensive. My apartment complex went condo and I couldn't afford to buy into it. Julie and I needed a place to live and since the tower had been sitting empty, Walt suggested we move in there."

Meredith lifted her chin in what he was coming to recognize as her defiant stance. "I've told you everything you need to know. The rest is for your father to explain."

She started to walk away then turned back. "By the way, when did you say you were leaving?"

Lee clamped his mouth shut to keep from saying something he would regret. Meredith might look soft on the outside but inside she was made of barbed wire.

It had been a long time since anyone had gotten under his skin and pierced his control. He prided himself on remaining cool and dispassionate under all circumstances. It had become the hallmark of his success as an attorney.

But in some strange and inexplicable way, sparring with Meredith was exhilarating. Taking a calming breath, he made another attempt to talk to her reasonably.

"Look, I know we got off on the wrong foot today and I'm willing to take some of the responsibility. But bickering like schoolkids won't get us anywhere. Neither one of us is leaving for the time being. Wouldn't it be better if we tried approaching this more like friends?''

"We could *never* be friends aga—'' Meredith's eyes blazed like blue flames with the intensity of her anger. "No. Not in a million years.'' With the dignity of a queen and the grace of an angel, she turned and went inside the tower, firmly shutting the door behind her.

Turning on his heel, Lee started back toward his room on the other end of the broad gallery. An unexpected sense of loss and loneliness settled around him. The moonlight didn't seem nearly as beautiful now, the breeze not as gentle.

In fact the night was downright cold and unfriendly. He stopped at the threshold of his bedroom door and looked back toward the tower.

Damn. Something about Meredith disturbed him. He didn't understand her anger or her fierce protectiveness toward Walt. He didn't understand anything about her at all except that she made him feel wary and on edge.

Running his hand along the back of his head, Lee turned and walked to the edge of the gallery, staring out into the night. The sound of the sea lapping gently on the manmade shore stirred an uneasy restlessness in his gut and brought vivid images of Meredith to his mind.

She was the most touchable woman he'd ever met. Her soft red-gold hair begged to be caressed by a man's hand. Her pixie face with its upturned nose had been colored by pale moonlight and morning's first dewy pink rays. She had the kind of sweet, endearing face a man would want to cradle frequently between his hands.

Even her body was softly slender and curvy where a woman was supposed to be, a body made for loving. Lee stared at his hand again, idly rubbing the palm where her hand, so soft and gentle, had rested.

Strange how his whole body had vibrated when she'd

touched him. Stranger still how he'd wanted to touch her from the moment he'd first seen her.

Then there'd been that moment of déjà vu. That sense of familiarity, of having experienced this all before. He'd felt a connection, a bond that he'd experienced only one other time in his life. It was the summer he was seventeen and, as usual, he'd come to spend his school vacation with Walt. He'd met some local boys and a girl—

Realization slammed into him with brute force. *Penny!* It couldn't be. But it was. Meredith Cole was Penny.

Dazed with shock, he wiped the palms of his hands over his face, struggling to digest his discovery. Meredith was Penny. Sweet, trusting Penny. He'd left her sitting on the platform inside the branches of the Friendship Oak after he'd won that damned bet.

Dear God, how could he have not recognized her? Those clear blue eyes, that childlike smile, that glorious red hair. She'd changed considerably since then. The shy, bookish young girl had grown into an incredibly lovely woman.

He cursed and bowed his head. He should have known in his heart it was her. He was a blind idiot. No wonder she was so angry and defensive around him. She'd expected him to recognize her in the kitchen today. Instead he'd dismissed her as a nuisance.

Lee sucked in a breath, feeling the strain of his constricted lungs. The realization was still exploding inside his head. Damn. He'd never thought he'd see her again. And now— He glanced back at the tower.

Guilt and remorse rapidly pushed through the shock, undermining the rigid control he held on his emotions. The sudden onslaught of painful and long-pent-up feelings was unbearable. He tried to retreat into his comfortable zone of indifference but he was only partially successful. He'd never felt so lonely, so empty inside as he did at this moment.

Penny. They'd been so close that summer. She'd been his only friend, the only one who understood and shared his sense of isolation and loneliness. But he'd been a young fool. He hadn't realized the value of her trust and friendship and he'd thrown them away for a fleeting moment of acceptance from a group of boys he never saw again.

Penny. His mind reeled at the magnitude of his sins. How could he ever make her understand why he'd chosen to win the bet over keeping their friendship? It had been more than a desire to fit in with the guys. Penny's lavish outpouring of affection had triggered unfamiliar and frightening feelings in him that he hadn't known how to handle.

Instead of being honest with her, he'd turned and walked away. Being alone had seemed easier, safer, and it was the one thing he understood completely. That was a poor excuse for betraying a friend.

Another sorrowful train whistle penetrated the night air, scraping sharply against his heart.

What could he say to her after all these years? He had no defense and an apology seemed so inadequate. But he couldn't ignore the past and pretend he didn't remember.

He had to think clearly, logically, and he couldn't do that when he was feeling guilty. He willed himself to concentrate on the core of the problem: how to correct this situation with Penny.

The best course of action was to be straightforward. He regretted his actions that summer but he could do nothing to change the past. He understood her anger but that was something she would have to deal with in her own way.

As for his part, he would go to her in the morning and apologize. Then it would all be set straight and he could put it behind him once and for all. With his control once again secure, he turned and went into the house.

The old kitchen was empty when Lee came downstairs the next morning, a fact that pleased him. Solitude suited him today. He felt like hell.

Between visions of Meredith tormenting his dreams and memories of Walt and his childhood staring at him from the walls of his room when he was awake, he'd barely slept all night.

Pouring himself a cup of coffee, Lee took a sip, remembering how Walt had always needed that first cup each day before he would even say good morning.

"Good morning there, fella. Did ya sleep good?"

Lee looked up at the woman who had clomped into the kitchen. He lowered his cup, staring dumbfounded at Florence. At least he thought it was Florence. She was dressed in black jeans and biker boots, a leather jacket with zippers, and a T-shirt that said Hot Hogs And Grandmas. Under her arm she carried a shiny black helmet.

"Let me guess," she said, holding up her hand. "You've never seen a grandma in leather before."

Embarrassed to be caught staring, Lee started to offer an apology but only managed to stumble over his tongue. "I didn't mean..."

"Don't bother trying to say something politically correct," Florence said, brushing him aside. "Here's the scoop. I always wanted to ride a motorcycle. So when my George died, I said, 'Hell's bells, life's too short. Why not give it a try?' So I joined a Harley club. Most fun I ever had."

"That's a...healthy attitude," Lee muttered, still struggling to find some correlation between Biker Grandma and the sweet-faced, flower-aproned granny from yesterday.

"Oh, and just so you won't think I'm some kind of wacko, Tuesday nights I go to my quilting class." She winked and grinned, fixing herself some coffee.

Lee couldn't resist a small smile. Florence was a unique

individual and he found his mind filling with questions about her.

"Well, go ahead. Ask me," Florence said with a knowing nod. "I can see the wheels of curiosity spinning in those green eyes of yours."

Lee raised an eyebrow at her insight. "All right. How long have you lived here at Sand Castle?"

"Well, actually I live in the old servants wing in the back. I ended up here after your aunt Ada left for Saskatchewan. Walt needed someone to look after things and Meredith recommended me."

"Have you known Meredith long?"

"Three years about. Ever since she adopted me."

"Excuse me?"

"Yep. Bless her heart. She picked me right out of a lineup, so to speak. It's another one of those things I wanted to do. Always wanted a family, lots of kids. But George and I never had any. So I signed up for a program where you could get adopted by people who didn't have grandparents. Meredith adopted me. That young woman has more love in her heart than she could give away in three lifetimes." Florence glanced at the clock. "Oops. Gotta scoot or they'll leave without me. We're riding over to Ocean Springs today."

Lee finished his coffee then walked out onto the back porch. Florence and Meredith were standing beside the cycle, deep in conversation. Meredith gave Florence a hug then started toward the carriage house.

Tension tightened Lee's chest when he thought about facing her again. He dismissed it as a slight case of nerves, nothing more. Perfectly understandable. From what he'd seen, Meredith had developed a lusty temper since they'd been kids and he wasn't anxious to be the recipient of it again. Even if he deserved it. He felt sure once he'd apologized for his behavior the animosity would end.

But as he watched Meredith walk gracefully toward her studio, his tension lifted. Warmth spread through him at the sight of her.

In her white blouse and flowered jumper she was as fresh and lovely as morning itself. The long skirt skimmed her slim hips and swished gently around her ankles as she walked. Her red-gold hair was held in place by a silly straw hat, the brim of which was folded back with a flower stuck in the middle.

She made him want to smile. She made him think of leisurely strolls through fields of daisies and long walks down country lanes and soft, romantic afternoons near a lake. He wanted to gather her softness against him to see if she tasted as sweet and fresh as she looked.

Thoughts of Meredith dissipated when a large white luxury car pulled up and stopped near the garage.

"Mr. Walt's home!"

Lee heard Julie's joyful shout and turned to watch as she and Meredith welcomed Walt home. Julie threw herself at Walt the moment he was out of the car, receiving a bear hug in response. A tightness formed in Lee's throat as Meredith stepped forward and receive a peck on the cheek and a warm embrace, as well.

Walt is like a father to me.

Burning hot discomfort filled Lee's chest. How had Meredith been able to elicit paternal feelings from Walt that his own son never had? Meredith, Julie and Florence all seemed more at home here than he did.

They welcomed each other like family, with laughter and smiles. To anyone else it would probably look like a living Rockwell portrait. Three generations of love, affection and devotion.

But Lee knew the portrait was a lie. It was *his* father, *his* home, but he was on the outside looking in. Strangers had usurped his place in the family. Like a stranger him-

self, he stood watching from the sidelines, a strange longing building inside him.

A familiar chill stole over him as he observed the little
scene being played out. With the ease of long practice he
slipped behind his strong gray walls of indifference. He
didn't need them. He hadn't needed anyone since he was
a kid.

Lee started to look away when his gaze collided with
Meredith's. In quick succession he read surprise, sympathy
and understanding in her clear blue eyes. A depth of understanding that reached deep down inside him to a place
so private even he'd forgotten about it.

He steeled himself against the realization that Meredith
knew what he was thinking, what he was feeling. He didn't
want anyone looking so closely at his heart and soul, root-
ing around in his private thoughts, probing parts of him
best left alone.

Lee pulled his gaze from Meredith's and went inside the
house. He stopped in the hallway, unable to shake the uneasy feeling in his gut that Meredith's penetrating stare
had caused.

He'd forgotten how easily Meredith had been able to
topple his defenses. He'd have to remember to be on guard
while he was here.

"Hello, son."

Lee spun around, coming face-to-face with Walt. He'd
been so preoccupied with thoughts of Meredith he hadn't
realized his father was in the house.

Suddenly tense and rigid, Lee faced Walt's disapproving
scowl. A painful awareness swept through Lee as he
looked closely at the older man. His father had always
been a big man, physically imposing, yet Lee suddenly
realized that he was a good head taller than Walt. Walt
was an old man now. His blue eyes were pale and faded,
his stature diminished.

The realization brought a heaviness to Lee's chest and he was filled with an unexpected impulse to reach out and embrace his father. Quickly he suppressed the idea. He knew from experience that a show of affection would be unwelcome and only prove embarrassing for both of them.

Lee cleared his throat. "Hello, Walt."

Walt grumbled and shook his head. "What brings you to this neck of the woods? You got some high-powered case going on?"

"No. It's personal," he said, resigning himself to the inevitable confrontation.

"Personal? I didn't figure anyone or anything here involved you personally anymore," Walt groused, walking on down the hall.

Lee followed along behind. "Are you saying I'm not welcome here anymore?" he asked, recalling how welcome Meredith and Julie were and realizing how closed off he felt at this moment.

"Did I say that?" Walt asked, stopping inside his study and facing Lee.

"It's what you meant."

"Bah." Walt waved the comment aside. "You always were argumentative as a boy. I should have figured you'd become a lawyer." Walt went to his desk and sat down. "So, what's this personal matter you're looking into? I don't suppose you've grown tired of that high-and-mighty law firm you work for?"

Lee exhaled in surprise at the unexpected wave of disappointment that had slammed into him. But he quietly steeled himself against it, angry at himself for still hoping for some show of affection from a parent who was incapable of it.

You're not capable of any real feelings. Doreen's words flashed through his thoughts.

"No," Lee admitted, swallowing his irritation for the moment.

Walt unzipped his New Orleans Saints jacket and tugged it off his broad shoulders, leaning back in his chair. "Yeah, I knew it was too much to hope you'd come back and take over the reins at Stratton Development."

"Yeah, right," Lee said sarcastically. He'd hadn't been home in five years and the first thing Walt did was drag out their oldest argument. "Carry on the family tradition. Fourth generation and all that."

"It was good enough for your great-granddad and for your grandpa and good enough for me."

Lee paced across the room, driven by a familiar restlessness. He *had* been growing more discontented with his job at Virgil, Mallory and Cox, but he certainly hadn't come home to be one his father's cronies.

Unwilling to go down that old road with his father again, Lee searched for another topic of conversation, one that held the least potential for argument. "What were you doing in New Orleans?"

Walt paused a moment, adjusting his ball cap. "I'm thinking about selling the business. I've got some people down in New Orleans who might be interested."

"Sell Stratton Development?" Lee couldn't believe he'd heard correctly. "It's the most important thing in your life."

"It's *not* the most important thing in my life!" Walt snapped, coming to his feet. He paused a moment, hiking up the waist of the baggy sweatpants he wore. "It's just no fun anymore, that's all. The casinos took all the adventure out of it. They come into town, plop down millions of dollars and it's all over. No challenge. Not like the old days when you had to be really creative to get a new development going. Besides, I'm getting too old for all this battling back and forth. It's time I slowed down. Maybe I'll retire to Florida and get me a little condo.''

"What about Sand Castle?"

"I might sell it. Or maybe donate it to some worthy cause," Walt said defiantly. "No one else seems to want the place."

Lee couldn't believe what he was hearing. He inhaled and found his lungs reluctant to comply against the pressure building in his chest. Sand Castle had been the Stratton family home for more than one hundred years. What could Walt be thinking of?

"If you're planning on selling, why did you spend a fortune restoring it?" Lee demanded.

"Because it was falling down around my damn ears!" Walt shouted. "Besides, a place this big needs a family and lots of kids running around. And it doesn't look like any more Strattons will be coming along to inherit."

"Is that why you became a landlord?" Lee asked, ignoring Walt's pointed glare. "You didn't see any grandchildren in your future so you decided to fill up the house with boarders?"

"What are you talking about?"

"I'm talking about the people living in this house, about renting the tower."

"It's my house. I can rent it or do any other damned thing I want with it. What business is it of yours, anyhow?"

Lee set his jaw, struggling to hold his temper. Walt was the most bullheaded, obstinate man he'd ever known. "You're right, It's none of my business. But it's damned awkward to come home and find a bunch of strangers in your house."

Walt came around the desk to stand toe to toe with Lee. "They aren't strangers. They're friends. In fact, we're kind of a family now."

The bitterness that pooled in Lee's mouth nearly choked him when he tried to swallow. They were family. *He wasn't.* The verbal slap in the face stung, but he masked it quickly with indifference. Why the hell had he come home? There was nothing for him here. There never had been and there never would be.

He turned and started from the room.

"Leland."

He almost didn't stop but respect forced him to respond.

"I'm sorry about the wedding."

Lee turned and stared at his father in openmouthed surprise. It sounded as if Walt was sincere. Lee had no idea how to respond to that. He wasn't used to Walt being sympathetic. He shrugged. "That's the way it goes sometimes."

Walt frowned and nodded. "Had my plane ticket bought. But I got my money back."

Lee was growing more and more confused. He'd never imagined in his wildest dreams that Walt would actually have attended his wedding. Doreen had insisted on inviting him.

"I'm glad." He wasn't sure if he was saying he was glad Walt got his money back or that he'd wanted to be there for his son.

"You know, not all women are like your mother and Doreen. They don't all walk off and leave you alone."

Lee turned and stared into the distance, wishing he'd stayed in Houston. He missed his structured, neatly controlled way of life. Being back at Sand Castle was like riding a damned merry-go-round. From one moment to the next he was thrust upward into the familiar, then plunged into sudden change, then spun around in circles. His insides were twisted in so many knots he wasn't sure he'd ever be able to sort them out.

"You know, son, my first marriage was a good one.

Alice and I were very happy right up until the day she died.''

Lee pulled his attention back to his father. He often forgot that Walt had another family—two daughters—Lee's half sisters. Maybe because it only reminded him that he didn't belong anywhere.

He'd been born too late to be part of Walt's first family and cast aside by his own. It seemed to be the pattern of his life, falling between the cracks, never belonging anywhere or to anyone. Lee quickly shut down the self-pity.

"What does your first marriage have to do with anything?" he asked.

"Nothing. I'm just making a point. Just because one woman threw you over doesn't mean they all will."

For a brief instant Lee thought he read affection in Walt's pale blue eyes. Lee turned away as a strange tightness lodged in the middle of his chest. Since when was Walt concerned with his son's well-being? He wasn't in the mood to hear any of Walt's theories on women.

"Take Meredith for example. She's one of a kind. She's caring, generous, and as loving a woman as you'll ever find. I'd be willing to bet there's not a person on earth she doesn't like."

The irony in Walt's remark almost made Lee laugh. "You'd lose."

"What? Why would I lose?"

"I'm her one exception."

"You? Why?"

Apparently, Walt knew nothing about the link between him and Meredith. So much the better. He wasn't going to try to make his father understand something he couldn't even explain to himself. "Let's just say I doubt if there'll be any warm friendships forming between your friend Meredith and me."

"You got something against her?"

"No." Lee sighed and ran his hand across the back of his neck. A familiar anger began to churn in his gut. It was always this way when he tried to talk to Walt. Lee was always at fault.

"I'm just saying, don't bet on us becoming buddies."

"Well, I say you're wrong."

Lee looked at his father in confusion. "What?"

"I'll bet you that you and Meredith end up friends before you leave here."

Lee shook his head. "I'm not a betting man."

"Damn it, boy, take a risk. If you're so all-fired sure, then you got nothing to lose."

Lee wasn't about to get into the details of his botched relationship with Meredith. But he recognized the determined note in his father's voice and he knew there'd be no moving the man until he got his way.

"Fine. How much are you willing to risk?"

"No money," Walt said with a smirk, heading for the door. "Just a big fat I-told-you-so when it's all said and done. Oh, and don't you do anything to upset that little lady while you're here or you'll have to answer to me."

Walt walked out of the study, leaving Lee trapped on the merry-go-round again, feeling frustrated and angry. Walt resented his own son coming home, but he took in strangers and called them family, then expected them all to become good friends. Something like hot ice formed around Lee's heart. He shoved the pain and the resentment aside.

The problems between him and Walt would have to wait. There were more important matters on his mind. He had to talk to Penny. It was important that he clear up the misunderstanding between them as soon as possible.

He'd been diverted by Walt's homecoming but now it was time to face up to his past. Lee headed straight for the carriage house stopping when he noticed the large sign outside the door.

Memory's Touch—Decorative Arts And Designs.

This must be the business she mentioned last night. The name was appropriate. Penny's memory had touched him and left its mark for eternity. He reached for the door handle but found himself reluctant to go inside.

He'd always been able to remain untouched by events around him. Jobs, friends, lovers, even family. But one thing he'd never been able to relinquish was that tiny spark of Penny's memory. No matter how cold or empty he'd felt, her memory had kept him from being totally alone.

He had to find a way to explain about his actions that summer. He had to make her understand. Gathering his courage, Lee pulled open the door and went inside.

Chapter Three

Meredith cursed softly to herself and pulled the stencil out, placing it in the right slot. In the past ten minutes she'd misfiled seven stencils because her mind wasn't on her job but on the two men in the main house.

What were Walt and his prodigal son talking about? She'd managed to warn Walt that Lee had come home but she hadn't been able to tell how that news had affected him. He had gone immediately into the house.

Now she was a bundle of nerves worrying about the outcome. She shoved another stencil into a slot only to take it out and shove it into the right one. She'd never get these things put away if she didn't concentrate, but that was impossible when she thought of Walt's condition and how Lee's presence could add to his stress.

Maybe she should go back up to the house to check on them. She discarded that idea almost as quickly as it formed. Walt might be her dearest friend, but it really was none of her business what went on between father and son.

"Hello, Penny."

Meredith froze at the sound of the once familiar name. A flurry of old memories and faded images breezed through her mind before she composed herself. She'd been so deep in thought she hadn't heard anyone enter the studio, but there was no doubt who it was.

Slowly she turned toward the door. Apparently Lee wasn't interested in getting reacquainted with his father. They couldn't have spent more than ten minutes together, but then, what else could she expect?

Lee stood just inside the double doors, his expression stony and unreadable. Obviously he'd finally remembered who she was, but it was also obvious it hadn't affected him in the least.

"I outgrew that name a long time ago," she said, turning back to her stencil drawer, attempting to focus on her task but unable to erase the image of Lee standing tall and imposing in her doorway.

Like the unerring lens of a camera, her mind had captured him in Technicolor detail. He was dressed casually today in a dark green sweater that heightened the broadness of his shoulders and defined the expanse of his chest. The painted-on jeans he wore outlined the muscled length of his legs.

"So I see," he replied. "That's why I didn't recognize you yesterday."

Meredith flinched slightly against the memory, but quickly braced herself. "It's been a long time. No reason you should remember someone you hardly knew."

"I thought about you a lot over the years."

Lee came closer and she caught a whiff of his tangy aftershave. It went to her head, dancing around in her mind, creating little pictures of them together. She moved away.

"Why would you?"

"Things between us ended…poorly."

"I didn't know there were 'things' between us," she said, shoving the stencil drawer shut with unnecessary force. "You were just a guy I met one summer."

Lee came toward her and she stepped behind her workbench.

"You know what I mean—that night at the Friendship Oak."

Meredith, tucking her hair behind her ears, faced him, her chin tilted upward. "I don't know what you're talking about."

"Yes, you do," he said firmly.

What was he trying to do, rub his cruel joke in her wounds? She searched his face for some sign that he was feeling regretful for what he'd done, but she could read nothing at all in his chiseled expression or his icy green eyes. So be it. He wouldn't humiliate her a second time.

"You mean, that little bet you made with your friends? I'd forgotten all about it."

"I wanted to explain about that."

"Don't bother," she said, forcing a smile. "I understand perfectly."

"Do you?"

"Of course. 'Boys will be boys,' I believe the saying goes."

Lee looked into her eyes, his gaze probing, questioning and creating an uneasy tension in her chest. She looked away.

An awkward silence settled heavily between them. Meredith wanted to say something to break the tension but she didn't want to give Lee the satisfaction of knowing his presence bothered her.

"Is this some of your work?" He stood beside her design board, examining a piece of stencil she'd been experimenting with.

"Yes."

"This is a very intricate design. Did you do this with a laser cutter?"

"No. By hand." Meredith couldn't help but be pleased by his compliment whether it was genuine or not. She was very proud of her skill and creativity. "A laser is out of my price range right now."

"I'm impressed. It's not what I expected."

Meredith reminded herself that the warm note of sincerity she'd heard in his voice didn't mean a thing. He'd always been able to turn up the charm when it suited him. "What did you expect?"

He shrugged. "Flowers, alphabet letters, that kind of thing."

"I do the flowers and letters, too. But many of my customers own historic homes and they want their original stencils duplicated or repaired."

Lee laid the stencil down and moved to another table in the far corner where she had several faux *marbre* picture frames in progress. "I looked at the fireplace in the front parlor, the one you said you repainted. I always thought it was real marble. I never knew it was wood."

There was a wistfulness in his voice that touched her heart. Quickly she pushed aside her sympathy. "All of the fireplaces in this house are pine, painted to resemble marble. Perhaps you didn't know that because you simply didn't care enough to be curious." It went against her nature to be curt but she had to remember she couldn't trust any of her impressions where Lee was concerned.

Lee looked at her with his paralyzing green gaze. "Or maybe it's because no one bothered to tell me."

An image of a lonely young boy standing on the beach burst into Meredith's mind and she wondered if there was some of that boy hiding within the broad shoulders of the man in front of her now.

"What does Mr. Cole think of your business?" he asked, resting his splayed fingers on his hips.

The sexy, wholly male pose caused her heart to skip a beat. She ignored it. "There is no Mr. Cole. I'm divorced." Meredith crossed her arms over her chest and faced him. "I'm sure you didn't come here to discuss the finer points of faux painting or my failed marriage. What do you want?" she asked, moving to the far counter. Her pulse was throbbing but she told herself it was caused by her own anger and not Lee's overpowering presence in her studio.

"I wanted to see you, Penny. I wanted to tell you—"

"Don't call me that! I told you I don't use that name anymore." Hearing that old nickname was like being plunged into icy lake water.

"Why not? It suited you."

"Worthless and dull like an old penny?" she quipped sarcastically.

"No," he responded quickly, taking a few steps toward her. "That's not what I meant."

"Isn't it?" Meredith tried to temper her anger but Lee was digging up feelings she didn't want to battle anymore. "I'm the girl you used to win a bet, remember? I'm the homely little orphan you left sitting in the tree after you'd found the courage to kiss her."

"That's not true."

Meredith choked back her anger. She refused to let him see how much his rejection still hurt, but she didn't know how much longer she could hold off the tears. "I told you to forget it. It's over and done with. In the past. I want to know why you suddenly came home after all this time."

For a moment Meredith thought she saw a flash of emotion in his eyes, pain maybe, or doubt. When she looked closer she realized it had only been the play of lights overhead. His expression was stony and unreadable.

"No particular reason," he said evenly. "I just decided it was time to come home."

Meredith didn't believe that for a minute. Rigid, unbending men like Lee didn't do anything on impulse. Every moment was planned. There was more to it than that. "So, you've come and you've seen. How soon will you be leaving?"

Lee stiffened slightly, causing Meredith to feel ashamed of her rudeness. But darn it, he had no right to drop in here and stir up trouble.

"I'm not sure how long I'll be staying."

"What about Walt?"

"What about him?"

She marveled at the callousness of the man. He really was made of ice. "Oh, forgive me for thinking that you'd come home to see your father. I mean, you haven't been home in five years. Why should you come now that he needs you?"

Lee's jaw flexed. "Walt doesn't need anyone."

"Oh, really? He's not well, you know. He's developed some problems with his heart."

"Heart? I wasn't aware that he had one."

"How can you say that?" she demanded angrily. "Your father is a dear man who's practically worked himself to death."

"It was his choice." Lee shoved his hands into his pockets.

"Now who's being heartless?"

"You're not the first one to point that out to me recently."

Meredith wasn't sure what he meant by that comment and could read little in his cool expression. Didn't he possess even one small fragment of feeling for his father? Maybe Lee didn't understand the full implications of what she was telling him. "He needs to retire or at the very least slow down, but he won't. The only reason he's home now is because his doctor forced him to take three weeks off or be admitted to a hospital.''

Lee started at the news, but said nothing, his brows drawn together.

"He should be relieved of some of the stress at work. He could use your help while you're here with the day-to-day running of the company.''

"No, that would only make things worse," Lee said with a firm shake of his head. "Walt and I could never work together. Even on a temporary basis. Besides, I know nothing about his line of work. I'm a lawyer not a developer." And he was the last person Walt would accept help from now, Lee thought to himself.

Meredith's anger burned fiercely. Lee hadn't changed. He still thought only of himself. She picked up the coffee carafe and poured herself a steaming cup, channeling her irritation into spooning in some cream and stirring up a whirlpool in her mug.

The last thing Walt needed right now was a prodigal son who didn't possess one grain of compassion.

The sooner Lee left, the better it would be for Walt. For all of them. Meredith clutched her cup between her hands and turned around, unaware that Lee stood at her side. Her arm collided with his hard chest, splattering hot coffee down the front of her jumper and over her wrist. "Oh!"

"Damn, I'm sorry." Lee grabbed a cloth and quickly wiped her hand. "Are you burned?"

Tears stung her eyes but she shook her head. The coffee had been hot but not scalding.

"Come here," Lee ordered, pulling her toward the sink and running cold water over her throbbing wrist. "Does that feel better?"

She nodded, acutely aware of his strong, hot hand wrapped around her wrist. The heat from the burn on her skin and the heat from the grasp of Lee's hand were indistinguishable. She stared at his long fingers, so strong yet gentle as they held her. The dark hair sprinkled across the back of his hand became thicker as it spread upward to his forearm.

Her pulse quickened beneath her skin as she glanced furtively at him. Could he feel it, too? Could he sense what his touch was doing to her?

Lee turned off the water and Meredith jerked her gaze from his hand to her own, watching as he dried her wrist with a clean towel.

"I'm sorry." He took the towel and started to dab at the spot on her chest.

Meredith looked down at her clothes. Coffee had soaked through the thin cotton blouse beneath her jumper, plastering it to her breast.

Lee made a second swipe along the damp area, inadvertently brushing across her nipple. The sensation was so unexpected she sucked in a sharp breath.

She met his eyes and saw the same awareness there. The cloth he held still rested against her breast. She could feel the heat of his fingers through the fabric. Her body responded to his nearness, to his touch, with shocking ease. Her breathing quickened. Her nipples ached and hardened. Her blood warmed in her veins and her thighs trembled.

She swayed toward him, feeling her core convulse and tighten. His eyes burned into hers for an eternity, then traveled downward, pausing at her mouth, then slid down to her chest.

Slowly he lifted the cloth, allowing a cold chill to touch her. She reached out and grasped his hand with her own, though whether to take the cloth from him or to keep it on her she didn't know. Her fingers touched his and she was surrounded by the warm scent of male and arousal and spice.

Neither of them moved or breathed. The air was charged, filled with the basic eternal chemistry that marked man and woman.

"Mom! You in there?"

Julie's intrusion jolted Lee from his sensual haze. He broke eye contact with Meredith and exhaled, struggling to clear his mind of the image of her damp white blouse plastered to the soft swell of her breast and the glimpse of a lacy bra beneath.

"Yes. I'm here."

The breathless quality in Meredith's voice confirmed that the sensual awareness hadn't been one-sided.

Julie darted through the door and stopped. Lee saw the curiosity bloom in her face and knew he had to lay it to rest. With as much nonchalance as he could muster he strolled away from Meredith.

"Mrs. Dixon called and wants to know if you can come over ASAP," Julie said after a long pause. "She wants to talk to you about some idea for tulips in the bathroom. You know what she's talking about?"

Lee glanced over his shoulder at Meredith, who was still attempting to wipe the stain from her blouse.

"I, uh, spilled my coffee. Yes. I know what she wants, but why didn't she call me here in the studio?"

"I don't know. She said the line was temporarily disconnected or something."

"That's impossible." Meredith picked up the portable receiver lying on the counter and held it to her ear. "Dead," she sighed in disgust. "I forgot to charge the dumb thing again. I'll run up to the house and call her."

Lee didn't trust himself to look at Meredith again so he stared blindly at a sample board until he heard the door close behind her.

Once again he'd ended up on the losing side against Meredith. He'd come to the studio to apologize for the past but instead found himself on trial and at the mercy of Meredith's sensuality. Whenever he touched her, his body behaved in a damned peculiar way. Every nerve still reverberated through him with a low-level intensity he couldn't shake.

Lee rubbed his hand down the back of his neck. Meredith was one of the most sensual women he'd ever met. Everything about her begged to be touched. The faint throbbing in his groin reminded him of the satin-soft feel of her wrist in his hand and the throbbing pulse that had beat rapidly under his thumb.

He wanted to stay close to her, to touch her, but the idea was as frightening as it was compelling. He felt as if he were sitting at the top of a roller coaster, eager to take the plunge yet at the same time fearful of the danger. The sensation was vaguely familiar. He'd always felt this tug of war with Meredith.

He understood why his body might have responded to her with little provocation. She was incredibly sensual. What disturbed him was the way she jostled vague sensations deep inside him. Feelings he couldn't name and was even more reluctant to examine.

He turned around and found himself facing Julie's inquisitive eyes. He shifted uncomfortably with unaccustomed embarrassment. What did you say to an eleven-year-old girl? Especially one who might have seen you with your hand on her mother's breast?

He had no experience with children. To him, they were as alien as any creature from outer space. He grappled with his problem until he remembered something Grandma Stratton had once told him.

Children are no different than adults. They may have less experience with life but they want to be respected, appreciated and liked just like everyone else.

Deciding to try Grandma's advice, he faced the young human. "Your mother's a very talented lady."

Julie beamed back at him. Apparently the compliment was the right thing to say. Infused with new confidence he ventured another comment. "I've been looking at some of her work. It's very impressive."

"She's pretty cool for a mom," she said, coming toward him, a sly smile on her cute face. "So, I guess you finally remembered her, huh?"

Caught off guard by her candor, it took Lee a moment to find his voice. "Yes, I did."

"She's changed a lot since she was a teenager. She's really pretty now."

Lee smiled. He couldn't argue that point at all. Meredith was indeed very pretty. "Yes, she is."

Julie hoisted herself up onto the broad worktable that stood in the middle of the room. "What did you do to her that got her so bent out of shape?"

"She didn't tell you?"

Julie shook her head and Lee breathed a sigh of relief. He wasn't able to deal with the past as it was, he didn't need to try to defend himself to both the Cole women.

"I made a bad decision that hurt her."

"Why did you do that?"

Lee frowned at her frank curiosity. "Sometimes we do stupid things when we're young."

"Did you apologize?"

Apparently Meredith wasn't the only one who could put him on the witness stand with ease. "Not at the time, but I tried this morning. She wasn't very receptive."

"Yeah, I figured that. It takes her a while to get over a mad."

"I wanted to explain but—" He shrugged.

Julie nodded knowingly. "But she told you it didn't

matter. It's all in the past and she's forgotten all about it, right?''

Her insight astounded him. "Yes, something to that effect.''

"Trust me,'' Julie said with a nod, "she remembers. She never forgets anything. She remembers everything I ever did from the time she picked me.''

Her choice of words puzzled him. "Picked you?''

"I'm adopted. Mom picked me when I was almost four.''

The surprise of Julie's announcement gave way quickly to admiration. Even as a young woman Meredith had an unusual capacity for giving of herself. He was glad that hadn't changed. "I didn't know. You look so much alike. The red hair and all.''

Julie smiled. "Yeah, that's why she picked me, because we're so much alike.'' She jumped off the worktable and tugged at her ear. "You know, I think you should talk to Mom again. She's usually pretty fair about stuff. You made her really mad but I'll bet if you were real nice she'd get over it.''

Lee smiled back at her, warmed by her concern. There were more similarities between mother and daughter than just their red hair. "Thanks for the advice. I'll take it under consideration.''

"See ya later.''

Julie dashed from sight, leaving Lee to wonder if her suggestion was worth trying.

Meredith made her call to Mrs. Dixon then headed for Walt's study. She had to know how things had gone and to make sure Walt was holding up all right. She refused to allow Lee Stratton to jeopardize his father's health.

She stopped just inside the door, waiting quietly when

she saw he was working. He looked up and motioned her to come in.

"Are you all right?" she asked.

Walt glanced at her briefly. "Why wouldn't I be?"

"Well, I know Lee's return was a surprise. I just didn't want you to be upset by it. I debated whether to call you at the hotel last night but I didn't want you driving home preoccupied. I'm sorry I couldn't have given you more warning."

"No problem."

"Did everything go all right between you two?" she queried, watching her friend intently.

Walt shrugged. "As well as can be expected. The boy's hardheaded as a mule." Walt rose and walked to the filing cabinet.

Meredith could see Walt was holding all his real feelings inside. While she admired his fortitude she knew suppressing his emotions could be dangerous to his condition. "Did he say why he came home after all this time?"

"Nope."

Meredith tucked her hair behind her ear. It was obvious from Walt's curt response that he was more upset by his son's arrival than he was willing to let on. She struggled to control her rising irritation. "He could have at least called or dropped a note in the mail first."

"He probably didn't think of it," Walt said, returning to his desk.

"No, I'm sure he wouldn't," she agreed firmly. "He figured he could just walk right in here as if he'd only been gone a few hours. He probably didn't give a second's thought to how you might feel about it. Never considered for an instant that to appear like some genie from a lamp might be a thoughtless way to show up after five long years."

Her irritation swelled and she paced the office, crossing

her arms over her chest. "All he probably thought about was what he wanted. How typical."

Meredith looked over at Walt who was watching her with narrowed eyes. Suddenly she had the feeling that her complaining was all one-sided. She shifted her weight and clasped her hands in front of her.

"Well, like I said..." Walt muttered absently, "I wasn't all that surprised to see him."

Now she understood, Walt was trying to downplay his true feelings and keep her from worrying. "You weren't?" she asked softly.

"No. I figured he'd end up here since the wedding was called off."

Meredith stared in surprise. "Wedding?"

"Yeah. His intended called it off two days before the big event."

Lee *jilted.* It was the last thing she expected to hear about him and it took some of the wind out of her sails. "Oh."

He didn't seem very upset for a man left at the altar. If it was anyone else she'd have figured he'd come home for some TLC but Lee the Ice Man Stratton wouldn't do that.

Walt frowned and came toward her. "What's got you so stirred up about Leland?"

"I'm not stirred," she replied, shoving any sympathetic feelings for Lee out of her mind. Why should she feel sorry for Lee? If he didn't care, neither did she. Walt was her concern at the moment. "There's no excuse for a son who hasn't been home in years to suddenly pop up like some jack-in-the-box with no warning at all."

"Uh-huh," Walt mumbled thoughtfully. "Well, like I said. I half expected him."

Bless his heart. He was trying to make her think he was taking it all in stride.

"Mom?"

"In a minute, Julie." She turned back to Walt. "I'm just worried about you. I don't want to see you hurt. He has absolutely no concern for your condition. All he cares about is himself."

Which is probably why his fiancée left him, she thought self-righteously. In fact, she was mildly surprised that any woman would even consider marrying him.

Walt frowned at her. "What does Leland have to do with my condition?"

Meredith frowned and tilted her head, puzzled. This conversation wasn't going at all the way she'd planned it. "I don't want you upset by his being here."

"I'm not upset," Walt said calmly, looking at her as if she'd lost her mind.

"Oh." She blinked with embarrassment. Apparently she had completely misread Walt's reactions. Feeling like a complete idiot, she smiled feebly at her friend.

"I like him," Julie interjected. "He's a pretty cool guy, Mom."

Meredith sighed in exasperation. She doubted his fiancée would think that. "Julie, he's not a very considerate person."

"Yes, he is. He's nice, and I don't see why you're so bent out of shape over something that he did eons ago."

Meredith winced. She'd have been perfectly content to have kept that little piece of news to herself for the rest of her life.

Walt was peering at her intently now. "You and Leland know each other?"

"No. Well, yes, sort of." Meredith shot her daughter an I'll-deal-with-you-later glare. "I mean, we did once, a long time ago," she said, playing with a strand of her hair nervously. "We were kids, teenagers actually. It was one summer."

She glanced at Julie, who was smiling in delight at her

discomfort, and then looked at Walt, who was frowning. "Oh, well, I just wanted to make sure you weren't upset." She backed toward the door, wishing she'd never set foot in Walt's study.

Walt shook his head. "I'm not."

"That's good," she said quickly, trying to mask her embarrassment with concern. "That you're not upset, I mean."

"I'm not upset."

"Yeah, Mom, he's fine."

"Good. Well." She glanced between Walt and Julie's puzzled expressions, feeling like the wicked witch who'd just had water poured over her—shrinking, shrinking.

She smiled tightly. "I'd better get back to work." Turning on her heel she beat a hasty retreat.

Meredith maneuvered her eight-year-old car along Pass Road, stopping at the light amid the heavy traffic. She glanced at her watch, impatiently tapping the steering wheel as she waited.

She had nowhere special to be but she'd been jumpy and irritable all morning. Truth was she'd been like this since Lee had shown up two days ago. She dreaded having to deal with him on a regular basis, seeing him around each corner, pretending she was unaffected by his presence.

But her heart never failed to skip a beat and her blood warm when he came near. Thoughts of him created a continuous current pulsating through her like a shorted-out wire.

The mere memory of his hand resting on her breast sent little prickles of excitement down her spine and turned her insides to mush. All she could think of was how he smelled like musky twilight, how strong his hand was and how the raw masculinity of him mesmerized her as completely as a sorcerer's spell.

She was an idiot! She wanted nothing to do with Lee Stratton. That included touching. All she wanted was for him to go away so she and Julie and Walt could return to their nice uncomplicated lives.

She made the turn onto Teagarden, mentally kicking herself for responding in any way to Lee. Yes, Lee was a very attractive, magnetic man but that was nothing more than human chemistry—pheromones or whatever. She was a grown woman and she could overcome this physical thing with a little willpower.

It was the man inside the sexy package she had to remember and be wary off. Lee was not the compassionate, understanding person she'd once believed him to be. He was cold and unfeeling back then and from what she'd seen of him so far, nothing had changed.

To her, the friendship with Lee had been a deep, personal, and special relationship. But to him it had all been a joke—something to do for laughs and to wile away those long hot days of summer on the Gulf Coast.

Even at that age, she hadn't been so naive as to believe Lee's interest in her was from pure attraction. At fifteen she'd been overweight and unattractive. Not at all like the skinny cheerleader types in their bikinis and long hair.

She'd known there was probably a reason Lee was paying attention to her, but he was cute and rich and she was living a fantasy.

But over the three weeks they'd spent together, she'd come to believe he liked her for who she was. Not what she looked like. Their friendship transcended physical beauty.

Meredith had shared with Lee things she'd never shared with anyone before—her greatest fears, her fondest hopes and her secret dreams. The wonder and the magic of it all was that he'd understood!

He'd convinced her he knew the pain of being different, shut out and always alone. Lee had told her things about himself, how he hated boarding school and how he disliked his stepfather and how his life had changed after his parents' divorce.

Lee had been so easy to talk to, so gentle and sweet. She'd discovered that underneath all the swaggering cool was a really nice, sensitive boy. She had truly believed with all her heart that they shared some rare kind of spiritual bond that would connect them forever.

But the fantasy had shattered like spun glass, disintegrated in her trusting young hands. The gentle hero had turned out to be a cruel villain.

Lee had taken her to the Friendship Oak, a place where, legend says, "Those who enter my shadow...remain friends through all their lifetime no matter where fate may take them in after years."

They'd climbed into the heart of the five-hundred-year old tree, sitting on the large wooden platform built high within its branches. They had talked easily, comfortably, then Lee had leaned toward her and she'd known he was going to kiss her. He'd hesitated for a long moment looking deep into her eyes, then lightly touched his lips to hers.

Lightning bolts had surged through her body and flamed in her cheeks. Her heart had threatened to explode in her chest. His kiss was thrilling, perfect, made ever more special by his endearing shyness.

So she'd thought, until the laughing and jeering erupted from below. His friends' cruel taunts echoed in her mind still.

"All right!"

"You did it, man!"

"He actually kissed her!"

She'd turned to him for an explanation. But he'd had none. Immobilized with shock and humiliation, she could only sit and watch as he'd walked away and joined his friends on the ground.

Everything that had happened between them had been a lie, a prank to win a bet by kissing the poor, gullible orphan girl. It had taken three weeks but Lee had finally overcome his reluctance toward kissing her and found the nerve to win the bet.

Pressing the accelerator with more force than was necessary, Meredith turned onto Beach Boulevard.

He'd left her sitting on the platform high in the branches of the tree, alone, rejected, and humiliated. She didn't know how long she sat there, numb and wanting to die, hoping to dissolve into nothingness and cease to exist.

Somehow she'd found her way home. Yet in spite of his cruel betrayal, for weeks afterward a small part of her kept hoping he'd come and apologize and tell her it was all a mistake and they really were friends. She was never the same after that. She changed her name, changed her outlook on life and shoved Lee Stratton into a deep, dark corner of her mind, buried him under all the pain and hurt and heartache.

Nothing had ever hurt her as deeply as Lee's rejection, not even the wounds from her brief disastrous marriage. Because of Lee's betrayal, she'd never allowed anyone to get close to her.

Over the years the pain of Lee's rejection that summer had evolved into a sadness in a corner of her heart. Scar tissue had formed over the wound but every now and again something would scrape against it and she would relive the betrayal. Sometimes she wondered if she'd ever get over it.

Meredith turned into the drive of Sand Castle, pulling

to a stop beside Florence who was lifting groceries from the trunk of her car.

"How did the meeting with Mrs. Dixon go?" Florence asked.

"Not well," she replied, shutting the car door. "She decided the tulips weren't realistic enough. She wants them bending as if blowing in the wind."

"Can you do that?"

Meredith exhaled heavily. "Yes, but our agreement was for still, upright, evenly spaced tulips on the bathroom wall. Now I'll have to start all over. So much for making a profit on this job."

"Little profit is better than none," Florence noted candidly.

"I know. But it seems like that's all I ever do is juggle dimes and nickels. Rob Peter to pay Paul."

"That's life, kiddo. But didn't you just tell me the other day that you had enough jobs lined up to see you through the next year? That's a brighter future than you had a while back when you were facing eviction and nearly lost your business."

A flush of humility touched Meredith's heart, reminding her that she had a lot to be grateful for. She gave her friend a hug. "Thank you for reminding me. What would I do without you?"

"Worry too much."

Chapter Four

"So, how do you like being a small fish in a big corporate pond?"

Lee looked up from his lunch in surprise. He'd barely seen Walt since he'd come home. When they did meet for a meal or in passing, the conversations were curt and brief. Now, suddenly, Walt was getting chummy.

"It's fine," he answered cautiously, taking a sip of his drink.

"Just fine? That's it? You like being a lawyer?"

A glib answer was on the tip of Lee's tongue but the frank curiosity in Walt's gaze prompted him to give a more honest response. "I'm good at it."

Walt leaned forward, his eyes narrowing. "I didn't ask you that. I'm good at balancing my books but I don't particularly like doing it. Do you like dealing with all that legal mumbo jumbo?"

Lee tapped the side of his cup nervously. His father's

unusual interest in his life was making him wary and uncomfortable, like waiting for the other shoe to fall. "Yeah, I guess. I like the structure, the basic dependability of it." He looked over at the older man, tensing for his response. But Walt merely nodded thoughtfully and took another bite of his sandwich.

"You always did have a lot of common sense," Walt said quietly. "Do you ever think about striking out on your own and going into private practice? You'd probably be damned good at it."

Lee stared in amazement. This was the second time in two days that Walt had behaved uncharacteristically. Walt never gave compliments. Criticism, Lee had heard frequently, advice had been offered with every breath, but praise had been nonexistent.

The damned merry-go-round was spinning again. Father and son camaraderie was foreign to Lee and he had no idea how to deal with it. "I've considered it. Maybe someday," he finally answered.

Silence hovered around them, growing more oppressive with each passing moment. Lee decided to tackle the subject that had been bothering him since he'd talked to Meredith in her studio.

"So, are you doing all right? Physically, I mean."

"Sure," Walt replied gruffly. "Not a damned thing wrong with me."

"Pen—uh, Meredith said the doctors found a problem with your heart."

"Meredith worries too much. One little spell of indigestion and everyone is ready to schedule me for quadruple bypass."

"Is it that serious?"

Walt frowned at him. "I'm as healthy as a horse."

A flicker of emotion clouded the pale blue eyes and Lee

realized with a jolt that his father was scared. He'd always thought of Walt as fearless, all-powerful and invincible.

But Meredith was right, Walt wasn't a young man anymore. Walt knew it, too, and whether his problems were minor or major, it must be hard for him to accept that some day his life would be over.

A tightness formed in Lee's chest and he took a deep breath, trying to chase it away. "Did your doctor run all the necessary tests? A man of your age should—"

Walt set his drink can down on the table with a bang. "What about my age? I can still work rings around you and anyone else half my age."

The defensive posturing did little to ease Lee's concern. Walt was worried and hiding it the only way he knew how—behind his tough-as-nails bravado. "I'm just concerned about your health."

"Well, don't be. I don't need anybody's damned concern. I know if I'm sick or not."

Walt clammed up after that, refusing to discuss the subject and leaving Lee with a heavy, pressing sensation in the center of his chest. Realizing that Walt was scared and therefore human was unsettling.

For some reason he didn't quite understand, he wanted to talk it over with Meredith. She was close to Walt. Perhaps she could help him understand the man a little better. Even as a teenager Meredith had been wise beyond her years. She'd possessed an ability to read people that he'd never developed.

Lee walked out to the edge of the upper gallery, watching the morning sun drench the beach. He'd been trying to connect with her since lunch yesterday but without success. She was either working on some stencil project across town, running errands or engaged in various activities with her daughter. Lee had been unable to find her alone.

Worthless like a penny.

It wasn't just Walt's health he wanted to discuss with her. There were other more personal things he wanted to discuss with her. Her words had ricocheted in his mind for days. Was it possible that Meredith truly believed that he hadn't wanted to kiss her? Nothing could be further from the truth.

Meredith had been different from all the other silly girls on the beach that summer. She was aloof, mysterious, and while she wasn't a beauty, something about her sweetness intrigued him. The guys had labeled her as stuck-up because she'd ignored them completely.

Lee had bragged to them one day that he could get any girl to fall for him, and it was that arrogant statement that had sparked the bet.

Somehow it had all gotten complicated. When the time came to kiss her, he'd found himself caught in a no-win situation. He'd never had a friend like her, someone he really cared about. He'd wanted to kiss her for himself, but he was scared.

Kissing her meant taking a risk and allowing her access to a part of himself he never shared. He would have been exposed and vulnerable, without the walls he'd created as protection from being hurt again.

He'd kissed her and won the bet, but then he'd walked away telling himself she didn't matter and he didn't care.

A yellow school bus stopped at the end of the drive and Lee watched Julie climb on board. Maybe this would be a good time to find Meredith, before she got too involved in her work. He had to make her understand that he never meant to hurt her.

He followed the porch around to the back of the house to see if Meredith's car was parked below. It was.

Quickly he descended the outside steps to the lower gallery, stopping abruptly at the sight that greeted him.

Florence was in the center of the breezeway, dressed in a loose blouse and pants, moving her arms and legs a in slow, controlled motion like a dancer underwater. No, he realized suddenly, she was going through the movements of Tai Chi Chuan.

A motorcycle club, quilting class and now martial arts. No one could accuse Florence of not living life to the fullest. He only hoped he was as active and adventurous when he was her age.

She smiled when she caught sight of him and temporarily halted her workout. "Hi, there. Care to join me? It's real relaxing. It's called Tai Chi."

Lee nodded. "I'm familiar with the discipline."

"Yeah, it's a great exercise. But that's not why I do it." She came toward him, lowering her voice. "You can kill someone with this stuff, ya know."

"Really?" He wasn't sure if she was serious or pulling his leg. "I was unaware of that."

"Yep. A woman my age can't be too careful, I say."

"You may have a point," Lee conceded.

"You looking for Meredith?"

Lee raised an eyebrow, mildly irritated that she'd guessed his mission so easily. "Is she here?"

Florence gestured toward the tower. "She's in there, I think. But I'm not sure this is a good time to be around her. You have a strange way of making her tense up. Mention your name and—*boing!*—she coils up like an overwound spring." Florence smiled and assumed another position. "Personally, I think it's the best thing to happen to her in years."

Lee wasn't sure how Meredith's being angry at him was beneficial but didn't ask. He knew why Meredith bristled. He was going to get this matter settled now. Getting the facts straight might not remove the hurt he'd inflicted so long ago but he didn't want her thinking he hadn't cared about her or that he'd deliberately hurt her to win that damned bet.

Everything would be fine once he explained it all to her. Then maybe this nagging sense of guilt would be gone from his shoulders.

Lee knocked on the wood frame of the screen door, organizing his thoughts, preparing his case.

Meredith came to the door, carrying a small brown dog in her arms. She stared at him for so long without speaking he wondered if she would refuse to let him in.

"What do you want?"

Lee saw the determined tilt to her chin and realized she wasn't going to make this easy for him. "I'd like to talk to you."

"About what?"

Just that quickly Lee found himself on the witness stand, trapped in the position of having to explain himself to her. But then, wasn't that why he was really here?

"I wanted to talk to you about something you said the other day in the studio. There's a few things I need to clarify."

He knew as soon as the words were out of his mouth he'd used the wrong approach. Her blue eyes turned a steel gray and her mouth became a hard, thin line. It was obvious she didn't want to discuss anything that concerned the two of them.

"I'm very busy."

"Meredith, it's important…it's about Walt." He cursed himself for being a coward. He did want to discuss Walt, but that wasn't the real reason he'd come.

"Is he all right? Has anything happened to him?"

He flinched at the concern that clouded her blue eyes. His falsehood had bought him some time but now it would take all his skill as a lawyer to turn the conversation back to their past. "He's fine, but I'd like to ask you a few questions."

Reluctantly she nodded, pushing the door open with her shoulder. "You'll have to talk while I give little Bucky here a bath."

Meredith stepped aside, allowing Lee to enter. He stopped just inside the room, inspecting her home intently with his sharp green eyes. She pursed her lips in annoyance. "Does it meet with your approval?"

"It didn't look like this when Grandma Stratton lived here."

"No, it didn't," she replied defensively. "I restored all of the original colors and patterns on the walls and ceilings. They were so thick with age and neglect you could barely make out the design in some places."

Meredith faced him, expecting to see a disapproving scowl on his chiseled features. But he didn't look irritated at all. Instead his expression was distant and thoughtful. She remembered then how close Lee had been to his grandmother. He'd spoken of her often that summer.

He probably hadn't been prepared for the drastic changes in the tower and was remembering the way it had looked when his grandmother had lived there.

The image of the Lee from that long-ago summer, the memory of his loneliness, engulfed her without warning. She wanted to believe that his feelings, his understanding of what it meant to be alone and unwanted, had been sincere. How could he have known the way it felt if he didn't feel it, too?

Some of the things he'd shared with her, the words he'd used, could only have come from the lips of someone who truly understood that kind of loneliness firsthand.

Or the person he was confiding in could have been a gullible fool who always believed everything she was told. She'd be wise to remember how her friendship with Lee had ended. She had to remember that everything Lee had said and done that summer had been for one purpose only—to win that bet.

With a sigh of exasperation at her own stupidity, Meredith walked briskly through the kitchen, out into the laundry room, and set the puppy in the warm water she'd prepared. Maybe she could wash away Lee's memory while she washed away the dirt from the little dog. But that lonely boy still peeked out at her from the shadows of the past.

"I didn't know you had a dog," Lee commented, stopping at her side.

"I do now. He's a stray. Julie brought it home."

"Someone must own him."

Meredith frowned. "Maybe. Maybe not. Sometimes people don't want the responsibility of a pet so they turn them loose to fend for themselves."

"There was no collar or tags on him?" Lee asked.

"No," she replied irritably. He was giving her the third degree over the legalities of a homeless puppy. She should have figured he'd completely miss the humanistic slant to this situation.

"Are you going to keep it?"

"Is this a cross-examination, counselor?" she asked pointedly. He started to respond but she cut him off. "If no one claims him, yes. The little guy needs a home and I'm going to see he gets one."

She sent a glare over her shoulder in his direction only to have her irritation vanish at the longing reflected in his green eyes. He looked every bit as lost and abandoned as the little brown dog. She wanted to touch him, hold him and chase away some of that sadness.

Quickly she turned her attention back to the dog. She wasn't about to fall for that again. Lee could look as lost and lonely as he wanted, he wouldn't sucker her in a second time. "So, what about Walt?" she asked, squirting a healthy amount of soap onto the puppy's wet head.

"I thought perhaps you could give me the name of his doctor." Lee slipped his hands into his pockets. "I spoke with Walt but he insists there is nothing wrong with him."

"Dr. Jay Baker." Meredith scrubbed the dog's neck and ears with more vigor than necessary. "Walt hides it well but he's scared. The truth is, he had a mild heart attack. He's been ordered to slow down, to cut back on his hours at the office and basically accept that he's not a young man anymore."

Lee nodded, leaning against the counter. "And as usual, he's too pigheaded to accept anyone else's advice, especially when it goes against his own plans. What did the doctors say? How bad is it?"

"That depends on whether he follows orders or not," she explained, scrubbing behind the dogs ears. "He's scheduled for tests at a clinic in New Orleans next week. But I don't mind telling you, none of us can get him to slow down much. I didn't want him to drive to New Orleans for that meeting but he insisted it was important."

"Yes, I'm sure it was since it involved Stratton Development."

The bitterness in Lee's tone was unmistakable and left a chill around her heart. "You have to tell him to slow down."

"I'm sure he values your opinion above mine," Lee suggested tightly.

"We're friends. That doesn't mean he takes my advice," Meredith replied. "Your father's a very proud man. To him, taking advice is the same as admitting failure."

"Then why would you assume he'd take advice from me?"

"Because you're his son."

Lee shook his head. "He won't listen to me."

"How do you know until you try?" she asked, turning on the sprayer and checking the water temperature.

"I know because he's never cared what I think."

There was a roughness in Lee's voice that drew her gaze to his face but he had turned away and all she could see were the tensed shoulders under his shirt. "That's not true. He loves you very much. He just has trouble showing it."

"You can't show what you don't feel."

Lee turned to face her and the bleakness in his emerald eyes was beyond her imagining. Her breath froze in her lungs and compassion tore at her heart.

For a fleeting moment, looking into those sorrowful eyes, Meredith had the feeling that Lee was talking about himself as much as about his father.

But even as she watched, Lee's expression hardened, becoming unreadable again.

Past experience forced her to doubt her impressions when it came to Lee. She had to wonder if she was seeing emotions that were truly there, frozen behind glacier green eyes, or nothing more than the cold, empty gaze of a man who cared for nothing and no one.

She turned the sprayer on the little dog, rinsing away the suds.

That was the question that had haunted her for fifteen years and continued to plague her since Lee's return. Which Lee was the real one? The warm, understanding boy she'd known those three glorious weeks or the callous young man who had used her to win a bet? She was no closer to knowing the truth now than she had been then.

Caught up in her ponderings, Meredith allowed her grip on the little puppy to slacken for a second. He slid from her grasp and leaped up onto the counter, shaking his drenched fur and spraying everything with soapy foam. Meredith let out a screech and held up her hands to ward off a shower.

"I'll get him," she heard Lee say, and opened her eyes. The little dog slipped through Lee's hands, pounced onto the chair at the end of the counter and down to the floor where it skidded on soapy paws. Lee bent to reach for it only to be hit in the face with a fresh shower when the dog shook itself again.

"Oh, no," she groaned.

Lee wiped his face with the palm of his hand and reached for the dog, this time succeeding.

Clutching the animal close to his chest, Lee brought him back to the sink and offered him to Meredith. "He's quite a handful."

He smiled and Meredith's heart plunged into the pit of her stomach. Lee Stratton's smile gave his air-force recruitment-poster features a boyish charm and rakishness that no female over five could possibly ignore. It had only taken one glance for her own daughter to develop a rabid case of puppy love.

The strong, straight white teeth flashing against his tanned skin had never failed to leave her weak-kneed and tingly. What made his smile even more devastating was the fact that he displayed it so rarely. It had been one of the things she'd teased him about during their friendship. He used his smile like a secret weapon to tip the scales in his favor when he was losing.

But against all her good advice she found herself returning his smile. Her gaze slid down his throat to his chest and the dark spot in the middle of his shirt. "I'm sorry you got drenched for your efforts."

He shrugged. "No problem."

She handed Lee a towel and their fingers touched. He seemed warm, almost vulnerable up close. She looked into his sexy green eyes and felt their hypnotic power drawing her in, making her remember things from that long ago summer. Those memories were still capable of stirring the cold ashes of her heart, ashes that no one had touched in a long time.

For a few weeks she'd known what it was like to be understood, to belong, to have someone care for her simply because they liked her for herself.

Lee had made her feel special.

The wet little dog squirmed in Meredith's arms, jolting her away from Lee's mesmerizing gaze.

"Shame on you, Bucky. You've made a big mess." She patted his head affectionately before dunking him in the sink again.

Meredith hastily finished the bath, drying the dog and setting it on the floor to play, hoping the activity would hide her still trembling fingers.

"Would you like a glass of tea or a cola?" she asked, masking her nerves by playing hostess.

"Cola would be nice."

If she didn't know better, she could almost believe they were friends again, that she could talk to him openly, honestly. She needed someone who understood her the way he had.

"There's something you said the other day that I would like to clear up."

"Oh, what's that?" she asked, handing Lee a soft drink.

"You implied that the reason I kissed you was to win the bet I made with those boys."

Meredith's good mood vanished. She should have seen this coming. Lee was determined to dig up those old bones. She'd gotten caught up in his eyes and that damned seductive smile of his and let herself forget what he'd done. "I don't want to talk about this. I told you it's over and done with."

"Not if you have a distorted view of what happened that night."

She turned to face him. "I was there, Lee. How could I possibly have distorted anything?"

"I can't let you go on thinking I didn't want to kiss you that night. I did, very much."

Meredith planted her hands on her hips. "Of course you did. It was the only way to win the bet."

"Yes, but there was more to it than that."

"I'm sure there was," she agreed sarcastically. "Now, can we please drop this issue?"

"I should have explained it all to you then but I wasn't sure I understood it myself. I want you to understand what happened."

It was obvious he wasn't going to be satisfied until he got this off his chest. So be it. Maybe then he'd go away. Meredith crossed her arms over her chest and faced him. "Well, here's your chance. Explain."

Her offer apparently caught him off guard. He looked surprised and uncertain. She reveled in her momentary triumph, watching as Lee hurriedly gathered his case. She wondered briefly if this was how he looked when he was in court.

"I spent every summer with Walt and my grandmother. I didn't enjoy it since I didn't know anyone here, but that summer I met some local guys and we started hanging around. You were at the beach nearly every day that summer, usually with a dark-haired girl."

"Mary Frances. She was my foster sister."

"Right. Well, you were so aloof, so indifferent to all of us. No matter what we did you completely ignored us. It became a crusade to see which one of us could get a reaction from you first."

An inner torment began to gnaw at her. God, she didn't want to hear this. She didn't want to relive that painful summer. "Did you ever think about just walking up to me and saying hello?"

"No. I guess we didn't," he admitted. Taking a deep breath, he continued. "I'd been bragging about my conquests back home, all of which were a pack of lies. So they bet me I couldn't get you to kiss me."

She bit her lip until it throbbed like her pulse. "I don't want to hear any more of this," Meredith said, holding up her hand.

"Meredith, I want to explain. Do you remember that day at the Blessing of the Fleet? I bumped into you and spilled your drink and then bought you another one?"

Meredith nodded, wishing she could say she didn't remember but the truth was she still remembered everything about Lee, every look, every gesture, every word he'd ever spoken to her. She stared at her glass, unwilling to let him see how well she remembered. "Vaguely."

"I took the bet because it was a good excuse to get to know you better. I'd at least gotten a smile and a thank-you from you. That was farther than any of the other guys had gotten. I figured that gave me a leg up on winning the bet."

She flashed him a look of disdain. "So you were looking at a sure thing?"

"No. I really wanted to get to know you."

"Why?"

Lee looked surprised at her frank question. "Because you were different. You didn't play any of those silly games the other girls did. And you were cute."

Meredith's heart winced against the sting of his lies. If he was trying to cleanse his soul, he was doing it at her expense. She knew what she'd been back then. "I was *not* cute."

"You were, and you became even more so after I got to know you."

She had heard enough. "Okay. I think I know how this story goes from here. Let's see, once you got to know me you discovered that you really did like me and you didn't want to go through with your practical joke but if you didn't the guys wouldn't be your friends. Didn't I see this plot on a TV sitcom once?''

"I know how it sounds, Meredith. But I did like you. You were special to me.''

"But you went through with the bet anyway.''

"Yes. Because I wanted to kiss you.''

"You could have kissed me without the bet," she said angrily. "You could have kissed me before that night.''

"I know," he admitted regretfully. "I wanted to tell you the truth but I didn't know how. I knew I was leaving the next morning and I'd probably never see you again.''

"I'll bet that was a relief, huh?" If she didn't know him better she would have thought he was truly sorry. But she did know him and she wasn't going to swallow his line a second time.

"Well thank you for setting the record straight. You can leave now.'' Meredith faced him, clenching her jaw against the tears that welled behind her eyes, determined to match his cold indifference with her own, despite the fierce trembling of her nerves.

"Meredith, are you sure you understand?" he asked, watching her intently. "I sincerely regret what happened.''

"Oh, I understand. But did you think that a simple 'I'm sorry' would wipe it all out? That a 'Golly gee, I didn't mean it,' would erase it all as if it never happened?" She took a deep breath, releasing some of her anger. "I'm afraid it's not that simple. The bottom line, Lee, is that I thought you were my friend. I thought we had something special. This isn't about the kiss, or the bet or whether you did or didn't tell me the truth. You betrayed me. You turned your back on a friend, someone who cared for you, and I will never forgive you for that.''

Trembling and near tears, Meredith walked out the door,

leaving Lee standing in the middle of her kitchen. How dare he think that a meaningless *I'm sorry* would magically change the past—that an explanation would undo the damage and the heartache.

"I wish he'd never come back here," Meredith complained as she paced the large kitchen in the main house. After conquering her tears and her anger at Lee she had come to the one person she knew would understand. Florence.

"I suppose you're talking about Lee. What's he done now?"

Meredith suddenly found herself reluctant to recount the story. "He's just upsetting everyone, that's all."

"Who's upset?" Florence asked, raising her eyebrows.

"Walt, for one," Meredith replied, picking up a dish towel and twisting it in her hands. "Oh, he's trying to hide it but I can see he's hurting inside at Lee's callousness."

"Oh, you can, huh? Walt seems to be his perfectly normal grouchy self to me."

Meredith shook her head. "That's just it. He's not grouchy at all. He's quiet and thoughtful. Almost withdrawn."

"I think he's tickled pink that Lee is home."

"Lee's coming home the way he did is the problem. The doctor said absolutely no stress," she reminded Florence.

"Having his son home isn't stressful, kiddo."

"Maybe not if he'd been expecting him, but Lee just waltzed right in here without so much as a phone call. He doesn't care one bit about his father or what happens to him."

"You don't know that."

"Don't I?"

Florence took the mangled dish towel from Meredith, smoothed it out and hung it up. "Seems to me the only one who's upset about Lee coming home is you. What did he do to you that you're still nursing that old wound after all this time?''

Meredith started to tell her, then decided against it. She'd dug up those bones so much lately she was beginning to feel like an archaeologist. "I'm not nursing anything. I'm just don't want Walt upset."

"You sure that's all it is?"

"Yes, of course."

"You're getting awfully prickly for no reason then."

"I didn't say I didn't have a reason. I don't like him or his frozen-tundra attitude. He's self-centered, unfeeling and heartless."

"Well, now, I don't get that feeling at all. I've talked to him several times and he seems more sad than cold."

Meredith kept getting the same impression but she was wrong and so was Florence. "Well, don't trust what you see. Lee Stratton is very good at convincing people he's sincere."

"Sincere or not, he's a good-looking son of a gun. You can't tell me you haven't noticed."

"Good looks mean nothing to me," she said, picking up the towel again.

Florence snatched it back. "Now who's being insincere? I know you. I know you'd like to have a man in your life."

"I don't need a man in my life to feel complete."

Florence spit out her favorite cuss words. "Don't sing that old song to me. You were born to have a family and until yours is completed you aren't going to be happy. And what you need to finish the job is a man."

Meredith sighed in irritation. "If the right man comes along, then of course I'll consider it, but I'm not going to grab the first eligible male who walks into the yard."

"Nobody's saying you should. All I'm saying is that

you won't even take the time to consider the men who come calling. You treat 'em as if they were annoying little gnats."

"I have no interest in them," she said, tucking her hair behind her ears.

Florence stood in the middle of the kitchen, arms akimbo. "One of them happens to be the most eligible man in the state!"

"He was a little too fond of the gambling boats."

"What about that nice doctor? The pediatrician, Doug something?"

Meredith shook her head. "Far too dedicated."

"The federal agent?"

"Too dangerous a job."

"The teacher?"

"No spark."

Florence threw up her hands. "Well who the hell does that leave, dearie?"

Meredith crossed her arms over her chest. "I won't commit to someone who doesn't want the same things I do. I have expectations that I refuse to compromise."

Florence frowned. "Just what do you expect from a man, anyway?"

Meredith lifted her chin. "He has to be moral, upstanding, and willing to fight for his beliefs. Have a good job and be supportive of my work. He has to be warm, tender and understanding. Devoted to his family first and foremost. He can never hurt me or let me down, he must be honest, forthright and never use people for his own advantage."

Florence stared at her for a long moment. "That's not a list of expectations, that's a fantasy hero. No one could live up that combination of James Bond and Dudley Do Right.

"Look, honey, my late husband George was a good

man, but he wasn't perfect. He was as thickheaded as a tree and as old-fashioned as they come. He didn't like me working or doing my crafts. He wanted me sitting by his side when he watched TV whether I wanted to or not."

Meredith shook her head in bewilderment. "That's horrible. Why did you put up with it?"

"Because I loved him," Florence said, patting Meredith's hand affectionately. "Football was his one weakness. Having me beside him to watch the game was his one quirk. Compared to what he could have been doing, it seemed a small compromise to make each Sunday afternoon."

"You had a right to do as you pleased."

"Honey, I always did my own thing. George just never realized it. He was a kind, gentle and generous man. He was faithful and hardworking and I never doubted for a moment that he loved me. He was what he was, and I loved him. What else really matters?"

"So where do you find the Georges of this world?" Meredith said wistfully.

Florence smiled and winked at her. "You don't find them, sweetie. They find you."

Chapter Five

He'd apologized. He'd explained. So why wasn't it enough?

Lee stared out at the murky water of the Gulf as it washed upon the sand, Meredith's last words lapping at the edges of his mind like the waves.

I will never forgive you.

He couldn't blame her. He'd never forgiven himself. He'd walked away, knowing he was turning his back on a friendship, knowing he was leaving her all alone, but unable to stop himself from leaving.

It was just the way he was. He walked away. He could walk away from anyone without a thought. It was something lacking in him. Some error in his DNA that prevented him from being able to care the way other people could. He'd never known a regret, never got homesick, never mourned the loss of a close friend.

Except once. He hadn't been able to completely remove

Meredith's memory from his mind or his heart. She was always there, in some dark, distant corner, her sweet face filled with disillusionment and shock, begging him for a reason for his betrayal.

He'd known his leaving would hurt her. It hurt him. But he'd just hoped the hurt would go away. He'd been wrong. He'd wished a thousand times he could apologize and explain about that night. But today, when he'd finally gotten the chance, it hadn't changed a thing.

Even to his own ears his explanation had sounded childish and superficial. He'd examined the events repeatedly in his own mind and come to the conclusion that if he could make Penny understand how the situation had come about then she would forgive him and everything would be all right between them again. He saw now that his mistake was in failing to look at that night through her eyes.

He'd hurt her more deeply than he'd ever imagined.

I'll never forgive you.

No one with her capacity for love and compassion would turn her back on a friend and refuse forgiveness. Not unless she'd been hurt beyond redemption.

The hell of it was, even if she gave him a second chance he didn't have a clue how to do things any differently. He was no more equipped now to handle her generous spirit than he'd been at seventeen. That's why he'd left her on that platform high inside the tree. The honest outpouring of emotions she'd lavished upon him had been too unfamiliar, too frightening to handle.

Love, joy, anger, and seemingly every other emotion in the spectrum came easily for Meredith. They were as natural to her as breathing. For him, even the smallest emotion was painfully difficult, if not impossible to conjure.

Lee pulled his gaze from the water and started back across the lawn toward the house. He stopped and looked up into the sky. Its brilliant blue color reminded him of

Meredith's clear blue eyes. In fact everywhere he looked signs of spring brought Meredith to mind.

The gentle teasing breezes were as soft as the touch of her hand. The vibrant color of the azaleas reminded him of the rich color of her hair. Even the beckoning warmth of the sun echoed the way Meredith warmed everything around her. He'd been home for four days and only now realized that the grass was turning green and the flowers were in full bloom.

He slipped his hands into his pockets as he continued on toward the house. Penny had always been able to open new worlds of sensation for him. For three short weeks he'd lived vicariously through her senses—seeing, hearing, tasting, touching life in ways he never had before or since.

But he'd walked away. Her vibrant, intense world was too foreign to him. Too different from the cool gray vacuum he inhabited. He'd known nothing of closeness then. He still didn't. He had many acquaintances but no real friends. While she adopted everything in sight, little girls, grandmas and dogs. And other people's fathers.

Everything concerning Meredith revolved around giving, loving. Things that made him uncomfortable. Physical passion was easy. It was the emotional passion he lacked.

He'd heard people talk of how they couldn't live if the woman they loved left them. It all seemed so melodramatic and childish. People didn't die from losing a spouse or lover. Love was an emotion. It wasn't vital element to life like air, water or food.

You're incapable of any real emotions.

Lee climbed the steps to the front porch, stopping at the top and turning to stare back at the shore in the distance. Maybe he should accept Doreen's assessment of him and live with it.

But part of him wanted to know what it was like to feel

joy, happiness and love. Something other than the cool gray vacuum of nothingness he knew.

If emotions could be learned then he could enroll in a class the way Florence learned Tai Chi or quilting and the way he'd mastered the practice of law. But how did you learn to love, to feel, when there were no textbooks and no directions to follow? How did you master something when you had no practical experience?

Lee walked out onto the breezeway and saw Julie sprawled across one of the wicker chairs, reading a book. The little stray dog, now more of a ball of brown fur, lay curled nearby on the floor.

"Hello, Julie. Good book?" He smiled down at her but she didn't budge. She continued to bury her nose in the book while one foot bobbed up and down absently. Lee lightly touched her shoulder. "Hey? That must be a fascinating story."

Julie looked up at him, a big smile lighting her face as she sat up. "Hi. I didn't hear you," she said, poking a finger in her ear. "I had my hearing aid turned off."

A terrible sinking sensation came over him as his mind balked at what Julie had told him. "Your hearing aid?" He wasn't certain he'd heard her correctly.

"Yeah, I turn it off sometimes when I read. I can get into the story better that way."

A sharp, cold pain scraped roughly against his heart. Now he understood why she was always tugging on her ear. She was adjusting the sound on her hearing aid. He'd never suspected.

Lee rubbed his forehead, searching for the proper words. He could find none. "I'm sorry, Julie. I didn't realize that—"

"It's no biggie," she said, cutting him off. "I can hear out of this ear okay but the other one is really bad. It happened when I was little. It comes in handy sometimes

though. You know, like when Mom's on the warpath?''
She rolled her eyes in adolescent disgust.

Lee grinned, amazed at her mature attitude. ''I guess
being able to tune people out could be an advantage at
times.'' The thought crossed his mind that so would tuning
them in. ''What are you reading?'' She handed it to him
and he glanced at the spine of the old book. It was faded
and worn as if it had seen far too many readings. *''Anne
of Green Gables.''*

''It's my favorite book ever. Want to know why?''

''Sure.''

''It's because Anne Shirley, the heroine in the book, is
an orphan just like me and my mom. She even has red
hair like we do.''

Lee smiled at her open enthusiasm. She was very much
like her mother. ''I guess that would make it more interesting to you.''

Julie nodded thoughtfully. ''Anne is really more like my
mother though because she goes around making everybody
happy. I'd like to be that way but I'm not.''

''You're not?''

''No, I'm too serious. I don't make people feel good or
anything like that. I make them think.''

There was a wistful, regretful tone in Julie's voice that
bothered Lee. ''There's nothing wrong with being that
way. I'm a lawyer. It's part of my job to make people
think. To make them look at things in a new or different
way and help them find the truth.''

Julie's brow knit in a thoughtful frown for a moment
then her green eyes began to sparkle and she smiled.
''Yeah. I'd never thought about it like that before. Cool!''

Lee felt a strange lightness deep inside that was unlike
anything he'd ever experienced before. For some reason
he didn't understand, giving Julie a better perspective on
herself had also given him a great deal of pleasure.

"So are you staying here a long time? I mean, like, are you moving back home or something?" she asked.

"I don't know. I just came home to..." To what? He still had no satisfactory explanation. "Well, I thought it was time to come home for a visit."

Lee sat in the wicker chair beside Julie, watching as she picked up her dog and hugged him. The sight unexpectedly tightened his throat. Such a simple gesture but one he realized he didn't know how to do—to reach out to another living being. Even a dog.

He was seized with the impulse to walk away but he fought it down, not wanting to be rude to this sweet young girl.

"Do you like living here?" he asked.

"Yeah. 'Course, I don't really remember the other places much. My mom *really* loves it here. She never had a home and this place has been here forever. Like since the town was built or something."

Lee reached over and scratched the small dog's head. It was warm and soft and it soothed him to touch the little guy. "My great-grandfather built Sand Castle in 1893."

"Did you live here when you were little?"

Lee nodded, remembering the years before the divorce and how his life had been secure and happy. "Until I was ten years old."

"Then what happened?"

"My parents got divorced and I had to go live with my mother and stepfather in Houston."

"Wow, bummer. That must have been really awful."

"I suppose it was." He hadn't really thought about it. He'd tuned it out the way Julie tuned out the world with her hearing aid.

"I'm really glad you came to visit us, Mr. Stratton."

Lee didn't know how to respond to her genuine gesture.

It was sincere, honest and freely offered. It felt good. "Thank you, but why don't you call me Lee."

Her smile widened and even the forest of metal that obscured her teeth couldn't diminish the brightness of it.

Well, at least someone was glad that he was here. How odd that it should be a child he barely knew. "Well, I'd better let you get back to your book." Julie looked at him with a guilty expression.

"Actually, I'm supposed to be doing my homework." She nudged a book on the floor with her foot. "History."

"Not one of your favorite subjects?"

"I hate history," she replied vehemently. "It's just a bunch of dumb facts about dead people."

Meredith stopped in midstride when she heard her daughter's loud statement. Julie seemed to grasp all her school subjects with ease, but when it came to history she either couldn't—or wouldn't—apply herself.

"Dead now but alive once."

That sounded like Lee Stratton's deep voice. Doubting her own ears, Meredith peeked around the corner and saw Julie and Lee deep in conversation.

"Yeah, a millennium ago," Julie complained.

Meredith stood immobile, watching and listening, ignoring the fact that she was eavesdropping.

"Not quite. They were people once, kids just like you."

Julie rolled her eyes. "Guys in curly white wigs and high heels. Bunch of sissies."

"Or a group of cutting-edge trendsetters," Lee suggested.

"Huh?"

Lee reached for her book. "What are you studying?"

"The Revolutionary War—1776. I'm supposed to be doing a report on the Declaration of Independence. Boring," she groused. "At least the War Between the States was romantic. I can go to the battlefields and tour the plantation homes. There's even a bunch of reenactments and stuff.''

''There was romance in this war, too. John and Abigail Adams have one of the greatest love stories of all time.''

Julie looked doubtful. ''A love story? You're not just making this up?''

''No. It's true. Did you know John Adams was able to tell the future?''

''What did he ever predict?''

''The Civil War. Adams proposed an antislavery clause but the other delegates refused to support him. He warned them that in a hundred years posterity would prove him right. And it did. Almost one hundred years to the day.''

''Cool. That makes him seem like a real hero.''

''History is about real people and real events,'' Lee explained. ''They were no different from you or me except they didn't have VCRs and compact disc players.''

Julie giggled. ''They played the harpsichord and rolled hoops down the road.''

''Exactly. Try this,'' Lee said, holding up Julie's history book. ''The next time you see the word history, cover up the letters *h* and *i* and think of the book as the rest of the word—story. A storybook.''

Meredith eased back around the corner, her mind spinning like she'd just stepped off a wild carnival ride. From moment to moment her emotions were slammed back and forth between the conflicting images of Lee Stratton before she could catch her breath and sort them out.

What was she to believe about him? One minute he was the ice man, seeing the world in emotionless black and white, unmoved by his father's illness, his treatment of her or anything else for that matter.

The next he was being sweet and thoughtful and helping Julie discover an interest in history, something no one else had been able to do.

Meredith walked into the kitchen in the main house still battling her confusion. The kind and patient man who'd helped Julie was the Lee she remembered. He was the kind and softhearted young man who shared her feelings of isolation and loneliness and made her feel valuable and special.

But was it a true picture of his character or a mask he donned to suit the occasion?

"What's bothering your mind, Mere?" Florence asked. "You still got your panties in a wad over Lee?"

"What? Oh," she replied, pulling her drifting thoughts together. "I guess," she admitted, tucking her hair behind her ears. Maybe what she needed was another opinion. Maybe she was too emotionally entangled to see clearly.

"How do you know when someone is sincere—that they're being themselves and not just being phony?"

Florence frowned as if she didn't quite understand the question. "Well, I suppose you just have to trust them. But I think most folks are what they appear to be. Being phony takes too much energy. Though sometimes," she said, peering over the rim of her glasses, "a person might behave a certain way because they're scared or insecure. The bottom line is that you have to trust your own gut feelings."

Meredith sighed. Back to square one. It all came down to trust and that was the one thing she couldn't do with Lee.

"I think I'll go for a walk on the beach."

"At this time of day?" Florence squawked. "It'll be dark before long."

"I'll be all right," Meredith assured her.

In a matter of minutes she'd crossed the busy highway, descended the seawall and was treading through the thick sand on the manmade beach. Only then did she allow her thoughts to focus on Lee Stratton again.

Trust your gut feelings, Florence had advised. But Meredith's instincts had led her astray before when it came to Lee. He'd deceived her once and she wasn't eager to repeat the experience.

So which one was the real Lee? The arctic man without feelings or the understanding, patient man who took time to help a little girl with her homework?

She stopped on the packed sand near the waves' edge, staring up at the seagulls as they circled the water. Their cries seemed to be asking, Why? Why?

Good question. Why did she keep seeing aspects of Lee that made her forget that he couldn't be depended on? He valued none of the things she treasured. Family, love, sharing. He didn't have staying power. When things got rough, or too intimate, he would walk away.

She wished there was some way to protect Julie from Lee's indifference. Her daughter already liked the man way too much. After the history lesson she knew her daughter's crush would worsen.

Meredith sighed, continuing her stroll down the beach, allowing the cool salty air to untangle her thoughts so she could see things more objectively. Lee had helped Julie discover an interest in history and for that she owed him at least a thank-you.

"What are you doing out here?"

Meredith whirled around at the sound of Lee's voice. His green eyes were narrowed and angry. His mouth a thin, disapproving line in his granite features. "How did you know where I was?"

"Florence told me. You shouldn't be out here all alone."

"I've walked here all my life. It's perfectly safe. Will you please go away. You should have lots of practice in that area by now." Meredith turned and started off down the beach at a brisk pace.

"I want to talk to you," he shouted.

Meredith inhaled loudly in irritation. Darn the man. Why didn't he understand that she didn't want to talk about that summer. "You said your little speech. You made your apologies. Now go away and leave me alone."

The man thought that all he had to do was explain his behavior and everything would be all right again. There was only one fact from that summer that mattered. Lee had used her. All the things he pretended to be were a lie. He wasn't nice, understanding or compassionate. He probably wasn't even lonely. It had all been a game to him, a way to win that bet.

After all, homely little orphans weren't supposed to have feelings. Only rich, handsome people had those. Ha. Lee Stratton couldn't find one decent emotion if his life depended upon it.

She pursed her lips angrily but for some reason that last thought didn't fuel her animosity toward Lee, it diminished it. All she could think of now was how sad it was that Lee would never know joy or disappointment, or even love.

Meredith slowed her pace, kicking at a small clump of sand at the edge of the waves. Why did she care about Lee's feelings? He'd made his own decisions on how to live his life. So now let him deal with it.

"Yee-haw!"

Meredith stopped in her tracks at the sound of the piercing yell. Coming toward her from up the beach was a group of six or seven men, drinking and laughing as they stumbled across the sand.

A small shiver of apprehension snaked up her arm when she realized with a jolt how alone and vulnerable she was. While it was true she walked the beach frequently, she rarely did so this close to dark.

The men drew closer and she saw one of them point in her direction. In an instant her apprehension became fear.

She had stupidly placed herself in a potentially dangerous position.

She was far from the house and there were no other people in sight. There were cars passing on the highway, maybe she should head toward the seawall. She backed up a step.

"Mind if I walk with you?"

Lee's voice came softly over her shoulder, flooding her with relief and gratitude. Thank God he hadn't left her alone as she'd asked.

"It's a public beach," she replied, hoping he didn't hear the tremor in her voice. She wasn't about to let him know how she welcomed his presence.

He fell into step beside her, not talking but lending quiet support. As the men drew near she felt him tense and move a little closer to her side. She'd been a fool to come out here so late alone.

"Howdy, folks!"

Lee nodded as the men passed by and Meredith breathed a sigh of relief. She glanced sideways at Lee. He'd always been thoughtful and considerate that summer. It was one of the things she'd liked best about him. Maybe he hadn't changed so much after all.

"Thanks," she said softly, without looking at him.

"You're welcome."

They walked on with only the gulls and the waves to break the awkward silence between them.

"The coastline has changed," Lee commented after they had walked some distance. "I think I liked it better before the neon and the glitz. You know, the cheap souvenir shops, the mom-and-pop shell stores and that ugly old goonie golf. This just isn't the same."

He was right. The once-empty beach was now clogged with rental stands offering everything from Jet Ski watercrafts and water bikes to parasailing rigs and catamarans. The gawdy lights of the casinos could be seen for miles.

But it was the wistful note in his voice that surprised her. Sentimentality was something she'd thought him incapable of. "You don't like change?"

Lee picked up a shell and tossed it out into the waves. "Not particularly."

"I must admit, I miss the way things were. Simple, uncomplicated. It's the life I wanted for Julie." Thoughts of her daughter reminded her of something else she needed to do. "I appreciate what you did for Julie today." Lee raised an eyebrow in surprise. "The history lesson. I overheard you talking to her. Maybe she'll find something about it she likes now."

"Julie is a good kid. She reminds me of you."

Meredith smiled. It always made her happy when people compared them. "It's the red hair," she explained with a grin.

"It's more than that. She has your spirit, too," he said softly. "She told me that you like living at Sand Castle."

"I do. There's a sense of permanence, peace and contentment here. I'm glad Julie is getting the chance to grow up in this kind of environment. I want her to feel safe and loved and to know a sense of connection with the past."

"And you think she'll get that here?" he asked, his tone sharply bitter.

"Yes, I do. Roots, knowing where you came from and having traditions to reinforce them is important to everyone."

"Always the optimist," Lee replied.

"Always the pessimist," she rejoined. Their opposing views on life had been one of the things they had joked about that summer. She always saw the glass as half full, he, as half empty.

Meredith was surprised he even remembered that. She

continued on, the gentle breeze and the lapping waves taking the edge off her tension. Walking with Lee on the beach and talking to him had always felt so comfortable, so right.

"I know you never understood my outlook on life but being hopeful and positive is the reason I have everything I always wanted. My daughter, my career and especially my home. When I was a child I used to walk by Sand Castle. I thought it was the most beautiful house on the coast. I used to dream that the people who lived there—"

"Were really your family and someday they would find you and give you a locket to prove you belonged to them," he said gently.

Meredith stopped and stared at him in surprise. "You remembered that?"

Lee looked down at her, a warm light shining in his emerald eyes. Time compacted. She was fifteen and he was seventeen. They were friends, soul mates bound by some golden, spiritual cord that nothing could ever break.

"Yes, I remembered. I didn't realize back then that it was my house you were talking about." He broke eye contact and started to walk again. "So, you got your wish."

"I guess I did," she replied, still trying to grasp why Lee would have remembered her childhood fantasy.

"You don't sound sure."

She shrugged. "I live here and I'm very contented, but I don't really belong. It's not my family or my heritage. It belongs to you."

"Does it?" Lee asked doubtfully.

Florence's observations about Lee suddenly came to mind. Maybe Lee was still the sad and lonely young boy she remembered. Maybe his stoic attitude was nothing more than a way to protect himself from being hurt and abandoned again. It was a possibility, but a dangerous one to embrace.

"Yes, because no matter how you feel about Walt, no matter what happens in the future, you'll always know where you came from, who you are. You will always be a Stratton. It'll always be your family."

"'Someday I'm going to have a real family and a home and I won't ever be alone again.'" Lee quoted with a faint smile.

Meredith stared at him in amazement. He really had remembered everything she'd ever said to him. "My husband didn't want children, so after the divorce I decided I would make my own family." She smiled, remembering the day she decided to adopt Julie. "I had to go out and handpick each one of them but I finally got what I wanted."

"Is that when you adopted Julie?"

"You should have seen her. She was such a sad little child. So shy and afraid, clutching this little torn piece of a blanket like it could save her life. I remembered what it was like to be passed over. To grow older and older and realize that you weren't ever going to have a real home. I couldn't let that happen to her. She reminded me so much of myself."

"Worthless and dull like a penny?"

Anger like a match flared inside her. She pulled Lee around by his arm to face her. "How dare you! My daughter is the most valuable thing in the world to me. She's beautiful and bright and special—"

"And so is her mother," he said softly, looking her in the eyes.

Meredith exhaled abruptly. Lee's gently chiding tone had punctured her anger and her defenses. She'd referred to herself in those words the first day he'd come to her studio. It was always the way she felt whenever anyone called her Penny. A penny was a throwaway coin, something people walked over without bothering to pick up because it was worthless.

But it was an old habit to think of herself that way. It was one of the reasons she'd changed her name. She was a different person now. A stronger person. A valuable person.

She let go of Lee's arm. Did he think she was special? Beautiful? He'd said so once. That summer.

"Your family isn't complete," Lee said pointedly. "Wouldn't it be better if Julie had a father?"

Meredith bristled. "A lot of children should have fathers but they don't. You have one and it doesn't seem to have made much difference to you."

A streak of pain flashed behind Lee's eyes. "Point taken."

Meredith regretted her words the moment they were out of her mouth. Shame and remorse washed through her. "I'm sorry. That was a mean thing to say."

Suddenly she was weary. Brushing her hair behind her ears she walked on. She'd been under a lot of stress with Walt being sick and her job and then Lee's return. It was all wearing her down. "You touched upon a sore subject," she said, sighing. "I know Julie needs a father but I'm not going to marry the first man that comes along just so Julie can have two parents."

"I would have thought the men would be beating down your door."

Meredith grinned sardonically. "I'm not the kind of woman men fantasize about."

Lee's eyes widened in surprise. "Then all the men here are blind fools."

She looked at him to see if he was sincere. Another compliment? She wanted desperately to believe that he

found her attractive and that it was desire she saw in his
smoldering, hypnotic green eyes.

If only she could believe that the real Lee Stratton was
that sweet, caring and compassionate young boy she'd met
that summer. But anything good that might have been in
him was tainted by the memory of the way he'd walked
away.

"Ouch." Meredith stopped and lifted her right foot,
looking down at the sand for the object that she'd stubbed
her toe on. An empty brown bottle lay half exposed. She
picked it up and started toward one of the many trash
recepticals along the shore.

"Why can't people at least pick up their own trash?
They act like this is their own private beach."

She dropped the bottle into the can with a loud clatter
and turned to go. "What's that?"

"I don't hear anything."

"It's—a mewing sound." Meredith followed the pitiful
cry to the corner of one of the nearby thatched roofed
picnic shelters. There in the shadows beneath the wooden
steps, huddled a tiny black kitten.

She picked it up and held it close to her heart. "Oh,
you poor thing. You must be starved."

"I suppose you're going to add this one to your menagerie, too," he said.

"Sure," she cooed, petting its head. "It's all alone,
aren't you, little one?"

"You just can't help it, can you?" Lee said roughly.

"What?" she asked, stroking the little kitten gently.

"Loving everything and everyone who comes close to
you."

She shouldn't expect someone like him to understand.
"Haven't you heard? Love makes the world go around,"
she replied tartly.

"I'd forgotten what a Pollyanna you are. The glass is

half empty, Meredith. I'm surprised you haven't learned that by now.''

Meredith could find no valid reason for Lee's sudden disapproval. Apparently he was just naturally sour. "Not only have I not learned it, I've discovered that the glass is overflowing if you know how to look at it properly.''

She walked out of the shelter and turned back up the beach toward Sand Castle, keeping the little lost kitten cradled close under her chin.

Lee followed her but she didn't bother to wait for him to catch up.

"That optimism is going to disappoint you someday.''

She stopped and turned to face him. "It hasn't so far, but then I don't expect you to understand.''

"No, I don't. You're divorced. Love let you down. How can you still believe in it?''

"Love is the substance of life.''

"Love," Lee scoffed. "I prefer to put my trust in things that have real substance. The kind I can hold in my hands and control with my mind and hands.''

Meredith spun around, shoving the little kitten at Lee. He took it, holding it out away from him awkwardly.

"There's substance for you. Now what should I do with it? Leave it here to starve? Or maybe get hit by a car? Or should I take it and give it a safe home and just a little bit of love?''

Lee's stunned and slightly frightened expression would have been comical if she hadn't been so irritated with him. "Here, give me that," she grumbled, taking the kitten back into her hands and nuzzling it against her neck.

"Love isn't perfect, but without it you might as well be dead.''

"You once told me that you weren't sure that love was real," he reminded her.

Meredith blanched. She *had* said that to him. They both

had wondered if love was real or just something they weren't entitled to.

"Love is real, Lee. I've seen it and I've experienced it. Some of the foster homes I was in were havens of love. I swore I'd have that kind of unconditional love in my life someday."

"And what about Julie? Shouldn't you be saving all your love for her and not wasting it on every stray critter that comes along?"

"What is that supposed to mean?"

"Isn't raising a handicapped child enough of a responsibility in itself. Do you really need more?"

His question fanned her simmering resentment. It wasn't the first time the question had been asked and she was getting thoroughly sick of having to defend her decision to adopt a handicapped child to people who didn't understand.

"You just don't get it, do you? You don't understand the first thing about people or love or giving." She started to walk away but Lee took her arm.

"Meredith, please." Lee stopped and rubbed his forehead. "I'm not criticizing. I think what you've done is admirable, but I hate to see you using yourself up this way. Giving all of your energy to Julie, Florence and Walt and every other damned thing that crawls past your door. What do you get back from all this devotion? Who loves you back, Meredith?"

"They all do," she replied, still finding it hard to believe that he didn't understand.

"Do they?" he questioned. "What will they do when they've used you all up?"

His question astounded her. "Love isn't a prescription, Lee. It's not something that can only be refilled once and then you're done."

Lee took a step closer, his gaze pinning her in place with its intensity.

"And what about you, Meredith? What about your needs?"

His unexpected consideration surprised her and at the same time touched something in her she rarely acknowledged. Underneath all the bravado, the commitment to others, the outpouring of love, there was a woman who'd been neglected for a very long time.

As much as she hated to admit it. It felt good to have someone worry about her for a change. To be concerned for her welfare. She really didn't take enough time for herself.

Lee pulled her around to face him, his hands gripping her shoulders. "You can't keep giving this way, Meredith. I don't want you to wake up one day and find yourself all used up."

She looked into his face, the sharp angles made even stronger by the shadows from the moonlight. She ached to let her head rest upon his broad shoulders for a moment, to place her burdens in his capable hands, and know the intoxicating freedom of no responsibilities, no worries.

Lee, the man who seemed so disapproving of everything, was releasing emotions and concerns she'd not looked at in a long time.

She closed her eyes, allowing the warmth of his strong hands to seep into her shoulders and deeper into her body. She shouldn't be confiding in Lee like this but it was so easy. So comforting.

"Ah, my little Penny," he said softly, tucking her hair behind her ears gently. "You spread yourself too thin, trying to be everything to everyone."

"I love them all."

Lee stroked her hair, then tilted her face upward. His

expression was a mixture of admiration and confusion. "How can you find so much love for so many?"

The bewilderment in his voice and in his eyes made her heart ache with sadness. He really didn't understand what she'd been trying to tell him. He didn't understand about love.

"Love is the easy part."

"No, Meredith, it's not. For some people it's impossible."

A stab of sorrow plunged into Meredith's heart. Was he talking about himself? Did he think he was incapable of loving anyone? Oh, how sad. "You can learn—" she began, but Lee looked away.

"Some things can never be learned. It's too late." He reached out and touched her cheek lightly with his fingertip.

She looked into his eyes and saw the lonely, sweet boy she'd fallen in love with. Lee's eyes had always been her weakness. She couldn't look into them and not feel herself inexorably drawn to him, connected.

She allowed herself to take a moment of comfort from him but the moonlight and the soft Gulf breeze and the smoldering glint in his eyes spoke of another kind of comfort she couldn't allow herself to consider.

"I'd forgotten what moonlight could do to your hair," he said softly, running his fingers through it and cupping her head in his hand.

She put her hands on his chest to push him away only to find his arms locked securely around her. "Lee."

Meredith's knees threatened to give way as his touch banished every sensible thought from her head. A cool breeze danced across her back, teasing her and urging her deeper into the warmth of his arms.

She looked up at him but his eyes were focused on her

lips. The realization scared and excited her. "No," she whispered with little conviction.

"Meredith."

There was a question in his voice, one she'd asked herself, one she wanted to explore at the moment. She wanted to know if his lips were as warm and firm as she'd imagined. If he tasted like spice.

He lowered his mouth, so close his breath floated over her cheek. Then he hesitated, as if seeking her permission and in that instant the past pushed itself rudely to the forefront of her mind.

The last time he'd kissed her, the last time he'd hesitated—the betrayal that followed washed over her like a cold wave. She pushed him away and turned around.

She wasn't any smarter now than she'd been at fifteen. A little moonlight, a little understanding, and she was ready to give her heart to anyone, even the man who'd taught her the hard facts of life.

"Meredith, wait."

"Just leave me alone."

Chapter Six

Lee watched as Meredith walked away, fighting down the physical awareness that permeated his senses. Every vein in his body pulsated with desire. His heart pounded and his fingers twitched at the memory of her softness in his hands.

"Damn."

He took a deep breath, and ran a shaky hand through his hair. She was getting under his skin. Each time he was with her, she infused all his senses with new life. He became keenly aware of sounds, sights and smells as never before. Meredith opened a new world of sensations, one he wasn't sure he wanted to inhabit.

But disengaging from Meredith's presence was like slicing off pieces of himself and leaving them behind. Away from her emotionally charged aura, he was deaf, dumb and blind. Lifeless. The thought scared the hell out of him.

Turning, he started to walk back down the beach. There

was no point in returning back to the house. He wouldn't be able to sleep. His mind was spinning with disjointed thoughts that would take hours to clear out.

For a man who made his living through logic and precedents she could confuse his mind with only a glance. She could upend his carefully controlled little world and make him question long-held beliefs and perceptions.

He'd always adhered to the belief that people should handle their own problems and responsibilities. But when he'd held Meredith on the beach and felt her tremble against him, he wanted nothing more than to protect her, to take her fears and insecurities upon himself and ease her burden for a little while.

He closed his eyes against the memory of her cradling the little kitten lovingly to her neck. She just couldn't help giving love to everything she touched.

But that lavish outpouring of love for a stray cat had angered him. He couldn't stand by and watch her waste that love when there were others who needed it more. Like Julie.

He'd tried to express his concern about her carelessly taking on unnecessary responsibility but he'd only succeeded in sounding disapproving.

He turned back toward Sand Castle. Meredith was out of sight; he was alone. The weight of that thought pressed down upon him heavier than usual.

That long, low whistle of a passing train seeped into his soul, mimicking his empty life.

Love is real.

Meredith almost made him believe it was true. He'd looked into her eyes and found himself yearning for things he had no business wanting, things like a home, a family and love.

It had been so long since he'd even wanted to care about

something other than his work he wasn't sure he could recharge those emotional batteries.

She'd been right about him. He didn't understand love. Her warmth tempted him to try. Each time he saw her with Julie, or Florence, even Walt, her love for them was so strong, so powerful that he had the feeling if he stood too close he would be caught up in it, as well.

The hell of it was, he wasn't sure which would be worse, being engulfed by all that warmth and emotion or being on the outside looking in.

He wished he could talk to Meredith about his confusion, the way he had that summer. He could use her help and advice on why he was incapable of feeling like everyone else.

I'll never forgive you.

The irony of the situation didn't escape him. He stared up into the starless sky, a cynical smile on his lips. The one person who'd understand his dilemma, who could help him get off this damned perpetual merry-go-round, had no desire to help him. And he had no one to blame for that but himself.

The fading train whistle echoed in his ears and reverberated inside his chilled heart. Maybe it was safer after all to be alone. A woman so full of love as Meredith could only reject a man who was as dead inside as he was.

"Then you'll come?" Julie asked eagerly.

Lee couldn't help but grin at her childish anticipation. He had been on his way to his car when she'd stopped him in the middle of the yard and asked him to come to supper the next night. While he was at a loss to explain why she would invite him, he was strangely warmed by her gesture. Like her mother, Julie was blessed with some unfathomable ability to make others feel good.

"I'd like that very much but..." he replied cautiously.

Meredith had made it clear she wanted no part of him. "Is it okay with your mom?"

"Oh, sure," she reassured him quickly. "No problem. Do you like spaghetti? That's all I can fix really good."

"Spaghetti is one of my favorites." He ignored the voice that taunted him, that whispered the truth about his eagerness to accept Julie's invitation. He wanted to be near Meredith. He wanted to bask in her warmth, in her softness, even if his hungry eyes were the only part of him that would be satisfied.

She smiled broadly. "Great."

"Julie!" Florence called, coming down the walk toward them. "Take this critter over to your house." She held out a small wire cage with something furry inside.

Julie took it gingerly. "What is it?"

"A hamster. The kindergarten teacher wants to find a nice home for it before school lets out for the summer. I figured your mother wouldn't mind."

"Gross," Julie groaned. "A rat."

"Hamster," Florence corrected, digging her keys from her voluminous purse. "Beauty is in the eye of the beholder, remember?"

Julie walked off toward the tower, muttering to herself. As Lee watched her go, he became aware of a growing irritation, not unlike what he'd felt the other night when Meredith found the cat.

"Why does she do that?" He turned to Florence for an answer. "Is it her mission in life to collect every stray on the Gulf Coast?"

Florence smiled at him. "I assume you mean Meredith and not Julie."

Lee nodded.

"Well, I suppose you could call it a mission. I like to think of it as a loving gesture. She just can't stand to see anyone or any thing without a place to belong."

His irritation increased. No one seemed to understand his concern. "This menagerie she's building takes time and energy and money. From what I can see she's in short supply of all three."

"So you think her little habit is a bad thing?"

"It is if she neglects herself in the process," he said firmly. "She has enough on her with Julie. She shouldn't throw away her love on stray cats and hamsters."

Florence peered at him over her glasses, nodded thoughtfully. "What if Meredith doesn't think she's throwing anything away?"

Florence's pointed stare made him uncomfortable. He felt like he was back in school facing a pop quiz from an eccentric teacher.

"She needs to take care of herself first."

"But that's who Meredith is. She gathers the homeless, the lost and the lonely to her heart and wraps them in love."

"Love." Lee shook his head. "I can understand her wanting to adopt a child, to share her love with another orphan, but taking on all these others."

"What are you scared of, Lee?" Florence asked.

Her blunt question sliced through him and made him wonder if he was so transparent that everyone could read his feelings but him. "Nothing," he said, looking away.

"Could it be you're afraid Meredith will use up all that love of hers and there'll be nothing left for anyone else?"

A tidal wave of fear and vulnerability crashed into him, threatening his control. He refused to look at Florence, to let her see the truth in his eyes.

"Don't worry," she said softly. "The sun will come up tomorrow and Meredith will always find more love in her heart for anyone who might come along and need it."

Lee stood on the porch a long time after Florence left, feeling lost and indecisive. He was usually a calm and controlled man who made decisions based upon logic and reason. But now he was increasingly tense and on edge. He constantly battled a feeling of being adrift and searching and there was a persistent tightness in his chest he'd never experienced before.

Was Florence right? Was he afraid Meredith wouldn't have any love left for him?

I'll never forgive you.

It was a moot point. Reaching into his pocket he unwrapped an antacid and popped it into his mouth, hoping to ease the persistent burning in his chest.

Stress. That's all it was. He had to stop reacting to the changes and regain his control. Closing his eyes he systematically began pulling on the cool gray armor that made him untouchable. But for some reason the fit had become uncomfortable.

The poignant wail of a train whistle intruded into his thoughts. He was almost used to the sound now. Perhaps he would adjust to this discomfort, as well.

Meredith scooped a can of cat food into a small dish and set it in front of the rescued kitten, remembering for the hundredth time the night she'd found it. If it had been left to Lee, the poor little thing would be abandoned on the beach. It was hard to muster any real indignation, though, because he'd seemed more puzzled than annoyed.

The look on Lee's face when she'd thrust the kitten into his hands had said it all. He was clueless about love. And that realization had erased much of her anger and left her feeling sorry for him. What an empty life he must have. No love. No family.

She filled the water bowl and stood staring at the floor. Why would Lee go to all the trouble to remember her dream about living at Sand Castle, about having a family of her own? Why had he filed away something so inconsequential?

She wanted to believe he remembered for the same reason she did—because he cared. Because their few weeks together had been important to him and their friendship had been more than a schoolboy prank at her expense.

If only she knew what to believe. When it came to Lee Stratton, her judgment was unreliable. She'd truly believed he had cared about her that summer but in the end he'd betrayed her.

Her heart wanted to believe the sadness she glimpsed in his eyes. The loneliness and the longing. But her head reminded her how he'd duped her once before. How painful his rejection had been and how she could never trust his words or his actions again.

Why couldn't she keep the three sides of him separate? Nice guy, bad guy, sexy guy. They kept intermingling, confusing her, each one intruding upon the other until she almost forgot her vow to never trust him again.

He'd been jilted by his fiancée. For all she knew he could be looking for a little comfort from the first willing woman with a warm bed.

Pouring a glass of tea she headed upstairs to the desk in the corner of her room. She'd been putting off figuring her sales tax and now it was going to be a rush to get it done on time.

Her gaze was drawn to the French door and the balcony beyond. Memories of that first night and her talk with Lee played in her mind.

If it were a simple matter of friendship, a truce for the length of his visit, she could handle it. But there was a new twist in their relationship now, physical attraction. She'd always found Lee disturbingly attractive. At seventeen he'd made her heart pound, her palms sweaty and her breath short.

Now at thirty-two he made her body sing and quiver to songs and rhythms she'd never known. His attraction was more powerful than her inexperience could withstand. If he touched her again she wasn't totally sure she wouldn't cave in and throw caution to the wind.

She couldn't let herself forget that Lee met none of her requirements for a man. He stood on the opposite side of the platform. Maybe, if she were alone, she might entertain the risk of becoming involved with him. But she had Julie to think of now. The girl worshiped the man and Meredith couldn't risk him shattering her daughter's dreams the way he had hers.

But despite everything she couldn't forget how wonderful it had been to have the emptiness chased away and the loneliness replaced with understanding. Lee was still the easiest person to talk to, to confide in.

There'd been that moment on the beach the other night, held in his arms, warm, safe, protected. The rapid beating of his heart under her hand had made her feel desirable as a woman, alive and sensuous, things she hadn't felt in a long time.

The problem was, she never knew which Lee she was dealing with. The tender, understanding boy who'd made her believe she was special? The cold, unfeeling rich kid who'd won his bet then walked away, leaving her heartbroken? Or the adult man, virile and potent, who could strum the strings of her physical being with little more than a glance from his dreamy green eyes? The man who knew nothing about love.

What had he meant when he'd said, *For some people it's impossible?* Did Lee believe that he wasn't able to love?

Then there was that cloud of sadness that drifted across his eyes and the huskiness that roughened his voice at unexpected moments—signs of a still-lonely man? She remembered vividly how it felt to be alone. She was beginning to feel sympathy for Lee that she didn't want to feel.

Whichever man was the real one, in the end it didn't matter. She wasn't getting involved. Focusing her attention on taxes again, she turned on the calculator and went to work.

"Mom," Julie shouted as she dashed into the room, "can I have a friend for dinner tomorrow night?"

Meredith didn't bother to look up from her desk. "I don't know, Julie, I have a lot of work to do."

"I'll do all the cooking. I'm going to make spaghetti and garlic bread and salad and maybe we could get some ice cream for dessert."

Meredith looked up at Julie and the eagerness in her eyes was hard to resist. She didn't want to refuse but she was so far behind she couldn't afford to be distracted. Lee was doing his share of that as it was. "Julie—"

"Please, Mom?"

It was always so hard to say no to her daughter. "All right, but you'd better promise to clean up afterward. No leaving the pans to soak overnight and no tomato sauce stains on the floor to scrape off in the morning."

"I promise."

"Julie, I mean it," she reiterated. "You will be totally responsible for the whole meal. You understand?"

"Yeah. I will." Julie nodded. "I promise."

Meredith pulled her close and gave her a quick hug. "Good girl."

"Can I have supper at seven?"

"Why so late?"

"It's more…sophisticated."

"I suppose. But tell Robin to be on time. I don't want this dragging out until all hours, even if it is a Friday night."

Meredith turned her attention back to her work, wondering about her daughter's sudden interest in cooking. Julie usually avoided the kitchen like the plague.

Reluctant to look a gift horse in the mouth, Meredith decided to enjoy Julie's domestic phase while it lasted.

"Mom, you're not wearing *that* are you?" Julie asked when Meredith came downstairs the next evening with her jeans and sweatshirt on.

"Can't you put on a dress?"

"Why? There's nothing wrong with what I'm wearing."

Julie's eyes filled with pleading. "It's my special dinner and I want to look good for...my company."

Meredith stared at her daughter wondering what had gotten into her normally levelheaded child. "Julie, Robin has seen me in jeans before."

"Please, Mom. I'm trying to set a mood here."

"For Robin?" Meredith asked in astonishment. Julie was positively obsessed with this meal being perfect.

"I have to practice sometime, don't I?"

Meredith's resistance crumbled in the face of Julie's desire. It was obvious that this evening meant a great deal to her daughter. "Okay. All right. Do you have something particular in mind that I should wear?"

Julie thought a moment. "How about that pretty blue dress. The one that you said matches your eyes."

"To eat spaghetti in? Julie—" She started to protest but didn't. "If it's that important to you, all right. But you'll owe me one, kiddo."

Back in her room, Meredith pulled up the zipper and walked to the mirror for a quick inspection. She had to admit, the blue dress with its simple lines and soft feminine fabric was flattering. It seemed a shame to waste it on Robin, though.

She shook off the thought and hurried back downstairs.

The doorbell rang at the same moment she stepped into the kitchen.

"Mom, would you get that?" Julie asked.

"Come on in," Meredith shouted.

"Mom!" Julie whined. "Can't you go to the door?"

"Julie, you're driving me nuts. Okay. Okay," she agreed at Julie's pleading expression. It was easier to give in than fight.

Meredith walked through the living room and pulled open the door. Her heart plunged into the pit of her stomach when she saw who stood there.

A positively drop-dead gorgeous Lee Stratton stared back at her.

Lee knew the moment he saw the stunned surprise in Meredith's eyes that accepting Julie's invitation had been a mistake. She either hadn't realized he was coming or had planned to be gone before he got there.

"I hope I'm not too early," he said, wondering how Meredith would react. A small frown furrowed her brow.

"Early. For what?"

"For dinner," he explained. "Julie said to be here a little before seven."

He watched the realization dawn in her blue eyes like the sunrise. He'd been right. She hadn't known he was coming.

"Is there a problem?"

"No. No problem," she said, masking her surprise and stepping back to allow him to enter. "Julianna. Your guest is here."

While he waited for his young hostess to appear, he discovered he was enjoying Meredith's discomfort. For the first time since he'd been home the tables were turned. He had the upper hand and he liked the feeling.

He enjoyed watching the swiftly changing emotions, like the flash of neon lights, reflect in her eyes.

"Hi!" Julie bounced into the room, stopping beside Meredith.

"Hello," Lee said, handing her the bouquet of flowers.

"For me?"

Julie's look of awe and surprise momentarily replaced thoughts of Meredith in Lee's mind. He'd brought the bouquet out of habit. Until this moment, he'd never realized how such a simple gesture could bring such joy to a young girl's eyes.

"Gosh. I've never had flowers before."

Julie's sincerity overwhelmed him and brought a strange warmth into his chest. "I'm pleased to be the first to bring them for you. I'm sure you'll receive many more."

Feeling a bit out of his league he looked at Meredith, pleased to see a begrudging gratitude in her blue eyes. Clearly the way to her heart was through Julie. He filed that information away for future consideration.

Meredith moved quickly to her daughter's side and when she passed him her fragrance wrapped itself around him with seductive embrace. Like walking through a spring garden, intoxicating.

While Meredith was distracted with her daughter, Lee took advantage of the moment to feast his eyes upon her.

The provocative blue dress accentuated every gentle curve, the small of her back, the rounded hips, the small, high breasts. The silky material whispered with every movement like a lover's voice in the night. The image of them together lodged in his mind and refused to leave.

As if sensing his eyes upon her, Meredith turned to look at him, tucking her hair behind her ears. He smiled inwardly at her revealing habit. She always did that when she was feeling uncertain of herself.

"Why don't you make yourself at home?" she said stiffly. "I'll give Julie a hand in the kitchen."

"No, Mom. I'm fine. I really want to do this myself. Please."

There was a moment of tension between the two Cole women, then Meredith stroked her daughter's hair and smiled. "All right."

The sight of them together never failed to bring warmth into Lee's heart. He wondered if Julie realized how lucky she was to have a mother like Meredith.

"That was very sweet of you to give flowers to Julie."

Her compliment seemed unnecessary. Lee shrugged and slipped his hands into his trouser pockets. "It's a simple matter of courtesy."

"Yes, of course."

Meredith turned instantly cool again. Though what he'd said to irritate her he didn't know.

"I take it you weren't expecting me?" he asked.

"No. I wasn't. Julie asked if she could have a friend for dinner and I assumed she meant Robin. I guess I should have been suspicious when she wanted me to dress up."

The annoyed look on her pretty face amused him. Some demon inside him urged him to nudge the annoyance to see what would happen. The tables were turned, he had her on the defensive and he found the idea intriguing.

"So if you'd known I was coming you'd have worn rags," he said, advancing on her.

"That's not what I said," she replied, backing away.

The wary look in her blue eyes excited him. He wanted her to be unsettled when he was close. He wanted her to feel a lot of things when he was close.

"I'm glad you made your daughter happy. You look lovely. You should wear that color all the time. It brings out the color of your eyes."

She looked at him, her gaze questioning yet hopeful.

Then her eyes filled with doubt and his gut tightened in regret, knowing he was the source of that doubt. He couldn't blame her for questioning his compliment.

But then he looked deeper and was shocked to see that she doubted her own attractiveness. The knowledge troubled him and he wondered how he could make her see how lovely she was, how desirable.

Suddenly he didn't feel like teasing her anymore. He was making her uncomfortable and there was no reason for it.

"Look, Meredith. There's no point in continuing with this. It's awkward for both of us. I'll just go. Tell Julie I had another engagement."

He started to turn away but she grabbed his arm, the warmth of her anger and passion flooded into him so fast he didn't have time to react. She was vibrating, furious, magnificently passionate and his body responded fiercely to her.

He'd never wanted any woman the way he wanted her now. He wanted to be the only man on earth who could tame that passion, to create it in her with his lightest touch, his deepest kiss.

"No! I will not lie to my daughter and I resent your suggestion. Is that your solution to everything? Just walk away."

She released him. The absence of her touch and her harsh but truthful words doused his rising desire. Plunged from Meredith's vibrant world back into his own cold gray one, he found it hard to respond without effort.

Quickly he pulled on his courtroom persona for protection, until he could regain his spinning thoughts. "I was only trying to make things easier for you."

"Disappointing my child doesn't make things easier for me. She's worked all day preparing this meal and you will not disappoint her."

"What do you want me to do?" he asked.

Meredith looked into his eyes, as if searching for something. He had no idea what she hoped to see. Didn't she realize there was nothing inside him?

"I want you to stay. Eat, enjoy every mouthful and then leave as soon as possible," she said firmly, crossing her arms over her chest.

"All right," he agreed with a curt nod. "It wasn't my intention to further complicate things."

"It's too late for that, isn't it?" Meredith turned away.

Lee harnessed his disjointed thoughts and tried to understand why Meredith was so angry. He had a feeling this was about more than his surprise appearance at the door.

"I think you should know," she said, confronting him again, "that Julie has a crush on you."

It was the last thing he expected her to say to him. "On me? No, I didn't know. Why?"

"Because she's eleven and she's romantic and she sees you as the long-lost hero who swoops into town to magically change everyone's lives."

"I don't understand," he said, frowning. "I've done nothing to warrant her affection."

The grim line on Meredith's mouth softened. "Maybe not. But then, Julie gives her heart easily. She sees someone she likes and they're her friend. No questions asked, no reservations."

"I remember her mother being exactly like that." His compliment brought a glow to her cheeks. Did she have any idea how much of her loving spirit she'd passed on to her child? Did she have any idea how breathtakingly lovely she was? He started to reach out to touch her but controlled the impulse.

As if sensing his intention she backed away, tucking her hair behind her ears. "She'll have her heart broken if she isn't more careful. But unfortunately that's part of life."

Coming from such an emotional woman, her matter-of-fact statement puzzled him. "Are you saying you don't mind?"

"Of course I mind. My heart will break with every crack that appears in hers. But I can't prevent it. All I can do is be there to pick up the pieces."

The helplessness of her position was clearly visible in her eyes. He thought he saw a flicker of pain appear, as well, the pain of knowing what it was like to have your heart broken.

His own heart turned cold and tight. He'd broken her heart and never given a thought to how she would deal with it. He would give anything to take back the pain he'd caused her.

"Who picks up the pieces when your heart is broken?" he asked softly.

Meredith met his gaze, and he could see the memory of that night looking back at him.

Her voice never wavered when she answered him. "I do."

Her remark sliced through him down to the bone, shattering his control like nothing else had. She knew how to hit him where it would hurt most. And he deserved every damn bit of it.

"Dinner is served."

Lee turned away, following Julie into the dining room and shoving his own feelings aside. He wouldn't allow anything to ruin Julie's evening.

Meredith absently swirled her spoon through the melted ice cream. She'd expected Lee to feel like the odd man out tonight, awkward and uncomfortable around the "family" dinner table. But instead she was the one who was feeling shut out and ill at ease. Lee had proved himself very adept at small talk. He'd lost none of his charm where women were concerned. Julie had beamed like a light-house for the last hour.

She wasn't proud of it but she found herself filled with feelings of resentment toward Lee and at the same time a begrudging gratitude. It was hard to dislike a man who was kind to your child.

He was making Julie's evening perfect. And her mother's hell. The kindness, the sympathy, was a trick. A tool he used in his life and in his profession. As for herself and her attraction to him, well that was physical, something she could overcome with a healthy dose of will-power.

True to her promise Julie dutifully began clearing the table after the meal was finished. Unfortunately that left Meredith in the unwelcome position of being alone with Lee again.

She walked into the living room determined to stay a safe distance from him. To her dismay he remained at her side, staring at her with those piercing, hypnotic green eyes. They were unusually green tonight, penetrating, vibrant with a hint of a smile that went straight to her heart.

Ignoring him was nearly impossible. She was disturbingly aware of every aspect of his presence. Everything about him drew her attention. She couldn't keep from noticing how his crisp, white shirt sharpened the angle of his jawline. The trim, dark trousers skimmed his well-muscled thighs with tantalizing perfection. The casual elegance of his sportcoat was a futile attempt to tame his savage sensuality. And the gold watch lay like a slice of civility and control across his strong forearm.

With great effort she forced herself to look away, willing her senses to ignore all that masculine power.

"I see you agreed to take on another boarder," Lee observed, glancing at the hamster cage across the room.

His tone was slightly less disapproving than when she'd

rescued Tweedy, the kitten, but at least he'd opened a safe topic of conversation.

"Its name is Sidney," she said, moving quickly toward the cage. "We weren't sure if it was a boy or a girl and that seemed like a name that could go either way."

"I had one of these once," he said softly.

Lee's voice came from directly behind her. She hadn't realized Lee was standing at her shoulder. She started to move past him, inhaling the strong scent of his musky aftershave. It seeped into her lungs with each breath, clung to her skin like a lover's touch. She forced herself to think rationally.

"What was its name?" she asked, unable to keep from quivering at his nearness and sternly scolding herself for behaving like a woman on fire.

"I think his name was Bogart."

His breath stirred the hair at her temple and when he reached around her and tapped on the cage, all she was aware of was warm strength and the memory of the comfort she'd found in his touch that night on the beach—how she always felt so incredibly feminine when she was with him.

"What happened to him?" She willed herself to remember that Lee's warmth was an illusion. No doubt an aspect of his personality he'd perfected over the years, a lawyer's technique, designed to instill confidence, trust and believability.

Her admonishments were useless. All she could think of was how tall Lee was, how he made her feel dainty and desirable and what a damned fool she was.

"I had to give it away when my parents divorced."

The huskiness in his tone penetrated her sensual fog, replacing it with sympathy and compassion. Lee had spoken often of the bleakness of his life after his mother had left Walt. Everything Lee had loved, everything that had anchored his existence, had been taken away. She ached for him, knowing personally the emptiness he'd experienced. She had so much in her life now. What did Lee have?

"I'm sorry," she said, turning and braving a look into his eyes. The little boy that looked back at her broke her heart.

She wanted to take him in her arms and chase away the loneliness. Wrap him in love and understanding the way she did Julie. She wanted to kiss those firm lips again and again until he forgot the pain—

Lee abruptly broke eye contact. "It was just a pet."

The flat tone in his voice rang false. She knew beyond a doubt that Lee was denying his own feelings, burying the hurt and sadness because dealing with it was too painful.

Sympathy and understanding swelled in her for him. If only he'd stop ignoring his emotions and learn to embrace them, he'd find the pain would start to go away.

Reaching out, she put her hand on his arm and felt his muscle flex. "Losing someone you care for, even a small animal, is painful, Lee."

"Is it?" he said, moving his arm from her touch. "I wouldn't know."

Lee's eyes were suddenly cold and unreadable, his face a mask of emotionless ice. The arctic wind had returned and Meredith marveled at her own susceptibility. She needed her head examined. Pushing past him, she walked across the room and rearranged the pillows for no reason at all.

The silence stretched between them, tense and uncomfortable. Then finally Lee spoke. "Why didn't you tell Walt that we knew each other?"

"Because it had no bearing on our friendship," she replied, punching the last pillow. "And because I didn't see any reason to tarnish his image of you."

Lee chuckled bitterly. "No danger there."

Meredith turned to look at him. The man was emotionally deaf. "Walt is very proud of you."

"No, he'd only be proud if I worked for Stratton Development the way he's always wanted."

"Is that so surprising? Don't most fathers want their sons to follow in their footsteps?"

Lee raised a skeptical eyebrow. "Most fathers want their sons to do what makes them happy."

Meredith had to agree that Walt could be bullheaded, but surely when it involved his own son— "Have you tried talking to him?"

Lee shoved his hands into his pants' pockets and turned away. "Walt and I don't talk."

His refusal to compromise stirred her irritation. One minute she ached for him, the next she was angry with him. "Lee, your father isn't getting any younger. You need to close this gap between you before it's too late. Pride isn't worth it."

"It's not about pride, Meredith."

The hard edge to his voice reminded her who she was dealing with. "No, you're right. It's about family."

"You're family," he said angrily. "I'm a rebellious outcast."

His resentment slammed into her with hurricane force, bringing with it the realization that his feelings were justified. Looking at Lee's visit from his point of view she saw how he could feel shut out. She'd done little if nothing to make him feel welcome.

But the truth was it was *his* home and *his* father, and she had to make him see that nothing had changed. He was the one who had turned his back on his family, not the other way around. "That's not true. Walt loves you."

"Your optimism is distorting your vision. You're not seeing the whole picture here."

"What I see is a couple of grown men acting like little boys because they're too stubborn to compromise."

"That's an interesting theory," Lee said sarcastically.

Meredith was at her wit's end. If she could only get them talking she was sure it would all work out. "Walt is going to New Orleans in a few days. That's a three-hour drive. You'll have plenty of time to talk to him then. Won't you at least try to work things out between you?"

Lee turned to look at her, his forehead deeply creased. "I'm not driving Walt to New Orleans."

Meredith couldn't believe what she was hearing. "You have to. He'll be there for three days and he won't be able to drive home after the extensive tests they'll be running."

"Florence is taking him," Lee said. And he doesn't want his son's help, Lee silently added.

It was all Meredith could do to keep from cursing. His attitude was completely abhorrent to her. "He's your father and he needs you. How can you be so cold and unfeeling?"

His icy green eyes chilled her to the bone.

"It's the way I am."

"No," Meredith said, anger burning deep into her throat. "It's the reason you're alone."

Meredith turned and went up the stairs, unable to look at Lee another moment without slapping his face.

She'd never met anyone in her entire life so completely lacking in feeling, so dead to emotions of any kind. Lee was right, her optimism was getting in the way of her common sense. She had to stop looking for qualities in Lee that simply weren't there.

When Meredith came downstairs a short while later, Lee was gone and Julie was curled up on the sofa, her blue eyes shooting daggers in her mother's direction. "Julie? What's wrong?"

"Why can't you like him?" Julie asked, her lower lip quivering and her eyes brimming with tears. "What did he do to you?"

Meredith should have expected this reaction but she'd been too preoccupied with her own problems with Lee. "Honey, Lee hurt me very badly once and it's hard to forget that."

"I like him. Why can't you be nice to him like you are everyone else?"

"I'm just concerned about you getting too attached to someone who's not quite as wonderful as you want to believe."

"He's nice to me." The tears began to roll down her cheeks.

Meredith moved to the sofa and sat down beside her daughter, taking her hand. "Lee can be nice but he can also be cold and indifferent to people's feelings."

"He's not cold," Julie stated, pulling her hand away. "He's sad and lonely just like I used to be before you picked me."

"Julie, you were only four years old when I adopted you," she reminded her.

"I remember lonely," Julie said firmly, glaring at her mother.

A sharp pang of understanding lanced through Meredith's heart. She remembered lonely, too. She'd never forget the cold, hollow ache that never went away.

Reaching out, Meredith smoothed her daughter's hair away from her face. Was she wrong about Lee? Were her fears clouding her perspective? Probably so, but it shamed her to have her own child remind her about an aspect of Lee Stratton she wanted to forget.

Unfortunately, Julie hadn't seen the other side of Lee's

personality. Meredith had. She remembered how he'd made her feel, how he'd pretended to be her friend and to understand her loneliness. Until he'd won the bet. Then he'd shed the friendship, the warmth and tenderness like a second skin and walked away.

It was the walking away that Meredith was trying to protect Julie from. Because as bad as loneliness was, being betrayed by someone you loved was worse.

Chapter Seven

"You got a minute?" Meredith asked, stopping inside Florence's small sitting room.

Florence frowned and continued her workout with her thigh buster. "Sure, but why do I have a feeling this is going to be one of those sticky topics. The kind where no matter what I say, it's wrong."

"No," Meredith reassured her, leaning against the door frame. Lee's bullheaded attitude had gnawed away at her all night and if she didn't talk about it with someone she was going to explode. "I just want to vent some steam, that's all."

"So vent."

"Julie invited Lee to supper last night and—"

Florence chuckled and nodded her head. "Clever young lady, that one."

"What do you mean?"

"Never mind. So how did it go?"

Tucking her hair behind her ears, Meredith sighed and continued. "The way things always go when Lee Stratton is involved. He is the most coldhearted iceberg I've ever known. I swear there's not one molecule of warmth in his whole body."

"Forty-one, forty-two." Florence continued her exercises as she spoke. "He seems pretty red-blooded to me. Forty-three, forty-four. He can still give me hot flashes when he looks at me with those sexy green eyes."

Meredith couldn't deny that Lee's hypnotic eyes could tempt her to throw over her common sense in favor of things that were dangerous. "It's an act. Don't believe any of it. He might have been warm and compassionate once, but not anymore."

"Once?" Florence stopped squeezing her exercise device and stared inquisitively at Meredith. "You mean, when you knew him before? Which, by the way, you never explained to me. Just what did he do to you that it can still ruffle your feathers after all this time?"

"I'm not ruffled," she replied, glancing down at the floor to avoid Florence's questioning stare. "But I learned my lessons. I won't be tricked again."

"Oh, come on, sweetie, what did he do? Don't leave me dangling like a horse thief at the end of a rope."

Meredith paced the room, sorting out what she was willing to share with her friend and what she should keep to herself. "He was supposed to be my friend but he betrayed me."

"How?"

"He used me to win a bet with his friends." Just the thought of his betrayal could still send tiny blades of pain rushing through her heart. "He's a cold, heartless, self-centered—"

"Whoa, there, slow that train down," Florence urged, putting away her exercise device and standing. "I've been around Lee quite a bit since he got home and the man you're describing doesn't sound like the one I know. In fact, he and Walt seem to be formed from the same mold, if you ask me.''

Meredith stared at her incredulously. ''He's nothing like Walt. Walt is warm, generous, hardworking. He's devoted to his family—''

''Crusty. Hardheaded. Gruff,'' Florence added.

Reluctantly, Meredith agreed. ''Sometimes, but that's just because he has trouble showing how he really feels. I remember when I first met him I thought he was so cold and disapproving, that he didn't care about anything but his work. But then, when I got to know him, I realized that he was really just sad and lonely and unsure how to reach out and—'' Realization struck like a blow.

''Like father, like son,'' Florence said pointedly.

As Meredith looked at the self-satisfied smirk on her friend's face, a layer of shame draped its heaviness around her shoulders. Lowering her gaze, she searched frantically for a reason to leave quickly. She needed time to think through this revelation. ''I have to, uh…call, go…check on, uh—I've got to go.''

She hurried out onto the breezeway, stopping at the railing as her thoughts tumbled wildly inside her head.

Like father, like son.

Florence was right. Julie had made the same observation last night. She'd challenged Meredith's opinion of Lee as cold and defended him as merely sad and lonely.

Oh, she'd seen moments of sadness, shadows of loneliness appear in his green eyes, but she'd refused to believe they were really there because it would neutralize the memory of the boy who'd hurt her and force her to look instead at the grown man. Without the clouds of his past sins she would have to judge him more honestly and fairly.

She didn't want to be unfair. Neither did she want to

think that she'd been ignoring the truth because it was safer for her.

On some level she'd always been aware of the similarities between the two men. She thought back to the time she'd first met Walt and her perceptions of his personality paralleled Lee's behavior exactly.

It had taken patience and understanding to coax Walt out of his shell. But the hard work had been worth it because under that granite exterior she'd discovered a warm, caring and devoted man.

But there was no guarantee that Lee was warm and tender beneath his icy facade. There was no way of knowing what kind of man would be coaxed from inside Lee's frozen world.

I remember lonely.

Julie's words came back to her, twisting her heart with their simplicity and her own memories of a life filled with too much loneliness. Memories of Lee's loneliness haunted her, too. She hadn't been able to turn her back on Walt. How could she turn her back on his son, knowing firsthand the isolation he felt?

Perhaps all Lee needed was someone to show him the way, help him find the part of himself that used to care. Maybe, like Walt, all Lee needed was a friend.

Damn!

She'd been Lee's friend once, and all it had earned her was heartache. Walt had never betrayed her and that, in the end, was still the main obstacle between herself and Lee. He couldn't be trusted.

If Lee Stratton needed a friend he'd just have to look someplace else. It wasn't going to be her. She was having enough trouble dealing with him as it was. Taking on his emotional revival was out of the question.

Meredith looked up at the sound of an engine roaring to life. She watched as Walt put the riding mower in gear and drove off across the lawn. Her heart smiled and her anger faded.

There was more at stake here than her feelings toward Lee. Walt's feelings were important, as well. She loved Walt like a father and she would do almost anything for him. But trying to repair the breech between father and son would put her in the middle and one way or the other she would get burned.

She'd reached Walt through their mutual passion for restoring the past. How could she reach Lee? They had nothing in common. Nothing except a strong physical attraction. An attraction that could be dangerous not only to them but to everyone they cared about.

Thawing Lee from his glacier could have more serious consequences than merely freeing his emotions.

"How did the dinner go, squirt?" Walt asked as he walked into the kitchen.

Julie rolled her eyes. "They fought. Like usual."

"Couple of hardheaded mules if you ask me," he grumbled.

"They're both too blind to see what's staring them in the face." Florence wiped her hands on a dish towel then draped it over her shoulder. "All they need is some enforced quality time together. I say we lock them in a closet until they learn to behave like adults."

"That's the first sensible idea I've heard," Walt conceded. "There's a nice big closet in the south bedroom."

"I've got an even better place," Julie said with a cunning smile, motioning her friends closer.

Meredith collected her date book and stuffed it into her briefcase, smiling as her daughter dashed into the studio. "Hi, sweetie. Wish me luck. I'm going to meet with Ms.

Cress in Mandeville about designing stencils for her new house. I'll be back late this afternoon.''

"Okay. Hey, Mom? Did you ever look around in Walt's attic for ideas for your stencils?"

"No. I've just been too busy but thanks for reminding me. I might find something I could use for Ms. Cress.''

"Why don't we look up there tomorrow?" Julie suggested. "I'll help.''

"Thank you, sweetheart, that's a good idea.'' She walked over and gave her daughter a hug. "You're better than a secretary.''

"Would you care to put me on your payroll?''

"Nice try but no.''

Julie shrugged. "Can't blame a girl for trying.''

Meredith kissed her goodbye and hurried out of the studio. She was looking forward to spending time tomorrow with Julie, just rummaging through the old junk.

Meredith moved aside the large oil painting from in front of a stack of boxes tucked away in a far corner of the vast attic. "Maybe there's something in here,'' she said, lifting the lid off the top box.

"I found a bunch of old wallpaper rolled up behind that chest over there,'' Julie called.

"Bring some over here.'' When Julie came to her side she noticed she was also carrying a rusted birdcage.

"Can I use this?''

"Why? We don't have a bird.''

"We might someday,'' Julie said hopefully, dropping the paper rolls on the floor.

"You'll have to ask Walt if it's all right,'' Meredith told her.

"Great. I'll be right back,'' she said, turning and hurrying toward the stairs.

"Julie, can't that wait?''

"I won't be gone long," she shouted.

Meredith sighed and reached down to unroll one of the faded papers. The first roll was a plain, unexciting green. The second was an ordinary stripe, but the third roll was an intricate and unusual pattern that sparked her imagination. She heard Julie pound up the steps as she set the paper aside. "What did he say?"

"He said he didn't care," Julie announced, poking her head over the rail at the top of the stairs. "I'll be back. I'm going to get a drink." She disappeared again.

"Julie, you're not being very helpful."

"I'll hurry."

Meredith shook her head. So much for having some quality time with her daughter. Lifting the lid from the dusty cardboard box, she inhaled softly with delight. Stacks of old cards dating from the turn of the century lay at her fingertips. There was a wealth of ideas for designs right here alone. Pulling up an old stool she began to sort through her treasure.

The creaking of the stairs penetrated her intense inspection. "Julie? Come see what I've found."

"It's not Julie."

The deep voice sent a current of recognition along her nerves. Lee. He stood at the top of the stairs, his seductive green eyes penetrating her defenses with ease.

"Julie told me you needed some help moving a trunk."

Puzzled, Meredith shook her head. "No. I was just going through some things. I don't know why she would have told you that."

"Perhaps I misunderstood," he said, making no move to leave.

Slowly Meredith rose to her feet, unable to stop herself from taking a quick inventory of him. A dark green knit shirt stretched across his broad chest, reminding her of how powerfully he was built. He wore faded jeans—the same pair he'd had on in her studio that first day—the ones that molded to every muscle and tendon in his long legs.

He looked less civilized today, more the rugged out-doorsman. The casual clothes brought out the savage angles of his jaw and the predatory gleam in those damned sexy eyes. She swallowed the swell of appreciation that crawled up her throat.

"I'm sorry. I don't know what she could have been thinking. She—"

A solid, foreboding thud suddenly shook the attic floor. Meredith refused to believe what she'd heard—the attic door had been slammed shut. Lee turned and hurried down the steps, but from the sounds he was making she knew the door wouldn't budge.

A flash of anxiety sliced through her heart. She was *not* going to be stuck here with *him.*

Quickly she made her way down the narrow stairwell, pushing in front of Lee. "Let me try," she said, twisting the doorknob. "Julie. Are you out there? Honey, come unlock the door. Julie!

"I can't believe this," she said, pounding against the hard panels. "The door has never jammed shut like this before."

She turned, unexpectedly caught between the solid wooden door and the solid male strength of Lee Stratton. Her mouth was suddenly as dry as the dust in the attic. She was exquisitely aware of how small, how helpless she was against the opposing forces that surrounded her. To her surprise the thought sent a thrill along her spine.

Perhaps it was the heavy warmth of the attic air or maybe it was the body heat emanating from Lee himself. He was so close to her she couldn't inhale without breathing in his scent.

He stood one step above her, his broad chest at her eye

level. The movement of his shirt as he breathed played tantalizingly over the sculpted contours of his body.

Meredith closed her eyes, willing her heart to stop beating so fast and her pulse to slow to a normal rate. Neither function paid any attention to her mental commands.

Her body temperature was rising and she wondered how someone had managed to suck the air out of the small space between them. It was hard to catch a breath.

She braved a look into his eyes, intending to ask him to move aside, only to have her remaining air syphoned from her lungs by the intimate light in his green eyes.

He stood above her, dangerous and predatory. Strong and powerful. But instead of being intimidated she caught herself wondering what it would be like to be wrapped in all that maleness, to be enfolded in all that masculine warm strength.

Her gaze drifted from his seductive eyes to his mouth and remained there. Thoughts of his kiss wedged in her mind, tormenting her with both the memory of their first kiss years ago and the promise of what his kiss would hold for her today if only she would—

Remember that he wasn't to be trusted. Ever. As much as she hated to admit it, her resistance to Lee, physically, was wearing very thin. Being trapped in this humid, stuffy attic for any length of time wouldn't be a good idea.

"Maybe we can get someone's attention from the windows in the dormers," she suggested breathlessly, ducking around him and hurrying up the stairs.

It had been a cool spring morning when she'd come up to the attic. The chambray shirt she wore over her cropped-off knit top had offered warm comfort. But it was past noon now and the temperature inside the airless attic was rising. She shoved the sleeves on her shirt up past her elbows.

Lee had done his part in raising the humidity factor up

here, too. How could a man who generated all that physical warmth be so damned cold inside?

Winding her way through the piles of cast-off junk in front of the dormer alcoves, she ducked her head and reached for the window latch. It was hard to see from this odd angle. The low-sloping ceiling prevented her from standing upright without bumping her head.

"Florence! Walt!" It was unlikely anyone would hear her from up here on the fourth floor of the old house, but she had to try. "I can't believe this," she complained, straining to see the lawn below. "Where is everybody?" There was no way she was going to be locked in a stuffy old attic with Lee. She'd get out if she had to gnaw through the door with her teeth.

She straightened, squealing loudly as her head impacted against the low ceiling. The pain buckled her knees and bolts of light careened inside her head. A strong arm grasped her around the waist, guiding her away from the dormer until she could stand upright.

"Are you all right?"

She nodded, still rubbing her head. "I think so."

"Here, let me have a look."

Turning slightly to her left, Meredith found herself practically in Lee's arms. She heard his quick intake of breath. When she braved a look into his eyes, the tenderness in his expression amazed her.

He looked her over seductively but something in his manner soothed her. Against her will she drank in the comfort of his nearness that wrapped itself around her like a warm blanket.

The attic of Sand Castle was large, with plenty of room to move around, but in the span of five minutes she'd managed to get herself trapped in the narrow stairwell and now the close confines of the dormer alcove.

Wedged between a rolltop desk and Lee, there was nowhere to go. Except through him. She pushed against his chest but before she could order him to move a razor-sharp pain pierced her skull and she gasped.

"Let me see."

He touched her head gently with his fingertips. His other hand cradled the back of her head to steady it as he inspected the lump. His fingers felt hot against her scalp.

She lifted her eyes and stared in fascination at the steady throbbing of the veins in his neck, the tempting angle of his throat. The warmth that radiated from him was mesmerizing, inviting. Her gaze traveled up his sharp jawline to his lips. A soft, interesting contrast to the planes of his face. She wondered if he tasted the way he had back then or if he had a riper flavor, a stronger, more mature taste.

"That's going to be one hell of a goose egg, but I think you'll live."

His eyes met hers, beckoning, luring her closer and closer. The thick, musty air swirled around them, closing in, heavily. She forced herself to breathe and inhaled his scent.

He reached out and gently tucked her hair behind her ear on one side. His other hand still firmly cradled her neck.

"Penny."

She closed her eyes and shoved past him, danger signs flashing blindingly in her mind. She had to get out of here. She ran down the steps, beating at the door. "Julie! Somebody! There has to be a way out of here. Can't we break the door?"

Lee stood at the top of the stairs. "It's no use. The hinges are on the outside and that door is made of two-inch-thick solid oak."

It wasn't what she wanted to hear. "Well, what do you suggest, then?"

His eyes twinkled as he looked down at her. "Lunch."

For a moment she thought he'd lost his mind. Then he motioned her to join him. She did so reluctantly and for the first time she noticed some new additions to the clutter in the attic.

Sitting on a lopsided table near the top of the stairs was a picnic basket, a bottle of wine and bouquet of flowers in a jar. "Where did this come from?" she queried.

"I think we're being manipulated," Lee said, inspecting the label on the bottle.

"Who would want to trap us up here— Oh. I get it," she said. A hot wave of embarrassment rushed through her. What if Lee thought this was her idea? She'd better set the record straight right now.

"Julie wants us to be friends. I guess she thought if we were trapped up here with some food and a little wine we'd come to some sort of understanding."

Lee glanced at her, his expression blank, but his eyes held a suspicious twinkle that unnerved her.

"I suspected as much."

"I just want you to know that I had absolutely nothing to do with this in any way." Crossing her arms at her chest, she faced him.

"I know that."

"Good." She was working on a list of appropriate punishments for Julie for this latest little escapade when the strains of romantic music began drifting through the air. A fresh wave of chagrin made her cringe. Julie was trying to start something between her mother and Lee that Meredith had been trying to prevent from the moment he'd come home. "Where's that coming from? Can you turn it off?"

Lee had already started searching, pointing to an air duct. "Probably a tape player placed close to the vent."

Apparently there was no end to Julie's little bag of

tricks. "Well, this is ridiculous. We can't stay up here until she decides to let us out. Try the door again."

Lee obliged but with no success.

"When I get my hands on that young lady I'm going to…" Words failed her.

"Are you hungry?" Lee asked.

"No," she answered, annoyed. Lee was taking this whole darned thing too lightly.

Dusting the table with a rag, he set the basket on top of it. "If you don't mind, I'm going to eat." He shoved up the sleeves of his shirt and reached for the wicker basket. "Is it stuffy in here?"

Meredith glared and stomped down the stairs again, trying the door. Not wanting to think about how the snug-fitting shirt drew her eyes to the perfectly developed pectoral muscles in his chest or how the tendons on his forearms rippled when he used his hands.

He was right about one thing, though. It was stuffy as a tomb up here. She flapped the fronts of her shirt to create a breeze then twisted the doorknob again. Hopeless.

Chewing on her frustration she went back up the steps. "I can't believe she did this to me. There has to be a way out of here." But looking around she knew she had to accept the truth. She was trapped in a steamy, empty attic with the last man on earth she wanted to be with.

"None that I'm aware of," Lee said, shaking his head. "Are you afraid?"

"Of what?" she asked, planting her hands on her hips.

"Of being alone with me?"

"Certainly not. Don't be ridiculous," she said, tucking her hair behind her ears. She knew better than to look him in the eyes, though, because she *was* afraid.

"Then come have lunch. I have a feeling we won't get out of here until we comply with Julie's little scheme."

He was probably right. The sooner she ate and made

nice with Lee, the sooner she could get out of here. "Fine. Since I have no choice."

Meredith watched as Lee began emptying the basket. Her daughter had thought of everything—plates, wine-glasses, sandwiches, fruit, cheese, napkins, even petits fours for dessert. The perfect romantic repast. She saw evidence of Florence's fine touch in this drama, too.

"So, what brought you up here today?" Lee asked, pulling up two chairs and dusting off the seats.

"Searching for ideas. I often get some of my best ones from old books, pictures, pieces of wallpaper."

"This place should be a gold mine." He glanced around the large open area. "I haven't been up here since I was a kid. My grandmother loved to dig around in all this stuff. She'd sit and talk about the good old days for hours." He pulled out a sandwich and offered it to her. "You sure you aren't hungry?"

She took it, forcing herself to take a bite. Under normal circumstances it probably tasted wonderful. At the moment, however, it had slightly more flavor than shoe leather. She put it down.

"So, what will we talk about?" she asked, shoving the sandwich aside.

"Whatever you want," Lee replied, pouring a small amount of wine into the glasses.

Her fingers were wrapped around the stem of the glass before she thought about the consequences of drinking the pale liquid. A steamy attic, a handsome man and wine. Not a good idea.

She plucked a grape from the bunch and put it in her mouth. Damn, but it was hot up here. She didn't really want to take off her shirt but the little knit top she wore underneath would be so much cooler.

Oh, what the hell. She was roasting! She shed the shirt, wishing she'd worn a top that didn't reveal her abdomen every time she breathed. She glanced at Lee and saw a faint light of amusement in his green eyes.

She lifted her chin. "Since you're in such an obliging mood, maybe I should ask you all the things I've wondered about."

"Be my guest."

She took a sip of wine to fortify herself. Nothing more. Maybe she was overreacting to this situation. She was, after all, an adult, not a naive little girl who swooned at every handsome face that walked by. There was no reason to let Lee put her on the defensive. "All right. Why was your wedding called off?"

Lee raised an eyebrow, obviously unprepared for that question.

"She changed her mind." His tone was carefully controlled and even.

His reply pricked her conscience. She remembered what he'd said on the beach that night about not liking change. She was beginning to understand why. First his fiancée and then all the changes at Sand Castle when he came home, including her own presence here.

"I'm sorry. It must have been painful for you."

He shrugged indifferently. "Not particularly."

A few days ago his cold indifference would have infuriated her, but now she realized that he was merely retreating from his pain and loneliness. Still, she found herself bothered greatly by his statement.

Compassion squeezed her heart. She longed to make him see that he was only making things worse by hiding and refusing to feel.

"Not particularly?" she repeated. "Didn't you love her?"

"I don't know," he admitted, avoiding her gaze.

"If you weren't sure, why were you going to marry her?"

There was a look of sad resignation in his eyes when he finally answered.

"Sometimes it's easier to think you're in love than accept that you're alone."

Lee's words pierced Meredith to her soul. She understood only too well what he was saying. "That's why I married John," she admitted, turning the stem of the wineglass as her thoughts traveled back to the past. "But I discovered there are many ways to feel alone. *You don't have to be an orphan to feel like one.*" Meredith quoted his own words back at him.

"You have a good memory, too." He grinned, a warm light filling his eyes. "I don't blame Doreen," he said quietly. "It wasn't her fault. She was a very special woman, everything I thought I wanted. I couldn't give her what she needed."

"Love?" Meredith guessed, and was rewarded with an icy glare from Lee's emerald eyes.

"I can't help the way I am, Meredith."

"The way you are or the way you want to be?"

The muscle in his jaw flexed as he shoved away from the table and stood. "I'm going to check the door again."

Meredith sighed and plucked another grape from the bunch, rubbing it between her fingers. Getting through to Lee might take a more forceful assault. She hadn't believed it possible but he was more hardheaded than Walt.

It wasn't hard to figure out what had happened. The divorce had wounded both Lee and Walt, and to protect themselves against the pain they had retreated inside themselves. What they should have done was reach out to one another.

They needed each other and she was determined to find a way to at least get them talking. Walt wasn't getting any younger and given his heart condition, neither father nor son could afford to lose one more minute to stubborn pride.

She would have to be careful, though, to protect herself in the process. She may understand Lee better now but that didn't alter the fact that he wasn't the kind of man she wanted in her life.

Lee pulled and twisted the knob but the door was still locked. He hadn't expected anything else. It had been a convenient means of putting some distance between himself and Meredith. He didn't want to fight with her again.

It's the reason you're alone.

Her painfully accurate assessment of him from the other night haunted his thoughts. He knew she was right. He also knew there was nothing he could do about it. He couldn't change. Rubbing a hand across the back of his neck, he glanced up the stairs. He couldn't stand here all day, either, even if he wished he could.

When he stood at the table again, he refilled his glass, fortifying himself for what was to come. Meredith wasn't one to give up easily so when she remained quiet he began to think something was wrong. "What, no more questions?"

"A couple," she admitted smugly.

He lifted his glass in a go-ahead gesture.

"Why do you call your father Walt?"

"It's his name." Lee braced himself against Meredith's probing. He hadn't anticipated her coming at him from that direction.

"Why don't you call him Dad?" she asked, reaching for a banana.

Lee took a sip of wine. "I used to. A long time ago."

"Why did you stop?"

"I don't remember." Lee poured more wine into his glass and lifted it to his lips. He didn't like the direction this conversation was heading. Her probing was arousing old fears and uncertainties.

"Don't remember or don't want to deal with it?"

Her insight made him chafe. How had she read so much in just a few words? Her blue eyes studied him intently. He looked away, afraid of what else she might see in him.

"Does it really matter?"

"Yes. I think you're taking the coward's way out. You hide behind this wall of ice, refusing to care, refusing to let anyone get too close because you're afraid of getting hurt."

"You don't know what you're talking about." He could have predicted she'd take this position. It was the same one she'd held that summer. She would try to convince him that all he had to do was open up and share his feelings and let love do the rest. He knew differently. Love might live in her world but it had never inhabited his. In his world love only led to pain, rejection and abandonment.

"Don't I? You're forgetting who you're talking to. I know that when we hurt too much we'll do anything to stop the pain. Even if that means refusing to feel. We think that if we ignore the pain, it'll just go away."

"What's your point?"

"It doesn't go away, Lee. It stays there, deep inside, like a piece of coal, getting harder and harder, never really disappearing. But you don't have to be alone. You don't have to feel isolated."

"Oh, and what's your answer, Pollyanna? Adopt a rodent a day?" he snapped sarcastically. She was getting too close, probing too deep and seeing things he didn't want her to see.

"It would be a start," she said angrily.

A wave of disappointment unexpectedly settled on his shoulders. Maybe Meredith had changed more than he'd realized. "You used to understand."

"I do, more than you think. Don't you see? The same

thing that kept you from loving Doreen is what's keeping you and Walt apart. You're both so afraid of getting hurt you turn off your feelings, but that only makes things worse."

Lee trembled, hating the way Meredith could read him like a damned book. "I'm not afraid," he said, knowing as he uttered the words he was lying.

Meredith sighed in disgust, planting her hands on her hips. "You and your father are so much alike."

"We're nothing alike." The last thing Lee wanted was to be like Walt.

"You may not want to believe it but it's true. You both love each other but you're so full of stupid male pride that neither one of you will make the first move."

"Spare me your optimism, please."

"And spare me your bullheaded pessimism. You have this blind spot where Walt is concerned. I would hate to be one of your clients. How do you represent them fairly with such a one-sided view of things?"

Lee shot her a fierce glare that had little or no effect upon her.

"Did you ever stop to think how much it must have hurt Walt to have you with him for only a few months each summer? Each time you left to go back to your mother must have ripped his heart out all over again. Maybe the only way he could survive that was to turn off his feelings."

"Maybe he was incapable of feeling anything at all." *Like me,* he thought to himself. Maybe he was more like Walt than he'd been willing to admit.

"I don't believe that about either one of you."

Meredith came toward him, stopping at his side. "Your father's feeling alone, too, Lee. All it would take is a gesture. Tell him you love him."

Meredith couldn't know that she'd plunged a knife into

an old wound. Lee swallowed the bitterness that rose in his throat. "I did," he said, struggling to keep his voice from breaking.

"And?"

Lee turned and glared. "He turned his back and walked away."

Sympathy bloomed instantly in Meredith eyes. "Oh, Lee, I'm sorry. Maybe he just didn't know how to say he loved you, too."

Lee walked away, shaking his head at her tenacity. "I thought we covered this love issue the other night on the beach."

"Listen to me, Lee. I know how you feel. I do. I remember. We were both at a crossroads that summer. We were questioning our identities and searching for our place in the world. It took me a while but I eventually learned the secret. You have to love yourself first. Then you can start giving love to others, and the more you give, the more you get in return."

"Love," Lee scoffed, marveling at how differently he and Meredith had ended up. They had felt the same once; alone, abandoned, different from everyone else. Yet she embraced emotions like a dear friend and he felt nothing inside.

"Love is the only thing that can fill the hole in your heart," Meredith said softly, coming to stand behind him. "It's the only thing that can chase away that cold emptiness inside you that reminds you every minute that you're different. It's the only thing that can conquer the fear that you'll grow old and die, never knowing the emotions that everyone else can feel."

Fear, tantamount to panic, seized his heart. Damn. How could she see inside him so easily? He'd built his walls high and thick, encased himself in cold numbing ice and still she could slice him open with a word or a look and expose his greatest fears.

He turned to her, anger sharpening his voice. "Love isn't the answer to everything, Meredith. That Pollyanna garbage may work for you but it doesn't wash with me, so back off."

He felt like a heel when he saw the tears start to form in her eyes, but he couldn't let her get too close.

"I don't know why I bother with you."

"Neither do I."

Meredith crossed her arms over her chest. "I had some crazy idea that if you and Walt would just talk to one another you could patch things up between you. I should have known from past experience that there's no compassion in your soul."

"Then stop looking for it," he said, turning away. But Meredith wasn't to be stopped so easily.

"You know when I decided that love was real and that it was something I could find for myself?"

He didn't answer her. There was no point. She would tell him regardless.

"After you walked away and left me alone in that tree. I knew if I didn't believe in love and learn to give it and receive it, I'd end up cold and hard like you. So, because of you I learned how to love."

Meredith's words were like an arctic storm blowing in the already frigid confines of his heart. He'd never felt more cold and alone. "I'm going to check the door." He heard Meredith swear softly under her breath.

"That's your answer to everything, isn't it? Just turn your back. You walked away from me, from your dad and from your future wife!"

Yes, he knew how to walk away. He was a damned expert at it. Everyone who ever claimed to love him had taught him how.

Julie pushed away from the attic door, turning down the volume on her hearing aid. She'd been listening to the loud voices coming from upstairs. "They sound like they're fighting again. Maybe we should let them out."

"Nah," Walt assured her with a pat on the back. "Things are going great."

Florence nodded. "All according to plan."

"When will we know when to unlock the door?"

"Well, we'll know when it gets real quiet, no talking at all. Then we'll wait one hour and let them out."

Julie tilted her head curiously. "Why an hour?"

Walt and Florence exchanged knowing looks. "That'll give them time to smooth out their differences," Walt explained.

"Oh."

"I'd sure like to hear how this experiment works out but I'm late for my auto repair class." Florence turned and started down the hall.

Chapter Eight

Meredith sorted through the cards, resisting the urge to glance at Lee. They hadn't spoken since they'd argued. And the standoff was stretching into forty-five minutes now.

They'd totally ignored each other for the first fifteen minutes. At the half hour point they'd graduated to curt phrases, the kind that don't really qualify as talking to one another. Things like "I'd better check the door" and "Do you want another drink?"

The last fifteen minutes had been spent playing the dare-you-to-look game. He'd glance at her, she'd glance at him, both gathering their courage to make the first move. She wasn't sure if she wanted it to be her or him.

Once her anger had dissipated, she realized she'd been impatient with Lee and pushed him too hard. She couldn't expect him to get in touch with his feelings simply because she told him to. More to the point, she shouldn't try to solve other people's problems. She had enough of her own to worry about. If Lee and Walt wanted to work out their differences it was up to them.

To her regret, it wasn't quite that easy. Lee's words kept running around in her mind like little cars on a racetrack.

Sometimes it's easier to think you're in love than accept you're alone.

She wished she could talk to him the way she had that summer. She wanted to make him see that he didn't have to be alone if he'd just allow himself to feel.

They'd been a comfort to one another once, giving support, understanding, things that made the loneliness, at least for a while, seem less terrifying. She was beginning to think that if nothing else, Lee had been sincere in his loneliness. She was even willing to consider that he may have been sincere in his friendship, as well.

Nevertheless when it came to the commitment, he failed miserably. He'd run from her, betrayed her because it was easier for him.

Meredith waved the old magazine she was using as a fan a little faster, sighing in disgust when it did nothing to stir up any cool air. Tossing it aside she gathered her hair off her neck and piled it on top of her head, holding it in place with her hands. The slightly cooler air felt deliciously good on her clammy skin.

The silence however was nerve-racking. This was really silly. They were behaving like children. Maybe she should be the one to break the tension.

She glanced at Lee out of the corners of her eyes. He was standing near the far end where his grandmother's furniture was stored. Meredith recognized several of the pieces she'd decided not to use when she moved into the tower.

He was looking through a book or something, turning pages. Her curiosity kept her watching him a moment too long. His intense emerald gaze met hers and she saw flames of desire flash in his eyes.

Her mouth went dry and her heart beat rapidly. His gaze slowly lowered to her chest and she realized with a jolt that her knit top barely covered her breasts.

She lowered her arms, unable to stop the blush from staining her cheeks and unable to look away from the invitation in his eyes.

He grinned and motioned her to join him. The battle was apparently over. She threaded her way through the clutter, stopping at his side.

"I found this in the dresser," he said, pointing to what she could see now was a very old photo album. "This is my grandma and grandpa Stratton on their wedding day."

Meredith couldn't help but smile when she saw the young couple captured on film on the happy occasion.

"They were married forty-eight years. My grandfather died when I was ten, right before I left here, but my grandmother lived to be eighty-seven."

Lee's comment brought a fresh wave of compassion into her heart. No wonder he had trouble feeling anything. In a short period of time Lee's life had been completely shattered. He'd lost his grandfather, his parents had separated and he was taken from the only home he'd known and sent off to a boarding school to live with strangers.

She longed to reach out and comfort him. She knew so well the bone-chilling numbness of feeling worthless and unwanted, shunted from one place to the other, rootless and drifting like a dandelion puff in the wind.

She looked up at him. The expression on his face clearly revealed the love he'd had for his grandmother. Maybe it wasn't too late for Lee after all. Her heart went out to him. But she was still hesitant to play the role of therapist again. Her last attempt had been a disaster.

Lee turned another page in the album and Meredith

smiled in delight at what she saw. "That's Sand Castle."
The photo showed the home the way it had looked before
the restoration. She had to admit, there was a certain charm
about the old shabbiness that appealed to her.

"This is the way I remember it," he said warmly.

Affection roughened his voice and touched her heart.
"You really love this place, don't you?" The discovery
surprised her. She'd always assumed the reason Lee never
came home was that he didn't like it here.

"Sand Castle is the only home I've ever known. My
relationship with Walt was always difficult but I could go
to the tower, to my grandmother, and feel like I belonged."

Now she understood the grim expression on Lee's face
the first day he came to the tower. What she'd seen as
disapproval had actually been sadness. Another unwelcome change greeting him. He'd been expecting the tower
to look the same—like a familiar friend waiting to welcome him home. She almost wished she'd never touched
the place.

She glanced at the photo again. At least Lee had his
memories. She envied him that. He may not realize it but
they were priceless treasures, things that had played a part
in defining who he was.

She had no such foundation to look back upon. She had
no past to connect with. After her divorce it had been more
important than ever to discover her lineage. She'd searched
her background as far as she could but the trail was a short
one. Her mother dead, her father traceable only as far as
Dallas. She'd found one set of grandparents, both head-
stones in a Pass Christian cemetery.

She knew names and dates of her immediate family but
there were no stories, no things that she could reach out
and touch that would connect her to anyone.

"Well, I'll be damned," Lee said softly, holding up a
small gold and ivory locket.

"Oh, how lovely." She reached out and laid it against her palm, marveling at the delicate design and the intricate detail. "It's the most exquisite thing I've ever seen."

"It was my grandmother's," Lee said with a warm smile. "It was very special to her. I wonder what it's doing in the pages of this album. It should have been in with her other valuables."

Lee touched the locket tenderly. "Her husband gave it to her on their wedding day. She was an immigrant. She used to say that her wedding ring made her feel married but the locket gave her roots and an identity. It bound her to the Strattons and to Sand Castle."

"Does it open?" Meredith asked.

Lee had a strange look on his face as he hesitantly pried opened the locket. Meredith was pleasantly surprised to see it unfold to reveal three hinged oval frames.

"Who are they?" She sensed something significant in the way he stared at the locket.

He angled the trinket so she could see the faces. "This is my father and this is his brother, Al. He died when I was a baby. You probably recognize this face."

Meredith smiled at the familiar image. "It's you." He looked exactly as he had that fateful summer, even the sadness in his eyes had been captured in the photo. The very same sadness she saw when she looked into his eyes now.

"She was always changing the pictures in this thing," Lee explained. "She said she didn't want anyone to feel left out. Sometimes she'd carry photos of Walt's two daughters, sometimes her sons or her husband and her father. It was a game to guess who was in the locket from week to week. But one picture never changed. It stayed in the locket no matter what."

"Whose?"

''Mine. She said I was the only Stratton heir. That I was special and I belonged in her locket always.''

Tears stung the back of Meredith's eyelids and a lump formed deep in her throat. Lee's grandmother must have realized how badly he needed to feel loved and had done what she could to reassure him. She must have been a very special lady.

''You loved her very much, didn't you?'' she asked, feeling closer to him than she had since that summer.

Lee shrugged. ''She was the only one who never changed. The only one I could count on.''

Meredith handed the locket back to Lee.

He gently placed it in the album, staring at it a long moment before he spoke again. ''I never meant to hurt you,'' he said quietly.

Meredith sighed and turned away, the sense of closeness fading like the images in the old photographs. ''Then why did you?''

''I'm not sure,'' he admitted. ''I've asked myself that a hundred times over the last fifteen years. You were the best friend I ever had. I missed you after I went home.'' He rubbed his hand across the back of his neck. ''I used to go over that night, trying to find a reason for my actions, one that made sense. I knew it was my fault but I didn't know why I'd thrown away something so important.''

Crossing her arms over her chest, Meredith stared at the floor, unable to muster the anger she had a few days ago. For the first time Meredith allowed herself to believe that Lee was genuinely sorry for what he'd done and that he'd been hurt as much by the loss of the friendship as she had.

She wanted to believe, but she was scared to trust him too far. His eyes held a question, seeking her forgiveness. She wasn't ready for that yet but... ''I missed you, too.''

His gaze caressed her face before he looked back down at the album. ''You were unlike anyone I'd ever known.

You were so alive, so full of energy and love. But we were so different. I didn't know how to react to you sometimes.''

It was hard to ignore the note of honesty in his voice. "It wasn't hard. Just be my friend."

"I didn't know how," he replied with a wry smile.

Meredith felt so sorry for him. It was such a simple thing and he was making it so complicated. "All you had to do was be honest and care about me as much I'd cared about you."

Lee shook his head. "I don't expect you to understand. It all comes too easily for you."

"It can for you, too," she said earnestly. "But it takes a willingness to give up the fear. You've got to let go and care about something or you might as well be dead."

He looked her directly in the eyes; the sadness reflected there tightened her throat.

"I've been dead too long."

She went to him, placing her hand upon his arm. "Lee, it doesn't have to be like this. You don't have to be afraid of life or the feelings that you have."

Lee pulled away. "Don't you understand? I don't know about those things. I know about honor and dedication to a job. I know how to be dispassionate in the courtroom. But I don't know about hope and love. I can't tell happy from sad, exhilaration from depression. Everything feels alike to me."

Meredith's heart was squeezed so tight with sympathy she thought it might break. "I wish I could help you."

"So do I. Because I have a feeling you're the only one who could."

He reached out to her, his eyes darkening, his gaze piercing deep into her already weak heart. Old fears pushed rudely to the surface and she backed away with a suddenness that surprised even her.

Lee studied her a moment, then lowered his hand. "You said I'm afraid of life. That may be true, but you're afraid, too, Meredith. You're afraid of love."

"I am not," she said defensively. "I love everybody."

"I'm talking about love between a man and a woman. You've denied the woman in you because you've had your heart broken. It's easier for you to be a mother, a friend and a businesswoman because those are things you can control. But to be a woman means you have to be held and petted and made to feel like the beautiful and desirable woman you are. It means you have to entrust your heart to a man and that scares the hell out of you."

Meredith tucked her hair behind her ears and shook her head, uncomfortable with the fact that he'd spoken the truth. "You don't know what you're talking about. I'm completely happy. I don't have a man in my life because I haven't found the right one. No other reason."

"You're lying and I'll prove it." He took a step toward her.

She backed up, connecting with the unyielding front of an old armoire. Lee smiled. There was a light in his eyes that sent shock waves rippling through her veins.

"You tremble every time I come close to you. You tense up whenever I touch you."

"You are so arrogant," she said with a shake of her head. He took another step closer and she breathed him in, unable to take her eyes off his neck, his lips.

"I frighten you because I touch something inside that you don't want touched. You don't want awakened." He stopped only inches away and placed his hands against the armoire, on either side of her head.

She refused to look at him, turning her head. "You're the most egotistical—" He moved even closer, the long, hard length of his body pressing into her.

"I don't understand it, either, but we both know that

when we get close something happens, and I'm tired of fighting it. I want to see where it takes us.''

The huskiness in his voice was nearly her undoing. She tried to push him away but when her hands lay against his broad chest her touch became more of a caress than a rejection. His shirt was sweat damp under her fingers and she could see every muscle beneath. "I don't. I know where it will lead and I've been there before.''

Lee smiled. ''Would it help if I told you it scares me, too?''

''No. And I'm not scared of you.'' She closed her eyes against the sight of him but blindness did nothing to stop the scent of him or the feel of him as he pressed against her.

''Look at me.''

She couldn't refuse.

He lowered his head, her eyes riveted on his mouth, desperate to know the taste. She wanted to turn away, to tell him no. She wanted to feel nothing. But she felt it all, the anticipation, the need and the hunger. She knew she could no more resist what was to come than she could resist taking air into her lungs.

If only his eyes weren't so green, his lips so tempting. She was trapped, but a willing captive. Surrounded, but with no desire to escape. Facing danger, but walking into it with her courage strong. There would be consequences, but she would face them later.

His breath coaxed her lips apart in a gentle foreplay. She inhaled and gave herself over to what was to come. His lips were hot, firm, and stole all the strength from her legs. Only the pressure of his body kept her upright.

He nibbled at the corners of her mouth, tasting her lower lip before sucking it into his mouth. She groaned softly and slipped her arms around his waist.

The kiss deepened, becoming more demanding. She

gave in to each request, anticipating, meeting and eager to surpass.

He released her, looking deeply into her eyes, then caressing her face with his smoldering green gaze before kissing her tenderly on her temples, her eyelids and her throat.

She clung to his shoulders as heat radiated from deep inside her. The warm confines of the attic wrapped them in steamy haze, stealing their breath.

He wrapped his arms around her waist, the heat of his palms branding her damp skin. The short top she wore gave no resistance as he hands slid up her back and along her spine. Tiny currents of awareness made her quiver in his embrace.

Lee pulled back and smiled at her as if reminding her of his earlier statement. She did tremble whenever he touched her. And she liked it.

The security of his arms gave her a courage she didn't normally possess and she pulled him closer, pressing herself against him. She could feel the hard heat of him against her belly and arched against it.

His hands moved down, cupping her, pressing her more intimately against him. She gasped for breath but the heavy, musty air absorbed most of it before she could take it into her lungs.

He whispered her name against her neck and she quivered. "It's so hot," she muttered, uncertain if she meant the airless attic or the mounting passion between them.

Lee slackened his hold, lifting his hands to rest on either side of her neck. He gazed at her a long moment as if unable to take his eyes from her face.

"Meredith, do you know? Do you have any idea how incredibly lovely you are? It almost hurts to look at you."

His words shocked her and pleased her at the same time, leaving a bewildering sense of elation. Slowly he slid his hands tantalizingly over her shoulders and across her chest, slipping under the short top and cupping her breasts in his palms.

She exhaled in pleasure, eagerly welcoming his probing tongue between her parted lips.

Cool air brushed across her chest briefly as he unfastened her bra and exposed her to his more intimate explorations. Gently and slowly he circled the rosy tips with his fingers, eliciting a sigh of delight and a silent plea to continue.

Forces raged within her. Needs and sensations that had been dormant too long, ignored and almost forgotten, suddenly burst from their confines and flooded her mind.

How long since she'd known this glorious celebration of life? How long since she'd known a tender touch, a burning need that she knew only he could satisfy? *Too long,* her heart whispered. *Too long,* her body confirmed. *Too long,* her soul exclaimed.

There were no doubts at this moment. No recriminations, no excuses, no obstacles—just the taste of him, the feel of him, the wonder of him.

Lee had never known such violent needs existed within him. Unrestrained, powerful desires to wrap himself in Meredith's softness, to drown himself in it. Sunlight flooded his soul and warmth infused his heart.

He was like a man starved for warmth. A man who'd been locked in a dungeon for years and suddenly set free. The unaccustomed light hurt his sensitive pupils but he craved its warmth, its brightness, even though to feel its heat, to see its light, was painful.

She was everything he'd ever dreamed and more. Her softness was more powerful a lure than anything he'd ever experienced. She'd given life to part of him he'd thought dead. He was Lazarus resurrected.

Before Meredith, he'd been deaf to the world around him, deaf to the emotions that lived inside him. Each taste of her soft, sweet lips renewed him, opened his ears to the sounds of life, his heart to the throbbing rhythm of the universe.

He needed her. All of her. She whispered to him and the temptation to explore her silken warmth was too powerful to withstand for long. He slipped his hand slowly up her rib cage to the soft swell of her breasts, eager to know their special softness but postponing the moment in favor of delicious anticipation.

He cupped the tantalizing mounds of flesh in his palms, exhaling sharply as her nipples pebbled at his touch. He marveled at how they seemed designed to fit his hands perfectly. He captured her lips again, devouring her like a starving man. He couldn't get close enough, couldn't probe deep enough.

One taste. That's all he needed. Just one taste and then he would be satisfied. He kissed her neck and felt her pulse throb behind her ear. She clung to him as he explored the hollow beneath her chin. In one swift motion he shoved her top aside and took one rosy tip of her breast into his mouth.

She arched against him, moaning softly with pleasure. His body bucked with the sudden agonizing need to possess her, even knowing with bone-chilling certainty that if he did he would be bound to her forever. His need for her was so strong he wondered if he could pull free.

The thought sent an icy knife of fear into his soul. He broke free, staring down into the blue eyes of heaven, gripping the form of a living angel as visions of hell danced in the back of his mind.

"Meredith, I can't..." What could he say? How could he explain his own confusion? She was everything he wanted, but he was afraid to ask for it. She gave, but he didn't know how to give back. She offered, but he didn't know how to accept.

He stepped back, inhaling a ragged breath, wiping his palm across his face. Her eyes were filled with confusion and as he watched, he saw doubt and pain darken her blue eyes to gray. It was as if he'd betrayed her all over again. Suddenly his cold gray world slammed shut around him.

The hurt in her blue eyes sliced his heart into shreds. She looked away, tugging her top into place, smoothing back the glorious red strands of her hair that had slipped through his fingers like spun silk.

She walked to the window and curled up in a chair, silent, withdrawn, and he had no idea how to pull her back. No idea how to tell her how she made him feel.

He had no skills at all to make her understand. They were from two different spheres. She was an angel of love. He, a demon from darkness.

He looked away, unable to still his labored breathing and the aftereffects of her softness upon his senses. He ached to hold her, to stir that fiery passion in her with his own hands, to watch her abandon herself to him, to hear her cry out his name in the heights of frenzied desire.

A woman like Meredith needed to be loved and cherished, to have all that pent-up passion stirred again and again.

Meredith possessed a boundless love that wouldn't be satisfied with a man who didn't know the first thing about love or warmth or caring. She deserved a man who would love her completely, a man who could match her fire and her endless capacity for giving with his own.

And he was incapable. He could never give her what she needed.

Meredith pulled her knees up to her chest and silently cursed herself for being a fool. A quiver of fading desire lanced through her and she exhaled involuntarily. She could still feel his hand on her, his lips. She'd done the unthinkable. She'd fallen for him again. She'd been suckered in by his charm and by those little-lost-boy eyes of his.

As before, he'd played on her heartstrings, manipulated her emotions and used his knowledge of her weaknesses to ensnare her.

Lifting her head, she caught a faint reflection of herself in a dusty mirror. No. She had to be honest. She was the one to blame because she realized that she still loved him. She'd never stopped.

All she'd accomplished with her digging and prodding into Lee's buried emotions was to resurrect all the things about him that had attracted her in the first place.

On some deep emotional level she'd been out to prove that she'd been right about him, that he really was worthy of her affection, of her friendship. She'd been looking for some sort of emotional vindication, some proof that she hadn't loved unwisely after all.

So where did that leave her now? She had a heart and body that cried out for him but a brain that warned her she was falling into the same trap.

A sharp click, like the sound of a bolt being drawn, echoed in the oppressive silence.

Meredith was instantly on her feet. Finally the door was unlocked. She hurried toward the stairs, eager to put some distance between herself and Lee and the still-lingering kiss that was trapped inside her.

She paused briefly at the top of the stairs, glancing, against her will, toward Lee. He stood in front of the old dresser again, and as she watched, he reached out and picked up the locket, slipping it into his pants' pocket.

The gesture brought an ache to her chest, replacing her scattered emotions with compassion. It proved that Lee still cared about some things. Still cherished some things even if he kept those feelings buried. Maybe there was hope for him.

She wanted to believe that his sadness was real. That his sincerity was genuine. More than anything, she wanted to believe that his embrace was for her alone. It had felt so good to be held and protected, to be wrapped in the warm strong arms of another human being who understood.

But did he really understand? It came back to the same problem. He'd fooled her once. How could she trust anything about him? She doubted his kiss, his touch, his words, and the things she read in his eyes. Now she doubted her own sanity because she was already losing her heart to him again.

Lee laid the gold and ivory locket on the dresser in his room, his mind replaying Meredith's every word, her every expression, as he'd explained about his grandmother's jewelry.

He could tell by the look in her eyes that she'd understood the significance of the locket and of having his picture in it. He didn't have to explain in detail how it made him feel as if he mattered, as if he was important.

It had always been that way with Meredith. She'd understood him beyond what mere words could convey. She understood things about him that he didn't understand himself.

This time, though, he understood completely what was happening to him. He was starting to care for her, more than was wise. Meredith needed more than he was capable of giving her.

There was Julie to consider, as well. She needed a father who would nurture her, build her confidence, and provide her with the sense of permanence and stability that a child needed.

He had nothing to offer either of them. If he was smart he'd back off before it was too late. There was no use in wishing for things that were out of his grasp.

Lee tugged off his damp shirt, the lingering scent of Meredith filling his nostrils as he pulled it over his head. He steeled himself against the memories of her, turning the shower dial to cold.

He groaned as the pulsating water pounded against him, washing away the film of sweat and the residue of desire that clung to him. But not everything could be rinsed off so easily.

Though he fought them, visions of Meredith filled him, chipping away at his foundation, working their way bit by bit into his heart until he couldn't get her off his mind.

He realized that she was in his thoughts night and day. He was always wondering where she was and what she was doing. He'd started to find inane reasons to be near her, schoolboy excuses to start a conversation. He'd even prefer an argument with her than no contact at all. And now he had the taste of her and the feel of her branded into his senses, as well.

Fear colder than the water beating down upon him punctured his heart. He couldn't allow himself to care for her. Couldn't risk exposing his heart again and having it rejected. He'd never known such conflicting feelings—the need to be with Meredith and the need to run away.

Lee turned off the shower and dried quickly. Pulling on a pair of khaki slacks, he went immediately to the closet and picked up his suitcase. Tossing it onto the bed, he zipped it open and began to pack.

Chapter Nine

Lee walked into the foyer and nearly tripped over the leather travel bag sitting in the middle of the floor. Walt was leaving for New Orleans today, a fact that had played a part in Lee's decision to remain in Gulfport a while longer.

He thought about his own partially filled suitcase still sitting in the corner of his room. He'd been prepared to return to Houston but Meredith's words refused to vacate his thoughts. Her painfully accurate observations about him had made leaving difficult.

Her words hit right on the mark. He did always walk away. It was the way he was made and there was nothing he could do about it. An uneasy feeling settled in his chest when another observation of Meredith's replayed in his ear. *The way you are or the way you want to be?*

Quickly, Lee tuned out her persistent voice. He hadn't seen Meredith in two days and in that time he'd been able to rebuild the defenses her kiss had demolished.

"Well, they aren't going to walk to the car by themselves," Walt snapped as he emerged from his study and glared at his son.

Lee allowed the gruff command to roll off unchallenged. He was beginning to understand that Walt was at his most defensive when he was worried or in this case, scared. Silently, Lee picked up the suitcases and carried them out to the car. When he returned Walt was standing at the window of his study staring out at the front lawn.

He turned as Lee approached.

"You'll be here when I get back?"

Lee nodded, wondering what was behind that loaded question.

"Good, then you can make yourself useful," he said, gesturing toward the desk. "There's some legal papers in that folder there that need looking at. If you can fit it into your busy schedule."

"Wouldn't you rather your own attorney look at them?" Lee asked. Taylor had been his father's lawyer for as long as Lee could remember. Walt never made a move without consulting him first.

"If I wanted John Taylor to look at them I would have called him! These papers concern you."

An old defensive mechanism suddenly kicked in and Lee responded accordingly. "I didn't think anything of yours concerned me anymore." As soon as the words were out Lee regretted them. He'd promised himself he wouldn't rise to the bait anymore.

"Mr. Hotshot Lawyer," Walt said sarcastically. "You think you have all the answers, don't you? Well, you don't." He walked to the desk and picked up the folder. "I'm not getting any younger. I've got things that need to be settled—legal matters that should be put in order. Sand Castle is one of them. Stratton Development is the other."

Lee studied his father closely, puzzled by his sudden attack of frankness. "What do they have to do with me?"

"Hell. I can't take it with me. The way I see it I have two choices. Sell out and divide the money between your stepsisters and you, or hang on to it and try to find a partner, someone who will fill my shoes when I'm gone and keep the company going for a another generation. My great-granddad started this business with a small land office back in 1822. I'd hate to see it end with me."

Lee was familiar with the story. He'd heard it nearly every day of his life. But this time, he seemed to hear it with new ears. This time the significance of it all made sense.

Meredith's voice intruded into his head again, reminding him about the importance of traditions, of family and of continuity.

He was hit with the deafening realization that he wanted permanence in his life. He wanted the peace and contentment that Meredith and Julie had.

He wanted it but he didn't know how to get it. Or what to do with it once he got it. That frightened him.

"Well, do you?" Walt shouted.

Lee jerked his head up and saw Walt looking at him with a deep scowl on his craggy features. "What did you say?"

"Do you want the house or not?"

Lee didn't hesitate. For the first time in years he knew what he wanted. "Yes."

He watched as his father's shoulders squared and his pale blue eyes softened. The corner of Walt's mouth moved in something resembling a smile. Lee couldn't be sure because Walt rarely smiled.

Did it really take so little to make his father happy? One word. One admission that he wanted Sand Castle?

All it would take is a gesture. Once again Meredith's understanding had hit home with pinpoint accuracy.

"That leaves Stratton Development," Walt continued. "First thing you should do is—"

Lee cut him off. "You know how I feel about that." Keeping Sand Castle was one thing. Taking over a company was a different issue entirely. "Stratton Development is your baby, not mine."

"The hell it is!" Walt bellowed. "You think I worked fourteen hours a day for myself? You think I stuck it out during the lean years for me?"

"Yes," Lee answered without hesitation. "It was more important to you than anything in the world."

"No, it wasn't! You were. I did this for you!"

Lee stared at Walt in stunned disbelief, unable to grasp the full implications of his father's words. Walt met his gaze for a moment then looked away as if embarrassed by his sudden admission.

"I couldn't give you anything else after your mother took you away," Walt said softly. "She used my child support payments to keep you locked in that damned boarding school instead of letting you live with me here where you belonged." Walt cleared his throat. "I wanted to at least keep the family business for you."

Shaken and confused, Lee ran his hand through his hair, at a loss to know how to respond or even how to feel about this his father's unexpected confession. "You never told me that."

"I tried to get you into the business," Walt replied gruffly, "but you were bound and determined to be one of them big-shot corporate lawyers."

Lee remembered the arguments and the you'd-better-or-else demands. "You didn't try. You ordered me. No one likes to be told how to live their life."

"Bah," Walt scoffed with a wave of his hand.

Walt moved from behind the desk and Lee was struck again by how frail his father had become. This wasn't the fierce, domineering man who had raised him, but a man facing the loss of the things he'd loved and worked for all his life. Walt was a man alone.

Meredith's words held new meaning. They were both alone, father and son. Alone because they were afraid to reach out. A sinking sensation settled around Lee's heart when he realized he was still afraid. But he wanted to try.

"I'll look over the papers while you're gone," he offered, watching his father closely for his reaction. "I could keep an eye on the business, too, if you want. Maybe even check in at the office."

Walt frowned and averted his gaze. "Least you can do since you can't be bothered to drive me to New Orleans."

Nausea swirled in the pit of Lee's stomach. He'd been a fool to think anything would change between them. "You never asked me," he replied sharply. "Just like you never asked me to join Stratton Development. You order people to do things and then expect to be obeyed. But you never ask."

"What if you'd said no?"

Walt's voice was so low, Lee wasn't sure at first he'd heard his father correctly. Then, as the realization seeped in, long-buried feelings of sadness began to well up in his throat, nearly choking him. His father was afraid to ask him for anything, the same way he was afraid to ask his father. What if the other would say no? Pride and fear had created the chasm between him and Walt and kept them from understanding the simplest things about one another.

Lee looked at the hunched shoulders of his father, his heart a confusion of fear, yearning and affection. The sensation was extremely unpleasant and he was at a loss to know how to proceed. It was what he'd tried to explain to

Meredith. He had no clue how to make a relationship work. He took a deep breath and plunged in.

"Dad," Lee said softly. "All you ever had to do was ask. I'd have done anything to make you happy."

The love and joy that appeared in the older man's eyes slammed hard into Lee's heart.

"Come on, Walter," Florence called as she barged into the room. "The bus is pulling out. If you want to make good time on the interstate we'd best be getting this show on the road."

Lee couldn't take his eyes off Walt. For the first time since he was ten he felt a bond with his father that he was reluctant to release. "Florence, maybe I should drive Walt down to the clinic."

"No can do, honey," Florence said. "I've made plans of my own. There's a big Star Trek convention at the airport hotel that I ain't about to miss. Besides, the dates and times all worked out perfect for Walt's tests. We'll be back sometime Monday."

Lee followed them to the back door. "Dad?"

Walt turned around, his blue eyes bright with affection. "Yeah, son?"

Lee smiled. "Don't worry about anything. I'll handle it all while you're gone. Take care of yourself."

Walt cleared his throat and tugged the ball cap on his head down tighter. "Just see to it you don't mess everything up. Won't be able to find a damned thing…"

His father's voice faded as he turned and headed toward the car.

Lee leaned back in the worn leather chair and stretched his arms above his head. He'd been going over his father's personal files for several hours now and was badly in need of a break.

Pushing himself out of the chair, he walked to the window and looked out, his mind filled with all he'd discovered during the last two days. He'd spent that time at Stratton Development's main office, getting acquainted with the staff and familiarizing himself with procedures.

Stratton Development had always been his last resort as a career. Not because he hated the business, but because he hadn't wanted to work with his father. Whatever Walt had been determined for him to do, Lee had been equally as determined to do the opposite.

But these last days, getting involved in the company, and now, going over Walt's personal affairs, had been surprisingly satisfying.

Lee had been fascinated by the projects Walt was planning, and excited about the possibilities for the future of Stratton Development. He even had several suggestions of his own he was anxious to discuss with his father when he returned.

Walking back to the desk, he was keenly aware of the eerie quiet that filled the old house in Florence's and Walt's absence. Meredith and Julie usually made their presence felt but since the attic incident, Meredith had kept to herself.

He missed her. He wanted to be with her, to talk to her, to hold her again. Fighting the edginess and frustration that plagued him incessantly was driving him crazy. It was nearly impossible to keep the memory of her softness, her voice and every other damned thing about her out of his head!

It was a exercise in futility. He and Meredith were total opposites, from two different worlds. Fantasizing about their being together was pointless.

With a deep breath he reached for a folder and flipped it open.

"Lee?"

He looked up, his whole body responding when he saw

Meredith standing in front of him. She was so lovely his throat tightened just looking at her.

"I'm sorry if I interrupted."

"No." He had to clear his throat before he could go on. "I'm just going over some things for my father."

A warm light appeared in her eyes but he had no idea what put it there.

"I just wanted you to know that Julie and I won't be home tonight. I have a business meeting that should run late and Julie is going to be at a slumber party with her friends. I left the numbers by the phone in the kitchen in case you should need me for anything."

He needed her now. He needed to hold her, to kiss her, to have her beneath him and— He corralled his wandering thoughts and glanced at the desk for fear she would see the desire in his eyes. Regaining control, he looked at her again.

"Thanks. I appreciate the consideration."

She nodded, tucking her hair behind her ears. "Well, I just thought that with Florence and Walt gone we should let someone know where we would be."

Lee stared at her, wanting her to come closer, wanting her to go away, not knowing what the hell he wanted her to do.

Meredith nodded, a small smile touching her lips. "Well, that's all I wanted. I'd better let you get back to work."

She backed toward the door, her gaze still locked with his as if willing him to say something. He didn't know what to say. He didn't know how to ask her to stay or how to ask her to come to him. So he said nothing at all, he just watched as she turned and walked away.

He sighed heavily, and massaged his neck. He had to stop letting her unbalance him. He had to regain control of his senses and accept the fact that Meredith wasn't meant for him. No matter how much he wanted her, no matter how fiercely his body responded to her, she needed all the things that were impossible for him to give.

The best way to regain control was to bury himself in work. Rolling up his mental sleeves, he focused all his energy on reviewing his father's affairs.

He was amazed when he looked up and it was dark outside. He'd worked straight through dinner. Standing, he stretched, pangs of hunger rumbling loudly in his stomach.

As he walked to the kitchen his thoughts returned to his ideas for Stratton Development. Lee gathered sandwich makings from the fridge and carried them to the counter. He was in the middle of spreading mayonnaise on his bread when he realized what he was doing.

He had to be out of his mind. He and Walt could never work together, even if Walt retired he would still be involved with the company and still making his presence felt.

Finished making his sparse meal, he sat at the table. It was his growing dissatisfaction with his career that was causing his irrational thoughts. Nothing more.

He took a bite of the sandwich but found little satisfaction in its taste. Damn. He didn't know how he felt about anything anymore. The thought of staying here scared the hell out of him one minute and intrigued him the next.

He was usually a man in complete control, able to make decisions based upon logic and reason. Now he battled a sense of being adrift, lost and searching, with a knot in his gut that he could only label as fear.

Dealing with Walt, and his growing attraction for Meredith, kept him tense and on edge. The daily loss of control, both mental and physical, was wearing him down.

He glanced around the kitchen, disturbingly aware of the cold, echoing emptiness of the old house. He needed someone to talk to. He needed Meredith.

Lee cursed under his breath and shoved his plate aside. No matter where his thoughts wandered they always came back to Meredith. God, how he missed the closeness he'd once had with her. For three short weeks that long-ago summer he'd known the comfort of a friend and the warmth of her special caring.

When the loud ringing of the phone intruded into his brooding, Lee was half tempted to ignore it. He was in no mood to talk to anyone. But with everyone gone, it might be important. Shoving back his chair, he went to the phone and picked it up.

"Hello?"

"Where's…my…mom?"

The question had been asked between hiccuping sobs and it took Lee a moment to realize who was speaking. "Julie?"

"Is my mom…home yet?" she asked with a loud sniff.

A damp apprehension touched Lee's skin. "No. She's still at her meeting. I don't think she'll be home until late. What's wrong?"

"I want to come ho-ome," she sobbed.

Lee's gut contracted with fear at the thought that the child might be hurt. "What's happened, Julie? Are you all right?" He was hit with the ridiculous desire to reach through the phone lines and pull the child safely to his side.

"I just want to c-c-come home."

Her pitiful wail tore at Lee's heart and sent a fierce protectiveness through his veins that shocked him. Quickly he ran down his options, discarding most of them as too time-consuming.

He knew he should call Meredith, but that meant hanging up on Julie and he was reluctant to lose contact with her in her distraught condition.

There was only one thing to do. He'd have to go get

her himself and call her mother when they got back to Sand Castle.

"Okay, Julie. Tell me where you are and I'll come right over."

The directions she gave him were sketchy but at least he had the address. The house was in a new section of town and it took him longer than expected to find it.

His stomach was churning like the Gulf waters before a hurricane as he waited for someone to answer the door.

"I've come for Julie," he said when a dark-haired woman finally appeared.

Julie nudged past the woman and started toward him, but the woman held her back. "I'm sorry, but I don't know you. I'm not sure I should let her go."

Lee reined in his impatience. "I'm Lee Stratton. Walt Stratton's son. Julie and her mother live in my father's house."

"It's okay, Miss Ann," Julie said, wiping her eyes. "I know him."

The woman looked hesitant. "I have identification," he offered, fighting his growing irritation. He understood her concern but he was more concerned about Julie, who had started to cry again.

"No, I guess it's all right. You look exactly like Meredith described you."

Lee didn't have time to wonder about her comment. He reached for Julie's hand then started to turn away.

"Mr. Stratton?"

Lee stopped and motioned Julie on to the car. "I'll be there in just a second," he told her with a smile.

The woman lowered her voice, concern evident in her tone. "I don't know what happened to upset her. Everything was fine and then suddenly she was in tears and begging to go home. I hope she's all right. Maybe she'll talk to you about it."

For the first time it struck him that he might have to step in and take over the parenting role. His mind spun wildly at the significance of the situation. He was totally out of his league. Completely incompetent to handle Julie's crisis. He didn't know where to begin to coax the story from her. Besides, Julie would never tell him her secrets.

Climbing into the car, he realized the full scope of the situation. His heart twisted like an auger in his chest at the sight of her forlorn little face. Anger and fear exploded in his gut and he couldn't tell which was stronger. His anger that she had been hurt or his fear that he wouldn't be able to fix it for her.

Dear God, is this what parents felt each time their child was hurt? How did Meredith live with this each day?

The need to help Julie was so intense his hands trembled. He looked over at her as he sorted through possible comments and came up empty-handed. She huddled in the corner of the front seat, her head resting against the window, crying softly.

"Julie, is there anything I can do?" It was all he could think of to say to her.

She shook her head, refusing to look at him.

"Are you hurt? Physically, I mean. Did someone hit you or..."

She looked at him and grimaced, as if to say, "Don't be ridiculous."

Stonewalled, Lee retreated and searched for another approach. He felt so inadequate, so helpless.

"I'm sorry your mom wasn't home, Julie. I know you'd rather she picked you up."

Julie sniffed and glanced over at him. "That's okay. I just wanted to come home."

He smiled at her. It's all he could think of to do. It must

have been somewhat helpful because she smiled feebly in return.

"I hate Joey McAlpin."

There was such vehemence in her tone that Lee was alarmed. His first impulse was to demand an explanation, to know if this Joey was the one responsible for her tears. But he suddenly remembered how he'd always hated it when Walt would demand an explanation. Maybe a less aggressive approach would get more results.

"Was he at the party?"

Julie shook her head. "No. It was a slumber party."

Lee waited for more information but Julie kept silent, huddled against the door until they pulled in at Sand Castle a few minutes later.

The moment the car stopped, Julie opened the door and started to run toward the tower. With Meredith away, Lee didn't feel comfortable allowing Julie to be alone in an empty house, especially considering her frame of mind.

"Julie, why don't you stay with me in the main house for a while, until your mother comes home," he called after her.

His suggestion only brought another wail from the child.

She stopped on the steps and turned back to him, her tears glittering in the porch light. "I just wanna go home."

Whatever was upsetting Julie, she obviously needed to be in her own familiar surroundings. She looked so pitiful, so little and forlorn, that Lee's heart ached for her. The sight of her brought the memory of her mother to his mind, and the way she'd looked when he'd left her at the Friendship Oak.

As he came to her side, he realized again that he had no idea how to comfort the little girl. He wasn't good at giving reassurance, or at physical expressions of affection.

The thought came to him that if Meredith were here, she would enfold her daughter in a warm hug and hold her close. Tentatively he reached, hesitating a moment in doubt. What if he did it all wrong?

One look into Julie's sad little face banished all his reservations. The child needed someone and he was the one available at the moment.

He pulled her close to his side, and she rested her small head against his waist as they walked up the steps to the back door. The warm little body, totally dependent upon him, sent a current of warmth surging through him. It wasn't an unpleasant sensation.

Once inside the kitchen, Julie left his side and went to sit at the table. She reached down and picked up her puppy and set him on the table in front of her, holding him close.

Lee was once again out of his element. He had her home, safe and sound. Now what? How could he fix the problem for her if he didn't know what it was?

He glanced at the clock wishing Meredith would come home and handle this. He couldn't go off and leave Julie here alone, but neither could he force her to tell him what had happened. What did that leave?

Then he remembered. When Grandmother Stratton had lived in the tower he used to come and talk to her here in the kitchen. Sometimes when he was troubled she would coax information from him by using an old family recipe.

"Do you like hot chocolate?" he asked Julie.

She nodded, hugging her puppy closer. "But I don't think we have any."

"No problem," he assured her. "I know where Florence keeps everything. I'll be right back. Will you be okay for a few minutes?"

When he returned, Julie was in the same position he'd left her. Sitting at the table, hugging her dog and looking like the end of the world was at hand. What if the chocolate didn't work?

He had to do something. He couldn't stand to sit by and see her so distraught.

He was in the middle of the preparations when Julie finally started to talk.

"How do you know how to make cocoa from scratch?"

Lee smiled at her, feeling hopeful at last. "My grandma used to make it for me and she showed me how once. It's been a long time, though. I'm not sure it'll be any good."

"That's okay."

Silence filled the room again and Lee began to fear he'd been overly optimistic.

"Thanks for coming to get me."

"Sure. I'm glad I could be there to help." He set the mugs of hot chocolate on the table, his gut tensed in anticipation. He wasn't sure if he was more worried that she wouldn't talk to him or that she would. Either prospect held frightening responsibilities.

He waited as Julie continued to stare morosely into her mug, now and then taking a small sip of the sweet liquid.

"It's good," she said quietly.

"Thank you."

Julie smiled and took another sip. "Why are boys so stupid?"

Lee paused with his mug halfway to his mouth. Was her question rhetorical? Or was he supposed to have an explanation for the behavior of his entire sex?

Something told him that how he answered her question would be crucial to helping Julie with her problem. But which way should he go? Agree, "Yes, boys are stupid?" Or disagree, "No, boys just seem stupid because you don't understand them?"

He took the diplomatic approach and prayed that Meredith would return soon. "Is this about the boy you mentioned earlier?"

Julie nodded, her lower lip puckering. "Joey McAlpin. He was supposed to be my friend."

A huge lump formed in Lee's throat as the tears in Julie's eyes welled up again. "You liked him a lot?"

Tears spilled over and rolled down her cheeks. "I thought he liked me, too, but…"

Lee reached for a napkin and handed it to her, not knowing whether to urge her to go on or remain silent. He'd never felt so useless and ignorant in his entire life.

"He promised to take me to Emily's party but he asked Christy instead."

Lee didn't quite grasp the significance of this but it was obviously extremely important to Julie. "I'm sorry," he said, wishing he had some magic words that would ease her sorrow. "I don't know why he would chose someone else over you."

Julie's eyes narrowed angrily and she reached up to her left ear and pulled off her hearing aid, throwing it down on the table. "Because of this stupid thing."

It skidded across the surface and Lee caught it before it fell to the floor. It was expensive and he knew it would be difficult for Meredith to replace it. He handed it back to her carefully and watched as she reluctantly put it back in her ear.

"What does this have to do with anything?" Lee asked, wishing he hadn't when he saw the disgusted grimace on Julie's face. Apparently he was supposed to put the pieces together from what she'd told him.

Julie crumbled into tears again as she tried to explain. "He said…he didn't want to…to…take someone with a han-di-cap to a p-party."

Her words pierced Lee to his soul. The rage he felt growing inside him was like nothing he'd ever known. It ripped open something deep inside him, something he didn't want to face. He gritted his teeth and focused on the child in front of him.

But what did he do? How could he comfort her? Reaching over, he took her tiny hand in his, squeezing it firmly. "He wasn't a very good friend to you."

"But I liked him," she cried. "I really liked him and I thought he liked me."

Her sobs were increasing and Lee rose and moved around the table, hunkering down at her side. Gently he patted her back, following some inner voice that told him touching equaled comforting. He didn't know what else to do for her.

"He was going to take me to the party until he met that new boy," Julie went on. "He told Joey he was a dumb for hanging around with a weirdo who was deaf as a p-post."

Lee felt as if he was being flayed alive. His agony for Julie was doubled by the agony he was experiencing himself. In a sense, Joey had done to Julie what he had done to Meredith all those years ago. He'd betrayed his friend.

Now Lee knew exactly what hell on earth was like. Julie was forcing him to relive his sins through the eyes of his victim.

How could he begin to explain to Julie the insecurities that ran rampant in young boys as strongly as it did in young girls?

"I'm sure he's sorry he hurt you, Julie."

"No, he's not," she said with a quick shake of her head. "He meant to. He never liked me."

"No, I'm sure he liked you. But sometimes boys are scared to let other people, especially girls, know how they really feel."

"I'd have understood. Why didn't he tell me?"

"Probably because he didn't realize what a special gift your friendship was. He didn't understand the value of your feelings for him. I know one thing for certain, though. He'll realize what he's lost and when he does, he'll feel so badly about how he treated you that he won't have any fun at that party and he won't enjoy being friends with that new boy."

Julie raised her head and sniffed, her forehead creasing as she contemplated what he'd told her. "You really think so?"

"I know so."

"You think he'll have an awful, miserable, slimy time at the party?"

"Guaranteed."

Julie wiped her eyes. "Good. I hope he feels like pond scum." Julie turned to him and wrapped her arms around his waist. "Thanks, Lee."

Caught by surprise he froze, uncertain how to accept her open affection. Slowly he embraced her, marveling at the sense of satisfaction he found in knowing he'd been able to help her.

Julie said good-night and went up to her room, leaving Lee with a collection of new emotions to struggle with.

Nothing in his life had given him such a feeling of accomplishment and fulfillment as this one childhood crisis with Julie. He felt victorious but at the same time drained and vulnerable.

It was the vulnerable part that sent bolts of terror to his heart. He was starting to care for Julie and her mother more than was wise. He wanted to protect them, care for them, but even that desire was shadowed by the more powerful need to protect himself. To run away.

He was thinking about his partially packed suitcase when he heard footsteps on the porch. He only had time to stand and face the door before Meredith burst into the room.

"What's going on? What are you doing here?"

The anxiety on her lovely face chilled his heart. He wanted her to never know a moment's fear or apprehension. He longed for the power to remove all pain and discomfort from her life and Julie's. The fact that what he wanted was impossible scared him.

"It's Julie," he said, watching Meredith closely. Before he could say more she paled and gripped his arm.

"Oh, God. What happened? Is she all right?"

Her blue eyes were wide with terror. Quickly, Lee took her arms in his hands and forced her to look at him. "Julie is fine, Meredith. She'd upstairs sound asleep in her own bed."

"I want to see her." She broke free and hurried up the stairs.

Lee wished he could have reassured her, but if he were in her place he'd want to see for himself that his child was safe. The irrational thought crossed his mind that he wished Julie was his child. But that was something he could never have.

"Is she still asleep?" he asked a few minutes later when Meredith returned to the kitchen. The terror was gone from her eyes. He saw only puzzlement and relief in her face now.

It hit him then that he'd have to relive the whole incident again when he explained it to Meredith. He wasn't sure he had the strength to go through it a second time.

"What happened? Why didn't she stay at the slumber party?" Meredith asked.

"Sit down and I'll explain."

Reluctantly she did as he asked. He poured her a cup of hot chocolate and joined her at the table.

"Was she sick? Did she get hurt? Was there a problem with one of the other girls?"

Lee understood her rapid-fire questions, more than he would have a few hours ago. "No. She was just a little upset about something that happened at the party and she wanted to come home.''

"Upset about what?" Meredith wrapped her hands around the mug. "Just start from the beginning."

Dredging up the shreds of his emotional courage, Lee recounted the tale again. "She called about eight-thirty asking for you. She was crying and very upset so I went to get her. The lady at the house—uh..." He fished for a name.

"Ann Conner," Meredith supplied.

"Didn't know what had happened. All she knew was Julie was determined to come home. Julie finally told me that a friend of hers, a boy named Joey, hadn't asked her to a party."

"He didn't? Oh, no, the poor little thing." Meredith bowed her head sadly, then lifted moist eyes to look at him. "She had her heart set on going to Emily's party with him. Boys can be such jerks."

"There's more."

Meredith looked at him closely and he could feel her tension transmitting itself to him. "Apparently the reason he doesn't want to take her is because she is hearing impaired."

"Oh, God," she whispered, placing a hand against her trembling lips. "It's bad enough when strangers tease her about her aid, but when a friend betrays you..." She shook her head slowly. "You never get over that."

Her words punctured his fragile defenses, flooding his chest with acid remorse and regret. There was nothing he could do but face his past yet again, seeing it first through Julie's eyes and now through her mother's.

Meredith rose and paced the small kitchen. "Why would he do this to her? They've been friends since the second grade. Joey knows all about her hearing impairment."

Lee rubbed his eyes against the pain building in his skull.

The repercussions of his thoughtless act that summer were coming home to roost and deservedly so. Lee knew he'd never be able to make Meredith understand why he'd betrayed her or why Joey had hurt Julie.

Glancing over at Meredith, Lee saw her huddled near the archway, her arms wrapped tightly around her waist as she cried.

"I should have been here for her."

Lee's heart twisted again, his gut wrenching at the thought of Meredith in pain. He hurt for her, not only because he was responsible for part of her pain but because she meant so much to him.

He went to her and slowly turned her into his embrace. "Shh," he whispered, not knowing if he was making things better or worse, only knowing he had to hold her and take away her pain if he could. "You can't be there for her every moment."

"I know, but everything that hurts her hurts me. I know you don't understand that, but seeing your child in pain is the most horrible feeling in the world."

"I know." He stroked her hair, wishing he could go back and redo the past. Wishing he would have gone back to the tree that night and comforted her the way he had Julie.

Meredith rested her head on his shoulder crying softly. The scent of her filled him, the warmth of her seeped deep into his soul, the softness of her consumed him.

"Meredith—"

"She's just a child," she said, looking up at him.

He looked into her tear-softened eyes, unable to pull himself out of their depths, unable to think of anything but Meredith in his arms, filling him, warming him, chasing away the darkness and the loneliness as no one else could.

He knew if he kissed her now there'd be no turning back. If he took this step he would never be the same again.

Fear like a glacier scraped against his soul, but the warmth of the woman in his arms melted it away. Gently he placed his fingertips under her chin, tilting her face upward to receive his kiss.

Chapter Ten

Meredith looked into Lee's eyes and saw desire smoldering in their green depths. His fingers were warm on her chin, his breath brushed softly against her cheek. She wanted his kiss. She wanted more than just a kiss.

Abruptly she moved away, putting distance between herself and Lee. She shouldn't be thinking of making love to him. She should be thinking about Julie.

Pulling a tissue from her pocket, she wiped her tears and sniffed, aware that she was lying to herself. Julie was fine. There would be long talks and comfort sessions in the days ahead, but Julie didn't need her at the moment.

Meredith was the one who need comfort and reassurance, and Lee's nearness was a fierce temptation. Especially tonight when she was feeling scared and vulnerable.

"Meredith," he said softly.

Looking at him would be a mistake. Gazing into those hypnotic emerald eyes would destroy what resistance she had left. But her body answered the call of her name on his lips.

He came to her, slowly as if stalking his prey, never taking his eyes from hers. When he stopped, inches from her face, he didn't touch her but held her captive with the force of his will.

Meredith's breath came quickly, matching her escalating heartbeat. His green eyes were warm with compassion, heavy with desire and she knew she couldn't stop the kiss he was about to give her.

She would give him whatever he asked because she wanted the same thing. She'd wanted this from the moment he'd come back into her life.

"I want you, Meredith."

The huskiness in his voice stroked her desire as if he'd physically touched her. But the ease with which he could arouse her set off an alarm, reminding her of the consequences of her actions.

"That's not a good idea." Her voice trembled.

Lee lifted his hands to her face, cradling it between his palms. "Let me comfort you tonight, Meredith. Let me carry your burden for a while."

Meredith fought to withstand his tender touch, his seductive offer. She really didn't want to spend another night alone, to lie in that bed and ache for someone to hold and touch. But it was dangerous to depend upon him for comfort. He could so easily let her down again. He wasn't always going to be here for her.

"It's irresponsible," she said, backing away, out of his reach.

"Are you saying you don't want this?" he asked, coming toward her again.

She couldn't lie to him, but what she wanted and what was right were two different things. "No, but—" She inhaled sharply as Lee reached out and touched the side of her neck.

"What about the attic? I didn't imagine what happened between us, did I?"

He was ruthless. Even now the memory of his warm hands upon her skin, the thought of his mouth covering her breast, sent a flash fire surging through her senses. Fear pushed its way to the surface of her mind again, turning down the flames.

"It was a mistake. It was hot and steamy up there. We were trapped. There was wine and music." She realized she was babbling. "It was a mistake."

Lee moved closer again, his eyes caressing her face hungrily. "You responded. I didn't imagine that."

"I got caught up in the moment."

He leaned toward her, kissing her temple. "Don't turn your back on what's happening with us."

She closed her eyes, aching to sink into the warm, hazy world of passion he was offering her. "I want to but I have to set an example for Julie. I'm her mother." She shivered as Lee kissed the sensitive spot behind her ear.

"You are a woman first, or have you forgotten?" he whispered.

She had forgotten. She'd closed off the part of her Lee was resurrecting and never looked back. Now she wanted to reclaim it in Lee's arms. Fear roared inside her head. Fear of the unknown. Fear of unleashing needs long ignored. Fear of repeating old mistakes.

Lee gathered her into his arms and all her fears began to disintegrate. She found the security she'd always longed for in his embrace and she relinquished herself to him, telling herself it was just for tonight.

"You were made for love," he said softly in her ear. "You were made to give it and to have it given to you. Let me love you, Meredith."

His lips were warm and gentle, his kiss was one of comfort and reassurance, of understanding and caring.

She melted against him, tentatively letting down her guard, allowing him access to passions that had been long dormant. Passions she'd buried under responsibility, motherhood, career aspirations. Passion she'd told herself she didn't miss.

But she did miss it, and each touch of his gentle hand reminded her of how much. He cradled her head in his hands, pressing her mouth hard against his as he devoured her lips. His kiss was demanding, ravenous and hot this time.

Lee deepened his exploration of her mouth, his tongue probing and teasing her to take him deeper within. All her senses were exploding, out-of-control fires rampaging through her body.

But it was happening so fast. Too fast. She wondered for one anxious moment if she could control them. It had been so long, so very long. What if she couldn't put the fire out?

Breathless, she broke off the kiss, scared yet every fiber of her being throbbed with life and need for him. She looked into his eyes. They were wild and hungry, green orbs of fire filled with desire for her.

"Oh, Lee." The realization convulsed through her. His raw hunger was for her. No one else but her. His passion was for *her*.

It was a heady sensation, having him find her desirable. He whispered her name and she trembled with a deep primal need.

Slowly, Lee slid his hand to her breast, his thumb coaxing the nipple to hardness beneath the thin fabric of her dress. She arched into him, feeling the heat, eager to plunge into the flames and feeling more alive than she had in her whole life. It was a terrifying and exciting sensation.

He groaned and took her mouth again, crushing her to him, the evidence of his need pressing hard against her stomach.

The clock chimed in the corner, a rude intrusion into her sensual intoxication state. Slowly she became aware of their surroundings. They were standing in the kitchen where anyone could come in on them, including Julie. It took great effort to pull out of his embrace and find her voice.

"Julie..." Her words were smothered by his mouth and she moaned. "What if—" she tried again "—she wakes..."

Lee cursed softly and straightened. "Your room?"

She nodded. Before she could say more he'd scooped her up into his arms and carried her upstairs. He set her on her feet near the bed then turned to hurriedly shut and lock the door.

His impatience stoked her inner fires and when he looked at her she could feel the heat of his fiery green eyes as his gaze raked her up and down.

"Do you know what you do to me?" His voice was thick with desire. "Making love to you is all that I've thought about since I came back, Meredith." He touched her hair, reverently drawing the strands through his fingers.

She swayed toward him and he dropped his hands to her hips, forcing her hard against him. The heat of him, hard and urgent, sent spirals of desire throbbing through her.

Then slowly he reached up and unbuttoned the first button on her dress, his fingertips brushing with tantalizing lightness against her skin. With each button he released he bent and kissed the warm flesh he'd exposed.

Meredith swayed in the midst of a fire. A fire she had no desire to escape from. With each button, each kiss, her need to have him inside her increased. His lips left burning brands down her chest and abdomen, and she moaned, clutching his shoulders to keep from falling.

Slowly he unfastened the button at her waist, slipping her bodice down, kissing each shoulder as it was revealed. Then he kissed her neck, her collarbone and the valley between her breasts.

"Lee." She ground out his name, quivering with delicious frustration. She reached for him but he captured her hands, holding them at her sides while his lips sought her mouth, his tongue a thrusting prelude to what was to come.

Limp, unable to do more than stand and let him explore her heated flesh at his leisure, she drifted upon the surging current of heat each touch brought to life.

She heard the faint snap of her bra as he released the clasp and felt the cool air on her fevered skin. His hands toyed with her eager breasts, circling them with his fingertips, kneading them then tracing agonizing circles with his thumbs.

Her knees buckled but he pulled her to him and covered her left breast with his mouth, soliciting a wild gasp of shock and pleasure. She held on to him, fingers digging into his shoulder, her insides pulsating with each lave of his hot tongue.

Lee took his fill of her flesh then eagerly sought her lips once more. He devoured her mouth with abandon, his tongue filling her, stoking that inner fire that was already well fueled.

The burning hunger in his eyes as he looked at her excited her naked breasts like nothing ever had. She felt beautiful, desirable and powerful.

His fingers worried the belt at her waist, disposed of it and began to hurriedly unfasten the remaining buttons. The dress slid down over her hips while his fingers probed her moist femininity, promising fulfillment. A wonderfully surreal feeling stole over her and she clutched him tightly to keep from collapsing.

"Oh, Meredith. You're so lovely. So beautiful."

She felt self-conscious now, her body intimately revealed to him while he was still fully clothed. She tugged at the zipper on his trousers, the raspy sound sending tingles of anticipation along her spine.

Her hand stroked him, feeling his heat, and the convulsive jerk of his body revealed her effect upon him. She reached for him again but he grabbed her hand, standing back and devouring her with his eyes.

"Let me look at you. Do you know how beautiful you are? How perfect? The moment I saw you that first day in the kitchen, I thought you were an angel. Now I know for certain that you are. The angel of love."

He crushed her to him, her breasts burrowing eagerly against his chest, the nipples hardening painfully as they rubbed his skin. Her hips curled toward him, inviting him to finish what he'd started.

He groaned deep in his throat and claimed her mouth with fierce possessiveness. Lifting her off the floor, he eased her onto the bed.

There was no turning back now. No reason to fear, no obstacles. Just the two of them, needing, wanting and sharing. She was desired, cherished and hungered for. She'd never known such complete happiness.

Lee discarded his clothes in a frenzy, desperate to hold Meredith against him again. Nothing in his life had ever felt as right as her in his arms, her heart beating in rhythm with his. He wanted her, all of her, like a man frozen to the core, he wanted to bury himself in her warmth and wrap himself in her softness.

But more than anything he wanted to chase away her loneliness and make her feel safe and protected. He didn't know how to do those things. He had no words, but here, in this intimate way, he could express all the emotions he denied elsewhere.

He wanted to go slowly, to make her understand that what he was feeling was special, important. He let his hands, his lips, his body tell her all the things his heart was too afraid to say. He told her of his regret, his need of her, his sorrow. But he also told her of his passion and the way she drove him wild.

Watching her bloom under his hand, hearing her cries of pleasure as his lips tasted every intimate throbbing part of her, excited him to a fierceness he'd never known. In some unfathomable way, the more pleasure he gave to her, the more pleasure he received in return.

She was an angel who penetrated his icy cave and shone the light of life into its dark corners, exposing him to emotions he'd not seen for most of his life, and setting them free.

He became part of her emotions, as well, until he was unable to tell where he ended and she began. Except for one tiny fragment lurking in the shadows of his soul that taunted him. Even if he gave Meredith everything he was and would ever be, it could never be enough to match her limitless love.

Meredith wrapped her legs around him and even those dark fears retreated in the glare of their burning passions.

Going slowly would be harder than he'd first thought. The silken feel of her under him, his desperate need for her were causing sensation to quickly build and throb in his loins. With supreme effort, he willed his body into a more manageable state, focusing on Meredith and putting her pleasure ahead of his own.

He kissed her forehead, feeling her pulse leap as his tongue left a trail on her temple and the side of her neck. Her lashes fluttered against his lips when he kissed her eyelids.

She was pliant in his hands now, no tension, no fear. Her languor fueled the protective urges in him and he wanted more than anything to be perfect for her.

Her eyes were mere slits, her lips soft and parted. Her small hand touched his chest and he gasped as her fingers burrowed beneath the dark hair and met his flesh. His hand sought the warm core of her, increasing his surging desire to bury himself in the center of her softness.

Meredith was helpless against the fierceness of Lee's passion. Her body burned, simmered, as he pushed her higher into the throes of delicious torture, sending her insides into coiling tightness.

He took her to heights of pleasure she'd never imagined. He anticipated her every desire before she realized it herself. He knew where and how to touch her to keep her teetering on the edge of oblivion. It was as if he were part of her soul.

His hardness teased at her center and she opened herself to him, crying out his name. She took him in fully, eagerly, and held on as they rode their rhythmic passion dance even higher. One hard thrust and they were careening over the edge into explosive satisfaction.

Her softness closed around him and his world erupted in laser bolts of hot color and mind-jolting currents of exploding release. Lee found where he wanted to be for the rest of his life. In Meredith's arms there was peace, joy, all the emotions he'd so fiercely denied, so doggedly suppressed.

He wasn't frightened of them here. He wasn't alone. He could face anything with Meredith. He was omnipotent.

Meredith filtered back through the world of mindless passion as Lee pulled her into the sheltering curve of his shoulder. Collecting her senses piece by piece, she settled against the warm, firm reality of Lee's hard chest beneath her cheek.

This was what it felt like to be loved. To be whole and connected. There was no Meredith, no Lee. Only them, making something more wonderful together than either of them could make alone.

In Lee's arms she was beautiful, treasured. No one else had ever made her feel those things and right now that was enough.

Dawn was touching the sky when Lee awoke. The night had been a blur of turbulent passion. He'd lost track of the times Meredith had aroused him to a fever with a touch of her hand or a glance from her blue eyes.

She was sleeping with her head in the hollow of his shoulder. The fragrance of her hair was in his nostrils when he breathed.

If only he could wake each day with her warmth in his arms and the scent of her filling him, to know this sense of connection with the world around him.

He touched his fingers to her tousled hair and felt the jolt of desire in his loins as her eyes opened and she smiled at him.

"Good morning," she whispered.

God, he could die at this moment. He knew what happiness was. He knew what love was.

He loved her.

Realization rumbled through him like an earthquake, toppling the last of his emotional barriers, swallowing the foundation of his control and unleashing a rampage of feelings.

Joy and terror, happiness and anguish, confidence and anxiety all crashed like storm-tossed waves upon his mind faster than he could comprehend.

Underneath the surging current one emotion remained constant. Love.

It was an unfamiliar emotion but he had no trouble recognizing it. He would do anything for Meredith. He would die for her, sell his soul, but the one thing she needed he wasn't sure he could give. His love.

Loving her was one thing. Knowing how to share that love was something else entirely. That was his eternal obstacle. He looked over at her, so warm, so beautiful in his arms. Everything he had ever dreamed of, alive and pulsating beneath his hand.

"Lee? Are you all right?"

She was still smiling. She reached up to touch his cheek and his fragile emotions screamed in protest. He tried to force them back into the icy tunnels from where they'd come, but it was futile. His lack of control scared the hell out of him.

He needed to time to think, time to examine his love for her. He couldn't do that with her in his arms. His body and his mind were in conflict. He needed to be close to her but wanted to pull away.

He reached out to stroke her hair, his hand trembling violently with the anticipated bombardment of raw emotions he would stir up.

"I'd better go," he said softly, pulling back his hand. "I don't want Julie to see me leaving. It would put you in an awkward position."

He didn't want her to know his fears. He didn't want her to think he was leaving because of her.

She must have sensed his confusion because he could read the question in her eyes, feel her slipping away.

Afraid to risk another look into her eyes, he rose, dressed and walked to the door. Only then did he trust himself to gaze upon her again. She was so lovely, so incredibly special and so far removed from his world.

He couldn't lose her a second time. But, God help him, he didn't know how to stop it.

* * *

Meredith watched him leave, sadness frosting her heart as the door closed behind him. She'd seen the fear darken his eyes, she'd felt him pulling away, retreating deep into his glacier where she couldn't follow.

She'd wanted to pull him back, draw him close and take him back into that perfect world of passion they'd explored all night.

A week ago she would have dismissed Lee's withdrawal as another sign of his indifference. But something had happened last night. She'd discovered that beneath Lee's icy facade there was a tender, gentle man trapped by his own fears. She wanted to release him from that cold existence and teach him how to express all the feelings he kept buried.

She'd found something else last night, as well, something she'd been searching for all her life. In Lee's arms she'd found where she belonged. She'd found a man who made her believe he wanted her for herself and no other reason.

She rolled over onto her side into the lingering heat of his body that still warmed the sheet. She'd fooled herself into thinking that one night of passion, of feeling special, was all she ever wanted. Now she wasn't so sure she could live without the feelings that Lee had awakened.

It was time to pay the consequences. She'd lowered her defenses, letting her soft heart override her head. The inferno of passion he'd unleashed in her arms had consumed them both.

But what had Lee felt? He'd said he needed her, that he desired her and he wanted to carry her burdens on his shoulders for a while. He'd said all the right things, but did he mean them or were they empty phrases muttered in the throes of desire? Words that held no substance in the harsh light of day? He'd never said he cared, never said he wanted more from her than last night.

She would be a fool to think something special happened between them last night. She'd be an even bigger fool to think that Lee had experienced it, too. But she was afraid it was too late. She was already in love with him and there was nothing she could do about it.

He loved her. Had always loved her, he could see that now. But giving that love to her, sharing the powerful emotion, was a mystery. Love was supposed to make you happy, but love was tearing him apart. He was losing his mind.

Meredith had weakened his once-impervious barriers until the walls were paper-thin. But he couldn't live with the fragile shell that encased his emotions, barely keeping them in check. He was terrified of what would happen if that last protection gave way. He'd be inundated with feelings and emotions he'd never learned to handle.

Every tiny feeling quivered inside him with acute awareness. He hadn't felt this confused and panicky since the day his parents split. Scared and at the mercy of emotions that were threatening to eat him alive, Lee had instinctively known if he was going to survive he'd have to shut down. Disengage from his feelings. He couldn't hurt if he didn't feel. If he stopped caring he could stop the pain.

You've got to care about someone or you might as well be dead.

Realization and understanding collided in his mind like full-steam locomotives.

Damn. Meredith had known from the beginning what he'd done. He'd always thought he was incapable of feeling. Now he saw that he'd chosen not to feel because he'd been afraid of having his love rejected. He'd thought there was something wrong with him that made everyone he loved shove him away, reject the love he wanted to give them.

Somewhere along the way, what started out as a means to endure the trauma of the divorce had become a way of life. His emotions had withered and died from lack of use.

Lee ran his hands through his hair, hastily examining this new revelation. That's why he'd left Meredith in the tree that night. Fear of her rejection. Fear that if she looked too closely at him she would see he was empty inside and turn away. So he'd turned away first even though he'd loved her.

Why hadn't he seen this before? It was all so clear to him now. But what now? What did he do with this new knowledge? He had a reason for his withdrawal but still no solution for it. Meredith had shown him how to feel, but she hadn't told him what to do with those feelings once he'd uncovered them.

In her arms he'd found peace, fulfillment and love. Without her, his newly unleashed emotions would slink back into their tombs. He couldn't go back and he was too afraid to move forward.

A momentary panic surged into his mind. What was he going to do? There was no one to turn to. No one to help him. He was trapped between his fear and his love for Meredith.

Love. It alone was the one thing he was certain of. If only he could tell her, confess how much he loved her, but he'd lost that right years ago. She would never believe him nor forgive him now.

Head bowed, Lee rested his palms on the secretary, staring blindly at the objects laid out there. Slowly, one came into sharper focus. His grandmother's locket. He picked it up, thinking of Meredith and remembering the silken feel of her beneath him.

He knew Meredith cared for him; she wouldn't have made love with him if she didn't. But how deep did her feelings run? Even if she could care, when she learned he didn't know how to love her the way she needed, she would reject him, too.

He tossed the locket down, cursing loudly. Dear God, he needed her, he needed her help. She was the only one who could guide him through the maze of feelings churning inside him. She was the only person who knew him better than he'd ever known himself. She made him feel whole and invincible and gave his life meaning.

How could he ever make her understand how much she meant to him? How vital she was to his existence? Meredith had said to find love you first had to give it. He wanted to give his love to her. He wanted to give her everything.

God forgive him. He didn't know how.

Meredith pushed open the French door in her room and strolled out onto the upper gallery, stopping at the rail. The picture-postcard view with its riot of colorful azaleas and sparkling Gulf waters barely registered on her troubled thoughts.

Her body still vibrated like a violin string whenever she thought about making love with Lee last night. Never had she known such a feeling of completeness, of oneness, as she had found in his arms.

She wanted to believe he'd found her attractive, that all his fierce passion had been for her alone. She knew she should regret giving in to her need for him but she couldn't. But neither was she so foolish as to ignore the voice that reminded her of his past transgressions.

Tucking her hair behind her ears, Meredith glanced toward the main section of the house. Walt had returned from New Orleans this afternoon. She was anxious to hear about his test results but unwilling to risk seeing Lee so she'd settled for secondhand information from Florence.

Meredith knew she couldn't avoid Lee forever, but before she saw him again she needed to think things through. Most importantly, how she felt about him and their night together.

Old doubts had begun to creep back into her head, replacing the earlier desire to comfort Lee. She wanted to believe he hadn't meant to hurt her that summer. She wanted to believe he'd wanted her last night because he cared and not because he was lonely and she was willing.

No. She'd needed comfort last night and he'd provided it in every way. His warm embrace, his gentle loving had touched a part of her long forgotten.

"Good morning, Meredith."

The blush was in her cheeks the moment she heard Lee's voice. She turned to face him, memories of her wild and wanton behavior in his arms scrolled rapidly across her mind, quickening her pulse and warming more than her cheeks.

"Hello," she said, silently willing her pulses to slow down. His eyes touched her and she felt her core clench reflexively. All her senses were attuned to him, responding with a will of their own.

"Is Walt okay?" she asked, hoping to divert her wandering thoughts. "I haven't had a chance to see him yet."

Lee nodded, coming toward her. "Not all the tests were back, but so far everything looks good. How's Julie?"

She wrapped her arms around her waist, trying to mask the shimmer of desire that his scent aroused. "She's fine. We had a long mother and daughter talk."

"She's a tough little kid," Lee said with a smile.

Meredith was pleased that Lee thought of Julie at a time like this. "Walt is tough too, Lee. There's not much can get him down."

Again Lee nodded, but the shadow of anxiety in his eyes gave her pause. She became aware of tenseness in his stance, a tightness around his mouth.

"What is it? Is anything wrong?"

"No. But I need to talk to someone. You're the only one who will understand."

A vague uneasiness moved deep inside her chest. The tone of his voice told her nothing. It was even, controlled, and without inflection. She braced herself for the worst.

"The other night, after we…" He took a deep breath and started again. "Something happened that made me realize you've been right about me."

Puzzled, Meredith peered at him more closely. For the first time she noticed how tired he looked. "What do you mean?"

Lee bowed his head a moment as if gathering his thoughts. When he lifted his gaze to hers, the look of confusion and fear in his eyes sent a chill along her spine.

"I did shut down my emotions. I guess it was a means of self-preservation." He shook his head slowly. "After a while, I got so used to not feeling it became normal to feel dead inside. I channeled all my energy into work and sustaining the illusion of being in control of my life." He looked at her. "But I wasn't born this way. I chose to become like this. I did it to myself. To keep people from getting too close."

Meredith smiled, setting aside her own feelings. Lee had made a significant discovery, one that could change his life. Happiness for him filled her heart. "Then you can choose to change how you are. You don't have to hold yourself aloof anymore from everyone who cares for you. Especially your family."

Lee turned and ran a hand across the back of his neck. "I may understand, but I don't know what to do about it. I've got a knot in my gut the size of a basketball, Meredith. My skin crawls like a thousand insects are on me. I feel like a dam about to burst, and I don't know how to stop it. I need your help."

His rising fear reached out to her, sending a shiver along her nerves. "What can I do?"

"Tell me how to handle these feelings," he pleaded, his eyes dark and tormented. "They scare the hell out of me."

Taking a deep breath, Lee walked a few feet away. "This is why I left you that night," he said softly.

Meredith wasn't sure she'd heard him correctly. "What?"

"The real reason I left you in the oak. I didn't understand it myself until a short while ago. But I was scared of this—" He pointed to his chest. "Scared of the feelings that you stirred inside me."

Meredith's heart went out to him. He was so confused, so lost. She searched for something comforting to say.

"God, Meredith, you were so giving, so willing to share yourself. You poured out all this attention, all this affection on me, but I didn't know what to do with it. You had so much love in you and I had nothing inside me."

The note of amazement in his voice touched her and brought a sting of tears to her eyes. "You could have given me your friendship."

"No, I couldn't." Lee shook his head, a sardonic grin on his face. "I didn't know how. So I took the coward's way out. I dumped you before you could dump me."

Meredith moved toward him, touching his arm lightly. The muscles in his forearm flexed under her fingers. "I wouldn't have dumped you."

"Yes, you would have. Once you found out I had nothing to give you in return." He reached out and briefly touched her hair with his fingertips. "It's like I've been emotionally deaf all my life, but in these last few weeks, being with you again, it's like having the sound turned on inside me. Meredith, you're the most amazing woman I've ever known. You have this capacity for love that washes over everyone you touch."

The look of wonder and affection in his eyes made her heart skip a beat. "Lee?"

Lee grasped her shoulders in his hands, squeezing them tightly. "I need you, Meredith. I've suddenly realized how much I need you. But you'll have to show me what to do, teach me how to handle all these feelings. Because if you don't..." He took a deep breath then rested his forehead against the top of her head. "I think I'll go out of my mind."

The serrated edge of disappointment pushed slowly into Meredith's heart. Lee needed her. Everyone in her life needed her. She didn't want to be needed. She needed to be *wanted.*

She realized in that instant that somewhere deep inside she'd harbored the hope that Lee loved her. She wanted to hear him say that he shared the special feelings she'd experienced last night.

A permanent sorrow weighed upon her heart. She bit her lip against the hurt. What else could she expect? She would always be overlooked.

"Well, looky here," Walt laughed good-naturedly as he came toward them. "Didn't I tell you I'd win the bet?"

Meredith pulled back, looking up into Lee's eyes, her heart pounding. "What?" The stunned and guilty expression on Lee's face sent wave after wave of shock slamming into her. *Dear God, please, not again.*

"Bet? What's he talking about?" She searched Lee's face for a sign of denial, knowing in her heart what had happened. Bitter nausea burned in her throat. Lee had used her again.

Her mind reeled and she backed away from Lee. He reached for her but she raised her hands to ward him off.

"There was no bet," he said quickly. "It was just an offhand comment. It's insignificant."

Shock yielded quickly to fury. "Insignificant? Like me?" she said, daring him to look at her.

"No, Meredith, let me explain."

He grasped her arm but she jerked away, trembling with rage. "I don't want any more explanations from you. How could you do this to me again?" She could hear the hysteria edging her voice but she couldn't stop from berating him. "You think because you're incapable of feeling, everyone else is, too? You think I'm some lifeless chess piece you can move about at will?"

"No, please—"

Pain clawed at her heart, slicing it into pieces. She backed away from both men, but her eyes were riveted on Lee. "What was it this time, Lee? Did you bet your father you could get me into your bed?"

"No, it wasn't like that. I meant what I said. I need you."

"I'm so glad I could put you in touch with yourself," she replied angrily.

Walt came toward her, his hand outstretched. "Meredith, this is all my fault. I made a bet that you and Lee would become friends, that's all. I'm sorry if I've created problems between you two."

"Problems between us started years ago, Walt." She turned and looked at Lee. "Congratulations. You won again."

Fighting spasms of anguish, Meredith managed to hold herself together until she was safely locked inside her bedroom. Alone, rejected and reliving the hellish nightmare of the past, she clutched her fists to her chest as the pain became unbearable.

"Oh, God." Stumbling to the bed, she curled up in a ball and gave herself over to the torrent of tears.

Chapter Eleven

After the tears had dried, after the pain had subsided, Meredith gathered her shattered emotions and sought refuge in the studio, isolating herself from everyone. All she wanted was to be alone with her pain and remind herself what a damned fool she'd been to believe Lee Stratton a second time.

She'd been an even bigger fool to let herself start to fall for him when she knew he couldn't be trusted. Actually, she should be grateful that it turned out this way. No real harm was done. Her ego was bruised and her heart was sore, but she would survive.

A shroud of melancholy draped over her. All she ever wanted was to be loved for herself. Apparently that wasn't meant to be.

Oh, sure, Julie loved her. She'd rescued her from an orphanage. Florence loved her because she'd given her a sense of belonging. Walt loved her because she filled the empty spot in his life Lee had left.

Did any of them love her because she was Meredith? Or only because of what she could do for them? Taking a deep breath she forced the self-pity into the back of her mind.

"Mom, why are you so mad at Lee?"

Meredith sighed in exasperation but didn't look up when her daughter approached the worktable. "I'm not mad."

"Mr. Walt said you and Lee had a big fight."

Walt was worse than an old woman when it came to telling tales out of school. "Well, he was wrong," she said. "We just had a difference of opinion."

"Mom, I'm not a kid anymore. I understand stuff. You can talk to me."

Julie's sympathetic tone pierced Meredith's defenses. Her little girl was growing up. Maybe it was time she treated her that way. Slipping her arm around her daughter's waist, she pulled her close. "I trusted him and he let me down again. The same way he did when we were young."

"Like Joey did to me?" Julie asked, resting a comforting arm across Meredith's shoulders.

"Something like that."

"Did you let him explain?"

She sighed and shook her head. "It wouldn't do any good. I heard it all the last time."

"That's not what you tell me," Julie reminded her. "You said that I owed the other person a chance to explain. You know, in case I'd misunderstood something."

Meredith shifted uncomfortably under Julie's righteous statement. "That was different."

"How?"

Meredith couldn't ignore her smarting conscience. Julie was right. There was no difference except that this situation concerned her personally.

"I let Joey explain. He said he was sorry and now we're going to the party together after all."

This was the first Meredith had heard about the shift in their relationship. "Julie, that's wonderful. I'm so happy for you."

Julie stared at her mother meaningfully and Meredith was forced to look away. "This is different," she repeated, rising and walking to the coffeepot. She poured herself a cup, only to be reminded of the day Lee had spilled coffee on her and the way the touch of his hand had sent tingles along her spine.

She set the mug down. "Even if I let Lee explain, it wouldn't change anything. He can't be counted on, Julie. Not when we were kids and not now. When things get too emotional he'll walk away."

"No, he won't. He likes us. You don't know him at all."

The tremor in her daughter's voice reminded Meredith of Julie's strong feelings toward Lee. She'd have to try to set aside her own wounded pride and deal with Julie's feelings more gently.

"Sweetie, I know you're hoping for something romantic to happen between Lee and me, but it's not going to."

Julie's lower lip quivered and her eyes were unusually bright. "It could if you weren't looking for Mr. Perfect."

"I'm not," Meredith denied, tucking her hair behind her ears.

"Yes, you are," Julie challenged, pulling away. "You keep telling me no one is perfect, but you want Lee to be—and I think that stinks." Bursting into tears, Julie fled, slamming the door behind her.

Meredith cursed under her breath, feeling as if she was losing her mind. No one understood her position at all. Was she the only one who saw how things really were between her and Lee?

Meredith had barely sat down at the design table when the door opened again and Florence came into the studio.

"All right. Talk to me," she demanded, planting herself in front of the table.

"About what?" Meredith asked, knowing full well what was on the older woman's mind.

"About what happened between you and Lee."

"Nothing. We just don't get along."

"Now that's the understatement of the year," she agreed in disgust. "I've seen the way he looks at you and you him. I'm not an idiot. I know when two people are hot for each other."

"Florence, I'm busy."

"You sure it's Lee that's got you so upset or are you angry because you're scared and he's an easy excuse?"

"I'm not scared of Lee Stratton," Meredith said with conviction.

"What is it, then? He couldn't pass the test for knighthood you devised for him? It was bound to happen sooner or later, you know. You can't expect people to meet your requirements, especially when they're so damned outlandish."

Meredith slammed her binder down on the counter. Was she the only one who could see this thing clearly? "Trust isn't outlandish."

"No, but lying to yourself is," Florence retorted.

Meredith sighed. There was no point in arguing with Florence. She had an answer for everything. It would be easier if she just explained it to her. Taking a deep breath, she set one fist against her hip. "He used me again. Just like before."

"Do you really believe that or are you looking for a reason to prove he's not worthy of your trust?"

"He's not," Meredith insisted. "He used his lost-little-boy routine to make me feel sorry for him so he could win

a bet with Walt. I was a fool for letting him get to me
again.''

"Nope,'' Florence said with a firm shake of her head.
"I don't buy it. Lee isn't a man who plays silly games.
He's a man looking for answers. A man trying to find some
missing piece of himself and I think he found it in you.''

"What he found was a sucker.''

"I think you're the one being unfair now.''

Meredith couldn't believe what she was hearing. "Me?
I trusted him. I fell in love with him again and he doesn't
care one bit for me.'' God help her, she sounded like a
petulant child.

"Don't believe that, either,'' Florence said, pointing a
finger in Meredith's face. "I think he cares so much it
scares the hell out of him. Everything comes so easy for
you. Your emotions are all out there for the whole world
to see, but not everyone is like you, Meredith.''

Meredith set her jaw. She didn't want to be preached
to. She wanted someone to understand her position. "I
don't want to be hurt again.''

"You can't avoid that, sweetie. Pain is part of life and
so is disappointment, failure and heartache.''

Meredith wrapped her arms around her waist and stared
into the distance. Hadn't she endured enough heartache in
her life already?

"You expect everyone to show their feelings the way
you do. You give love freely, you want them to do the
same. Maybe it's time to cut the other guy some slack,
kiddo. Or do you want to be alone the rest of your life?''

"This has nothing to do with being alone. I was putting
the past behind me. Trying to give Lee a second chance,
despite all my common sense that warned otherwise. I told
myself we were young, it was a long time ago. Get over
it.'' Meredith tucked her hair behind her ear. "Then I'd
look into his eyes and see such sadness, such confusion

and pain and I couldn't stand it. I wanted to help him. I wanted to help Walt, too, and get them back together.''

"And it worked," Florence said. "You weren't there, but you should have seen the way they acted when Walt came home this afternoon. They didn't exactly hug one another but there was a bond there, a warmth that I'd never seen before."

Meredith felt a pang of jealousy cut deep into her, then quickly chided herself for being selfish. Lee and Walt's reunion was one of the things she'd hoped for, she shouldn't feel shut out now that it was coming to pass.

"I'm happy for them. I really am. But that doesn't change anything between Lee and me."

"Just what did he say that prompted this?"

"He said he needed me," Meredith answered.

"So what's wrong with that?"

"He didn't say he loved me or even that he cared about me. Only that he needs me. Don't you understand? I chose everyone in my life. Julie. You. Walt. I want someone to pick me for myself. Because they think I'm special, or lovable. Not because I can do something for them."

Florence leaned closer, her eyebrows raised expressively. "What if he did pick you but you're too afraid to believe it? Set aside your emotions a moment and look at the facts. Forget the Lee that hurt you. He was a kid then. Look at the man he is today. Measure him against what you know about him now and his behavior toward you now. And keep in mind that he's not a saint, Meredith. No man is."

"I'm not looking for a saint," Meredith said defensively.

"Aren't you? Think about this. If Lee walked out of your life tomorrow and then you found out he truly loved you, how would you feel?"

* * *

Alone in the studio again, Meredith's anger boiled and her frustration coiled until she wanted to scream from the pressure. Instead she kicked an empty waste can and watched it slide across the floor.

As much as she resented Florence's and Julie's unsolicited advice and intrusion into her studio, she hated being alone now even more.

Because in the wake of their visit, Meredith was forced to do the thing above all else she'd told herself she'd never do again. Think about Lee.

Both Julie and Florence had made the same observation. That she was looking for Mr. Perfect. Nonsense. She merely wanted someone dependable, someone to stand by her and comfort her, to make her feel loved and cherished and complete.

The way she had felt in Lee's arms.

She kicked herself mentally for allowing Lee to intrude. Now, where was she? Oh, yes. She wanted a man who loved her, who gave her that sense of oneness and belonging like she had that summer and just the other night in bed with—Lee.

Damn. There was an uncomfortable pattern developing that her recalcitrant mind wasn't eager to confront.

Meredith walked to her design table, staring at the intricate pattern she was developing. Fine lines, minute cutouts evenly spaced, nicely balanced. Not perfect but very good. One of the first lessons she'd learned when designing stencils was not to strive for perfection because she would always be disappointed.

The imperfections gave each piece a charm and interest of its own. She smiled slightly, pleased with her accomplishment.

It was hard work and it required intense concentration.

This design was going to be as close to perfect as she'd ever come.

Mr. Perfect. Standards of perfection.

Meredith stared at the stencil, a window of understanding beginning to open in her mind.

No man had ever measured up to her standards. Why not?

It was the first time she'd ever asked herself that question. No matter how wonderful, or wealthy, or handsome, or generous, they always fell short. Why?

Because none of them had made her feel the way she had that summer—the way Lee had...

A soft gasp escaped her as she began to see what she'd done.

She'd been holding up her image of Lee as a standard for other men, comparing them to him when what she really wanted was Lee himself.

She'd been holding out for the perfect man, a man who didn't exist. A man she'd invented to keep her safe and free from being hurt again.

She realized she'd been in love with Lee all this time. She'd fooled herself into believing she'd nurtured Lee's memory out of resentment, but she'd really held his image in her heart from love.

She loved Lee Stratton.

Realization of her love didn't come in a blinding flash or a roll of thunder. It came as a soft, quiet truth that unfolded like a flower nestled near her heart. It had always been there.

But the discovery did little to soothe her now. Lee didn't love her in return. He didn't care for her at all. Did he?

Florence thought he did. Dare she believe it was true?

He'd lost her again.

Lee stared out the gallery door with unseeing eyes, the cold ache in his chest his only comfort. In the distance a train whistle moaned woefully and he closed his eyes against the additional torment to his already scoured soul.

He tried to retreat behind his cold facade, hide in the icy cave of indifference, but there was nowhere left to go. She'd robbed him of everything, down to his heart and soul.

She'd opened up his emotions, then left him alone to deal with them. Like an infant, unprepared, incapable and vulnerable.

The hell of it was he couldn't even blame her. It was all his fault. He'd brought it upon himself. None of this would have happened if he hadn't been so scared of his own emotions.

No. That was nothing more than wishful thinking. He could never give Meredith all the love she and Julie needed. Even if he gave all he had it would still not be enough.

Besides, there was no hope of regaining her love or trust now. He'd ruined every chance he'd had. How could he ever convince Meredith he loved her, that he'd always loved her? If he said the words at this point they would be meaningless. He should have said the words that night when she'd lain in his arms, but he'd been too scared, too afraid she'd turn away.

The whistle sounded again. "Damn you!" He smacked his hand against the door and gritted his teeth in despair.

God help him, he couldn't go on like this. He couldn't stay here with Meredith so close, knowing he could never have her, knowing he'd hurt her again.

He ran his shaking hands through his hair and paced back across the room, his gaze falling on the suitcase still sitting on the floor.

A powerful urge to flee bombarded him, burning like fire in his chest. He was sinking in emotional quicksand. If he stayed he'd be sucked down into it. He had to get out. Get away and gain some perspective on all this. Lee tossed his suitcase onto the bed and pulled open the dresser drawer, grabbing a handful of shirts.

A knock on the door stopped him midstride.

"Lee, it's Julie. Florence wants to know if you can come downstairs for a minute."

Lee opened the door, realizing he'd made a mistake the moment she caught sight of the clothes in his hand and the open luggage.

"Why are you packing? Are you going away?" Julie asked.

Lee found it difficult to face her. He didn't want to lie but he didn't have the strength to tackle the truth, either. "It's time. I've been here longer than I planned as it is."

"I thought you liked us."

The hurt and disappointment in her voice hit him hard in the chest. How could he ever explain this to her? "I do like you, Julie. This has nothing to do with you. I have a job I need to get back to."

"I want you to stay here."

Lee closed his eyes against her sincere plea. He didn't dare look at her or he'd fall apart. "I can't, Julie." His voice nearly betrayed him. He realized that leaving Julie would be almost as hard as leaving Meredith. He loved them both. But for the love of God he didn't know what to do about it.

"This is because of the fight with my mom, huh? Can't you talk to her? Please?" Julie begged.

"I tried. There's more to it than this one disagreement, Julie." There was no way he could make her understand. He was in over his head and he had to get out before he lost his mind.

He turned to the young girl but she backed up a step, the look of sadness on her face becoming one of defiance and anger.

"My mom was right. She said you didn't care about us. She said you'd walk away."

Lee's heart was being shredded, his inside were threatening to explode. His desire to grant Julie her wish and his strong instinct for self-preservation were pulling him apart.

"Julie, let me explain."

With her eyes narrowed in anger and brimming with tears, she reached up and turned off her hearing aid. "I hate you!"

Pierced to the heart, Lee could only watch helplessly as Julie turned and ran away. Everyone he cared about was turning against him. Didn't they understand it was better this way? He couldn't give them the kind of love they needed but so help him God, if he could he would gladly sell his soul to do so.

He turned back toward the bed. The half-empty suitcase mocked him. Meredith and Julie were right about him. Walking away was all he knew how to do. He avoided and ignored his feelings because confronting them was too terrifying a prospect.

How did you confront something so fierce and life-threatening?

Meredith had released his emotions but those feelings now bound him to this place and to her, making it impossible for him to leave without leaving part of himself behind. He was boxed in. He couldn't stay. He couldn't go.

What the hell was he going to do?

Lee guided his car around to the back of Sand Castle, nearly running into Florence as she ran toward his car. Slamming on the brakes, he cursed as the vehicle skidded sideways on the brick surface.

Florence was shouting at him before he could get the window halfway lowered.

"It's your daddy. Hurry!"

Lee's blood turned to ice. "What happened?" He shoved open the car door and got out, jogging beside Florence as she tried to explain between anxious gulps of air.

"I don't know. He came out into the kitchen, complaining about his arm hurting and then he just fell on the floor."

Lee's fear imploded, sending ragged shards of pain scraping on every nerve. "Did you call the paramedics?" he asked, bounding up onto the back porch.

"They're on their way. I didn't know what to do for him. Meredith and Julie are at the mall...and you were gone...."

Florence's voice broke but Lee didn't have time to offer her comfort now. He yanked open the back door and stepped into the kitchen.

The sight that met his eyes sent a tidal wave of fear crashing over him, bringing him near blackout. His father was lying on the floor unconscious, pale and deathly still.

An unholy war of emotions waged full-force inside Lee's gut. Panic, terror, and horror all clawed relentlessly at his being.

Blood surged in his ears and his heart pounded violently in his chest. He fought for some semblance of control. He couldn't cave in now. Not while Walt needed him.

He knelt beside his father, scared, lost and helpless to know where to turn. His walls had finally given way, leaving him vulnerable and completely exposed. "Where's the damned ambulance?" he growled, tasting acid bile in his mouth.

Lee took his father's hand in his, but the contact did little to ease his nightmare. Walt's fingers were cold. As cold as the overpowering fear that possessed his son.

"Oh, God, please," Lee whispered softly. "Don't die, Dad. Please, don't die."

From somewhere deep inside a prayer formed and he gave himself over to it.

He wanted to smash something. He wanted to scream at the top of his lungs. He wanted to cry. He wanted to *run!*

He'd never felt so alone in all his life. Or so terrified. Stripped of every protective device he'd ever used. There was no place to go, to hide.

Wave after wave of long-buried feelings swamped him; the cacophony of emotions impossible to sort out let alone conquer.

Lee paced the waiting room, running his fingers over his scalp repeatedly as the nervous tension ate slowly away at him.

Stopping at the window, he stared out into the parking lot but in his mind's eye he saw images of Walt and Meredith and Julie. In little more that twenty-four hours he'd lost the woman he loved and maybe the father he'd adored.

In the past two days he'd known the glorious heights and depths of his emotions. He'd known the rapture of falling in love, the spiritual connection with the other half of his soul.

He'd experienced the trauma of losing that love and knowing he alone was responsible for destroying the thing he loved most. He'd faced the devastating truth of his inadequacies.

He'd known the piercing agony of seeing a child he'd come to love hurt by the thoughtlessness of someone who was supposed to be her friend, reminding him painfully of what he'd done to Meredith. He'd been introduced to the aching helplessness of not being able to take that pain upon himself.

Now he was battling the horror of death, the specter of permanent loss, of final separation from someone he'd loved his whole life. A separation that could have been eased by the simple bending of a proud neck or the forgiveness of a stubborn heart.

Lee cursed savagely and turned away from the window, cursing silently again when he saw the people who filled the waiting room. He couldn't stand to have anyone around right now. He wanted to be alone with his pain, to try to protect the few fragments of control he still possessed.

Quickly he sought a corner of the room as far from the others as possible. A fresh wave of fear raged through him and he inhaled sharply. God, he was going insane.

"Lee."

Meredith's voice vibrated like a tuning fork upon his raw sense and he recoiled. He knew she wanted to comfort him but he was afraid if she touched him he would shatter. His emotions were sitting on the outside of his skin.

Lee held up his hand to ward her off. "Don't."

It was all he could manage to say. The hurt in her blue eyes stabbed him but he didn't have the strength to try to deal with her now. With a shake of his head, he turned and fled.

Meredith watched Lee walk away, feeling as if a knife had scraped each nerve in her body raw. She ached to comfort him but he'd spurned her help, curling in on himself and turning away. She'd never felt so helpless in her life.

He looked like hell. His eyes were dark, haunted green pools sunken into his face. There was a pallor to his skin that told her he was consumed with fear.

She closed her eyes, inhaling raggedly, her heart writhing in agony for him. For love of him.

"Mere, you okay, kiddo?"

Meredith turned and nodded to Florence. "I'll be all right. It's Lee I'm worried about."—

"Did you talk to him?" Florence asked, gently guiding Meredith to a chair and urging her to sit down.

"He wouldn't let me," she replied, brushing the tears off her cheek. "Florence, he looks so awful. I know he's terrified that he might lose Walt. I could see the fear in his eyes. I could *feel* it radiating from him when he walked past me. I wish I could do something to help him."

"I know you do, honey, but the truth is, getting through this ordeal is something Lee will have to handle all by himself."

"But I could make it easier if he'd let me."

"You might be able to comfort him a bit, but Lee's the kind who handles his problems privately. Handling his fear in his own way may be the only bit of control he still has. Don't take it away from him."

"He was going away, you know," Meredith said, glancing at Florence. "Julie saw him packing."

"I know," the older woman nodded. "But he didn't and I don't think, when it came down to it, he would have left."

"I wish I could believe that. If only for his father's sake."

Meredith's own fears for Walt surged inside her. "If Walt doesn't come through this heart attack…" She shook her head. "I don't know what will happen to Lee."

Florence patted her hand. "No more talk like that now. That old goat is going to be just fine. You've got to believe that. Just like you've got to believe that everything will work out for the best when all's said and done."

It was a nice thought but Meredith wondered if anything would ever be all right with any of them ever again.

There was nowhere to go to escape the terror. Watching his father through the ICU window offered no comfort, it only reminded Lee of how precarious life was.

Sitting in the small hospital chapel had proved impossible. It reminded him of his own failures and shortcomings.

Desperation had finally brought him here, sitting in his car in the parking lot, rapidly losing his last tenuous hold on his emotions.

His feelings were swirling around him like a raging whirlpool. He was afraid to let go and afraid to hang on. He'd lost everything he loved because he was afraid. Meredith, Julie, and maybe his father.

He was tired of fighting, tired of trying to maintain control over things he didn't understand. Closing his eyes, he lowered his head to the steering wheel where his hands clutched tightly.

He didn't want to let the tears fall, didn't want to give in to that last humiliating weakness, but he knew it was hopeless. He was disintegrating piece by piece.

Defeated at last, he relinquished who he was and cried, deep, racking groans of long-buried pain.

Time held no meaning in the quiet confines of the car. But after a while a new force began to take over in his despair. A quiet, slow-moving river began to replace the raging torrent of fear.

Slowly the sobs gave way to a shudder, a raggedly drawn breath. When he opened his eyes he felt strangely at peace. The fear was still there but it was manageable now. The sorrow was there, too, but he could control it.

Stunned at the change, Lee rested his head on the back of the seat and tried to make sense of what had happened to him.

Two days later Lee entered his father's room and noticed the familiar scowl on the craggy old face. Walt had come through his ordeal exceptionally well, but Lee couldn't entirely shake off his concern.

"So, you talked to Meredith lately?" Walt asked the moment he saw Lee.

Lee avoided looking at his father. He knew his feelings for Meredith were written in his eyes and he didn't want to get into the subject at the moment. Dealing with Walt was his first priority. He'd deal with Meredith later.

"No. I haven't seen anyone but you for the past few days."

Walt was quiet so long that Lee grew concerned. He walked to the bed and looked closely at his father. "Is something wrong?"

Walt looked up at him, a sad, regretful expression on his face.

"Don't make the same mistake I did, son," he said quietly.

"What do you mean?"

"Shutting down your feelings, trying to bury the hurt and the pain in your work, thinking you can live your whole life without ever getting close to someone else, without ever risking your heart. It's no good."

Lee sighed and pulled up a chair near the side of the bed. It was ironic that Walt should address this subject now, after Lee had finally succumbed to his emotions. He still didn't know how to deal with his new feelings. They still scared the hell out of him but they were under control for the time being. "I know," Lee said softly. "I found that out."

"You did? Good," Walt said, signaling his approval with a nod. "It's amazing what almost dying will do for you. I wish I would have figured it out sooner. Look what it's done to you and me. You were the most important thing in my life. When your mother took you away—" he sighed heavily "—something in me snapped."

Lee remembered vividly the abrupt and frightening

change in his father's attitude. "I always thought you were mad at me for coming home."

"Hell, no, boy. I lived for your visits," Walt barked. "It was just so damned hard to look at you, knowing I'd have to give you up again in a few months. That first summer was pure hell. It was like going through the divorce all over." Walt closed his eyes and rested his head against the pillow. "And each summer got worse."

"I never knew that." Lee's heart twisted with regret for all the things they'd missed, for all the years of loneliness they'd both endured when they could have been comforting one another.

"I took the coward's way out. I pulled back and kept an emotional distance between us because it hurt too damn much to see you go back to Houston," Walt admitted quietly.

Lee understood how difficult this confession was for his father. But his courage gave Lee the confidence to open up, as well. "I thought you didn't love me. I told you that once, that I loved you, and you turned and walked away without saying a word."

"I remember," Walt said, clearing his throat. "I wanted to say the words, son, but I was afraid of falling apart in front of you."

The tremor in Walt's voice sent a warm flush of love through Lee's heart. "It wouldn't have mattered to me, Dad. I'd have loved you anyway."

"I know," Walt said with a wave of his hand. "I know that now. Forgive me, son. I never stopped to consider how that would make you feel. I was so damned selfish and bullheaded."

"Like father, like son?" Lee said quietly.

Walt's eyes were suspiciously moist when he held out his hand to his son. Lee swallowed past the lump in his throat and clasped the hand in both of his. Then he leaned forward and pulled his father into a firm embrace.

Nothing had ever felt so good to Lee in his whole life.

Walt cleared his throat again and pulled back, patting Lee on the shoulder affectionately. "Well, now, what are we going to do about you and Meredith?"

Lee straightened, turning away briefly to gather himself. It took a moment to clear his eyes and find his voice. "What about us?"

"I know you love her, son. It's written all over your face."

"It's one-sided," Lee attested.

"Bah," Walt scoffed. "You're blind and bullheaded to boot. She may be hurting right now, but she loves you. I'd stake my life on it."

Lee shoved his hands into his pockets, staring at the floor. "I hurt her, more this time than before. She'll never forgive me now."

"Haven't you learned anything about that young woman since you've been here? She doesn't know how to carry a grudge."

If he didn't hurt so much Lee would have laughed out loud at his father's statement. "Where I'm concerned she makes a firm exception."

"One of these days you'll have to tell me just what you did to her. But I don't have the time or the energy to hear about it now. Have you told her how you feel?"

Lee nodded, remembering the moment before Walt had come up and spilled the beans about their bet. "I tried to tell her how much she meant to me. How much I needed her, but then she found out about that damned bet." He shrugged, unable to trust his voice to continue.

"Everyone *needs* Meredith, son. Maybe what she wanted to hear from you was that you loved her."

"I don't know how to tell her," he admitted, a dull

sadness shrouding his mind. "I don't know how to love the way she does and I can never give her all the love she needs."

"Leland," Walt said gently, "why don't you let her be judge of what she needs?"

Chapter Twelve

Meredith had managed to avoid Lee at the hospital for the past two days. But today her luck ran out. He stepped from the waiting room just as she walked up.

Her heart leaped when she saw his handsome face. He looked tired and drawn but there was a light in his green eyes that reached out to her. Was it for her? She loved him so much, but she meant nothing to him. A small part of her hoped that Florence was right, that Lee did love her. But what if he did and she was too blind to see it?

Her feelings were so confused. She loved him, she was mad at him, and a small part of her still couldn't bring herself to completely trust him.

He came toward her hurriedly, his hands grasping her shoulders when he drew close. The contact sent a tremor through her body that she tried valiantly to mask.

"Where have you been? I needed to talk to you," he said, his eyes searching her face.

Needed.

The spark of hope Meredith had been carrying in her heart quickly extinguished. He hadn't said he missed her or that he wanted her. Only that he needed her.

It was all she could do to hide her bitter disappointment behind a smile she didn't feel. "I've been here at odd hours. Between work and Julie's school activities—" She left the sentence unfinished, finding it hard to keep her voice from betraying her inner turmoil.

"I wanted to tell you about Walt." Lee glanced at the waiting room full of people and shook his head. "Come on." He steered her toward the small chapel at the end of the corridor.

Something about his urgency stirred her concern for Walt. "What's happened?" she asked as soon as they were in the quiet sanctuary.

"Exactly what you predicted," Lee said, a strangely puzzled smile on his face. "Walt and I had a long talk, Meredith. The first real conversation we've had since I was a kid. He told me how he felt after the divorce and how hard it was for him to send me back to my mother at the end of the summer."

Lee sighed and ran a hand down his neck. "He even explained why he walked away that day I told him I loved him."

Meredith's joy for Lee temporarily overrode her own broken heart. "That's wonderful, Lee. I know how much this means to you."

"It's all because of you, Meredith. You made this possible." He took a deep breath, his expression one of amazement. "God, when I think of the time wasted. The years lost. But you gave them back to us, Meredith. You've given me back my family. I can never repay you for that."

The pressure squeezing her chest threatened to crush her

heart. Meredith stoically endured it, determined not to let him see how she felt.

Nothing would ever change for her. Every time she did a good deed there was a price to pay. She'd helped Lee and Walt but ultimately she'd left herself out in the cold. Alone and unwanted again.

"I'm glad, Lee. But I didn't do all that much. You're the one who took the risk and had the courage to face your emotions."

"But I wouldn't have if it hadn't been for your help. You've changed my life. You've made me see so many things." He reached out and touched her face. "There so much I want to say to you. So much I want to ask you."

"Mr. Stratton?" the nurse asked, coming into the chapel.

"Yes." Lee turned to face her.

"Your father wants to see you."

"Thank you. I'll be right there." Lee looked into Meredith's eyes. "Come with me."

Meredith shook her head, pulling out of his reach. "No. You go. I'll check back with Walt a little later."

"All right," he said softly, placing a light kiss on her forehead. "Think of me."

Meredith held her smile until Lee disappeared into the hallway, then she raised trembling fingers to her lips. Think of him? Dear God, that's all she ever did. Every minute, every hour, every day.

No, what she needed to do now was learn how to *stop* thinking about him. Slowly she walked out of the chapel and toward the exit doors. Despite her own anguish, she couldn't deny her feelings of happiness for Lee and Walt. Finally, Lee had what he'd always wanted—his father's love.

Unfortunately, Lee didn't love her. Not in the way she'd hoped. Unlocking her car, she got in. But once behind the steering wheel she could only stare into the distance, her troubled thoughts consuming her.

She couldn't go on like this, seeing Lee, being close to him, being a part of his family yet always an outsider. And above all, she couldn't go on loving him and knowing that he didn't love her.

It would be a slow, torturous death.

There was only one solution. It would break her heart and Julie's, too, but it was the only decent thing to do. She would have to leave Sand Castle. Move her business and find another place to live.

The thought brought an unbearable sadness into her heart. Walt had been her family for the past five years. He'd given her the only sense of permanence and belonging she'd ever known. But the bitter truth was, he wasn't her father. Walt was Lee's father and it was Lee's relationship with Walt that was important. Not her own.

Lee's happiness meant everything to her. Nothing else mattered. She knew better than anyone how he felt, the loneliness, the sense of abandonment that haunted him. That he'd regained his sense of belonging was the most wonderful gift she could give him.

If it meant giving up her own relationship with Walt, it was a small price to pay. She loved them both. Lee and Walt needed each other more than she did.

But the best thing she could do now was to give father and son time to reacquaint with one another and they couldn't do that with her in the way. Besides, it wasn't as if she were alone. She had Julie. Walt would still be her friend. Florence, too.

With Walt out of the woods physically, there was no need to postpone the inevitable. She'd call a real estate agent today, before she changed her mind.

Numb and unable to find even the strength to cry, Meredith started the car and headed home.

* * *

"You're not serious about this?" Florence questioned later that afternoon when she heard Meredith on the phone with an agent.

"Yes, I am," she replied, holding the phone to her ear as she waited for a response. "It's time I got on with my life and stopped relying on other people to be my safety net."

"You aren't making any sense at all. What safety net? Walt?" Florence huffed in disgust. "He may have provided a place for you to start your business, but that's all he did. The rest was because of you and a lot of hard work."

"He gave me advice and support." She paused as the agent picked up the line again. "Yes, I need help in finding a location for my business." Meredith turned her attention to the woman on the phone, grateful she didn't have to defend her decision to her friend.

"Anyone can give advice and support, Mere. That's what friends are for."

"Yes, thank you." Meredith hung up the phone and scribbled a number on the table. She should have known Florence wouldn't let it rest without a fight. "It's no use trying to talk me out of it. My mind's made up."

"This is because of Lee, isn't it?"

The sound of his name lanced through her, bringing fresh regret and pain. "No. It's because of me," she said, walking away. This decision was hard enough without having people rub salt in her wounds.

"Don't you think this move is a bit sudden? It's not like you to make rash decisions."

Meredith avoided Florence's penetrating gaze. "It's not rash. I've been thinking about it for a while now."

Florence laughed skeptically. "Oh, right. Let me guess. You decided all this when you were at the hospital this morning. Right?"

Tears stung her eyes at just the memory of seeing Lee in the chapel. She shook her head, not trusting her voice.

Keenly attuned to Meredith's moods, Florence placed an arm around her shoulders. "Sweetie, don't do this to yourself. Give it some time. Let the dust settle before you go cutting off your nose to spite your face."

Meredith sniffed and quickly brushed tears from her eyes. "It's better for everyone this way."

"Better for who?" Florence asked softly.

"For Lee." Meredith met Florence's sympathetic gaze and saw realization dawn in the brown eyes. Her friend understood that she loved Lee and that her sacrifice was for him.

"Well..." Florence sighed in resignation. "Have you told Julie?"

"No," Meredith admitted, growing sick with dread at the thought of confronting her daughter. Walt and Sand Castle were the only life she'd ever known.

"She'll be crushed."

Meredith nodded, her heart threatening to shrivel and die inside her. "I know."

Florence bent and hugged Meredith's head to her chest. "Why don't you come with me for a little ride? You could use some time away from here to clear your head."

Meredith pulled out of the comforting embrace and shook her head. "No, I don't feel like going anywhere."

"Nonsense. It'll do you good. We'll take Julie and Robin, too."

Reluctant, but filled with a need to have her little family close around her, Meredith agreed. It wasn't until they were in the car and headed down Beach Boulevard that she asked where they were going.

"To Long Beach," Florence replied. "I'm going to sign up for a summer class on how to write a romance novel. The university is having a two-week-long workshop with some famous agent, Alice something or other, from New York.''

The University of Southern Mississippi. The home of the Friendship Oak. The irony of their destination would have been humorous if Meredith hadn't been so buried in sadness.

She'd never been back to the tree since that summer. Maybe this was as good a time as any to put all those ghosts to rest. Provided she had the courage to face them.

He found the note propped up on his dresser when he got home that afternoon, his name scrawled in large letters and underlined at the top. Hurriedly, he scanned the message, his heart growing tighter with each word he read. Meredith was leaving Sand Castle.

According to Florence, who'd written the note, Meredith had decided it would be better for everyone if she moved out, business and all.

Lee struggled to control the whirl of emotions the news had unleashed. Fear at losing Meredith, the heartache of his own failures, and the dark prospect of being forced back into his cold, gray world spiraled inside him.

She couldn't leave. He needed her. They all needed her. Lee closed his eyes, visions of life without Meredith filled his mind. It was a life cold, barren and grey. He'd lived in that world and he didn't want to return to it.

He wanted the vibrant world Meredith inhabited. Even with its frightening emotions and unpredictable events, it was life at its best. And he knew now that he liked it that way.

Lee inhaled a ragged breath, his mind searching frantically for a way to stop his world from slipping away. He had to find a way to make her stay. Make her see that she belonged here with them.

He ran a hand down the back of his neck, frustrated and

helpless. Damn. He didn't know what to do. He needed advice but he couldn't discuss this with Walt. His dad would be crushed to learn that Julie and Meredith were leaving.

If only his grandmother were still alive. She had been one of the wisest women he'd ever known. His gaze came to rest on the locket, still lying on his dresser. He picked it up.

"Tell me what to do, Grandma. Do I drag her back? Beg her? Make her feel guilty? Tell her how much I need her?"

Words began to fill his head but it wasn't the wisdom of his grandmother that echoed in his ears, but that of his father.

Maybe what she wanted to hear was how much you loved her.

He was well aware that he'd been unable to bring himself to say the word *love* to her. Shamefully he admitted that a part of him was still scared. The feelings he'd uncovered weren't as frightening now that he'd brought them out into the light, but he'd only explored them tentatively; they were still too new, too sensitive to explore too deeply.

One emotion he was sure of was that he loved Meredith. What he wasn't so sure of was how to deal with that love. He had nothing to give her but his woefully inadequate love.

He'd handled the whole thing like a rank amateur. She'd said once she would never forgive him and he'd done nothing to convince her she should.

Another idea formed in his mind, one that he didn't want to face. Maybe the best thing he could do for Meredith was to let her go. Her happiness was more important to him than his own. If leaving was what she really wanted then maybe he had no right to interfere. Maybe the most loving thing he could do was to stand aside without making a scene, without bombarding her with his feelings, his desires.

Walt's words echoed again. What if all she needed was to hear the words? Fear of saying the words had kept him and his father apart for fifteen years. Fear of having his love rejected had cost him the relationship with Walt.

He didn't want to face life without Meredith because he was still too scared to tell her how he felt.

Pain augered upward into his chest. Right or wrong, he couldn't let her leave without first telling her how desperately he loved her. Somehow he had to make her believe that he loved her for herself. No other reason. Because she lit up a room when she entered. Because she warmed everyone's life she touched. Because her beauty was of the soul as well as of the body.

Lee glanced at his watch, checking the time against the time Florence had written in the note. They'd only been gone a short while. He still might be able to catch them at the campus if he hurried.

The last afternoon traffic clogged the highway and it took nearly thirty minutes to drive the few miles up the coast to Long Beach. Lee's impatience had been stretched to the breaking point by the time he pulled to a stop near the green.

He had no idea where to start looking for them. Florence had given him the name of one of the buildings but he had no idea where it might be. He started to stop a passing student when he realized the significance of where he stood.

He gaze traveled to the far end of the green and the gigantic live oak that had stood on this spot since 1487. He saw her then, her red hair shining like a beacon in the shadows of the old tree. She was sitting on the bench inside the platform.

They had come full circle, back to the scene of his

crime. His insides tightened with an acid sting and his heart beat furiously with the old fear. Dear God, what if she turned him down?

Meredith stood in the middle of the platform, a sense of nervous expectation gnawing in her mind. It had been a long time since she'd stood within the sprawling limbs of the Friendship Oak. She'd forgotten how large the outdoor room actually was. It was big enough to hold fifty people with ease. As she recalled, it had often served as an outdoor classroom.

She walked to the far edge, her hand reaching out to touch the five-foot-thick trunk. She had loved coming here when she was growing up, protected underneath the dense foliage, safe from both rain and sun.

Sadness at all that had been lost lay heavily upon her heart. She closed her eyes, giving in to the hopelessness that had plagued her, knowing she should feel ashamed of her weakness but hurting too much to care.

She was doing the right thing in leaving Sand Castle. She just hadn't expected her sacrifice to be so painful. She wondered now if even staying in Gulfport was a mistake. Maybe she should move farther away, to Slidell or La-Place. Someplace far from Sand Castle and Lee.

Tears welled in her eyes but she didn't bother to wipe them away.

"Meredith, are you all right?"

She started, a soft gasp escaping her when she looked into his intense green eyes. He walked toward her and, for a moment, she was transported. It was that long-ago summer and she'd been waiting for Lee to meet her.

Only this time she was able to look past the end of the memory. All she could see now was the man she loved.

"Don't go," he said softly.

She didn't have to ask him what he meant. "It's necessary,'' she replied, struggling to speak past the constriction of her throat. Her heart was pounding so hard in her chest she feared it might explode.

She turned away from him. It was impossible to speak with his hypnotic eyes piercing her fragile facade. ''You and Walt have years to catch up on. You need time together to get reacquainted, to rebuild your relationship.''

''I need you here. With me.''

She braced herself against the tenderness in his voice. The last thing she wanted was for him to be understanding and sympathetic. It would only make what she had to do more difficult. ''No, you don't. You're just feeling insecure with all the new emotions you've started to experience. They were buried for a long time. It'll take some time to adjust but it'll get easier. I promise.''

Lifting her chin she turned to faced him. ''Just don't be afraid of how you feel.''

''Penny, I want you to stay.''

The old nickname slashed cruelly across her already aching heart. It took all her strength to keep from crying. ''Why, Lee?''

''Because I love you.''

Stunned, she could only stare in astonishment at him. She'd never expected to hear him say those words to her. That he should finally say them now, when it was too late, tore her heart out. The toxic irony of it ate away at her.

Lee came to her side, reaching out as if to touch her, then allowing his hand to drop to his side.

''I've never said that to anyone since I was ten. I never thought I could or that I'd want to,'' he explained quietly.

''Oh, Lee.'' Meredith wrapped her arms around her waist, moving away from the warm nearness of him. A few days ago those words would have been enough. But she'd had time to think. Love and commitment were two different things. Lee might love her but it was his ability to commit that had always been lacking. When love got rough, when love was tested, would he still walk away?

"What is it?"

The hurt in his voice rubbed against her sore heart. "I don't know."

Lee turned her to face him, his eyes dark with confusion and anxiety. "You're afraid to trust me again, aren't you? I don't blame you for that. I've made a mess of everything since I've been back. But you can trust this, Penny. I do love you. I've always loved you. Just please stay and give us a chance to work things out. I don't have anything else to give you. I can't even promise that my love will be enough."

"Lee. It's no use. You don't know what you're feeling right now. You've got all these emotions churning inside you, confusing you—"

"I'm not confused about you," he said firmly. "I know you can never completely forgive me for what I did to you that summer…"

Meredith touched her fingertips to his lips. At least this was one thing she could put to rest. "No. I forgave you a long time ago for that. But yesterday, you were ready to walk away again. How can I believe you won't leave me again?"

Lee's eyes widened in surprise. "How did you—"

"Julie told me. I know you're sincere at the moment. But it's not just me to consider now. It's Julie. She loves you, too. If our relationship shouldn't work out then there'd be two hearts broken. I don't want you to have to deal with that responsibility and I can't survive another heartbreak like that."

Meredith pushed past him, fighting to hold on to what little self-control she still had. "You and Walt have finally found each other after all these years. Focus on that, Lee. Nothing else is important."

"Penny, please, don't leave."

She stopped at the top of the steps and turned back to him, the sadness in his eyes wrenched her heart. "Don't you understand? We both have what we've wanted all our lives. I have a family. I have Julie and now you have your father. Neither of us can ask for more than that."

Meredith blinked back her tears, determined to see this through. She had to go, before her love for Lee caused her to make a mistake. "Goodbye, Lee."

Lee stood helpless as his whole world walked away. With each step Meredith ripped another piece of his heart from his body and there was nothing he could do to stop her. The past and the present merged and he knew with vivid intensity how Penny had felt that night when he walked away. He knew now, how deeply the wound had penetrated.

He would give his life a thousand times over if he could go back and change the past, erase the pain and give her what she always wanted.

He watched her moving farther away, his soul screaming in protest. How was he going to live without her?

A bitter laugh formed in his throat at that question. There'd been a time when he hadn't understood feeling that way. Now he did.

He'd come to realize something else, too. That wanting what was best for Meredith was more important than what was best for himself. She'd been willing to leave to give him happiness. Could he do less for her?

He would return to Houston, resume his practice and leave Meredith's world intact. She could stay at Sand Castle with Julie and her business. As for him and his father, they had been through the worst of their troubles and he would visit Walt as often as possible.

It was a small sacrifice to ensure Meredith's future happiness. Resigned, he slipped his hand into his pocket, his fingers closing easily around the locket. He pulled it out and stared at it, thinking of how Meredith had always wanted family and a heritage like he'd been blessed with.

Stratton roots ran deep in the Gulf Coast soil. Suddenly it all became clear. He could give Meredith what she'd always wanted. It was his to give. His to pass on. If he had the courage. If he was willing to take the risk. If he was willing to give all of his heart and damn the consequence.

Lee's heart pounded violently in his chest. It wasn't fear that surged through him but hope. Nothing mattered but loving Meredith. If she turned him down then he would learn to live with it.

Moving to the edge of the platform, Lee shouted to her. "Penny. Wait!"

She stopped at the far rim of the tree branches, where the shade met the green lawn, and turned to look at him. With her red hair blowing around her face, she was the most beautiful woman he'd ever seen.

"Come back. Please. For just a moment."

Meredith stared at Lee, regretting her decision to stop and answer his shout. Didn't he understand that it was better this way? It would prevent heartache for both of them.

"No," she called. "It won't do any good."

Brushing the hair off her face, she turned around, vaguely aware of the students assembled on the green.

"Penny!"

Her eyes stung with renewed tears and she brushed them quickly away. "Lee, I have to find Julie and Robin." She couldn't believe she was shouting at him like a fishwife.

"Here we are," Julie called, running to her mother's side. "Why's Lee up in the oak, yelling at you?"

"Penny!"

Meredith turned, her face warm with embarrassment

from the stares of the curious students. She took a few steps closer to the platform so she could lower her voice. "Lee, you're causing a scene."

"I don't care," he shouted. "Tell me what you've always wanted more than anything in the world."

Utter astonishment froze her to the spot. "What?" The man had lost his mind. She glanced around, painfully aware of the increasing interest on the faces of the students. "Not now," she refused, lowering her head and tucking her hair behind her ears.

"Yes, now! Tell me. Tell me everything. They want to hear it, too," he said, gesturing to the small crowd.

"Yeah, tell us about it," a young man shouted.

"This is so cool," a female voice cooed beside her.

Meredith was beginning to think he really had gone mad. He'd caved in under all the stress of Walt's heart attack and discovering his emotions. It was the only explanation, and apparently the only way to get him to shut up was to play along. "A home," she called to him.

"What else?" he demanded.

Feeling exposed and vulnerable, she almost didn't answer. But underneath her insecurity was a strange current of excitement she couldn't ignore. "A family and place to belong."

Lee's smile brightened the shadows beneath the old tree. "Then marry me. I can give you all of that."

Meredith gasped. Marriage. Was he serious? A thrill of hope cascaded through her, sending her spirits soaring into the heavens.

"Marry me. I love you."

He'd said it again, but her brain was having trouble accepting it. The crowd on the green, however, jumped eagerly into the drama.

"Go, girl."

"Say yes, lady. Don't let that hunk get away!"

"Mom, this is so romantic," Julie squealed, bouncing on her toes.

"He's lost his mind," Meredith muttered, but her heart was beating wildly with the thought that her dreams might be coming true.

"I want to give you what you've always wanted, Penny. A name and roots and tradition and all the love you never had."

In a daze, all Meredith could see was Lee's smile and his green eyes drawing her to him. Drawing her home. Somehow she found herself moving toward the tree, the encouraging shouts of the crowd urging her on.

She climbed the platform, unable to take her eyes from Lee's and the love she saw there. She didn't realize she was crying until his image blurred and she felt wetness on her cheeks.

Lee pulled her to him, tilting her chin upward with gentle fingers.

"I've been searching for you all my life, Penny." He slipped his grandmother's locket over her head. "You belong to us. To the Strattons and to Sand Castle. Forever." He took her shoulders in his hands. "Marry me. I love you, Penny. I want to spend the rest of my life loving you. I want to give you everything you ever wanted, and I want to be a father to Julie."

Meredith grew apprehensive. Was this real? Faced with having all her dreams come true she was suddenly afraid to reach out and take them.

"If you can't love me, I'll understand," Lee said, his voice raspy. "But you can't leave here. It's the only home you've ever known and I can't let you give it up. If you want, I'll go back to Houston so you can—"

Her fears vanished in the wake of the love she saw in Lee's eyes. Quickly she pressed her fingers against his lips. "I don't want you to leave. I love you. I always have."

"You'll have to help me, Meredith," he said, enfolding her in his arms. "I don't know if I can give you all the love you need, but I can give you all the love I have."

The radiance of pure happiness filled her heart. He understood. There was nothing he could have said that could have banished her lingering doubts so completely.

"That'll be enough," she whispered, touching the locket. "That's all I ever wanted—you to love me."

His kiss smothered her last word as he pulled her into a crushing embrace. She wrapped her arms around his neck knowing she was finally complete.

Lost in a world of their own, Meredith didn't hear the roar of approval that accompanied their kiss. But when the kiss ended and she looked down at the shouting and laughing crowd below them, she realized the old nightmare was gone forever.

Lee had erased the past, replaced it with a new memory. The touch of this memory would bless their lives forever.

* * * * *

Five unforgettable
couples say 'I Do'...
with a little help
from their friends!

Always a Bridesmaid!

The Engagement Party by Barbara Boswell
Silhouette Desire®, May 1998

The Bridal Shower by Elizabeth August
Silhouette Desire, June 1998

The Bachelor Party by Paula Detmer Riggs
Silhouette Sensation®, July 1998

The Abandoned Bride by Jane Toombs
Silhouette Intrigue®, August 1998

Finally a Bride by Sherryl Woods
Silhouette Special Edition®, September 1998

Always a Bridesmaid!
is coming to every Silhouette® series
so don't miss any of these
five wonderful weddings!

COMING NEXT MONTH

ALISSA'S MIRACLE Ginna Gray

That's My Baby!

He'd told her he couldn't have a child and she was so in love that she'd agreed to a childless marriage. But then the pregnancy test was positive! Suddenly, she was in for the fight of her life—her man or her child. Alissa wanted both!

THE MYSTERIOUS STRANGER Susan Mallery

Triple Trouble

A mystery woman with amnesia washed up on his beach and marriage-shy millionaire Jarrett Wilkinson was suspicious. Was this another new tactic to get him to propose? He had to let her stay, but he was going to watch her like a hawk!

THE KNIGHT, THE WAITRESS AND THE TODDLER
Arlene James

The Power of Love

Lawyer Edward White was as reliable...and...romantic as granite. Then a desperate waitress heiress sought his protection for her secret son and suddenly he was all rumpled.

THE PRINCESS GETS ENGAGED Tracy Sinclair

Hired to impersonate a missing monarch, Megan Delaney became engaged to a handsome prince! She wanted the perfect fairytale to end happily ever after, but how could it when Prince Nicholas's real bride was bound to return?

THE PATERNITY TEST Pamela Toth

She'd gone from riches to rags, then from nanny to mistress, but now Cassie Wainright was going to be a mother! How was powerful businessman Nicholas Kincaid going to react to the fact that he was going to be a father again?

JUST JESSIE Lisette Belisle

It was a marriage of convenience, but his virginal wife's charms were driving bad boy Ben Harding crazy. She was too hard to resist...

On sale from 22 May 1998

COMING NEXT MONTH FROM

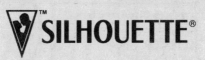

Intrigue
Danger, deception and desire

ANGEL WITH AN ATTITUDE Carly Bishop
FATHER AND CHILD Rebecca York
THE EYES OF DEREK ARCHER Vickie York
STORM WARNINGS Judi Lind

Desire
Provocative, sensual love stories for the woman of today

NOBODY'S CHILD Ann Major
JOURNEY'S END B J James
HOW TO WIN (BACK) A WIFE Lass Small
THE BRIDAL SHOWER Elizabeth August
LONE STAR KIND OF MAN Peggy Moreland
ANOTHER MAN'S BABY Judith McWilliams

Sensation
A thrilling mix of passion, adventure and drama

MIND OVER MARRIAGE Rebecca Daniels
LOVING MARIAH Beverly Bird
PRIME SUSPECT Maggie Price
BADLANDS BAD BOY Maggie Shayne

On sale from 22 May 1998

SUSAN WIGGS

The Lightkeeper

Lighthouse keeper Jesse Morgan's reclusive life is
changed forever when he finds Mary Dare washed up on
the shore one morning—unconscious and pregnant.
She's keeping a secret—one that puts them both in
terrible danger.

"A classic beauty and the beast love story...
A poignant, beautiful romance."
—bestselling author Kristin Hannah

1-55166-301-5
AVAILABLE NOW IN PAPERBACK

MIRA®

INTERNATIONAL BESTSELLING AUTHOR

Karen Young

Good Girls

When they were good...

Jack Sullivan is an ambitious and painful presence in
the lives of three prominent Mississippi women.
He made Suzanne a prisoner of violent memories,
used Taylor as a lonely trophy wife and drove
Annie's mother to suicide. When Jack is murdered,
each wonders who finally pulled the trigger...

"Karen Young is a spellbinding storyteller."
—Romantic Times

MIRA®

1-55166-306-6
AVAILABLE NOW IN PAPERBACK

DEBBIE MACOMBER

The Playboy and the Widow

A confirmed bachelor, Cliff Howard wasn't prepared to
trade in the fast lane for car pools. Diana Collins lived life
hiding behind motherhood and determined to play it
safe. They were both adept at playing their roles.
Until the playboy met the widow...

"Debbie Macomber's stories sparkle with love and laughter..."
—*New York Times* bestselling author, Jayne Ann Krentz

1-55166-080-6
AVAILABLE NOW IN PAPERBACK

SPOT THE DIFFERENCE

Spot all ten differences between the two pictures featured below and you could win a year's supply of Silhouette® books—FREE! When you're finished, simply complete the coupon overleaf and send it to us by 30th November 1998. The first five correct entries will each win a year's subscription to the Silhouette series of their choice. What could be easier?

E8C

Please turn over for details of how to enter ⇩

HOW TO ENTER

Simply study the two pictures overleaf. They may at first glance appear the same but look closely and you should start to see the differences. There are ten to find in total, so circle them as you go on the second picture. Finally, fill in the coupon below and pop this page into an envelope and post it today. Don't forget you could win a year's supply of Silhouette® books—you don't even need to pay for a stamp!

Silhouette Spot the Difference Competition
FREEPOST CN81, Croydon, Surrey, CR9 3WZ
EIRE readers: (please affix stamp) PO Box 4546, Dublin 24.

Please tick the series you would like to receive if you are one of the lucky winners

Desire™ ❑   Special Edition™ ❑   Sensation™ ❑   Intrigue™ ❑

Are you a Reader Service™ subscriber?   Yes ❑   No ❑

Ms/Mrs/Miss/Mr ....Initials ....
(BLOCK CAPITALS PLEASE)

Surname..

Address ....

....

....Postcode..........................

(I am over 18 years of age)   E8C

Closing date for entries is 30th November 1998.
One application per household. Competition open to residents of the UK and Ireland only. You may be mailed with offers from other reputable companies as a result of this application. If you would prefer not to receive such offers, please tick this box.   ❑
Silhouette is a registered trademark used under license.

MEGALITHIC
Mysteries

MEGALITHIC MYSTERIES

AN ILLUSTRATED GUIDE TO EUROPE'S ANCIENT SITES

MICHAEL BALFOUR

WITH PHOTOGRAPHS BY **BERND SIERING**

FOREWORD BY JOHN MITCHELL

PARKGATE
BOOKS

For Elizabeth and Calandra, companions in the field

ACKNOWLEDGEMENTS

I would like to thank the following very much for their valuable advice and
help during the compilation of this book: Colin Burgess, Celia Dearing,
Tom Deas, Paul Devereux, Lesley Ferguson (Royal Commission on the
Ancient and Historical Monuments of Scotland), Michael Gibbons (Office
of Public Works, Dublin), Cherry Lavell, Teresa Marques (Department of
Archaeology, Instituto Patremoneo Cultural, Lisbon), Jenny Mulherin,
Susan Vaughan for the Index, and the Librarian and staff of the Institute of
Archaeology, University College, London. My special thanks to Aubrey
Burl, and Sean O'Nuallain (Ordnance Survey Office, Dublin).
M.B.

COVER ILLUSTRATIONS:
Front: Stonehenge, Wiltshire
Back, main picture: Pentre Ifan, Dyfed
top right: Gavr'inis, Morbihan
below: Nuraghe Su Nuraxi, Sardinia

First published in 1992
This edition published in 1997 by
Parkgate Books Ltd
London House
Great Eastern Wharf
Parkgate Road
London SW11 4NQ
Great Britain
1 3 5 7 9 8 6 4 2

Editorial: Jenny Mulherin
Editorial Director: Pippa Rubinstein
Design: Tom Deas
Art Director: Dave Allen
Picture Editor: Celia Dearing

The catalogue record for this book is available from the British Library.

ISBN 1 85585 355 8

Typeset by Bookworm Typesetting, Manchester, England

Printed in Italy

Contents

VISBEKER BRAUT, the Bride of Visbek, one of a pair of hünengraben *in Oldenburg, Germany. The Bridegroom lies just to the south-west.*

HAVELTE WEST, one of the many hunebedden *in the Dutch province of Drenthe. They are all numbered, and this* ganggraf *is D. 53.*

Foreword

BY JOHN MICHELL

When the subject of megalithic monuments crops up, everyone knows about Stonehenge and many people have at least heard of Avebury, Newgrange, Callanish, and one or two other famous sites, mostly in the British Isles. In Brittany, the stone alignments of Carnac have become a major tourist attraction, but the thousands of other wonderful relics of French prehistory are comparatively neglected. Further afield, in eastern Europe, Scandinavia, Portugal and the Mediterranean lands, including North Africa, the very existence of their great megalithic structures is sparsely recognized, even in some cases by the natives. Who, for instance, would first think of Holland as a likely place for megalithic explorations? Yet, as we learn from this book, the 'unique and remarkable' *hunebedden* (Huns' beds) in the north-eastern Dutch province of Drenthe outdo in size and interest many of the better known British monuments. We also learn that in little Denmark the number of listed and protected prehistoric sites, some 24,000, is greater than in any other country, and this number represents only a fraction of the total sum.

There is no one obvious reason why modern visitors are increasingly attracted to ancient sites and sanctuaries. These are often located in remote, desolate regions far from any 'facilities' and, once found, they convey little direct information about the lives and thoughts of their founders. Unlike the great cathedrals and galleries they have no history to teach and offer no explicit images. Their aesthetic is simple and minimalist to a degree. Prehistoric sites are certainly an acquired taste, but those who happen to acquire it, whether as archaeologists, historians, artists, pilgrims or antiquarian ramblers, come to experience more satisfaction among the ruins of ancient stones than at the famous historical showplaces.

Far more than is generally realized, local cultures and countrysides are largely formed on patterns laid down by the megalith builders. The early Christian practice of taking over and reconsecrating the sites of pagan shrines and temples has ensured that virtually every old church stands on a place of long pre-Christian sanctity. The calendar round of festivals and saints' days, which England lost at the Reformation but which continues elsewhere in traditional country districts to mark the stages of the agricultural and social year, derives many of its locations and customs from prehistoric times. Even the familiar shapes of hills, adapted by mounds, cairns and earthworks, bear the marks of ancient workmanship.

The megalith builders were the same people as we are and they are separated from us in time by a mere 3,500–4,000 years, but the beliefs or understandings which inspired them to structure wide landscapes with a vast system of inter-related monuments in earth and stone are still deeply mysterious. The mystery deepens further as one reads through this book. Despite its extensive contents, it scarcely does more than scratch the surface; for every site described or mentioned there are thousands of others, a fair number of them still unknown even to archaeologists. And all these great works, both individually and as a whole, were raised up for an unknown purpose!

In this revelation of the wealth and variety of megalithic sites both within and beyond the British Isles, Michael Balfour is continuing a career which he began as a publisher in 1966. In that period of archaeological fervour, when studies by Hawkins, Thom and others were demonstrating the astronomical and scientific skills of the megalith builders, his Garnstone Press published a series of books on the mysteries and folklore of ancient sites, the alignments which they form across country and their possible connection with astrological powers and the subtle energies of the earth.

This is an informative rather than a speculative book, but like the author's previous *Stonehenge and its Mysteries* it stimulates a host of speculations about the riddle of the megaliths. One would like to be able to follow in Balfour's footsteps to the ancient, sacred and often secret places which he has discovered and brought to view, but his geographical range is too wide to be covered in most people's busy lifetimes. The best possible use of this book is as a practical guide for travellers, but those who cannot make the journeys are compensated as far as is possible by these stirring accounts and images of the spots where all traditional cultures had their mysterious origins.

John Michell

Introduction

> Till antiquaries are agreed whether the circles are temples or
> tombs or observatories, whether the dolmens are monuments
> of the dead or altars for sacrificing living men, and whether the
> mounds are tombs or law courts, it seems impossible, without
> arguing every point, to write anything that will be
> generally accepted.
>
> – from James Fergusson's Preface to his *Rude Stone Monuments In All Countries :*
> *Their Age and Uses, 1872*

This book is intended to be a general introduction to over 200 archaeological sites in Europe and North Africa, which present clear, exciting evidence of the craft of the megalith builders. Map references and travel instructions are provided, with illustrations and accounts of all these monuments.

Far more megalithic sites exist than could be encompassed by any one volume. Denmark, for example, boasts more than 24,000 listed, protected sites. This selection is necessarily eclectic – but I hope that this adds to its interest. There are even included non-megalithic sites, such as SILBURY HILL, Wiltshire, England, because I cannot believe there is no stone structure within its vast pile, and SIDI SLIMANE, Meknès, Morocco, because it is a contemporary replica in mud of a prehistoric North African mortuary house. (NOTE: The use of SMALL CAPITAL LETTERS indicates that the site has its own account in this book).

It is conceivable that no one researcher has visited every one of these sites; I have not been able to do so. Authors must rely upon existing books and publications, archaeologists' reports, and myriad secondary sources. This is why, whenever possible, I have given the names of excavators; they are the heroes. That said, any errors occurring will, I trust, be mine alone. Most facts can be verified, but legends cannot, except for their age, and they are attached to so many megalithic sites across the world. Some of the legends repeated here are among those that I have taken on a degree of trust; but one entirely bogus one is included, just to see how it makes its way in the world!

The language of the megaliths

It was a Dane, Jacob Worsaae (1821–85), an amateur archaeologist, lawyer and politician, who first reached for labels to describe the stages of toolmaking art which were becoming increasingly recognisable. Worsaae is credited with coining the names of the Three Ages : Stone, Bronze and Iron, to describe a National Museum collection by Christian Jurgensen Thomsen (1788–1865) in 1819. The word 'megalith' was devised by an Oxford don, Algernon Herbert, in 1849, for use in his book *Cyclops Christianus*; he had quite logically Anglicized the two Greek words 'megas' (great) and 'lithos' (stone).

The term 'Prehistoric' first appeared in English in the title and text of *The Archaeology and Prehistoric Annals of Scotland*, by Daniel Wilson (1816–92). This was first published in 1851, and Wilson's new word was a welcome replacement for the clumsy 'antehistoria'. The innovative Danes had already evolved 'forhistorisk' in 1837.

General interest in prehistory was really first sprung by a paper read to The Royal Society in London in 1859 by Joseph Prestwich (1812–1896), a Clapham-born wine merchant who became Oxford Professor of Geology at the age of 62. The subject was flint implements and their relationship with extinct animals. *The Origin of Species by Means of Natural Selection* by Charles Darwin (1809–82) was published in the same year to a wide, though initially sceptical, public. The recognition of Early Man, as he was comfortably known, as a toolmaker was widening, within his overall evolution through various cultures, to ever higher levels of manual, intellectual and social achievements.

A few years later, Sir John Lubbock (1834–1913; later the first Lord Avebury), a banker and politician, invented two more words which remain in the archaeologists' vocabulary. They made their appearance in his book *Prehistoric Times as Illustrated by Ancient Remains and The Manners and Customs of Modern Savages*, published in 1865; these words were Palaeolithic and Neolithic.

This book covers sites in more than 20 countries and the descriptions incorporate their indigenous terms for those structures unique to them. Thus we meet some striking nomenclature within the six groups of countries into which they are divided.

Across these countries some epithets recur in the names of sites: those of Devils, Druids, Fairies, Giants, Knights, Huntsmen, Maidens, Pipers, Priests, Trolls and many others. In this way, folk memories from the ancient past remain embedded in the present language of the megaliths. The monuments bearing them in this book are almost all Neolithic, to use Lord Avebury's word. The term is indicative of a certain cultural stage, not a fixed period of time. Very broadly, it implies food producing as opposed to gathering, and the manufacture, export and use of ground and polished stone implements and weapons.

The latter are among the most common finds during an excavation and have much to tell archaeologists. For example, a certain honey-coloured flint is found all over Europe at tomb sites; 'Le Grand Pressigny' constantly appears in excavation reports and it proclaims its presence in tombs far from its quarry south of Tours in Indre-et-Loire, France, which is over 250 miles (400km) south of the coast of England. Those reports also note pottery finds, and these too have a story to tell.

The broken pottery mystery

From America, the islands of the Pacific and Indonesia, as well as all over Europe, has come evidence that, in Neolithic times, the body of a deceased person appears to have gone through two entirely separate rituals. In the first, it seems that all bodily fluids were drained from the corpse into pottery vessels. The corpse was then allowed to decay through putrefaction to the ultimate state of total discarnation. This stage may have taken place on top of a chamber or passage capstone, which could explain why they are so often made flat on top as well as beneath. This natural process was sometimes hastened by the deliberate removal of flesh: evidence for this has been found, for example, on bones in Michelsberg culture burials at the Belgian sites of Spiennes and Furfooz.

The ritualistic act which came next was one of celebration. The spirit of the dead body had by now departed on the next stage of its journey and the purified bones were finally interred in their sepulchre (most often megalithic in Europe). At the same time the used vessels were smashed into pieces and the sherds were buried either with the skeletal remains (together with other burial goods) or near the entrance of the grave. 'Broken pottery near the entrance' is a frequent refrain in the accounts of sites throughout this work. Complete vessels are found very rarely, indeed almost never. In today's world this funerary procedure is reversed. First comes the funeral service (a kind of celebration in remembrance), followed by cremation or burial, and sometimes both. A separate and later service of thanksgiving may follow in a third stage.

In Neolithic times death was believed to be but one stage of the soul's eternal journey. As accounts in this book show, inhumations in burial chambers frequently took place in succession; the disarticulated bones from earlier rituals were unceremoniously piled up in corners or against walls to make room for the next arrival. Odd facts persist. The last arrival is the one an archaeologist discovers with the keenest interest, but even he cannot prove why one skeleton often lies on its left side, with its head to the west, or why another skeleton is in an extended position or flexed. It does seem that if inhumations occurred in succession, they were very rarely collective, but one by one, as if of the same family, tribe or clan. Thus the origins of different pottery sherds at the same location can be so instructive.

Sites and the public

Professor Stuart Piggott has written: 'Archaeology comprises a constantly elaborating set of techniques for obtaining knowledge of communities by means other than the use of written records.' (Piggott 1982). Ever-improving standards of excavation, as well as dating and photography techniques, contribute to this elaboration; site dates are on the retreat, leading to exciting revisions to earlier assessments of the capabilities of prehistoric man.

Were the leaders of these tribes astronomers, priests, surveyors, blood-thirsty thugs with territorial ambitions or perhaps simply men with natural authority elected by the bodies of their communities? In this so-called New Age, public interest in archaeology is greater than ever before. The works of respected archaeologists such as Aubrey Burl and Colin Renfrew have contributed much to this happy situation. There is inevitably a lunatic fringe, but this is healthy in its way. The founder and Editor of *Antiquity*, O.G.S. Crawford refused to publish a review of *The Old Straight Track* by Alfred

---

MEDICINE WHEELS AND EARTH MOUNDS IN NORTH AMERICA AND CANADA

In North America the Indians in the first millennium BC were living as hunters and food gatherers, with some plant cultivation. They did not use stone in the making of their ceremonial and burial sites. They used timber to construct mortuary houses which were then buried beneath enormous earth mounds. The earthworks of the Hopewell culture, which started about 300 BC and came to an end about AD 700 in Newark, Ohio, and the Illinois valley are notable. The Serpent Mound, of the Adena culture (about 1000 BC to 300 BC) is near Locust Grove, Ohio. It is 1300ft (396m) long, and up to 3ft (0.9m) high; the uncoiling serpent holds an egg-shaped object in its mouth. Is this a dragon enclosing the sun – the place for ritual acts?

Another Adena mound is in Mason County, Kentucky; it is 120ft (37m) in diameter, 17ft (5m) high, and contained 55 cremations and burials. The remarkable settlement site at Koster, Southern Illinois, was continually in use from the extraordinary date of 8000 BC (Early Archaic period) right up to AD 1200; then the Mississippian people built great ceremonial squares, defensive walls and earthen temple mounds. At one edge lies one of North America's oldest cemeteries (about 6400 BC); in one grave an infant was found to be dusted with red ochre (*see* SKARA BRAE, Orkney Islands). Again, no large stones were used: so, no megalithic mysteries at Koster.

South of this site, in Missouri, is the Cahokia 'Woodhenge', which has been proved to be a solar observatory of great sophistication. Also in the Cahokia Mounds State Park, is the massive Monks' Mound; it is no less than 1000ft (303m) long, 700ft (213m) wide, and 100ft (30m) high.

Cahokia was undoubtedly a Neolithic-type settlement, but the existence of some 50 medicine wheels on the plains of western America and Canada can only have been created by nomadic hunters; moreover it has been shown that they were in use since about 2500 BC. They are confined generally to Alberta (which has most of them), Saskatchewan, Montana, North Dakota, Idaho, and Wyoming. This last state is home to the Bighorn Medicine Wheel, on Medicine Mountain. It is set 9640ft (2938m) up, and is snowfree for only three months in the year. One of the most recently made wheels, it was in use from about AD 1250 to 1750, as a lunar, solar and stellar obsevatory. It has 28 radiating 'spokes' – the days in a lunar month.

The older and larger Moose Mountain Medicine Wheel, in Saskatchewan, Canada, is similar to Bighorn in that both use stone rubble cairns for co-ordinating points around the wheel 'rims'.

Some of the 1099 menhirs forming the MÉNEC alignment in Carnac – north-west France's 'megalithic wonderland'.

Watkins in the late 1920s; that book remains in print to this day. One champion of Watkins and his ley theories has been John Michell. His own publications have proved very popular as well, and he was one of the first writers to bring the surveys and their accounts by Professor Alexander Thom to the general reader's attention.

Archaeo-astronomy is a discipline of its own these days. See the accounts here, in Thom's native Scotland, of THE RING OF BRODGAR, Orkney Islands, CALLANISH, Western Isles (the 'Stonehenge of the North'), THE HILL O' MANY STANES, Highland Region, and KINTRAW, Strathclyde. Where there is an elliptical stone ring there is a megalithic mystery; there is even one in Morocco (*see* M'ZORA). Interest in archaeo-astronomy in this century can be traced back to the publications of Sir Norman Lockyer (1836–1920); Alfred Watkins read his observations on the apparent alignments between ancient sites. Indeed it was Colonel Johnston, Director-General of the Ordnance Survey in the 1890s, who alerted Lockyer to an alignment upon which STONEHENGE occurred!

The ever-increasing popularity of archaeological sites does, of course, create problems. STONEHENGE, Wiltshire, can no longer be touched. Some monuments near Carnac, Morbihan, France, are having the past trampled out of them but some are now being protected by wire-netting. The solution would

appear to be to have a few principal sites in each country, which, once archaeologists have finished with them, are fitted out with car parks, toilets, visitor centres, multi-language guide books and a full range of facilities for a curious public. This has been done at Lough Gur, Co Limerick, Ireland, not far from THE GREAT STONE CIRCLE there, and at BARNENEZ, Finistère, France.

In general people do not regard megalithic monuments as dead, inanimate things. They may bring to them preconceptions – indeed misconceptions – but I have found that people often express a liking or disliking for a monument. And yet how is it possible to 'like' a chamber tomb in other than architectural terms? Why is a much-restored site held to have 'lost something'? How can it be so, assuming that the restoration was sound? As with many man-made constructions, the answers are linked to the level of personal attention brought to a site. Truly to 'see' is to feel and understand the strength or spirit of the place. Conversely, some monuments seem to lack presence and atmosphere. Two of my nominations for this mysterious latter category are TUMULUS ST MICHEL, Morbihan, France, and ST. LYTHAN'S, South Glamorgan, Wales.

What is certain is that megalithic monuments *always* evoke responses *of some kind*; I have heard them whenever I am not alone at a site, and indeed children join in the opinionating.

DROMBEG, Co Cork, Ireland, evoked very mixed emotions and views when I was last there. Personally, I would give this most interesting assembly of stones only two stars out of five – if this was that kind of guide book!

Christianization of megalithic monuments

Controversy about monuments is nothing new. From the earliest days of the Christian church, its leaders have concerned themselves with the problems of dealing with places of so-called pagan worship. In AD 392, the Roman emperor Theodosius I The Great, a Spaniard, ordered such shrines to be dedicated as Christian churches. In 408, Honorius, his second son, issued an edict forbidding the demolition of 'heathen temples' in areas of high population. In 574, St Martin, the first Archbishop of Braga, asked in a famous sermon : '. . . what is lighting candles at stones . . . but the worship of the Devil?' But old ways continued. An edict issued from the Breton city of Nantes in 655 was firm in its direction that 'bishops and their servants . . . dig up and remove and hide in places where they cannot be found those stones which in remote and woody places are still worshipped and where vows are still made'.

St John's Church at YSBYTY CYNFYN, Dyfed, Wales, is a well-known example of a Christian place of worship which incorporates parts of a stone circle. Another is the recumbent stone circle in the churchyard of MIDMAR KIRK, Grampian, Scotland. The best-known churchyard standing stone in Britain is probably the one at All Saints, RUDSTON, Humberside, England. The stone with ogham notches and a cross at BRIDELL, Dyfed, Wales, in the churchyard of St David's is a wondrous curiosity.

The stone standing at the western end of Le Mans Cathedral, Sarthe, France, has a legend that women wishing to bear children should dip a finger in its deep cup-shaped hollow. Jersey's LA HOUGUE BIE carries a chapel on top (which replaced an earlier medieval one), and so does TUMULUS ST MICHEL, Morbihan, France.

The *département* of Morbihan has very many Christianized megaliths. A strange legacy of those early days of doubt among Christian leaders is in La Chapelle de Les Sept Saints, Le Vieux-Marché, just east of Plouaret, Côtes-d'Armor (known as Côtes-du-Nord until 1991). Its southern transept has as its crypt an *allée-couverte*, and the seven saints are inside it. Even more curious is the fact that they are the object of an annual pilgrimage by Islamo-Christians!

There is a similar arrangement in north-west Spain, 40 miles (64km) east of Oviedo, in the Asturias. Below the church of Santa Cruz de la Victoria at Cangas de Onis is a passage-grave, of which the capstone is the altar. Portugal has the remarkable ANTA DE PAVIA, Mora.

LEFT: *The GARYNAHINE stone circle, on the Isle of Lewis, Scotland, is in fact oval-shaped. It is noted for the unusual low rectangular stone in its centre.*

RIGHT: *Three of the four remaining STONES OF STENNESS in the Orkney Isles. The stone in the foreground, with its strange, steeply sloping top, is 16½ ft (5m) tall.*

FAR LEFT: *STONEHENGE is one of the most important megalithic monuments in Europe. It was constructed over about 1800 years.*

Areas to visit

In England, the Wessex Group (AVEBURY, STONEHENGE and others) would provide many days of happy exploration. To the north, the beautiful Western Isles in Scotland, which include CALLANISH, would be a perfect week; so would a stay in the Orkney Islands. They contain such fine monuments as MAES HOWE, THE RING OF BRODGAR, SKARA BRAE and THE STONES OF STENNESS, (where my very early childhood was spent).

In south-west England, a week touring Cornwall, with another one on the Scilly Isles, would make a worthwhile package. The Boyne Valley group, in eastern Ireland, which contains 25 of the country's 300 and more passage-tombs, offer study for half a lifetime. A whole life's study is to be found in France's Morbihan (the setting of Carnac). In the north-east of the old East Germany, the island of Rügen is littered with megalithic tombs. For an exotic break, and if North Africa appeals, I suggest the vast cemetery of DJEBEL MAZELA — and the services of a guide!

In the end

This book does not pretend to offer solutions to the mysteries displayed — so few are founded on universally accepted facts. Migrations across continents, leaving dateable structures behind them, have been zealously tracked for a few hundred years. Diffusionist theories come and go. The linkage between archaeology and language has been brilliantly explored by Colin Renfrew (1987), who asks if modern European languages are derived from just one Indo-European tongue.

It is no longer conventional to assume that those food-producing stone users, the people of the Neolithic age, spread from south-east Europe in the sixth millennium BC, west into the Mediterranean countries, perhaps across the coastal Mahgreb to Iberia, and also up the Danube into central Europe, and as far as The Netherlands by the end of the fifth millennium BC. Or that they reached Brittany northwards on land, or by sea to its south-west coast, and then moved on to England and Ireland at the same time. The possibility of simultaneous tomb and temple design and construction all over Europe might yet emerge as a plausible fact.

'Dates and Dating', which follows this Introduction, gives a brief account of radiocarbon dating. By the 1970s, the dates being thrown up served to transform our conceptions of the so-called diffusion of megalithic cultures from the Near East (*tholoi* 'beehive' chambers notwithstanding).

The time had come to put on one side the famous reference by Professor Gordon Childe (1892–1957) to 'the irradiation of European barbarism by Oriental civilization'. We now know there are monuments in Brittany and Portugal, for example, which are vastly older than their supposed models in the Near East. The importance of the carving of a Mycenaean-type dagger, which Professor Richard Atkinson so famously discovered on the inner face of Stone 53 in the Great Trilithon Horseshoe at STONEHENGE during the late afternoon of 10th July 1953, became a victim of the calibration curves. Ancient Britons, whether or not covered in paint, were at work with their stones millennia before the dawn of the Mycenaean glories.

In the end, it is perhaps best to think of megalithic monuments as prehistoric handwriting. They were evidence set up to record, forever as we see, rights to territory. Around 7000 years ago these were assumed by a commonly felt instinct, by whole communities, which then related the area of their claims to their own numbers. Such megalithic markers were, we must never forget, most often places of burial. Thus they were dignified with the aura of life, in which death was almost suddenly acknowledged to be merely a stage, as archaeological finds demonstrate.

If such a cognition of this eternal passage of man's spirit did occur at broadly the same time all over the world, then we have the context for the building of physical structures which represented newly formed social orders. I would call it the Society Age.

Michael Balfour LONDON

Dates and Dating

High up in the White Mountains of California there grows the bristlecone pine (*pinus aristata*), which can live for more than 4000 years. This tree plays a central role in the very important story of how the dating of archaeological sites has, in recent years, been drastically revised.

Carbon, together with hydrogen, is an element found in all organic matter and is fundamental to life. Examples of pure carbon are graphite (the lead in a pencil) and diamonds. The possibility that radiocarbon might be detected in living matter was realised by Willard F. Libby (1908–), a Professor of Chemistry at the University of Chicago, in 1946. For his work he was awarded a Nobel Prize in 1960. Here 'C14' signifies one of the three elemental carbons, with an atomic weight of 14. It is not stable, and therefore very slightly radioactive – which is why it is called radiocarbon.

Everybody knows that a tree adds a ring for each year of its life. Once it is felled it ceases to 'exchange' its carbon, in the form of carbon dioxide, with the biosphere (the animal and vegetable worlds), and consequently will not add further rings. Conversely, human bone continues to exchange with the biosphere for about 30 years; animal bones do so for a shorter time span.

The science of the use of tree rings for the calculation of dates is called dendrochronology. Thomas Jefferson (revered for many reasons, and also as a founding father of American archaeology) long urged the use of this science. Their yielded dates, in the early years of research (notably by another American, the astronomer A.E. Douglass, who was investigating the Pueblo Bonito ruins earlier in this century), were then compared with analyses of radiocarbon dates. Considerable discrepancies constantly appeared in calculations which should have matched up. So-called C-variations were responsible for the differences between C14 dates and known historical or calendar dates (from Egypt's Old Kingdom, for example).

The Californian bristlecone pine was used by Wesley Ferguson and other Americans to establish a dendro-chronological sequence about 8000 years long. This was possible because these pines survive when dead, as it were, because of the very dry environment at their altitude of about 9800ft (3000m) and their high content of resin. Thus both dead and living trees were used – with the living samples being acquired by means of bore holes in their trunks. An important dendrochronological factor is that rings in trees do not exchange C14 among themselves, in the same trunks.

Hans Suess's name is forever associated with the first curve he produced, using the pine rings for true calendar dates, and which gave calibrated sets of dates. His curve showed major variations; at the beginning of the fourth millennium BC the variation was about 900 years. Curves using other organic matter followed by the hundred. But why that variation?

The strength of the earth's magnetic fields fluctuates. This strength (called the geomagnetic moment) has a direct effect upon the production of carbon, because cosmic rays are particles which are charged. Therefore, as they arrive, on their spiral path, they are deflected by the earth's magnetic field. So if the geomagnetic moment (the fluctuations) is low, production of carbon on earth rises. It is a fact that the whole direction of the earth's magnetic field is known once to have been reversed. Long ago there was a Magnetic South, but well before the 8000 year old start to Suess's curve. During that time it has been assumed that the C14 level in all living organisms has been constant.

Short term variations also occur on calibration curves – they are known as Suess wiggles or the de Vries effect (after the Dutchman, H. de Vries). These are the results of sunspot activity, which goes in long cycles of 200 years and short ones of 11 years. Wiggles affecting calibrations show decreases in C14 production during times of high sunspot activity. This is because it enlarges magnetic fields between planets, which in turn increases the deflection of cosmic rays.

During such times short wave radio transmissions and indeed communication on a global scale (through computers) are affected; the aurora borealis (the Northern, flickering showers of light) become visible as far south as the tropics. Violent sunspot activity can also cause the magnetic pole to 'wander' by two or three degrees, naturally disturbing the accuracy of compass readings. It is likely that Neolithic man had a need to know when sunspot activity was likely to occur, bearing in the mysterious presence of quartz stone at so many sites (including many that follow in this book).

Man-made alterations to the atmosphere has meant that no post-1950 organic matter can be used in the calibrations for curves. The neutrons in nuclear bomb tests, for example, briefly and sharply increase production of radiocarbon. Some human and natural agencies therefore require a process called fractionation in the correction of the C14 dates which are so essential to archaeologists. Contamination of the earth's atmosphere *is* serious!

There are two main methods used for the detection of C14 in archaeological finds: conventional radiocarbon dating, and the now less acceptable accelerator mass spectrometry (AMS), which can permit dating back through at least 70,000 years.

It is conventional to follow C14 dates, for the years before the birth of Christ, by the lower case bc and the plus and minus symbol ±. BP or bp is also used for an uncalibrated radiocarbon date (where the year 0 BP is taken as AD 1950, the last acceptable year for test matter). Think of it as standing for Before Present. In these ways, the probable time range within which the organic sample material 'died' is indicated. A calibrated or corrected calendar date (using the bristlecone pine curve tables) is stated using the upper case BC.

Passage-grave G in the primary cairn at BARNENEZ, Finistère, France, can provide an example. Charcoal found in it yielded a C14 date of 3800 ± 150 bc (ie: between 3950 and 3650 bc). The corrected calendar or true historical date was found to be about 4600 BC (one of the earliest in this book).

A very simplified C14 calibration table is as follows:

bc	BC
4500	5350
4000	4845
3500	4375
3000	3785
2500	3245
2000	2520
1500	1835
1000	1250

A useful check on C14 dates can be provided by a thermo-luminescence dating technique, commonly referred to as TL. It involves the use of crystals, and is particularly useful for dating pottery.

The dating of obsidian artefacts, both tools and decorative, is easily established. A date of manufacture can be calculated from a measurement of the thickness of the hydration layer on a thin section of a piece. This is because it absorbs water at a rate which depends on its source and the temperature.

Dates for archaeological 'Ages' tend to move about a little, and particularly in different countries. The following table for the British Isles gives a general indication of their spans:

Age	BC
Early Neolithic	5000–4500
Middle Neolithic	4500–3750
Late Neolithic	3750–3000
Final Neolithic	3000–2150
Copper	2150–1700
Early Bronze	1700–1500
Middle Bronze	1500–1150
Late Bronze	1150–1050
Final Bronze	1050–875
Early Iron	875–400

The Council for British Archaeology, London, publishes *Archaeological Site Index To Radiocarbon Dates For Great Britain and Ireland*, with occasional Supplements.

Recent research at the Belfast Conservation Laboratory is expected to provide final confirmation of a tree-ring chronology for the Irish bog oak, going back to the year 5289 BC; radiocarbon dates for between 800 bc and 400 bc are however now being shown to be unusable.

Measuring the Megaliths

In ancient civilizations parts of the human body were used for short measurements – forearms, palms, fingers, feet, etc. In Greece, four fingers' breadth (*daktyloi*), equalled one palm (*palaste*); three palms (*palastai*) equalled one span between thumb and little finger (*spithame*); four palms equalled one foot; one and a half feet equalled one cubit.

In ancient Rome, the smallest unit of measurement was also the breadth of a finger (*digitus*), and 16 of them equalled a foot. Early Egyptians measured the rise and fall of the River Nile in cubits; they regularly surveyed land areas after floods, and this gave rise to 'geometry', which means 'measuring the earth'.

The Rhind mathematical papyrus (bought in Luxor and now in the British Museum) is dated at 1849–1801 BC. It reveals knowledge of some of the properties of right-angled triangles, which were used in the construction of the pyramids. These were square, and positioned (in practically every case) with each side facing a compass point.

Sumerian writing in about 3000 BC recorded numerals, as did the Babylonians (about 2000 BC onwards). Ptolemy (c.90–168 AD) noted that records of eclipses were maintained by them from about 747 BC. More than 200 years late the Babylonians had established the Metonic (19 year) cycle for their astronomical calculations.

It was knowledge of such sophisticated facts that brought the mind of Professor Alexander Thom (1894–1985) to the question of just how Neolithic megalithic builders went about their tasks. Britain has more stone circles than any other country in the world, and when Thom retired as Professor of Engineering Science at Oxford in 1961 he started to survey in the most rigorous fashion several of their number. He established that they had an astronomic function, being set to be aligned on significant risings and settings, of (at different sites) the moon, the sun and first order stars. Some were apparently capable of predicting the occurence of eclipses – plainly terrifying events in the prehistoric world.

Alexander Thom's great bequest is his establishment that one unit of measurement was most commonly used. He called it the megalithic yard, and it equalled 2.72ft (0.829m). No summary here can do justice to the scale and detail of his surveys, and the reader is therefore directed to his publications which are listed in 'Further Reading' at the end of this book. Some of his findings and conclusions have been questioned, but he opened out a subject to the general public as well as to the academic archaeological world, and for this he will be remembered for a long time to come. To discover that stone circles are in fact enormously subtle ellipses is to realize that Neolithic man was himself a remarkable instrument. The circles at AVEBURY in Wiltshire are set to an accuracy approaching 1 in 1000.

I

British Isles

Historians through the ages consistently ascribe to the British Isles a possession of 'special' qualities. A map shows them to be tucked away off the massive peninsula of north-west Europe, on the way to nowhere, and with no great natural resources worth the journey to plunder. However, 'this other Eden' (Shakespeare; King Richard II) is home to perhaps the oldest Christian church in the world, at Glastonbury, and its foundation was only the latest (though the most lasting) of a long series of stone constructions across the land which incorporated ancient knowledge. This knowledge is all but lost to us, but enough remains for evidence to be discovered of highly sophisticated engineering. Between four and six thousand years ago more than 1000 stone circles, and countless standing stones and burial chambers were erected with stunning precision in large groups all over the British Isles, from the Shetland Islands in the north to the Isles of Scilly in the south-west of England, and in most parts of Ireland. Britain has a concentration of megalithic remains which is comparable only with Brittany and Denmark.

The legacy of Christianization

For the fact that there still are megalithic mysteries we have partly to be grateful for the Roman attitude to the old places of so-called worship. Until Constantine died in AD 337, the earliest Christian missionaries and their converts destroyed the Britons' existing temples, shrines and idols – and set up their churches elsewhere. But the powers of these sites and the ancient beliefs in them remained considerable, and could be used. So Rome changed its mind, and in AD 601 Pope Gregory gave to Abbot Mellitus a letter to take to Bishop Augustine in England: '. . . I have come to the conclusion that the temples of the idols in England should not on any account be destroyed . . . smash the idols, but the temples themselves should be sprinkled with holy water and altars set up in them'.

That new policy left alone much for us to enjoy and puzzle over today. There are many hundreds of circular, raised churchyards in Britain; it is not difficult to spot unusual, large or alien stones incorporated into their walls or indeed the fabric of churches themselves. Witness the five large stones, one 11ft (3.3m) high, in the churchyard and wall at YSBYTY CYNFYN, Llanbadarn Fawr, Dyfed, in Wales. The huge standing stone in All Saints churchyard in RUDSTON, Humberside, survives to this day, as do the stone circle in MIDMAR churchyard, Aberdeen, and the fine altar table, with strange carvings on the supporting stones, in the churchyard of St Nicholas, Trellech, Gwent. Tremendous sarsen stones

which once topped the elliptical mounded churchyard in Alfriston, East Sussex, are long since broken up and lie ignored beneath a nearby tree – the still visible reason for the very existence of beautiful Alfriston and 'The Cathedral of the South Downs'. Perhaps that Roman policy was responsible for a dramatic fact: there is not a stone circle to be found to the east of a line between Scarborough on the North Yorkshire coast and Southampton on the Hampshire coast.

In the beginning

The story of Britain's prehistory could be said to start with the gradual ending of the Ice Age, about 12,000 years ago. At that time there was no English Channel; remains of mammoth and woolly rhinoceros have been found in the Cheddar Gorge, Somerset; bones of bears, lions and hyenas were discovered in Kent's Cavern, Torquay. Over the next 4,000 years the English Channel, as we know it, slowly came into existence; the Isles of Scilly were one land mass as recently as 2,000 BC, easing the tasks of the megalithic workforce there, in that great concentration of tombs. A distribution map showing the numbers and grouping of burial chambers, circles, standing stones and alignments is more eloquent than words, but it does not betray one remarkable fact; this is that at the time when STONEHENGE I was being made (before the Great Pyramid was even started) it has been estimated that the population of the British Isles may have been no greater than about 20,000. This implies discipline of a very high order, which is why a kind of priesthood must have attained, preserved and passed down the necessary mathematical and astronomical knowledge enshrined in Britain's monuments. It is unsafe to assume that druids had anything to do with them; through the years they have been called up as the true inheritors of the ancient traditions, but they are best left in their sacred groves, where Julius Caesar found and recorded them as such.

Anglesey

Megalith hunters heading for Ireland would do well to leave a day spare for this Welsh island. The carvings in BARCLODIAD-Y-GAWRES are well worth examining, beneath their modern dome overlooking Trecastell Bay. BRYN CELLI DDU, in its restored state, is very instructive, and the blue-green pillar in the chamber (actually a replica) is one of the strangest stones in the British Isles; one puzzle is its height of only 4ft (1.2m). Free-standing pillars are also found in Breton V-shaped passage-graves, such as Ty-ar-Bondiquet, Brennilis, Finistère.

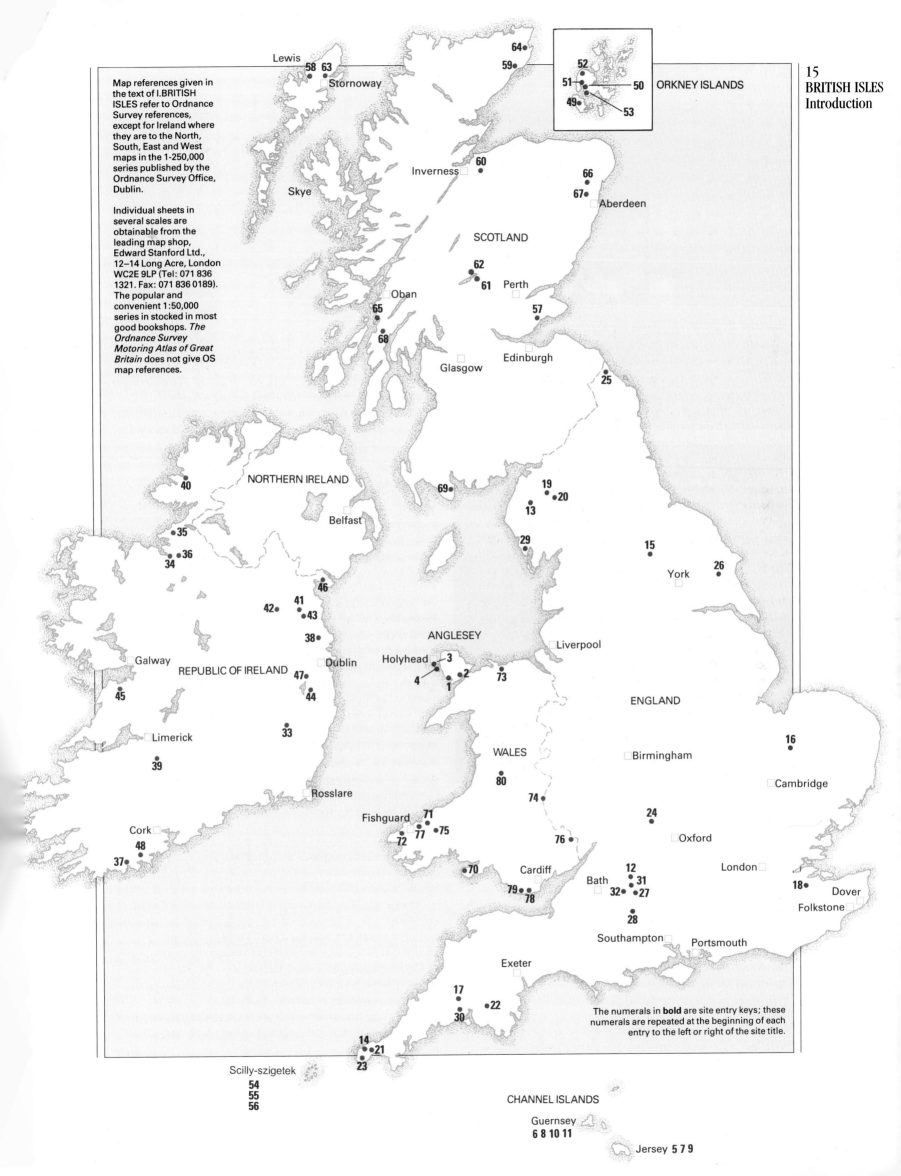

Map references given in the text of I. BRITISH ISLES refer to Ordnance Survey references, except for Ireland where they are to the North, South, East and West maps in the 1-250,000 series published by the Ordnance Survey Office, Dublin.

Individual sheets in several scales are obtainable from the leading map shop, Edward Stanford Ltd., 12–14 Long Acre, London WC2E 9LP (Tel: 071 836 1321. Fax: 071 836 0189). The popular and convenient 1:50,000 series in stocked in most good bookshops. *The Ordnance Survey Motoring Atlas of Great Britain* does not give OS map references.

ORKNEY ISLANDS

Lewis

Stornoway

Skye

SCOTLAND

Inverness

Aberdeen

Oban

Perth

Edinburgh

Glasgow

NORTHERN IRELAND

Belfast

Galway

REPUBLIC OF IRELAND

Dublin

ANGLESEY

Holyhead

Liverpool

York

ENGLAND

Limerick

WALES

Birmingham

Cambridge

Rosslare

Fishguard

Oxford

London

Cork

Cardiff

Bath

Dover

Folkstone

Southampton

Portsmouth

Exeter

The numerals in **bold** are site entry keys; these numerals are repeated at the beginning of each entry to the left or right of the site title.

Scilly-szigetek

CHANNEL ISLANDS

Guernsey
6 8 10 11

Jersey **5 7 9**

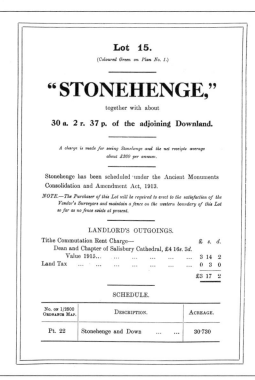

ABOVE LEFT: *A tranquil scene at* AVEBURY, *Wiltshire.*

LEFT: *This natural rock outcrop at* ROUGHTING LINN, *in the far north-east of England, is covered with more than 60 cup-and-ring marks. These mysterious carvings have never been deciphered.*

ABOVE: STONEHENGE *was auctioned by British agents, Knight, Frank & Rutley, on 21 September 1915. This great megalithic site fetched £6600.*

RIGHT: *The Neolithic hut settlement at* SKARA BRAE, *Orkney Islands, revealed after a violent storm in 1850.*

kind in the world – and it is a dominating presence among the country's 21 sites described in this first section of the book. Much has been written about this giant calendrical instrument, and it correctly lies towards the centre of any attempt to understand life and times in Neolithic days. As a small, contemporary aside it also lies on a ley (*not* ley line); this is an invisible straight line which connects prehistoric sites; moreover, this fact was first announced in the 1890s by the then Director-General of the Ordnance Survey, Britain's official map-making organization. Parts of the thrilling and important AVEBURY monument complex, also in Wiltshire, also fall on a ley. Single monuments of mysterious purpose are included here: the carved rock face at ROUGHTING LINN, Northumberland, the huge and lonely RUDSTON MONOLITH in Humberside, and the vast yet empty SILBURY HILL, Wiltshire.

Channel Islands

Jersey and Guernsey were still joined to France in about 7500 BC. Four and a half millennia later the huge passage-grave of LA HOUGUE BIE was going up in Jersey. Much later on it was truly Christianized, with the arrival of a church on top of it (in the manner of TUMULUS ST MICHEL, Morbihan, France. On neighbouring Guernsey, at CÂTEL, stands a 6ft 6in (2m) high statue-menhir, showing a necklace and two breasts. It is about 3000 years old, and its carvings are distinctly similar to others in different parts of France and as far away as Corsica (see FILITOSA). LES FOUAILLAGES is perhaps the oldest of the 60 or so megalithic tombs on Guernsey.

England

England's greatest single glory is of course STONEHENGE, Wiltshire – the most complete megalithic monument of its

Ireland

The Emerald Isle possesses an embarrassment of riches. The capstone on BROWNE'S HILL, Co Carlow, is unforgettable; it is fat and weighs 100 tons! Had more care been taken of it, then CARROWMORE, Co Sligo, might today be rivalling Carnac as a megalithic site; at the last official count it had 42 stone circles, 14 burial chambers, and five cists. There are several indications here which suggest that passage-graves and other tombs in the east and west of Ireland were not the work of migrant north-west European builders, but of local device. The greatest wonder of Ireland is NEWGRANGE, in the Boyne Valley; here there is a description of the unusual stone ring, the massive kerb, the shining quartz roof, and of course the carvings within.

Orkney Islands

In the north of Scotland, among these beautiful islands, lie some of Britain's finest monuments. They include the very rare rock-cut tomb, DWARFIE STANE on Hoy, THE RING OF BRODGAR, Mainland (which Professor Alexander Thom believed to be a prehistoric observatory), the Neolithic settlement of SKARA BRAE, Mainland, and its story of ancient Britons as 'the painted ones', and the romantic 4900 year old STONES OF STENNESS, Mainland.

The stone circle and rows of CALLANISH, in the Western Isles, form a distant yet popular venue for megalith hunters. In its very beautiful setting, there was carefully constructed, so the native Professor Thom argued, a lunar observatory. CLAVA CAIRNS, near the bloody battlefield of Culloden, outside Inverness, provides a set of very unusual features in stone. The recumbent stone circles are unique to Scotland, and one of the most striking of them is probably MIDMAR KIRK, in Grampian. In 1914 a graveyard was established around this ring of stones!

Wales

One of the most moving megalithic landscapes in Britain lies near the foreboding Preseli Mountains (of bluestones fame), in Dyfed. The perfect stone circle and standing stones of GORS FAWR, among the sheep and gorse on the land that has always been common, make a remarkable scene. The village of Trellech, in Gwent, contains HAROLD'S STONES (three of them), a holy well, an earth mound, and a stone table (or pagan altar) in front of a preaching cross in the churchyard. PENTRE IFAN, Dyfed, may be some 5500 years old and has yielded many archaeological secrets; yet one feels there is more to know about this well-excavated megalithic site.

I.1

BARCLODIAD-Y-GAWRES

Trecastell Bay,
Gwynedd

CHAMBER TOMB

SH 328708

This site's name 'The Giantess's Apronful' derives from the legend that the stones were scattered here when the strings of a giantess's apron broke; she had been carrying the stones to build a fortification nearby.

There is a car park above this popular beach, on the Bordorgan Estate. The tomb is well signposted, guiding you some 500yds (457m) along a cliff path. Take a torch. This tomb has locked iron gates at its entrance; for a deposit and a small fee the key is obtainable from The Wayside shop up the road in Llanfaelog.

Spirals and circles highlighted in red chalk on the fourth stone to the left inside the chamber.

The name of this fascinating tomb is Welsh for 'The Giantess's Apronful'. After excavation in 1952/53, a concrete dome (now topped with earth and turf) was installed to shelter this apparent jumble of stones, which was clearly so arranged for some purpose.

Just beyond the 23ft (7m) passage, which faces north-north-east and out across a bay, a cruciform chamber contains six or more carved stones (among the 23 and capstone) of great antiquarian interest. They feature chevrons, lozenges, squares, arrows, spirals, grooves, cup marks, a hexagram, and even an ankh-like carving. When last seen by the author in August 1990, these were outlined in red chalk, and they made a dramatic show. Symbolic art such as this connects its creators with the builders of the Irish Boyne Valley cruciform tombs.

In the central hearth of the chamber, the excavators found a most odd collation of burnt remains, including eels, a frog, a hare, a mouse, part of a pig's vertebra, a shrew, a snake, and whiting. A meal for a coven perhaps, but no legends of witches are to be found in these parts.

This is an ideal site at which to study prehistoric carvings – but remember to take a wide-beam torch. With the key you may be left alone in the tomb with the megalithic puzzles.

I.2

BRYN CELLI DDU

Llanddaniel Fab
Gwynedd

PASSAGE-GRAVE WITH
CHAMBERED CAIRN

SH 508702

Leave the Menai Bridge on the A5 to Holyhead; then turn left on to the A4080, and right towards Llanddaniel Fab. Park, as directed there, just past the school on the verge. Then walk as signposted, along the broad farm track for about 750yds (686m). Take a torch.

The restored entrance, with kerbstones in the former henge ditch.

Much has been written about this famous megalithic site, which about 4000 years ago was marked with a stone circle, bank and ditch. These were then replaced by a chambered cairn with a 27ft (8.2m) long passage, and the whole was covered by a mound of earth. The present kerb stones stand in the former henge ditch. Beside the unusual pit beyond the chamber lies a carved stone; this is in fact a cast of the original which, together with other finds from the site following the 1928 excavations, is now in the National Museum of Wales in Cardiff. Deliberately smashed white quartz stones were one of the interesting finds here (they also feature in other sites in north Wales). Carvings can also be seen on the inside face of one of the entrance stones.

The chamber itself is about 10ft (3m) wide and 6ft (1.8m) high. Within is discovered a standing stone, one of the most mysterious stones in Britain; it is a 5ft 6in (1.7m) tall column, exceptionally smooth, and of a local blue-green stone.

Fragments of cremated and unburnt human bones were found in the passage and chamber; outside the present mound, post sockets, the skeleton of an ox and a human ear-bone were uncovered. Experts describe this site as a ritual place, and many regard it as a temple rather than a tomb.

PENRHOS FEILW

*Penrhosfeilw,
Trearddur Bay,
Gwynedd*

STANDING STONES

SH 227809

*In Trearddur, turn left off the
B4545; proceed north along
the coast road, and take the
third lane on the right.*

*The two remaining stones (right) of
a possible stone circle, the
colloquial term for a ring.*

This attractive site raises many questions, and answers none. It
consists of two Early Bronze Age (2000–1500 BC) standing
stones, each 10ft (3m) tall, and placed 11ft (3.3m) apart.
Although of the same stone, quarried yards away, they are
different in outline yet have the same thickness, and vary only
8ins (20cm) in their base lengths. Weathering could not have
produced such a difference. And why are they placed on a
north-east-north/south-west-south axis?

Tradition says that these two stones were once part of a
circle, a belief which often recurs around the country. Farmers
have been known to take down one of a pair of stones, leaving
the other as a rubbing post for cattle – but not here. Farmers
are also known to erect such a post – but surely not two, so
closely together in the same field? Whatever their original
purpose, they are an excellent antidote to the horrors of nearby
Holyhead, the ferry port.

TREFIGNATH

*Trearddur Bay,
Gwynedd*

BURIAL CHAMBER

SH 258805

**Excavations have revealed
both decorated and plain
pottery fragments at this site.**

This heavily restored burial chamber is almost literally
overshadowed by nearby huge smoking factories and, with
excavation, has definitely lost some of its mystery. However, it
is an unusual and technically interesting site, and excavation
has revealed that there were three constructional phases, each
represented by a separate chamber.

The first was at the west end of the present site; its entrance
is very short and faces due west, and the chamber was square
and simple. Then came the now collapsed rectangular, central
chamber; only an entrance stone and the back stone remain
standing, but the fallen and broken capstone is there. Its
rounded forecourt once had a drystone retaining wall.

The third and final burial chamber is the best preserved.
Five uprights support two capstones (with the help of a
recently installed plinth); there are two tall and impressive
portal-stones (associated with the second building phase) at the
south-facing chamber entrance, and these were probably not
covered by the original stone mound. They opened on to a
horn-shaped, recessed forecourt.

*Travel from Holyhead south-
east along the B4545; turn
left just before the Shell petrol
station, and the site is 1 mile
(1.6km) along the road, past
the houses, on the right, where
it is signposted.*

*There were three different
construction phases at Trefignath.*

LE CÂTEL

I.5

Couperon,
Jersey

EARTHWORK

WV 68915464

On the north-east of the island
between Pot du Rocher and
Couperon; on the left down a
lane. On private property, so
ask for permission to cross the
farmland.

This is the finest earthwork in Jersey. Its date is uncertain, but probably late Iron Age. With a height of 19ft 9in (6m), and a width of 32ft 9in (10m), sections of the earthwork survive to a length of 219yds (200m). Like others in the Channel Islands, it was obviously planned to fortify a spit of land jutting out between Bouley Bay to the west, and Rozel Bay. Roman occupation also seems evident since coins from Gaul have been found at this site, which was once known as Caesar's Wall.

Near the north side of the entrance to Ste Marie du Câtel Church, on Guernsey, stands a Neolithic statue-menhir. It is, of course, far older than the church itself, but probably just as old as the churchyard site which may have been used in pagan rituals. The menhir, which is roughly though distinctly human in outline, is about 6ft 6in (2m) high, has no face, but shows a necklace and two breasts.

The best-known statue-menhir on Guernsey is La Gran'-Mère du Chimquière, which has a clear carved face; it stands 5ft 6in (1.7m) high and was remodelled in Roman or medieval times. In France, there is a carved stele of some similarity at the end of the short passage of the *allée-couverte* of CRECH-QUILLÉ at Saint-Quay-Perros, Côtes-d'Armor.

The 3000 year-old statue-menhir in the churchyard of Ste Marie du Câtel.

LES FOUAILLAGES

I.6

Chouet,
Guernsey

PASSAGE-GRAVE WITH
STATUE-MENHIR

WV 33578314

Take L'Ancresse Road north
from St Michael Du Valle,
and then the second turning on
the left towards Chouet. The
site is on the right.

Possibly the earliest passage-grave on
Guernsey, in the first of its four
stages.

Since excavations in the early 1980s this important site has been thought to pre-date, in its early Neolithic period, all the 70 or so Guernsey tombs. It was found to have been constructed in four stages.

In the first, four structures were built, on a north-east/south-west alignment, and covered by a triangular kerbed earth mound, 65ft 6in (20m) long and 32ft 9in (10m) wide, with a narrow entrance at the east end. There was a small chamber, a rectangular chamber, a cairn over a cist, and, at the east end, a small anthropomorphic statue-menhir. Sherds of Bandkeramik pottery, giving this first stage its rough date, were found on a circular platform.

Next, the whole interior of the grave was filled in with stones and closed. Then the façade at the eastern end was levelled and an oval shrine erected within concentric kerb-stones. Finally, about 2000 BC, use of the shrine is shown by the presence, in pairs of two, of eight superb barbed-and-tanged flint arrowheads. Four of them came from the central French quarry at Le Grand Pressigny, which is 224 miles (360km) away.

LA HOUGUE BIE

*Grouville,
Jersey*

PASSAGE-GRAVE

WV 68205038

*Take the A6 north from St
Helier, and turn right at Five
Oaks on to the B28. The site
is signposted nearly 1 mile
(1.6 km) along on the left.
The Museum of the Société
Jersiaise is on the site.*

*The massive lit interior of this
remarkable passage-grave.* Inset:
*The second chapel to be built on top
of the enormous mound.*

The features, size and fine condition of this 5000-year-old monument place it among the most exciting in north-west Europe. A medieval chapel was built on top of the tomb, and then another adjoining it: hefty pieces of Christianisation! These were removed during the excavations and restoration in 1924, along with a more recent house built on top of *them*.

The mound is a huge 180ft (54.9m) in diameter, and is 40ft (12.2m) high.

The single cruciform grave within is 70ft (20.4m) long, and lies broadly east to west, towards which end the Great Chamber is set. It is 29ft 6in (9m) long, 9ft 9in (3m) wide, and 6ft 6in (2m) high. There are two small side chambers outside the main one, just to the east on either side of the passage. Roofing is provided by rectangular, flat capstones.

All the stones here came in groups from well-spread sources, which is something of a mystery, unless conjecture is correct that very small local 'communities' brought their own materials and labour.

Hougue means 'mound' or 'barrow', from the Old Norse *Haugr* (eminence), which also provided 'How' in northern England and Scotland. 'Bie' stems from *-by*, Old English and Scandinavian for a settlement.

LA LONGUE ROCQUE

*Les Paysans,
Guernsey*

MENHIR

WV 26527717

*In a field to the west of Les
Paysans. On private property,
so ask for permission to visit
the stone at the house opposite,
Val des Paysans.*

The largest menhir in Guernsey.

This is the largest menhir in Guernsey. Its total height is known because the site was excavated in 1894; the slim granite column measured 14ft 9in (4.5m) in length, of which 11ft 6in (3.5m) is visible above the ground today and has a circumference of 12ft 6in (3.8m). Although a Bronze Age burial was found under Britain's tallest standing stone (*see* PUNCHESTOWN, Naas, Co Kildare), no burial was found beneath this menhir.

In a garden in St Stephen's Lane stands another smaller granite menhir which, according to the island's Ancient Monuments Committee, is probably La Petite Longue Rocque. It was recorded as long ago as 1793.

MONT UBÉ

St. Clement,
Jersey

PASSAGE-GRAVE

WV 6769 4742

This somewhat mutilated grave was discovered in 1848, when W C Lukis, the father of archaeology in the Channel Islands, heard that an unusual group of stones was being quarried. He arrived too late to save the capstones.

The site was originally covered by an earth mound; the sad chamber we see today measures 24ft by 9ft 9in (7.3m by 3m). It is reached from the south-east through a tapering passage, which is 16ft 6in (5m) long and 6ft (1.8m) at its widest point. There is a small side chamber to the south and possibly there were others. A very small cist, or replica dolmen, has been found at the 'neck' of the passage, and objects found in Mont Ubé have included polished axes, stone rings and numerous pottery sherds.

This site has suffered for a long time because it is known to have been used almost continuously from late Neolithic to early Roman times. Possible fragments of the capstones lie around, but the drystone walling has all vanished.

Turn north off the A5 (La Grande Route de St Clement), on to La Blinerie. At the top of the hill a sign on the east side of the road indicates the path to the site.

The passage here is 16ft 6in (5m) long and 6ft (1.8m) at its widest.

LA ROCQUE QUI SONNE

Rue de l'Ecole,
St Sampson,
Guernsey
PASSAGE-GRAVE
WV 34978236

North of the harbour at St
Sampson, in the grounds of
Vale School.

The remains of this passage-grave lie in school grounds. This once substantial site was originally the largest chamber and passage-grave in the Channel Islands but was broken up in the last century so that the stone could be incorporated in a new house here; the sounds of the breakers' hammers could be heard many miles away – hence its name. Soon after, the newly completed house burnt down and its owner, who had dared to tamper with a prehistoric burial place, died horribly on board ship a few years later.

Today, the dead are honoured and left to rest in peace. After all, the old passage-graves were built to be secure.

Sufficient stone was removed from this site to load a 150-ton vessel. Other stones were used in doorposts and lintels.

Excavations in the 19th century revealed plain and decorated pottery beakers, a small bronze bracelet and a fragment of a jet band.

The passage-grave in school grounds.

LE TRÉPIED

Perelle Bay,
Guernsey
PASSAGE-GRAVE
WV 25987889

On the coastal road, north of
Perelle, overlooking Perelle
Bay at Le Catioroc Point.
Signposted between Saumarez
Fort and Richmond Fort.

A beautiful location, but one to be
avoided on Friday evenings.

Legend has it that Le Trépied is a place to avoid on Friday evenings, because witches had this day as their Sabbath and held covens among the stones. There are records of witch burning in the 17th century in this area of Guernsey; but elsewhere in the British Isles old practices have not died out entirely. It is reputed, but may not be true, that a stone circle in Oxfordshire can be rented for covens.

Perelle means 'rock'. The passage-grave here is 18ft (5.5m) long and has almost parallel walls, which is rare. Three times restored, there are modern supports in the chamber, which is 19ft 9in (6m) long, 6ft (2m) wide and 4ft 9in (1.3m) high. There are 12 uprights on this slightly raised site and its entrance faces north-east. Arrowheads, sherds of pottery and human bones have been found in this Late Bronze Age grave.

AVEBURY

A view of one of the majestic stone circles. Avebury is one of Britain's most important Neolithic sites; the outer circle of megaliths is probably the largest in the world.

*Avebury,
Marlborough,
Wiltshire*

STONE CIRCLES AND
EARTHWORKS

SU 103700

*The Avebury circles are
'among' a village. It is
therefore well signposted
6 miles (9.6km) west of
Marlborough, and 8 miles
(12.9km) north-east of
Devizes (where some artefacts
from and records of the Wessex
Group of megalithic
monuments can be seen in the
Museum, in Long Street). The
Alexander Keiller Museum in
Avebury is well worth a visit.*

*A stone outline with a familiar
shape: was that angled top surface a
foresight to the stars?*

Avebury has been called the 'metropolis of Britain' of 4600 years ago. Today it is the name of a Wessex village, but to prehistorians it is the nomenclature for an extraordinary array of monuments both in the village and nearby, including SILBURY HILL and WEST KENNET LONG BARROW.

The famous diarist and biographer John Aubrey is credited with 'discovering' Avebury on 7th January 1649, while he was out hunting foxes. He recorded that it 'does as much exceed in greatness the so renowned Stoneheng (*sic*) as a Cathedral doeth a parish Church' (*see* STONEHENGE, Wiltshire, and its Aubrey Holes). The first detailed account of the Avebury complex of Neolithic monuments was William Stukeley's *Abury, A Temple Of The British Druids* of 1743. In 1724 he attempted a reconstruction drawing, as would be seen obliquely looking northwards, of the area around Avebury. It depicts at its centre the majestic outer Great Circle of monoliths, which is the largest in the British Isles, and dates back to about 2600 BC. At that time Windmill Hill camp, also shown north-west of the Circle, was still in use. Within the stone ring, he shows two sets of concentric circles, parts of which remain today. Leading away from the circles were two avenues of stones, like great dragon features in the landscape, one curling away south-west, and the other to the south-east. The first he called Beckhampton Avenue, and the other Kennet Avenue, which swirled away to The Sanctuary and Overton Hill. South of the circles he showed Silbury Hill, and further south West Kennet Long Barrow.

Avebury lies on a mysterious alignment of sites. Taking Silbury Hill with its sighting notch as a centre point, a meridian line can be traced north through the churches at Avebury and Berwick Bassett; to the south, the same invisible straight line runs through the Milk Hill earthwork to Wilsford Church.

The most comprehensive account of this thrilling area is Aubrey Burl's *Prehistoric Avebury* (1979). The brief facts of the village circles are that they lie within a 28½ acre (11.5 hectare) site, enclosed by an outer bank, which is between 14ft and 18ft (4.2m and 5.4m) high. This was constructed from

The ditch inside the outer bank is up to 30ft (9m) deep.

RIGHT: *Avebury village, the ditch, bank and stones.*

N

Northern Inner Circle

Museum

øCove

Pub

Church

High Street

Southern Inner Circle

Ditch

Bank

Metres 0   150

Feet 0   500

● Standing stone
● Fallen stone
▫ Stone hole
▫ Stone hole (probably)

the contents of a massive ditch; this was up to 30ft (9m) deep and an estimated 3,950,000 cu ft (111,864 cu m) of chalk and rubble was dug out from it. In Stukeley's 1724 engraving of the Great Circle, about 100 stones are shown, of which 27 stand today. The inner two stone circles were probably put up afterwards, though some question this; indeed a wooden structure and stone setting might have been constructed first, at the middle of the Great Circle. Avebury has suffered badly in the past, particularly at the hands of insensitive neighbours who seemed not to have appreciated its beauty and importance. In the 1930s, its condition greatly improved during the ownership of Alexander Keiller (of Dundee Marmalade fame),

his excavations of the western half between 1934 and 1939 revealed most of what we know of the circles and avenues today.

Like so many megalithic monuments, Avebury will probably conceal its secrets for a long time to come. Recently the earliest known drawing of the Great Circle (made by John Aubrey sometime between 1648 and 1663) was discovered in a library in London. It clearly shows four concentric circles within the outer bank, and also pairs of portal stones at entrances to the north, east, south and west. Thus the possibility is raised of there having once been not two avenues but four, leading away from the Avebury circles.

CASTLERIGG

*Keswick,
Cumbria*

STONE CIRCLE

NY 292236

The best time to visit Castlerigg is soon after dawn or at dusk, when the circle looks particularly imposing. However, its level site high on Chestnut Hill is accessible at all times and the views all around are stunning, but particularly to the north towards Skiddaw and Blencathra.

This Type A flattened circle has 38 stones, of which five have fallen, and is nearly complete in the form in which it was constructed in about 3000 BC. Its average diameter is 100ft (30m). Its entrance, towards the best view to the north, is marked with two fine portal stones.

Unique to this site is a rectangle of nine stones (known as The Cave) which are 'attached' to two more on the inside of the ring on the east side.

There are stones all around and in hedges, and one notable one is an outlier by the stile to the south-west, but it may have been moved there.

The late Professor Alexander Thom, who made a detailed survey of Castlerigg, concluded that it was a prehistoric observatory and capable of a number of calendrical functions. It is sometimes known as The Carles, apparently relating to a familiar old legend – that the stones are petrified men – but in fact, this is based on a mistaken reading of William Stukeley's word Carles (castle) in 1725.

Very clearly signposted by English Heritage east of Keswick, on the A66 and A591. Park at the field gate.

One of the most beautiful stone circles in Britain.

CHÛN QUOIT

*Morvah,
Cornwall*

BURIAL CHAMBER

SW 402339

Take the B3306 west from St Ives, turn left at Morvah, towards Madron. Take the lane on the right, leading to a farm. The chamber is uphill north-west of the farm.

A Cornish quoit, once covered by an earth mound.

This is a great and handsome monument. A quoit is a dolmen or cromlech, and not always identifiable as a burial chamber. Chûn Quoit is set high on a ridge, above Chûn Castle hillfort, and was originally covered by an earth mound, of which much evidence abounds.

It was a closed chamber. The mushroom-domed capstone measures 11ft (3.3m) by 10ft (3m), with a maximum thickness of 2ft 7ins (0.8m). It is supported about 7ft (2m) from the ground by four substantial slabs. There is evidence of an entrance passage to the south-east within the mound area.

This part of Cornwall is ideal for megalithic visits; in the same vicinity there are Chûn Castle hillfort (very near, off the same track), Lanyon Quoit (The Giant's Table), MEN-AN-TOL, and Mulfra Quoit.

THE DEVIL'S ARROWS

*Boroughbridge,
Ripon,
North Yorkshire*

STANDING STONES

SE 391665

turn left (after the Three Arrows Hotel) up Roecliffe Lane, passing Druids Meadow. The Arrows are either side, one on the left and two in the field to the right.

Going north on the A1, take the turning off (A6055) for Boroughbridge. Immediately cross over the road east and carry straight on for Boroughbridge. In the town,

One of the three remaining Arrows, with the distinctive grooves at the top.

The famous line of three standing stones, intersected by a lane, is 190yds (174m) in length. A fourth stone was pulled down in the 16th century. Their heights are 22ft 6in (6.8m), 21ft (6.4m), and 18ft (5.5m). The purpose for which they were erected will probably never be known, although one theory was that the unusual grooves running down the stones provided a system of sight lines to the stars, since it was considered unlikely that the millstone grit stones would have weathered over millennia in such precise and matching ways. But weathering marks on the stones are now confirmed. The name of the stones comes from the story that the Devil aimed and shot arrows at nearby Aldborough, but that they fell short and landed on this site.

GRIMES GRAVES

*Weeting-with-Broomhill,
Norfolk*

PREHISTORIC
MINESHAFTS

TL 817898

*Travel north on the A134
from Thetford to Mundford
for 2 miles (3.2km), then
turn left where the Graves are
signposted. Park along the
track on the left.*

*One of the galleries beneath the many
mineshafts.*

This is the best known source of flintstone in Britain. The Neolithic mineshafts were first worked between 3300 BC and 1650 BC, and it is estimated that nearly 4000 mines of different classes were dug. The origin of their group name is uncertain, since this was never a graveyard for human or animal remains, but may have Scandinavian roots. They were first discovered by a Reverend Greenwell in 1868 who, when exploring a circular depression, came across a gallery at a depth of 32ft (9.7m). Today you can climb 30ft (9m) down an iron ladder, and examine the elaborate gallery system below.

Shaped red-deer antlers were used as picks to dig a shaft and gallery, which took about six months. It has been estimated that one such mine would have yielded some 50 tons of flint. The stone was roughly shaped at the minehead into the required axe and arrow shapes, to save weight, and these implements were then 'exported' all over Britain.

At Grimes Graves which is a 34 acre (14 hectare) site, there are three flint layers, and the best material lies at the lowest. All these centuries later, hundreds of 'capped off' shallow craters can still be seen.

THE HURLERS

*Minions,
Liskeard,
Cornwall*

STONE CIRCLES

SX 258714

*On Bodmin Moor. Travel
south from Launceston towards
Liskeard; take the right
turning to Minions and park
there.*

*A well-known group of Cornish
circles on Bodmin Moor.*

These three dressed, granite circles were set high on Bodmin Moor in about 1850 BC, close together, and so carefully that all their stones appear to be the same height. As with most circles, they are on a north-north-east/south-south-west alignment on a slope.

The northern circle is 115ft (35m) across; 15 stones remain, of which four have fallen, and there were probably a further nine there. A paved path led directly south to the slightly egg-shaped circle; its average diameter is 139ft (42.5m), and 14 stones are here, with 14 marker stones. The southernmost

circle has only nine stones left around its diameter, which measures 107ft 6in (32.8m).

The two 6ft 6in (2m) tall Pipers stand to the west, and there are doubts as to their authenticity. Petrification is part of a legend here. The famous historian William Camden, for example, recorded in his *Britannia Descriptio* (1610 edition) that: 'The neighbouring inhabitants terme them Hurlers, as being by devout and godly error perswaded that they had been men sometime transformed into stones, for profaning the Lord's Day with hurling the ball'.

KIT'S COTY HOUSE

*Aylesford,
Kent*

BURIAL CHAMBER

TQ 745608

*Take the A229, going north
from the M20 to the M2*

*towards Blue Bell Hill. Turn
left for Burham, park at the
footpath on the right for the
short walk to the signposted
site.*

*One of the few megalithic monuments
discovered in Kent.*

The close steel fencing around this burial chamber would not
have amused Samuel Pepys, the famous 17th-century diarist,
who saw it in happier times; he was, he recorded, 'mightily
glad to see it'. Three upright stones topped by a capstone ('of
great bigness') measuring some 13ft (4m) by 9ft (2.7m) are all
that remain of this Neolithic burial chamber.

In Pepys' time and before, there was a long barrow here
with an isolated recumbent stone at its western end; it was
called 'The General's Tomb' but was destroyed by a farmer
who wanted more acreage in 1867. There may also have been a
forecourt façade at the eastern end. It has even suffered in
name. Stow's 1580 *Chronicles of England* calls it 'Cits cotihous',
and Camden's *Britannia* (1610 edition) mentions 'Keith-coty-
house'.

To the south of the road leading north-west to Burham,
about 500yds (457m) away, lie The Countless Stones. Now
just a jumble of about 20 leaning or fallen stones, they once
formed a burial chamber, sometimes called Little (or Lower)
Kit's Coty House.

LITTLE MEG (MAUGHANBY)

*Glassonby,
Penrith,
Cumbria*

**STONE CIRCLE WITH
CARVINGS**

NY 577375

*Take the A686 from Penrith
to Alston. After about 4 miles
(6.4km), turn off to
Langwathby, then through
Little Salkeld. A little further
on towards Gamblesby, go
past the signposted track on the
left to Long Meg And Her
Daughters. This site is then
on the left in a field. Park at
the gate.*

This Early Bronze Age site was once one of Cumbria's smallest
circles, but today it is a half-hidden pile of disconsolate stones,
with many of them aliens. An 1875 plan shows 11 stones in a
ragged ring (enclosing a central cist in which a cremation was
found), but there are many more now, including the largest
stone, placed there in the relatively recent past. However,
there are large early stones on the site, and one, lying just east
of north, bears carvings of five concentric circles and a spiral.

Interestingly, among the 50 or so circles in Cumbria, LONG
MEG, Little Meg, and the Glassonby stone circle, 1m (1.6km)
away, are the only ones sporting carvings. The late Professor
Alexander Thom proposed that Little Meg is on an alignment
of considerable significance, involving his 16-month calendar.

**Professor Thom proposed
that, in the years 2000–1600
BC, megalithic man divided
the year into 16 parts for the
purposes of solar prediction.**

*Carvings on the remaining part of
one of the stones in this small circle.*

Long Meg and her Daughters

*Hunsonby,
Penrith,
Cumbria*

STANDING STONE AND
STONE CIRCLE

NY 571373

Recent (1988) aerial photography has revealed a huge earthen enclosure, hitherto invisible, to the north of the circle, which meets with and fits exactly the flattened northern segment of the ring.

This was a large family! Originally there were about 70 stones, the Daughters, standing in a ring here; today 27 still stand, and 42 lie fallen. This is the third largest stone circle in Britain (the outer circles at AVEBURY, Wiltshire and Stanton Drew, Avon are bigger), and is a Type B flattened circle, set on ground which slopes to the north-east, and measuring 119yds (109m) by 102yds (93m). The stone is local granite, and the largest Daughter has a tremendous waist measurement of 10ft 9in (3.3m) and tips the scales at about 28 tons. Nothing of significance has been found at the centre of this unexcavated circle — any goods would have been easy to steal, because sadly a road runs right through it.

Long Meg, which is 12ft (3.6m) tall and of local sandstone, stands just outside the south-west entrance, 238ft (72.6m) from the circle's centre: this is the alignment of the midwinter sunset. Long Meg has a cup-and-ring, a spiral and an incomplete concentric circle carved on her 'best side', which faces north-east, back along that line.

Take the A686 from Penrith to Alston. After about 4 miles (6.5km), turn left to Langwathby, then through Little Salkeld. A little further on towards Gamblesby a signposted track to the left leads to the site.

A dramatic view of Britain's third largest stone circle.

MÊN-AN-TOL

I.21

*Madron,
Penzance,
Cornwall*

STANDING STONES

SW 427349

Take the B3306 west from St Ives, turn left at Morvah, and park after the next left turning. Signposted.

The Stone with A Hole

The name of this group is Cornish for 'stone with a hole', and refers to the now central, circular stone. It is famous for its smooth hole, which is in the middle of the stone as it shows above the ground, and occupies about half its size. The stone is about 4ft 6in (1.3m) across its centre. The three stones are now aligned, but were once in a triangular formation, which makes certain astro-archaeological claims for it difficult to support.

Centuries ago, the holed stone was known as The Devil's Eye. Legends persist of strange rituals which involve crawling (often three times) through the carved-out aperture to conjure up cures, fertility, prophecies, etc. Cures for rickets in children were always a popular request. Elsewhere in Cornwall, in a private garden in Gweek, is a tall, triangular slab with a circular hole in it, 17¼ins (44cm) in diameter. These are two Bronze Age puzzles yet to be solved.

MERRIVALE

I.22

*Princeton,
Tavistock,
Devonshire*

STONE CIRCLE, STONE
ROWS AND CAIRNS

SX 555744

Not signposted. The hamlet of Merrivale is midway between Tavistock and Princeton (Dartmoor Prison) on the B3357; the rows are on the right, about 400yds (365m) to the east of the pub.

An exciting megalithic complex on Dartmoor.

Mysteries abound at this bleak Bronze Age site. It is one of the most accessible among more than 70 or so stone rows on the vast area of Dartmoor, and features a multiplicity of megalithic remains. In this single respect it rivals the stone rows at KERMARIO and MÉNEC in Brittany.

Here there are two double rows and one single one. Both double ones are 'planted' east to west. The northernmost is 596ft (182m) long, and has some 170 stones. To the south of it is a 865ft (264m) long row, containing more than 200 stones. The third, single, row is only 140ft (43m) long, and is directed to the south-west.

At Merrivale there is also a fine standing stone, nearly 11ft (3.3m) high, a very incomplete stone circle oval in plan, and the remains of a small cairn-circle, which is located for some inexplicable reason about halfway along the second double stone row.

THE MERRY MAIDENS

*St Buryan,
Penzance,
Cornwall*

STONE CIRCLE

SW 432245

Signposted. On the B3315, 4 miles (6.5km) south-west of Penzance.

This is Cornwall's prettiest stone circle. It is believed to be complete, which is rare, is 77ft 10in (23.7m) in diameter, and has 19 stones in its ring. They range in height from 4ft 6in (1.4m) in the south-west to 2ft 6in (0.8m) on the north-east side. The gap, exactly at the east, was either an entrance or the site of a missing stone. This delightful site has also been known as the Rosemodress circle, and as Dans Meyn, which is the Cornish for 'stone dance'.

According to legend, these Maidens were turned to stone for making merry on the Sabbath to the music of two Pipers – the two tall stones standing like naughty non-identical twins in another field to the north-east of the circle. The same legend attaches to THE PIPER'S STONES, Co Wicklow, Ireland. The north-east Piper is the tallest Bronze Age Cornish menhir, at 15ft (4.6m).

A peculiarity here is that when a line is drawn from this menhir through the second Piper, to its south-west, and continued onwards, it just touches the north-west edge of The Merry Maidens – forming yet another mysterious alignment of stones in Cornwall.

THE ROLLRIGHT STONES

*Little Rollright,
Chipping Norton,
Oxfordshire*

STONE CIRCLE,
STANDING STONE AND
BURIAL CHAMBER

SP 296308

Travel north on the A34 from Oxford. Pass the turning for Chipping Norton and Banbury. Turn left opposite the second turning for Great Rollright. Well signposted.

This splendid and accessible group consists of a stone circle (The King's Men), a standing stone (The King Stone), and a burial chamber (The Whispering Knights). The King's Men is privately owned and a small fee is charged (which goes to animal causes) for a visit to stones which have distinctly anthropomorphic shapes. Dating back probably to 3000 BC, there are about 77 stones around the 103ft (31.4m) diameter. Early in the 17th century only 26 were standing; this captivating circle, tucked into its wooded glade, has been much tinkered with, and there was a major re-erection of stones in 1882.

The King Stone is across the road from the circle to the north-west; this twisted, pitted menhir is certainly prehistoric, but undated. It was probably once connected to a barrow to the west of it. Clearly visible from The King's Men, due east over rolling farmland, stands The Whispering Knights. This burial chamber was probably part of a long barrow in about 3750 BC. The steel fencing tightly encloses the mounded remains of a fallen capstone and four other stones leaning together around the south-south-east facing entrance.

The Rollright Stones have been popular for many centuries. The many legends attached to them involve Danish kings, druids, petrification, fairies, witches and covens, sacrifices and fertility. One such legend tells how the King's Men go down to a spring in Little Rollright spinney at midnight to drink; the King Stone goes to the spring too, but starts his journey only when he hears Long Compton church clock strike midnight (*see* FOUR STONES, Walton, Powys).

ROUGHTING LINN

CARVED ROCK FACE

NT 984367

South of Berwick-upon-Tweed, leave the A1, after Scremerston, on the right on to the B6525. Do not turn left at the crossroads for Lowick, but continue, take the first right turning signposted to Milfield, and then park near the track for Roughting Linn Farm. The rock is tucked away, just up the track, on the right in a clearing.

One of over 60 mysterious carvings on this natural stone outcrop.

This important site can truly be called megalithic. The natural rock outcrop measures about 60ft by 40ft (18m by 12m), and is covered with over 60 cup-and-ring marks and other motifs. The grinding of holes in stone to produce these marks was an ancient, almost universal, practice in Neolithic times, commonly associated with funerary rites of some kind. They have been found all over Europe, Russia, Australia and America.

It could be argued that cups carved into horizontal slabs may have held oil, blood, or holy water but since they also occur on vertical stone faces, they may simply have been a form of exterior decoration, or fashion designs or paint boxes for 'the painted ones' (*see* SKARA BRAE). With megalithic mysteries such as these, one feels, surely, that a code, a Neolithic Linear B, is involved and will soon be deciphered.

RUDSTON MONOLITH

I.26

*All Saints Churchyard,
Rudston,
Bridlington,
Humberside*

STANDING STONE

TA 097677

Rudston is about 5 miles (8km) west of Bridlington on the B1253.

The tallest standing stone in Britain, measuring 25ft 9in (7.8m) high, above ground.

This is the tallest standing stone in the British Isles, and it is to be found only 12ft (3.6m) away from the north wall of one of the Church of England's places of worship, in its graveyard. It is therefore probable that the site of All Saints Church has been a sacred one for more than 4000 years continuously. The crumbling top of the 25ft 9ins (7.8m) high stone is possible evidence of an early attempt to 'christianize' it; this was common practice in Britain in the first centuries AD, and indeed elsewhere in Europe. As with so many monuments of this type, the source of its stone was not the nearest available, but gritstone known to have been quarried about 10m (16km) away on the coast south of Scarborough.

SILBURY HILL

*Beckhampton,
Marlborough,
Wiltshire*

EARTH MOUND

SU 100685

*5 miles (8km) west of
Marlborough on the A4. Park
in the lay-by at the base of the
mound.*

Silbury Hill is Europe's tallest prehistoric monument, and one of the world's largest man-made mounds. About 4600 years ago some 500 people slaved for approximately 15 years, under very sophisticated direction, to put 8.75 million cu ft (248,000 cu metres) of earth and aggregate on top of a 3.75 million cu ft (107,000 cu metres) natural hill. The base of the Hill is 550ft (167m) in diameter – and is perfectly round, like a bowl barrow. Its summit, 130ft (40m) high, is flat-topped and 100ft (30m) wide. It has a distinct notch, near the top, best seen from the east, and the whole is surrounded by a huge, causewayed moat.

What the Hill's significance, or purpose, was remains a mystery – for it is an undisputed fact that there is nothing and nobody buried inside Silbury Hill.

It may indeed be shaped like a bowl barrow, but the next highest of Wessex's bowl barrows (of which there are approximately 380) is only 25ft (8m) high; moreover, the Hill occupies 5½ acres (2.2 hectares) of chalky Wiltshire valley floor, unlike all the other barrows.

A large-scale excavation during 1967–70, led by Professor R.J.C. Atkinson, was televised by the BBC in the hope that dark secrets or a magnificent burial would be revealed. There were none. The writer Michael Dames has suggested that the mound and moat might be a sculpture of The Great Goddess, but he finally acknowledges that the monument remains 'a stupendous enigma'.

An aerial view of one of the world's largest man-made mounds; the extraordinary crop circles in the corn field behind it appeared overnight.

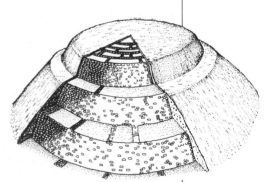

The complex stepped construction of Silbury Hill (towards the top), which is one of the world's largest man-made mounds and 'a stupendous enigma'.

STONEHENGE

*Amesbury,
Wiltshire*

STONE CIRCLES,
HENGE, AVENUE,
CURSUS AND STANDING
STONE

SU 123422

Stonehenge is the most complete, the most important, and the most famous prehistoric site in Europe. There is no single answer to the first and inevitable question 'what was it for?'. This is mainly because the complex was constructed in six broad phases; these have been very fully described at book length, and made the subject of commentaries literally for hundreds of years.

In about 3200 BC, the circular, non-defensive ditch was dug providing, over some 28,000 man-hours, about 3,500 cu yds (2,700 cu m) of chalk rubble for the bank inside; the 56 Aubrey Holes (white-painted markers today) were made, and (probably) the famous outlier, The Heel Stone, was put in place; the midsummer solstice sunrise occurs almost over this stone, an event celebrated by latter-day Druids since 1906. A

A familiar view of one of the most famous megalithic monuments in the world.

timber building may have been at the centre of the earth ring.

Around 2200 BC a double blue stone circle was erected (*see* GORS FAWR, Dyfed, for the amazing source of these stones). Then the Altar Stone arrived, a companion to The Heel Stone (a recent discovery), as well as two more entrance stones, and the first stage of The Avenue.

About 100 years later the main construction phase took place: the Altar Stone was moved, and the Sarsen Circle of 30 stones was put up (17 remain today), as probably were the four Station Stones and the five Great Trilithons which make up the Sarsen Horseshoe. Stone 56 stands alone in the middle of the Great Trilithons, its tenon visible on top, and is without doubt one of the most beautiful dressed stones in the world. In approximately 1800 BC, the Altar Stone was placed in its present position, the 29 Z Holes and 30 Y Holes were dug (the Aubrey Holes were once called the X Holes), and a bluestone setting of at least 19 stones was erected but then dismantled.

Take the A303 west from Amesbury, and then the A344 to the right. The stones are fenced off from the public. *The site is open from 10.00am to 6.00pm in the summer, 10.00am to 4.00pm in the winter (1st October – 31st March). Kiosks at the entrance sell multi-lingual maps and guides to Stonehenge and other local Wessex prehistoric monuments. Toilets and parking. Admission charges (but free to English Heritage members).*

A view towards one of the inner Sarsen Trilithons, of Stones 57 and 58. Note the tenons on the tall Stone 56 on the left.

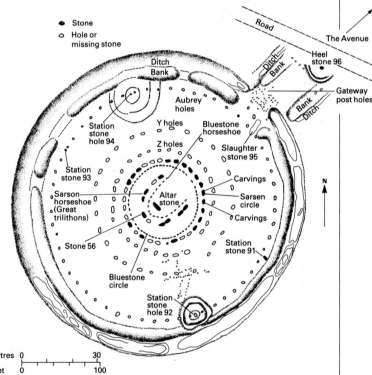

Stonehenge as it never was. Several construction phases, shown in one plan, from about 3100 BC to about 1550 BC. The Avenue was extended in about 1100 BC.

In about 1550 BC the Bluestone Circle (60 stones) and the Bluestone Horseshoe (19 stones) were raised into position, and, finally, in about 1100 BC The Avenue was extended south and then eastwards. This brief account necessarily omits many details which alone confirm that Stonehenge was mathematically an extremely sophisticated set of calendrical devices.

Stonehenge, the first stage of which predates the Great Pyramid at Giza, was first mentioned in literature by Geoffrey of Monmouth in his famous 'history' of 1135. His account of Merlin the wizard and the plan to 'fly' some great stones over from Naas, Co Kildare, was the first of a very long and often brilliant and entertaining collection of speculations about the origins of the stones and their settings. In summary, serious attempts have been made to prove that Stonehenge has been a sunrise, a moonrise, and an eclipse predictor.

Books such as Gerald Hawkins' *Stonehenge Decoded* enormously widened public interest in this extraordinary set of

A close-up view of the morticed and tenoned Trilithon comprising Stones 57, 58 and their lintel.

stones. But he was merely a recent entrant into the list of those who have felt personally involved with them, and a need to bring their own interpretations to the subject. Such a list would include Professor Richard Atkinson (the excavator and greatest authority on Stonehenge), John Aubrey (he of the Holes), William Blake, William Camden, Thomas Carlyle, William Caxton, Charles I and II, John Constable, Daniel Defoe, Ralph Waldo Emerson, John Evelyn, John Flamsteed, Jacquetta Hawkes, Henry VII and VIII, Henry of Huntingdon (who quoted Geoffrey of Monmouth's vanished history), Sir Fred Hoyle, Inigo Jones (who named The Altar Stone), Ben Jonson, Alexander Keiller (*see* AVEBURY, Wiltshire), the firm of Knight, Frank & Rutley, London (which auctioned off Stonehenge on 21st September 1915 as Lot 15 in a public sale; it went for £6600), Paul Nash, Samuel Pepys, Sir William Flinders Petrie, John Speed, John Stow, William Stukeley, Professor Alexander Thom (and probably every other serious archaeologist who has ever lived).

Countless times through its very long history, Stonehenge has been threatened by all kinds of authorities (even the Royal Air Force, which wanted to flatten it during World War I). Recently, there has been much public and professional controversy about how to cope with more than 700,000 annual visitors and all their needs. A new Visitors' Centre, much further away from the stones, is a welcome likelihood. To all newcomers, an unexpected warning: Stonehenge, at first sight, *always* appears much smaller than imagined. This is partly a trick of the landscape, and is a common impression.

The mighty Sarsen Stones (from the right) 29, 30, 1 and 2, with their three lintels, as seen from the Heel Stone. Stone 56, with its tenon, stands majestically in the background.

SWINSIDE (SUNKENKIRK)

*Broughton in Furness,
Millom,
Cumbria*

STONE CIRCLE

SD 172883

*32 stones survive in this beautiful
ring; 23 more have all fallen
inwards.*

*Travel west to Broughton in
Furness on the A595 past
Duddon Bridge. Take the
next road on the right, where
it is signposted; on foot, fork
left at Craig Hall up a
private track towards
Swinside Farm. The site is
about 1 mile (1.6km)
along on the right.*

This Late Neolithic circle has been called the most beautiful in England. Originally, there were a probable 55 stones, set closely together, almost like a defensive palisade, in stone rubble. Only 32 of them still stand, all of which have strangely fallen inwards. The palisade effect recalls CASTLE-RIGG, also in Cumbria.

The diameter of the ring is about 94ft (29m), and its entrance is at the south-east. This is guarded by two tall portal stones against the outside of the circle; this arrangement is also seen at LONG MEG AND HER DAUGHTERS, again in Cumbria, and far away at Ballynoe, County Down.

Swinside was excavated in 1901 and although little was found, there were fragments of red iron-stone which could have been used as pigment for body painting (*see* SKARA BRAE). The alternative name of Sunkenkirk derives from an old story that the local grey slate stones were foundation stones for a church under construction, and that the Devil came each night to re-bury them.

TRETHEVY QUOIT

*St Cleer,
Cornwall*

BURIAL CHAMBER WITH
PORT-HOLE IN
CAPSTONE

SX 259688

*Take the B3254 south from
Launceston to Liskeard. Pass
the right turn to Minions;
take the next right to the
hamlet of Darite and travel
½ mile (0.8km) south.
The Quoit is in a field behind
cottages on your right.*

*This dramatic burial chamber is
famed for the hole in its capstone.*

The wonder of this dramatic chamber (once known locally as The Giant's House) is not so much the size of the capstone, which is 12ft (3.7m) long and, in its half-fallen state, 15ft (4.6m) high in the air, but that the natural hole pierces it at its now highest point. It was probably chosen for this aperture.

The function of port-holes is a mystery; experts speculate that they were used for astronomical observation or, perhaps, to allow good or evil spirits to come and go. Whatever their purpose, they are rare in Britain. The rectangular chamber, which is 6ft 6in by 5ft (2m by 1.5m), is made of seven uprights. averaging 10ft (3m) in height, and is divided by a large doorstone at its eastern end. There is a puzzling 'doorway' cut out of the entrance stone, which may have been for the passage of bodies, but, curiously, the sloping angle of the top of this hole is reminiscent of many free-standing stones (for example, THE STONES OF STENNESS, Orkney Islands).

WEST KENNET AVENUE

*Avebury,
Marlborough,
Wiltshire*

STONE ROWS

From SU 103699
(Avebury) to SU
118679 (The
Sanctuary)

All through history, ceremonial avenues have been erected to someone's greater glory (in Paris over 100 years ago; in Bucharest in modern times) or for ritual of unknown origins. Some are literally straightforward; others have recently been shown to be astonishingly subtle astronomical instruments (*see* KERMARIO and MENEC, both in Morbihan, France).

West Kennet Avenue was originally almost 1½m (2.4km) long and connected the south-south-east entrance of the earthwork at Avebury with the concentric circles at The Sanctuary on Overton Hill. Some 30 pairs of stones in the northern section have been re-erected, and missing stones are indicated by markers.

There is a mysterious fact about this 'stone row'. In Late Neolithic times (as confirmed by grave goods and burials), it was decreed that the shapes of the 100 pairs of stones should alternate, both down each row and in their opposites, so that tall narrow pillars are followed by wide 'lozenge' shapes – thus suggesting male and female forms. They average 10ft (3m) in height, and stand, within their giant puzzle, about 80ft (24m) apart. Perhaps the raising of a form of energy, through coils and spirals, was involved.

The shapes of the 100 pairs of stones in the Avenue mysteriously alternate.

The Avenue runs roughly parallel to the B4003, going south-east from Avebury village towards West Kennet village.

WEST KENNET LONG BARROW

*Avebury,
Marlborough,
Wiltshire*

LONG CHAMBERED
BARROW

SU 104677

This is the most famous of Britain's 260 or so long barrows, of which 148 are to be found in the county of Wiltshire alone. In many parts of Europe long barrows have been given giants' names, as a reminder of their size and presence. But one of their puzzling aspects is that they are very long, for no apparent reason; the chambered tomb in West Kennet Long Barrow occupies just an eighth of the barrow's 340ft (104m) length. Nevertheless, it is the longest chambered tomb in England and Wales.

The Barrow is similar to many long, raised enclosures in Germany and Denmark, and particularly to GROENJAEGERS HOEJ ('The Green Hunter's Mountain'), Denmark. Construction commenced about 3600 BC, which surprisingly is some

Signposted about ¹/₂ mile (0.8km) west of West Kennet and 1 mile (1.6km) east of Beckhampton. Some parking space there. Then walk up path around fields for ¹/₂ mile (0.8km). Take torch.

The largest chambered tomb in England and Wales, and one of no less than 148 in Wiltshire.

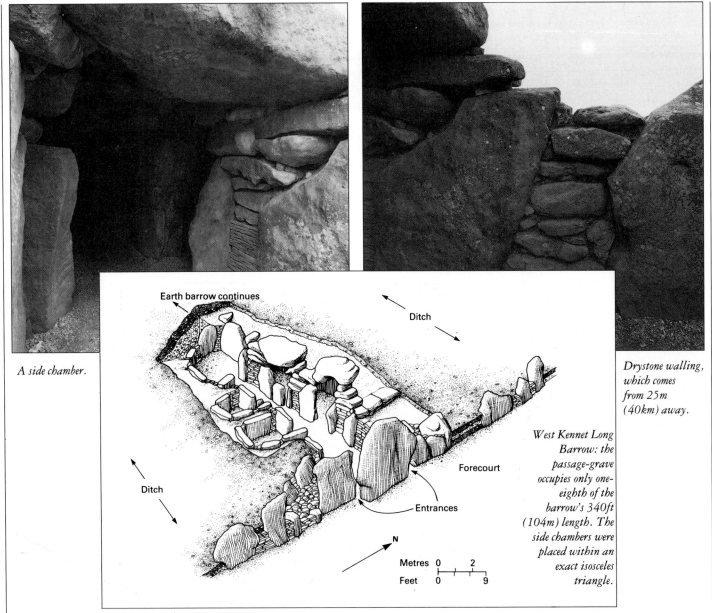

A side chamber.

Earth barrow continues

Ditch

Ditch

Forecourt

Entrances

N

Metres 0   2

Feet 0   9

Drystone walling, which comes from 25m (40km) away.

West Kennet Long Barrow: the passage-grave occupies only one-eighth of the barrow's 340ft (104m) length. The side chambers were placed within an exact isosceles triangle.

400 years before the first stage of STONEHENGE. It was finally closed by the Beaker people in about 2500 BC.

As one looks along its green and bumpy spine, even the exterior presents an impression of design and effort on a scale which must tell us how important the site was in Neolithic times. Entering the tomb beyond the forecourt past the three massive upright sarsens (the biggest of which stands 12ft (3.7m) above the ground and weighs 16 tons), there are two burial chambers either side and a larger polygonal one at the end of the passage. The sarsen stones used for the interior uprights, capstones and corbelling are undecorated (unlike, for example, some of those at the mighty NEWGRANGE), and are local. However, the drystone walling is known to come from the Frome area, which is 25m (40km) away.

Why, therefore, was more than a ton of either Forest Marble or oolitic limestone purposefully hauled over such a distance? The probable answer does not involve magnetism, healing powers, or a false druidical significance, and is a surprisingly sophisticated one, given that it was spotted more than 5500 years ago: it was the right stone for the job, being comparatively easily worked and known to withstand weathering. Indeed, the stone is still used for house building today, as visitors to the Cotswold area can see.

The interior of West Kennet Long Barrow has an attractive geometry. Excavations in 1955–56 revealed that the side chambers occur inside an exact isosceles triangle, the height of which is twice the length of its base. Within were found the scattered remains of 40 to 50 people, although not all were buried at the same time. The chambers also contained relics and artefacts, some of which may be seen at the Devizes Museum, Devizes, Wiltshire. Those included later Neolithic Peterborough and grooved-ware, knives, scrapers, flint arrowheads, jewellery, and animal remains, such as a carefully sharpened boar's tusk, and a beaver's tooth.

The pottery was, as always, in pieces, and it is entirely reasonable to assume that a pot is totally unlikely to remain in its complete form for more than 5500 years. And yet the assumption may not be a sound one.

The destruction of pots over the dead in their place of burial used to be common all those years ago in very widely scattered cultures; the act was seen to symbolize the liberation of the spirits of the dead from perfect vessels, the former bodies, and it also provided sherds as utensils for the journeys thereafter. The burials at West Kennet Long Barrow, together with their magnificent housing, elucidate some mysteries but hide others.

Browne's Hill

I.33

*Kernanstown,
Carlow,
Co Carlow*

PORTAL-TOMB

Map 3 (East) 275176

Very well signposted as you approach. Park by the signpost there, and then walk for 5 minutes around the fenced perimeter of the fields.

The capstone of this portal-tomb weighs about 100 tons, and is one of the heaviest in Europe.

The sight of this tomb, from the small car park looking south-west over fields, is magical. From this distance, the rough-hewn eastern vertical face of the capstone proclaims a sort of bullish majesty. It is named after a large local house, but must surely have been called The Giant's-something in the past. That stone reputedly weighs more than 100 tons, and is one of the heaviest capstones in Europe.

Browne's Hill (closely fenced in) is set on a slope, from west to east. Unusually, it was probably never covered in earth, as were almost all tombs of this type. Beyond the southern entrance, just to the west, there are three uprights, and two recumbents lie beneath the fallen western side of the capstone. A fourth upright stands nearby. From the west, up the slope, the capstone looks like a huge pudding, unsubtle in outline and yet smoothed to perfection all over; and its belly, the underside, a massive 41ft (12.5m) in girth, has been shaped to a completely flat surface. This must have been a tomb of an important figure, and in need of very secure protection.

Carrowmore Group

I.34

*Sligo,
Co Sligo*

CEMETERY; PASSAGE-TOMBS, DOLMENS AND STONE WITH PORT-HOLE

Map 2 (West) 166333

Well signposted. In fields 2 miles (3.2km) south-west of Sligo.

An antler pin and a walrus bone ring were found in Grave 27.

Ireland's largest concentration of megaliths is at Carrowmore. The legendary Queen Maeve's Grave is in the far distance.

This huge site is 1 mile by 1½ mile (1.6km by 2.4km) in area, and possesses the largest concentration of megaliths in Ireland. It is possible that it was once the largest cemetery in Western Europe but, because tragic and scandalous quarrying has destroyed vital evidence, we will never know. One recent count produced 42 stone circles, 14 burial-chambers, and five other cists.

The necropolis is dominated by Queen Maeve's Grave (or Cairn or Lump) on Knocknarea. One of the largest tombs is Listoghil; the site is typical of the group, and of a type which spread west and north from the Boyne Valley, via LOUGHCREW

and Carrowkeel. The recently excavated Grave 27 is a very early version of the passage-tomb, in a cruciform shape; this is important because its probable construction date (before 3750 BC) controversially proposes that passage-tombs in western and eastern Ireland were not initiated by Brittany's megalith builders at all, but instead were developed independently by an already existing Neolithic population. Furthermore, Tomb 4, in the field on the Sligo side of the car park, contains the remains of a passage-tomb which may be the earliest in the country — pre-4500 BC. Diffusionist theories which suggest links between early cultures may yet be found wanting.

CREEVYKEEL

I.35

*Cliffony,
Co Sligo*

COURT-TOMB

Map 2 (West) 172354

Signposted near the Creevykeel crossroads. Up a path behind a house east of the road from Sligo to Bundoran.

Looking east across two burial chambers to the huge oval open court.

There are about 350 known court-tombs in the whole of Ireland, but only five of them are in the south of the country. Creevykeel is one of the most impressive, and has been finely restored so is well worth a visit.

It is located within a clear wedge-shaped cairn, and was originally about 200ft (61m) in length. The entrance is at the eastern end through a small passage, which leads into the oval forecourt; this has the extraordinary dimensions of 56ft by 33ft (17m by 10m), and was, of course, originally paved. The tomb continues on beneath a lintel stone through two successive chambers, where four cremations have been found. Sealed off, but even further on, are the remains of a possible three more burial chambers, of which one plainly has a side entrance.

One of the most exciting discoveries at Creevykeel came in 1935; a chalk ball, similar to ones found in Brittany, provided further confirmation that court-tombs, such as this, often slightly pre-date passage-tombs. It also highlights fascinating questions about the migration of cultures. But much of this history remains undiscovered.

DEERPARK (MAGHERAGHANRUSH)

I.36

*Sligo,
Co Sligo*

COURT-TOMB

Map 1 (North) 175336

Signposted 'Leacht con Mhic Ruis' 4 miles (6.5 km) east of Sligo on the road from Leckaun to Sligo; then a ten-minute walk south on a footpath.

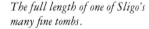

The full length of one of Sligo's many fine tombs.

This is just one among many prehistoric sites in Sligo which merit attention. It is situated on the top of a limestone ridge with splendid views of Lough Gill. The 50ft (15m) long central court lies within a cairn twice as long. One two-chambered gallery is off the west end, and two more lie off the eastern end of the court. They were originally roofed, of course, and the line of the kerb indicates a trapezoidal construction, dated at 3500–3000 BC.

DROMBEG

*Skibbereen,
Co Cork*

STONE CIRCLE, HUT
AND COOKING PLACE

Map 4 (South) 124035

*Signposted. 1 1/2 miles
(2.4km) east of Glandore. To
the east of a side road, find the
400yd (366m) path.*

*Drombeg is noted for its prehistoric
cooking area.*

RIGHT: *The neat stone circle at this
megalithic complex.*

Drombeg was built around 1500 BC. It is full of interest as a collective site in reasonable condition.

Entering the site from the north, one comes to the stone circle 30ft (9.1m) in diameter on its natural rocky terrace. Of the original 17 stones, 13 remain in this well-ordered place. To the left of the entrance, one fine portal stone is 7ft 2in (2.2m) high; its opposite number is recumbent, measures 6ft 10in (1.9m), and has two egg-shaped cup-marks (one with a ring around it).

Excavations in 1957/58 revealed cremated bones in a deliberately broken pot near the centre of the circle. There is an additional interest for followers of Professor Thom, in that the axis of the circle points to the setting sun at the winter solstice.

A few yards to the west there are two adjoining huts; the smaller had a cooking place 5ft by 3ft 6in (1.5m by 1.1m), on the east side, which was still in use in the 5th century AD; this prehistoric kitchen had a trough in which water was boiled by dropping hot stones into it, and there was a well and a hearth for cooking. Drombeg has a functional but rather bleak feel about it.

FOURKNOCKS

A decorated lintel stone.

*Naul,
Co Meath*

PASSAGE-TOMB

Map 3 (East) 310262

*Signposted. 2 miles (3.2km)
north-west of Naul and 17
miles (27.2km) north of
Dublin. Obtain a key from the
first house on your left going
down the hill, going east from
the stile. Ten minutes' walk
up the path.*

This tomb with the puzzling name is only about 9 miles (14.5km) south-west of NEWGRANGE, the most famous of them all, and it has been dated to 1900 BC by the radiocarbon method but may well be 500 or more years older. The stretched oval main chamber is 21ft (6.4m) long – unusually long for an Irish tomb. Today it is covered and preserved by a concrete dome. It has some similarities to Portuguese passage-tombs, but most experts believe that it was the work of migrants and their successors from Brittany, and not from the Iberian peninsula.

Most unusually, the main chamber has probably never contained burials – although 60 or more of them were found during the 1950/52 excavations elsewhere on the site. It could have been a safe and protected meeting place for unknown ritual practices, celebrations of seasonal changes, and so on. It is notable also for its 12 decorated stones, one of which bears a crudely carved 'funny' face which is probably the earliest Irish portrait!

There are two other sites on this slate ridge: a crematorium, about 150yds (137m) east of the passage-tomb, with five cists containing infants, and two urn cremations; and there is a 50ft (15m) round barrow with a cremation and Bronze Age pots.

THE GREAT CIRCLE/LOUGH GUR

Lough Gur,
Co Limerick

STONE CIRCLE WITHIN
HENGE

Map 4 (South) 164140

12½ miles (20km) south of
Limerick, east off the R512
near Kilmallock. Well
signposted.

Near the east-facing entrance to this
huge, elegant earth-banked circle of
contiguous stones at Lough Gur.

Lough Gur, in terms of its location, is one of the most important prehistoric sites in Britain. Within the vicinity are more than 30 places of separate interest to anyone concerned with 'the way we lived then', and 15 of them make a full day out, with the assistance of the excellent Visitors' Centre.

Easily the most exciting of them is The Great Circle, a full orchestra of a place. The ring of contiguous orthostats (all stones touching) is 148ft (45m) in diameter, and is literally backed up by an earthen bank which averages nearly 33ft (10m) in its width. The flat, slightly raised area within this mighty, densely palisaded construction conveys prehistoric activities of high importance. On the north-east is a dressed stone of volcanic breccia which weighs about 50 tons. The impressive paved entrance to the circle, dated at about 2000 BC, is at the east.

Nearby and worth visiting is The Giant's Grave, a wedge-shaped gallery grave. Excavations in 1938 (preceding those at The Great Stone Circle by a year) revealed remains of at least four children and eight adults; Neolithic and Early Bronze Age pottery was also found. These are but two attractions in a huge area which was a major Stone Age dwelling place and was then used in parts right into early Christian times.

KILCLOONEY MORE

Ardara,
Co Donegal

PORTAL-TOMBS AND
COURT-TOMB

Map 1 (North) 172396

¼ mile (0.4km) up the lane
behind Kilclooney Church, 4
miles (6.5km) north-west of
Ardara.

The 'flying' capstone of this fine Irish
portal-tomb presents a memorable
picture.

Here are two portal-tombs within what remains of an 82ft (25m) long cairn. Both their chambers face eastwards and are about 29ft (9m) apart. The larger is visually impressive, and has a bird-like appearance to its capstone, which is some 13ft (4m) long and about 20ft (6m) across. It is supported by twin uprights 6ft (1.8m) high. The western chamber is almost identical but smaller.

About 66yds (60m) to the east of the road lies a corbelled court-tomb. It is well preserved, but very small, the maximum diameter of its mound being only 36ft (11m).

About 5½ miles (8.8km) to the north-east on the road to Trusklieve (near the northern tip of Toome Lough) is a long cairn containing two portal-tombs called Dermot and Grania's Bed; one wonders where such a cosy name came from, to come to rest on such flat and lonely moorland. About 160 portal-tombs are known to survive in Ireland; many are dramatically sited.

KNOWTH

Signposted, off the N51 Slane to Drogheda road 2 miles (3.2km) south-east of Slane. NOTE: Knowth is closed to the public while excavations continue.

*Slane,
Boyne Valley,
Co Meath*

DOUBLE PASSAGE-TOMB
TUMULUS WITH
CARVINGS

Map 3 (East) 299274

One of the carved kerbstones.

A remarkable flint macehead, probably a ritual object since it is beautifully marked but unused, was one of the finds inside Knowth.

Knowth is one of the grandest of the 300 or so passage-tombs in Ireland (even though presently laid bare). About 25 tombs are in the Boyne Valley, the huge and impressive necropolis about which much has been written in recent years. Knowth is broadly contemporary with NEWGRANGE (middle of the fourth millennium BC). Excavations began here in 1962, and have gone on ever since under the direction of Professor George Eogan; interesting and valuable information continues to be published.

Site 1 is the great centre mound and covers an amazing 1½ acres (0.6 hectares). It is nearly oval in shape and measures between 262ft (80m) and 312ft (95m) across with its maximum height about 40ft (12m). Thrilling discoveries were made here in the late 1960s, revealing that this great mound contains two passage-tombs; they were probably built facing away from each other at the same time, on a precise east-west axis. These orientations have suggested to archaeologists that they had special functions at spring and autumn equinoxes and were designed to produce very accurate times for, among other

activities, sowing and reaping.

The western undifferentiated tomb passage is 111ft (34m) long; outside its entrance lies a large kerbstone, 10ft 2ins (3.1m) long, decorated with concentric rectangles, and featuring a vertical groove carved into it. The slightly longer kerbstone at NEWGRANGE, which has more elaborate carvings, also has such a groove. A sill stone was placed where the passage widened into the chamber, and a carved stele was at one time there.

Its eastern counterpart is cruciform in shape, and is perhaps the longest tomb in north-west Europe: it measures just over 131ft (40m). Its right-hand recess is the largest of three and contains a heavily carved and decorated stone basin. Cremation remains have been found in all three recesses. Chamber stones at Knowth bear intricate carvings of familiar motifs, such as crescents, concentric circles, labyrinths, serpent shapes, spirals and zigzags. They constitute one of the great collections of passage-grave art in the world, and have been the subject of many theories.

Excavations at Knowth have continued since 1962.

LOUGHCREW

*Oldcastle,
Co Meath*

PASSAGE-TOMB
CEMETERY

Map 3 (East) 258278
(marked as Megalithic
Cemetery)

Loughcrew is part of the famed Boyne Valley group of megalithic tombs. The tombs here were probably, but not definitely, the work of Breton migrants as they passed west from their landing point at the mouth of the River Boyne, via the great sites of Dowth, KNOWTH and NEWGRANGE. The Loughcrew Hills have in the past been generally called Sliabh na Caillighe (The Hill of The Witch), but this is actually the name of a cairn in Carnbane East.

The sadly vandalized and neglected Carnbane sites are on two hill tops on a 3 mile (4.8km) east-to-west ridge. More than 30 tumuli are scattered about; a variety of tombs lie within them, and often their stones are decorated. The carved sunray motif occurs at Loughcrew, and is yet another piece of evidence of solar observation in Ireland. On Carnbane West, the decorated Cairn L (the third largest) contains a standing stone; it can be found to the left of the first left turning below the car park. Its purpose is still a matter of speculation.

LEFT: *Rayed, possibly solar,
carvings in one of the Loughcrew
tombs.*

BELOW: *Loughcrew passage-tomb
cemetery.*

*Signposted. Marked as
Carnbane East and Carnbane
West in the Loughcrew Hills
3 miles (4.8km) south-east of
Oldcastle, and then up tracks.*

The writer Martin Brennan found that the rising sun on November 8 (an important date in the ancient eight-fold year) had its light beam so narrowly sculpted by the entrance of Cairn L that it enters like a laser beam to illuminate just the top of the white standing stone.

NEWGRANGE

*Slane,
Boyne Valley,
Co Meath*

PASSAGE-TOMB

Map 3 (East) 301274

*The entrance to Newgrange,
showing the rectangular light
entrance hole above it. A massive
carved stone lies in front; it is
famous for its unfathomable spirals
and lozenges.*

In three square miles (7.8sq km) overlooking the historic River Boyne there are 20 or more passage-graves; the great tombs of KNOWTH (to the north-west of Newgrange) and Dowth (north-east) are nearby, and there are standing stones, barrows and enclosures in abundance. Along with Carnac in Brittany, the Boyne Valley offers one of the greatest megalithic feasts in Europe.

In its much restored form, Newgrange is perhaps the most spectacular prehistoric cemetery in the world; detailed, comprehensive accounts of it are widely available. Here, it is sufficient to state that the monument took some 30 years to construct some time towards the end of the fourth millennium BC. It consists of a mound, containing a passage leading to a

*About 28 miles (45km)
north-west of Dublin. Travel
6 miles (9.6km) west from
Drogheda on the N51; turn
south 2 miles (3.2km) before
Slane, following the signposts.*

These linked spirals exemplify the great megalithic art at Newgrange.

The notable corbelled roofing.

RIGHT: *The covering mound at Newgrange was originally 40ft (12.2m) high; 12 of the surrounding circle of stones survive. (After M.J. O'Kelly)*

Newgrange, one of the great Boyne Valley tombs in section and plan. The dashed lines indicate the path of the midwinter sunrise rays for about 20 minutes through the unique roof box. {After a diagram in 'Midwinter sunrise at Newgrange', Nature, 249 (1974)}

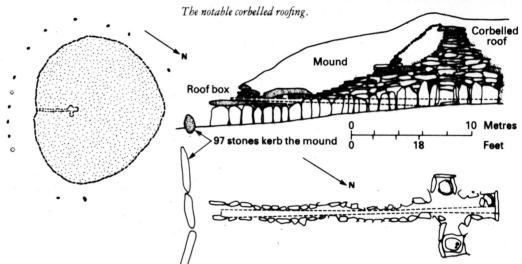

burial chamber, which has most of a circle of stones surrounding it; inside and out, some of the stones have been decorated with carved motifs of different kinds. But this simple description is misleading.

To begin outside, the ring of standing stones is almost unique in Great Britain and Ireland, with CLAVA CAIRNS, Culloden, being the other notable example (but also *see* LOANHEAD OF DAVIOT, Grampian). Though consisting today of only 12 stones, the Newgrange circle is one of the largest, with a diameter of about 340ft (104m). Inside it, the immense mound was originally 40ft (12.2m) high, made up of alternate layers of small stones and earth turves, rising to a formerly flat top with sloping sides, with the entire mound dome once covered in white quartz pebbles. The entrance façade was also walled with quartz, as it is again today. From far-off Tara, the ancient seat of Ireland's high kings, the monument must have presented a dazzling sight.

The huge covering mound is kerbed by no less than 97 stones; the largest and heaviest of them (up to 10 tons) are in the south-east entrance arc. The passage is 62ft (19m) long (not nearly as long as that at KNOWTH). Set above its entrance is a small rectangular hole, which is one of the best known

small stone holes in all Ireland. This is because it is precisely orientated to the midwinter sunrise; for about 20 minutes, one morning a year, eerie golden rays of light shine through and reach the very back of the chamber tomb. The corbelled roofing, the top flat slab of which stretches 20ft (6.1m) high above the floor, must be one of the most photographed megalithic interiors anywhere. The chamber itself measures 21ft 6in by 17ft (6.5m by 5.2m) across the three recesses; they have been badly looted over the centuries – but wonders remain.

The megalithic art at Newgrange is of a very high order indeed; here are cascades of arcs, chevrons, circles and half-circles (both single and concentric), cup marks, cup-and-ring marks, loops, lozenges, serpent shapes, spirals (single and double), triangles, wavy lines, and zig zags. About 40 per cent of the decorations at Newgrange are lozenges (much higher than at, for example, LOUGHCREW and KNOWTH nearby, or at GAVR'INIS, Morbihan). Zig zags were the next most constantly depicted motifs, followed by circles and (surprisingly low on the list) spirals.

There are a number of particularly fine decorated stones here. The roofstone of the right-hand recess, for example, has a beautifully precise spiral, that most challenging of motifs which to some represents the Mother Goddess of Earth. The entrance stone is justly famous for its five intertwining spirals and borders of lozenges. Knowth also has a magnificent entrance stone, and both have vertical grooves down them. At Newgrange the patterns cease above ground level, and so the stone was perhaps set into earth elsewhere, a prehistoric carver's studio, for the work to be done.

Many of the 97 kerbstones have carvings; K52 bears curious bordered rows of three holes. These are somewhat reminiscent of the rows of round protuberances, within borders, depicted on slate plaques, which have been found as far apart as ALTAMURA, Italy, TARXIEN, Malta, and FILITOSA, Corsica. Most oddly some of the kerbstones have carvings on their inside faces, against the mound and out of sight; K13 is a veritable sketch pad, of which all artists have need.

The much restored tomb today, with part of the ring of remaining huge kerbstones.

THE PIPER'S STONES

Hollywood,
Co Wicklow

STONE CIRCLE

Map 3 (East) 293203
(marked as Athgreany
Stone Circle)

Signposted as 'The Piper's Stones'. 1½ miles (2.4km) south of Hollywood, to the left on the road to Baltinglass. Park by the roadside.

The massive Piper, with a carved cross on its back.

The outlying stone at this impressive megalithic site is a Falstaffian 25ft (7.6m) in circumference. This massive, smoothly-dressed, squat, grey granite boulder which lies down a steep slope 68yds (62m) to the north-east of the circle, must surely be the Piper, with the 18 stones in this Leinster-type ring being his players; 14 are large, and there are supporting pillars or erratics among them. Moreover, many large stones litter the banks and ditches of the meandering footpath that leads to the group. West of the circle, over a small valley, a probable burial group can be seen; a detailed survey of the whole area would perhaps reveal a prehistoric settlement.

Legend has it that The Piper's Stones were petrified for the sin of playing on the Sabbath. THE MERRY MAIDENS and The Two Pipers in Cornwall carry the same legend, which may be a reflection of puritanical thinking 350 years ago, but more likely there is a much older explanation. Perhaps our Piper here did indeed call a tune — one of great importance to his community — for he bears a giant cross all over his back, and one of the lines is deeply incised. This is a mystery worth looking into.

POULNABRONE

Ballyvaughan,
Co Clare

PORTAL-TOMB

Map 2 (West) 123200

Signposted. 5 miles (8km) south of Ballyvaughan, on the way to Corofin. The tomb is clearly visible from the road, where you park. The Burren Visitor Centre is nearby.

The ever popular portal-tomb on The Burren.

This is said to be the most photographed site in all Ireland. The Poulnabrone portal-tomb is a singularly dramatic site across the fissures of the stark, karstic limestone pavement of The Burren. The thin capstone has a somewhat insolent tilt to it as it sits protectively on two fine 6ft (1.8m) high portal stones (the eastern one is a replacement, following a discovery in 1985 that it was hopelessly cracked), to create a ragged chamber in a low cairn measuring 30ft (9m) across.

Excavations during the repairs showed that this was clearly a special burial place in about 2500 BC. Discoveries highlighted the importance in Neolithic times of precision in burial, and, most likely, timing, and the central role of the megalithic tombs as protectors against disturbance and robbery.

Uncremated remains were found in the chamber, its portico and in the grykes (crevices in the limestone floor). A detailed analysis of all the fragments of the disarticulated bones revealed exact planning — but for what purpose or reason we shall never know.

All the main body bones of one newborn baby, six juveniles, and probably 19 adults (of whom only one lived past 40) were discovered, as was the sex of eight adults; there were four of each. The bones indicated a hard physical life and a coarse diet. Ritual was obviously involved in their final journey, because the analysis further proved that the bones were naturally defleshed elsewhere, and only then moved, in a complete but disarticulated state, to be roughly scattered within the chamber at Poulnabrone.

Remarkably, visitors have made hundreds of miniature tombs nearby, perhaps in recognition of the burial and as unconscious votive offerings.

Proleek Dolmen

*Ballymascanlon,
Co Louth*

Portal-tomb

Map 3 (East) 308311

This modest but cheerful tomb is often known as 'The Giant's Load' – doubtless a reference to the massive capstone, which weighs 40 tons and is one of the heaviest in Ireland. It is supported by a tripod of uprights: two matching portals 7ft (2.1m) high and another upright of 6ft (1.8m), with the smaller one providing the ever-familiar slope to the capstone profile.

In this case, the pleasing slope has a legend attached to it. It has long been said that if you throw a small stone about 13ft (4m) up and on to the top of the capstone – and it remains there – then you will be married within the year.

If this fails to interest, take a walk 100yds (91m) to the south-east, and there on the flat pasture you can examine the few merits of the remains of a wedge-tomb.

Situated in the grounds of the Ballymascanlon House Hotel, from whence it is signposted – as it is also on the road from Dundalk, 3½ miles (5.6km) to the south-west.

Stone pebbles on top of the capstone are evidence of an ancient belief.

PUNCHESTOWN

*Naas,
Co Kildare*

STANDING STONE

Map 3 (East) 291216
(not marked; find
racecourse)

*Not signposted. Take the
R410 from Naas to Blessington
and turn right to
Punchestown. The stone is
clearly visible ½ mile
(0.8km) along the road to the
left, just before the racecourse
entrance. Park at the nearest
field-gate.*

This is the second tallest standing stone in the British Isles (see RUDSTON MONOLITH). The exact height of this beautiful standing stone (the tallest in Ireland) is known, because it fell down in 1931; it was measured to be 23ft (7m) high, and 9 tons in weight; three years later, 3ft 6in (1.1m) of the granite were put back into the earth on its re-erection. The almost square base is 11ft (3.3m) in circumference, and an identification notice sits unhappily against its west face, spoiling an otherwise elegant sculpture.

From the base it gradually turns wedge-shaped as it rises, and towards the top it tapers finely to the south. Its function was probably as a memorial stone to the Bronze Age burial found beneath it; no role as a marker stone has yet been ascribed to it, unlike some of the huge menhirs in Brittany.

The tallest and most beautiful standing stone in Ireland, which measures 23ft (7m) above and below ground.

TEMPLEBRYAN

I.48

*Clonakilty,
Co Cork*

STONE CIRCLE; nearby
ORATORY, WELL,
STANDING STONE AND
BULLAUN

Map 4 (South) 138044

*Not signposted. 2½ miles
(4km) north of Clonakilty,
turn left (signpost:
Shannonvale 1 mile). At
crossroads (by Noel Phair
pub), turn left; the stone circle
is in a field about 300yds
(274m) up the hill on the
right, opposite modern houses.
Parking there and access by a
steep stile.*

This marvellous megalithic site includes a fine slender stone. The cow has been drinking from a bullaun on the ground beside it.

This is a very ancient site with an enticing variety of features, although there is not a lot left of the sloping circle today. A 1743 survey shows nine stones and a central monolith but it is thought that the original number of stones was 13; today five flat-topped stones survive, of which one is recumbent, and the old centre is now occupied by a unusual semi-embedded flat, white quartz stone. White central stones occur in a number of other Irish circles. The entrance to the circle was set at the south, the internal diameter is 30ft (9m), and these impressive stones are some of the very biggest in the area, suggesting an important megalithic site.

Two fields away, to the north-west (on a working farm, so

remember the usual courtesies), is the ancient Teampull na mBrienach, the now ruined church of the O'Briens, within a ring fort (whose moat has now gone). At the south of the enclosure lie the remains of a building, a well-head, and a notable, slender standing stone. It is more than 11ft (3.3m) tall, has faint ogham marks on its southern edge, and a pattee cross on the west face, thus indicating use of the site through to early Christian times.

Near it there lies a beautifully carved tri-cornered bullaun, which resembles a pillarless font with a deep, smoothly dressed bowl. Bullauns have been known as wart wells; this one seems to work as a cow's drinking place.

The Dwarfie Stane

Hoy,
Orkney

ROCK-CUT CHAMBER
TOMB

HY 243005

Take the 9047 south from Linksness, and then the road on the right to Rackwick. Before it bends westwards, look for the sign on the left.

The only rock-cut tomb in Britain outside Ireland.

This is probably one of only two chamber tombs in the British Isles ever to be hollowed out from solid rock (the other is at Glendalough, Co Wicklow). In fact, it most resembles a hermit's cell and has been called as much by travelling antiquaries; it even has a small spring near it. The Dwarfie Stane is of the late Neolithic or Early Bronze Age and is the only prehistoric site on the most hilly island in the Orkneys.

A vast rectangular block of local red sandstone from the nearby Dwarfie Hamars, it is 28ft (8.5m) long, a maximum of 14ft 9in (4.5m) wide, and 6ft 6in (2m) high. The narrow entrance is in its west face; inside, on either side, are two small recesses. The smaller is to the north and measures just 4ft 3in by 2ft (1.3m by 0.6m); the chamber to the south is 5ft by 3ft (1.5m by 0.9m). The roofing has been holed for centuries.

Maes Howe

I.50

Orkney,
Mainland

CHAMBERED CAIRN

HY 317127

Signposted. 5 miles (8km) east of Stromness, just north of the A965. A key is obtainable from the local farmhouse during normal hours.

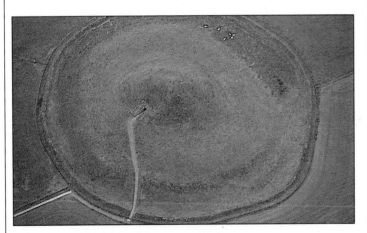

This fine cairn dates back to about 2100 BC. It stands on a levelled platform, and is covered by a huge mound 24ft (7.3m) high and 115ft (35m) in diameter. The 36ft (11m) long passage leads to a high 15ft (4.6m) square chamber, with a marvellous corbelled roof, at the centre of the mound. Ahead and on both sides lie small chambers, their square openings being just 3ft (1m) above the floor. Two huge fully dressed stones stand as supporting pillars for the corbelled roof.

The present appearance of the site was completed in the 10th century AD, when the low outer earth ring was added. Then, in the 12th century, Vikings broke into the tomb leaving 24 runic inscriptions and also pictorial carvings (including a splendid one of a dragon); they also referred to buried treasure, but alas none has been found so far!

The dressed 36ft (11m) long passage.

THE RING OF BRODGAR

*Orkney,
Mainland*

STONE CIRCLE and
HENGE

HY 294134

Fabulously situated, this is one of Britain's most majestic stone circles. Here, in about 2500 BC, 60 stones were originally set up on a slope facing east. Today, there are 27 left around the diameter of 113yds (103.3m), and the circle has two entrances, at the north-west and south-east.

Four of the stones bear different carvings – of an anvil, a cross, an ogham and a runic inscription. Between the ring and an outer earth bank lies a ditch which, in terms of man-hours devoted to its construction, rivals most in the British Isles. Quarried from solid sandstone bedrock, it was once no less than 12ft (3.6m) deep and 30ft (9m) wide.

To the south-east, 449ft (137m) away, stands the Comet Stone. The late Professor Thom believed The Ring of Brodgar to be a prehistoric observatory. Some 18th century antiquaries regarded Brodgar as the sun and STENNESS as the moon.

Travel east from Stromness on the A965 for 4 miles (6.5km), then turn left along the B9055. The site is nearly 2 miles (3.2km) north-west along the road on the left.

This impressive circle was probably a prehistoric astronomical observatory.

SKARA BRAE

*Bay of Skaill,
Orkney,
Mainland*

NEOLITHIC SETTLEMENT

HY 230187

In the winter of 1850 a violent storm ripped off a covering sand dune at this site to reveal what had been covered by another terrible storm about 5000 years previously – a Neolithic hut settlement of nine dwellings in remarkably fine condition. Because the Orkney Islands have always been virtually treeless, the domestic 'fittings' were carved from stone, not wood – hence their excellent state of preservation. They included beds (also used as seats), hearths, shelves, storage compartments, and water tanks.

The important excavations at Skara Brae were begun by the eminent Professor Gordon Childe in 1926; he emphasised the importance of the flat-based grooved ware uncovered there. It linked this Late Neolithic site with Woodhenge (and later Durrington Walls) and other southern sites. This distinctive pottery is principally found, curiously, only in sites in

Travel north from Stromness on the B9056 for about 7 miles (11km), park at the signpost, and follow the path around the south of the bay.

This Neolithic hut settlement, overlooking the Bay of Skaill, was revealed by a storm in 1850.

Stone domestic 'furniture' at Skara Brae.

Curiously scratched stones with geometric lines have been noted at Skara Brae, and geometric stone balls uncovered.

The nine huts and alleyways at the Neolithic settlement at Skara Brae, overlooking the Bay of Skaill.

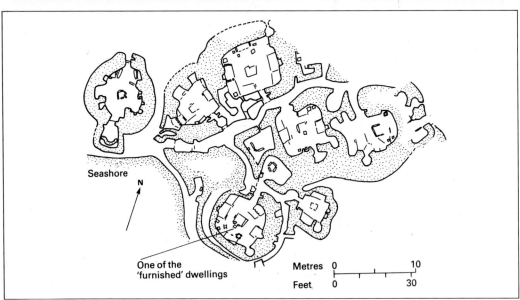

Seashore

N

One of the
'furnished' dwellings

Metres 0   10
Feet   0   30

Northern Scotland and the Orkneys in the north and in south and south-eastern England: little or none until recently was discovered in the hundreds of square miles in between. Its form and the 'spiral and lozenge' motifs link this settlement with the Irish Boyne Valley tombs (such as NEWGRANGE) and burial chambers in southern Spain and Portugal.

Among the domestic 'houseware' uncovered here were dishes, some of which contained traces of blue, red and yellow pigments. Now Julius Caesar recorded that 'all the Britons painted themselves'. Moreover, the Greek explorer Pytheas (as quoted by Strabo) referred, in the fourth century BC, to Britons as *Prettanoi*, ancient Greek for the Celtic word *Pritani* ('the painted ones'), from which comes the Latin *Britannia* ('land of the Britanni'), and so Britain. Evidently, ancient mainland Britons did not use vegetable dye (woad) at all, but a mixture of clay, metal carbonates and oxides, and the evidence is here at Skara Brae. Recent analysis of skin fragments from The Lindow Man (Pete Marsh) has provided scientific evidence of this interesting habit of body painting, which is still practised by many tribal societies today.

The nine huts and alleyways that make up Skara Brae today probably formed the third settlement on the original site. Early Neolithic settlements such as this, which imply high degrees of intelligence and discipline in their leadership, are quite rare in Britain, but Skara Brae is one of the most complete, and has provided valuable information.

However, it is not as large a settlement as, for instance, Carn Brae in Cornwall, which held about 200 people and dates back to 3900 BC. Another fine and similar site, where most of the nine houses even had their own small gardens, is Chysauster, also in Cornwall.

These Neolithic villages perhaps housed the astronomer-priests of the day – a privileged class whose job it was to keep an eye on the heavens in order to predict the terrifying occurrence of an eclipse, or to maintain a constant watch on the 18.6 year cycle of the moon.

THE STONES OF STENNESS

Orkney,
Mainland

STANDING STONES AND
HENGE

HY 306125

The four stones left standing in this 104ft (31.7m) circle of originally 12 stones have most distinct slanted tops, each at a different angle; the tallest remaining one is 16ft 6in (5m) tall. It has been proposed that they were once part of a huge astronomical observatory, with Britons constantly stationed to look up along the smooth angles of sight in order to note movements in the night sky.

The site dates back to about 2970 BC, but the ditch and outer bank are now almost gone, and the three stones of the Cove were reconstructed early this century. Although the site today may seem a slight disappointment, in its time it was clearly very important. Thousands of man-hours must have been devoted to hewing the 3ft (1m) deep ditch from solid sandstone bedrock, as at the neighbouring RING OF BRODGAR.

To the north-west of The Stones stands the Watch Stone: 18ft 6in (5.6m) tall and with an interesting name.

About 4 miles (6.4km) east of Stromness, along the A965, on the left, just past the B9055 turning.

Two of the four remaining stones at this beautiful Orkney Islands site.

BANT'S CARN

*Halangy Down,
St Mary's*

ENTRANCE GRAVE

SV 911123

The kerbed mound of this impressive tomb is about 39ft (12m) in diameter, 6ft (1.8m) high, and has inner and outer rings of kerbstones. The cairn on top is some 26ft (8m) in diameter, and its existence indicates two periods of construction. The passage, just north of east, is 15ft (4.6m) long, and turns due east at the chamber which is handsomely roofed with four large capstones. Unhappily, a modern wall slices through the south-west section.

Excavation has given the tomb a construction date of around 2000 BC, after which it was continuously used for about another 500 years. Neolithic and Late Bronze Age pottery found at Bant's Carn indicates contact with Cornwall. Remains of a lower collar at this site also link it with Scillonian chamber tombs. There is a remarkable total of 50 or more such tombs in the Isles of Scilly.

The remains of an ancient settlement nearby, excavated in 1935 and 1964–70, revealed a site occupied from Bronze Age to Roman times.

*Beside the coastal path at the northern end of the golf course on Halangy Down.
Signposted from Macfarland Downs.*

Four large capstones are prominent at this tranquil location. Remains of a lower 'collar' of stones can be seen to the right.

INNISIDGEN CARN AND LOWER INNISIDGEN

*Helvear Down,
St Mary's*

ENTRANCE GRAVES

SV 921128 and
922127

*North-west of Block House
Bay, beside the coastal path,
between Bar Point and
Watermill Cove. Signposted.*

*Innisidgen Carn is the finest
mounded passage-grave in the Scilly
Isles.*

Innisidgen Carn, also known as The Giant's Grave, is the finest mound in these beautiful Isles. It is located at the top of a slope and has a diameter of about 27ft (8.2m). Remains of an outer ring of kerbstones can be seen to the north; within is a kerb of three courses of stones. It has one more capstone than its similar neighbour, BANT'S CARN, and they are most likely to be contemporary.

About 109yds (100m) along the path to the north-west lies Lower Innisidgen, below a slope and virtually at sea level, which is most unusual (although it is true to say that the level at the time of its construction, when most of the Isles were one land mass, was much lower). Its mound is a rough oval, and is slightly squeezed at its waist.

The chamber faces precisely due south, and has been dated at approximately 2095 BC. Deposits found in Scillonian graves indicate rituals involving both the living and dead.

PORTH HELLICK DOWN

*Porth Hellick,
St Mary's*

ENTRANCE GRAVE

SV 928108

*Signposted on the A3110 at
Carn Friars to the north-east
of the Down.*

*The Down of Porth Hellick on the
island of St Mary's, with the
largest mound in the group clearly
visible.*

The 40ft (12.2m) diameter mound here, the biggest of five in this group, has a flattened appearance – but this is probably due to careless restoration, which has all but destroyed a lower, surrounding kerb or 'collar'. The three-course, high kerbstones contribute to the illusion. A roofless passage entrance is at the north-west, and approaches the chamber at a distinct angle; at the point where it turns, a protective upright slab stands guard. As with BANT'S CARN, the roof of the chamber consists of four capstones, with the edge of the first above the guardian slab. The site was excavated in 1899 and Late Bronze Age pottery was found; this indicates the ever-familiar re-use of the grave which is much older.

SCOTLAND

BALBIRNIE

Markinch,
Fife

STONE CIRCLE

NO 285030

6 miles (9.6km) north of Kirkcaldy off the A92: 1 mile (1.6km) north-west of Markinch. Park at the Balbirnie Craft Centre.

This site was excavated in 1970-71, prior to being moved 137yds (125m) to the south-east because of a road-widening scheme. The eight stones are accurately and cleanly reset, and the place, albeit shifted, is of unusual interest.

The stone circle of local sandstone is actually an ellipse, indicating that higher mathematics were used in the astronomical observations clearly conducted here, and is between 46ft and 49ft (14m and 15m) in diameter. The longer axis lies to the south-west.

Originally, a rough square of thin stone slabs was placed in the middle of the circle, but about 100 years later they were moved by another group of settlers, who used them for lining three new burial cists. There is also a paved rectangle there.

After that, cremations and burial goods, including already broken pottery (*see* WEST KENNET LONG BARROW, Wiltshire, for a possible explanation), were covered by a cairn (today removed). Cremated bones have been found beneath the four eastern stone holes; grooved ware in another hole gave a probable date for the circle of about 2000 BC.

After excavation in 1970–71, this elliptical setting of stones was moved 137yds (125m) south-east, due to a road-widening scheme.

CALLANISH

Stornoway,
Lewis,
Western Isles

STONE CIRCLE AND ROWS

NB 213330

Well signposted; 14 miles (22.5km) west of Stornoway on the A858. Turning on the left after Garynahine.

'The Stonehenge of the North', as Callanish is known.

This is a visually satisfying site but a tantalising one archaeologically. It dates from about 1800 BC, but precise dates and proven functions have been hard to establish.

The site consists of a circle, 43ft by 37ft (13.1m by 11.3m) in diameter, of 13 tall slender undressed stones, with another at their centre which is the tallest of all at 15ft 6in (4.75m). Four incomplete avenues lead away, with single rows of stones to the east, south and west, and a double row just east of north. Had all the rows been completed the axial alignments of them would have converged at the centre stone. A second outer concentric circle was probably also intended.

The central standing stone is at the west of a later chambered tomb, the radius of which extends to the east of the circle. It has a short passage, and then two successive small chambers, now ruined. Professor Thom believed that Callanish was a lunar observatory. A popular legend says that marriage vows have been taken there – and yet it is also known as Tursachan, meaning a place of pilgrimage or mourning!

CAMSTER

*Camster,
Lybster,
Caithness*

CHAMBERED CAIRNS

ND 260442

Take the A9 south-west from Wick. At Lybster turn directly north on the minor road; after Camster, the cairns are on the left.

RIGHT: *Camster Round, with Camster Long to the north-west.*
BELOW: *One of the two entrance passages in Camster Long.*

There are two quite different outlines in plan to these tombs (also known as The Grey Cairns of Camster). Camster Round is roughly oval, but flattened at the south-east where the entrance lies. It is about 11ft 9in (3.6m) in height, and some 60ft (18.3m) in diameter. Here is yet another entrance passage which, at just over 2ft 6in (0.8m) along its eight-slabbed 19ft 9in (6m) length, is very low. Its central chamber, reached through a small antechamber, is more agreeable for the megalith hunter with a height of 9ft 9in (3m) to its corbelled roof; it contains three compartments, separated by slabs.

Camster Long lies 220yds (200m) to the north-west. It shares a similar ground plan to the Tulloch of Assery cairn not far away in Halkirk. Both are double-horned. At Camster Long, the two entrances and chambers have very different shapes. They were constructed quite separately, and covered by their own unconnected mounds.

Later, today's distinctive, long, double-horned cairn was put over both of them. The cairn is now over 200ft (61m) at its longest, and a maximum of 65ft 6in (20m) across its horns.

CLAVA CAIRNS

Culloden battlefield and area,
Inverness,
Highland Region

CHAMBERED CAIRNS

NH 757444

This group is one of the most notable in Scotland, and has some unique features; they, and the battlefield nearby, combine to offer a fascinating visit. The tomb group as a whole consists of about 30 cairns in three main areas. Six of them, some of which are described here, are around the Beauly Firth, north of the River Ness; 17 are on riversides in Strath Dores and Strath Nairn, and at least seven are to be found in Strath Spey.

Three tombs at Balnuaran, Clava, in the first group, provide the chief interest, because the heavily-kerbed ring-cairn and passage-graves are surrounded by stone monoliths in a formation nearly unique in the British Isles (but *see* LOANHEAD OF DAVIOT, Grampian, and NEWGRANGE, Co Meath). More-

5½ miles (8.8km) east of Inverness, and ½ mile (0.8km) south-east of Culloden battlefield, by a lane between Clava Lodge and Balnuaran Farm. Signposted.

A view along the megalithic alignment at Clava Cairns.

LEFT: *Balnuaran North-East
passage-grave at Clava Cairns.*

*The unusual oriention of the
passage-grave entrances point to a
midwinter sunset at* CLAVA CAIRNS.
*There are cup marks at all four
constructions.*

over, they all contained cremations and have cup marks.

The northernmost is Balnuaran North-East; this passage-grave is in a stone-covered and egg-shaped cairn, with large kerbstones measuring 103ft 6in by 97ft 6in (31.6m by 29.7m). One of the kerbstones, which are largest at the south and west, is heavily indented with cup and cup-and-ring marks, and grooves. A cup-marked stone in the passage can be spotted on the north-west side. The central and roofless chamber is 13ft (4.0m) in diameter; the passage to it is orientated to the south-south-west, in contrast to most other chamber tombs in the British Isles which face in an easterly direction. The ring of stones surrounding the cairn is not completely circular, as Professor Thom has shown; they too have cup marks.

Balnuaran Central is a circular ring-cairn, 104ft (31.6m) in diameter, and again kerbed. It has nine stones in its circle, one of them cup marked, and three of them are mysteriously attached to the cairn by thin earthen banks, like spokes to a hub. The remains of a cist were found in the middle during Stuart Piggott's excavations in 1952/53.

Balnuaran South-West is the other passage-grave here, and also now roofless. Twelve cup marks can be seen on the boulder at the west side of the chamber entrance which, also unusually, faces south-south-west. It had a diameter of 104ft 6in (31.8m).

On the western perimeter of the Clava Cairns site, at the foot of a tree, there is a small Late Bronze Age 12ft (3.7m) stone circle. Its stones are fallen or recumbent, and contiguous, and they bear cup and cup-and-ring marks. Scattered fragments of white quartz have been found inside the circle here, as they have at the well-preserved, huge, kerbed Corrimony passage-grave 25 miles (40.2km) away at the west end of Glen Urquhart. It has been proposed that the Clava Cairns represent a fine flowering of a type of tomb which originated in south-western France or Iberia, then migrated north-west to Ireland, east across the Irish Sea to the Firth of Lorne, up the Great Glen here, and thence onwards to Denmark.

Dr Johnson and his amanuensis James Boswell visited one of the Clava Cairns in 1773. Boswell wrote: 'About three miles

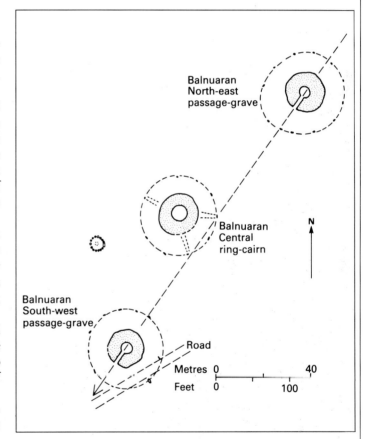

beyond Inverness, we saw, just by the road, a very complete specimen of what is called a Druid's temple. There was a double circle, one of very large, the other of smaller stones. Dr Johnson justly observed "to go and see one druidical temple is only to see that it is nothing, for there is neither art nor power in it; and seeing one is quite enough"'. Dr Johnson clearly did not do enough 'seeing'; if he had, 'believing' would surely have followed. This is a remarkably moving place.

The three chambered cairns at Clava have bequeathed puzzles. There were cremations in each tomb, but no pottery has been found. They were evidently not family mausolea, but were used for favoured individuals of both sexes.

CROFT MORAIG

*Aberfeldy,
Tayside*

STONE CIRCLE

NN 797472

Although somewhat hidden away, Croft Moraig is a very important site. Like STONEHENGE, Wiltshire, and The Sanctuary, Wiltshire, it has seen a succession of constructional phases, and like them the first, in about 2850 BC, involved wooden posts – in this instance, a horseshoe-shaped setting of 14 posts.

After subsequent repair, the site was levelled and 'planted' with a horseshoe setting of eight undressed stones. A bank of earth and huge stones was then erected behind it. No less than 23 cup marks are to be seen on the top of a supine stone, lying along the line of the midsummer full moon at the south-west; it may have been a decorated entrance stone, in the manner of the magnificent one at NEWGRANGE in the Boyne Valley, Ireland.

At a third stage, more than 800 years after the first, 12 huge stones encircled the horseshoe, but within the bank, and two more formed an entrance at the east. As elsewhere in Britain, quartz pebbles and fragments have been found here; they are a true minilithic mystery.

Just south of the A827, 4 miles (6.5 km) west of Aberfeldy on the way to Kenmore, at the north-eastern head of the Tay Valley.

The complex henge and circles at Croft Moraig evolved through several phases.

FORTINGALL

Fortingall,
Aberfeldy,
Tayside

STONE CIRCLES

NN 745469

There were once three stone circles at this Early Bronze Age site. They were then virtually destroyed, although three stones were left standing – apparently – in each. However, when two of the three (Fortingall East and West) were excavated by Aubrey Burl in 1970, it was discovered that deep inside each five more stones had been buried. The original settings had been rough rectangles of eight stones each; an unusual arrangement in this region. The third circle, Fortingall South, could possibly have been a recumbent stone circle in the Aberdeenshire tradition.

Ten stones, remnants of three stone circles on the eastern edge of Fortingall village, above the River Lyon.

Travel west from Aberfeldy on the A846; take the second road on the left, signposted to Fortingall.

GARYNAHINE

Stornoway,
Lewis,
Western Isles

STONE CIRCLE

NB 230303

12 miles (19.3km) west of Stornoway on the A858, at the junction with the A8011.

The supine rectangular centre stone within this ovular setting is located on the left.

This circle is very near the majestic CALLANISH complex, and serious megalith hunters should allow for a three-day visit to this endlessly fascinating island. Here is a compact oval setting measuring 42ft 3in by 30ft 3in (12.9m by 9.2m); the five remaining stones in it surround a low rectangular central one. This was placed in a cairn, which was not always the case.

The establishment of a focal point in a circular stone setting seems a perfectly natural idea from a design point of view. Much taller central pillars have an obviously totemistic role (*see* BRYN CELLI DDU, Anglesey, Ty-ar-Boudiquet, Brittany, and LOS MILLARES, Almeria, Spain). Ritual and celebration around maypoles and sacred trees are very ancient occurrences. It is possible that central stones which were not associated with burials (as is the case at Garynahine) were command posts, or positions for the conduct of rituals, religious or otherwise, like preachers' crosses (*see* HAROLD'S STONES, Gwent).

Notable sites with centre stones in their circles are at nearby CALLANISH and at TEMPLEBRYAN in Co Cork. The most famous supine centre stone of all is The Altar Stone at STONEHENGE, and the mystery about it is that this blueish-grey micaceous sandstone, heavy with quartz grains, does not occur anywhere else at the monument.

THE HILL O' MANY STANES

Lybster,
Wick,
Caithness,
Highland Region

STONE ROWS

ND 294384

Leave Lybster on the A9;
before Wick take the farm lane
going north-west. The rows,
about 650yds (600m) from
the A9, are to the south-west
of it. Signposted.

The site of 22 fan-shaped stone
rows, perhaps an observatory.

This famous and unusual site consists of 22 or more splayed rows of more than 200 stones. Unlike those in the Carnac alignments (*see* KERMARIO and MENEC, Morbihan, France), these stones are small, less than 3ft 3in (1m) high, and mostly only a few inches wide. They are set on a south-facing slope, below a cairn lying on top of it. The stones are in fact set in a slight fan shape, and were analysed meticulously by Professor Alexander Thom.

He showed that the stones at the site (which he designated Mid Clyth) must have been set up in about 1900 BC for the purpose of identifying the exact maximum moonrise in summer and winter by plotting the movement of certain stars. A standing stone, now fallen, 147ft (45m) to the west of the cairn, might well have been associated with this prehistoric observatory.

KINTRAW

Kintraw,
Argyll,
Strathclyde

CIRCLE, CAIRN AND
MENHIR

NM 830050

Near Kintraw Farm. On a
plateau off the road from
Craignish to Bealach,
Kilmartin and Lochgilphead.

The standing stone, viewed from the
large kerb cairn, looking towards
the Jura hills.

Kintraw is an important and exciting site, and its place in the history of megaliths is assured as a result of Professor Thom's survey of the site in the early 1960s. In 1967 he wrote that Kintraw ' . . .may be another solstitial observatory capable of giving a very accurate value of the obliquity of the ecliptic' (that is, the sun's declination down through the sky). From his detailed survey, he was able to date the site at about 1800 BC.

Kintraw consists of a ring cairn, a menhir 12ft (3.7m) high, then (on the same north-easterly alignment) a large ruined cairn 48ft (14.6m) in diameter, a further large stone and, finally (across a gorge and stream), a ledge.

In 1970/71, excavations proved that Thom's deduction was probably correct. The ledge was likely to have been a Late Neolithic observation platform of stones which provided a line of sight 26¾ miles (43km) long over the gorge, cairn, menhir and circle to the col between Beinn Shiantaidh (one of the Paps or hill peaks of the island of Jura) and Beinn a' Chaolais. Air and eyesight were much clearer in Neolithic times.

LOANHEAD OF DAVIOT

*Daviot,
Inverurie,
Grampian*

RECUMBENT STONE
CIRCLE AND CEMETERY

NJ 747288

This circle is in line with New Craig stone circle (visible from Loanhead of Daviot) and the site of a former stone circle in the churchyard of nearby Daviot.

This elegant grouping is set on ground which slopes to the north-east between two rivers; it is one of more than 15 megalithic sites in this lovely area. The circle has a diameter of 67ft (20.5m), and is dated at approximately 2500 BC. A strange feature recurs here; the huge recumbent stone and its flankers were set just inside the line of the circle (*see* MIDMAR KIRK, also in Grampian).

Professor Thom, who surveyed his native country in his long retirement years, was able to show that the distance from the circle's exact centre to the edge of the inner cairn is precisely 20 megalithic yards, and, further, on to the circle edge was another five megalithic yards. Two outliers to the south-east confirm a probable role in the prediction of midwinter sunrises.

During 1934 excavations, broken pottery sherds were found around the bases of most of the monoliths, indicating single burial cairns at each. In the middle of the low Bronze Age cairn within the circle lay a rectangular mortuary pit, which might be the oldest part of the site. The recumbent stone and its pair of flankers stand in great state at south-south-west, watching over eight further equally spaced uprights at this fine prehistoric place.

The nearby circular-banked cemetery, of about the same age, consists of a 950sq ft (88sq m) cremation site. There is one prominent central burial, and several burials with grave goods in urns.

Inverurie is 13 miles (20.8km) north-west of Aberdeen on the A96. Leave the town north-west on the B9001; take the fourth turning on the right for Daviot, and the first left. The circle is signposted on the right.

The huge recumbent stone in the circle near Daviot.

MIDMAR KIRK

Midmar,
Aberdeen,
Grampian

RECUMBENT STONE
CIRCLE

NJ 699064

The church in tiny Midmar is 15 miles (24km) west of Aberdeen on the B9119, beyond Echt.

Part of the recumbent stone circle at Midmar Kirk; modern graves can be seen behind, to the left.

In 1914 a graveyard was established around this 57ft (17.4m) diameter stone circle and today it is a most manicured place, with a neat disc of grass within the circle, and a gravel path between and around the ring of stones. This is clearly saying that it was here first, and the cheerleader in the matter is without doubt the massive recumbent stone, lying, as it always has done, between two tall portals.

Recumbent stone circles are peculiar to the Aberdeen area (though there are others in the south-west of Ireland), and in many cases, as at Midmar, the recumbent stone is placed a little inside the circle; their top surfaces are almost always horizontal.

Professor Thom has pointed out that the left-hand portal stone, looking from the centre, is almost always about 1ft 6in (0.46m) nearer the centre. Such odd facts define this circle as having been a delicate instrument of some kind – another monument to the wonders of prehistoric engineering.

TEMPLE WOOD

Kilmartin,
Strathclyde

STONE CIRCLE AND
STANDING STONES

NR 826979

Travel south from Oban on the A816, past Kilmartin and the turnings for Slockavullin. The signposted circles are now on the right. The standing stones are not generally accessible.

The central cist and its kerb within a boulder-strewn stone circle.

This is a small, somewhat lonely, but beautiful circle, with 20 stones in its setting among trees. Its diameter is 44ft (13.4m), and boulders, small and various in shape, are strewn over the inside. Excavations in 1928 and 1974–76 revealed a much smaller inner ring, 11ft 6in (3.5m) in diameter, and, inside this at the centre, a large open cist. There were several burials in the cairn, which dates back to about 1750 BC. A second small cist, with a burial and goods, was located just outside it.

The standing stones to the east were, according to Alexander Thom, set in such a position as to make the Temple Wood site a lunar observatory using a notch in a nearby ridge; his exhaustive and highly accurate surveys confirm that the stone circle's dimensions can be expressed in terms of round figure megalithic yards (*see* 'Measuring the Megaliths'). The several 'temple' or 'teampull' sites in the British Isles are each held by archaeo-astronomers to be of special significance.

A notable feature at this one is the circle stone exactly to the north of the cist. In 1973 a large though faint double spiral was discovered on it by Aubrey Burl; what is more, this most mysterious of motifs continues down into the ground below the packed stone surface. This means, of course, that it was carved before the monolith was erected, and therefore could have been used before elsewhere.

Other decorated stones are to be found in the Kilmartin Valley, at Nether Largie cairns, and among the standing stones at Kilmartin and Ballymeanoch, all close to Temple Wood. The 'Bally' prefix to the latter place name implies an Irish connection: the incredible megalithic art in the Boyne Valley tombs (*see* KNOWTH and NEWGRANGE, Co Meath) is not far away across the sea.

TORHOUSEKIE

*Wigtown,
Dumfries and Galloway*
STONE CIRCLE

NX 383565

One of the cairns near this circle was opened in the 19th century. Soon after, locals observed a mysterious light repeatedly emerging from the open cist. Such light phenomena have been reported in other copper-rich areas.

This unusual circle is all nicely fenced and neat, when you get there, but it also feels a little lonely. It is supposed to be the nearest stone circle to Ireland, and it does have affinities with sites across the North Channel.

Its 19 stones are set on a gently raised platform of stones and earth, and they are carefully graded towards the south-east in height. The tops of the now lichen-covered boulders were mostly hammered into smooth, round shapes; this could indicate former funerary rites in their midst, rather than astronomical observation of some kind. The circle probably stands on an artificial earth platform. There are three outliers 1094 yds (1000 m) to the east of it. On the other side of the road, west of the circle, lies a curious circular stone structure.

Two large stones and one small one (of local granite, like the rest) are aligned in the centre of this circle, which is 60ft (18m) in diameter, and Aubrey Burl has suggested that such a grouping may possibly indicate a variant of a recumbent stone circle. These are mostly concentrated in north-east Scotland and south-west Ireland (Torhousekie lies in between) and associated with copper and gold mining, together with ritual celebration. Copper mining goes on today near Wigtown which is about 4 miles (6.4km) away from this site.

3 miles (4.8km) west of Wigtown, on the B733; on the left and signposted.

The 19 graded boulders which make up this beautiful circle, with its central setting of three further stones.

ARTHUR'S STONE

*Llanrhidian,
West Glamorgan*

STONE CIRCLE WITH
BURIAL CHAMBER

SS 491905

*The burial chamber and part of the
circle.*

*On the Gower Peninsula.
Take the A4118 west from
Swansea. At Upper Killey,
take the right fork on to the
B4271. At the village of
Crickton, turn left at the
signpost and go along the
trackway. Park and walk as
directed.*

According to the ancient Welsh texts, *The Welsh Triads*, this site is one of Britain's 'three wonderful things'. The other two were SILBURY HILL and STONEHENGE. Inspired by this tribute, travellers and antiquarians have for many centuries subjected it to the indignities of false reportage. Legends have grown up around it including the familiar one about how the stones go down to the sea nearby to drink at midnight. Indeed, a new one appeared in print as recently as 1973!

The facts are that the ring cairn here is 75ft 6in (23m) in diameter. Unusually, a burial chamber lies at its centre, and it is in two sections. The capstone is supported by four of the 10 uprights, and is part of the original 30-ton stone: today it measures 13ft (4m) long, and 6ft 6in (2m) wide, and 7ft (2.2m) thick. There are very many erratic stones spread all around this famous group which is perhaps the most in Wales. It is also called Maen Ceti and The Big Stone of Sketty.

BRIDELL

*St David's Church,
Bridell,
Cardigan,
Dyfed*

STANDING STONE WITH
OGHAM NOTCHES AND
CROSS

SN 176420

RIGHT: *The remarkable stone at
Bridell.*

FAR RIGHT: *A detail showing the
circled cross with ogham marks
visible down the left edge.*

*3 miles (4.8km) south of
Cardigan on the A478. On
the right, at a junction where
you can park. Church
generally locked.*

This is a strange and fascinating site. For a start, the porch and door (the only one) into the church are placed, unusually, on the north side. And the most likely reason is to be found within a few feet of the south side: a standing stone, a prehistoric relic from pagan days which might have offended newly converted Christians arriving at their place of worship.

Its cup marks give a broad Bronze Age date although the

ogham notches on the north-east edge of this 7ft 3ins (2.2m) tall stone, opposite the smooth, dressed side, date from AD 5-6. They read as *Nettasagru Maqui Mucoi Breci*, and translate as 'Nettasagus son of the descendants of Breci'.

Soon after, the Christians incised a big, broad cross within a circle on the side facing their church. Thus thousands of years of worship are manifest in this one single spot.

CARREG SAMSON

Abercastle,
Fishguard,
Dyfed

BURIAL CHAMBER

SM 848335

Take the A487 south from Goodwick (north-west of Fishguard). At the junction with the B4331, turn off north-west, through Mathry and Abercastle. The drive to Longhouse Farm is on the right, and the chamber is signposted. It is 200yds (180m) into a private field.

A handsome burial chamber, overlooking Strumble Head. Carreg is Welsh for rock; St Samson was born in South Wales in about AD 490.

This handsome Neolithic chamber occupies a wonderful site overlooking Strumble Head. Three of its seven remaining uprights support a large chunky capstone – all of which were once covered by an earth mound. It is a fine burial place, although little is known about it.

What it does have is an ancient and interesting name. *Carreg* is Welsh for 'rock'. Samson refers to the remarkable saint of that name who was born in South Wales in about AD 490 and became successively a monk, an abbot, a hermit, and finally a bishop in what today is Dol de Bretagne, Ille-et-Vilaine (*see* DOL). He ministered in Cornwall, The Isles of Scilly, Ireland, Jersey, Guernsey and Brittany (where he died in AD 565). Such was his fame, and reputation for miraculous deeds and his ability to communicate with birds, that his biography was written soon after his death. Some Arthurian experts have proposed that he was the original Sir Galahad.

THE DRUIDS' CIRCLE (MEINI HIRION)

Penmaenmawr,
Dwygyfylchi,
Gwynedd

STONE CIRCLE

SH 722746

The hillside site, near Cefn Coch, is reached by a signposted footpath which starts on Graiglwyd Road, south of Penmaenmawr and the A55.

Only 10 of about 30 large dressed stones survive here.

This circle, containing some of the largest dressed stones in Wales, stands on a rocky bank about 85ft (26m) in diameter. According to one authority, there were originally 30 stones; 10 have survived and they are almost 6ft (1.8m) high. One of them has been called The Deity Stone, and another is still called The Stone of Sacrifice. The entrance to the stone circle is at the south-west, and is marked with two big portals. The circle is sited beside a Bronze Age trackway; northwards along it, at Graig Lwyd 765yds (700m) away, was once a well-known axe factory.

There are remains of many other circles and cairns in this area, and a number of cremations. Three cremations of children have been found in The Druids' Circle; two were close to the centre, and the other to the west where the cremation was found in an enlarged food vessel, with a bronze knife. Another cremation and pot has been found about 164yds (150m) south-west in a ring cairn. Evidence for the sacrifice of children within several circles in North Wales and Anglesey, and directly across the water in Co Down, is plentiful. A macabre feature is that children's ear bones frequently occur.

FOUR STONES

*Walton,
Presteigne,
Powys*

FOUR-POSTER

SO 245608

*Travel west from Kington on
the A44. Take the next road
on the right after the B4357
to Walton. Park at the first
trackway (which completes a
crossway) on the left. The
Stones, which cannot be seen
from the road, are in the field
to the left of the field gate.*

*This 'four-poster' is a rough,
rectangular setting of surprising
attraction.*

This rough rectangle of stones lies on ground which slopes sharply to the east; each of the four is precisely placed on an axial line of a quadrant. The internal circumference is about 15ft (4.6m), and the distances between the stones varies between 8ft 10ins (2.7m), from the tallest stone at north-west to the smallest at north-east, to 5ft 8ins (1.75m); the largest stone has a well-fed girth of 15ft (4.6m). Though apparently not part of a circle, the stones have 'presence'; 76 similar examples occur in Scotland, and at least eight in England.

An ancient legend relates that the stones go down to Hindwell Pool, 200yds (183m) to the east, to drink at night, perhaps to the sounds of the bells of Old Radnor Church, which is located on a high and ancient site nearby; similar legends are attached to many stones around the British Isles.

In a great, flat field 300yds (274m) east-north-east of the Four Stones lies the Walton Stone. This attractive little stone is 2ft 7ins (0.84m) high and is visible to the north-west of the field gate there (one of a pair), about 100ft (30m) in.

GORS FAWR

I.75

*Mynachlog-ddu,
Cardigan,
Dyfed*

STONE CIRCLE AND
STANDING STONES

SN 134294

*The circle and two standing stones
have a wonderful setting; the dark
Preseli Mountains can be seen to the
right in the distance.*

*Going south from Cardigan
on the A478, take the first
road on the right
(unnumbered), signposted to
Mynachlog-ddu. Go straight
through the village, ignoring
the right turn. The signposted
stones are over 1 mile (1.6m)
south, on open moorland on the
right. Park at the sign there.*

This is one of the most beautiful megalithic sites in the British Isles: it is on gorse-covered moorland where sheep and cattle graze and is watched over by the dark Preseli Mountains to the north. Here there are square miles strewn with prehistoric circles, stones, chambers, and doubtless sight and ley lines. From the Mountains, 'bluestones' (as they appear in the rain) were apparently hewn, shaped and then transported 240m (386km) to STONEHENGE (though some experts disagree).

The delightful stone circle here is a perfect ring 73ft (22.3m) across, and its 16 stones have been designed to rise gradually in height towards the south. The entrance looks away to the south. Two standing stones, 7ft (2.1m) tall and 15yds (13.7m) apart, have been placed 109yds (100m) to the north-east. Their purpose has yet to be divined although they were perhaps outliers in some giant scheme, which may yet be revealed at this magical site.

HAROLD'S STONES

Trellech,
Monmouth,
Gwent

STANDING STONES

SO 499051

Trellech (variously spelt) is 6 miles (9.6km) south of Monmouth, on the B4293. There is an excellent framed map of the village and its prehistoric attractions in the main street.

The stone table, or outside altar, in the churchyard at Trellech. The three Harold's Stones are nearby.

Trellech takes its name from these three huge stones which are set on a slope in a line 34ft 6in (10.5m) long, and have stood there for about 3500 years. They were first recorded in 1689, in stone, on a remarkable sundial which is now in St Nicholas' Church there. They are depicted on one face and mysteriously bear the numbers 7, 10, 14, which may well be their former height in feet; today the two upright stones measure 15ft (4.6m) and 9ft (2.7m); the leaning stone is 12ft (3.7m).

Nearby, in the grounds of Court Farm, sits Tump Terret, a three-tiered earth mound. The notice there states that it 'dates back to the thirteenth century', but very probably it is pre-Christian. So, most certainly, is a stone table in the two-acre Churchyard of St Nicholas nearby, set in front of a medieval preaching cross. This enthralling little village holds yet more secrets. Over the crossroads from Harold's Stones there is a holy well; it is now labelled The Virtuous Well, but it has been appropriately called The Red Pool, and, very long ago, St Anne's Well, implying the place of a beacon fire.

PENTRE IFAN

Newport,
Dyfed

BURIAL CHAMBER

SH 099370

Clearly signposted, on the right going east from Newport on the A487. Turn off it southwards at Temple Bar. Park at the footpath.

The famous Welsh burial chamber, perhaps part of a larger setting.

This is one of the most popular tomb sites in Wales; it is easy to find yet in remote countryside, and well-presented with a storyboard at the gate into the area. The lasting impression that one carries away is without doubt of the huge, almost flying capstone, most delicately poised on its three uprights. The quality of the engineering feat is plain to see. The stone, which is dressed on its south face, weighs over 16 tons, it is 16ft 6in (5m) long and 8ft (2.4m) high off the ground.

This chamber, which dates back to about 3500 BC, was once covered and at the end of a long barrow about 120ft (36m) long. The recessed south-facing forecourt once had stones closely packed between the portals, and these would have been laboriously removed every time there was a fresh burial. The north-south axis is rare. Some of the original kerbstones around the barrow can still be seen. Excavations took place at Pentre Ifan in 1936–37 and in 1958–59.

All around the area there are large stones which pose unanswered questions. Were the stones at the gate in the field to the east once associated with the tomb? What of the enormous dressed stone against the drystone wall in the field 140yds (128m) directly to the west? Was there perhaps an enormous circle of stones around the site, enclosing a settlement? Possibly, since *pentre* means 'village'.

St Lythan's (Maes-Y-Felin)

Duffryn,
Barry,
South Glamorgan

CHAMBER TOMB

ST 101723

This chamber's name translates as
The Mill in the Meadow.

West of Cardiff. Turn off the
A48 at St Nicholas, at the
sign to Duffryn Conference
Centre and Gardens; pass the
entrance and continue to the
road junction. Turn left, and
it is signposted on the right.
Park there.

There is a tradition that the field in which the remnants of this tomb stand is cursed, and that nothing will grow there. The site certainly feels uncomfortable; constant visitors to mega-lithic monuments gradually acquire 'a sense of place'.

The chamber, which faces almost due east away from the downward slope, measures 8ft (2.4m) by 6ft (1.8m) and is 6ft (1.8m) high. The insides of the two portal stones have been smoothed, and the back stone has a port-hole near its top. Externally, the brown stones are very heavily pitted; huge they are, and eminently sited, but as nothing compared with the neighbouring TINKINSWOOD in general attraction.

St Lythan's capstone is 14ft (4m) long, 10ft (3m) wide, and 2ft 6in (0.7m) thick: it is said that on Midsummer's Eve it spins around three times, which must be an awesome sight! This story fits with the chamber tomb's Welsh name, which translates as 'The Mill in the Meadow'.

TINKINSWOOD

St Nicholas,
Barry,
South Glamorgan

HORNED BURIAL
CHAMBER

ST 092733

West of Cardiff. Turn off the
A48 at St Nicholas, at the
signs to Tinkinswood and the
Duffryn Conference Centre
and Gardens. The site is
shortly before the Centre, on
the right. Walk south across a
field, and then over the
signposted small wooden
footbridge.

RIGHT: *The horned forecourt of*
Tinkinswood, which is a rare
feature in Britain.

The 40 ton capstone here is like a giant slice of home-made brown bread, and has suffered only one crack since 4000 BC when it was first placed here to shelter burials. The horned entrance beneath it faces north-east, and indeed towards a radio transmitter (which will interest fans of quartz at ancient sites). The earth mound either side and to the south-west of the chamber is 130ft (40m) long and is 60ft (18m) wide. On it, on the west side, there is a pile of stones beside a pit.

Following excavations in 1914, the whole site was greatly restored; the horned entrance is most impressive, though spoiled a little by the close fencing. A depression exactly at the south-east marks the site of a possible side entrance. There are standing and fallen stones all around, including two uprights south-east of the chamber, just inside the entrance gate.

More than 50 burials have been found at Tinkinswood, which has attracted the attention of archaeologists ever since the first excavations. In 1925, Sir Mortimer Wheeler recorded the old legend that anyone who spent a night in the chamber on a pagan spirit night (such as Beltane or Hallowe'en) would die, go raving mad or become a poet.

YSBYTY CYNFYN

St John's Church,
Ysbyty Cynfyn,
Devil's Bridge,
Dyfed

STONE CIRCLE AND
CHURCHYARD

SN 752791

2½ miles (4km) north of
Devil's Bridge on the A4120,
as it leads up to the A44.

Two standing stones in the wall of
St John's Church.

Early Christian missionaries in Britain, Europe and elsewhere, soon learnt that their aims were best served if they did not destroy the pagans' ancient places of worship, but converted them. Here there is a circular churchyard with a circle built into part of its wall. Five stones remain of the circle that previously tenanted the site; two serve as gateposts (perhaps they were formerly portals) at the church's east entrance, two are incorporated in its churchyard wall, and one, the tallest at 11ft (3.3m), is in its original position among the graves.

Other churches with standing stones in their graveyards include Ste Marie du Câtel, Guernsey (*see* LE CÂTEL, Jersey); St Gwrthwl's Church, Llanwrthwl, Powys; St Brynach's Church, Nevern, Dyfed (with ogham markings); and St David's Church, Bridell (*see* BRIDELL, also with ogham markings, and others). The largest British example of the overt Christianisation of a site is the huge ditched earthwork at Knowlton, Dorset, where a Norman church now stands right in the middle of it.

Raised circular or oval-shaped churchyards (but not those with deeply sunk church foundations) often indicate a probable prehistoric place of worship. Old Radnor Church, Powys (*see* FOUR STONES, Walton, Powys) is a fine example. Such church sites are very often found on leys (invisible straight lines which criss-cross the landscape, with ancient sites occurring along their ways). A single piece of stone lying in a churchyard can, in fact, be the remaining stump of a standing stone, and a clue to a ley. There is one at Lenham, Kent — and they are quite common all over the country.

II

France

France is a megalithic wonderland. There are literally thousands of stone structures in most parts of this huge country, and the study of passages of its successive prehistoric cultures among them can be relied upon to provide both popular and academic controversy for many years to come. The 33 sites described here offer a cross-section of megalithic sites; many of them are located in Brittany which is easily the most popular area of the country (and probably in Europe) for their enjoyment and study. Less accessible areas are also rich in monuments; for example, the southern *département* of Aveyron has more of them than are found in England and Wales together.

There are some outstanding sites therefore to be explored. For megalithic art, GAVR'INIS, Morbihan, rivals NEWGRANGE, Ireland, with mysterious, detailed carvings on 23 of its uprights; they have similarities with those on stones in Malta and Spain as well as Ireland. The broken colossus LE GRAND MENHIR BRISÉ, Morbihan, may never have stood; KERLOAS, Finistère, is Europe's tallest standing stone, at 31ft (9.5m) above ground. The stone rows at KERMARIO and MÉNEC, both in Morbihan, each offer a long walk among more than 1000 stones, standing in serried ranks and posing some very difficult questions. Down in the south, the Neolithic camp at VILLENEUVE-TOLOSANE, just outside Toulouse, Hâute Garonne, is a sophisticated works site.

The language of stones

The word dolmen was invented by a French archaeologist, Carnet, in 1796. He put together the Old Breton words *tôl*, *taol* or *dol* (table) and *maen*, *mên* or *men* (stone) to describe the archetypal megalithic monument which occurs over many parts of France. About two hundred years of commentary have produced terminological confusion! Consider the following.

A dolmen in France, three or more uprights supporting a capstone, is the same as a cromlech in parts of Britain; TRETHEVY QUOIT, Cornwall, and CARREG SAMSON, Dyfed, Wales, are generally marked as cromlechs on maps. But the word cromlech also occurs in France. It comes from the Breton word Kroumlec'h derived from *kromm* or *kroumm* (curved) and *lec'h*, *leac'h* or *liac'h* (sacred stone or circle of stones), and means stone circle (of which, incidentally, there are remarkably few in the whole country). The Cornish and Breton languages were very similar, and it is possible that in fact Carnet derived the word dolmen from the Cornish word *tôlven*, which unfortunately refers to one natural boulder supported by others, without human intervention. A *dolmen simple* in France is not, when translated into English, a simple dolmen, but a open-ended rectangle of stone slabs probably featuring false corbelling over its passage or chamber. It is an odd fact that the first published reference to a French chamber tomb was by Rabelais (c.1494–1553) in his Pantagruel, Book V; he was referring to La Pierre Levée, St Saturnin, Poitiers, one of many dolmens bearing this name.

The French term *allée-couverte* is in many ways preferable to the English gallery grave (which 50 years ago was called a long stone cist) because it more precisely defines the absence of a distinct chamber (as at La Chaussée-Tirancourt, Somme). A chamber tomb in France may be covered by an earth mound or cairn (like the many-chambered LES MOUSSEAUX, Loire-Atlantique), and is unconnected with the non-megalithic British tumulus. The lone vertical stone in Britain is a standing stone; in France it is a menhir. Legrand d'Aussy coined the word in 1796 from the Breton *méan* or *men* (stone) and *hîr* (long or tall). In the British Isles, Cornish has supplied MÊN-AN-TOL, Cornwall, but this is a group of standing stones; Welsh has contributed to THE DRUIDS' CIRCLE (MEINI HIRION), Gwynedd, where there are stone circles and cairns. One of the great menhirs of France is the 31ft (9.5m) DOL (though KERLOAS was once higher) in Ille-et-Vilaine – but, as previously mentioned, the Breton words *tôl*, *taol* and *dol* mean table which it manifestly is not (unlike, for example, the Minorcan *taula*). But then DOL might not even be a true menhir in any case; there is a controversial record that about a century ago a large area of ground around it was stripped of its top soil, revealing that the stone is in fact carved directly out of the broad granite plateau which lies beneath the soil. This is an entertaining tale, but the plateau is schist, and the menhir was probably quarried (and dressed) about 2¾m (4km) away.

Even apparent facts can confuse. The massive BAGNEUX, Maine-et-Loire, is widely referred to as an 'Angevin' chamber tomb, but it is very doubtful that it ever received a burial. Adding to the language problems, guide books sometimes resort to idiosyncratic nomenclature; for example, the English Michelin green guide to Brittany goes to the trouble of translating LES PIERRES PLATES, Morbihan, as Dolmen of Flat Stones!

The first monuments

The 5000 or so burial chambers and other megalithic monuments in France are mostly grouped in a few large areas. They are dense in the Paris basin, northern Normandy, west of Caen, the north-west peninsula of Brittany, from St Malo west

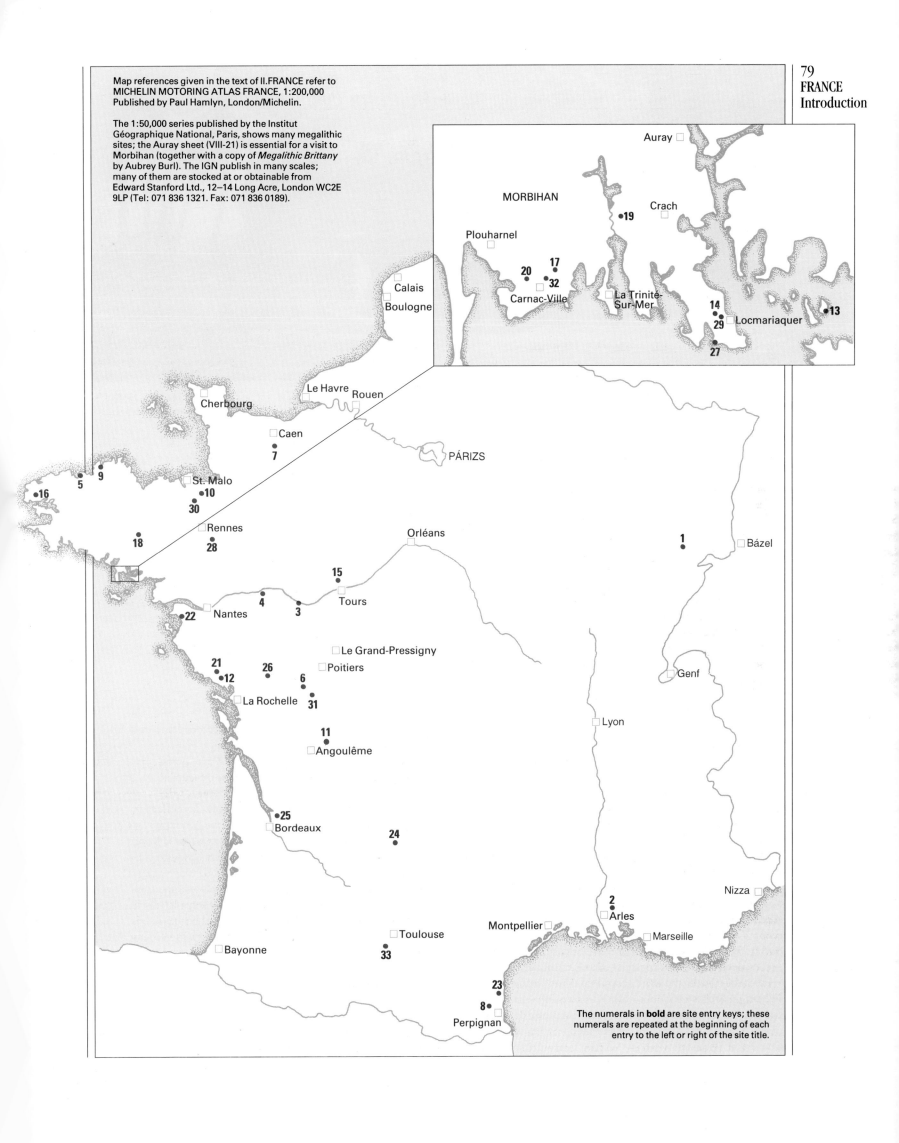

Map references given in the text of II.FRANCE refer to
MICHELIN MOTORING ATLAS FRANCE, 1:200,000
Published by Paul Hamlyn, London/Michelin.

The 1:50,000 series published by the Institut
Géographique National, Paris, shows many megalithic
sites; the Auray sheet (VIII-21) is essential for a visit to
Morbihan (together with a copy of *Megalithic Brittany*
by Aubrey Burl). The IGN publish in many scales;
many of them are stocked at or obtainable from
Edward Stanford Ltd., 12–14 Long Acre, London WC2E
9LP (Tel: 071 836 1321. Fax: 071 836 0189).

Auray

MORBIHAN

Crach

● 19

Plouharnel

20   17

32

Carnac-Ville   La Trinité-
Sur-Mer

14

29   Locmariaquer   ● 13

27

Calais

Boulogne

Le Havre   Rouen

Cherbourg

Caen

7   PÁRIZS

9

5   St. Malo

16   10

30

Rennes

18   Orléans   1   Bázel

28

15

Nantes   4   Tours

3

22

Le Grand-Pressigny

21   26   Poitiers   Genf

12

6

La Rochelle   31

11

Angoulême   Lyon

25

Bordeaux

24

Nizza

2

Arles

Montpellier

Marseille

Toulouse

Bayonne

33

23

8 ●

Perpignan

The numerals in **bold** are site entry keys; these
numerals are repeated at the beginning of each
entry to the left or right of the site title.

ABOVE: *The 25-ton entrance lintel stone is a dramatic feature of* LA ROCHE AUX FÉES, *Ille-et-Vilaine, one of France's finest chamber tombs.*

RIGHT: *Two of the four pairs of 'breasts' at* TRESSÉ, *Ille-et-Vilaine. Both are in the end cell. Together these measure 13ins (33cm) across; traces of necklaces can be seen beneath each pair.*

LEFT: *A café in Montguyon, Charente-Maritime, celebrates in its name the local prehistoric attraction,* LA PIERRE FOLLE. *Note the 'M'.*

and south down the Atlantic seaboard as far as Chârente Maritime, and from there in a broad belt across central southern France, through Aveyron towards Montpellier. There are further concentrations west of Cannes over to the east of the French side of the Pyrenees.

In the north, the earliest farming communities appeared on the left bank of the Rhine in about the middle of the fifth millennium (the cemetery at Rixheim, Alsace, for example). The old and difficult question of indigenous spontaneous tomb construction in several parts of France (indeed, in different countries) is highlighted by a date of 4600 BC obtained from Tomb G at BARNENEZ, far to the west in Finistère. A very similar date (4675 BC) has come from Kercado in Morbihan; this is a fine, mounded burial chamber with a menhir on top. So here is a funerary construction in Brittany which predates STONEHENGE, Knossos and the Great Pyramid at Giza.

The early Neolithic Bandkeramik culture (named after the swirling patterns on its pottery) came to north-east France, and even as far as the Channel Islands, from east of the Danube, also spreading all over Germany and the Low Countries. Its people were not intense farmers however, and it is likely that the practice of agriculture reached Brittany from south-west France.

From about 3400 BC to 1800 BC the Paris Basin culture held sway. It was clumsily named Seine-Oise-Marne (SOM), after the rivers, in 1926 by two Spanish archaeologists, P. Bosch-Gimpera and J. de C. Serra Raffols. Its collective chamber tombs, mostly *allées-couvertes*, are generally distributed north of Paris and on river sites. Some have port-hole slabs, and most are sunk in trenches with their capstones showing just above ground level; they were rarely covered by earth. Though probably of local origin, some have argued that the origin of the *allée-couverte* may well lie in southern Spain, following north the routes of the earliest farmers on the way; these tombs are earlier than the somewhat similar versions found to the north, in Germany, Denmark and Sweden.

In the south
The first Neolithic farmers settled in south-western France in the century or so before 5000 BC. A date of 4830 ± 200 bc has been obtained from one of the deepest hearths in the Grotte

Gazel, Sallèles-Cabardès, Aude, where Impressed Ware occurred. This is also called Cardial Ware; *cardium* is Latin for cockle, the shell of which, once it contents were consumed, was used to effect a serrated style of pottery decoration. This pottery probably originated in Yugoslavia, spread west to Italy, across to Sicily, and thence by way of Provence, to Spain.

Early Impressed Ware sites in Provence include Châteauneuf-les-Martigues, Bouches-du-Rhône, where Hearth 5 produced the date of 5570 ± 240 bc, which is very much earlier than other Midi sites. The succeeding culture, that of France's first intense farmers, has left the date of 3810 ±140 bc in Level 8B in the upper network of Grotte de l'Eglise, Baudinard, Var. It is found in many different types of burial sites and settlements, including, for instance, La Grotte des Fées, in the ARLES-FONTVIEILLE GROUP, Bouches-du-Rhône, which dates back to about 3100 BC.

The Chasséen culture reached the Paris basin just before the start of the third millennium BC, leaving behind few satisfactory dates in western and central France for a tracking exercise. On the other hand, this could indicate broadly contemporary indigenous tomb development – but some pottery assemblages go against this argument. The Chasséen culture was named by the eminent Australian archaeologist Gordon Childe (1892–1957) after the fortified hill site of Chassey-le-Camp, near Chagny, which is south west of Beaune, Burgundy's wine capital.

Brittany

All around the Breton *départements* of Finistère, Côtes-d'Armor, Morbihan (where Carnac is), Ille-et-Vilaine and Loire-Atlantique lie many hundreds of megalithic structures: dolmens, menhirs, chamber tombs within and without stone cairns and mounds of earth, passageless or otherwise – with entrances frequently facing the midwinter sunrise.

And then there are the oddly disturbing stone rows (*alignments*); at KERMARIO, Morbihan, over 1000 menhirs are set up in seven main rows over a distance of 1230 yds (1125m). The site's name means Village of the Dead, but the Scottish surveyor Professor Alexander Thom has, less prosaically, concluded that the stone rows constituted a giant eclipse predictor.

AILLEVANS GROUP

Aillevans,
Villersexel,
Vesoul,
Haute-Saône

HORNED CHAMBER
TOMBS

76 C 2

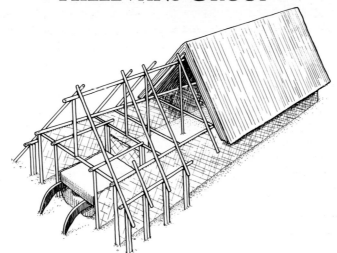

Take the D9 south-east from
Vesoul towards Belfort. After
16 miles (26 km), turn
north, through Villersexel, on
the D486. Aillevans is
signposted on the left.

A conjectural reconstruction of Tomb
I, one of three horned chamber-tombs
forming the Aillevans Group.
(After P. Pétrequin and J.-F.
Piningre, 1976)

The three monuments here date, through successive use, from the Late Neolithic to the Early Bronze Ages. Each of them is small, about 6½ft (2m) square, set east to west precisely, with the antechamber and horned entrance at the east.

In Tomb I, at least 23 bodies were deposited; the tomb's mound was circular at first but, in a second stage, the tomb was covered by a long wooden trapezoidal hut about 65½ft (20m) long, and partly paved. In Tomb II, at least 100 burials took place; animal bones, flint arrowheads and a dagger blade have also been uncovered there.

Tombs I and II were re-used a number of times, and on occasions the bodies were placed complete, and not in the more familiar foetal position, with the heads facing west, away from the entrances.

ARLES-FONTVIEILLE GROUP

Sainte Croix,
Fontvieille,
Bouches-du-Rhône

ROCK-CUT TOMBS
(HYPOGÉES)

158 A 2

Among the finds at Castelet were arrowheads, beads, axes and pottery; at Bounias, a copper dagger was found.

Leave Arles northwards on the
N570; turn right on to the
D17 towards Fontvieille. The
group is at Sainte Croix and
beyond the ruined L'Abbaye de
Montmajour, on the right of
the road. Somewhat
inaccessible.

The smoothly dressed interior of La
Grotte Arnaud-Castelet.

There are five tombs at this important site, and, in the general Provençal tradition, they are all orientated to the setting sun. Within their earth mounds, they are beautifully carved (with the exception of the drystone walled Coutignargues) and smoothly finished, and each is covered by a large capstone. Other rock-cut tombs or *hypogées* such as these are found in Mediterranean regions such as Malta, Sardinia and Sicily.

The largest here, with a length of 141ft (43m) in a mound 230 ft by 165 ft (70 m by 50.3 m) is La Grotte des Fées on the north side of Montagne de Cordes, which dates back to about 3500BC (human remains and radiocarbon dateable artifacts have been found in most of these tombs). Carved stone stairs lead 11ft (3.3m) down to an antechamber, with one small chamber on each side, and then on through a doorway to the main chamber. This is 80ft (24.4m) long, about 11ft (3.3m) high, but only 9ft (2.7m) wide; it gradually tapers like a hilted sword, from which fact the tomb's alternative name, L'Epée de Roland, might have been derived.

La Grotte Arnaud-Castelet (the only site on the other side of the road) is somewhat similar to La Grotte des Fées, but smaller; over 100 skeletons were found here during excavations. La Grotte Bounias and La Grotte de la Source share similar findings, including arrowheads, axes, beads and pottery sherds. The tomb of Coutignargues, on the Plateau de Castelet, is not a true *hypogée,* since it is constructed of drystone walling.

BAGNEUX

*Bagneux,
Saumur,
Maine-et-Loire*

'ANGEVIN' CHAMBER
TOMB

81 D 1

*The massive 'Angevin' chamber tomb
in the café courtyard in Bagneux.
Locally it is called Le Grand
Dolmen.*

This tomb belongs in any book of records; it is the largest tomb of its kind in France – alas it cannot be used as a dance hall (floodlighting already installed). 'Angevin' graves are often found grouped together in this area, and they are not generally set on high or prominent places; even among them this monster is unique.

At almost 65ft (19.8m) long, and 25ft (7.6m) wide, it bears some resemblance to LA ROCHE AUX FÉES, Ille-et-Vilaine, which is a little longer but otherwise smaller. The entrance, which faces just south-south-east, leads into a veritable hall of stone; four massive capstones cover the entire length of the tomb, and the largest of them is 25ft (7.6m) long. They support four opposing pairs of massive flat slabs, square or

Leave Saumur south-west on the N147. The tomb is in a café courtyard in Bagneux (a suburb of Saumur), nearly 1 mile (1.6km) along on the left.

rectangular and leaning slightly inwards. The largest capstone weighs no less than 86 tons, as compared with the weight of an unladen red double-decker London bus which is a meagre 9¾ tons.

First excavated in 1775, Bagneux was never covered by an earth mound on its slight slope in the entrance direction, and nothing is known with certainty to have been found inside it, though there are reports of some finds in 1849. Called a tomb, perhaps it never was one.

Inside, its ceiling height is 10ft (3.1m) – just the place for a prehistoric party, for celebration, for rituals of unknown significance, then as now.

This 'Grand Dolmen' is located in the gravel courtyard of a modest family-owned café/bar/tabac, and is probably the largest private megalithic monument in the world. Entrance is free only if you spend in the café!

The interior of the Bagneux tomb – 'a veritable hall of stone'.

La Bajoulière

*Saint-Rémy-la-Varenne,
Angers,
Maine-et-Loire*

'ANGEVIN' CHAMBER
TOMB

66 B 4

This is one of the most impressive tombs of its type in France, and in terms of its sheer size can be compared with BAGNEUX, Saumur, which is not far away. In plan it is similar to the sole of a man's shoe, with a trapezoidal surrounding mound.

Inside lies a simple, most elegant and almost completely symmetrical chamber. Two square boulders stand guard at its south-east facing entrance. An antechamber leads to an enormous square chamber, measuring no less than 23ft by 23ft (7m by 7m). This 58½ sq yds (49sq m) area is covered by a single capstone; like many Angevin chamber-tombs, it is divided inside by a curtain wall of six stepped uprights with a door space left in the middle. This Late Neolithic grave appears 'younger' than it is because of the neat squared-off finish given to the capstone and chamber uprights.

Leave Angers south-east on the D952, along the River Loire. After about 12½ miles (20 km), at St. Mathurin-sur-Loire, turn right, southwards, over the bridge on the D55. Immediately turn left to St. Rémy-la-Varenne, then right on to the D21. Now take the first left, and then fork right towards La Roche. The tomb is on the left, before the small village.

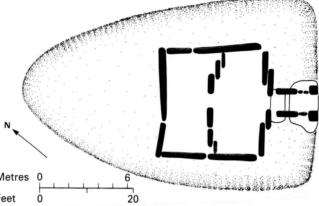

The peaceful setting of La Bajoulière. There may be remains of further tombs in the nearby wood.

Metres 0   6

Feet   0   20

La Bajoulière is famed for its size and symmetry; two ditches reach out from the entrance like horns. (After Gruet)

BARNENEZ

*Plouézoc'h,
Morlaix,
Finistère*

CAIRN WITH MULTIPLE
PASSAGE-GRAVES

27 E 2

This is one of many magnificent monuments in Brittany, the land of megalithic superlatives. Here there are an incredible eleven passage-graves, and they demonstrate almost all the forms of grave construction in Neolithic times.

The massive stepped cairn, aligned north-east/south-west atop its dramatic hilltop site, was built in two distinct stages, and using different stone (green dolorite to the east, granite to the west). The first, at the north-east, is dated at about 4600 BC; it is 115ft (35m) along its north-east/south-west axis, and 26ft (8m) at its widest. In its south-east flank there are five passage-graves, with their entrances in a row. From south to north-east, they are labelled today as Tombs G, Gi, H, I and J. A few centuries later, another cairn was literally attached to

Take the D76 north from Morlaix along the estuary. Go through Plouézoc'h. At the next fork, take the lane on the left to Kernelehen. Ticket office, exhibition and bookstall. Closed in the winter, midweek, and, of course, lunchtime. Only two of the graves (C and D) can be visited. Take a torch.

RIGHT: *This impressive complex at Barnenez of 11 passage-graves was built in two stages, and discovered as recently as 1954 (when excavators were seeking stone aggregate behind tombs A, B, C and D). (After P.-R. Giot and Y. Lecerf)*

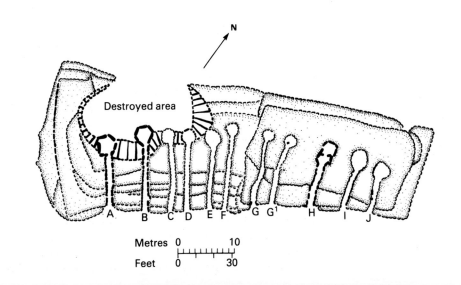

Barnenez from the air. The dark area to the left, at the back of the passage-graves, is where 'stone' was taken for road building.

Looking north-east along the restored cairns at Barnenez. Some entrances can be seen.

A legend has it that this site was built by fairies and that an underground passage led out from the cairns to the sea.

it to the south-west, together with another six passage-graves joining the row. From the south they are called Tombs A, B, C, D, E and F. In its entirety, the present cairn measures 230ft (70m) long and 82ft (25m) deep.

The whole site was only discovered in 1954, when contractors seeking stone aggregate for a new road in the area tore the backs off Tombs A, B, C and D, exposing the splendid chambers to the elements. Quarrying was immediately halted and in 1955 P.R. Giot commenced a two-year excavation of the site.

The Barnenez passage-graves were without doubt just that, even though there were few human remains among the amazing finds. Tomb A is dated at about 4400 BC; its corbelled roof was partly destroyed in 1954, its passage is lined with orthostats and broken pottery, indicating burial, was unearthed. Of interest are seven carved wavy lines on one of the uprights.

Tomb B has a megalithic chamber, now partly ruined, in which human bones were found, as well as pottery sherds.

Tomb C, in contrast with its southerly neighbour, has a passage of drystone walling. The partly destroyed corbelled roof is topped, not with corbelling, but with a capstone, in keeping with the capstones roofing the passage. Among the finds here have been a copper dagger and flint arrowheads.

Tomb D is constructed like C, but has drystone walling in between orthostats; burnt human bones, Beaker sherds and flint arrowheads have been discovered in this tomb. E is constructed in the same way as C.

Tomb F is the longest at the site, with a passage and chamber stretching 46ft (14m); it has two small stelae at its entrance, and has been dated at about 4500 BC.

Like C, Tomb G is of drystone walling and has the oldest date here at about 4700 BC. Tomb Gi is likewise similar to C except that a thin rectangle of granite stands near the entrance to its chamber.

Of all the tombs, H proved to be the archaeological treasure house. It is the most elaborate and important megalithic structure, with a huge capstone over its back chamber. Stones inside bear carvings of axes, triangles, wavy lines and zigzags, and small stelae in its antechamber are very similar to those at LOS MILLARES, Almeria.

A further variation in passage construction is seen in Tomb I, which is half uprights and half drystone walling. The chamber is exclusively drystone with a corbelled roof. Finally, Tomb J is notable for the rough carving, which probably represents a female form, beneath the capstone.

*Bougon,
St. Maixent-L'Ecole,
Niort,
Deux-Sèvres*

CEMETERY

94 C 2

In Tomb C four skeletons were found seated along the wall, and attached to it with stone brackets.

Archaeologist Jean-Pierre Mohen considers that some of the stone chambers at this site were not used for burials.

This very important Neolithic site was first discovered as long ago as 1840. It consists of six tombs in a tight cluster. Serious excavations commenced in 1968, and then in 1972, under the direction of Jean-Pierre Mohen.

Tomb A is enclosed in a circular mound which is 130ft (40m) in diameter, and dates back to about 3750BC. The passage leads to a divided rectangular chamber measuring 24½ft by 16½ft (7.5m by 5m); in the 1840 excavations, some 200 skeletons were uncovered in three distinct, separated layers. Complete pots were also found, which is unusual.

Tomb B contains two small stone cists in a 115ft (35m) long mound, which is dated at approximately 4250BC; later two passage graves with four-sided chambers, and two others, were constructed. Tomb C has a diameter of 185ft (56m), and a height of 13ft (4m); inside the mound is a squarish chamber at the west end. Tomb D is not in any way prehistoric but is a 275ft (84m) long mound.

Tomb E, which had a round, corbelled-roofed chamber when first constructed, shows two virtually parallel passage-graves to the east.

The final Tomb F is notable for its substantial capstone over a rectangular chamber tomb at the north; it weighs 32 tons and measures 19¾ft by 11½ft (6m by 3.5m); at the other end of the extended mound there is a second, round corbelled chamber.

In July 1979 the Tomb F capstone was the object of a famous experiment by Jean-Pierre Mohen. With a team of 200 able-bodied men, a 32 ton replica of the stone was pulled along by 170 men, with the help of the other 30 levering the slab along over 30 rounded oak trunks on 'railway lines'. As a result, Mohen estimated that it would have taken one and a half months to bring the stone about 2½miles (4km) from its original source to the Bougon site. In those prehistoric times, the disciplines involved in this exercise alone must have been of an amazingly high order.

St. Maixent is about 15 miles (24km) north-east of Niort on the N11. After the town turn right on to the D737. After 6¾ miles (11km), at La Mothe, turn left on to the D5, then take the second turning on the right for Bougon. Marked 'tumulus' on the map, just north of the village.

One of the six tombs, after excavation and restoration by Jean-Pierre Mohen.

Cairn de la Hogue and Cairn de la Hoguette

*Fontenay-le-Marmion,
Caen,
Calvados*

CAIRNS WITH MULTIPLE
PASSAGE-GRAVES

32 A 2

*There are 12 entrances to passages in
Cairn De La Hogue*

*Leave Caen southwards on the
D562. After 6¼ miles
(10km), at May-sur-Orne,
turn left on to the minor
D41b. Cairn de la Hogue is
soon seen on the left.*

This type of cairn was invariably placed on a prominent, high site, and from the time of construction always incorporated passage-graves. These two are roughly contemporary, late Neolithic, and are not strictly megalithic in that they are made of drystone walling.

De La Hogue is almost rectangular – 140ft (42.7m) long, 102ft (31.1m) wide, and some 30ft (9.1m) high. There are no less than 12 entrances to passages leading to small round chambers at the end of each; six disarticulated skeletons were uncovered here and, in 1829, a small primitive altar, made of

chalk, and a perfect miniature dolmen, were found in one of the chambers.

De La Hoguette is 650 yds (595m) away, dates back to about 2300BC, and is almost 98½ft (30m) long by 65½ft (20m) wide. Its excavation, begun in 1964, has revealed an interesting find. It contains seven round chambers (there was once an eighth); in six of them, remains of 56 complete skeletons have been identified, and there are, unusually in late Neolithic tombs, almost exactly equal numbers of men, women and children.

La Clape Group

*Laroque-de-Fâ,
Aude*

CEMETERY

172 B 3

Eight chamber tombs make up this site, which dates from about 2000BC. Tomb 1 is a passage-grave within an oval mound; the teeth of 15 people have been found there in the two side chambers. Tomb 2 is a three-sided burial cist. Tomb 3 is a rectangular grave, which contained the remains of two people (a child and a young adult), and a flint knife; it is in the same mound as Tomb 5, nearer the centre. This is an open-ended passage-grave, where 24 people were buried. Only one was a man. Tomb 4 is a simple passage-grave.

Tombs 6 and 7 lie within the same kidney-shaped mound, the longer 6 to the south, and 7 to its north, where another 24 people, mainly youngsters, were laid to rest. Tomb 8, the most symmetrical, has an unusual, almost circular chamber with two well-placed portal stones without, and all inside a round mound 16½ft (5m) in diameter.

*Laroque-de-Fâ is a mountain
village on the D212, which
runs south from the A61
autoroute between Narbonne
and Carcassonne. The tombs
are just south of the tunnel
through Col de Bedos.*

CRECH-QUILLÉ

*Saint-Quay-Perros,
Côtes-d'Armor*

ALLÉE-COUVERTE WITH
SIDE ENTRANCE

28 A 1

*The side entrance of Crech-Quillé,
looking towards the carved stele.*

This passage-grave was discovered only in 1955, and it was excavated in 1963-64. The late Neolithic long mound is aligned almost east-west, measures 98ft by 36ft (30m by 11m) and the large kerbstones around it are in-filled with drystone walling. On the south side of the grave towards the eastern end, the short side entrance passage is set, and a single stone stands there.

The chamber is 53ft by 6ft (16.2m by 1.8m), and contains a Breton mystery in the form of a large stele, facing the passage entrance, like a sort of guardian; upon it are carved two breasts, in relief, with a necklace or collar looped below them. Perhaps it was a string of token beads, an indication of wealth, and thus of power.

Such an image has been found elsewhere in passage-graves in France, and also at CÂTEL, Guernsey. Graves of this type are similar to the *hunebedden* in The Netherlands and passage-graves in northern Germany.

2½ miles (4km) north of Lannion on the D788, turn right to Crech-Quillé.

Excavators found a stone cist containing five pots and some pendants in the passage.

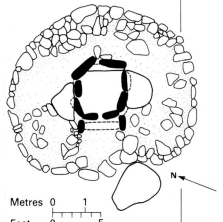

Metres 0   1

Feet 0   5

N

DOL

*Champ Dolent,
Dol de Bretagne,
Ille-et-Vilaine*

MENHIR

48 B 1

Take the D155 coastal road from St Malo south-east to Le Vivier-sur-Mer, and then south to Dol de Bretagne. Leave the town southwards on the D795, and then, after about 1 mile (1.5km), turn right, as signposted. The menhir is now visible on the right.

Champ Dolent means 'Field of Sorrow', recalling a legend of a great battle here between good and evil. Today however this is a most pleasing spot with no air of sadness about it.

The splendid menhir is 31ft (9.5m) high; and almost square (unlike KERLOAS, Morbihan, although the faces of the stones are similarly aligned, east-north-east/west-south-west). Dol's surface has been dressed to a smooth finish (doubtless at its quarry source to lose weight), so that, in ever-changing weather, it would be less likely to fragment and crumble (like the top of RUDSTON, England, for example, though of granite, a different stone). It has two strange holes at shoulder height.

St Samson, whose name is attached to two menhirs in Côtes-d'Armor, died in Dol de Bretagne, and the cathedral there is dedicated to him (*see* CARREG SAMSON, Wales).

The giant menhir standing in the 'Field of Sorrow'; there are now picnic tables all round it and a storyboard of the area.

DOLMEN DE LA MOTTE DE ST. JACQUILLE

Chateaurenaud,
Mansle,
Angoulême,
Charente

PASSAGE-GRAVE

108 B 1

The remarkable 'swinging door'.

Travel northwards from Angoulême on the N10 for 16 miles (26km), then turn left for Mansle. In the town, turn north over the River Charente and then left along the river to Chateaurenaud. Then turn north-west towards Villesoubis on the D61. After about ½ mile (1km), at La Motte, the site can be seen on the left.

'Too little too late' was probably the sad verdict of the 1981/82 excavators at this unique site. The tomb had been much robbed, and just a few bones, flint arrowheads and pottery were found. On the other hand, they were able to report a quite remarkable feature in the tomb – what may have been the world's oldest known swinging door.

A circular mound, 98½ft (30m) in diameter covered the now roofless chamber. The long passage bends to the right just before the chamber entrance, which consists of an inner, two piece port-hole, and is closed off on the passage side by a stone door, 4ft high by 3¼ft (1.2m high by 1.0m). It swung by means of the tenons at the top and bottom which still survive, fitting mortices set in the lintel and threshold. Close by this Late Neolithic doorway is La Motte de la Garde, with a polygonal chamber, just to the south-west towards Luxe.

LA FRÉBOUCHÈRE

II.12

Le Bernard,
Avrillé,
Les Sables d'Olonne,
Vendée

'ANGEVIN' CHAMBER TOMB

92 B 2

The almost complete 'Angevin' chamber tomb, with its immense capstone, which is now split into two.

Le Bernard is a hamlet, 15 miles (24km) south-east of Les Sables d'Olonne. Take the D949 eastwards out of Les Sables d'Olonne. After 17 miles (27km), after Avrillé, turn right on the D91 towards Le Bernard; the site is on the right.

This 'Angevin' chamber tomb (sometimes called Le Bernard), about 3 miles (4.8km) from the Atlantic, was once used as a sheepfold, which seems perfectly sensible. After all the 2½ft (0.75m) thick and handsome capstone (which was split in two by lightning in the 19th century) is 27½ft (8.5m) long and 10½ft (3.2m) wide.

Supporting this huge megalithic covering are nine uprights: one great endstone, three pairs of opposing ones (though one has now fallen inwards) and two doorway stones. The capstone also has the help of two fine portal stones at the south-east. Most of the monoliths have rounded tops. A little mystery exists inside La Frébouchère: a betyl (a small stone pillar, probably of sacred significance) stands in the chamber, and no-one knows exactly why.

GAVR'INIS

*Larmor-Baden,
Golfe du Morbihan,
Morbihan*

PASSAGE-GRAVE WITH
CARVINGS

62 C 2

One of the 23 carved upright slabs.

Here is a megalithic art mystery on a grand scale. Inside this most beautiful of passage graves there are 29 upright slabs of stone, 23 of which have been heavily carved. What secret prehistoric codes involve the following patterns and shapes? Axeheads, bucklers, chevrons, ships, single and concentric half-elipses, crooks like walking sticks, hafted axes, serpent or snake forms, spirals, shield/idols, suns (or rayed circles or spoked wheels), whorls, yokes and zigzags? The answers are unknown. Many of the patterns continue from one upright to the next – and yet more are on the stones' reverse sides, hidden from view, indicating perhaps a re-use of certain stones. We know that the chamber's capstone is 'secondhand'.

Gavr'inis has a number of remarkable similarities with

Leave Vannes south-west on the D101; continue on the D316 to Larmor-Baden, and then its harbour. Very frequent sailings, from mid-May to mid-September, take less than half an hour to the island. Visits on request at other times. Take a torch.

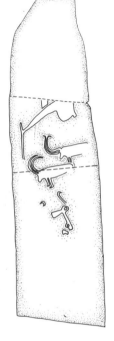

Further examples of megalithic art at Gavr'inis.

LEFT: *This 46ft (14m) high menhir once stood near* LE GRAND MENHIR BRISÉ. *Today its central section is the chamber capstone at Gavr'inis; the top is incorporated in the nearby Er Vinglé Tomb, and the lower section is the capstone of* LE TABLE-DES-MARCHANDS.

This extraordinary passage-grave is most noted for its art; 23 of its upright slabs bear carvings. (After Z. Le Rouzic)

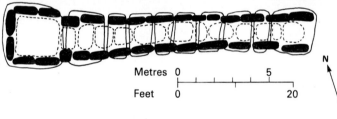

NEWGRANGE, Boyne Valley, Ireland, which lies across sea and land some 250m (402km) away to the north-west. Carvings of spirals are few in number, but do not occur anywhere else among Brittany's hundreds of megalithic monuments. Both use quartz stone (there is a single slab of it here). The Irish monument is the only equal of Gavr'inis's in the world for artistic richness, and it features many spirals. Most remarkable of all is the fact that both tombs have entrances exactly aligned to the mid-winter sunrise. It has also been calculated that Gavr'inis can accommodate an alignment to the southern moonrise at 'Major Standstill' (every 18.6 years). The solar and lunar lines intersect at the quartz stone.

This astonishing passage grave has been dated back to about 3500BC. The entrance is 6½ft (2m) high and 5ft (1.5m) wide; the passage, the longest in Brittany, at 38¾ft (11.8m), is paved with 11 flat slabs, and roofed with nine mighty capstones. Among the most notable of the carved uprights either side of it are the single white quartz stone, which is the seventh on the right; the next one along, with its crooks, coiling snake forms, possible human outlines and axeheads; and the fifth stone along the left, which bears the mysterious spirals, and further crooks and human outlines. Beyond the irregularly paired 23 uprights lies the rectangular chamber. It measures 9ft by 7½ft (2.7m by 2.3m) and is topped by a granite capstone, 12ft by 9ft (4m by 3m), which rests on the

last two passage uprights and the six chamber uprights. The grave is covered by a stepped, sand gravel, revetted cairn, 197ft by 177ft (60m by 54m), and 26¼ft (8m) high.

Gavr'inis was first excavated in 1832 and explored in the early 20th century by Zacharie Le Rouzic. During 1979-84, a substantial excavation was directed by Charles-Tanguy le Roux who, in 1983, made a remarkable announcement. Megalithic detective work led him to believe that a 46ft (14m) high menhir once stood near LE GRAND MENHIR BRISÉ, also in Morbihan; it then either fell or was pulled down, and broke or was broken into three parts. The smallest and the most heavily decorated central piece showed an ox with massive twin horns, curling away from each other at the top. The lowest part of the menhir bore another pair of horns, curling in the same backward direction. On the top piece parts of an axe plough were carved. Today, this top, mostly undecorated, block is incorporated in the nearby tomb of Er-Vinglé, and the bottom piece is now the capstone of LA TABLE-DES-MARCHANDS. The liveliest, central part is to be found on top of the chamber, as its capstone, at Gavr'inis.

The mystery of those realistic carvings is the only one to be solved. The others, on the 23 uprights, are similar to some found in Ireland, Malta and Spain, but are more abstract than literal, suggesting elemental forces rather than still depictions; the mysterious spirals possibly represent the forces of life itself.

Le Grand Menhir Brisé

*Locmariaquer,
Morbihan*

Menhir (fallen)

62 B 2

*The four remaining pieces of the
giant menhir; it weighed about 250
tons, according to the most recent
estimate.*

This astonishing Neolithic stone is broken (*brisé* in French) into (probably) five pieces, most likely by a fall durings its erection. Four pieces remain on the site. Its image is of a doomed submarine lying on a sea-bed, split into four and lifeless, with the longest bow section twisted away from the rest of the craft. Professor Thom proposed that had it ever stood, it would have been a marker for observing early March and October moonrises from TUMULUS ST. MICHEL, Morbihan.

Like all great menhirs it tapers towards its summit, a distant 66½ft (20.3m) from its exposed base; it would have been the tallest in the world. This 250 ton (latest estimate) giant is of dressed local granite, though not the most readily available: it comes from a quarry 2½m (4km) away to the north-west and why such a long haul was necessary may never be known. There was formerly a huge tumulus called Er Grah just to the north-east of this monster menhir's base, and LA TABLE-DES-MARCHANDS lies just to the north-east.

*Take the D28 south from
Auray. At Crach turn south-
west on to the D781. Before
entering Locmariaquer, turn
right for Keriaval. The stone
lies 100yds (91m) ahead on
the right.*

La Grotte des Fées (Mettray)

*St Antoine-du-Rocher,
Tours,
Indre-et-Loire*

Allée-couverte

67 F 4

The sylvan setting for an allée-
couverte *which may never have been
covered.*

*Leave Tours north on the
N10, over the Cher and
Loire. In St Cyr, fork left on
to the N138, and then take
the turning on the right
towards Mettray. From this
village travel north on the
minor road towards St
Antoine-du-Rocher. After
about ½ mile (1km), the site
and its car park is signposted
about 220yds (200m) along
on the right.*

Fée (fairy) comes from the Latin *fates* or *fatidica* (from *fatum*, which means fate or destiny, and *dicere*, to say) – so were Grottes des Fées megalithic tombs taken over by soothsayers, which became popular places to visit for discovery of the future? Where better than in a safe, rainproof, venerated prehistoric room? Grottes des Fées are found in many parts of France (see, for example, ARLES-FONTVIEILLE GROUP, Bouches-du-Rhône).

This one is sometimes known also as Mettray or St Antoine-du-Rocher (St Antony was a wise hermit). It is uncovered . . . and very probably it always has been. It is 30ft (9.1m) long, 11ft (3.3m) wide, and 6ft (1.8m) high, with an entrance vestibule at one end. A distinct feature of this *allée-couverte* is the middle one of the three capstones. It has been estimated to weigh over 55 tons, enough to remind any soothsayer of the potentials of cracks of doom.

KERLOAS

*Kervéatoux,
St Renan,
Finistère*

MENHIR

26 B 3

This is the tallest standing stone in western Europe (though less than half the length of the fallen LE GRAND MENHIR BRISÉ). It measures 31ft (9.5m), from top to ground level, and another 4½ft (1.4m) or more of stone is probably beneath the earth. At PUNCHESTOWN, Co Kildare, Ireland, 15 per cent of the stone was established as being below ground (and held with stone packing). Kerloas was once even taller, but a piece broke off the top some two centuries ago; it weighs about 100 tons, roughly the equivalent of the capstone of BROWNESHILL, Co Carlow, Ireland.

On the two narrowest sides of the menhir, east-north-east and west-south-west, two 'breasts' protrude about 3ft (1m) from the ground. They have given rise to legends, which may well go back to the Early Bronze Age. One states that newly-wed, sometimes naked, couples on the adjacent sides of the stone joined hands and embraced the menhir—rubbing themselves against the breasts as they made wishes for fruitful marriages with many sons.

Leave St Renan south-west on the D67; take the first road on the right to Kervéatoux. The menhir is signposted about 1¾ miles (3km) along the road, on the left.

The top of this immense menhir broke off about 200 years ago.

KERMARIO

II.17

*Carnac-Ville,
Morbihan*

STONE ROWS

62 B 2

These are the longest of the remarkable 'alignments' in the Carnac area. Over 1000 stones are set in seven main (and smaller ragged rows) over a distance of 1230yds (1125m). They seem to march like undisciplined, poorly clothed, yet determined foot soldiers, along the rising and falling terrain through gorse and past farmhouses. Predating these rows is the Lann Mané burial chamber, at the sharp bend (see right); finds in the chamber have put it at 3500BC. Kermario means 'village of the dead'; perhaps these are indeed memorial stones of long fallen and forgotten soldiers.

Leave Carnac-Ville north on the D119; turn right on to the D196 towards Kerlescan. The stones soon come into view, nearing a very sharp bend in the road to the right.

LISCUIS

*Laniscat,
Gouarec,
Côtes-d'Armor*

ALLÉES-COUVERTES

46 C 1

The site is north-west of Pontivy, and not too easy to locate. Leave Gouarec, which is on the N164, north on the D76 towards Laniscat. Turn right at the sign for the Gorges du Daoulas. Continue on the R47 to Cranach' Leron. After ¾ miles (1.25km), turn

This rewarding group of tombs is set high on the lonely, beautiful Landes de Liscuis overlooking the River Daoulas. They form part of the distinctive Breton *allées-couvertes* (see CRECH-QUILLE, Côtes-d'Armor).

Liscuis 1 is the odd one out here; it is about 500ft (150m) down the path from Liscuis 2. This V-shaped *allée-couverte* passage-grave was excavated by Charles-Tanguy Le Roux in 1973-74, and is dated at about 3950BC. The whole was enclosed by an oval rubble mound with kerbstones to keep it in place; signs of both can be seen today. It had a fine false entrance at its north end and the uprights surrounding it are each quite different in shape; one kerbstone has shoulders, suggesting to one expert that it is anthropomorphic. Beyond the antechamber and its transversal entrance slab, the long gallery passage was once lined with six pairs of upright slabs, with one extra on the east side. The gallery is 39ft 9in (12m) long; it is lower at the entrance end, and also narrower at 5ft (1.5m). As is common with this grave type, it widens towards

right at the junction; after about 500yds (460m) turn left on to a minor road. Park after 220yds (200m), and walk up the trackway on the left. At the top of the hill, walk left along the grass track. At the sign indicating St Gelven turn right. Pass a path on the left just before reaching the site. There are information boards.

Liscuis 1, a V-shaped allée-couverte, was built in about 3950BC.

Liscuis 2, another fine allée-couverte *on this high heath, is made of thin schist slabs. The end cell has been dated at 3245*BC.

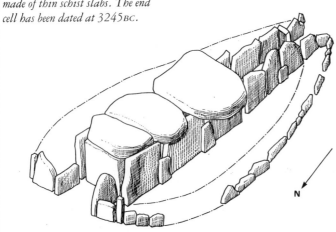

the end of the chamber to 6ft (1.8m). Three large capstones covered the passage.

Liscuis 2 is a long *allée-couverte*, and was excavated in 1974-75. It has an open-ended vestibule directly at the north end. The gallery commences past two entrance stones, and consists of five parallel matching pairs of uprights. This central part of the tomb was roughly paved with large, thin, shaped slabs, which is a rare sophistication in such tombs. The grave as a whole measures 49ft 3in (15m) long and at the southern chamber end is 7ft 3in (2.2m) wide. The end cell has a confirmed date of 3245BC.

Liscuis 3 was built later and was in use from about 2900-2150BC, and is located on the path to the right of Liscuis 1. There are seven parallel pairs of uprights with two capstones walling the gallery. The tomb lies east-west, measures 47ft 6in (14.5m), and has its entrance vestibule at the western end. A marked septal slab separates the chamber of the tomb from the antichamber.

This group presents an ideal opportunity for a day's archaeological exploration. Basic requirements are stout footwear, windproof clothing, binoculars, a local guide book, the largest scale map available, a camera, a compass, a measuring tape, and a pencil and notebook. A walking stick is very useful for poking about.

The point here is that however thorough a site's excavation, objects can be missed; moreover, many which occur in great profusion are discarded by archaeologists who select only the most interesting specimens.

Pottery sherds, for example, abound in and at the entrances of many tombs; it is entirely probable that the pots were broken deliberately by relatives and friends to accompany their recently departed to the next stage of what was then regarded as a natural event on the great journey through life. Such pottery remains all over the world help archaeologists to establish the migration routes of cultures, and the dates when they were taking place.

It is important, of course, to report to the nearest museum any unusual discovery, such as a statuette or a complete pot or a weapon in good condition. That way the day out will have been worth it in many more ways than one.

LUFFANG

II.19

Carnac-Ville, Morbihan

ALLÉE-COUDÉE WITH CARVINGS

62 B 2

Although unroofed and rather ruined today, this angled Neolithic passage-grave contains carvings which are ancient, unfathomable and therefore exciting. A cast of the famous shield/idol found here and elsewhere, notably GAVR'INIS, is in the admirable museum in Carnac-Ville.

Other carvings are to be seen here, as in other allée-coudées in this magical area, among them another hafted axe (similar ones are underneath the capstones at LA TABLE-DES-MARCHANDS, Locmariaquer, and Kercado, Carnac-Ville). In many respects this grave closely resembles LES PIERRES PLATES, Locmariaquer, and the western passage-grave at KNOWTH.

Take the road west from Crach to Luffang. The tomb is just beyond the village on the left.

*Carnac-Ville,
Morbihan*

STONE ROWS

62 B 2

Ménec at dawn.

At each end of the approximate north-east/south-west axis of these rows are remains of quite similar stone circles (*cromlechs*). The one at the east is almost ruined; only 25 stones are here now, from an original huge, egg-shaped space, measuring 351ft by 295ft (107m by 90m).

The stone rows commence immediately to the west of the circle. Eleven (and possibly 12) of them fan out slightly towards the west. This is the usual local configuration. An impressive 1099 granite menhirs have been set up here over a distance of 1276yds (1167m), the tallest of them being 12ft (3.7m) off the ground. At the western end of the 'alignments' lies the other egg-shaped circle.

Although in a poor state, and with the hamlet of Ménec 'among' it (like AVEBURY, Wiltshire, England, though on a much smaller scale), this is a substantial site covering an area 298ft by 233ft (91m by 71m). Though two large gaps exist, 70 large stones still stand, and they are often contiguous, or very close together, implying a kind of prehistoric village hall.

Leave Carnac-Ville north-west on the D781, and turn right on to the D196, to Ménec. Park 550 yds (503m) along on the right. The KERMARIO rows are the same distance again further east along the road.

These rows were identified by Thom as possibly being a calculator grid on which the lunar observations using LE GRAND MENHIR BRISÉ were extrapolated. He made a similar suggestion for HILL O'MANY STANES (Scotland).

Menhir du Camp de César

*Avrillé,
Les Sables-d'Olonne,
Vendée*

Menhir

92 B 1

This stone's local name is Le Roi des Menhirs.

Leave the coastal town of Les Sables-d'Olonne east on the D949. The small town of Avrillé is nearly 15 miles (24km) along the road. Park near the Hotel-Restaurant Le Menhir; the stone stands in the well-kept municipal gardens of the Mairie, which is close by.

All around Avrillé there is a rich selection of monuments to be enjoyed. A century and a half ago there were more than 150 known dolmens, menhirs, stone rows and tumuli. Tragically, from then on, and right up to 1960, many were destroyed to provide stone for the port of Les Sables-d'Olonne. Of the once existing 48 menhirs, some 37 survive. This is still an enticingly high number and undoubtedly the grandest of them all is this one. Locally, it is known as Le Roi des Menhirs.

The stone is delightfully located in gardens in the town centre, where guidebooks, leaflets and postcards are everywhere on sale, showing every facet of the menhirs and dolmens. The huge LA FRÉBOUCHÈRE is in the little village of Le Bernard, just to the south-east of Avrillé.

The Menhir du Camp de César is 23ft (7m) high, with fissures down its smooth worked surfaces. Two hundred years ago, it is sad to learn, there were three more stones like this at the site. What a majestic sight they must have made, even in an area with so many monuments.

Les Mousseaux

*Pornic,
Loire-Atlantique*

Mound with Two
Passage-Graves and
Cup-marks

78 B 1

Travel west from Pornic on Avenue de General de Gaulle, turn right on to Rue Mermoz, and then right on the Chemin de la Motte. Look for the sign Les Pierres Druidiques.

The third, and only accessible, cairn at this site, after restoration.

There are three cairns at this site; the first two are on private property, and therefore cannot be visited. Les Trois Squelettes was excavated at the end of the last century; several chamber tombs were within but, alas, no human remains were found. The second, large, 230ft by 98ft (70m by 30m) cairn is covered by buildings.

The third cairn is Les Mousseaux, which is known locally, as signposted, as Les Pierres Druidiques. It is rather beautiful in plan – the plurality lies within, because it contains two parallel, cruciform Neolithic graves. The cairn has stepped exterior walls in an oval 78ft 9in by 65ft 6in (24m by 20m).

The entrances are at the south-east; sherds of votive pottery were found there, as at so many grave entrances, placed after they had been sealed. The right-hand portal stone of the northern tomb has a line of cup-marks along its edge. Today, we leave flowers on graves in remembrance. Les Mousseaux was excavated and restored in 1975-76 by Jean L'Helgouach; it is a monument that is a delight to visit.

LE PALET DE ROLAND

The port-hole gives on to a probable compartment.

Leave Carcassonne on the N113 eastwards. Fork left over the River Aude to Trèbes, and continue eastwards on the D610. After 17½ miles (28km), turn left for Olonzac. In the village, turn left for Pépieux; the grave is 2 miles (3.2km) along on the left.

Names of tombs sometimes tell tales. *Palet* is French for 'quoit', the heavy flat ring used in the game of quoits; it is frequently found in Cornish sites (see CHÛN QUOIT, Morvah, and TRETHEVY QUOIT, St Cleer, Cornwall), where it refers to a different type of burial chamber from this one. Le Palet de Roland is also known as 'Moural de Las Fades', which means 'Fairies' Hill'; prehistoric place names commonly incorporate fairies' names, with old legends attached to them.

This grave is one of the most important of the surviving Aude tombs. It was excavated first in 1891 and again in 1972, after which it was restored. It is set on a hill top in an oval cairn which, at its longest, measures 120ft (36.6m). The parallel-sided gallery is set south-west to north-east, where the entrance is, and, as so often, it is lower at that end. A port-hole slab leads to a probable compartment and the higher end-chamber. It appears that this Late Neolithic grave was often re-used, but not, of course, until Charlemagne's time. His nephew, Roland, was killed nearby, hence the site's name.

LE PECH DU GRAMMONT

Le Pech du Grammont; only the tops of a few stones are visible today.

Today unseen there are two simple chambers within a huge beautifully shaped oval earth mound set on the vast limestone plateau of Gramat (home of truffle markets). The site was constructed in three distinct stages.

In the first, a rectangular stone chamber was enclosed by a circular earth mound, with kerbstones around it. Next, a second and larger chamber of the same shape was built to the east of the first, on the same axis, and covered with a roughly square kerbed mound; its easterly endstone has a port-hole in it. Finally, a fine, large oval mound was put up, all but burying the chambers. A few stone tops can be seen.

Gramat is just south-east of Rocamadour. Leave the town on the N140, and take the D15 lane (the Avenue du Tumulus) on the left. Marked 'tumulus' by Michelin, it is on the right before the left turn to Lavergne.

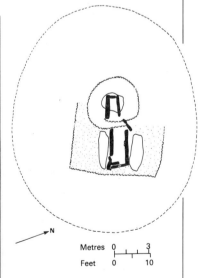

Following excavation, these chambers forming Le Pech du Grammont lie buried beneath a huge earth mound, in a most tranquil setting. (After J. Clottes)

LA PIERRE FOLLE

Montguyon,
Libourne,
Charente-Maritime

ALLÉE-COUVERTE

121 F 1

Take the D910 north from
Libourne, as far as
Montguyon. Then take the
D158 north-east out of the
town towards Neuvicq. Pass
two turnings on the left, and
then the grave is on the left
just before a road junction,
1¼ miles (2km) north of
Montguyon.

By far the larger of the two capstones
at this complicated and interesting
site.

This fine, long-galleried grave (also known as Dolmen les Maines) was first excavated as long ago as 1850 by C. Duteil. The passage is over 30ft (9.1m) long and its axis lies exactly east-west, with its entrance at the east. The gallery is typical of its type, consisting of parallel orthostats with one small and one very large 35 ton capstone. The latter rests on a cross slab to the west, after which there is a shorter passage. Off this to the north there is a side chamber, and there may possibly have been three more chambers, all lying on the axis or to the north. Challenge: find the horse carving on an orthostat exterior! Finds here include human bones, and the usual axes, flint blades, arrowheads, a dagger, and decorated Beaker and Chassey ware, as well as undecorated pottery sherds. This site should not be confused with La Pierre-Folle, Thiré, Vendée.

LA PIERRE-LEVÉE

II.26

Nieul-sur-L'Autise,
Vendée

CHAMBER TOMB

94 A 2

Leave Niort north-westwards
on the N148. After nearly 12
miles (19km), turn right on to
the D104 to the village of
Nieul-sur-Autise.

Among the finds here were three gold leaves folded spirally, a copper knife, an incised bone and early beakers.

Beneath one large capstone there was a single chamber here, once clearly divided into compartments although only eight of many stones remain. The entrance faces south-east and is cut into a long trapezoidal mound extending to the north-west. Here is another example of the mysterious long wedge of empty earth (see WEST KENNET LONG BARROW, Wiltshire, England). During the 1972/73 excavations, many pottery sherds and flints were found, and the indications are that the tomb was in use, for successive burials, for 1000 years or more.

Avrillé, Vendée, makes an admirable centre for touring the many tombs and menhirs around the town. This Pierre-Levée is not to be confused with others such as those at Saint-

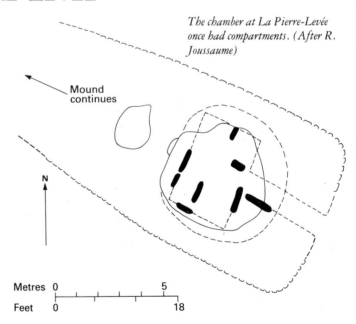

The chamber at La Pierre-Levée
once had compartments. (After R.
Joussaume)

Mound
continues

N

Metres 0   5
Feet 0   18

Georges-La-Pouge, Creuse, at Saint-Jory-de-Chalais, Dordogne, at Brétignolles, Deux-Sèvres, at Jugon, Côtes-d'Armor, or at Poitiers, Vienne (first described by Rabelais).

Near this site and worth a visit is the impressive Neolithic fortified, triple-ditched camp of Champ-Durand, one of several of its type in central-western France.

LES PIERRES PLATES

*Locmariaquer,
Morbihan*

ALLÉE-COUDÉE,
MENHIR AND
CARVINGS

62 B 2

*Looking north-west along the
passage, in which 13 of the upright
slabs are carved.*

Revolver-shaped in plan, this classic *allée-coudée* (dated at about 3200 BC) contains some fascinating features. Like GAVR'INIS, it is artistically important.

The grave entrance faces south and, past a 'sentry', a cupmarked menhir. The 'handle' of the gun is the 19ft 9in (6m) low passage; it then turns to the north-west, and on the inside bend there is an open chamber, the 'trigger guard'. The ever-widening passage (covered in flat slabs, thus its name) continues for a further 49ft (15m), and ends with a small chamber. Other Morbihan graves constructed on a similar plan include Goërem, LUFFANG and Rocher au Bouc.

Down the passage and in the side chamber are 13 uprights with carved decorations. Shield/idols, most showing vertical lines, abound here and, with their somewhat practical designs, are not dissimilar to those at LUFFANG, in the immediate area. The place is like a deserted teaching hospital; the reception area is in on the left, and prehistoric medical illustrations have been left on the walls – ribs, hearts, lungs, livers, stomachs, below collar bones and neck recesses, with spinal cords, channels of life.

*Leave Locmariaquer on the
western road south to the coast,
heading first for Kerlud, and
then left for Kerhéré. At the
coastal junction turn right,
and park just along the cul-
de-sac lane by the sea-shore.
Take a torch. Beware: the
English language green
Michelin Tourist Guide
(otherwise admirable) indexes
this site as Flat Stones.*

LA ROCHE AUX FÉES

*The grandest of the French tombs
incorporating Fées (fairies) in their
names. The entrance, with its huge
lintel stone, is on the right.*

*Take the D178 north from
Châteaubriant, turn north-
west on to the D94. In Retiers
(from which the site is clearly
signposted) turn left, on to the
D41, and then right in ½
mile (1km) on to the D341
towards Essé. The tomb is just
beyond the village on the
right. There is a well-stocked
shop and large car park at the
site.*

This is one of the finest tombs in the whole of France – if it ever was one, because there have been no finds here! Its statistics are as mighty as its external form. The building is 64ft (19.5m) long, 19ft 6in (6m) wide, with an internal ceiling height of 7ft (2.1m).

The entrance lintel stone is set lower (as in contemporary Japanese restaurants, one has to bow), weighs a tremendous 25 tons, is perfectly horizontal and its outfacing side is sheer and immaculately dressed. Nine capstones (one very small) provide the roof, and the walls are made up of 42 stones, of which six weigh up to 45 tons.

In 3300 BC, the construction was covered in earth. Local stone was not used; the purple palaeozoic schist came from over 2½m (4km) away and, according to legend, was carried to the site by fairies (*fées*). Consequently, it was endowed with special powers which is why couples wanting to marry come here on nights of a new moon; the man counts the stones walking in a clockwise direction, while his prospective bride counts anticlockwise. If their totals differ by more than two, then they have no future together.

LA TABLE-DES-MARCHANDS

*Locmariaquer,
Morbihan*

PASSAGE GRAVE WITH
CARVINGS

62 B 2

*Take the D28 south from
Auray; at Crach turn south-
west on to the D781. Before
entering Locmariaquer, turn
right for Keriaval. The grave
is about 150yds (137m) on
the right, near the fallen
GRAND MENHIR BRISÉ. Take
a torch.*

The headstone, with crook carvings.

This grave was first excavated in 1811, when the mound was removed from the chamber, and many times thereafter. Art, in the form of some remarkable carvings, was the reason.

The small entrance faces south-east; the 23ft (7m) passage within leads to a veritable 'living' museum of prehistoric rock art. A large capstone, which weighs about 40 tons and measures 21ft 3in by 13ft (6.5m by 4m) covers an 8ft 3in (2.5m) high chamber; the floor area is 11ft 6in by 10ft (3.5m by 3m). The sandstone backstone (unique to the site and easy to work) is justly famous for its anthropomorphic and other carvings; and there are further examples on the stone's back.

The chamber capstone comes from another local menhir (*see* GAVR'INIS, which used another part of it while a further fragment contributed to Er-Vinglé not far away). The headstone here is covered in crooks, like walking sticks, carved in four rows either side of a space down the middle. There are also carvings on the back of the headstone. This site is currently being excavated.

Leave Dinan north-east on the N176; turn right southwards on the N137, and then first left on the D9 to Tressé. Continue through the village into the Forêt-du-Mesnil. A little way along park at the picnic space on the left at the signpost, and walk northwards into the forest, over a small wooden bridge, for about 275yds (300m).

*Tressé,
Dinan,
Ille-et-Vilaine*

ALLÉE-COUVERTE

48 B 1

The elegant restored allée-couverte in the Forêt-du-Mesnil.

The often-quoted alternative name for this fascinating grave is 'La Maison-des-Feins', but an ancient 's' has been wrongly transcribed as 'f', so that *Feins* should read *Seins*, meaning 'breasts', four pairs of which were carved here.

The site was excavated in 1931 by a Scottish woman, the archaeologist V.C.C. Collum, at the behest of Sir Robert Mond (a co-founder of ICI) for his friend Baron Robert Surcouf of St Malo, the owner of Le Forêt-du-Mesnil. She was an expert on sculptured stones as symbols of the Earth Mother Goddess.

The grave entrance is at the south-south-east. There were nine pairs of parallel uprights leading north-west, with eight capstones, of which seven remain, in the chamber, which measures 35ft 9in by 4ft 6in (10.9m by 1.4m). The roofless end cell at the north-north-west is now open, but was perhaps once closed, because an 1883 engraving shows a large supine transversal stone lying in the appropriate position. A skeleton was found in the main chamber, as well as more than 60 pots, beads and Grand Pressigny flint daggers.

The four pairs of breasts make this site very interesting. The first two pairs are on the outside of the gallery's end slab, but were damaged by vandals in about 1961. Within one oval cartouche, there was carved in relief a small pair, perhaps of a young girl, measuring 3½ins (8cm) in diameter. To the right and slightly higher is a fuller pair, those of a mother. Exactly the same pairing and small differences are to be found on the inside of the upright to the west of the end-stone.

Similar sets of carvings can be seen at Kergüntuil and Prajou-Menhir (both Côtes-d'Armor).

TUMULUS DE MONTIOU

*Ste Soline,
Couhé,
Deux-Sèvres*

CAIRN WITH MULTIPLE
PASSAGE-GRAVES

95 D 3

This well-restored site was probably fairly complete before its partial destruction, at the north-west end, in about 1920 for its stone. Two graves and the entrance to a third remain; there were perhaps five originally. Broken pottery has been found in the passages and in the southernmost chamber. Both of them contained complete and disarticulated skeletons.

Excavations started in 1975. The original rectangular cairn was orientated north-west/south-east, and was 164ft (50m) long and 79ft (24m) wide. The passage of the southernmost grave is 36ft (11m) long, with five pairs of opposing uprights, each separated by drystone walling, and roofed with contiguous stone slabs, 4ft 3in (1.3m) above the partly paved floor. Its chamber is polygonal and lined with smooth rectangular contiguous slabs up to 7ft 3in (2.2m) high. The obviously huge capstone has disappeared. It has a notable carved 'dog kennel' entrance, and the site is well-known for the anthropoid shape of the first upright in the chamber on the right. The neighbouring chamber is almost square in shape, and, as in the first, and so often, it is higher than its passage. The capstone of this chamber has also gone.

Leave Poitiers southwards on the N10; after 22 miles (36km), at Couhé, turn off on to the D14 to Rom. Then take the signposted minor road south-west through Vérrines to Ste Soline. Now take the D55 road to Vanzay eastwards. After 1 mile (1.6km) the cairn will be visible on the left of the road.

TUMULUS ST. MICHEL

Carnac-Ville,
Morbihan

CARNAC MOUND

62 B 2

This is one of the great monuments of Brittany, but perhaps not the most popular, being closed for six months of the year and also unavailable for solo visits. The enormous mound consists of at least 26,000 cu yds (20,000 cu m) of stone, clay, earth and rubble and has been dated at around 3500 BC. The original mound was 410ft (125m) long, 197ft (60m) wide, and (before the chapel was constructed), 33ft (10m) high.

Its Christianization took the spectacular form of a chapel built right on its top (*see* LA HOUGUE BIE, Jersey), together with a calvary; from earliest Christian times chapels on high places were dedicated to St. Michael, hence its name. The two long galleries are modern. At the centre of the passageless mound was a cairn, with two central large cists surrounded by 18 to 20 smaller ones.

The viewing table on top of the tumulus (courtesy the Touring Club de France) offers a magnificent overview of this unique megalithic landscape.

Travel east from Carnac-Ville on the D781. Pass over the first crossroads, and take the next road on the left. Car parking. Guided tours only. Closed October to March (inclusive).

One of the chambers inside the mound.

A Christian chapel sits on top of the prehistoric mound, and provides the second part of the site's name.

VILLENEUVE-TOLOSANE

*Villeneuve-Tolosane,
Toulouse,
Hâute Garonne*

NEOLITHIC CAMP

152 C 3

*The 74 acre (30 hectares) Neolithic
camp at Villeneuve-Tolosane
was partly excavated in 1978.
Almost circular pit hearths are
clustered to the south-east; the strips
are cobbled. (After Clottes, Giraud,
Rouzaud and Vaquer)*

*The camp is situated in what
has become a suburb of
Toulouse, immediately west of
the A6 autoroute (which must
be avoided). Leave the city on
the modest D15, going south-
westwards. At the turning for
Cugnaux, after 6 miles
(10km), turn left on to the
D24, and the site is on the
left.*

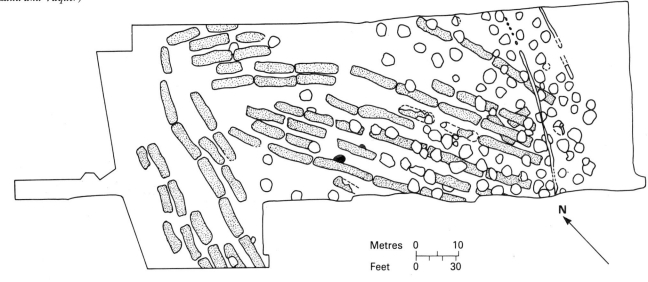

Metres 0 — 10
Feet 0 — 30
N

This is *not* a megalithic site, but it is of the greatest interest to archaeologists because it provides fascinating insights into how Neolithic man lived when he was not foodgathering or putting up megaliths. It was used more or less continuously between about 4000 BC and 2500 BC, and has yielded plentiful evidence of an amazing degree of order and discipline in the daily lives of the prehistoric people who used the area.

This Chasséen site is on a promontory in the middle valley of the River Garonne and it covers no less than 74 acres (30 hectares), making it one of the biggest Neolithic camps ever uncovered.

The camp (the nomenclature is perhaps questionable) at Villeneuve-Tolosane was first explored in 1962, and then more thoroughly in 1978 by Clottes, Giraud, Rouzand and Vaquer. These four distinguished French archaeologists agreed to differ in certain details about the uses to which the site was put through the centuries, but they found, or reconfirmed, more than 700 shallow hearths of basically two kinds.

The first are what one might call broken strips, or rough rectangles, which are up to 6ft 3in (1.9m) wide and up to 36ft (11.0m) in length. The second shape is broadly circular, with an average diameter of about 8ft 3in (2.5m); the latter are mostly congregated in the south-east of the sub-rectangular site; each is a shallow pit, containing charcoal and above it burnt pebbles.

These pits are placed far apart, up to 330ft (100m) from

each other, which gives the appearance of a hut site. However, no holes for wooden support posts have been found, nor any obvious signs of human habitation. Clearly, the site was not a crematorium, as no bones have been found in these pit-hearths; moreover, burials have been located in the ditches placed in a defensive position on the promontory.

The area was most probably a giant field kitchen, a central feeding station, a food support system for a working community, which spent some of its days and all of its night elsewhere. It could literally have been a take-away or a food delivery service for scattered tribal communities. It was evidently a tidy operation; many storage and refuse pits have been discovered by the excavators. Indeed, one contained an astonishing 50,000 snail shells: some French eating habits go back a long way! A well, some 24ft 6in (7.5m) deep and 5ft (1.5m) across, has been found some distance from the centre of the site; in it were cast the usual detritus of a prehistoric kitchen — bone and stone tools for food preparation, broken pots, animal bones, and also many thousands of cereal grains, most of which were wheat.

Such orderliness reminds archaeologists of their constant backdating of Neolithic achievements, but the puzzles remain. Why is it that the circular pits at Villeneuve-Tolosane, unlike the rectangular ones, appear to have been used for only one fire? And why was this extraordinary site suddenly and completely abandoned in about 2500 BC?

III

Northern Europe

Northern Europe is here taken to encompass Belgium, Denmark, Germany, The Netherlands and Sweden. It has been necessary to omit, for reasons of space, Norway and Finland and even Poland, whose Kujavian (triangular) barrows are full of relevance to European archaeological contexts.

The First Danubian culture, beginning in about 5300 BC, brought to the centre and west of Europe, but not to France or Britain, early Neolithic farming practices. Animals were domesticated and crops cultivated, settlements became permanent (though still with strictly seasonal agriculture), the trade and barter of flint, pottery and produce grew, newly localized populations increased, social orders became established, and tribal ritual and practices took root. The need for funeral ceremonies evidently grew generally within a thousand years or so, and the stone buildings that evolved for them, sometimes indigenously, also became recognized as territorial markers. In Denmark, for example, the broad timescale was that agriculture appeared in about 4200 BC, and the first megalithic monuments some 600 years later.

In about 2800 BC a second wave of Neolithic immigrants (following the Late Danubian culture, of about 3400–3000 BC) reached the Low Countries, and then, it is supposed, most of north-west Europe, from the east of central Europe. Whilst their Funnel Beaker (TRB) culture spread widely, that of the closely related Michelsberg people was more narrowly confined to central Germany and the great river valleys of the Rhine, Necker and Main; in the south it reached eastern Switzerland and the Upper Rhine.

Belgium

To the west the Michelsberg people apparently stopped short of what were to become the borders of The Netherlands by just a few miles. In Belgium they left a habitation site at Watermael-Boitsfort, in today's south-east suburbs of Brussels, just north of the Forêt des Siognes; interestingly it was never a cemetery or a fortified camp. The odd fact is that Belgium has only a handful of megalithic monuments, and they are grouped together in the province of Luxembourg; they derive from the Seine-Oise-Marne culture (c. 3400–1800 BC). The WÉRIS GROUP, on its unusual alignment, is described here.

Denmark

The statistics of Danish archaeology are astonishing. In a country of 16,614 sq miles (43,031 sq km) there are nearly 24,000 listed and protected prehistoric monuments. The total

still existing, regardless of condition, is thought to be nearer 85,000, and about 150,000 sites have been identified. The great survey of 1956 produced 2067 cists, dolmens (of which about 1800 remain out of 5000 recorded) and passage-graves — and no less than 19,902 round mounds, from the Stone Age through to the Iron Age, and other sundry monuments, like standing stones and stone ships.

It is therefore hardly surprising that Denmark produced one of northern Europe's first great archaeologists, Ole Worm, whose major book 'Danicorum Monumentorum Libri Sex' was published in 1643. Another prominent archaeologist, Christian Thomsen (1788–1865) divided later prehistory into the Stone, Bronze and Iron Ages (The Three Age System, which has subsequently been refined). 'Danmarks Oldtid', a book published in 1843 by one of Thomsen's former students, Jens J.A. Worsaae (1821–85), was the first to use the words diffusion and typology; he is regarded as the father of the science of prehistoric archaeology.

It is thought that the first farmers arrived in Denmark in about 4200 BC, succeeding the Ertebølle kitchen midden culture (first identified by Worsaae). Their dolmenic chambers (*dysse* in Danish) so frequently seen, were once covered by earth mounds. These have mostly gone, leaving their familiar circular revetment of boulders to delineate the boundaries of the tomb area.

In about 3500 BC the great passage-graves began to appear, accompanied by the beautiful pottery of the Funnel Beaker (TRB) people. These graves had oval or rectangular chambers, with passages leading off at right angles. Again, they were covered by earthen mounds. Later there developed, particularly in the Jutland area, long dolmens (*langdysse*) for multiple burials. In the Late Neolithic period, large and small cists were in use, for both single and multiple inhumations, while the construction of the dolmens and passage-graves ceased. The Bronze Age, beginning in about 2000 BC, saw the creation of thousands of burial mounds, enclosing single coffins and then urns, always in prominent locations (see MOLS GROUP, East Jutland).

Germany

The megalithic legacies of the Funnel Beaker people (in German *Trichterbecher*, commonly abbreviated to TRB), carriers of the earliest Neolithic culture, are widespread in northern Europe from about 3800 BC. A particularly handsome and famous example of the succeeding passage-grave builders is VISBEKER BRAUT, Oldenburg, south-west of

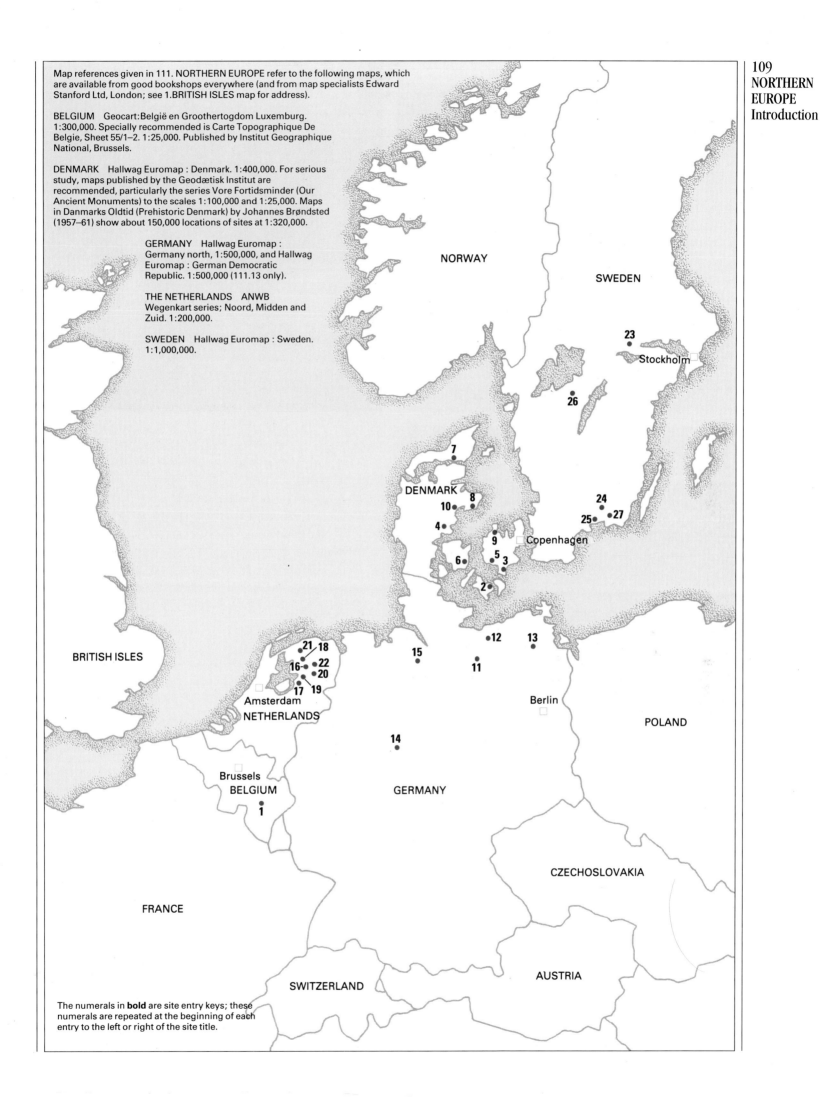

Map references given in 111. NORTHERN EUROPE refer to the following maps, which are available from good bookshops everywhere (and from map specialists Edward Stanford Ltd, London; see 1.BRITISH ISLES map for address).

BELGIUM   Geocart:België en Groothertogdom Luxemburg. 1:300,000. Specially recommended is Carte Topographique De Belgie, Sheet 55/1–2. 1:25,000. Published by Institut Geographique National, Brussels.

DENMARK   Hallwag Euromap : Denmark. 1:400,000. For serious study, maps published by the Geodætisk Institut are recommended, particularly the series Vore Fortidsminder (Our Ancient Monuments) to the scales 1:100,000 and 1:25,000. Maps in Danmarks Oldtid (Prehistoric Denmark) by Johannes Brøndsted (1957–61) show about 150,000 locations of sites at 1:320,000.

GERMANY   Hallwag Euromap : Germany north, 1:500,000, and Hallwag Euromap : German Democratic Republic. 1:500,000 (111.13 only).

THE NETHERLANDS   ANWB Wegenkart series; Noord, Midden and Zuid. 1:200,000.

SWEDEN   Hallwag Euromap : Sweden. 1:1,000,000.

NORWAY

SWEDEN

Stockholm

DENMARK

Copenhagen

BRITISH ISLES

Amsterdam
NETHERLANDS

Berlin

POLAND

Brussels
BELGIUM

GERMANY

CZECHOSLOVAKIA

FRANCE

SWITZERLAND

AUSTRIA

The numerals in **bold** are site entry keys; these numerals are repeated at the beginning of each entry to the left or right of the site title.

ABOVE LEFT: *The restored* ganggraf HAVELTE WEST, *Drenthe, in The Netherlands. It has been dated at about 2750 BC.*

LEFT: *A deplorable though amusing defacement of a standing stone at Süntelstein, near Osnabruck, Germany.*

ABOVE: *The much visited Dutch* hunebed PAPELOZE KERK *('Priestless Church').*

RIGHT: *The massive front capstone of* DE STEENBARG. *This is the only* hunebed *in the Dutch province of Groningen.*

Bremen. It was originally kerbed by no less than 105 upright carefully selected natural boulders, which were graded in size along the grave's axis, from north-east to south-west. This Bride of Visbek has an even longer Groom 2½ miles (4km) away. This truly enormous *hünengrab* measures 354ft by 33ft (108m by 10m), and is testimony to the abilities of that remarkable culture.

A *steinkist* (stone burial chamber) in Germany (treated as united in this book) often has distinct similarities with the SOM culture's *allée-couverte*. LOHNE-ZÜSCHEN, Hesse, is, in the typical manner, sunk in a trench so that the tops of its 24 uprights show above ground level, along its north-east/south-west alignment. Its entrance vestibule is separated from the main gallery chamber by another typical feature, a port-hole slab (*seelenloch*). Another form of German passage grave is the *einteilige galeriegräber*, a long rectangular megalithic chamber sunk in a trench, with access through the top, via a wooden covering or opened stone slab. There is a surprisingly large number of standing stones in Germany; a concentration of them is within a broad circle drawn through Luxembourg,

Bonn, Koblenz, Frankfurt-a-M, Mannheim, Karlsruhe and Saarbrücken.

The Netherlands

The Funnel Beaker (TRB) people spread all over The Netherlands and flourished during about 4000–2800 BC. Their predominant megalithic bequest is however confined to the north-eastern province of Drenthe and, in fact, only three monuments are known to have been outside it. The reason is simple. Glacial moraines are plentiful down through Drenthe; big round erratic boulders were everywhere. A brief account of the unique and remarkable Dutch megalithic chamber tombs, which are called *hunebedden* (Hun's Beds), and their different types and characteristics are given below under NOORDLO and elsewhere in this part.

A drive southwards from Groningen to Emmen on the N92 provides an excellent introduction to Dutch archaeology. The *hunebedden* mostly date from about 3300–2800 BC (a date for HAVELTE WEST, for instance). This produces a puzzle, because the earliest of them predate the oldest Danish passage graves to

the north; SCHIMMERES has been placed early in the fourth millennium. Another odd fact is that there is not a single French-type dolmen in all The Netherlands, *Hunebedden* were constructed for collective burials, although single burials did occur. Because their total number is so small (only 53 still exist today, out of 76 recorded), and through the exhaustive efforts of Professor Albert E. van Giffen from the beginning of this century for some 40 years, all of the tombs have been carefully accounted for. and most excavated. Generally the grave goods were the usual flint flakes, broken tools and pottery sherds (with very simple decoration). After the Beaker period, megalithic construction all but ceased – although, strangely, this was certainly not the case in northern France and Britain, where great monuments were going up.

Sweden

The Slate Culture, named after some of its tools, arrived in northern Sweden in about 4000 BC, probably from the far east. About 1500 of their sites have so far been identified in Norrland, where rock carvings and cave paintings also occur,

in very inaccessible locations. One amazing site, and not remote, is at Nämforsen, Ådals-Liden, Ångermanland; here there are some 1500 naturalistic stone carvings all around the river bank, rapids and islets.

The Funnel Beaker people probably arrived in Sweden in about 3350 BC; traces of their early farming practices have been found on the west coast and in Västgotland. The first megalithic structures were simple four-sided dolmens – in Swedish *dosar* (singular *dos*). This is the first of the three classes of Swedish tomb pronounced by the famous Oscar Montelius (1843–1921) in 1898; the other two were *grafvar med gang* (or *gänggrift*) and *hallkistor*.

In the Middle Neolithic period, passage-graves (almost always with collective burials) were being built, and often in clusters. Some 234 of the country's 330 or so occur on the high plain of Falbygden, in the east of Västgotland. Others are found, in descending order of numbers, in Skåne, Bohuslän, Halland and Oland. In these, and the other 4500 or so megalithic tombs in Sweden, very few grave goods have been found, apart from broken votive pottery at their entrances.

—— **BELGIUM** ——

WÉRIS GROUP

*Wéris,
Erezée and Oppagne,
Marche-en-Famenne,
Luxembourg*

ALLÉE-COUVERTE,
GALLERY GRAVE AND
STANDING STONES

20 I·

Belgium occupies 11,778 sq m (30,513 sq km) of Europe but only three megalithic tombs are known to exist today in the whole country (compared with 2067 in Denmark out of a total of 23,774 known prehistoric monuments). Two more are known to have existed, and for some strange reason, they are all in the neighbouring provinces of Namur and Luxembourg. This group in the Ardennes has been thoroughly explored and written about by Sigfried J. De Laet; he has also drawn attention to two unexplored long mounds in Brabant. The Wéris group of graves share the Seine-Oise-Marne (SOM)

Leave Liege southwards on the A26 autobahn. Take Exit 49, then take the N651 westwards, and continue to Erezée on the N807. Beyond the village take the minor road north to Wéris.

Two of the stones at Bouchaimont.

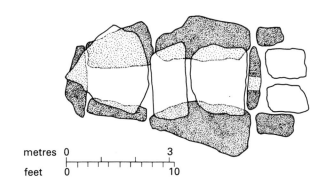

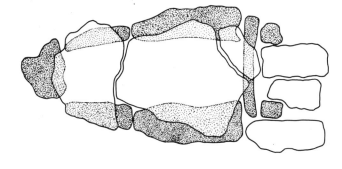

Two graves in the Wéris Group, Dolmen d'Oppagne (left), a sunken allée-couverte *was discovered in 1888 and restored in 1906. Dolmen de Wéris (right), an above ground gallery grave, was discovered in the same year. (After De Laet).*

metres 0   3

feet 0   10

culture (2400–1600 BC), and are connected with the *allées-couvertes* of the Paris basin through the West German *einteilige galeriegräber* (sunken gallery graves without compartments).

In the same area a group of three menhirs and a single one also occur – and the remarkable fact is that the tombs and menhirs, all made from the same local puddingstone, are placed in a straight line. The 5000–4500-year-old Wéris alignment commences at Tour, Heyd, north of Wéris, where a standing stone is known to have existed (and to have been broken up about 100 years ago); the total length of the alignment, which extends south-west from this point, is about 3 miles (5 km).

The next monument is the Dolmen de Wéris (known as Le Grand Dolmen). This above-ground gallery-grave was restored in 1906, with virtually no finds. Now fenced off and among trees, it was once covered by an earthen mound and measured 36ft (11m); its internal chamber length is 18ft (5.5m), and its width is 5ft 6in (1.7m). The larger of its two capstones is badly cracked; there may have been a third, consisting of the three present substantial paving slabs at the entrance. The chamber is walled with two pairs of uprights and an endstone, and in separated from its antechamber by a slab which has a doorway hole carved out of it.

Next in the alignment is an unnamed, 10ft (3m) tall standing stone, which was found buried in a field and clumsily re-erected beside the road in 1947. The rather ugly, lower part of the stone which was once below ground is now visible.

Approximately 1 mile (1.6km) away from the Dolmen de Wéris, among trees, lies the Dolmen d'Oppagne (known as Le Petit Dolmen). This one is an *allée-couverte* of the SOM type, in a trench, so that only the three capstones are above ground level. It was discovered in 1888, and excavated in the same year by A. Charneux; all his finds have now sadly vanished, but reportedly included human and animal bones. This dolmen was restored in 1906, a great year of activity in Belgian archaeology, following these monuments' acquisition by the nation. The internal chamber length is 15ft (4.6m), the width 4ft (1.2m) and internal height 2ft (0.6m). It has two pairs of uprights and an endstone, with the interstices being filled with drystone walling. There is an antechamber, of which two uprights survive. Again, the two paving slabs might have formed part of a fourth capstone over it. As at the Dolmen de Wéris, a septal slab, this time with a large port-hole, separates the chambers.

At the end of the line, about 650 yds (600m) away, at

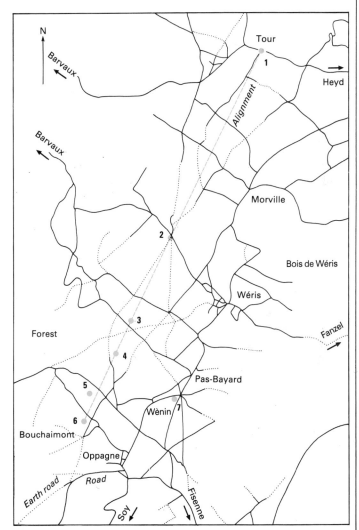

The Wéris group of megalithic sites. 1 *Standing stone, destroyed about 100 years ago.* 2 *Dolmen de Wéris (Le Grand Dolmen); gallery grave.* 3 *Standing stone, beside road.* 4 *Dolmen d'Oppagne (Le Grand* Dolmen d'Oppagne (Le Petit *Standing stone; just west of alignment.* 6 *Bouchaimont group of three standing stones (not shown in IGN map no. 55/1-2; 1:25,000).* 7 *Puddingstone fragment.*

Bouchaimont near Oppagne, is a tight group of three standing stones; they are visible from the road. The tallest of these Belgian stones, beneath the tree, stands about 8ft (2.4m) above the ground. They too were found buried, and erected again in 1906.

Although not in the Wéris alignment and some distance

away, remains of a third megalithic burial chamber were identified in 1976, near Jemelle, Namur; two now-destroyed graves were also located: Bois des Lusce, a gallery grave at Jemeppe-Hargimont, Luxembourg; and La Pierre du Diable (The Devil's Stone) at Velaine-sur-Sambre, Jambes, Namur. At the latter site there is also a standing stone called La Pierre Qui Tourne which, according to local legend, spins three times during nights of the new moon. There is another Pierre Qui Tourne at Baileux, and two more standing stones complete the list of Belgian megaliths; Pierre Brunehaut (between Bléharies and Hollain) and Zeupîre (at Gozée).

A visit to the Wéris area could be completed with an inspection of the large piece of puddingstone which lies beside a street in the hamlet of Pas Bayard, just south-west of Wéris. It has the approximate shape of a capstone, thus presenting another megalithic mystery.

The Bouchaimont group of standing stones, at the south-western end of the alignment of the main Belgian megalithic sites.

III.2

DENMARK

115
NORTHERN
EUROPE
Denmark

Frejlev Skov Group

Nysted,
Lolland

Neolithic Burial
Complex

J 9

Leave Nykøbing west, take the
first left and then the minor
road south, just before
Kettinge, to Nysted.
One of the four round dolmens, with
a passage-grave capstone behind.

Denmark has more prehistoric monuments than any other country in the world. The smallest village has 'something', whether part of a standing stone, the remnants of a barrow or a complete long dolmen; pride in the preservation of monuments is shared with visitors, with the well-stocked museums, guide books and signposting.

This forest site on the island of Lolland possibly offers a greater variety of so-called monuments than any other in this

book. The area faces Guldborge Sund, and is roughly 2½m (4km) long and 1m (1.5km) wide. Among the trees are four round dolmens, five passage-graves (dated at about 3000 BC), nine long dolmens, more than 100 Bronze Age barrows (most of them fairly small), and a somewhat spoiled stone circle with a tall monolith beside it. The greatest concentration of monuments is the middle section of this huge site, among fields and either side of a lane, which is good for parking.

Grøn Jaegers Høj

This long dolmen is 335ft (102m) in length.

Fanefjord,
Stege,
Møn

Long Dolmen
(langdysse)

K 8

The dolmen is about 8m
(13km) south-west of Stege,
and ⅓ mile (0.5km) south of
the church at Fanefjord. Car
park beside a farm barn.

The name of this delightful Neolithic dolmen on the west of Møn island, translates as 'the Green Huntsman's Mound', and it reflects its still sylvan setting. It is one of Denmark's finest long dolmens (*langdysser*), and the second longest. The rectangular mound measures 335ft by 33ft (102m by 10m). It is bounded by no less than 134 huge kerbstones up to 6ft (1.8m) tall, with drystone walling between them. It lies on an east-west axis, and beyond the western end three large stones are set, for some unknown purpose (unless as a triumvirate guard representation). Inside the mound there are three burial chambers; today only the westernmost retains its capstone.

Long dolmens, mounds, tumuli or barrows, containing megalithic chamber tombs, either in a primary or secondary

context, are found all over Northern Europe (*see*, for example, WEST KENNET LONG BARROW, Wiltshire, England, and LISCUIS, Côtes-d'Armor, France). Not a single long mound has ever been found on the Iberian peninsula.

Nearer Denmark, famous similar tombs are VISBEKER BRAUT, Visbeck, Bremen, Germany, and SCHIMMERES, Emmen, Netherlands. In the north-east of England, there are nearly 40 trapezoidal-shaped long barrows. The same shape of long mound is found in Denmark with chambers; Bygholm Nørremark, Jutland, for instance, which is dated at about 4000 BC, is 197ft (60m) long, and only much later acquired a megalithic burial chamber inside an extension. However, most Danish long dolmens are rectangular.

GRØNHØJ

Bygholm Park,
Horsens,
Jutland

PASSAGE-GRAVE

E 6

The grave is situated in a
hedged enclosure about 330ft
(100m) south of Lake
Bygholm, in Bygholm Park,
just west of Horsens (finds are
in the Museum there).

The well-worn entrance to the 'green
mound'.

Grønhøj means 'green mound', and this is a large one: 10ft (3m) high and 82ft (25m) in diameter. Its revetment has 60 kerbstones, mostly about 3ft 3in (1m) high, with drystone walling between them. The passage to the chamber is a very narrow 3ft (0.9m) and 13ft (4m) long. The chamber at its end measures 11ft 6in by 8ft 9in (3.5m by 2.7m) and is formed by seven uprights and two capstones.

Grønhøj was excavated in 1940 by Knud Thorvildsen, and subsequently repaired. Two levels of burial were found. In and around the grave Thorvildsen discovered 7,000 Middle Neolithic sherds of pottery in a 1ft (0.3m) deep pile, and also 20 complete vessels, dated at about 3000 BC. These pots had been carefully placed upside down, together with some serving ladles, outside the grave entrance. There was evidence that they had originally been positioned in rows on top of the forecourt uprights, or just behind them.

GUNDERSLEVHOLM

Gunderslevholm,
Zealand

LONG DOLMEN
(LANGDYSSE)

J7

Leave Naestved northwards on
road 14; fork left soon on to
the 239, and left again at
Skelby to the site.

One of about 1200 long dolmens in
Denmark.

About 2000 long dolmens or mounds have been recorded in Denmark, the country where methodical cataloguing of megalithic remains began earlier than in any other country in the world. About 1200 remain to be seen today. Round dolmens (*runddysse*) (see MOLS GROUP, East Jutland) invariably have a single burial at their centre, whereas long dolmens may have up to five in their extended rectangular confines.

Here, 61 kerbstones have survived, packed with drystone walling, as is almost always the case. The stones were probably local erratics, carefully selected for rounded shapes. The largest of them, as usual, are at one end only. There was probably a vestibule at the opposite end. Inside the grave there are three chambers, two side by side, and each of a size to accommodate one adult flexed burial.

Similar long dolmens are sometimes found in pairs, such as the remarkable group at Blommeskobbel, Mommark, on the island of Als in the south of the country, and at Steneng, Bredebro, Tønder. A pair of long dolmens actually joined down a long side can be seen in the woods on the coastline at Oleskoppel, near Blommeskobbel, on Als.

LINDESKOV

*Lindeskov,
Ørbaek,
Funen*

LONG DOLMEN
(LANGDYSSE)

G 7

*On the Ørbaek to Ringe road,
1¼ miles (2km) west of
Ørbaek. North of the small
village of Lindeskov a minor
road leads off to the north,
over a railway, to the site.*

Denmark's longest dolmen.

The island of Funen is often called the Garden of Denmark. Its city of Odense is the country's third largest and attracts tourists as the birthplace of Hans Christian Andersen.

Funen is also host to Denmark's longest Neolithic dolmen. It is 551ft (168m) long, and is kerbed with 126 boulders. At the north end there is a small roofless chamber, and there is speculation that more may lie within the huge length of raised earth. Perhaps this is because at nearby Ellested, north-west of Lindeskov on the main road south-east of Funen, there is another long dolmen, which, most unusually, contains five megalithic chambers, over four of which capstones survive as do many of the kerbstones.

Lindeskov Hestehave, about 655ft (200m) away, also has dolmens, but they are mostly in poor condition.

LINDHOLM HØJE

*Nørresundby,
Aalborg,
Vendsyssel,
Jutland*

CEMETERY WITH STONE
SHIPS AND MOUNDS

E 3

*A large site beside the
Limfjord on an undulating
hill overlooking farmland.
Leave Aalborg north on the
bridge over Limfjord. Take
the A17 north-west for 1¼
miles (2km), turn right into
Viaductrej, left at the traffic
signals and then right at the
next site signpost.*

*There are about 200 'stone ships'
here, among more than 700 tombs.*

This is the most impressive of Denmark's early historic sites, created in the early years of the Christian era, and therefore not megalithic in this book's sense. In about 1100 AD it was covered by sand, which accounts for its fine state of preservation (as at SKARA BRAE, Orkney Islands).

It is largely Viking (about 700–1100 AD), but, during excavations in 1952–59, parts of an associated earlier settlement were uncovered, including a square-shaped house and courtyard. There was also evidence of metal working. Lindholm is justly famed for the extraordinary sight of more than 700 stone-kerbed tombs, of which some 200 are shaped like ships in plan, recalling the ancient concept of death as the start of a journey.

The oldest burials date back to the 6th century AD, and they were almost all cremation burials, marked by mounds. Further burials, over 300 years later, were inhumations and bounded by stones; they are in various shapes, such as triangles (the earliest), circles, ovals, pointed ovals and squares.

The ship-shaped burials came later in the Viking period. At the end of it about 30 more inhumation graves marked by mounds were grouped in the south-east of the site. The cremation graves also contained burnt burial goods such as glass beads, knives, personal ornaments, counters for playing games, and also animal bones – everything needed for a safe trip to the Great Beyond.

Finds are in Aalborg Museum.

MOLS GROUP

Knebel,
Mols,
Djursland,
Jutland

ROUND DOLMEN
(RUNDDYSSE)

F 5

The huge round dolmen near Knebel.

Take road 15 north-east out of Aarhus as far as Tastrap. The village of Knebel, overlooking Knebel Vig, is about 6 miles (9.6km) to the south-west.

Porskjaers Stenhus is a magnificent round dolmen (*runddysse*), which is often called 'Knebel', after the village of that name, just over ½m (1km) to the south-west. It is one of the largest of its class in Denmark among the 300 or so remaining; they represent the earliest type of passage-grave, with a passage as here of just two portal stones.

On top of a natural hillock, 23 huge roughly (and probably naturally) rounded boulders are set in a circle measuring 65ft 6in (20m) in diameter. Originally an earth mound covered two chamber tombs. The surviving one is positioned off-centre in the northern part of the round enclosure; its five uprights, 7ft (2.1m) high, are topped with an enormous capstone which is perfectly flat underneath.

By the road to Agri, 1¼m (2km) to the north of Porskjaers Stenhus there are three more burial chambers. The one with the polygonal chamber has nine Bronze Age cup marks on its capstone. In the vicinity there is another fine polygonal tomb with a large capstone; it is called Stenhuset (the Stone House) and lies to the north of the road between the villages of Strands and Torup. A cup-marked capstone is also to be found on the square chamber tomb just west of Torup.

To the north-west of Agri lie the Stabelhøje group of Bronze Age barrows, dramatically sited on two neighbouring chalky hilltops overlooking Kalø Cove. Shaped and close together, they are known (like all such pairs) as 'maiden mounds'.

The Julingshøje group of ten barrows is 1¼m (2km) north-east of Agri, and the three Trehøje are just to the south, by the road to Vistoft. These barrow sites are all worth visiting for the views from them alone.

TROLDSTUEN

Stenstrup,
Ods Hundred,
Nykøbing,
Zealand

DOUBLE PASSAGE-
GRAVE

J 6

Nykøbing is on the road 21 in the north Odsherred, overlooking Isefjord. The site is signposted.

Inside one of the 'Siamese twin' chambers.

These prehistoric Siamese twins (the Trolls' Chambers) were excavated as early as 1909, and are among the finest of the many passage-graves in Zealand. They are joined at the broadest ends of their chambers beneath their shared mound.

The northern grave has its entrance at the east, and the southern one at the south-east. The dimensions of each are the same. The separate passages are 23ft (7m) long, with massive uprights leaning slightly inwards and gradually increasing in height; as usual they are packed with drystone walling. They give on to very broad chambers, measuring 23ft by 6½ft (7m by 2m). Even the dimensions are shared.

Each chamber has four capstones, including a contiguous pair, which is why the chambers are most unusual; they come from the same boulder, which was split in two by fire and water, and the halves placed with their internal flat face downwards. All the capstones rest on a single course of flattish boulders running along the tops of the leaning uprights. The chambers look like vaults, which is what they are; remains of more than 100 skeletons were found here. Other finds here included Late Neolithic pots and flint daggers.

TUSTRUP GROUP

*Tustrup,
Aarhus,
North Djursland,
Jutland*

BURIAL CHAMBER,
ROUND DOLMEN
(RUNDDYSEE), PASSAGE-
GRAVE, AND 'TEMPLE'

F 4

*The burial chamber in the Tustrup
complex.*

This famous complex was discovered in 1954 by Poul Kjaerum, and excavated by him over the next three years. The site is broadly semi-circular, measuring about 164ft (50m) across. Within this area a burial chamber, a round dolmen (*runddysse*), and a passage-grave were identified, forming an isosceles triangle; north of its base lies a so-called temple.

The burial chamber is polygonal in shape, and now without a capstone (which may, however, be the large slab lying not far away). The remaining uprights lean inwards and are 6ft (1.8m) high. The round dolmen is a very hefty affair; its mound (if there was one) has gone, as has the capstone; what is left is a set of two concentric circles of rough and ready boulders. The outer ring was, of course, a revetment. The

Park at the sign Stendyssene (Stone Dolmens), which is on the southward road between Fjellerup and Vivild, nearly 1 mile (1½km) west of the village of Tustrup. A few minutes' walk on the footpath, down through a wooded valley and on to open heathery heath, leads to the site.

The round dolmen.

Burial chamber

Temple

Possible fallen
capstone

Round dolmen

N

Passage grave

*The Tustrup Group, in a broadly
semi-circular setting, about 164ft
(50m) across.*

interior five uprights forming the polygonal chamber lean inwards, and are some 6ft (1.8m) high, making the construction as a whole a squat one. A single stone stands just outside the outer ring.

The passage-grave (in Danish *jaettestue* meaning 'Giant's Tomb') is within a round, grass-covered, earth mound, today partly revetted around its passage entrance at the south-east. Part of the once covered passage lies open. The rectangular chamber opens out to left and right, giving dimensions of 32ft 9in (10m) by 6ft (1.8m). A second, much smaller rectangular chamber is joined by a deep stone passage to the other longer side of the first chamber. Votive pottery has been found, as is usual, around the entrance. Finds are now in the local Aarhus Moesgaard Museum.

The fourth structure in this wonderful place, to the east of the others, is variously described as a temple, sanctuary ossuary, mortuary house, and 'house of the dead' (or funeral parlour). It is roughly horse-shoe shaped, with a very wide gap at the north-east, the direction of the midsummer sunrise. It had a revetment of contiguous small blocks which stretched 16ft 6in (5m) along each side, and was about 2ft 6in (0.8m)

high, of which many are now missing. Against them, on the inside, is a line of piled stones up to 5ft (1.5m) thick, like an embankment, surrounding an area 18ft by 16ft (5.5m by 4.9m). A small shallow depression can be seen in the middle of the enclosed space. This was an oval pit of sand which could have been the location of an altar or shrine, or the penultimate resting-place of a great tribal chieftain before he was buried in one of the tombs. Around this spot Poul Kjaerum's excavations uncovered 28 attractive clay pots of different shapes and designs, together with eight spoons or ladles, of the Middle Neolithic period.

In the middle of the open end there is a block of stone, which might have been the support, originally 5ft 3in (1.6m) high, for a wooden roof, which was destroyed by fire, probably deliberately, after one great funerary ceremony. It is unlikely that cremations were involved, as the place is too early for this practice (as the charred timbers have proved).

What is so interesting is that here was a wooden-roofed building in use at the same early date of about 3200 BC as the nearby megalithic burial tombs. Other such compounds have been found more recently at Ferslev, Herrup and Foulum.

The remarkable 'temple' at Tustrup.

The passage-grave.

--------- **GERMANY** ---------

EVERSTORFER FORST GROUP

*Barendorf,
Kr. Grevesmühlen,
Schwerin,
Mecklenburg*

TOMB COMPLEX

M 3

One of the ten urdolmen *in the forest.*

Leave Lübeck eastwards on the 105. Grevesmühlen is about 19 miles (30 km) along the road, near the forest.

This astonishing group of monuments is mainly located in the northern part of a beautiful forest in the far north of what was East Germany; it lies half-way between Lübeck and Rostock. There are ten *urdolmen* (simple burial chambers), three *erweiterte* dolmens (extended burial chambers), one *grossdolmen* (large burial chamber, rectangular or trapezoidal in plan), five *rechteckig* (rectangular) graves, two trapezoidal mound graves, one *ganggrab* (gallery grave), and one *steinkreis* (stone circle) – making a veritable megalithic academy! No dates have been calibrated for this site, but, for guidance, one can note that of 2216 ± 120 bc (c.2900BC) for the complicated ringed *erweiterter* dolmen, Serrahn, Kr. Güstrow, about 40m (64km) to the west.

As usual, none of the tombs is complete but, oddly, stones are generally missing from either one end or the other of the long compartmented graves. The burial chambers within the long rectangular or trapezoidal above-ground or entrenched earth mounds are rarely centrally placed and are now open in most cases; some of them are set on earth mounds as well, and, like KATELBOGEN, Kr. Bützow, situated upon a hillock.

One *erweiterte* dolmen near Naschendorf in Everstorfer Forst is especially impressive; 14 of the original 24 boulders set in a ring around it are still to be seen. Another strange fact about this site is that although it is quite compact, there is no consistency in the entrance directions at all. The peaceful sylvan setting for these stone chambers and arrangements, in their mostly excavated clearings, provides a memorable megalithic outing.

KATELBOGEN

*Kr. Bützow,
Güstrow,
Mecklenburg*

GANGGRAB IM HÜNENBETT (GALLERY TOMB IN MEGALITHIC GRAVE)

N 3

Leave Güstrow, northwestwards. Immediately after Bützow turn directly west; the site is soon on the left of the road, before the windmill on the left.

This splendid site is one of several monuments in what is known as the 'Mecklenburg Group'; it is on a hillock, isolated in ploughed farmland, with trees growing on and around it. Set amid the trees is a long domed mound containing an almost complete burial chamber. The rectangular mound has a north-east/south-west axis. Surrounding the rectangle of earth there were once 36 upright boulders, including five at each end; 22 remain today, of which all five at the north-east have gone. Inside, the rectangular burial chamber shares the same alignment. Its length is 26ft 3in (8m), width 7ft 6in (2.3m) and height 6ft (1.8m); its condition is very good.

Originally, above earth level there were five capstones across five pairs of opposing uprights, packed in between with much smaller stones. One capstone, the south-westerly one, is now missing; this allows daylight into some clearly delineated burial compartments which were continually re-used. Over the short 9ft 9in (3m) passage on the southernmost long side, there are two more smaller capstones over three more uprights. Finds here, including 127 potsherds, helped to establish the tomb's date as Late Middle Neolithic.

KRUCKOW

Kruckow,
Demmin,
Mecklenburg

GROSSDOLMEN
(CHAMBER TOMB)

H 3 (Hallwag GDR
Map)

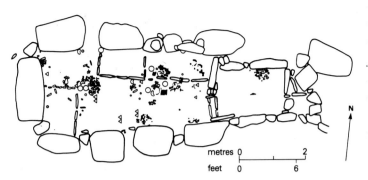

Leave Neubrandenburg north
on road 96. After 25 miles
(40km), turn left at Völsehow
for Kruckow. Fork left on to
the 110; go past the turning
on the left to Vro Marienfelde.
The site is signposted on the
right past the woods.

This trapezoidal site, another in the Mecklenburg Group, is 82ft (25m) long, and is aligned north-south, with its internal chamber entrance facing east. In the course of its length it narrows from 37ft 9in (11.5m) wide at the south, before the vestibule, to 21ft 3in (6.5m) at the north.

The kerbstone boulders retain a flat earth platform, and they originally numbered 40, of which only five are missing (two were once at the north, within another small vestibule only one pair of stones deep). Two vestibules in a *grossdolmen* is most

unusual. The chamber here is in remarkably good condition. It has four pairs of uprights each supporting a capstone; the westernmost also has the endstone beneath it and is the biggest, measuring 9ft 3in by 5ft 6in (2.8m by 1.7m) and over 3ft 3in (1m) thick.

This *grossdolmen* has a short passage in the long side, giving a total tomb length of 37ft 9in (11.5m), which is comparatively large. It also shows a number of compartments inside, separated with thin upright very low slabs.

LOHNE-ZÜSCHEN

III.14

Fritzlar Züschen,
Hesse

STEINKIST (BURIAL
CHAMBER) WITH PORT-
HOLE SLAB

H 8

Leave Kassel (north of
Frankfurt-a-M)
southwestwards on the 231;
after 2½ miles (4km) turn
south onto the 450, and take
the second right to Züschen 14
miles (23km) down the road
to Fritzlar.

The handsome port-hole is sometimes
called a spirit hole.

This is a handsome and unusual *steinkist*. The 62ft (19m) long rectangular trench is sunk in earth to the level of the tops of its 24 boulders. The axis is north-east/south-west. At the north-east there is an entrance vestibule (thus it is also known as a *portikusdolmen*); separating it from the main gallery stands a slab with a large smoothed, round access hole. These are sometimes known as spirit holes, although this one is rather large merely for escaping vapours!

Towards the south-west lies an internal chamber, and

beyond it, a single huge endstone at the end of the rectangle; it is the biggest stone at the site. No capstones have survived at a grave which has many similarities with SOM tombs.

Remains of 45 people were uncovered here, along with bone, stone and flint tools, ornaments and Neolithic vessels. Another point of interest at this site are its 'decorated' stones which depict interlinked, broken horizontal lines, and one possible and another definite oxen outline. The mystery of why 'spirit holes' are not more common remains.

VISBEKER BRAUT

Wildeshausen,
Visbek,
Oldenburg

HÜNENGRAB
(MEGALITHIC GRAVE)

F 5

The Visbeker Braut (bride of Visbek) was constructed by the Funnel Beaker people (in German *Trichterbecher*; thus the common abbreviation TRB for them), who represented the earliest Neolithic culture in Northern Europe.

This stretched rectangle of stones measures 262ft by 23ft (80m by 7m). It was originally kerbed by 105 upright boulders, which increase in size from the north-east to the south-west end of the axis. It does, in fact, narrow slightly at the north-east end where the three middle endstones are missing. Altogether 23 stones are gone, including a line of eight directly south-west of its chamber, and two to the north of it (perhaps evidence of tomb robbers). Others have fallen outwards. The passageless chamber towards the south-west end of the kerbed mound is 19ft 9in by 5ft 3in (6m by 1.6m); the capstone is missing, and the tops of the upright stones forming the burial chamber are level with the earth inside the long monument.

Visbeker Bräutigam (the bridegroom) lies 2½m (4km) to the south-west of his bride. It is longer and wider along its almost east-west alignment, being 354ft by 33ft (108m by 10m). The earth platform inside the kerbstones, which are higher – up to 8ft (2.4m) – at the east, has gone, but five great capstones still reside on the ground towards the western end.

There are many other dolmens in this beautiful wooded area, including notably the Pestruper Gräberfeld, a few miles directly south of Wildeshausen. But the bride and her groom should be at the start of a day's German megalith hunting.

5 miles (8km) north of Visbek. Take the 213 west from Wildeshausen, which is 30 miles (48km) south-west of Bremen, towards Cloppenburg. Turn left at the sign to the site, pass beneath the E37 Bremen-Osnabrück autobahn, and park at the sign by the woods on the right.

Visbeker Braut (the bride).

Visbeker Bräutigam (the bridegroom).

THE NETHERLANDS

BORGER

Hunebedstraat,
Borger,
Emmen,
Drenthe

RIJKSHUNEBED (D.27)
Noord Nederland B.7

There are no simple 'French dolmen' burial chambers at all in The Netherlands. The country is however renowned for its *hunebedden* (see NOORDLO, Drenthe). This *hunebed*, D.27, is one of 11 in and around the village of Borger. Although hugely impressive in size, it is in a very dilapidated condition. An 1833 drawing shows it as it is today – all traces of an earthern covering gone, forlorn, but immensely climbable for children! It is, in fact, quite a moving experience to wander in and out and beneath this massive megalithic skeleton, along the enormous 80ft (24.4m) length, set in a charming clearing among trees.

The axis of this *rijkshunebed* lies, as most do, north-east/south-west. It consists of 26 uprights (*draagstenen*) and two endstones (*sluitstenen*); above them at now odd angles lie nine capstones (*dekstenen*) of huge size, their top surfaces some 12ft (3.7m) from the ground and their underbellies levelled to a flat smooth surface, to form what must have been a formidable internal long chamber.

The chamber's entrance, at the south-east, now has four portal stones (*poortzijstenen*) and one remaining entrance capstone (*portal dekstenen*). To the north-west of the tomb, two kerbstones (*kransstenen*) reside, indicating a long gone earth covering mound, which must have been one of the most substantial one in The Netherlands.

Travel northwards from Emmen on the N34; 5 miles (8km) north of Odoorn turn right on the road towards Stadskanaal. Turn left immediately for the village of Borger on the minor road towards Gasselte. Follow the signposts to Bronneger round to the east. Continue straight on to Hunebedstraat (and not north-east to Bronneger). The monument is signposted on the left.

All hunebedden *in The Netherlands are numbered. D.27 at Borger is one of eleven in and around the village.*

HAVELTE WEST

*Havelterberg,
Havelte,
Drenthe*

RIJKSHUNEBED
(GANGGRAF)
(D.53)

Noord Nederland B.5

This ganggraf dates back to about 2750BC, and is covered with nine large capstones; only their undersides were roughly dressed.

Though now in a somewhat dilapidated state, this megalithic monument has been admired since at least 1732. It was excavated by Professor van Giffen in 1918 and restored to its present appearance in 1954. It is dated at about 2750 BC.

At least five stones survive from a former revetment around a broadly ovular mound. The entrance to the central long chamber is at south-south-east; either side and all around it there was once an ovular circle of 48 stones, of which 23 remain today. A capstone resting on two uprights form the passage.

The central chamber, lying about north-east/south-west like its surroundings, consists of 23 uprights along its sides, which lean inwards over once paved flooring. Most of the inside faces have been dressed to present flat smooth walling, with drystone packing; there are also stone slabs at each end. They support nine very thick capstones.

This D.53 *hunebed* is almost identical in plan to the German *grosssteingräber* of Gross Bersen, Emsland, just over the border, and Thuine, Emsland; the latter has an extra ovular ring of stones inserted between the outer and inner ones. All three *hunebedden* share the same axial direction. Two more remarkably similar *grosssteingräber*, but with entrances at the south-west instead, are Gross Stavern, also in Emsland, and Gandersee, Oldenburg, a little further to the east in the former West Germany.

Leave Meppel northwards on the N.32 motorway; at the Havelte exit turn off north-eastwards on to the N371. After 2½ miles (4km), at Overcinge, turn left north-west towards Tuinbouwschool. Turn right at the Café Hunebed and park where indicated. Walk past the next field on the right and then turn right, as signposted, to the site.

The chamber lies on a north-east/south-west axis and is lined with 23 uprights.

Noordlo

*Annen,
Groningen,
Drenthe*

Provinciaal hunebed
(D.9)
Noord Nederland A.7

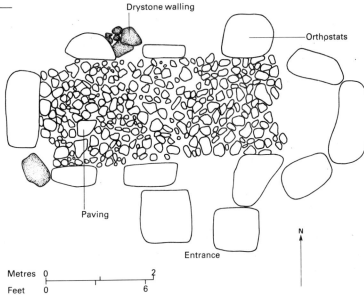

Drystone walling

Orthostats

Paving

Entrance

N

| Metres | 0 | | | 2 |
| Feet | 0 | | | 6 |

*Leave Groningen southwards
on the E232 motorway. After
7½ miles (12km) leave at the
Zuidlaren exit, and take the
N34 to the south-east. After 3
miles (5km) the monument is
on the left, just before the
crossroad connecting Annen
with Anloo.*

In 1878 reports reached
London of over-zealous
excavation and restoration of
hunebedden in The Netherlands.
As a result, the leading
British archaeologists
William C. Lukis and Sir
Henry Dryden were
despatched to the country to
investigate by The Society of
Antiquaries. They visited and
recorded this site – which is
how finds from D.9 come to
reside in the British Museum,
London.

Hunebedden (Hun's beds) are typical of the northern part of The
Netherlands, and are megalithic tombs of the Funnel Beaker
(TRB) culture which flourished about 3400–2200 BC. They
have round or oval kerbed earth mounds which cover
rectangular burial chambers; these have entrances on one of the
long sides, sometimes accompanied by a very short passage-,
which relates them to Danish passage graves (*jaettestuer*). The
burial chambers are normally long, and lie on a north-east/
south-west axis (though not always). Sometimes the chambers
are below ground in a shallow trench, with pairs of opposing
uprights carrying capstones (above ground) like a succession of
trilithons. They can be as long as 80ft (24.4m), like *hunebed*
D.27 at BORGER, which sports ten capstones. They were often
placed on a slope, with taller uprights above ground, and were
used for multiple collective burials.

There are 53 *hunebedden* still existing (in 1990) in The
Netherlands (all but one of which are in the province of
Drenthe), from a total recorded of 76. The first *hunebed* to be
recorded in about 1570 was called Duvels Kutle, which means
'Devil's Cot' or 'C**t'. It is thought to be D.6-Tinaarloo. The
first complete list of these tombs was drawn up in 1818–20
and in 1925 the famous Dutch archaeologist Professor Albert
E. van Giffen gave all extant *hunebedden* a letter for its province
(D is for Drenthe) and a serial number. Van Giffen, by design
or chance, was the excavator of D.6-Tinaarloo in 1928, a year
after it was re-discovered.

This partly destroyed Neolithic *hunebed* (D.9) is totally
accessible, on a surburban village roadside next to a modest
bungalow. It lies in flat countryside in a province which is
easily the richest in *hunebedden*. It was excavated in 1952 by
Professor A. E. van Giffen, very much the father of Dutch
20th-century archaeology. It looked then much as it did in
that first depiction of it in about 1570: two pairs of uprights,

an endstone at the west side, with partial drystone walling in
between the megaliths. The capstones were at one time taken
down by villagers of Annen because they were considered
unsafe but they are now back in place. Since then this
monument has been thoroughly researched by D. J. Groot and
his findings published. *See* BORGER, Drenthe, for the main
'megalithic words' in Dutch; they are useful for reading the
details of site notices.

The eastern end of the grave is now destroyed, but it once
consisted of a further five uprights placed in a semi-circle to
the east, and two more to the south, in the style of two portals.
It is thought that there may have been an upper floor; this
would have been most unusual, and the evidence for it is not
fully accepted. More dependable are the distinct traces of an
earthen mound which most likely once covered the whole
long chamber.

Most of the finds at Noordlo are now to be found in the
Provinciaal Museum at Assen 20½m (33km) up the N371 to
the north-east. They included 870 potsherds, of which 810 are
TRB and the others Early Bronze Age ware. At least 101
vessels were identified after laborious examination and partial
reconstruction. There were 41 funnel beakers (naturally), 23
bowls, ten tureens, six amphorae, one pail, five collared flasks
and 15 others. There was no sign of any cremation at the site,
or indeed of any funerary practices. There could of course have
been burials, articulated or otherwise, but the acidity of the
soil here would have destroyed the bones. In any case, no soil
stains were noted.

To the west of this *hunebed*, on the other side of the road,
north of Anloo, there are *hunebedden* D.8 -Anlo-N (Kniphor-
stbos) and then D.7 (Schipborg), roughly equidistant, and
worth visiting. These would be two more to add to the list of
53 *hunebedden* which could be visited in a fortnight's holiday.

PAPELOZE KERK

Schoonoord,
Sleen,
Emmen,
Drenthe

RIJKSHUNEBED
(GANGGRAF)
(D.49)
Noord Nederland B.7

RIGHT: *The roofed entrance to the 'Priestless Church'.*

A view of the chamber showing the undersides of some of the six capstones.

The name of this interesting burial chamber means 'priestless church'; it is a kidney-shaped *ganggraf* (similar to a *portaalgraf*, but with its entrance passage roofed). Professor van Giffen's excavation and restoration here was on a large scale.

About a third of the earth mound at the south-eastern end is open to the sky, and so some of the replaced uprights can be examined. Giffen restored 24 missing kerbstones; at the beginning of this century there were only four, and there were no portal stones or capstones on top of them.

The central chamber tomb lies along a north-west/south-east axis, which is most unusual; it is lined with 12 uprights and six enormous capstones (the biggest is the one just past the entrance, and weighs 25 tons). In addition, there are two endstones, and two pairs of portal stones with a capstone over them make the entrance at the south-west. Such a thoroughly complete restoration has much to demonstrate to megalith hunters, and its woodland setting has been left in such a way that the site's name gains a mysterious significance.

Take the main road west from Emmen's centre. After 5 miles (8km), turn right north-westwards towards Schoonoord; the site is only 1¼ miles (2km) along on the left, down a pathway.

III.20

129
NORTHERN
EUROPE
The
Netherlands

SCHIMMERES

*Emmen,
Drenthe*

MOUND WITH TWO
BURIAL CHAMBERS AND
SIDE ENTRANCES
(*LANGGRAF*) (D. 43)
Noord Nederland B.7

This is one of ten *hunebedden* in and around Emmen, but it is the only *langgraf* in The Netherlands. It was partly restored in 1870 and boulders from the demolished *hunebed* D.43a nearby were incorporated into it. It was again excavated in 1913 by J.H. Holwerda, and in 1960 by Professor van Giffen, who dated the site to the early fourth millennium.

The 131ft (40m) long grave is set in sparse, tranquil woodland on a north-north-east/south-south-west alignment, nearly a direct north/south one though. It is shaped like a huge longboat; around a raised earth platform 52 uprights remain, with drystone walling in the wide gaps between them. The larger stones, up to 6ft (1.8m) high above the ground, are at the northern end. The triangular boulder at the southern pointed end has a slightly raised 'spine' on its outward facing back. There are several free-standing stones west of the grave.

This unique *langgraf* contains two burial chambers. One is at the northern end, with an entrance at the east-south-east beneath a flat earth covering. Its rectangular chamber has six uprights at its sides, two endstones and three capstones; the entrance consists of a pair of portal stones supporting two smaller capstones, which now lie close by. To the south, near the centre of the enclosure, lies the second, longer chamber. Strangely, there is no outer sign of a passage connecting the inner tomb with the outer kerb, and so perhaps it was entered from above after the entrance was blocked. Above the now slightly domed earth cover, lie nine uprights, two endstones, and just two of a probable seven. There is cobbled paving, both in and around both chambers, and more to the south-west near a fallen internal slab, possibly once the capstone of a third chamber in a logical position.

There are two burial chambers inside this unique langgraf *in the Dutch* hunebedden *province of Drenthe.*

From Emmen's market place and main cross roads, take the Grongingen road to the north. Pass Weerdingestraat and then Walstraat on the right; the site is then signposted to the left, down a path. This is the only megalithic site in this book which is within a few minutes' walk from a railway station!

DE STEENBARG

Noordlaren,
Haren,
Groningen

Rijkhunebed (G.1)
Noord Nederland A.7

The front capstone of this monument, the only *hunebed* in Groningen province, looks preposterously large, and must surely be the largest natural boulder ever to be heaved on to supporting stones for funerary purposes in The Netherlands. It covers a very wide opening and is supported, along with a much smaller stone behind it (they both have small, round holes drilled through them), by two pairs of uprights and an endstone.

Professor van Giffen and others thoroughly explored the eastern part of De Steenbarg in 1957; they established that originally there were ten uprights, five capstones, two endstones, and two portal stones with their own capstone. There is an unattractive small replica of the monument on Zuidlaarerweg in Noordlaren, which is to be found south-east of the real thing.

The stones were already missing by 1768, according to a Petrus Camper drawing. Early in the next century the two capstone holes were drilled; they were to receive gunpowder, in preparation for the demolition of the already partly ruined monument. Fortunately for posterity, this foul plan was halted at the last moment.

The interesting part of this near-tragedy is that it is fully recorded by the contemporary historian J. Boeles, in the *Groninger Volks-Almanak* for 1845. He did this in order that, in his own words 'over time people will not fill their heads with conjectures as to the origin and meaning of these stones. After all, people already fool the small children with the story that giants put their thumbs in the holes so that they could throw the stones at each other'. The moral of this true tale should be noted by propagators of legends 'from the old days'. Facts are usually more interesting.

The same historian also noted a recollection from his clergyman father of an excavation at the beginning of the 19th century. Between two layers of pebbles under the grave was a layer of sand, into which had been placed urns containing human ashes and small bones.

Leave Groningen southwards on the E232 motorway. After 6 miles (10km) take the Eelde Airport Exit east and then southwards towards Zuidlaren. After 2 miles (3km), past the windmill, just to the south of Noordlaren, the signposted site is on the right at a crossroads about 550yds (500m) down a lane.

DE TWEELING VAN BRONNEGER

Bronneger,
Borger,
Emmen,
Drenthe

Rijkshunebedden (D.21 and D.22)
Noord Nederland B.7

These two *hunebedden*, only yards from each other, translate as 'the twins of Bronneger'; D.21 is sometimes called simply Bronneger-W, and D.22 Bronneger-O (East). The site is beside a road, and trees there, no doubt self-seeded, stand very close to both graves, rather spoiling their appearance.

The first is much the more complete today, and is a *portaalgraf*. It has seven uprights (one of the pairs is missing), two endstones, and three immense, craggy capstones. One portal stone survives at its south-east entrance. Inside, the boulders are smoothly dressed, and the floor is paved with small loose stones; among them 600 potsherds of the Funnel Beaker culture have been found. This monument seems to have had successive periods of use.

D.22, a moment's walk to the south-west and set among trees, is a miserable thing today. Only three uprights are still standing, together with two endstones and two capstones, one of them huge and uneven in shape. Clearly, the twins are not identical!

North of Emmen join the N34 towards Borger. In the village turn north-east to the signposted site.

ANUNDSHÖGEN

*Badelunda,
Västerås,
Västmanland*

STONE SHIPS, MOUND AND RUNE STONE

F 5

*The site is only 3³/4 miles
(6km) from Västerås. Leave
the town north-east on the
minor road towards Tortuna
following the signs. Instead of
turning left for Badelunda,
turn right; the site is
immediately on the right.
Local guides.*

*A 174ft (53m) long stone burial
'ship', with the 'stern' in the
foreground.*

This marvellous wooded site, on the shores of Lake Mälaren, compares not unfavourably with the more famous stone ship cemetery of Gamla (Old) Uppsala but lacks its historical associations. Here is one of Sweden's longest stone ships: stone bounded, ship-shaped graves, often containing a wooden boat and burial. It is 174ft (53m) long, with a large triangular stone lying at the prow, and a tall rectangular one marking the stern. Either side of them, forming the sides of the boat, lie matching lines of smaller boulders, 11 in each, with gaps between them. The majestic Late Bronze Age ship at Boge, Gotland, has its lining of stones placed in a contiguous fashion. Other stone ships can be seen at Anundshögen, and a further group of eight at nearby Tuna Alsike, where one excavated Viking boat revealed a large wooden boat, bearing what probably were the remains of a chieftain's wife. Very few

such grand burials have been discovered. Close to the mound there is a fine standing rune stone.

Anundshögen means 'Anund's mound', and it is one of Sweden's largest, being 49ft (15m) high. It is dated at about 600–700 AD and was the location of a court (*thing*), as found all over Europe. This is why 'court' appears so frequently in house and place names near prehistoric raised earth mounds.

This mound is 16ft 6in (5m) higher than any of the three famous mounds at Gamla (Old) Uppsala, north of today's city. Gamla evidently flourished as a centre of pagan worship and ritual from about 500 AD until the end of the 11th century. *Beowulf*, the Anglo-Saxon epic, relates the story of the three Swedish kings buried there beneath the mounds – Adils, Aun and Egil of the Ynglinga family, as does the famous chronicle *Ynglingatal* in the eleventh century.

CARLSHÖGEN

The entrance to this burial chamber is unusually placed off-centre, to the south-east.

*Hagestad,
Löderup,
Skåne*

**BURIAL CHAMBER WITH
PASSAGE ENTRANCE**

D 1

Leave the south coastal Skåne town of Ystad travelling east. After 5 miles (8km), take the first right fork to Hagestad. Not signposted.

Högen means 'mound', and this site was named after Carl Wulferona, a local landowner, by its first excavator, Baron Arvid Kurck in 1875. Flattened oval in shape, the mound is located on a gentle slope surrounded by farmland. The earth is banked as high as the top of the entrance capstones; within it the burial chamber and its entrance are set slightly and strangely off-centre to the south-east.

The entrance is on the east side of the internal chamber and and its passage, which is 21ft (6.4m) long and up to 3ft (0.9m) wide, aligned east-north-east. The passage retains the only three capstones here, about 3ft 3in (1m) above the original floor. The one nearest the chamber measures 3ft 6in by 5ft 6in (1.1m by 1.7m), and its top surface is covered with 92

cup marks, 80 of which are round with diameters of up to 3½ins (9 cms). There are four pairs of portal stones, closed by a square boulder at the outer entrance.

The axis of the chamber is broadly north-west/south-east, and is a rectangular 17ft (5.2m) long and 7ft 6in (2.3m) wide, with rounded corners. There are ten uprights around the chamber, interfilled with drystone walling (with curious tall thin stones inside it).

Finds here include the remains of several skeletons, of which some may have been buried in a sitting position (concentrated at the southern end of the chamber), potsherds, flint heaps, flakes, and a knife. These were discovered at two different floor levels, demonstrating a long period of use.

RAMSHÖG

The absurdly large capstones are a famous feature of this site.

*Hagestad,
Löderup,
Skåne*

**BURIAL CHAMBER AND
PASSAGE IN MOUND**

D 1

Leave the south coastal town of Ystad travelling east. After 5 miles (8km), take the first right fork along the coast a few miles to Hagestad.

This marvellous site (the old name of which was Ramsbjer) was first excavated in 1875, and then more thoroughly, before restoration, in 1961–69. The earth tumulus is in the shape of a flattened circle, and contains a smallish chamber and, by comparison, a long passage. The entrance passage is orientated east-north-east; it is 21ft 6in (6.6m) long and up to 2ft 6in (0.8m) wide. It has five pairs of opposing boulders, dressed on their insides and packed with drystone walling and smaller stones. There are also 14 fine paving slabs, and two of the capstones nearest the chamber survive.

The oval chamber to the south-west is aligned north-west/south-east. It has nine uprights, dressed on the insides, and measures 17ft by 8ft 6in (5.2m by 2.6m), at the widest inner

points. Its three massive capstones seem to perch in dramatic profile on top of the earth mound.

Some interesting finds here, uncovered to the left of the chamber entrance and to the right and far right of it, were several potsherds, amber beads, flint tools and flakes, a knife blade, and, from a later period, cattle and horse bones. Around the entrance, there were 5214 ceramic pieces. The fascinating human remains in the burial chamber, in piles and very mixed up, consisted of seven to nine individuals, including one or two children, two or three young people, and four adults.

One adult bone at Ramshög has produced a radiocarbon corrected date of 2590 BC.

RÖSSBERGA

Valtorp,
Falköping,
Västergötland

PASSAGE-GRAVE

C 5

This grave was excavated by C. Cullberg in 1962. The chamber is 29ft 6in by 6ft 6in (9m by 2m), and it was found that the floor had two strata. The older one revealed a 1ft (0.3m) deep pile of disarticulated human bones from about 40–45 individuals. This confirms that skeletons in a burial were simply swept to one side if space was needed for further inhumations (the adult body has 206 separate bones in its body, so piles soon build up!). The discovery of a complete skeleton therefore usually indicates a last use of the site.

Here the secondary floor level was found to contain no less than 17 compartments, some as small as 3ft 6in by 1ft 6in (100cm by 50cm); this could imply that each was made to fit an individual, and for various positions. Their 33 dividing slabs were 12in–19¾in (30cm–50cm) in length, and averaged 1ft 6in (0.5m) high.

According to early reports of similar graves to Rössberga, skeletons were found in a sitting position. If this was true, it would establish the constructions as true Funnel Beaker Culture (TRB) graves, and not just simple ossuaries or depositories for bones. However, most likely the bones arrived here as already disarticulated skeletons.

Take the 184 south-east from the north coastal town of Lidköping for 31 miles (50km), through Skara, to Falköping. There turn north-east on to the minor road through Torbjörntorp, just west of Valtorp. The signposted site is on the right.

TÅGARP 5

This passage-grave received considerable restoration, following its excavation in 1970.

Tågarp Östra Tommarp,
Skåne

PASSAGE-GRAVE

E 1

Near the south-east coast in Skåne; Tågarp is 6¼ miles (10km) west of the port of Simrishamn after Östra Tommarp.

This Middle and Late Neolithic site yielded much that was unusual and fascinating during its excavation in 1970. It was in bad condition, and the restoration thereafter was on a considerable scale.

The central grave alignment is north-south; its 12 uprights and the drystone walling between them, in a stretched ovular setting, surrounded an area of 18ft by 6ft 6in (5.5m by 2m) Outside this is a low, kerbed cairn. The insides of the uprights were dressed, and lined a floor holding 13 compartments (perhaps for specific ranks in the community), made with both small, thin slabs (as for individual cists) or lines of piled up stones.

A strange stone and the only one of its kind on the site was found here: it was of arrow-shaped quartzite, measuring 17in by 5in by 3in (42.5cm by 12cm by 6.5cm); an exactly similar one was found at another local grave, and also in drystone walling between two uprights here.

The short passage to the entrance faces east, is 16ft 6in (5m) long, and consists of three pairs of portal boulders, septal stones, and a single capstone. In front of the entrance and either side of it, soot-filled ditches were uncovered which contained Middle Neolithic potsherds and burnt human bones. There were also six hearths, all of different ages.

In the chamber, below the secondary level (the compartments), there was found, in the northern section, a heap of firestones, together with a single unburnt rib bone. At the secondary level, in only one of the compartments, there were small piles of tiny shreds of red cloth (which has also occurred at RAMSHÖG, Löderup). Unhappily, the oxide content in the material was so low that dating by radiocarbon methods was impossible. In this same compartment lay a Funnel Beaker pot lid.

There were two exciting conclusions here: it has been proved that flint was not used for cutting or dressing the stones at this site. And charcoal remains have indicated the intriguing possibility that the primary pebbled floor of the chamber could have been partially boarded over. This is another example of the use of wood within Neolithic tombs.

IV
Iberia and the Balearics

There is still no certainty about the origin of the first Neolithic settlers on the Iberian peninsula. Were they indigenous – spontaneously commencing agriculture about 7500 years ago? Or did the builders of, for example, ANTA DE POÇA DA GATEIRA in Portugal's Evora province in 4510 ± 360 bc, come from the eastern end of the Mediterranean Sea, and by way of the Balearics, or not? Both may be true. On the other hand, at the beginning of this century it was proposed that the early Iberian megalithic monuments were erected by Atlanteans from Libya inter-married with native Iberians!

Minorca (Menorca in Spanish) has, over its 271 square miles (702 sq km), an astonishingly diverse array of monuments to offer a megalith hunter – and all of them can be seen in a day or so. Yet similar monuments are not found in the countries nearest to the island, although the distances between them are not great: Majorca an intervisible 30 miles (48km), Spain 124 miles (200km), Algeria 199 miles (320km), Sardinia 211 miles (340km) and France 230 miles (370km). Majorca (Mallorca in Spanish), the largest of the Balearic Islands with 1405 square miles (3639 sq km) of land, is only 104 miles (167km) from the Spanish mainland, yet it did not export the *talayot*; nor did Minorca the *naveta* to Majorca.

It can be surprising to discover that the Iberian peninsula and Balearic Islands possess thousands of megalithic tombs, some of which are among the oldest in the world. The *antas* (dolmens) and *cuevas* (corbelled chambers) in Evora, for example, date back to about 5500 bc, and even then succeeded a tradition of megalithic single cist building.

Iberian passage-graves
In spite of the scarcity of radiocarbon dates for Iberian megalithic sites, it now seems clear that passage-graves with single chambers were evolving around that time (*c*.4500–4000 bc) in both the north-west and south-west with no discernible direct cultural influences from northern Europe. They are detached from the passage-grave's traditional forms in western France, because no covering mound in Portugal or southern Spain has ever been found to contain more than one primary (as opposed to a later second) passage-grave. *See*, for instance, BARNENEZ, France, and elsewhere.

In spite of this, the temptation to award contemporaneity to passage-grave construction in northern Europe and the Iberian peninsula can be resisted. The French corbelled roofing systems appeared in Brittany and many parts of Britain at the time of the earliest Evora *antas*, but not for several hundred more years in Portugal and southern Spain (to the north of Almeria). The absence of corbelled roofed chambers in northern Spain appears to rule out such a route south.

The most spectacular of the corbelled passage-graves which followed is CUEVA DEL ROMERAL, near a sugar refinery outside white-walled Antequera, north of the southern Spanish tourist centre of Malaga. It is dated at about 3500 bc, and its enclosing mound is about 285ft (87m) across. This is one of the three best known *cuevas* of a type that does not exist in northern Spain. The others are CUEVA DE MENGA (where one of the capstones weighs 180 tons) and CUEVA DE LA VIERA, which is a *tholos* type, over 100ft (30m) long, and containing three port-hole slabs.

Tholoi tombs arrived in southern Iberia later still, around 3000 bc: *see* LOS MILLARES, Spain, and REGUENGOS DE MONSAREZ, Portugal, for example. The Greek name invented by the famous archaeologist Louis Siret for these beehive-shaped tombs should not persuade one to look to the east of the Mediterranean Sea for their inspiration; most likely they were an indigenous variation by talented builders.

Los Millares
The most famous type-site in Iberia and the Balearics is LOS MILLARES, on its bleak and rocky prominence, some 14 miles (22km) north of the coastal resort of Almeria. Although sometimes marked as a necropolis, this huge site was also a fortified settlement, complete with an aqueduct and forts. Here was one of the first great copper mining centres in Europe. Between about 3100 and 2600 bc, before the Beaker culture succeeded it, the Millaran culture spread throughout southern Iberia. Unfortunately treasure hunters, with their metal detectors, and other human predators, have in recent years made a tragic nuisance of themselves. The consequence for such an important site came in 1990, with the erection of a 1¾ miles (3km) long wire fence all around it. Access is therefore now restricted to bona fide visitors.

Megalithic art
The most famous megalithic art in Iberia is in the 886ft (270m) long Altamira cave, which is 18½ miles (30km) west of Santander, and 1¼ miles (2km) south of Santillana-del-Mar, on the northern Spanish coast. The cave was discovered by accident in 1868; a local girl was the first to spot the artwork eleven years later. It was only accepted as genuine

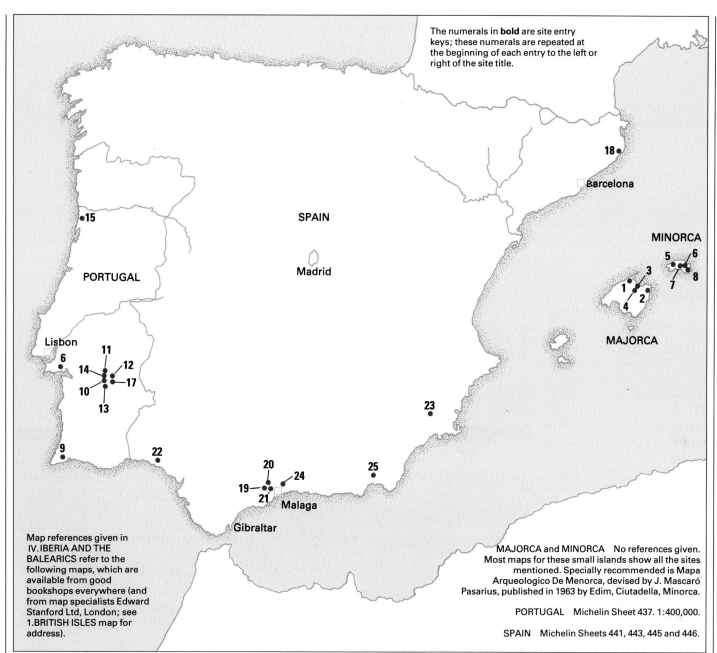

The numerals in **bold** are site entry keys; these numerals are repeated at the beginning of each entry to the left or right of the site title.

SPAIN

Barcelona

18

MINORCA

5 6
3
1 2
4
7 8

MAJORCA

PORTUGAL

Madrid

15

Lisbon
6
11
14 12
10 17
13

9

22

23

20
19 24
21 25
Malaga

Gibraltar

Map references given in
IV. IBERIA AND THE
BALEARICS refer to the
following maps, which are
available from good
bookshops everywhere (and
from map specialists Edward
Stanford Ltd, London; see
1. BRITISH ISLES map for
address).

MAJORCA and MINORCA   No references given.
Most maps for these small islands show all the sites
mentioned. Specially recommended is Mapa
Arqueologico De Menorca, devised by J. Mascaró
Pasarius, published in 1963 by Edim, Ciutadella, Minorca.

PORTUGAL   Michelin Sheet 437. 1:400,000.

SPAIN   Michelin Sheets 441, 443, 445 and 446.

Quaternary art (dating back to 30,000 BC) after discoveries of paintings and engravings at La Mouthe, and Font de Gaume and Combarelles, in the Dordogne area of southern France (in 1895 and 1901 respectively) and their subsequent verification by the abbé Henri Breuil. The cave at Altamira, which has 150 or so paintings, is now closed to the public most of the time because of the effects of its popularity (like France's Lascaux caves), but the nearby Cueva de la Estalactitas can be visited.

Majorca and Minorca in the Balearic Islands

On both Majorca and Minorca, the earliest third millennium burials were in settlement caves. At first they were in natural openings, such as Cueva de Muleta, Majorca, where a radiocarbon date of 3984 ± 109 bc has been obtained. Rock-cut tombs followed, such as CALA SANT VICENÇ, Majorca, with corridors, side chambers, and ledges inside. There are many more of these in Majorca than in Minorca.

The successive Talayotic cultures in both islands were broadly contemporary, stretching from about 1500 BC through to Roman times, though there were variations in them. A

talayot (or watchtower) is a round cyclopean construction which was either solid or contained a single round chamber with a corbelled roof. Later versions were sometimes square, and with a second chamber above the first. The 72 well-excavated tombs in the cemetery of SON REAL, Majorca, have three different chamber shapes. At SES PAÏSSES, Majorca, a *talayot* can be seen within a walled settlement, and also at TALATI DE DALT, Minorca, though in some cases they occur just outside enclosing walls. At the latter site an indigenous megalithic Minorcan monument is also to be found. This is a *taula*, a T-shaped structure consisting of a dressed, almost rectangular upright supporting a cross beam, also dressed. The largest of these on Minorca is TREPUCÓ.

The first-ever study of prehistory to be published in Spanish, in 1818, took Minorca as its subject; this bestows a fitting pedigree on a small island crammed with megalithic riches. Its author, Juan Ramis y Ramis, gave the cleverly logical name *naveta* (boat) to its most famous single monument, ELS TUDONS. This extraordinary boat-shaped chamber tomb is claimed to be the oldest above-ground building in either the Balearics or Spain.

136
THE
BALEARICS
Majorca

MAJORCA

IV.1

CALA SANT VICENÇ

ROCK-CUT TOMBS

Majorca is 62 miles
(100km) east to west,
and 46 miles (74km)
north to south.

These tombs were the natural successors to caves as settings for burials, in the pre-Talayot period (*see* SES PAÏSSES). They were an obvious and common development throughout the Mediterranean, although the kinds of entrances varied widely in accordance with local geology, as did the layouts of the passages and chambers.

There are nine tombs in this group (as they generally occur), and quite the most interesting of them is Tomb 7. Its rectangular carved façade and forecourt face directly south. A short passage leads to a rectangular antechamber; another short passage leads on to a second chamber of the same shape but the other way about, and with one chamber at each side. Its principal gallery is 29ft 6in (9m) long, has a rounded roof, and has a rare but sensibly utilitarian ledge running along each wall. Even as far back as 2000 BC the islanders were showing signs of order.

2½ miles (4km) west of Port de Pollença on the 710, turn right, north-east, towards Cala de Sant Vicenç. The tombs are 1¼ miles (2km) along on the right.

SES PAÏSSES

TALAYOT SETTLEMENT

Leave Artá south-west on the 715. The site is almost immediately on the left.

Part of the settlement's still complete oval wall, and the large south-east gateway.

The Talayotic culture in Majorca (*talaia* means watchtower) produced a form of housing within walled settlements, with *talayots* (round, tapering stone towers) either inside or adjacent to them. It possibly commenced around 1400 BC, lasted no more than 1500 years and was first identified by Emille Cartailhac, who held that the slightly different *talayots* in neighbouring Minorca were broadly contemporary.

This fascinating site on a hill by a spring was excavated not long ago by the Sardinian archaeologist Giovanni Lilliu. The settlement's containing wall, roughly ovular in shape, is complete; this is extremely rare for a Bronze Age site. The area within it, at its widest points, measures 348ft by 308ft (106m by 94m). It has four unevenly spaced gateways, of which the main one on the south-east is hugely impressive. There are very small housing 'units' in the centre, built over more than a millennium, a small passage and a solid *talayot*, which today is 14ft 9in (4.5m) high. It must once have had an external winding stairway to a platform area at the top.

SON REAL

*Take the 712 coastal road
south-east from Alcudia; after
7½ miles (12km) turn left
into the town of Can Picafort.
Park, and walk less than 1
mile (1½km) south-east
along the beach. Wear rubber
boots.*

*The burial chambers in the cemetery
on the Bay of Alcudia have many
different shapes.*

Son Real is one of the few Majorcan examples of a substantial mass burial site. It dates back to about 8–6 BC, the end of the Talayotic period. It was built in three approximate stages at today's water's edge in the Bay of Alcudia; at that time the level of the sea was several metres lower (as more tombs on a nearby islet indicate).

Extensive excavations since 1957 have revealed that the earliest burial chambers were boat-shaped, somewhat in the manner of the Minorcan *navetas* in plan (*see* ELS TUDONS). These are distinctive for two unusual features. In some of them, two or three very small rectangular holes occur side by side. In others there are shallow trenches at each end, between which crouched skeletons were laid, always with their heads facing to the east, and to the carefully dressed stone 'bows'. Collective burials have been found in the second oldest, circular, stone chambers.

The slightly more recent rectangular tombs vary in their methods of construction and form. More than 100 of all these types were built, and sometimes so close together that they share common stretches of wall. Disappointingly few grave goods have been uncovered at this remarkable cemetery, although many 'tools for the job', such as fragments of axes, blades, chisels, daggers, knives and swords, have been found. The tombs here are relatively young.

VERNISA

Majorca has been inhabited for nearly 7000 years, as evidence of inhabitation and use in these caves has proved. Burials commenced here in the Late Neolithic period, being, as ever, one of ancient man's major preoccupations.

The cave culture was succeeded in about 1400 BC by the Talayotic way of life and, judging by pottery finds at this site, the caves were in almost continuous use for a further 1000 years. Flint flakes, buttons, a bronze dagger, and both plain and decorated pottery sherds have been found here.

Other natural caves in Majorca, similar in basic respects to the Vernisa cave are Cas Hereu, Cueva dels Bous, Sa Canova, Son Marroig, and Son Torrella.

Leave Artá (on the east of the island) on the C712 north-west towards Puerto de Alcudia. After 9¼ miles (15km) turn left on to the PM340. Take the first turning on the right, then right on to the PM341, then left towards Muro. Vernisa is now on the right.

138
THE
BALEARICS
Minorca

MINORCA

IV.5

ELS TUDONS

Minorca is 30 miles (48km) east to west, and 8½ miles (14km) north to south.

A *naveta* is a form of chamber tomb which is unique to Minorca. The name was invented by Spain's first serious prehistorian, Juan Ramis y Ramis, when he explored this tomb in 1818; at the time he concluded that it was a temple of Isis, the moon goddess of ancient Egypt. It was then the only known construction of its kind on the island, and it had the clear outline shape of an upturned boat. In Minorca today, *navetas* are sometimes confusingly called 'talayetas'. Els Tudons means the wood pigeons; perhaps they wisely used it, when all burial activity had ceased. It is held to be the oldest

Leave Ciutadella eastwards on the island's only major road, the C721. The naveta is signposted at the second track on the right.

Els Tudons is easily the finest of Minorca's 50 or so remaining navetas.

above ground 'building' in the whole of Spain and the Balearic Islands; it is also the Balearics' grandest monument.

From its exterior, the multicoursed stone mound tapers slightly inwards towards the entrance, as the chamber does within. The high and unique, inward curving façade contains a small, very low outer doorway; it faces almost south-west and has a great lintel stone above it, which projects slightly outwards. It leads into an antechamber or narrow corridor. From the outside, Els Tudons is 46ft (14m) long and 21ft 3in (6.5m) wide at the middle. Large, squarish semi-dressed stones form its foundation; eight layers of flatter stones lie above, tapering inwards as they rise. A big, flat, stone slab forms a platform at the back of the chamber and there is also a remarkable low, upper chamber, entered from the antechamber.

Navetas were constructed as tombs, and today some 50 are known to survive in Minorca. There is a fine group of these remarkable *navetas* around Alayor; they include Biniac 1 and 2, Cotaina, Llumena, Rafal Rubi 1 and 2, Torralbet, and Torre Llisa Vell. Els Tudons, in the area of the greatest concentration of them, has yielded the remains of more than 100 humans on pebble layers, as well as associated grave goods. Among the mysterious finds were discs bearing circular patterns.

The closed end of the monument, at the north-east, completes a spectacular piece of architectural design; its semi-dressed 'upturned prow' is most beautifully made. Els Tudons is roofless today, and exactly why is part of the monument's fascinating history. Some 30 years ago it was in terrible disrepair – mostly fallen, with many stones plundered for the ubiquitous Minorcan field walls, and with olive roots tearing at its great foundations. After much fund raising,

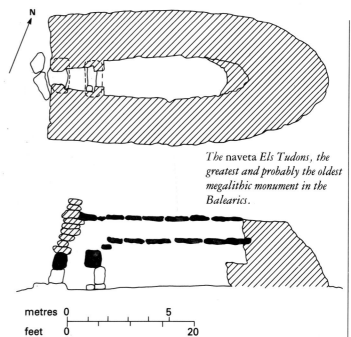

The naveta *Els Tudons, the greatest and probably the oldest megalithic monument in the Balearics.*

excavations took place in 1958. Then restoration commenced in 1959–60 under the direction of a remarkable servant of Minorcan archaeology, Maria Luisa Serra Belabre, who died before her time in 1967. She was never convinced by an original drawing of the site by Ramis, lodged in archives in Mahon, and therefore refused to accept unconfirmable conjecture about the roof's construction beyond the vestibule (it was probably corbelled). And so today Els Tudons is finely restored, after two years' work, but remains without a roof.

TALATI DE DALT

IV.6

---

*Algendar,
Mahon*

TAULA AND TALAYOT

The T-shaped taula *might represent a bovid (cattle-like) head.*

Leave Mahon westwards on the main C721; after 2½ miles (4km) turn left for Algendar. Take the first right fork, and then the site is on the left, about ½ mile (1km) from the main road. Not signposted.

This sloping, heavily-wooded and hard-to-find site disguises its megalithic excitements. Within a D-shaped enclosure there are remains of a stone circle around a fine *taula* (which has a tall stone leaning against it, cushioned by another). Its

rectangular, horizontal capstone has the same wonderfully dressed shape as the one at TREPUCÓ (see the reference to Stonehenge), and is the largest in Minorca; it measures 13ft by 5ft by 2ft (4m by 1.5m by 0.7m).

This site also contains buried chambers, standing stones (possibly supports for wooden roofs), and one distant, individual stone with a port-hole. Added to this, the remains of a substantial *talayot* dominate the prehistoric hamlet. Quite a building site over 3000 years ago!

Whatever the elegant and mysterious *taulas* were used for, it is generally accepted that they were neither roof supports nor sacrificial altars. One authority, J. Mascaro Pasarius (whose archaeological map of Minorca is recommended), has suggested that *taulas* were emblems of bull worship.

TORRE D'EN GAUMÉS

From the town of Alayor, 7½ miles (12km) west of Mahon on the main C721, take the road south-west to Son Bou. After the hamlet of San Isidro, take the turning south, as signposted.

A fine view of this prehistoric village in its rural setting.

This prehistoric settlement is sometimes referred to as 'Sa Comerma de Sa Garita', which is actually the name of the tomb at this site.

The village contains one of the four chamber tombs on Minorca, and, like the others, it is in a pitiful state with its capstone gone; its chamber measures 13ft 9in by 8ft 3in (4.2m by 2.5m). Also in the enclosure are standing stones, a stone pillared hall, three *talayots*, and a *taula* which has no capstone, but a candidate lies nearby – although the tomb may have had a wooden covering.

Dated between 2000 BC and 1000 BC, the site yielded, during excavations in 1974, an Egyptian bronze statue of Imhotep, the god of medicine, along with primitive surgical instruments, and also a bronze spearhead – a unique artefact in the Balearics.

This is a most tranquil place, and is watched over by a huge and brooding farmhouse, shutters ever closed against the elements.

TREPUCÓ

Take the main road PM702 south from Mahon to San Luis. After 1¼ miles (2km), turn left for Trepucó, and then left again; the round tower is now visible.

The most elegant of about 50 taulas on the island. Its top surface is 15ft (4.6m) above ground level.

This is the largest *taula* on Minorca with a pedestal 13ft (4m) above the ground and 9ft (2.7m) wide. Its rectangular, horizontal capstone measures 12ft by 6ft by 2ft (3.7m by 1.8m by 0.6m). The shape of the capstone is distinctly similar to the lintels of the Sarsen Trilithon Horseshoe (c.2000 BC) at STONEHENGE, Wiltshire, England.

Other impressive *taulas* on Minorca with the same capstone shape include Torralba d'en Salort (with a 'spine' running up its pedestal on one face – a familiar sight on standing stones around the world), Torre Trencada (with a separate stone 'spine' behind it), and Torre Llafuda.

There are some 50 *taulas* on the island; like many of the others Trepucó is enclosed by a stone wall, within which there are also tables stones and standing stones. A mostly ruined round tower stands nearby. Funerary practices have not been traced.

The site was excavated during 1928 and 1930 by the English archaeologist Margaret Murray.

IV.9

ALCALÁ GROUP

Monchique

CHAMBER TOMBS

4 U

Monchique is 15 miles (24km) north of the south-western port of Portimao.

BELOW: *Tomb 7 at Alcalá.*

This important group consists of 13 clusters of beehive-shaped chambers or *tholoi* (*see* LOS MILLARES, Almeria, for the origins of the term) which date back to about 3500 BC. Their first great excavator was Estacio da Veiga. In most of them the chambers average 8ft 3in by 9ft 9in (2.5m by 3.0m).

Tomb 1 at the site is unlike the others in the group, in that a double ring of stones forms the chamber. Tomb 3 has a handsome closed vestibule at its south-east facing entrance and two compartments within its passage, the last part of which has a septal slab before its chamber is reached. This has a niche to the east of it, which was found to contain seven long flint knives. Chisels, four daggers, awls, pieces of ivory and phallae made of clay were among other finds.

Two niches were found in Tomb 4, which contained two pieces of thin gold, probably finger rings. Tomb 7 is notable for the double rows of drystone walling all around it. Its entrance, as usual, faces the south-east, and the narrowing passage is punctuated, as in Tomb 3, with three pairs of opposite slabs. The chamber here is set lower than the entrance, as is the case in Tomb 9. It has a corbelled roof, the heavy top slab of which is broken. A 'cell' opens off either side of the chamber, at right angles to the axis of the passage. This grave also features the arrangement of double stones along its 14ft (4.3m) passageway.

ALMENDRAS

Guadalupe,
Evora

CROMLECH (STONE
CIRCLE)

5 Q

This is generally considered to be the
largest and most complete cromlech
in Portugal.

Take the N114 westwards out
of Evora towards Montemor-o-
Novo. After 6¼ miles
(10km) turn left for
Guadalupe 1¾ miles (3km)
down the road. At the
crossroads in the village,
continue over on to the good dirt
road, and follow the site signs
thereafter. Turn right almost
immediately, and then left just
over ½ mile (0.8km), until it
reaches Almendras Farm.

farm the road turns left and follows a winding route through
woodland. After another ¾ mile (1km), the *cromlech* (as a
stone circle is called in Portugal) can be seen to the left of the
road.

Almendras is the largest and most impressive *cromlech* in
Portugal, so it is claimed. It lies on an east facing slope with
panoramic views, and is made up of about 95 stones, up to
8ft 3in (2.5m) high, with the enclosed area measuring about
197ft by 98ft 6in (60m by 30m). They are arranged in a main
double oval setting, with a small 'lobe' at the western end and
a larger one to the east.

Recent excavations and restoration (which caused the dirt
road approach to be created) have cleared away vegetation,
raised some of the fallen stones and revealed several more
decorated stones, to add to those already known. The
decoration ranges from simple cup marks on the flat top of one
stone (near the road), to more elaborate compositions of
circles, curves, zigzags, and wavy and straggly lines. Overall
the designs fit into the general range of Portugese megalithic
art, with the cup marks in particular providing a link both to
standing stones and passage-tombs. This is a most rewarding
site, and a visit should be completed with a picnic.

At the farm, in the directions above, a fine standing stone,
10ft 6in (3.2m) high, can be visited; it is in an olive grove near
the grain silos to the south of the farm. This pleasurable
megalithic quest now continues back on the road, which turns
north through the farm. Along the way, a Roman altar and
milestone can be seen. After another 220yds (200m) from the

ANTA DE PAVIA

Pavia,
Mora,
Evora

PASSAGE-GRAVE
(REMAINS)

5 P

In the small square in the centre of the modest town of Pavia
there is to be found one of the more startling sights as well as
sites in this book! The massive chamber of a passage-tomb
rears up some 13ft (4m), to the level of surrounding rooftops.
Hidden from view on the far side, where the passage would
have led off, a tiny chapel (dedicated to St Dennis) has been
built up against the chamber – and indeed using its interior.

The chamber is characteristic of central Portugal, with its
tall pillar-like stones abutting and curving in towards the top,
kept in place by a massive capstone.

A true megalithic curiosity!

Take the N4 north-east from
Montemor-o-Novo for 15½
miles (25km) to Arraiolos;
then turn north on to the
N370 to the town of Pavia.

Anta de Poço da Gateira

---

*Reguengos de Monsaraz,
Evora*

Passage-Grave

---

7 Q

Anta is the Portuguese word for a burial chamber, and this is one of the most important of its type in the Iberian peninsula. It has an astounding thermoluminescence date of 4510±360 bc, which makes it one of the earliest monuments in this book

Leave Evora south-eastwards on the N256. The site is near Reguengos de Monsarez, about 23 miles (36km) along the road. Guide books and maps to the monuments in the area are on sale locally.

(*see* DATES AND DATING *pages 12–13*). The first serious excavation of this grave was conducted in 1948–49 by archaeologists Georg and Vera Leisner.

The covering circular cairn, kerbed in places, was 39ft (12m) in diameter. The short, low passage was lined with just two upright slabs and leads to the central chamber, which measures 10ft by 6ft 6in (3m by 2m). The most unusual discovery in the chamber was a line of 11 plain pots and one other – corresponding possibly to 12 corpses destroyed by acid soil – which doubtless once contained human remains. Many other pottery sherds were uncovered, along with polished axes, flint cutting blades, and a beautiful plain hemispherical Neolithic bowl.

Anta Grande do Zambujeiro

---

*Valverde,
Evora*

Passage-Grave

---

5 Q

Take the N114 westwards out of Evora towards Montemor-o-Novo. After 6¼ miles (10km) turn left for Guadalupe, 1¾ miles (3km) down the road. At the crossroads in the village turn left and proceed south continuing on a good dirt road. Valverde is reached in

2½ miles (4km). Now turn left down the hill through the village in the direction of Evora, cross the river, turn left past the agricultural station on the right. The site is signposted on the left, and a car park is soon reached to the north.

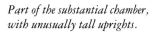

Part of the substantial chamber, with unusually tall uprights.

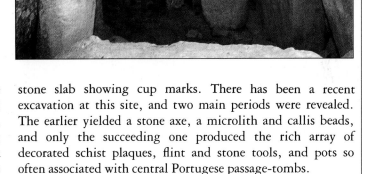

The huge mound, which lies across a stream (dry in the summer), is now protected by tin roofing. Much of the mound has been removed, leaving exposed an enormous chamber, constructed of typical in-curving pillar-like uprights reaching 19ft 9in (6m) in height – perhaps the tallest to be recorded in this book. The vast passage is well preserved, and contributes to the 'monumentality' of this extraordinary site.

About 65ft 6in (20m) to the south of the mound lies a long

stone slab showing cup marks. There has been a recent excavation at this site, and two main periods were revealed. The earlier yielded a stone axe, a microlith and callis beads, and only the succeeding one produced the rich array of decorated schist plaques, flint and stone tools, and pots so often associated with central Portuguese passage-tombs.

This site is not to be confused with the village of the same name, 21 miles (34km) east of Evora and south-west of Redondo.

Cabeças

---

*Arraiolos,
Evora*

Passage-Grave

---

6 P

This 28ft (85m) long grave has some interesting characteristics. Its entrance vestibule is just south of east and the passage is lined with upright slabs, which increase in height towards the chamber at the north-west. This passage is 8ft (2.4m) long but its maximum height, before the antechamber, is only 2ft 3in (0.7m) high. What a gloomy crawl! There were probably seven capstones. The largest and domed slab covers the four-sided chamber, the uprights of which lean inwards; the chamber's entrance was through a narrow gap at the north-east. A large paving stone on the chamber floor reflects the 6ft (2m) high roof area.

Leave Evora north-westwards on the N114-4, and then turn north on to the N370. Arraiolos is about 13½ miles (22km) from Evora. Local guides and maps on sale.

CUNHA BAIXA

Espinho,
Oporto

PASSAGE-GRAVE

J4

This dolmen, with its chamber and corridor, is one of the largest and best preserved to be found in Portugal. The polygonal chamber, which is surrounded by nine orthostats carrying one capstone, is 10ft 6in (3.2m) high by 9ft 9in (3.0m) wide. There is evidence of ochre painting on the orthostats, and the chamber was once paved.

The passage, which is about 5ft (1.5m) lower than the chamber, is bounded by a double row of eight uprights carved with incised cup marks and other engravings. These uprights are still partly covered in the area next to the chamber by one of the large stone slabs which originally covered the whole corridor.

The majority of the artefacts found on the site are now in the National Museum of Archaeology in Lisbon; they consist mainly of polished stone axes, flint blades, microliths, pottery sherds, and a granite supporting stone. This stone, which is 4ft (1.2m) tall, has 15 parallel incisions carved on its sides.

Beside the bridge over the brook (castelo) on the road from Cunha Baixa to Espinho, a concrete footpath is on the left of the road; this leads directly to the dolmen, about 650ft (200m) from the road.

PALMELA

Quinto do Anjo,
Palmela,
Setubal

ROCK-CUT TOMBS

3 Q

The entrance to one of the tombs, now badly desecrated. Finds have though been of importance.

This site is about 31 miles (50km) south-east of Lisbon, over the Tagus estuary, and some 5 miles (8km) north-west of the coastal town of Setubal. Leave this town north-west on the N252, then take the second turning on the left, on to the N379. The signposted site is about 3 miles (5km) along the road, off to the left.

This small group of tombs (sometimes spelt Palmella) has given its name to a type of fine developed Beaker pottery, dated about 2500–2000 BC. Four of them (two complete and two sliced in half) have been excavated. Three of their entrances face to the east, and one is aligned almost north/south, with its entrance just east of north. Their kidney-shaped chambers are reached through long, very low passages, which probably had one or more door slabs at their entrances, or through roof manholes, which are unique to the Iberian peninsula. They were used for successive multiple burials, then sealed; afterwards they were entered, almost emptied and, finally, it seems, deliberately and badly damaged.

Finds have happily been made, however. Notable among them is a unique arrowhead design; it has an almost circular blade and a long tang, and its type is known now as the Palmela point. The later Beaker burials brought copper daggers and flat axes. Remains have also been found of reddish and brownish decorated vases, sherds of low wide bowls, hanging vases with inturned rims, a small beautiful mixing bowl, a strange carved ball of limestone with a recessed waist around it, and beads for a necklace, perforated discs and other sundry amulets.

There was also a thin cylindrical idol-like figurine, which tapers towards its 'head'. It has four incised bands around the top, five more a third of the way down, then an inverted crescent less than the width of the object, followed by six bands all around, like the others and, finally, at the base but above a single band, what may be a representation of a human face. This may be artistic licence or mathematics expressed.

REGUENGOS DE MONSARAZ

*Reguengos de Monsaraz,
Evora*

PASSAGE-GRAVES

7 Q

*A tall menhir stands at the centre of
the large Xarez stone sanctuary.*

There are several important tombs here, set to the west of and among the tributaries of the Rio Guadiana. As a group they are well worth a visit (*see* also ANTA DE POÇO DA GATEIRA).

The *Antas* of Da Comenda Da Igreja, to the west of Evora, and away from this group, are fascinating. The circular cairn here, Anta Grande (which was excavated in the 1930s), contains a primary passage grave with very large upright slabs, and a secondary *tholos*, like POÇO DA GATEIRA near this site. The earlier grave is approached from the south-east by a low passage 34ft 6in (10.5m) long and at one point only 20ins (50.8cms) high. The once capstoned megalithic chamber is 8ft 3in (2.5m) high, with a maximum diameter of 11ft 6in (3.5m). This tomb has been tentatively dated back

*Leave Evora south-eastwards
on the N256. Reguengos de
Monsaraz is about 23 miles
(36km) away. Guide books
and maps to the monuments
are on sale locally.*

Anta 2 da Olival Da Pega, near this Evora group.

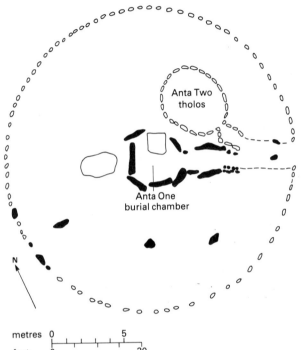

RIGHT: *Antas One and Two within the circular mound at Farisoa, one of a group at Reguengos de Monsaraz, Evora. (After G. and V. Leisner).*

The crook motif is thought by some to be a symbol of authority. It may also have been a horizon-measuring device and in this respect the apparent association with sun symbols is interesting. Crooks with zigzags were found at Anta Grande de Olival da Pega, close to this site.

to before 3500 BC.

Many centuries later a *tholos*, Anta 2, was built into the enclosure to the south of it but at a distinctly lower level. This chamber, which once had a corbelled roof, in accordance with its type, is 11ft 6in (3.5m) long and 9ft (2.7m) wide and is reached by a 6ft 6in (2m) long passage, which is actually parallel to the passage of Anta 1.

Nearby, there is a standing stone known as Abelhoa. Although the bottom part has been replaced, the top two-thirds of this typically-shaped menhir has some intriguing carvings on its surface. A crook is clearly discernible, with its handle to the right; this motif was often carved (*see* GAVR'INIS, Morbihan) and is a puzzle. More explicable is a representation of the sun shining above it, and there are also wavy lines, which possibly represent the ripple effect of water. The stone stands 8ft 9in (2.7m) above the ground. Other standing stones in the area include the 19ft 9in (6m) high Outeiro to the north, and Xarez, which stands at the centre of a huge stone sanctuary.

In plan, Antas 1 and 2 Da Farisoa (a few miles south-west of Da Comenda) are rather beautiful. The round mound which encloses both is perfectly circular and about 65ft 6in (20m)

across. At its centre, the passage and burial chamber was constructed first and, secondly, a *tholos* to its north. The oval chamber, Anta 1, is approximately 10ft (3m) in diameter, and seven uprights survive. Anta 2, with a diameter of 14ft 9in (4.5m), is the *tholos*, which shared an entrance at the south-east with the passage of the earlier grave; dated at about 2750 BC it is a neat oval, some 15ft (4.6m) at its widest, and is set, as customary, lower than the earlier grave. Its narrow orthostats are unusually thin and are shaped to fit their contiguous neighbours almost perfectly. They average 4ft (1.2m) in height, and would have been a fine sight beneath the corbelled roof of the *tholos*. Mysterious slate plaques have been found in both graves.

The earliest passage-grave in the Reguengos De Monsaraz Group is Anta 1 Dos Gorginos, which was excavated in 1949 by the Leisners. It has yielded a thermoluminescence date of 4440±360 bc. Its almost round, kerbed mound is some 40ft (12.2m) across. Other early graves in this remarkable area include the two Antas Da Pega, where more than 60 fragmented, engraved slate plaques were found; their patterns were mostly abstract, but some were anthropomorphic in design. These were probably prehistoric good-luck charms.

IV.18

Cova d'en Daina

Romañyá de la Selva,
Sant Feliu,
Gerona

GALLERY GRAVE

Sheet 443:38 G

Take the C250 from Sant Feliu on the coast north-west towards Llagostera and Gerona. After about 3 miles (5km) turn right along a minor road to Romañyá de la Selva. The site is to the north of the village.

The interior of the gallery grave, with its remarkable doorway.

This grave is set within a kerbed circular mound, which has a diameter of about 36ft (11m). The ring of stones, even if most are fallen, make an impressive sight. The parallel sets of orthostats inside are reminiscent of the French *allées-couvertes*. A single capstone, measuring 27ft (8.25m) in all, with a width of 5ft (1.5m), remains over the end of the gallery.

To the west, at the right of the entrance, stands the distinguishing feature of the site: a huge slab, second in size only to the endstone. The slab is the first of seven (one of which has fallen) around the quadrant. Finds here have included plaques – notably a bone plaque which is beautifully incised with abstract patterns and dated at 1500 BC, plain Almerian bowls, awls made of copper and Beaker sherds.

IV.19

Cueva de Menga

Antequara,
Malaga

UNDIFFERENTIATED
PASSAGE-GRAVE

Sheet 446:16 U

Take the N351 northwards from Malaga towards Antequara. At the junction with the C337, turn left towards Antequara; the site is signposted on the right.

One of the three monolithic supports.

This has long been one of the most famous chamber tombs in Spain; its main features are its huge length of over 82ft (25m), and the monoliths in its passage. Three large roughly square stones of slightly different dimensions stand in a row at approximately equal intervals down the centre of the passage, supporting capstones. There are five of these, and the end one over the chamber is estimated to weigh an incredible 180 tons.

The chamber's trilithon entrance faces north-east, with a vestibule; the passage is lined with twelve upright slabs on each side, averaging 9ft 3in (2.8m) in height. This great gallery is 20ft 3in (6.2m) at its widest, and the central pillars undoubtedly add to the grandeur of the interior. The tomb was once covered with a mound some 164ft (50m) across.

Being well-known over many centuries, it must have been thoroughly plundered, because no finds are recorded. But there are traces of carvings and paintings on the insides of the uprights; they include faintly human cross shapes, and one of them sports a kind of skirt.

Cueva del Romeral

Take the N351 northwards from Malaga towards Antequara. At the junction with the C337, cross over on to the minor road, and the site is signposted on the left.

A drystone passage leads to the narrow trilithon doorway and on to the round tholoi *chamber.*

Here is perhaps the most impressive passage-grave in Spain, and it has been dated at about 3500 BC. For a start, the enclosing mound is some 285ft (87m) across, and reaches 30ft (9m) in height. There are only six upright megaliths here, plus three near the entrance.

Regular drystone walling lines the 5ft (1.5m) wide and 6ft 6in (2m) high passage, this leads north-east towards a lower narrow trilithon doorway. This gives on to a drystone walled circular *tholoi* chamber, the first and larger of two here at 15ft (4.6m) in diameter. A capstone, 12ft 6in (3.8m) high above the ground tops the vaulted corbelled roof. A second, short, funnel-like passage, slightly west of the main passage axis, leads to the much smaller chamber between two uprights, ‚beneath roofing capstones in the walling. Again, a capstone lies astride the corbelling. Del Romeral is a typical *cueva*, of a form that does not exist in northern Spain.

Cueva de la Viera

IV.21

Take the N351 northwards from Malaga towards Antequara. At the junction with the C337, turn left; the site is signposted on the right.

The entrance down into this fine passage-grave.

This is another handsome tomb in the Antequara group which, archaeologically, is very important. Its mound is some 200ft (61m) across, and within it lies an 80ft (24.4m) long passage. This is lined with a parallel set of contiguous uprights, of which 22 survive. The entrance vestibule is at the south-east, and a port-hole transversal slab gives on to the passage.

A second, four-sided, port-hole stone slab gives access to the 2 sq yds (1.7 sq m) end chamber. This is covered by a massive 170-ton capstone which slightly overhangs an open area in the mound behind a huge capstone. This ambulatory space is reached by a third port-hole entrance in this endstone.

Port-holes are, incidentally, a particular feature of the Alcaide rock-cut tombs nearby; there are seven of them and each incorporates this almost square-shaped, carved access. The chamber here is most notable for its security, derived from some impressive vertical grooving on those port-hole stones – a Late Neolithic design triumph for a clearly important client.

DOLMEN DE SOTO

The so-called 'dolmen' is called Cueva del Zancarrón de Soto on some maps. This communal tomb with a stone rubble cairn is now partly depleted, but this does not detract from the majesty of the place. Indeed, light pouring down into the roofless end of the gallery adds to its drama.

There are about 32 pairs of contiguous uprights, (the final seven have lost their capstones) which gradually rise away from the entrance. The odd one is the twenty-second on the left; it is easily twice the width of the others except the endstone, which is about 9ft 9in (3m) in width.

The gallery is some 69ft (21m) long and is partially covered by a remarkable 19 capstones of which the penultimate one is by far the largest. Beneath the seventh capstone from the entrance, about a quarter of the way along the passage, two internal uprights act as portals, to produce a narrowing or neck; just ahead of them is another upright, just off-centre, and its purpose is difficult to guess at. Of the uprights, 21 bear carved decorations some of stylised human faces. In terms of tonnage, this is a mighty megalithic monument indeed.

Leave Huelva north-east on the N431. At San Juan del Puerto turn left north on to the N435 to Trigueros 3¾ miles (6km) away. A trackway leads south-east to the site. Take a torch.

LOMA DE LOS PEREGRINOS

This name literally means 'pilgrims' mound', and about 20 skeletons of them have been found in articulated form inside this rock-cut tomb. The entrance is, typically, at the south-east. After a short passage, two lateral side cells occur before the main chamber opens out; this is oddly elongated to the south-west and measures 13ft by 10ft (4m by 3m). This arrangement is very similar to the rock-cut tomb Praia Das Maçás (Estremadura, Spain) now mostly destroyed.

Finds have included rectangular Millaran copper awls, which are rare in tombs of this date (about 3400–3100 BC), plain Almerian pottery, and flint arrowheads.

Leave Murcia northwards on the N301. After 8¾ miles (14km) turn left over the River Segura, to Alguazas, where the site is signposted.

LOS CASTILLEJOS

IV.24

Montefrio,
Granada

CHAMBER TOMBS AND
SETTLEMENT

Sheet 446:17 U

The directions here guide you into a beautiful limestone valley, with great cliffs rising along the right hand side of the road. Eventually a track is signposted on the right, and this leads to a parking place (and picnic area). From here begins a memorable archaeological ramble along the foot of the cliffs. Amidst a jumble of crags and meadows, with fine views across the valley, megalithic tombs are strewn over more than ½ mile (1km). At least 20 sites are known, not individually large or spectacular, but often with splendid 'dog kennel' and port-hole entrances. They are generally simple passage tombs, with short passages widening into small, low, wedge-shaped chambers. In their midst, on a defensible crag detached from the main scarp, is a deeply stratified settlement. Excavation, penetrating to a depth of 16ft 6in (5m), revealed a lengthy sequence of Neolithic and Copper Age layers, followed by long abandonment in the Bronze Age. During the final, Iron Age, phase the settlement was defended at one end with a fine bastioned, ashlar wall, probably of Greek inspiration.

Leave Granada westwards on the E902. After about 21 miles (34km), at Loreto, turn north on to the C335. Montefrio is then 15½ miles (25km) along the road. In the village take the road for Penas de Los Gitanos.

LOS MILLARES

This wild, desolate site certainly does not provide an easy-going day's outing. In the summer months it is very hot, the stream, Rambla de Huechar, is dried up, and a quick glance across the rocky spur might not reveal any man-made constructions. But they are there, and in great numbers.

The Los Millares site, which is 790ft (240m) above sea level, consists of a 12-acre (4.8 hectares) cemetery attached to three or more forts, which are to the west of an ancient partly-walled hut settlement. Los Millares was a seat of great power from about 3100 BC for some 500 years thereafter; the scale of the place and the fortifications make this clear. There was even a long aqueduct running east and then northwards to the village ramparts to meet the needs of the village inhabitants on the harsh spur overlooking the confluence of the Rio Andarax and the Rambla de Huechar.

There are up to 100 individual burials in passage and circular graves, spread about either side of the aqueduct, to the

Models and finds from this important site can be seen in the Archaeological Museum, Almeria. Take the N340 north from Almeria, on the coast. At Benahadux, turn left north-westwards on to the N324. The large mountainous site is over on the right on the spur between the river valleys of Andarax and Rambla de Huechar. This signposted site has been fenced in recently, but there is a manned entrance.

A partially restored area at this vast famous site.

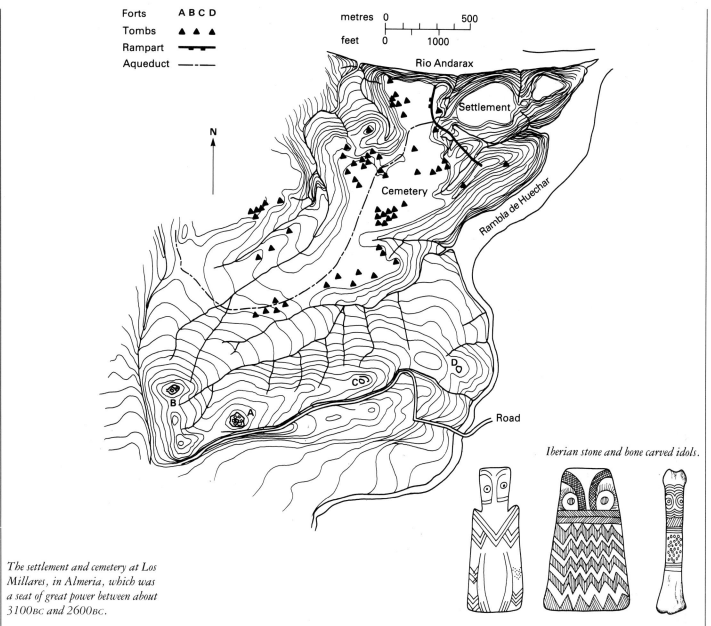

Forts   **A B C D**
Tombs   ▲ ▲ ▲
Rampart
Aqueduct

metres 0 — 500
feet 0 — 1000

N

Rio Andarax

Settlement

Cemetery

Rambla de Huechar

Road

Iberian stone and bone carved idols.

The settlement and cemetery at Los Millares, in Almeria, which was a seat of great power between about 3100 BC and 2600 BC.

north of the forts and, naturally, outside the village ramparts. The site was first seriously excavated at the beginning of this century by Louis Siret who was able to demonstrate the copper mining industry at Los Millares, to the astonishment of archaeologists at that time.

Among the 80 or so circular chamber tombs here, there are distinctive, beehive-shaped, drystone walled, corbel-roofed chambers; to describe them in one word, Siret came up with the Greek word *tholos* (plural *tholoi*). He had related such tombs to Mycenaean equivalents, but, as radiocarbon dating has subsequently proved, Los Millares graves are far too old for such a design influence. However, the corbel-roofing can be related to architecture in the Mediterranean basin – to the Sardinian *nuraghi* (*see* LI-LOLGHI and SANT' ANTINE, Sardinia), the *sese* of Pantelleria (the often-ignored island lying between Sicily and Tunisia) and the *talayots* of Minorca (*see* TALATI DE DALT).

Los Millares was next excavated by M.J. Almagro Gorbea and Antonio Arribas, and also examined during 1953/55 by Georg and Vera Leisner who designated the tomb numbers used here. Many have notable features. Tomb 7, for example, yielded the usual copper artefacts but at the south side of the entrance ten small betyls (flat topped, cone-like stelae), about

1ft (0.3m) high, stood in a group – a mysterious minilithic huddle. These were often painted with a red substance, and elsewhere have measured up to 2ft (0.6m) high.

Tomb 17 is a well-known *tholos*. The flat-topped circular cairn was probably constructed in two stages and had four levels of kerbstones, with a semi-circular entrance forecourt at the east breaking into the first two levels. The passage was equally compartmented by septal port-hole slabs; most unusually two rectangular side chambers open out either side of the third western compartment. The circular chamber is 11ft (3.4m) in diameter, with contiguous uprights and a corbelled roof. A low monolith was set at the centre, and was perhaps once a platform for a wooden roof support.

Tomb 19 has provided the important date of 3100 BC. Tomb 40 was revealed to contain about 40 burials, and Tomb 63 was rich, not in bones, but in grave goods, behind its square port-hole slab at the chamber entrance. Los Millares has been well served over the last 100 years or so by both architects and publishers. Settlements and camps which are set on hill spurs at the confluence of rivers (*see* also VILLENEUVE-TOLOSANE, Haute-Garonne) have proved to be major contributors to an increased understanding of interactions between small local prehistoric communities and their ways of life.

V

Southern Europe

In cultural matters richness can lie in diversity. The basin of the Mediterranean Sea contains islands and mainlands which are strewn with megalithic remains of the greatest interest. Iberia and the Balearic Islands are dealt with separately in this book, as are France and the coastal African Maghreb countries of Morocco, Algeria and Tunisia.

Early burials and pottery

Rock-cut tombs present the earliest evidence of single and double burials only, perhaps as far back as late in the fifth millennium BC, throughout the central and western Mediterranean. It is an odd fact that no rock-cut tombs have been found in Corsica, although a few miles to the south lies the island of Sardinia, where well over 1000 such tombs have been recorded.

Equally strange is the fact that none occur north of Tuscany, 51 miles (82km) across the sea from Corsica. In Campania, south-west Italy, near the walled coastal town of Paestum (famed for its Greek temples), are three of the most sophisticated rock-cut chamber tombs (*hypogea*) in Italy. They have yielded corrected radiocarbon dates ranging from 3350 BC to 2500 BC. This type site of Gaudo was discovered in 1943, when United States military bulldozers were seeking rock for an airfield after the Salerno landings; it was quickly explored by the British Army's Mobile Archaeological Unit. There were 25 graves, clearly used in succession, as their earlier occupants were disarticulated and simply piled up in a corner. Around the walls of a kidney-shaped tomb, 25 complete skeletons were found (almost equally male and female). There were 33 pots and other vessels of great beauty. They included a double cup, made by fusing the handles together, and an *askos*, a vessel with a top opening off-centre and a carrying handle extended to the middle of the pot top. The same pottery, now known as Gaudo ware, was found in a tomb nearby, Mirabello Eclano, where a chieftain was buried with many primitive weapons at his side for the great journey, and a dog at his feet. Sadly, this site at Paestum cannot be visited today.

Also in Campania, but very much open to those hardy enough to explore it, is the site known as LA STARZA, or sometimes Ariano. It is outside the village of Ariano Irpino, but best reached from Benevento. This huge rocky gypsum hillock overlooking the Ariano Pass was excavated in 1957–61 by David Trump, a notable contributor to European archaeology. He established that the site was in human occupation from the Early Neolithic to the Early Iron Ages, and that trade in those far-off days was vigorous.

There are no megaliths and no mysteries here, but plenty of remarkable pottery finds to demonstrate such trading. They included Lagozza ware (from near Milan in the north, and dating back to 3800 BC), Piano Conte (from the island of Lipari, north-east of Sicily), Connelle (from the Marche, east-central Italy), Rinaldone (from a Copper Age site near Lake Bolsena, north of Rome), and Gaudo ware. There was also the site's own pottery; this has a distinctive white band around the waists of the pots – bands made of gypsum from the hill itself.

As usual, in southern Europe, natural and then artificial cave and rock-cut burials were succeeded by interments in single stone cists. At about 2500 BC the building of megalithic chamber tombs commenced.

Corsica

This rugged island of 3368 square miles (8722 sq km) lies only 7½ miles (12km) north of Sardinia, across the strait of Bonifacio, and yet their two cultures differed in many ways. Some remarkable megalithic monuments remain from the Chalcolithic Age (c.2800–1700 BC). Chief among them are the two rows (remains of seven) of some 90 statue-menhirs at PAGLIAIU (or Palaggiu). These are the survivors of 258, out of an island total of about 450 (and not one of them shows any part of the female body). The Middle Bronze Age statue-menhirs, unique to Corsica, reached their zenith at FILITOSA, south of Ajaccio. Although spoiled, this is one of the more instructive as well as beautiful archaeological sites in southern Europe. The statue carvers were succeeded here by the Torreans – builders of circular cyclopean towers (which are also unique to Corsica) of which there are 120 dotted around the island. Chamber tombs, known here as *dolmens* (as in France, of which the island is a *département*), include SETTIVA. It is unusual in having two stones standing outside its forecourt entrance.

Italy

Rock-cut tombs in mainland Italy have already been mentioned. Later came the builders of *specchie*, Italy's own form of burial chamber. One spectacular example, even if tragically harmed during its discovery, is GIOVINAZZO, near Bari. It is counted as one of the so-called Bari-Taranto group of tombs in the region of Apulia, on Italy's heel. Almost all of these collective grave sites mysteriously feature an associated standing stone (*pietrafitta*), though not at Giovinazzo. *Specchie* is also the name given to larger non-burial cairns.

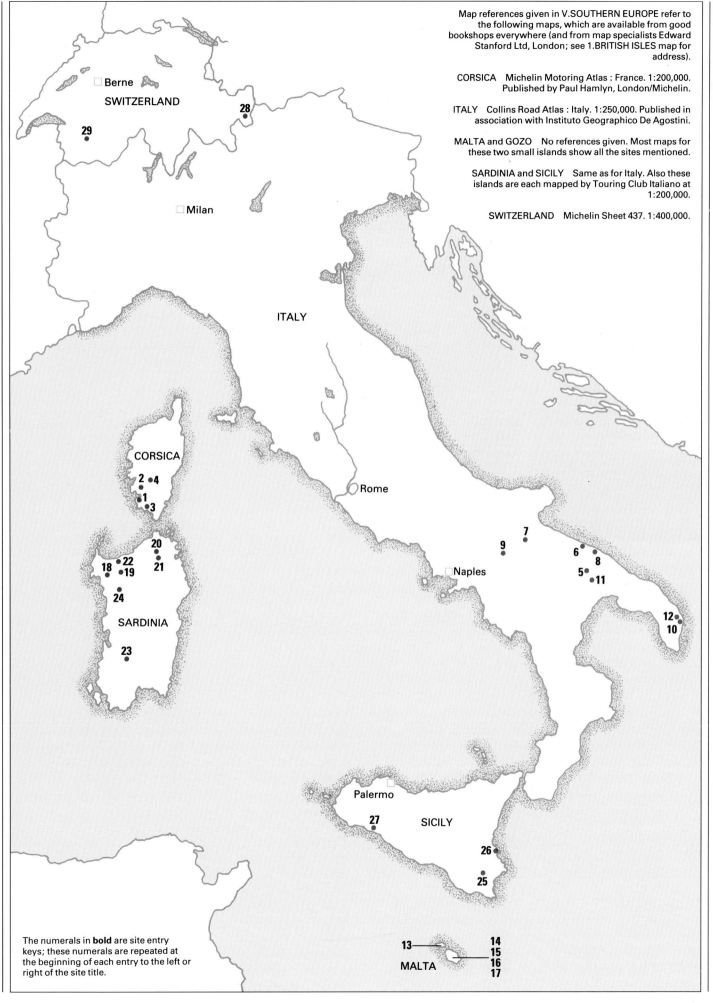

Map references given in V.SOUTHERN EUROPE refer to the following maps, which are available from good bookshops everywhere (and from map specialists Edward Stanford Ltd, London; see 1.BRITISH ISLES map for address).

CORSICA   Michelin Motoring Atlas : France. 1:200,000. Published by Paul Hamlyn, London/Michelin.

ITALY   Collins Road Atlas : Italy. 1:250,000. Published in association with Instituto Geographico De Agostini.

MALTA and GOZO   No references given. Most maps for these two small islands show all the sites mentioned.

SARDINIA and SICILY   Same as for Italy. Also these islands are each mapped by Touring Club Italiano at 1:200,000.

SWITZERLAND   Michelin Sheet 437. 1:400,000.

□ Berne

SWITZERLAND

28

29

□ Milan

ITALY

CORSICA

2 ●4
1
3

○ Rome

20

18 22
19
21

7

9

□ Naples

6
8
5 11

24

SARDINIA

23

12
10

13

14
15
16
17

MALTA

○ Palermo

27

SICILY

26

25

The numerals in **bold** are site entry keys; these numerals are repeated at the beginning of each entry to the left or right of the site title.

LEFT: *One of the 'holes' at* MNAJDRA, *Malta. The southern temple at this site is the best preserved on the island.*

ABOVE: *One of the most interesting chamber tombs in Corsica is Fontanaccia, south of Sartène in the south-west of the island on the remote Cauria plateau.*

RIGHT: *The dramatic, well-preserved Nuraghe Su Nuraxi at Barumini, south-east of Oristano, in Sardinia.*

Although there are no rock-cut tombs north of Tuscany (nor indeed in Corsica to the west), they occur in the south. In one at ALTAMURA, Bari, a strange bone plaque has been found, showing six bosses (possibly breasts). Similar plaques have been found elsewhere in southern Europe, at TARXIEN, Malta, for instance, and CASTELLUCCIO, Sicily.

Apulia has a concentration of tombs worth visiting. BISCEGLIE, Bari, is typical of the Bari-Taranto Group, and 12 in the different Otranto Group are located near Lecce. Of the latter, SCUSI was the first to be recorded in the whole region, in 1867, and it has been broadly dated between 2500–1800 BC.

Malta and Gozo

The islands of Malta and Gozo attract thousands of visitors each year to their 30 or so rock-cut and cyclopean temples. Their construction started in about 3500 BC and suddenly ceased for ever in about 2400 BC. Some are in pairs, such as HAGAR QIM and MNAJDRA. Perhaps the most extraordinary is HAL SAFLIENI (partner TARXIEN), south of Valletta. Twenty chambers were accidentally discovered in 1902, hewn out of solid rock; there were about 7000 disarticulated skeletons, red ochre paintings, and curious oracle holes (perhaps the world's earliest confessionals). There are also dolmens on the islands.

Sardinia

This is another island with unique megalithic monuments. The oldest site is LI-MURI, near Arzachena, in the north, which has five intersecting stone kerbed circular platforms. In the centre of each is a *coffre* (an open-ended high-sided rectangular stone slab cist). Near them are the remains of a Giant's Tomb – one of the many *tomba di giganti*, collective burial chambers, in Sardinia. They were constructed by the *nuraghi* builders for well over a millennium starting in about 1900 BC and perhaps as early as 2300 BC.

Nuraghi are Late Neolithic high round stone defensive towers, built from about 2500 BC; there are more than 6500 of

them spread over this 9,301 square miles (24,089 sq km) island (*see* SANT' ANTINE, near Thiesi). One of the most extraordinary and complex of them all is Nuraghe su Nuraxi, at Barumini in Cagliari, with its 13 towers, surrounding walls and a hut settlement; it is dated at about 1800 BC. Not to be missed in Sardinia are well temples, such as SANT' ANASTASIA, near Campidano, and the atmospheric so-called temple mound of MONTE D' ACCODDI, near Porto Torres, with its stone egg.

Sicily

This fascinating country, a fifth larger than Wales, is known for its rock-cut tombs, such as the coastal THAPSOS, near Siracusa, and the huge inland site of CASTELLUCCIO. The Castelluccian culture has been placed in the First Siculan period (about 2500–1700 BC), but may be earlier; it gives its name to the buff-coloured pottery with black linear patterns found there. More than 200 small, round oven-shaped (*a forno*) chambers were cut into the hillside for collective burials. Some of the doorway slabs bear decorative motifs which are unique in Sicily. Seven bone plaques have been found here (with six bosses or breasts) out of the ten discovered so far on the island.

Switzerland

One of the most interesting Swiss megalithic sites is LE PETIT CHASSEUR, Sion, in the Valais; here there are chamber tombs, statue-menhirs and cists. A date of 4000 BC has been obtained from one of the two excavated stratified levels. There was a very early re-use of anthropomorphic statue-menhirs here which is unusual (but which also occurred at FILITOSA, Corsica).

Physically-fit megalith afficionados might enjoy trekking up to the rock carvings at CARSCHENNA in the canton of Graubünden. The ten carved surfaces are well worth reaching. The eventual pause for breath would be a good moment to reflect upon the fact that every single motif carved here is also found in every other country in this book.

CAPU-DI-LOGU

Belvédère-Campomoro,
Propriano

CHAMBER TOMB WITH
CARVINGS

180 C 3

This is one of about 100 chamber tombs in Corsica, where (as in France) they are called *dolmens*. They are mostly in the south of the island, where such building commenced in about 2900 BC.

Usually, dolmens were simple rectangles formed by stone slab uprights, but one or two have short passages facing east and some were covered by an earth mound. Most Corsican examples are in a ruined state, because of looting by treasure hunters through the ages.

This dolmen, with incised decoration, has a horned forecourt, which is similar in design to TINKINSWOOD, South Glamorgan, Wales, and, much nearer, to many Sardinian *tomba di giganti*, such as LI-LOLGHI, Arzachena.

Take the N196 south from Propriano. Turn right onto the D121 along the Golfe de Valinco. After 10 miles (16km) just beyond Belvédère-Campomoro, the site (also known as Capo di Luogo) is down a signposted track on the left.

FILITOSA

Filitosa,
Sollacaro

STATUE-MENHIRS AND
TORRI

180 C 2

Three of the many statue-menhirs at this site. None of them are 'female', and nor are there any in Corsica.

Take the N196 south from Ajaccio. 6¼ miles (10km) south of Petreto-Bicchisano, take the next turning right on to the D757 running south-west along the Taravo to Sollacaro, and on to the site of Filitosa, which is signposted. Car park and museum.

Though a much disturbed site, Filitosa is easily the best known in Corsica, and one of the most famous in the Mediterranean basin. In its beautiful setting above the Taravo river, it has a lasting 'presence' which perhaps recalls its original use as a sanctuary. (Prehistoric sites without question possess characters of their own; some are simply 'not nice': ST LYTHANS, South Glamorgan, Wales, is, the author feels, one example). Filitosa was discovered as recently as 1948, and led to a modest flurry of interest and activity in Corsica's prehistoric monuments under the direction of Roger Grosjean.

The sanctuary site was probably occupied in three different stages between about 4000 and 500 BC. For the first 2000 years, it was in the hands of Neolithic and then Early Bronze Age tribes, who were megalith builders. During the next 1200 years, from about 1800 BC to about 800 BC, it was the province of indigenous creators of Corsica's *torri*.

A *torre* is a circular tower constructed of cyclopean masonry, with a large entrance giving on to a short access passage which leads to a large single chamber, with a false-corbelled roof. Variations incorporated small niches within the chamber and additional passages, especially if they were built around natural rock formations (as one is at Filitosa). There are about 120 *torri* on the island, and tourist literature rightly displays them as Corsica's principal contribution to Mediterranean prehistory (just as Minorca has *navetas* and *talayots*, Sardinia *nuraghi*, Italy *specchie*, and so on). Here they date to the Middle and Late Bronze Ages.

The final period of Filitosa's active occupation saw the 'arming' of some of its many statue-menhirs, with daggers, swords, coats of chain mail with strange grooves, and depictions of helmets carried on the menhirs. These helmets have two holes which may have accommodated horns.

The site is approached along a path past the museum. The East Monument, the first *torre* of three, incorporates a narrow gateway in a wall of cyclopean blocks which encircles the site on its rocky spur. The Central Monument is reached through hut remains. This consists of a ruined *torre* (dated at about 1800 BC) resting on a larger low round cyclopean platform.

Today statue-menhirs almost surround it; they were excavated from the *torre's* foundations and date from about 2000–1500 BC. Unlike France, Spain, and elsewhere, there are no 'female' statue-menhirs, showing breasts, at Filitosa or anywhere in Corsica (among a total of about 450 carved and uncarved menhirs).

Further to the north-west on the spur lies the West Monument, a *torre* dated to between 1400–900 BC. This soft stone 20ft (6.1m) high outcrop with deep, rounded fissures driven into it by weathering, is surrounded by now ruined cyclopean walling. Below it and nearby are five intriguing statue-menhirs of great age. But their positions in the peaceful sylvan arena are modern, like statues in a public park – which is just what they are.

A vividly carved statue-menhir from the group opposite, with the familiar necklace. Below it are rare symbols of defence or attack, which were perhaps carved during the fifth of their six development stages.

RIGHT: *The sanctuary site at Filitosa, notable for its statue-menhirs (one shown) and its Torrean monuments.*

BELOW: *There are about 450 carved and uncarved statue-menhirs in Corsica. A carved dagger can be seen below the mysterious visage.*

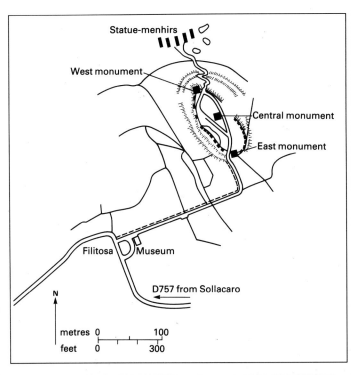

PAGLIAIU

Sartène

STONE ROWS
(ALIGNMENTS) OF
STATUE-MENHIRS

180 C 4 (marked as
Alignements de Palaggiu)

*Standing and fallen stones among
the rows. About 90 of them are
carved.*

These two stone rows, or *alignments*, are sometimes collectively referred to as 'Palaggiu'; there were originally 258 carved granite standing stones placed in seven groups, out of an island total of about 450. Unusually, not one depicts the female body, or any of its parts. They are dated around 2000 BC, and seem to have developed, according to R. Grosjean, in six broad stages; only in the fifth stage were weapons depicted.

Recalling the stone rows of Brittany (*see* KERMARIO and MÉNEC, Morbihan, France), many of the 90 or so statue-menhirs here are placed in alignments oriented north-south, with the carved surfaces facing east. The Carnac rows are uncarved, and are set east to west. It has been proposed that the Carnac rows formed an astronomical instrument; perhaps these Corsican menhirs are simply memorial stones.

At Pagliaiu there is also a cup-marked cist (known here as a *coffre*), with a small stone circle around it, which probably acted as a revetment around a covering earth mound; it could date back to 2500 BC. Rare for Corsican sites, this cist yielded artefacts in the form of Beaker-type fragments. Carved dolmens are also to be found here.

Leave Propriano in the Golfe De Valinco southwards on the N196. Sartène is 8 miles (13km) south. South-west of the town, turn right on to the D48; after 5½ miles (9km), take the right fork on the D48. The rows are signposted on the right.

SETTIVA

Petreto-Bicchisano

CHAMBER TOMB
(DOLMEN)

180 C 2

This is one of three Corsican dolmens which have port-holes in their entrance slabs. Its wide outward curving forecourt faces south-east, and unusually two stones, rather than one, stand a few feet in front of the entrance.

A tiny antechamber leads into a square chamber, which has an extra rectangular upright slab in its north-west corner. The original cist (dated at about 2250 BC), from which the tomb evolved, was in this chamber.

Remains of five individuals were found here, as well as beads, pottery sherds, obsidian and flint blades, axes, and also 20 cups from the earliest layer of deposits. They are of a type which indicates 3250–2750 BC as the probable date for the first use of Settiva.

Petreto-Bicchisano is 14 miles (22km) up a winding mountain road, the N196 north of Propriano on the road to Ajaccio. Ask in the town for local directions.

ITALY

V.5

*Altamura,
Bari,
Apulia*

ROCK-CUT TOMBS

62 B 4

ALTAMURA

These tombs are set in to the side of a hill. Neolithic sherds of pottery have been found, coming from the Diana-Bellavista period, (4th millennium BC), and from the Bronze and Iron ages, in the higher tombs. Lower down, disturbed deposits have occurred from the Late Paleolithic period; there were also stones carved with distinct geometric patterns, and both impressed and painted pottery.

In the vicinity of the tombs, a bone plaque with some intriguing characteristics has been discovered. It is 3½ins (8.9cm) long and has six protuberances, bosses or breasts. Exactly similar plaques have been found at Troy, TARXIEN, Malta, and CASTELLUCCIO, Sicily.

Leave Altamura south-eastwards on the S171 towards Santéramo in Colle. The tombs are 5½ miles (9km) along the road on the left before the station at Casal Sabini.

V.6

*Corato,
Bisceglie,
Bari,
Apulia*

GALLERY GRAVES

61 J 1 (Chianca); 63 G 4 (Tavole dei Paladini)

BISCEGLIE

Near the seaside town of Bisceglie, just to the west of the ferry port and city of Bari (capital of Apulia; its archaeological museum is in the Piazza Umberto), are a dozen burial chambers, which are sometimes (thanks to John D. Evans) called the Bari-Taranto group. They are all collective grave sites, housed in parallel-sided, narrow, galleried structures, with endchambers of the same width. In this respect they are like the French *allées-couvertes*, and similar Neolithic tombs are found all over Europe, including the Mediterranean basin. In this group, rather mysteriously, almost all of them have an associated standing stone or menhir, some of which are statue-menhirs.

Chianca was discovered in 1909. It lies on an exact east/west axis in a shallow trench.

Take the straight road south from the coastal town of Bisceglie, beneath the regional road, towards the E55 autostrada. Turn left before it, and Dolmen Di Chianca (as marked on the map) is on the right. Albarosa is just over ½ mile (1km) away. Tavole dei Paladini (as marked on the map), is south-east of Bari, just north of the S16, between the towns of Fasano and Ostuni.

The chamber of Chianca at the western end is unusually tall at 6ft (1.8m).

The finest grave in this group is Chianca (not to be confused with another Chianca, at Maglie, south-east of Lecce). It was discovered in 1909, excavated by M. Gervasio and A. Mosso and dated at 2300–1750 BC. The whole tomb is 24ft 6in (7.5m) long, set exactly on an east/west axis, with its entrance at the east. The western chamber is particularly tall at 6ft (1.8m), and measures 12ft 6in by 8ft (3.8m by 2.4m) beneath a thin capstone. The chamber and passage are set in a shallow trench, and were most likely once covered by a stone cairn. Such cairns, and other stone towers (often with exterior spiral stairways) which were never tombs, are known as *specchie* and are characteristic of southern Italy. *Specchie* apparently never had compartments; here, handsome pairs of uprights line a passage now open to the sky.

There have been many finds in and around Chianca, including the usual broken votive pottery, a strange bronze disc and amber beads. There were also 13 skeletons, one of them complete and in a flexed position. This individual was no doubt the last to arrive. Chianca is set in a delightful olive grove, but is now bounded by unattractive stone walls.

Tavole dei Paladini, though not in the immediate vicinity of Chianca, is counted as one of the Bari-Taranto group. This gallery grave has a very short passage, with a vestibule facing east; a septal slab gives on to the antechamber. The sloping capstone survives, as do the huge side slabs.

Albarosa, another notable gallery grave about ½m (1km) away was also enclosed by a huge *specchia*. Curiously, its height in the chamber, at 6ft (1.8m), is the same as at Chianca; the length of the whole is only slighter shorter, at 23ft (7m), and its entrance also faces east (though this is very common).

Frisari, nearby, is a good example of a simple burial chamber, with just four uprights; the widest of them is 11ft 6in (3.5m), and one of the others has fallen. Dolmen di Giano was once in this loose group, but it has now vanished without trace, due to the economic demands of agriculture and therefore for big flat fields for farmers.

Man has been in the area of Bisceglie for a long time. Neanderthal human remains have been found in the nearby Grotta S. Croce, which is somewhat similar to caves in the Cheddar Gorge, Somerset, England; bones of rhinoceros and hyena were found there by L. Cardini during excavations in 1939, and again in 1954–56. During the following six years he explored a similar inhabitation, Cave di Mastro Donato. Its quaint name seems to be unconnected with the astonishingly long period of its use – its excavator uncovered both Neanderthal remains and SERRO D'ALTO pottery.

V.7

CASTELLUCCIO DE' SAURI GROUP

161
SOUTHERN
EUROPE
Italy

Castelluccio De' Sauri,
Foggia,
Apulia

PREHISTORIC
SETTLEMENTS AND
STATUE-MENHIRS

56 D 6

RIGHT: *A statue-menhir from the*
prehistoric settlement at
Castelluccio De' Sauri. (After
Philip Howard)

This site, on the huge plain of Tavoliere (which means 'chessboard' and is a reference to its Roman field system) is one of a number of prehistoric settlements in the area for those with sharp eyes. Others include La Quércia (to the north-east), which is ringed by no less than eight ditches, and Passo di Corvo, which is a veritable township of 100 dwelling places. Another important prehistoric settlement is on the Adriatic coast, north-west of Foggia, outside the village of Manfredonia.

There are three statue-menhirs from the Copper Age from this site in the Archaeological Museum in Foggia. The early ones are primitive and mostly faceless, as in Sardinia (*see* FILITOSA). They become more elaborate and detailed as the centuries pass, very often featuring necklaces – or are they token belts, displays of wealth and status (see CRECH-QUILLÉ, Côtes-d'Armor, France, and LE CÂTEL, Channel Islands).

Other recurring decorations, both incised and in low relief, are weapons such as daggers and axes and anatomical features such as breasts, arms, heads and eyes, and also navels. Grave goods or local finds are very rarely found with statue-menhirs, and yet they must have been megalithic memorials.

Leave Foggia southwards on
the S655. After about 12½
miles (20km), turn right on to
the S161 for the village of
Castelluccio De' Sauri, 3¾
miles (6km) away. Then ask
for local directions.

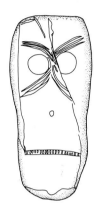

GIOVINAZZO

One of the most impressive specchie *in Italy.*
It was inadvertently discovered by a farmer.

Giovinazzo,
Molfetta, Bari,
Apulia

GALLERY CAIRN
(SPECCHIA)

62 B 2 (marked *dolmen*)

Leave the coastal town of
Giovinazzo south-westwards
on the largest road towards
Terlizzi. Cross over the S16,
and then over the E55
autostrada and the site is
visible on the right. It is 11
miles (18km) from Bari, and
not signposted.

This splendid *specchia*, sometimes called San Silvestro, was only discovered in 1961, when a farmer attempted to flatten what he thought was simply a long high mound of earth. Smashed in two though it is, it is still regarded as one of the grandest *specchie* in their native southern Italy and forms one of the Bari-Taranto group (*see* BISCEGLIE, Bari).

It has been dated at about 1750 BC, but is probably earlier. Most likely it was constructed for a tribal or family group, and was in use for some 1500 years. It boasts a substantial semi-circular forecourt, the walling of which is so thick that it is difficult to believe that its top surfaces were not used, in conjunction with the courtyard below, for some ceremony or ritual, perhaps involving votive offerings.

The original covering cairn of dressed drystone was 90ft (27.4m) long and set on a north/south axis, with the grave entrance at the south – which is extremely rare. The round antechamber consists of inward leaning square stone blocks. Beyond this lies the 53ft (16.1m) long gallery passage, topped by six surviving capstones and lined with substantial leaning flat slabs; it measures only 3ft (0.9m) at its widest, and is divided into compartments by septal slabs. In one, human bones of nine adults, two adolescents and at least two children were found. The roof of the chamber, now destroyed, was probably of the *tholos* type.

Many skeletons have been identified at this *specchia*, and also pottery from the Mycenaean I and II periods. This is an archetypal southern Italian megalithic site, although it has no associated standing stone (*pietrafitta*). Many of these are to be seen around the nearby village of Terlizzi. Apulia offers an excellent 14 day megalith hunting holiday.

LA STARZA

Ariano Irpino,
Benevento,
Avellino,
Campania

PREHISTORIC CAVES

59 I 2

Sometimes called Ariano, this huge and dramatically situated site is a rocky gypsum hillock overlooking and commanding the Ariano Pass. It was excavated in 1957–61 by David Trump, a notable contributor to European archaeology. He established that the site was in human occupation from the Early Neolithic to the Early Iron Ages, and that trade in those far-off days was vigorous.

There are no megaliths and no mysteries here, but plenty of remarkable pottery finds. They included final Lagozza ware (from near Milan in the north, and dating back to 2850 BC), Piano Conte (from the island of Lipari, north-east of Sicily), Connelle (from the Marche, east-central Italy), Rinaldone (from a Copper Age site near Lake Bolsena 50 miles (80km) north of Rome), and Gaudo – all implying considerable movement.

On one terrace there was a large rubbish heap, giving 16ft (4.9m) deep of stratified finds, including the site's own Ariano pottery; this has a distinctive white band pressed around the waists of the pots – bands made of the gypsum of the very hill.

Leave Benevento eastwards on the E842 autostrada; turn off northwards at the Grottaminarda exit on to the S90 going northwards to Ariano Irpino. Then ask for local directions.

SCUSI

Minervino di Lecce,
Otranto,
Lecce,
Apulia

CHAMBER TOMB

69 I 4 (marked *Dolmen di Scusi*)

This charmingly situated dolmen is one of 16 in the Otranto area (*see also* TERRA D'OTRANTO). It was, in fact, the first such tomb to be recorded in Apulia, in 1867, and has been dated between 2500–1800 BC. It was thought by its excavator, M.A. Micalella, that its name might have been derived from a local dialect word *scundere*, measuring 'hiding place'. It is very similar to other Otranto group sites, which have clear affinities with Maltese and Sardinian tombs.

Its thick flat, perforated capstone, which is 12ft 6in (3.8m) across, rests on one upright slab and eight piles of up to four courses of large stones, all of which stand on a platform of natural limestone. In this platform, near the tomb, there is a small rectangular hole, which once almost definitely held a menhir; this would have been consistent with the tomb's type.

Leave Otranto south-westwards for 3¾ miles (6km). At Uggiano la Chiesa turn right towards Minervino di Lecce. The signposted site is 1¼ miles (2km) beyond the village on the left.

This charmingly situated chamber tomb was the first Apulian megalithic site to be recorded. The capstone pillar supports are unusual.

SERRA D'ALTO

*Serra d'Alto,
Matera,
Basilicata*

CAVES, ROCK-CUT
TOMBS AND OPEN
VILLAGE SETTLEMENTS

62 B 4 (marked
Villaggio Neolitico)

Caves hewn out of rock faces in valley ravines are known as *sassi* in this region which forms the arch in the foot of Italy. The *sassi* La Murgecchia and Tirlecchia to the north and east of Matera, below the 13th-century cathedral, number more than 3000 and, incredibly, more than 17,000 people occupied this honeycomb until the beginning of this century, when American funds sponsored their removal. Some were excavated by D. Ridola in 1900–10 and by U. Rellini in 1919.

High on a limestone escarpment a hut settlement, dated at about 3750 BC, was found. Pottery, now known as Serra d'Alto, was made here. In design terms it was amazingly advanced for the Neolithic period; its painted detail varied but often featured meanders and spirals, while always conforming to a simple yet distinctive general style. The museum at 24 Via Ridola in Matera displays fine examples of this classic prehistoric ware.

Leave Matera north-eastwards on the S271. The site is signposted about 1¾ miles (3km) on the left.

V.12

TERRA D'OTRANTO GROUP

*Otranto,
Lecce,
Apulia*

BURIAL CHAMBERS
(DOLMENS) AND
STANDING STONES
(PIETREFITTE)

69 I 4 Giurdignano;
69 H 3 Gurgulante and
Placa (all as marked)

The coastal town is the most easterly in Italy. It is reached by the autostrada running south-east from Brindisi to Lecce, and then on the S16 to the town.

The Gurgulante dolmen, one of the smallest in this book.

There are 12 tombs (out of 16 recorded) in the so-called Otranto Group, and they are markedly different from the Bari-Taranto tombs (*see* BISCEGLIE, Bari). Here there are menhirs (called *pietrefitte* in south-east Italy) which are almost always associated with *dolmens*. They are generally about 10ft (3m) tall, slender and finely dressed rectangles, with their longer faces to the east and west.

The chambers much resemble French dolmens in construction. They consist simply of a sub-rectangular capstone (sometimes with a port-hole), about 6ft (1.8m) across, supported by uprights and pillars of stones, with no passage. They were probably covered with earth. There are few carvings, and, oddly, no finds have been recorded. This is disappointing, because associated radiocarbon dates might have provided links with similar French Atlantic-seaboard megalithic tombs.

Prominent among the Otranto tombs is a group of seven, with standing stones, outside the village of Giurdignano near a farm called Masseria Quattro Macini. On one of the *pietrefitte*, about 4ft 6in (1.4m) from the ground, there are carvings of two differently shaped crosses, one above the other, indicating modest attempts at Christianization.

Other tombs in this coastal area include Gurgulante, next to a wall in an olive grove, and Placa, with a tree growing against it, just west of the village of Melendugno (between Otranto and Lecce, via the coastal road). SCUSI is also in this group.

GGANTIJA

Xaghra,
Gozo

TEMPLE

Malta and Gozo are only 121sq m (313sq km) in total land area.

Malta is justly world famous for its unique temples, of which there are about 30 on Malta and its smaller neighbour Gozo. They were all built between 3500 BC and about 2400 BC, when all work abruptly ceased: just why is one of the great megalithic mysteries yet to be solved.

The temples were generally built in pairs. The two here are side by side in a great cairn 50yds (46m) long. The southernmost is the earlier, and has five apses. Like its partner, it has a fine curved forecourt at its entrance with enormous stones around the bases and cyclopean drystone walling above. The length of the southern temple is 86ft 3in (26.3m) and its width is 77ft 9in (23.7m).

The temple tomb to the north has only four apses and is altogether smaller, being 61ft (18.7m) long and 57ft 6in (17.5m) wide. The apses are rounded, have virtually no entrances and in plan are rather beautiful, spreading like the petals of a flower.

Cyclopean walling looms over small trilithons in the temple.

Take the road (no numbers used) directly east from Victoria; take the first left for the village of Xaghra. The temple is signposted on the right. A hypogeum was discovered opposite this site in 1991.

Many authorities now accept that the temple ground plans depict the Great Goddess in outline. The Earth Mother is, of course, a key motif in Maltese archaeology.

Hagar Qim

*Zurrieq,
Malta*

TEMPLE

This superb temple's pair is the neighbouring MNAJDRA. Hagar Qim was constructed in two stages between 3500 BC and 3300 BC. Four giant stones, irregular and much gnarled by the Mediterranean elements, form the curved frontage together with some lintels. The great trilithon entrance survives, together with the base course of huge dressed stones; the other courses and roofing are long gone. There is a stone kerb all around the temple.

The two lobed chambers inside are of different periods and contain altars, a slab with a port-hole, a betyl, and a huge central passage lined with dressed uprights and a few lintels, but no roofing. The central four apse chamber is 56ft 3in (17.1m) long and 65ft 6in (20.0m) wide. The northern chamber is much narrower, but has five apses; it measures 52ft 6in (16.0m) in length and 24ft (7.3m) wide.

Seated female figures, carved in local limestone, have been found here; their greatly exaggerated proportions suggest a Mother Goddess depiction of about 3000 BC. They manifest a mystery: why are they virtually always headless? Perhaps their neck holes were for receiving the latest Goddess's head?

Take the road south from Zurrieq, near the south coast; turn right, north-east, before the Blue Grotto. The signposted temple is down the next track on the left.

A seated figurine from Hagar Qim (now in the National Museum of Malta, in Valletta).

166
SOUTHERN
EUROPE
Malta
and Gozo

V.15

HAL SAFLIENI

ROCK-CUT TEMPLE
(HYPOGEUM)

Go south from Valletta,
through Marsa to Paolo.
Continue straight on; the
temple is signposted a few
streets along on the left in
Burials Street.

The dramatically lit interior of the
underground temple.

The *hypogeum* at this site is one of the most remarkable prehistoric monuments in the whole of Europe – and yet surprisingly little is known about what went on inside it. The three-level site was discovered accidentally by workmen in 1902 while they were working on a drainage system for this suburb of Valletta. Its nearby partner, TARXIEN, was not discovered until 1914. The excavations of 1905–09 produced a date of between 3500 BC and about 2400 BC, the now accepted period for all Maltese temple building.

In the 20 chambers cut out of the rock, reached by one entrance shaft, remains of some 7000 disarticulated human skeletons were found. The *hypogeum*, at the lowest level and reached through a carved 3ft 3in (1m) high doorway, reflected many of the characteristics of the buildings above it.

It contains shallow port-hole niches surrounded by trilithon entrances, amazing paintings of cattle in red ochre, local pottery, personal ornaments, animal bones, carvings in relief, and strange so-called 'oracle holes' connected to hidden chambers like confessionals. One of the most spectacular finds here was of two terracotta 'sleeping women' statuettes.

Although its specific uses may still be a mystery, this temple was being carved out of solid rock to a pre-planned design of great sophistication probably before the beginning of STONEHENGE or the Great Pyramid at Giza.

MNAJDRA

TEMPLE

Take the road south from
Zurrieq, near the south coast;
turn right, north-west, before
the Blue Grotto. The temple is
down the next track on the
left, past Hagar Qim by the
coast.

The north temple.

These three temples are set in a hollow, just below their 'pair', HAGAR QIM. The southern and central temples are faced with the familiar and substantial dressed base-stone courses, with courses of cylopean drystone walling above; they share a common wall between them.

The southern one is 49ft 9in (15.2m) in length, and 45ft (18.7m) in width; it has a substantial 'reception area', with four apsidal chambers leading of it. One of them containing two betyls (pillar altars), and another two port-hole slabs.

Its central partner to the north is the largest here, with a length of 59ft (18.0m) and a width of 54ft 6in (16.6m), and also four apses. The third, north-eastern temple has three apses, and is the oldest, at about 3400 BC, and the smallest, at 27ft 3in (8.3m) long and 38ft 6in (11.7m) wide.

As the best preserved temple complex in Malta, the one to visit here is the southern one; it bears witness to an astonishing period in megalithic history, which was most likely a completely indigenous occurence.

TARXIEN

Tarxien,
Valletta,
Malta

MEGALITHIC TEMPLES

The four temples at Tarxien were built in succession, and became the best decorated temples in Malta and Gozo. The 30 or so were all built between 3600BC and 2400BC.

This famous group of temples has HAL SAFLIENI as its pair, a few hundred yards away in this built-up suburb of the island's capital. Dating from about 3300 BC, this is the only Maltese site of the time of the temple builders (3600–2400 BC) which was subsequently used after they were gone, in the Bronze Age. The site was discovered in 1914 and excavated by Sir Themistocles Zammit in 1915–17; it covers about 59,200 sq ft (5500sq m). The four temples, which adjoin each other, were built from the island's fairly soft limestone – and not all at once, but in succession. They were once all roofed.

The southernmost, at the west and called Tarxien South, (also Tarxien West!), is 74ft (22.8m) long and 60ft (18.3m) wide. It has two pairs of opposing chambers (known here as

Go south from Valletta, through its suburbs to Marsa and Paola. Continue straight on to Tarxien, turn left, and then left again at the signpost into Old Temple Street.

Part of an altar carving at the temple of Tarxien South.

apses), many abstract and literal carvings, a font and a most unusual altar. This is robustly carved in sunken relief with an interleaving swirling pattern of great beauty; it is 4ft (1.2m) high, and has a mysterious recess in the front in which a flint sacrificial knife was found. Another surprise in this astonishing temple, is a massive and rather unattractive Goddess (of fertility?) statue (today in replica: the original is in the National Museum of Malta in Valletta). It is broken off horizontally across the waist (the top part has never been found); two grotesquely swollen legs descend from a voluminous pleated skirt and seem to rest upon tiny feet that one expects to be cloven.

In the same period the four-apse East temple was constructed, containing the finest decorated stones in Malta, often with the enigmatic spiral motif prominent. It is 51ft (15.6m) long, and 41ft (12.6m) wide. The adjoining Far East temple here is smaller at 39ft (12.0m) long, and was probably once 19ft (6.0m) at its widest. In about 3200 BC, the largest temple, Tarxien Central, was inserted between the South and East ones. Its entrance led from the southern end, and it features six apses within a total length of 75ft (23m) and a width of 61ft (18.6m).

Megalithic temple architecture on Malta and Gozo is unique to the islands and justly famous. Although Sicily is only some 62 miles (100km) away, there is nothing of it to be found there. The Maltese builders used their stone in an amazingly sophisticated manner from about 3600 BC, some 1400 years after the first Neolithic farmers settled on the island. No more than 20 foreign pottery sherds (of Sicilian origin) have ever been found, compared with thousands of fragments of indigenous ware.

Skorba, another Maltese site, has produced an early date of about 4000 BC. Rock-cut tombs were probably being used for collective burials at much the same time as at TRANCHINA, Sciacca, Sicily, and were probably inspired by Sicilian immigrants. By this time large-scale temple building was commencing, with the subterranean trefoil plans made of massive cyclopean masonry going up above ground. Skorba West is a trefoil temple where the end apse later acquired an internal open doorway. Five-apsed temples followed (see GGANTIJA, Gozo).

In later temples, the end apse shrank in size, so that, by the time of the unique six-apsed Tarxien Central, it had become a cupboard-like extension only, perhaps a sanctuary, the innermost sacred shrine. There seems little doubt that the Tarxien constructions, like most of the 30 or so on the island, were never used for funerary purposes. They incorporated, from the beginning, altars, statues, 'oracle holes', and shrine areas. The earliest are believed to be among the oldest above-ground, roofed buildings in the world.

Although constructed soon after the very earliest megalithic tombs in north-west Europe, these temples were immensely more sophisticated in their design and layout. It seems that there really were architects and master carvers at work, at least at Tarxien, which is the best decorated temple group on Malta or Gozo. Interestingly, a fragment of a clay model for a building (now in Valletta Museum), showing rectangular rooms and doorways, has been discovered at Tarxien. Perhaps it was too advanced for its time, because no such building has ever been found. Nevertheless, the main façade at Tarxien, with its raised trilithon doorway and courses of immaculate cyclopean masonry, was once a mighty and beautiful thing.

V.18

S. Marco,
Alghero

CEMETERY

86 B 6

ANGHELU RUJU

This cemetery is one of the best-known in Sardinia. On this site, which was formerly a quarry, more than 35 tombs have been found, made from sandstone extracted from the fields around. They share some common design features – such as steps down from the entrance, and then a descending passage to a large burial chamber, with small chambers leading off it. The main chamber's closing slabs were often decorated and were surrounded by a sort of trilithon carved in relief.

A particular feature of the carvings are long-horned bulls' heads in low relief, and they were sometimes painted in red ochre. These cult symbols, which occur in Tombs 19, 20 and 30, for example, have been interpreted in different ways. Mycenaean influence is naturally detected, but the finds here date at around 2900 BC, which is too early for that theory.

The exotic array of artefacts include obsidian, barbed and tanged flint arrowheads, an axe and awl from Ireland, maceheads and a ring from East Europe, copper-tanged daggers from Spain (*see* LOS MILLARES, Spain), spiral wire beads, buttons, small marble statuettes, and stone bracers.

Pottery finds included Beaker ware, Chassey ware (Neolithic pottery found all over France; the type site, Chassey-le-Camp, is west of Dijon in central France and the ware reached Sardinia during the Ozieri culture), and Ozieri (or San Michele) ware (Copper Age Sardinian pottery showing links with the Maltese Tarxien Cemetery phase [about 2500–1500 BC]). Some of these finds can now be seen in the Museo Nazionale, Sassari.

Marked on the map 'Necrop Anghelu Ruiu'. Leave the coastal north-west town of Alghero northwards towards Porto Torres. The cemetery is on the left after about 5½ miles (9km).

The antechambers and oval main chambers were originally roofed in this cemetery of more than 35 tombs. Most had steps leading down to their entrances.

ENA'E MUROS

*Ossi,
Sassari*

LONG CIST (TOMBA A
POLIANDRA)

86 D 5

This is one of over 200 such cists in Sardinia, dating from the early nuragic period. In Sardinian this site's name implies a large number of bodies, and, indeed, more than 30 skeletons were found at this site. A most unusual feature here is the fine collection of pottery found with the burials. It was Bonnanaro ware, dated to about 1750 BC, and named after the rock-cut tomb in which it was first discovered.

What today would be regarded as a full set of kitchenware was evidently carefully designed, manufactured, sold or exchanged, and also exported to Italy. It has been found in giants' tombs on this island (*see* LI-LOLGHI, Arzachena). Although the surfaces are undecorated, there is a definite style in the basic shapes of upturned handles, drinking cups, cooking and serving pots; one notable example is a fine, handled serving bowl supported on three square legs. The pottery's brown finish has a 20th-century look, and is in striking contrast to the much more decorative and colourful Monte Claro ware (local Sardinian pottery dated to about 1850 BC but perhaps earlier), of which sherds have also occurred at Ena'E Muros.

*Take the minor twisting road
southwards out of Sassari,
under the 131 main road, to
Ossi. In the village turn left
for Muros, just down the road.*

LI-LOLGHI

Arzachena

GIANT'S TOMB

87 I 3

*Signposted, and near
Li-muri – see below.*

Giants' tombs (*tomba di giganti*) were constructed all over Sardinia by the *nuraghi* builders for some 1000 years from about 1900 BC until the destructive invasion by Carthage. Their collective burial chambers were long, with upright slabs, and covered with stone or earth, and robustly kerbed.

The tombs generally featured a horned semi-circular forecourt, which, as elsewhere in both the Mediterranean and north-west Europe, was doubtless used as an open arena or meeting place for ritual, forms of worship and/or celebration.

The boat shapes of the wedge ends of the tombs are reminiscent of the Minorcan *navetas* (*see* ELS TUDONS, Ciutadela), which some think might have inspired them; others believe that giants' tombs are indigenous developments of the earlier dolmens.

Construction probably began at Li-lolghi in about 1500 BC; the passage-grave is about 88ft 6in (27m) long in total. Its gallery is 49ft (15m) long, and some 5ft (1.5m) in width. The paved, raised chamber at the end of it is a further 13ft (4.0m) long, and, most interestingly, cathedral-style, has an ambulatory around it.

LI-MURI

*St Oddastru,
Arzachena*

STONE PLATFORMS
WITH CISTS AND
GIANT'S TOMB

87 I 3

*In the far north-east of the
island, a third of the way
along the road from
Arzachena leading to
Luogosanto, and signposted to
the right; far up a trackway,
through farmland, over a
wall to the right. 20 mintues
from the car park.*

This is a high, remote and dramatic site. Though tentatively dated at 2500 BC, work probably began here some 1000 years earlier, making it the oldest megalithic site in Sardinia.

There are four distinct but intersecting circular stone platforms here (and remains of at least one more), which recall common walls elsewhere, notably at the large cemetery at SON REAL, Majorca. Each of them has a *coffre* (an open-ended high-sided rectangular stone slab cist) at its centre, the open ends of which, in three, lie in the northerly direction. There are another eight or so around the circles.

The largest circle is the western one at about 25ft (7.6m) across. Finds here include human bones in one *coffre*, and the usual motley hoard of pottery sherds, beads, polished axes, perforated maceheads, flint knives, obsidian flakes, and a steatite cup. It is impossible to say whether or not collective burials took place here.

Near the Li-muri circles is a Giant's Tomb which is worth viewing. It must have been a massive structure when its original earth mound covered it. However, all the stone constructions in this area are now in poor condition, partly due to the simple passage of time in the harsh, baking Mediterranean climate, and also because of the islanders' ancient belief that treasures still lie hidden in these resting places.

Monte D'Accoddi

*Porto Torres,
Sassari*

Temple Mound

86 C 5

*The temple mound area is also host
to a mysterious stone.*

This is a puzzling place. The high, broad and most peaceful setting is host to an earth mound with nothing inside it. It is just possible that there may be a concealed entrance, but it remains to be discovered. It is two-tiered, square, 29ft 6in (9m) high, and its very substantial cyclopean drystone walling is 121ft (37m) along a side. A similarly kerbed broad earth ramp leads to the top of the mound from the south. Perhaps it was a sighting platform, or a place for initiation or fertility rituals (with spectators standing on the surrounding tier ledge).

A number of standing stones are to be found in the area around the mound, but their association, if any, is unclear. Just to the east of the ramp lies a beautiful dome-shaped stone, like a flattened planet.

*Take the 131 south-east from
Porto Torres (on the north-
west coast) towards Sassari.
After about 3¾ miles (6km),
take the signposted track on the
right to the site.*

SANT' ANASTASIA

Sárdara,
Campidano

WELL TEMPLE

90 D 2

Not marked on the map. Take the 131 north from Cagliari for 33 miles (53km), and then turn off for the village of Sádara where the church is.

Campidano is the undulating farmland which stretches from the River Tirso in the north to Cagliari in the south. This is a prehistoric spa, and the earliest of many in Sardinia. It takes its name from the nearby church, which is dedicated to a saint now rarely commemorated except in Byzantine churches. The church dates back to about 7th–8th century AD, but the tradition of healing at the waters goes back at least a thousand years before them.

Steps beneath ground level descend to the well, which was once covered by a stone roof in the form of a cupola. A stone building stood at ground level. The area around the well was quite large and paved – implying the 'use' of the waters by many people at the same time.

Finds have been made in a pit in front of the well; they include nuragic pottery sherds, animal bones and much decorated pottery, which confirm its long use. Also, excavated was the rough outline of a stone bull's head, which perhaps clarifies the dedication of that church. Other fine sacred wells in Sardinia (among 30 or so) include Santa Vittoria, Serri, and Su Tempiesu, Orune.

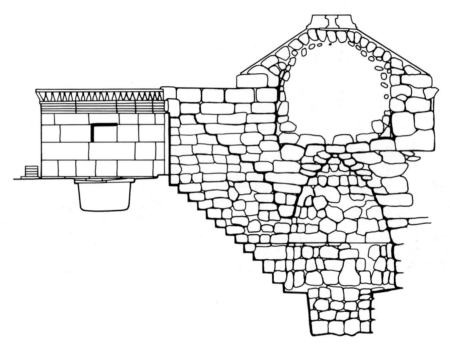

SANT' ANTINE

Torralba,
Thiesi

NURAGHE

88 D 2

Nuraghi are Late Neolithic high, round, stone defensive towers, peculiar to Sardinia; this is one of about 6500 on the island, and in better repair than most. They are somewhat similar to, but more elaborate than the *talayots* of the Balearic Islands and the *torri* of Corsica. (The medieval peel towers on the borders of England and Scotland served similar purposes.) This one is set on a larger, triangular tower, and, like most, it is built of cyclopean drystone.

Some *nuraghi* were quite complex, such as Palmavera, Alghero. The formidable stonework gave adequate defence for the chambered living quarters in these towers. The cyclopean walls surrounding their settlements complete a profile of a warring people, intent on preserving territorial gains.

The *nuraghi* culture on Sardinia reached its height during 1100–600 BC. Other *nuraghi* near Sant' Antine are Ránas, Monte Longo, two separate Tres Nuraghes, Póltolu, S'Ena, Sant' Sisto, and Oes (very near this one). The Italian Touring Club 1:200,000 map is recommended to *nuraghi* hunters.

Take the 131 road south-east from Sassari. Nuraghi are visible either side of the road. Turn off the road at Mores, and take the minor road west and south. Go through Torralba village, and take the third turning left, under the 131. The nuraghe is now on the right, before the railway station.

V.25

CASTELLUCCIO

Castelluccio,
Noto,
Siracusa

ROCK-CUT CHAMBER
TOMBS

85 G 5

The useful Italian Touring Club 1:200,000 map labels this site a prehistoric village which it never was. The present village occupies the top of a rocky spur. According to Professor Bernabo Brea the Castelluccian culture flourished broadly between pre-2000–1400 BC, but it may well have started earlier. This site gives its name to a buff-coloured pottery, bearing simple linear patterns painted in black, which perhaps betrays Greek inspiration. It is physically related, not to the present village at all, but to the cemetery cut into the limestone walls of the nearby Cava della Signora valley.

The first excavations here were conducted by Professor Paolo Orsi in 1891–92. More than 200 small round oven-shaped (*a forno*) chambers (called *Cava della Signora*), which average 4ft 6in (1.4m) in diameter, were cut into the hillside, often with vestibules beneath galleries 'hanging' over them. One such gallery is supported by four portal stones with carved double spiral motifs. They were collective burial tombs and, after use, were sealed with either drystone walling or blocking slabs.

Some of these have finely carved decorations on them, and they are the only examples of prehistoric carving to be found

Leave Noto (near Avola on the south-east coast of the island) on the 115 main road south-west towards Ragusa. After 4¼ miles (7km) turn right, north-west, for 8 miles (13km). Then turn right to the signposted village of Castelluccio.

LEFT: *A carved stone slab from Castelluccio; now in the Museo Nazionale Archeologico in Siracusa, where many examples are held. This 3ft (0.9m) high stone may have blocked a chamber.*

One of more than 200 a forno tombs cut into the limestone in the Cava della Signora valley.

Some tombs had less elaborate entrances in the valley cemetery.

anywhere in Sicily. Why this should be is a mystery, unless one allows for a 'closed' community, entirely self-sufficient. These doorway slabs feature a fascinating variety of motifs, but their creators must have travelled, or else been employed outside any such community or tribe, because similar incised and relief designs such as spirals and lozenges are found throughout Europe (*see* GAVR'INIS, Morbihan, France).

Some of the stone slabs here display heads, breasts, and arms uplifted; such captured poses, in an apparent worshipping position, have been found in the Near East, Crete, Malta, Spain, Brittany and Guernsey. The Museo Nazionale Archeologico in Siracusa holds examples. One slab in particular, some 3ft (0.9m) tall, can be closely compared with one at TARXIEN, Malta, and another at ALTAMURA, Italy. Finds, apart from human remains, have included pottery sherds with clear Aegean connections. There were also seven (out of ten found so far in Sicily) of the mysterious, carved bone plaques, found at FILITOSA, Corsica, and elsewhere. Like others, they are 3½ins (8.9cm) long, but showing six, not seven, oval breast-like protuberances, surrounded by finely incised line decorations. Such amulets were burial objects and no sign of human inhabitation has been found here.

THAPSOS

V.26

Thapsos,
Penisola Magnisi,
Siracusa

ROCK-CUT TOMBS

85 I 4

Leave Siracusa (Syracuse) north-west on the coastal road. After about 9m (14km), at Priolo Gargallo, turn east for Thapsos which is 2³⁄4m (4½km) away. The site is signposted.

Sicily is the largest of all the Mediterranean islands, with almost exactly 10,000 sq miles (25,900 sq km), which is 20% larger than the land area of Wales. Several millennia ago this promontory site was an island in the Golfo di Augusta. Professor Paoloa Orsi, the first great Sicilian archaeologist (who devised the Siculan periods) excavated this perhistoric trading post in 1894; it evidently flourished around 1800–1300 BC. Below the old village, he found hundreds of rock-cut tombs, for which Sicily is famed. There were two types. Those away from the shoreline had vertical entrance shafts, with a convenient carved step. The typical tomb let into the cliffs facing the sea mostly had grooves to accomodate a sealing stone, and then a short passage (*dromos*) giving on to a recessed door case. Beyond was the cool, dark tomb, where pottery was found among the detritus of centuries.

Thapsos is the type site for a local incised grey pottery; it is highly distinctive – delicate bowls set on tall thick cylindrical pedestals, with handles placed high up beneath the rims (excellent examples can be seen in the Museo Nazionale Archeologica, Siracusa). Also occuring in the tombs at Thapsos were Borg in-Nadur pottery from Malta and Mycenaean pottery (dated at 1400–1200 BC).

At Pantalica, north-west of Siracusa (between the villages of Sortina and Ferla), there is a cemetery of some 500 rock-cut tombs on a plateau site overlooking the River Anapo.

TRANCHINA

V.27

Tranchina,
Sciacca,
Agrigento

ROCK-CUT CEMETERY

79 F 5

Tranchina is 7 miles (11km) from Sciacca, on the south-west coast.

There are 36 tombs at this hillside cemetery (sometimes called Sciacca), which was excavated by S. Tinè in 1959. It has subsequently been calculated that it was in use for some 1000 years from about 3300 BC.

Of the total number of tombs, 33 had mostly single and some double burials in carved-out holes in their floors. The other three, of a later date, were used for collective burials. The usual range of grave goods was found, and they included broken Bell beakers, flint flakes and metal weapons of war.

Rock-cut chamber tombs, out of all classes of burial place, are the earliest in the central Mediterranean area, and moreover they were used for the longest period of time. Inexplicably, none occur in Corsica. In Sicily, the most common type to be carved out of rock was oven-shaped, *a forno*, which was entered either through the rock face, or through a roof shaft.

V.28

CARSCHENNA

Sils,
Thusis,
Graubünden

ROCK CARVINGS

Michelin sheet 427:
M 5

There are no less than ten separate rock surfaces at this hard-to-find site, and they are well worth discovering (which, naturally, can only be achieved in the summer months). They are located on the northern side of a mountain overlooking Carschenna and the farmland around. This is no doubt a most difficult megalithic site to locate, but a most attractive one for keep-fit enthusiasts!

The rock surfaces were accidentally uncovered in 1965 by a forest surveyor. Here there are horsemen, cup marks, cup-and-ring marks, concentric circles (plain and divided into quadrants), bulls' eye marks, semi-circles, sun-wheels, both straight and wavy lines — and, of course, spirals, the most ubiquitous and mysterious motif of all.

That these sets of carvings may be maps of sacred places, such as springs, or local spots where lines of an earth energy may intercross, have to remain pure speculation. But the simple fact persists that every one of these strange patterns occurs in prehistoric sites all over the world (see ROUGHTING LINN, England).

Leave Chur (west across the mountains from Davos) on the motorway, going south-westwards, and then south beside the Hinterrheim for about 14 miles (23km). Leave it at the Thusis exit for the short distance east to Sils. Ask for walking directions in the town.

Many authorities think that spiral motifs are related to celestial, especially solar, motions.

LEFT AND BELOW: *Rock surface carvings.*

LE PETIT CHASSEUR

*Sion,
Valais*

CHAMBER TOMBS,
STATUE-MENHIRS AND
CISTS

Michelin sheet 427:
G 7

One of the many simple four-sided cists at the second level.

This important site, by the Rhône, in the Valais, was thoroughly excavated by Olivier Bocksberger, and then by Alain Gallay (with Geneva University). At this oddly-named site ('the little hunter'), there are two stratified levels. The lower has been dated at about 4000 BC, one of the earlier dates in this book; it consisted of a hut settlement, a cemetery of cists, and an alignment of standing stones. The later, higher level has over ten, perhaps 12 cists and megalithic tombs.

The earliest and most impressive is Tomb 6, dated Late Neolithic. It is an extended triangular horned grave, 52ft (15.8m) long, built along a north-south axis, with an antechamber and single capstoned chamber. The entrance, however, is through a holed stone in its eastern flank, and the

The N9 autoroute south from Lausanne, through Montreux and Martigny, ends at Sion. Enter the town on Avenue de France, turn left along Avenue de Petit Chasseur. The restored site is in the courtyard of St. Guérin School, past church. Finds are in the Musée d'Arhéologie, 12 Rue des Chateaux.

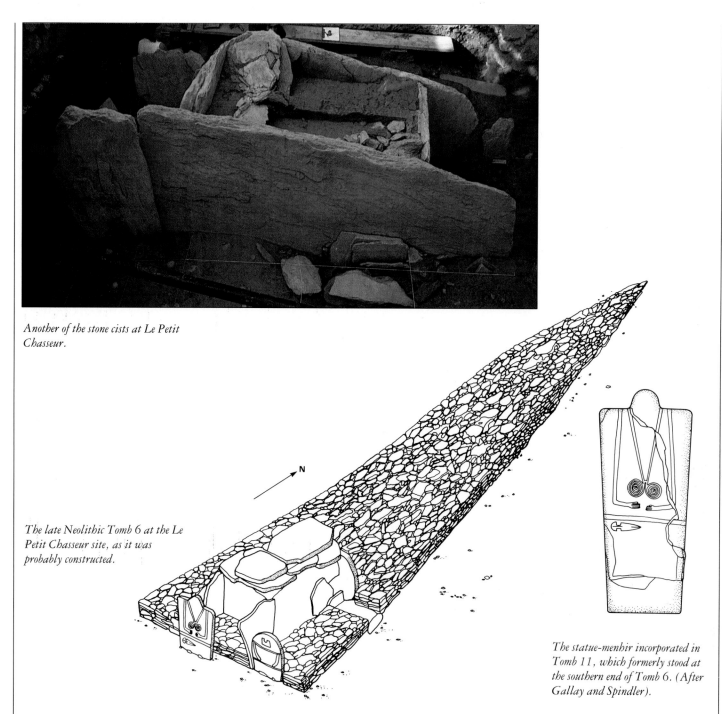

Another of the stone cists at Le Petit Chasseur.

The late Neolithic Tomb 6 at the Le Petit Chasseur site, as it was probably constructed.

The statue-menhir incorporated in Tomb 11, which formerly stood at the southern end of Tomb 6. (After Gallay and Spindler).

general plan shows great affinities with Scandinavian long dolmens. The tomb was later abandoned, and then re-used by the Beaker people in about 2500 BC. Flint daggers have been found here from the great mine and factory of blank and finished pinkish flints at Le Grand Pressigny, Indre-et-Loire, France, which exported flint for megalithic builders' yards all over Europe.

The stone-covered cairn over Tomb 11, on the same site, incorporates decorated statue-menhirs, taken from Tomb 6 and re-used in Tomb 11's construction. Tomb 11 is particularly known for them, and they probably originally stood at the southern end of Tomb 6. They date back to about 3200 BC, and perhaps further. The more elaborate of them (which stands apart from the revetment) features a lower neck, at the top of the stone, and carvings of two arms and hands, a necklace with two ornaments with spiral shapes hanging from it, and finally a dagger.

This secondary placing of anthropomorphic statue-menhirs occurs elsewhere (*see*, for example FILITOSA, Corsica), but this

is one of the earliest dated re-uses.

Stone cists were later dug in against the south-west and south-east sides, and Early Bronze Age pottery vessels were found in the traditional votive position. The capstone has a hole in it, the damage of tomb robbers no doubt, after it was, like Tomb 6, re-used by the Beaker people.

Finds from their burials, apart from human bones, included carvings on boars' tusks and silver earrings; these demonstrate the more elaborate nature of Early Bronze Age burial customs.

There is also evidence, from revealed post-holes, that the tomb site was probably once covered with a wooden roof, and almost certainly ringed with wooden posts.

It is only when such roofing timbers are burnt, and the charcoal remains subsequently preserved in the right soil conditions, that radiocarbon calibrated dating techniques can be applied (*see* DATES AND DATING, pages 12–13). This was possible at a site in Denmark (*see* TUSTRUP GROUP), where the 'temple' was burnt down after, it is thought, a single funerary ceremony.

VI

North Africa

The root of the word Maghreb, which comprises Morocco, Algeria and Tunisia, is the spoken Berber word *gharib*, meaning to travel to the unknown. Tourists are, in ever-increasing numbers, attracted by the harsh and ancient ways. Nomadic life continues away from the great cities, kasbahs and ksour (fortified Berber villages) in accordance with the seasons and market days. Pottery for sale at roadsides is likely to be decorated in styles which are literally thousands of years old. It is a different world on a different continent – and yet the ferry boat takes only 75 minutes to cross from Gibraltar to Tangier. This is the passage where the Mediterranean Sea becomes the Atlantic Ocean, between the two Pillars of Hercules. One of them is the Rock itself; the other is Mount Acho (Abyla), the highest of the seven hills at Ceuta, a visible 14 miles (22.5km) away. Over this short distance many cultural influences and practices have passed.

In comparatively recent times, the contribution of the French Army to the archaeology of its North African colonies has been notable. French tomb builders, some thousand years ago, had brought their funerary habits to the whole of the old Maghreb, and so there still survive local versions of *allées-couvertes*, such as Aït Garet on the Algerian coast, for example, which has a 41ft (12.5m) long, narrow, paved chamber. Egyptology is widely published, but less is known about Libyan megalithic tombs and cemeteries. There are of course riches in stone throughout the African continent; Ethiopia is a scholar's lifetime; the name Zimbabwe means chief's graves and comes from the Shona for stone houses.

Second millennium BC chamber tombs in Morocco, Algeria and Tunisia are concentrated in two broad areas. Those in two coastal districts in northern Morocco are very early in that millennium and unsurprisingly derive from the Iberian peninsula. Then there are the Algerian cemeteries on the central coastal area, and the Tunisian groups to the north. Compared with the coverage of European sites, little has been published in English about them. Even popular accounts of a well-known tourist attraction such as, for instance, DOUGGA (THUGGA) in Tunisia, virtually ignore the 13 Neolithic graves just outside its massive walls.

Berber *djoulas* are fairly simple above-ground dolmenic burial chambers, consisting of uprights and drystone walling, or only the walling, which support capstones (as found throughout Europe); they were not covered by mounds. They are, however, often set on stepped revetted plinths (up to four in number); this makes them reminiscent of Mediterranean island tomb structures, such as the Sardinian *nuraghi*. Berber tradition has them built by giants, manifesting a common worldwide belief about megalithic monuments which is often reflected in their names.

Berber *redjem* are present in their thousands all over North Africa in raised places. These are simple stone cairns, sometimes shapeless, sometimes made in distinct cones, covering burials, which may be within cists. On precarious sites, such as steep slopes, these may have a revetment of bigger boulders, always undressed. The burials were single or multiple, and with or without poor grave goods. In summary, they varied in both structure and purpose; indeed the more recent Moslem *marabouts* were even placed to mark tribal territorial bounds.

Most countries have indigenous kinds of megalithic burial chambers and other forms of monument. Cyclopean constructions, using very large, precisely fitted, mortar-free blocks of dressed masonry are common throughout the Mediterranean basin and yet, strangely, are almost unknown for funerary purposes in North Africa. There is though a fascinating cyclopean burial chamber at DJEBEL MAZELA, Algeria. *Bazinas* occur at the same site, and Bazina XXII is a beautiful example. Its concentric stepped circles of stone retaining walls, on its sloping position, show great similarities to cairns as far away as the Orkney Islands (Wideford Hill, for example, though this has an entrance passage).

The Algerian *chouchet* (singular *choucha*) are unique to the north-east and Kabylia regions of Algeria and northern Tunisia. These are stone-walled cylinders, rising to about 10ft (3m), capped by one slab, and containing a four-sided chamber just large enough to accommodate a single contracted burial (unlike *bazinas*). The other north African burial tomb is the *hypogeum* (sometimes charmingly called *haouanet*, Arabic for small shops). These Late Bronze Age cliffside tombs greatly resemble Sardinian and Sicilian sites; the oldest African ones have a short passage in front, with a shaped ceiling above it. They are common in northern Tunisia, and on Cap Bon, which faces Pantelleria and Sicily.

Most North African guide books cater for the needs of young travellers. They form much the same market that crowds the Wessex complex of megalithic monuments in England and the hundreds around Carnac, in Brittany, but rarely do guides mention these fascinating sites, lying unregarded a few miles from Europe.

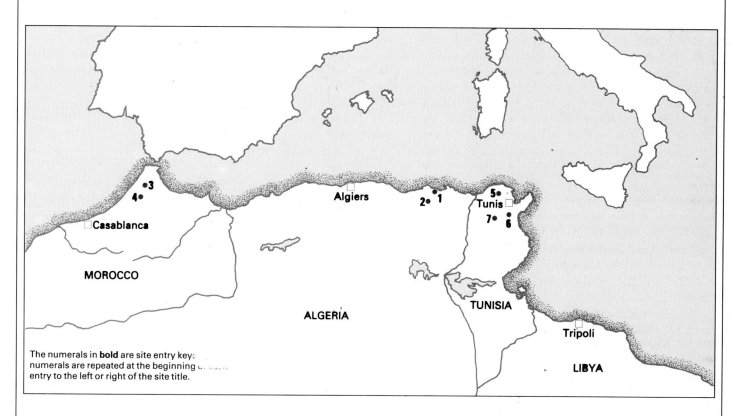

The numerals in **bold** are site entry keys
numerals are repeated at the beginning of each
entry to the left or right of the site title.

Map references given in VI.NORTH AFRICA refer to the following maps, which
are available from good bookshops everywhere (and from map specialists
Edward Stanford Ltd, London; see I.BRITISH ISLES map for address).

ALGERIA   Michelin Sheet 972. 1:1,000,000.

MOROCCO   Michelin Sheet 969. 1:1,000,000.

TUNISIA   Michelin Sheet 972. 1:1,000,000.

DJEBEL MAZELA

VI.1

Bou Nouara,
Oued Berda,
Constantine

MEGALITHIC CEMETERY
(BAZINAS, DJOUALA
AND THE CYCLOPEAN
MONUMENT)

Michelin Sheet 972

Leave Constantine south-east
on the N3. After 9¼ miles
(15km) turn left on to the
N20. Bou Nouara is about
26¾ miles (43km) away
from Constantine. Ask for
local directions.

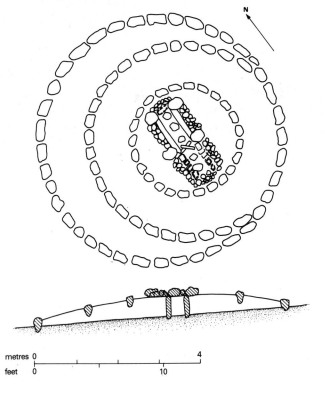

Bazina **XXII** *at the megalithic*
cemetery at Djebel Mazela. Its
sloping site is 220yds (200m)
north-east of the Cyclopean
Monument. There were many finds
in the chamber and antechamber,
including (not noted anywhere else
in this book), bird bones. (After G.
Camps).

metres 0   4
feet 0   10

The Djebel (mountain range) Mazela stretches from west to east and south-east, north of the lowland village of Bou Nouara. Lying along it, and a little to the north, east and south of the ridge, is a cemetery which is not only the largest in Algeria but also contains a greater number of tombs than almost anywhere in the world. It is perhaps more important than ROKNIA, located not far away, and is much larger than the other Algerian cemeteries of Beni Messous and Gastel.

Bou Nouara was so-named by Général Faidherbe in his 1868 account of the site, but he was actually referring to a small area on the southern slope near the present village. He could not have known then that the cemetery extends over more than 1000 acres (400 hectares). What is known today about the area is derived from the definitive account by Gabriel and Henriette Camps, following their exhaustive surveys and restoration work in 1954 and 1963. They estimated that there are between 3000 and 4000 tombs, but point out that it is difficult to spot sites from aerial photographs, when they are only 9ft 9in (3m) or so in diameter. Many sites have also been completely destroyed on the lower levels of Djebel Mazela.

The greatest concentration of tombs is in the centre of the range, along the ridge called Chabet-El-Ameur (sometimes Kef-El-Ameur on maps). The Camps actually located a rather grand megalithic entrance to this huge area – and so, again, one is faced with the incontrovertible facts of a high degree of design, order and discipline of Neolithic times. These thousands of tombs would appear to be randomly distributed; often they are only a few feet from each other. Material was easily managed, because the plateau consists of stratified limestone. Finds have been few; through the centuries Berbers have taken all they could find, and even today one is offered potsherds from the tombs.

In their survey the Camps gave an account of only a small number of tombs, the sophistication of which is most impressive. Their Dolmen VIII, for example, is set on a fairly steep slope on a circular platform 13ft (4m) in diameter and has two surrounding stone boulder walls. The exterior one has two courses: apparently the builders put one huge upright wall stone in place and decided not to trim it down to the size of its neighbours, so up went another course of stones to match the height of its top surface! The exterior western faces were neatly dressed, and the whole provided for a horizontal surface into which a dolmenic chamber was placed, so that the capstone alone showed. It measured 7ft 6in (2.3m) in length, and 3ft 3in (1m) in width.

The chamber is rectangular, measures 4ft by 1ft 6in (1.2m by 0.5m), and is orientated exactly north/south (which is *not* dictated by the topography). The rectangular shape is standard here – at ROKNIA, not far away, polygonal chambers are seen. Finds in Dolmen VIII included snail shells, a bowl, potsherds, and, beneath them, human bones (but in poor condition, as always here), and skull fragments. One body had been placed on its side, with its face to the east.

Algeria's chamber tombs are called *bazinas*. They are basically similar to the *djouala* of the Maghreb (that is, a revetted mound, with one or two stepped platforms as it rises, and containing a dolmenic chamber). The *bazina* has a high retaining exterior wall, its shape in plan may be circular or four-sided, and it most often has multiple burials. The Algerian *chouchet*, on the other hand, contain single burials in their 10ft (3m) high cylindrical stone towers.

Bazina XXII on Djebel Mazela overlooks the railway (the construction of which led to the ruin of so many of the tombs on the lower slopes). It is very beautiful in design, taking

perfect account of its location on a slope. The lower platform is 19ft 9in (6m) in diameter. Inside this walled exterior are two concentric stone revetments all to provide rising flat surfaces. The rectangular north/south, chamber measures 4ft 3in by 1ft 3in (1.3m by 0.4m). Its uprights are all surrounded by drystone walling, and there is a small antechamber as well. Finds included disarticulated human bones and teeth, bird bones (an unusual find), and, lower down, a heaped up skeleton. Pottery was found at the south entrance.

The unique Cyclopean Monument lies 220yds (200m)

south-west of this *bazina*; it is a most striking construction, half way down the southern slope on the edge of the ravine. It is rectangular, with walls 6ft 6in (2m) high, 26ft 3in (8m) long and 6ft 6in (2m) wide and its southern wall has three huge courses of boulders, each measuring about 6ft by 3ft 3in by 1ft 9in (1.8m by 1m by 0.5m). It is bordered at the east by large stone blocks 13ft (4m) long, and at the west by blocks 26ft 3in (8m) long: cyclopean indeed!

Djebel Mazela is an ideal candidate for the world's first megalithic park.

ROKNIA

Hammam Chellala (formerly Meskoutine), Constantine

MEGALITHIC CEMETERY (BAZINAS, CHOUCHET AND DJOUALA)

Michelin Sheet 972

Take the N3 south-east out of Constantine near the coast. After 9¼ miles (15km), turn left on to the N20. After another 45 miles (73km), turn off northwards before Guelma on to the W122 to Hammam Chellala (until recently Meskoutine). The signposted site is about 6¾ miles (11km) of twisting road further on.

This remarkable megalithic cemetery lies on the western edge of a plateau, near a precipice overlooking the Oued Roknia. The 'oued' (river bed) runs between Djebel (mountain range) El Grar and Djebel Debar.

This 500ft (153m) high cliff is made of tufa, and is the same dimension in horizontal thickness. This unique stone has been curiously shaped into cones and cliffs, over many millennia by the action of the famous hot springs in the valley below the cemetery. The sulphurous water bubbles up from great fissures in the ground at about 97° Celsius, making it the hottest spring water in the world outside Iceland. Its most famous source is at nearby Hammam Chellala. Until recently this village was called Hammam Meskoutine, meaning 'the

accursed baths'. Hammam is a bathing place and a natural site for settlements. The Romans called the hot spring baths there Aquae Tibilitinae, and they gloried in the great falls of the waters (which are still to be seen today) down the cliff below the Roknia cemetery.

At this site (which was excavated in 1875), it has been estimated that some 3000 burial chambers are made of tufa. This extraordinary estimate dates from the very birth of Algerian archaeology. Before 1859 no dolmens were thought to exist in North Africa (the Maghreb), but in that year a paper was given to The Society of Antiquities, London, entitled 'Ortholithic Remains in North Africa'. Four years later an intrigued archaeologist, Henry Christy, travelled to Algeria, where an Algerian army interpreter led him to Roknia and a personal count of over 1000 dolmens in three days. A report of the expedition by M Féraud was subsequently published which awakened the interest of the academic world.

The cemetery at Roknia mostly comprises simple *djouala*; these chambers consist of a large capstone supported by two or three upright megaliths or drystone walling and are typical of the Maghreb, but reminiscent of the French dolmen or the Welsh cromlech. Burial chambers may also be resting on a one- or two-stepped platform (the Berbers' *choucha*, pl. *chouchet*), or within a close variant (*bazina*). They are not covered by earth mounds or stone cairns. Dated at about 2600 BC, their discernible design influences are from southern Italy, through Malta, and from Sardinia, home of the *nuraghi*. The early estimate of 3000 tombs is probably too high, but as Roknia is littered with megalithic wreckage, the original number will never be known.

— **MOROCCO** —

M'ZORA

Chouahed,
Asilah,
Larache

STONE CIRCLE [WITH
TWO STANDING STONES]
Michelin Sheet 969

Leave Larache (El Aräiche)
on the west coast, and take the
coast road northwards towards
Asilah (Africa's first fully
pedestrianised town). After
15½ miles (25km), take the
turning east towards Tétouan.
Cross the railway line, take

Here is a megalithic surprise! The so-called circle of stones is in fact a perfect ellipse, and is claimed to be the only one in the world outside the British Isles and Brittany, where there are many hundreds. Its dimensions of 177ft (54m), north to south, and 190ft (58m), east to west, indicate the use in the design of Alexander Thom's megalithic yard and the Pythagorean right-angle (long before his time!). There are three or more groups of stones outside the 'circle' as well as a curious earth platform, all of which makes it practically certain that M'zora was a prehistoric lunar or solar observatory, perhaps in use about 4000 years ago. The major axis of the ellipse is directly aligned to the summit of Djebel Si Habib, the highest mountain on that horizon. It is no wonder that M'zora in Arabic means holy place.

This site is also variously spelt M'Sora, M'Zorah, Mçora, Mezora, and Mzoura. It was excavated in 1935–36 by Cesar Luis de Montalban. Strangely, he left no account of his findings; worse, his trenches were not filled in, bequeathing a

the first left, and travel 2½
miles (4km) to a village called
Souk Tnine de Sidi el Yemeni.
With the aid of either a very
detailed map (obtainable in
Rabat or Tangier), or a guide
hired here, make your way 3
miles (5km) north-east over a
maze of rough tracks to the
very small village of
Chouahed and the site.

Part of the ellipse of 167 dressed
stones.

certain disarray inside the circle. There were rumours at the time of a possible sepulchral structure at its centre, but there is no trace of one today.

The elliptical setting consists of no less than 167 dressed monoliths, of varying shapes, mostly circular, ovular and rectangular, with domed tops; their average height is 5ft (1.5m). One of them is heavily cup-marked. On the north side of the 'circle', there is an extraordinary feature; in place of a standard monolith stands El Outed, narrow and 16ft 6in (5m) tall. Its name, which means stake or post (according to local tradition, for a god-king's horse) is sometimes given to the whole site. Beside it is a similar stone, 13ft 9in (4.2m) high. This setting of monoliths is surrounded by a huge wall, made of several courses of precisely shaped rectangular stone blocks. There is a model of this marvellous site in the museum at Tétouan in case you don't feel like reaching it.

VI.4

SIDI SLIMANE

Sidi Slimane,
Meknès

MORTUARY HOUSE
Michelin Sheet 969

The market in Sidi Slimane had to be enlarged in 1939 and, soon after work commenced, workmen revealed a strange rectangular structure to the south of what had appeared to be an earthen mound. It turned out not to be made of stone, but was very similar to the Cyclopean Monument at DJEBEL MAZELA, Algeria. Excavations soon started, led by A. Ruhlmann.

The exterior dimensions are 43ft (13m) long, nearly 28ft (8.5m) wide, and nearly 7ft (2.1m) high. The circular mound in which it was enclosed was made of clayey mud, and was 154ft (47m) in diameter and 19ft 6in (6m) high. It is made of mud bricks in precise courses, with earth as mortar between them, and is in three parts. The antechamber is 17ft (5.2m) long, 4ft (1.2m) wide at the entrance, tapering to 3ft 3in (1m) at the other end. Inside there are vertical grooves which held wooden posts, and an extended skeleton, lying on its left side was found. Was it perhaps a sleeping guard?

Next came the sepulchral chamber; on the wooden threshold to this lay another extended skeleton, without weapons. The chamber is 9ft (2.8m) long, 4ft (1.2m) wide, and 6ft 6in (2.0m) high. At the end was the funerary chamber, 10ft (3m) long and 9ft 9in (3m) wide. At the far end of this almost square chamber there was a shelf, similar to an altar and the floor was paved. The ceiling was formed by six tree trunks, covered in beaten earth. Two skeletons were found here, under the paving.

The distance from Tangier to Meknès, via Ksar-el-Kebir and Sidi Kacem, is 165 miles (265km). Sidi Slimane is north of Sidi Kacem; ask for local directions there.

Skeletons have been found in this mortuary house.

TUNISIA

ÄIN EL HADJAR

Mateur,
Bizerte
TWO DJOUALA
(DOLMENS)
Michelin sheet 972

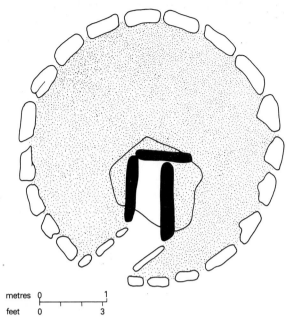

metres 0   1
feet 0   3

Mateur is on the GP11 which leads south-westwards from the northern coastal town of Bizerte.

These two *djouala* are the most westerly to be found in Tunisia, and they probably represent the earliest form of North African burial chamber. This type (the simplest dolmen form) has a circular mound with a roofless passage leading to a central chamber, and *djouala* like this are also found in the cemetery of Tayadirt, Moyen Atlas, Morocco.

One at this site has 20 boulders in a circle enclosing the mound. Unlike its companion, the very short entrance passage (three stones on the left and just one large one on the right) is angled south-west to the rectangular chamber.

The other *djouala* is also circular, with a neat revetment of 56 small boulders and a straight, longer passage to the rectangular chamber. The unroofed passage is partly paved and has eight pairs of opposing small uprights. The tomb is sealed at the chamber entrance with drystone walling. Four slabs, which include a particularly large one directly opposite the entrance, form this late Neolithic capstoned chamber.

Berbers believe *djouala* were constructed by giants.

DOUGGA (THUGGA)

Téboursouk,
Tunis
MEGALITHIC CEMETERY
Michelin sheet 972

Dougga (its Latin name *Thugga* is still often used) is justly famed for some of the finest and most extensive Roman ruins in all North Africa. They are set on a plateau and steep hillside overlooking the Oued Khaled valley to the west of the old road from Carthage to Theveste. The site goes back to Neolithic times, but eventually became a Numidian settlement, under Carthaginian influence, until the third century AD. Roman colonists came, and Septimus Severus united the populations, and created a beautiful city. Visitors passing through it to the megalithic cemetery can see many of the splendid remains.

The only surviving wall section of the earlier Numidian settlement is at the northern and highest part of the plateau. Its 426ft (130m) length overlooks a cemetery of 13 dolmens, located north-east of the Temple of Minerva. They naturally predate the classical ruins all around, probably at about 1500–1000 BC. Among the finds in the cemetery have been human bones, funerary urns, Italian potsherds, unguent bottles and Punic coins and are in the Bardo Museum, Tunis.

Among the grave sites, there is one with two chambers inside a ring of 17 stone boulders; one of the chambers is directly north of the other. Both consist simply of three upright slabs forming three sides of a square, with the fourth sides open precisely to the east.

Take the GP5 south-west out of Tunis. After about 37 miles (60km) follow the same road off to the south at Medjez-El-Bab. About 22 miles (35km) later, turn right on to the MC75 to Téboursouk 4½ miles (7km) away. Dougga (Thugga) is clearly signposted there just to the south of the town.

ELLÈS

*Ksour Toual,
Maktar*

DJOUALA (DOLMENS)
Michelin Sheet 972

This is the most important group of *djouala* in Tunisia, and perhaps in North Africa. An 1882 report by the archaeologist Professor J. Poinssot mentions 15 of them; today, just three, may be four, survive. They were first discovered by an American explorer, Frederick Catherwood, in 1839; his published plan of the best preserved of them was not very accurate, but a single accompanying comment rings true: 'I found this edifice inhabited by two Arab families, and the tradition is that it was always thus'.

This 'edifice' apart, the *djouala* are very similar in design and construction to the French *allées-couvertes*. They are up to 13ft (4m) in length and incorporate broad slabs and porticos.

The incomplete tomb mentioned by Catherwood is set on a slope, with compensating foundations. Either side of a narrow passage there are side chambers; five to the right and three to the left. At the passage end is a closing stone; there was also a now-vanished perambulatory apse beyond the stone, and possibly also an altar stone.

The exterior uprights supporting the roofing slabs in the style of trilithons, are huge dressed rectangular stones, with their broader faces inwards/outwards. The present structure measures 57ft 6in by 41ft (17.5m by 12.5m). This really is a unique megalithic structure, a second millennium BC achievement that is truly monumental in its formality.

Leave Tunis on GP3, via the very beginning of the motorway (which runs south-east to Hammamet). After 33 miles (53km), at El Fahs, turn south-west on to the GP4. After 62 miles (110km), before reaching Maktar, turn north-west on to the GP12 towards Le Kef. After 17 miles (27km), at Ksour Toual, turn directly south to Ellès as signposted.

The most monumental of the Tunisian djouala, *discovered by the American Frederick Catherwood in 1839.*

A Glossary of Terms

POULNABRONE, *a fine restored portal-tomb on The Burren, a famous limestone pavement south of Ballyvaughan in County Clare, Ireland. It has been dated at about 2500 BC.*

Alignment More or less straight row of standing stones.

Allée-coudée Allée-couverte with passage leading off at right angles before one end.

Allée-couverte French for stretched rectangular Late Neolithic megalithic burial chamber, beneath long mound.

Anta Portuguese for burial chamber.

Antechamber First section of tomb, with same width and height as chamber.

Anthropomorphic With human attributes.

Archaeo-astronomy Science of prehistoric astronomy, using megalithic sites. (Preferred to Astro-archaeology).

Arrowhead Made of bone, metal or stone (flint); occurs in many shapes, such as barbed-and-tanged, hollow-based, and tranchet.

Artefact Man-made object.

Assemblage Group of different but associated objects.

Avenue Two parallel rows of standing stones.

Awl Sharp point of bone, flint or metal, for making holes.

Barrow Round or long mound of earth over burial chamber or deposit. Many different shapes and often surrounded by a ditch.

Bazina North African concentric stepped circle of well-built stone walls over burial.

Beaker folk Prehistoric makers and distributors of distinctive pottery and copper artefacts all over Europe. Origins still uncertain and controversial.

Beaker Ware Generally handless deep pottery drinking vessels, or beakers, with many designs.

Betyl Small stone pillar, probably sacred, and often conical.

Bossed bone plaque Long animal bone with row of carved round or oval bosses, or 'breasts', in varying small numbers. Often finely decorated; function unknown.

Broch Scottish circular drystone fortified homestead.

Bronze Alloy of copper (dominant) and tin or lead.

Cairn Round or long mound of stones, often covering chamber or burial (sometimes used for earth mound).

Calibration Mathematical calculation in radiocarbon dating (see 'Dates and Dating').

Callais Western European greenish stone bead.

Capstone Horizontal stone on top of chamber or passage; dressed or otherwise.

Cardium Latin for cockle; shell edge used for decorating Impressed Ware.

Carination Distinct beaked profile of vessel and spout.

Chalcolithic Age between Neolithic and Bronze (sometimes Copper); used outside Britain.

Chambered cairn Chamber tomb covered with stones.

Chamber tomb Common form of tomb, comprising orthostats, sometimes with interstices filled with drystone walling, and megalithic capstone over burial chamber approached by passage.

Chassey French Middle Neolithic culture with several phases and pottery decoration designs.

Chevron V-shaped carving motif.

Chouche North African stone-walled cylinder containing four-sided burial chamber.

Cist Small box-like square or rectangular burial place.

Coffre Open-ended cist (Sardinian).

Collective tomb Contains more than one burial.

Compartment Internal sub-division of burial place.

Contiguous Adjoining, touching.

Corbelled Beehive-shaped style of roofing; each rising stone course projects inwards over one below, until one or two stones close it.

Court cairn Kind of long chamber tomb occurring in northern Ireland and south-west Scotland. Generally more elaborate than horned cairns.

Cremation Burning of the dead, before burial or disposal. Ashes often placed in urns.

Cromlech Dolmen in Wales; stone circle in France.

Crook Megalithic art motif, like walking stick handle.

Cueva Spanish for chambered mound.

Cup mark Cup shaped depression carved out from stone.

Cup-and-ring mark One or more concentric rings around a cup mark; sometimes with groove slashed out from cup centre.

Cursus Generally very long Middle Neolithic rectangular enclosure formed by parallel earthen banks with external ditches. Function unknown.

Cyclopean Substantial stone walling of large blocks fitted together, in courses, without mortar.

Danubian culture One name for first farming culture of eastern and central Europe.

Diffusion Spread of cultural influences

from places of origin. Subject of continual debate among archaeologists.

Discarnation Divestiture of flesh, by natural or manual means.

Djoula North African above ground burial chamber, without mound, often set on revetted plinth.

Dolmen Simple megalithic burial chamber with three or more uprights and one or more capstones.

Dressed stone Manually shaped and smoothed.

Dromos Entrance passage to tholos burial chamber.

Drystone walling Without any form of mortar.

Dun Small Scottish and Irish fortified structure with internal galleries and rooms.

Dyss Danish burial chamber.

Eclipse Partial, total or annular interception of light of sun by moon to earth, or of light of moon by earth's shadow before sun. Very important event in prehistory, and probably much feared.

Enclosure Area bounded by stones or earth banks.

Entrance grave Sometimes called Undifferentiated Passage Grave; no distinction between passage and chamber, within round mound.

Faience Baked clay and sand, becoming glass-like, in blues and greens.

False entrance Dummy entrance opposite real one in chambered long barrow.

Fogou Cornish name for souterrain.

Forecourt External concave entrance area of tomb.

Funnel beaker Vessel with expanded neck. In German Trichterbecher (TRB), which gave its name to early Neolithic culture in north Europe.

Gallery grave Stretched rectangular megalithic burial chamber, beneath long mound.

Ganggrab German passage grave.

Ganggrift Swedish passage grave.

Grave goods Artefacts buried with dead.

Grooved Ware Type of Late Neolithic pottery pre-dating Beaker Ware.

Hallstatt Austrian salt mines and cemetery which gave name to European Late Bronze Age periods (A and B).

Head stone Faces tomb entrance.

Henge Almost unique Late Neolithic British earth enclosure of bank and ditch (usually internal). Class I has single entrance; Class II has two or more entrances.

Horned cairn Partly enclosed façade of cairn; can be at front and back.

Hugel German tumulus or mound.

Hunebed Burial chamber type most often found in The Netherlands; long narrow chamber of trilithons, within kerbed mound, with entrance on one long side.

Hünengrab German equivalent of hunebed.

Hougue French dialect word for tumulus or mound, from Old Norse haugre (eminence); howe in Scotland.

Hypogeum Large underground

chamber, often carved out of rock; generally for burials.

Incised pottery Decorated by deep cuts in soft clay before baking.

Inhumation Burial of dead body (as opposed to exposure or cremation). Position may be extended, flexed, or crouched, and prone, supine, or on side.

Impressed Ware First Neolithic farmers' pottery.

Interstice Intervening space.

Jaettestue Danish passage grave.

Jet Black soft stone.

Kerb Ring of retaining stones against mound or cairn base.

Lagozza Italian Neolithic culture type site.

La Tène Swiss type site providing name of post-Hallstatt European Iron Age.

Lateral chamber Chamber set in side of tomb.

Le Grand Pressigny Unique French source of fine, honey-coloured flint.

Lintel Horizontal stone across tops of two orthostats (forming trilithon).

Lozenge Diamond-shaped carving motif.

Lug Handle on pottery.

Megalith Great stone; sometimes wrongly used to describe megalithic monument.

Megalithic yard Alexander Thom's proposed prehistoric unit of measurement, equivalent to 2.72ft (0.829m).

Mesolithic Middle Stone Age, between Palaeolithic and Neolithic.

Menhir French word for single standing stone, but sometimes used loosely for other megalithic monuments.

Michelsberg Low Countries' Neolithic culture.

Microlith Very small stone implement.

Midden Domestic or food refuse heap.

Monolith Single stone block, monument or pillar.

Mortuary house Sepulchre in shape of building made of stone or wood; for temporary body storage.

Mound Of either earth or stone pebbles or rubble, generally covering burial chamber or deposit.

Naveta Minorcan cyclopean upturned-boat-shaped chamber.

Neolithic Period when settled farming superseded nomadic life.

Nuraghe Sardinian round cyclopean tower.

Obsidian Very hard volcanic glass used for tools. It can be dated by measurement of thickness of its hydration layer on surface.

Ochre Natural red or yellow oxides of iron, used for art, and most probably body painting.

Oculus Common eye-like carved motif of paired spirals and circles.

Ogham (ogam) Ancient alphabet, in which letters are formed of parallel lines which meet or cross a base-line. Possibly of Irish origin.

Orientation Positioned to face a certain direction, not only the east.

Ossuary Place for human bones.

Outlier Single stone away from main setting (generally a circle).

Passage grave Passage (sometimes with lateral chambers) leading to broader burial chamber, often roofed, within round mound (which may be kerbed). Façaded forecourt entrance common.

Paving Stone slabs on passage and chamber floors.

Pecking Hammered shapes or decorations on stone.

Peristalith Retaining kerbstones around barrow or cairn.

Pietrafitta Italian standing stone (plural pietrefitte; sometimes two words).

Plaque – see Bossed bone plaque.

Portal dolmen Rectangular burial chamber which is narrower and lower towards back, with two portal stones at entrance. Mainly Irish and Welsh.

Port-hole Circular hole, often in entrance stone to chamber tomb, or made by semi-circular holes in facing contiguous stones. Also in orthostats and capstones.

Portico Entrance porch.

Post hole Socket for wooden post.

Potsherd Fragment of pottery.

Primary burial (or interment) Burial for which surrounding structure was initially created.

Quoit Cornish name for burial chamber.

Radiocarbon date Derived from techniques for measuring Carbon 14 remaining in organic matter. See 'Dates and Dating' at the beginning of this book.

Recumbent stone circle Unique Scottish and Irish circles with one large stone lying horizontally between two uprights.

Redjem Simple North African stone cairn covering burial (sometimes within cist), often on raised site.

Revetment Retaining wall of stones around base of mound.

Rock-cut tomb Chamber tomb cut out of solid rock.

Roofing slab Another name for capstone.

Sarsen Sandstone lying on Wiltshire Downs; used for Stonehenge and Avebury, though not exclusively.

Schist Fine-grained rock, altered after formation by heat or pressure or both, so that mineral content is in roughly parallel layers. Can therefore be split into thin plates.

Secondary burial Follows primary or first use of grave site.

Segmented cist With internal compartments.

Seine-Oise-Marne (SOM) culture Latest Neolithic culture phase in Paris Basin; gallery graves with port-hole slabs, which occur elsewhere.

Septal slab Slab set in ground dividing internal chamber compartment.

Serra d'Alto Southern Italian type site for pottery with geometrical patterns.

Sese Bronze Age tomb on island of Pantelleria.

Severn-Cotswold tomb Early Neolithic gallery-type grave, located east and west of Bristol Channel, England.

Shaft-and-chamber tomb Burial

chamber opening to side of pit bottom.

Sherd Sometimes shard. Broken piece of pottery.

Shield/idol Carved abstract version of anthropomorphic figure, as idol.

Slab Flat thinnish dressed stone.

Socket hole For holding orthostat.

Souterrain Underground megalithic storage room in prehistoric settlements.

Specchia Southern Italian stone cairn monument, sometimes with burial.

Spiral Common decoration motif carved on stone; sometimes interconnected. Meaning unknown.

Standing stone Lone vertical stone; see Menhir.

Statue-menhir Stone slab or pillar with anthropomorphic carving.

Stazzone Sardinian dolmen.

Stele Small stone slab or pillar, sometimes carved with abstract or literal decoration.

Stone circle Ring, which may not be circular, of spaced or contiguous standing stones; sometimes roughly (and very rarely completely) dressed.

Stone row Sometimes alignment. Line of regularly spaced standing stones.

Stratigraphy Interpretation of layered deposits.

Talayot Balearic circular cyclopean tower, sometimes with internal chamber, and corbelled roofing.

Taula Catalan for table. Minorcan vertical dressed pillar supporting dressed horizontal block.

Temple General term for megalithic buildings; used especially in Malta.

Thermoluminescence (TL) – see 'Dates and Dating' at the beginning of this book.

Tholos Greek for corbelled roof. Now name of bee-hive shaped burial chamber so roofed.

Three Age System Division by Thomsen in 1816–19 of prehistory into Stone, Bronze and Iron Ages.

Timber lacing Wooden framework strengthening earth or stone structure.

Tomba di giganti Sardinian chamber tomb.

Torre Corsican round cyclopean tower with single room.

TRB Commonly used initials for Trichterbecher (German for funnel beaker), the first northern European Neolithic culture, which developed in several phases and directions.

Transept Side chamber.

Trilithon Two orthostats with lintel across them.

Tumulus Latin for mound or barrow; generally covers a burial, in a chamber (as in French use of word) or not.

Upright Colloquial term for orthostat.

Vitrification Fusing together of stones by heat.

Wedge tomb Irish type of chamber tomb which tapers slightly from entrance inwards beneath mound; sometimes with parallel outer walls either side.

Wheelhouse Scottish Iron Age circular stone house with internal walls radiating from the centre.

Further Reading

Alimen, H., *The Prehistory of Africa*, Hutchinson, London 1957

Atkinson, R.J.C., *Stonehenge*, Pelican, London (2nd Ed.) 1979

Baillie, M.G.L., *Tree-ring Dating and Archaeology*, Croom Helm, London 1982

Balfour, Michael, *Stonehenge and its Mysteries*, Hutchinson, London (2nd Ed.) 1983

Barber, Chris, *Mysterious Wales*, David & Charles, Newton Abbot 1982

– , and Williams, John Godfrey, *The Ancient Stones of Wales*, Blorenge Books, Abergavenny, Wales 1989

Bender, Barbara (with Cailland, Robert), *The Archaeology of Brittany, Normandy, and the Channel Islands*, Faber and Faber, London 1986

Bord, Janet and Colin, *Ancient Mysteries of Britain*, Grafton, London 1986

– , *A Guide to Ancient Sites in Britain*, Paladin, London 1979

Bray, W. & Trump, D., *A Dictionary of Archaeology*, Allen Lane, London 1970

Brea, L. Bernabo, *Sicily Before the Greeks*, Thames and Hudson, London, Rev. Ed., 1966

Brennan, Martin, *The Boyne Valley Vision*, The Dolmen Press, Portlaoise, Ireland 1980

– , *The Stars and the Stones*, Thames and Hudson, London 1983

Burgess, Colin, *The Age of Stonehenge*, J.M. Dent, London 1980

Burl, Aubrey, *The Stone Circles of the British Isles*, Yale University Press, London 1976

– , *Prehistoric Avebury*, Yale University Press, London 1979

– , *Rings of Stone*, Frances Lincoln/ Weidenfeld & Nicholson, London 1979

– , *Megalithic Brittany*, Thames and Hudson, London 1985

– , *The Stonehenge People*, J. M. Dent, London 1987

Camps, Gabriel, and others, *Atlas Préhistorique de la Tunisie*, Vol.8, Maktar, Rome 1985

– , and Camps- Fabrer, Henriette, *La Nécropole Mégalithique du Djebel Mazela à Bou Nouara*, Arts Et Métiers Graphiques, Paris 1964

Cartailhac, M. Émile, *Les Ages Préhistoriques de l'Espagne et du Portugal*, Ch. Reinwald, Paris 1886

Champion, T., Gamble, C., Shennan, S., and Whittle, Alasdair, *Prehistoric Europe*, Academic Press, London 1984

Chippindale, Chris, *Stonehenge Complete*, Thames and Hudson, London 1983

Collum, V.C.C., *The Tressé Iron-Age Megalithic Monument*, Oxford University Press 1935

Crawford, O.G.S., *The Eye Goddess*, Phoenix House, London 1957

Daniel, Glyn, *The Prehistoric Chamber Tombs of France*, Thames and Hudson, London 1960

– , *The Megalithic Builders of Western Europe*, Hutchinson, London (2nd Ed.) 1962

Darvill, Timothy, *Prehistoric Britain*, B.T. Batsford, London 1987

De Laet, S.J., *The Low Countries*, Thames and Hudson, London 1958

Dyer, James, *Discovering Archaeology in Denmark*, Shire Publications, Princes Risborough 1972

– , *The Penguin Guide to Prehistoric England and Wales*, Allen Lane, London 1981

Ellis Davidson, H.R., *Pagan Scandinavia*, Thames and Hudson, London 1967

Evans, J.D., *Malta*, Thames and Hudson, London 1959

Farinha dos Santos, M., *Pre-Historia de Portugal*, Editorial Verbo, Lisbon (2nd Rev. Ed.) 1974

Feacham, Richard, *Guide to Prehistoric Scotland*, B.T. Batsford, London (2nd Rev. Ed.) 1977

Fergusson, James, *Rude Stone Monuments in all Countries*, Murray, London 1872

Gibson, Alex, and Woods, Ann, *Prehistoric Pottery for the Archaeologist*, Leicester University Press 1990

Glob, P.V., *Danish Prehistoric Monuments*, Faber, London 1971

Guido, Margaret, *Sardinia*, Thames and Hudson, London 1963

– , *Sicily : An Archaeological Guide*, Faber and Faber, London 1967

– , *Southern Italy : An Archaeological Guide*, Faber and Faber 1972

Hadingham, Evan, *Ancient Carvings in Britain : A Mystery*, Garnstone Press, London 1974

Harbison, Peter, *Guide to the National Monuments in the Republic of Ireland*, Gill & Macmillan, Dublin 1970

– , *Pre-Christian Ireland*, Thames and Hudson, London 1988

Hawkins, Gerald, *Stonehenge Decoded*, Souvenir Press, London 1966

Henshall, Audrey, *The Chambered Tombs of Scotland*, 2 Vols, Edinburgh University Press 1963 and 1972

Johnson, Walter, *Byways in British Archaeology*, Cambridge University Press 1912

Johnston, David E., *The Channel Islands : An Archaeological Guide*, Phillimore, Chichester 1981

Joussaume, Roger, *Dolmens for the Dead*, B.T. Batsford, London 1988

Klok, R.H.J., *Hunebedden in Nederland : Zorgen voor Morgen*, Fibula-Van Dishoeck, Haarlem, 1979

Leisner, Georg and Vera, *Die Megalithgräber der Iberischen Halbinsel*, Berlin 1943 and 1946

Lockyer, Sir J. Norman, *Stonehenge and other British Monuments Astronomically Considered*, Macmillan, London (2nd Ed.) 1909

MacKie, Euan, *The Megalith Builders*,

Phaidon, Oxford 1977

MacSween, Ann, and Sharp, Mick, *Prehistoric Scotland*, B.T. Batsford, London 1989

Malagrino, Paolo, *Dolmen E Menhir di Puglia*, Schena Editore, Fasano 1978

Mallory, J.P., *In Search of the Indo-Europeans*, Thames and Hudson, London 1989

Marshack, Alexander, *The Roots of Civilization*, Weidenfeld and Nicholson, London 1972

Michell, John, *City of Revelation*, Garnstone Press, London 1972

– , *The View Over Atlantis*, Garnstone Press, London (Rev. Ed.) 1972

– , *The Old Stones of Land's End*, Garnstone Press, London 1974

– , *Megalithomania*, Thames and Hudson, London 1982

– , *A Little History of Astro-Archaeology*, Thames and Hudson, London (Rev. Ed.) 1989

Milisauskas, Sarunas, *European Prehistory*, Academic Press, London 1978

Mithen, Steven, *Thoughtful Foragers : A Study of Pre-historic Decision-making*, Cambridge University Press 1990

Mohen, Jean-Pierre, *The World of Megaliths*, Cassell, London 1989

Morris, Ronald W.B., *The Prehistoric Rock Art of Argyll*, Dolphin Press, Poole, Dorset 1977

Munksgaard, Elisabeth, *Denmark : An Archaeological Guide*, Faber and Faber, London 1970

Over, Luke, *Visitor's Guide to Archaeology in Scilly*, St. Mary's, Scilly 1974

Paget, R.F., *Central Italy : An Archaeological Guide*, Faber and Faber, London 1973

Paturi, Felix R., *Prehistoric Heritage*, Macdonald & Jane's, London 1979

Pearce, Susan M., *The Archaeology of South West Britain*, Collins, London 1981

Peet, T. Eric, *Rough Stone Monuments and their Builders*, Harper & Brothers, London 1912

Pericot, Garcia L., *The Balearic Islands*, London 1972

Phillips, Patricia, *The Prehistory of Europe*, Allen Lane, London 1980

Piggott, Stuart, *The Neolithic Cultures of the British Isles*, Cambridge University Press, 1954

– , *Scotland Before History*, Edinburgh University Press 1982

Poinssot, Claude, *Les Ruines de Dougga*, L'Institut National D'Archéologie et Arts, Tunis 1958

Ponsich, Michel, *Nécropoles Phéniciennes de la Region de Tanger*, (Études et Travaux D'Archéologie Marocaine : Vol.111), Éditions Marocaines et Internationales, Tanger 1967

Radmilli, Antonia Mario (Ed.), *Guida Della Preistoria Italiana*, Sansoni Editore, Florence 1975

Renfrew, Colin, *Before Civilisation*, Jonathan Cape, London 1973

– , (Ed.), *The Megalithic Monuments of*

Western Europe, Thames and Hudson, London, Paperback Edition 1983

– , *Archaeology and Language*, Jonathan Cape, London 1987

Roche, Denis, *Carnac*, Tchou, Paris 1973

Savory, H.N., *Spain and Portugal : The Prehistory of the Iberian Peninsula*, Thames and Hudson, London 1968

Scarre, Christopher (Ed.), *Ancient France: Neolithic Societies and their Landscapes : 6000–2000 BC*, Edinburgh University Press 1984

Schirnig, Heinz (Ed.), *Grossteingräber in Niedersachsen*, August Lax, Hildersheim 1979

Schuldt, Ewald, *Die Mecklenburgischen Megalithgräber*, VEB Deutscher Verlag der Wissenschaften, Berlin 1972

Service, Alastair, and Bradbery, Jean, *A Guide to the Megaliths of Europe*, Weidenfeld and Nicolson, London 1979

Souville, Georges, *Atlas Préhistorique du Maroc*, Vol.1, 'Le Maroc Atlantique', Éditions Du Centre National De La Recherche Scientifique, Paris 1973

Sprockhoff, Ernst, *Atlas der Megalithgräber Deutschlands*, 4 vols., Rudolf Habelt, Bonn 1966, 1967, 1975

Stenberger, Mårten, *Sweden*, Thames and Hudson, London 1962

Strömberg, Märta, *Die Megalithgräber von Hagestad*, CWK Gleerups Forlag, Lund, Sweden 1971

Thom, A., *Megalithic Sites in Britain*, Clarendon Press, Oxford 1967

– , *Megalithic Lunar Observatories*, Clarendon Press, Oxford 1971

– , and Thom, A.S., *Megalithic Remains in Britain and Brittany*, Clarendon Press, Oxford 1978

Thomas, Nicholas, *Guide to Prehistoric England*, B.T. Batsford, London 1976

Trump, David, *Central and Southern Italy Before Rome*, Thames and Hudson, London 1966

– , *Malta : An Archaeological Guide*, Faber and Faber, London 1972

– , *The Prehistory of the Mediterranean*, Allen Lane, London 1980

Twohig, Elizabeth Shee, *The Megalithic Art of Western Europe*, Clarendon Press, Oxford 1981

Waterhouse, John, *The Stone Circles of Cumbria*, Phillimore, Chichester 1985

Watkins, Alfred, *The Old Straight Track*, Methuen, London 1925

Weatherhill, Craig, *Cornovia : Ancient Sites of Cornwall and Scilly*, Alison Hodge, Penzance, Cornwall (Rev. Ed.) 1989

Weir, Anthony, *Early Ireland : A Field Guide*, Blackstaff Press, Belfast 1980

Whitehouse, David & Ruth, *Archaeological Atlas of the World*, Thames and Hudson, London 1975

Whittle, Alasdair, *Problems in Neolithic Archaeology*, Cambridge University Press 1988

Wood, John Edwin, *Sun, Moon and Standing Stones*, O.U.P., Oxford, 1978

Index

Picture credits
The publisher thanks photographers and
organizations for their kind permission to
reproduce the following photographs in this
book.

A: *Above* B: *Below* L: *Left* R: *Right* C: *Centre*
18(L) Michael Balfour; 18(R) Janet & Colin
Bord; 19 Michael Balfour; 20(A) A. Weir/
Janet & Colin Bord; 20(B) Bob Burns; 21(A)
The Jersey Museums Service; 21(B) Bob Burns;
22 Robin Briault; 23 Bob Burns; 24–27 Bernd
Siering; 28(A) Robert Estall; 28(B) Bernd
Siering; 29(A) English Heritage; 29(B) Bernd
Siering; 30(A) Robert Estall; 30(B) Janet &
Colin Bord; 31 Bernd Siering; 32(A) Bernd
Siering; 32(B) M. Jenner/Robert Harding;
33(A) Bernd Siering; 33(B) Robert Estall;
34(A) Bernd Siering; 34(B) Janet & Colin
Bord; 35 Kevin Redpath; 36–42 Bernd
Siering; 43(A) A. Kennedy/Janet & Colin
Bord; 43(B) David Lyons; 44 David Lyons;
45(A) Bernd Siering; 45(C) H.M. Brown/Janet
& Colin Bord; 45(B) A. Weir/Janet & Colin
Bord; 46(A) Michael Balfour; 46(B) A.
Kennedy/Janet & Colin Bord; 47(A) A. Weir/
Janet & Colin Bord; 47(B) Office of Public
Works, Ireland; 48–51 Bernd Siering; 52(A)
Michael Balfour; 52(B) Bernd Siering; 53
Bernd Siering; 54 Michael Balfour; 55(A)
Werner Forman Archive; 55(L) Patricia
Macdonald; 55 (R) C. Tait/Ancient Art &
Architecture Collection; 56–59 Bernd Siering;
60 Frank Gibson; 61(A) Frank Gibson; 61(B)
Cornwall Archaeological Unit; 62(A) David
Lyons; 62(B) Bernd Siering; 63(A) David
Lyons; 63(B) Mick Sharp; 64–65 Bernd
Siering; 66 David Lyons; 67(A) David Lyons;
67(B) Bernd Siering; 68(A) Bernd Siering;
68(B) David Lyons; 69 David Lyons; 70(A)
Janet & Colin Bord; 70(B) David Lyons; 71
David Lyons; 72(A) Chris Barber 72(B)
Michael Balfour; 73(A) Bernd Siering; 73(B)
Aubrey Burl; 74(A) Janet & Colin Bord; 74(B)
Michael Balfour; 75(A) Michael Balfour; 75(B)
Bernd Siering; 76 Bernd Siering; 77(A)
Michael Balfour; 77(B) RCAHM, Wales; 80–
81 Michael Balfour; 82 Colin Burgess; 83
Michael Balfour; 84 Robert Estall; 85 Michael
Balfour; 86–88 Jos Le Doaré; 89–90 Chris
Scarre; 91(A) Aubrey Burl; 91(B) Michael
Balfour; 92(A) Colin Burgess; 92(B) Chris
Scarre; 93–94 Bernd Siering; 95(A) Ronald
Sheridan/Ancient Art & Architecture
Collection; 95(B) Colin Burgess; 96 Bernd
Siering; 97–98 Jos Le Doaré; 99 Bernd
Siering; 100(A) Michael Balfour; 100(B)
Aubrey Burl; 101(A) Colin Burgess; 101(B)
Michael Balfour; 102 Michael Balfour; 103
Mick Sharp; 104(A) Michael Balfour; 104(B)
Robert Estall; 105 Michael Balfour; 106(A) Jos
Le Doaré; 106(B) Colin Burgess; 110–114
Bernd Siering; 115–116 Ministry of the
Environment, Denmark; 117(A) Ministry of
the Environment, Denmark; 117(B) T.
Spiegel/Rapho; 118(A) James Dyer; 118(B)
Ministry of the Environment, Denmark; 119–
120 Ministry of the Environment, Denmark;
121(A) Forhistorisk Museum, Denmark;
121(B) Minsitry of the Environment,
Denmark; 122 Landesmuseum, Schwerin; 123
Pfaltzer/Roger Viollet; 124–129 Bernd
Siering; 131 S. Andersson/Scandibild
Bildbyra; 132(A) Märta Strömberg; 132(B)
ATA/Märta Strömberg; 133 Märta Strömberg;
136 Oronoz/Artephot; 137 David Trump; 138
Nimatallah/Artephot; 139 Robert Estall;

140(A) N. Saunders/Barbara Heller; 140(B) X.
Miserachs/Firo-Foto; 141 Chris Scarre; 142–
143 Colin Burgess; 144 R.J. Harrison; 145–
146 Colin Burgess; 147(A) Firo-Foto; 147(B)
Oronoz/Artephot; 148(A) Oronoz/Artephot;
148(B) Ministry of Culture, Spain; 150
Oronoz/Artephot; 154(L) Bernd Siering;
154(R) Percheron/Artephot; 155 Ziolo/
Artephot; 156–157 Bernd Siering; 158
Petcheron/Artephot; 159–162 Ruth
Whitehouse; 163 Caroline Malone; 164–165
Bernd Siering; 166(A) Percheron/Artephot;
166(B) Bernd Siering; 167 Robert Estall; 168
Bernd Siering; 169 David Trump; 171 Fabbri
Editori; 173–174 Caroline Malone; 175
Archaeological Photo Service, Canton of
Graubuenden; 176–177 Alain Gallay; 180 G.
Camps; 182 Bernd Siering; 183 A. Ruhlmann;
185 G. Camps; 186 Bernd Siering.

Every effort has been made to trace
photographers. In the event of any
unintentional omissions the publishers invite
copyright holders to contact them direct.

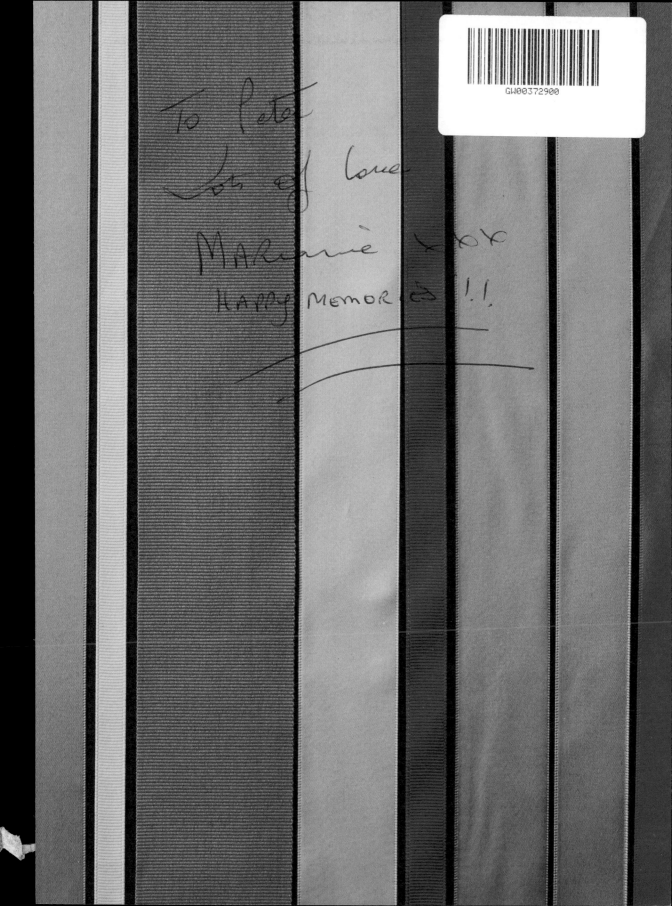

PROVENCE

AND THE CÔTE D'AZUR

Discover the Spirit of the South of France

Text and photography by
Janelle McCulloch

plum   Pan Macmillan Australia

CONTENTS

Introduction:

Discovering the spirit of
the South of France 8

Note: Apologies to French speakers and Francophiles, but we've decided to follow the English convention of capitalising street names, geographical place names, days of the week, etc. Thus, Place du Général de Gaulle (not place du Général de Gaulle), Baie des Anges (not baie des Anges) and Gare de Nice Ville (not gare de Nice Ville).

CONTENTS

005

DISCOVERING THE SPIRIT OF THE SOUTH OF FRANCE

The South of France is the stuff of travel hyperbole. The region may not have invented the word 'glamour', but it has certainly adopted it as its mission statement. This famous part of the Mediterranean coast is a glorious, almost painterly swirl of spectacular, sun-filled landscapes, seductive villages, sublime beaches, secret coves, scented gardens, high-octane cars, beautiful people and a blissful climate.

Adding further interest is the fact that there are two sides to the South of France. There is the coast, an area that encompasses the Riviera with its charming coves, bobbing yachts, Belle Époque architecture, bougainvillea-draped lanes, grand villas and waterfront promenades buoyant with life.

PROVENCE
AND THE CÔTE D'AZUR

And there is the countryside, an area that encompasses Provence; a gentle and charmingly photogenic scene of winding roads, weekend markets, sleepy villages, Roman ruins, enchanting châteaux, fields of lavender and sunflowers, babbling fountains and dapper gentlemen chatting or playing boules in ancient squares, all enveloped in a light that seems almost Impressionist in quality.

SAY HELLO TO PROVENCE AND THE CÔTE D'AZUR

Now something needs to be clarified before we tie our hair in a silk Hermès scarf and start our sky-blue Sunbeam convertibles. The terms 'Côte d'Azur', 'Provence' and the 'French Riviera' are, well, they're not so much strictly defined geographical areas as they are states of mind: each a shift in spirit that happens once you get past a certain point on the road from Paris to Nice. The official name for this region is Provence-Alpes-Côte d'Azur. But as that's a bit of a mouthful, shorter phrases have crept into the vernacular. Some people like to use Côte d'Azur or the French Riviera if they're visiting the Mediterranean coastline along the south-east corner of France, or they'll say Provence if they're visiting the hinterland and countryside further inland. Other people see the entire south-eastern corner of France as Provence. It's complicated, I know.

To be precise, this region comprises six major *départements*. However, for the purposes of this book we have decided to simply split the region into two areas: Provence and the Côte d'Azur. Easy.

That's the admin done; now for the potted history and glamorous anecdotes. Like much of Europe, the history of this part of France is long and complicated. It begins 40,000 years ago with prehistoric settlements, Greek colonies in 600 BC, Roman influence from around the 3rd century BC, endless 'barbarian' invasions, and the incredible fortifications of the medieval period that form the core of many of the regions' breathtakingly beautiful villages. Unfortunately, space does not permit me to delve into such a complex past, but I will attempt to offer some insights into the history of each town as we go.

For now, let us focus on the more recent legends who have passed through this area: F. Scott and Zelda Fitzgerald in Juan-les-Pins; Picasso and Graham Greene in Antibes; Matisse in Nice; Béatrice de Rothschild, David Niven and Somerset Maugham in Cap Ferrat; Cocteau and Chanel in Menton, and Bardot in Saint-Tropez. They came for the garden parties, the soirées, the people, and the experiences they'd later immortalise in print, or with paint and canvas. They came for the sun and fun, the decadence and indiscretions, the swimming coves and beaches, and all the sights in between.

Yet it wasn't always like this. The South of France only really became popular at the end of the 18th century when the British and northern European upper classes saw its potential as a winter resort. When the new railway arrived in the mid-19th century, the area rapidly became the playground of the European well-to-do and, soon after, the wealthy American set. And it is still one of the most popular places in the world for stars to escape to. Elton John loves it so much that he's bought a home in the hills above Nice. Bono has one on the beach at Èze-bord-de-Mer. Sting and his family like to come here and hang out each year, as do Naomi Campbell, Kate Moss and Giorgio Armani. And Jack Nicholson often cavorts here, although it's usually on a yacht with a few beautiful models. Some days, particularly in May during the Cannes Film Festival, half of Hollywood seems to have decamped to the Riviera.

The South of France does, however, have a flip side. Over-development has ruined some of the beautiful coastline and in the height of summer the roads are often jammed

with cars. Even in Provence, the lines of summer tourists can become an eyesore on the lavender-etched landscape. But you can still find 'old Provence' and 'the classic Riviera' in many places: the coastal paths around Cap Ferrat and Cap d'Antibes, the pretty side streets of Cannes and Nice and, of course, the back roads of Provence.

So sit back, refill that glass of wine, and get comfortable. Because we're about to explore two of the most beautiful places in the world: the enchanting villages of Provence and the magnificent coastline of the Côte d'Azur.

INDIVIDUALISING YOUR ITINERARY

The key to enjoying the South of France is to focus on what you love. Although tempting, it is not a good idea to try to cover all of the South of France in one holiday: you'll just become exhausted. The distances are greater than you think. Instead, go to just two or three areas that offer what you really want and explore them in depth. So if you prefer the quiet of the countryside, the winding lanes without traffic, the fields of wildflowers and lavender and the quaint ancient villages, then spend most of your time in Provence. If you love lively streets, shopping, sheltered swimming coves, and an endless view of yacht sails and the elegant blue of the Mediterranean, stick to the coast.

Wherever you go, don't discount the lesser-known parts of the region. Cap Ferrat is extraordinarily beautiful and Menton, with its Italian feel, brightly coloured architecture and profusion of gardens, will charm and delight. So go off the beaten path if you can; it may just surprise you.

Another thing to consider is your level of expectation – some of the so-called 'famous' places may not quite live up to their reputations. When I first saw what one friend described as 'the sexy, sybaritic village of Saint-Tropez', I wondered if I'd missed something. Where were the celebrities? The chic sidewalk fashions? The famous Saint-Tropez spirit? Admittedly I was visiting in early May, before the season was in full swing, but I was still slightly taken aback by the empty, wind-blown beach and the incongruous sight of dozens of über-cruisers from the Cayman Islands squished into a tiny harbour. Don't be too disappointed if parts of the Riviera don't look like you might imagine they did in the glamorous heydays of the 1950s and '60s. Things do change.

This leads me to the third consideration: timing. Just as some places have looked better in the past, some will be more appealing at certain times of the year. Provence looks glorious in spring and summer, when all the flowers are out. Cannes seems to sparkle in May, when the film festival brings the stars to town. Ditto Monaco during the Grand Prix. Many other places have festivals throughout the year that turn the streets into one long party, so if you love a festive atmosphere try to time your visit with these. Personally, I prefer the quieter coves and villages, which is why I fell in love with Paloma Beach and the coves of Cap d'Antibes. But you'll no doubt find your own favourite hideaway.

HERE ARE SOME WAYS TO SEE THE GLAMOUR AND GRANDEUR OF THIS GLORIOUS PART OF FRANCE

By foot. Some of the most beautiful parts of the coast and countryside in this region are off the main roads and even off the village lanes. Look for the many walking paths (they'll usually be marked 'sentier'). Be sure to take lots of water and proper walking shoes, but even if you want to stroll along in casual sandshoes, there are plenty of paths along the coast that offer a quick walk and fantastic views. The path from Nice to Villefranche and Cap Ferrat is one such walk. If you prefer to stay in the towns, there are many great walks, such as the one along Nice's famed Promenade des Anglais that follows several kilometres of stunning Belle Époque-era architecture and azure blue sea.

Follow the stars. Many parts of the Riviera attract big Hollywood names in May during the Cannes International Film Festival. Hang around Cannes during the festival and you'll likely see a few famous faces. Or head to Saint-Tropez in July and August for some more celeb sightings, where they often sail in on mega-yachts before lunching in town. Some places, such as Les Caves du Roy and Club 55 in Saint-Tropez are perennial star-pleasers, so the odds of seeing a 'name' there are high.

Follow the artists. Many painters have made their names from settling in the South of France and capturing the light and landscapes on canvas. You can still see where many of them lived and worked, and if you can't visit their villas, there are museums (musées) that showcase their lives. These include the Musée Matisse in Nice, the Musée Picasso in Antibes, the Musée Marc Chagall in Nice and the Fondation Maeght in Saint-Paul de Vence. Some people even opt for a 'painting holiday', where they bring their watercolours and spend leisurely afternoons trying to capture the gentle light and landscapes on paper. I can't think of a better way to experience this place – or remember it.

Explore it from behind a wheel. The South of France has long been known as one of the world's great driving destinations. There are the famous corniches (the roads that hug the cliffs along the coast), the touring roads of Provence and all the lanes in between. Hire a classic car or even a convertible (but make it a small one; some roads can be tiny; and don't wear a long scarf or you may end up like Isadora Duncan). This is the way to see the coast as it's meant to be seen: from behind the wheel of a beautiful motorcar.

See it from two wheels. Cycling holidays are an increasingly popular activity in Provence (no doubt influenced by the Tour de France), though less so on the Riviera, where the traffic is horrendous and drivers are downright scary. But on the back roads, cyclists are a common sight – and what better way to see the countryside? Sure there are hills and mountains, but they only mean that the bottle of wine at the end tastes even better.

DISCOVERING THE SPIRIT

LE HAMEAU *Soulier*

PART ONE
▚ PROVENCE ▞

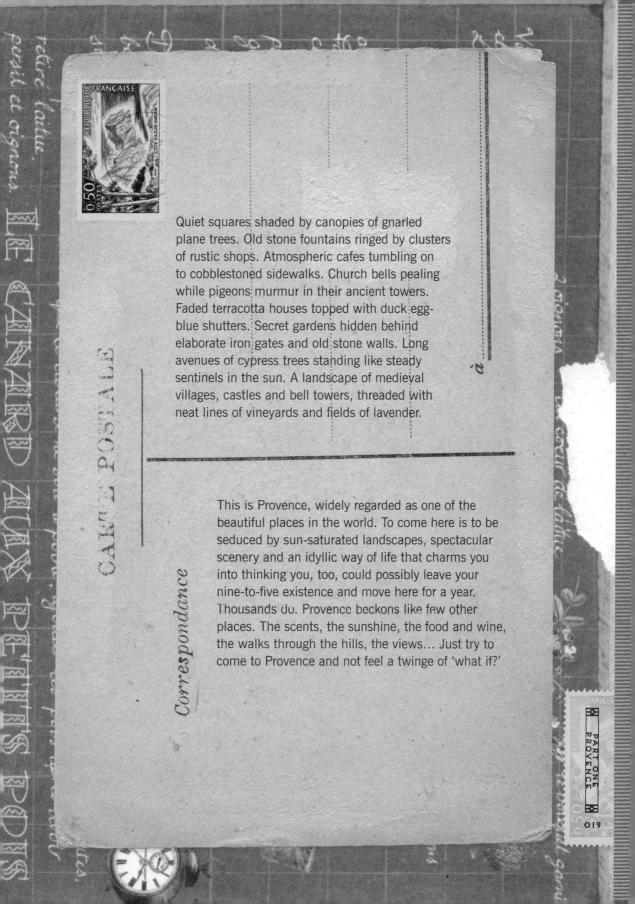

CARTE POSTALE

Quiet squares shaded by canopies of gnarled
plane trees. Old stone fountains ringed by clusters
of rustic shops. Atmospheric cafes tumbling on
to cobblestoned sidewalks. Church bells pealing
while pigeons murmur in their ancient towers.
Faded terracotta houses topped with duck egg-
blue shutters. Secret gardens hidden behind
elaborate iron gates and old stone walls. Long
avenues of cypress trees standing like steady
sentinels in the sun. A landscape of medieval
villages, castles and bell towers, threaded with
neat lines of vineyards and fields of lavender.

Correspondance

This is Provence, widely regarded as one of the
beautiful places in the world. To come here is to be
seduced by sun-saturated landscapes, spectacular
scenery and an idyllic way of life that charms you
into thinking you, too, could possibly leave your
nine-to-five existence and move here for a year.
Thousands do. Provence beckons like few other
places. The scents, the sunshine, the food and wine,
the walks through the hills, the views... Just try to
come to Provence and not feel a twinge of 'what if?'

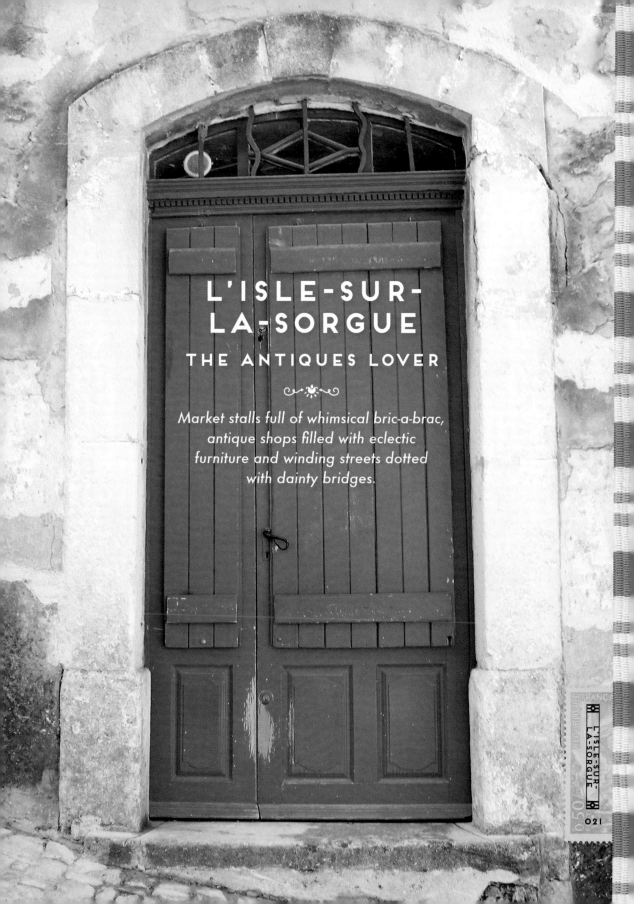

L'ISLE-SUR-LA-SORGUE

THE ANTIQUES LOVER

Market stalls full of whimsical bric-a-brac, antique shops filled with eclectic furniture and winding streets dotted with dainty bridges.

Known simply as 'L'Isle' by the locals, this pretty Provence village is often dubbed 'The Venice of the South'. While that's a bit of a stretch, the curious canals that run through the town – five mini tributaries of the river Sorgue – do make for a watery oasis.

L'Isle is a truly lovely place, although (and this is going to get me into trouble) it used to be lovelier. Before the masses of tourists came and before the famous Sunday markets began to attract the cheaper dealers. Yet it's still wonderful. You just need to ignore the tacky pockets and focus on the beautiful parts, of which there are plenty. Let me show you.

Firstly, L'Isle is a naturally pretty town, so it doesn't really matter how you approach it. Simply find your way to the city centre and follow one of the five waterways. You can cross and re-cross the various bridges (all very Venetian). In fact, the tiny bridges are one of the nicest ways to explore the place. You'll soon see how the river is the heart and the soul of the town.

L'Isle was originally known as 'Insula' and grew from a medieval settlement on the river Sorgue. The river, whose headwater is at Fontaine-de-Vaucluse several kilometres away, served a defensive purpose as a moat around the settlement and a valuable source of both food (fishing) and industry (artisan mills for paper, silk and other materials). In 1890, inspired by the waterways, the town officially adopted the name L'Isle-sur-la-Sorgue. Over the next century, the town's chiefs took pains to preserve a great deal of the town and its river tributaries, knowing its importance for L'Isle's survival. Look out for the lovely waterwheels scattered around town, some of which still turn.

The main reason people visit L'Isle is for the **markets**. There have been markets here since the 16th century, but the modern ones are so well known that they attract buyers from all over the world. Every week, regardless of the weather, there are stallholders here on Thursdays and Sundays, but summer attracts a larger crowd of both stallholders and tourists. Stretching from Place Gambetta all the way along Avenue des Quatre Otages there are stalls full of delicious produce from local farms and provedores – walnuts, olives, cheeses, breads, spices, charcuterie – all of it great picnic fare if you're heading off to the countryside afterwards. There are also stalls selling typical Provence-style wares – bright tablecloths, candles, soaps and so on. However, what most people really come for is the antiques. L'Isle has become the antiques capital of the south.

Some even believe it has the largest *marché aux puces* (flea market) outside of Paris. While I can't verify that, I was amazed at the range of goods. There was even a stand devoted to antique greenhouses and conservatories.

If you want to see the markets on Thursdays and Sundays, the key is to arrive early, ideally before 9 a.m. Most of the stalls will be set up, or in the process of setting up, and at that time you'll be able to find a park more easily, as well as stroll along without the crowds.

A good plan is to start at the Tourist Office on Place de l'Église in the middle of town. (A word of warning: the Sunday market can become especially crowded, so watch your bag.) If you need a coffee to kick-start the day, the beautiful Café de France is around the corner, on 14 Place de la Liberté, behind the church. This is a show-stopper of a cafe that also offers a great position from which to enjoy the sights.

Walk east a few blocks along Rue Raspail, and you'll soon reach Le Bassin, where the river splits into four canals. It's a truly lovely scene, and the swift current is a reminder of how powerful the water is, and how it could generate so much industry.

Cross the northern bridge, stopping for a photo if you need to, and then you have two options. The first is to continue forward and follow the tourist throng along Avenue Fabre de Sérignan. This will lead you through some of the market stalls. If you wish for some tranquillity, turn left onto one of the tiny footbridges that cross the river and you'll be on the quieter side. Stroll along the quays of the River Sorgue and admire the waterwheels (at one point there were around seventy). There are always some bric-a-brac dealers around here, but if you want more 'serious antiques' you'll have to head for Avenue des Quatre Otages and Avenue de la Libération. Most of the antique stores are along these streets and in courtyards behind them.

There's a good group of antiquarians at Hôtel Dongier (15 Esplanade Robert Vasse; hoteldongierantiquites.fr), and yet another group at Passage du Pont (formerly L'Isle aux Brocantes) at 7 Avenue des Quatre Otages. There is also a good range at Le Quai de la Gare (4 Avenue Julien Guigue).

Some antique stores are open all year, others only from April to October. If you really want to be sure of finding some great antiques, time your visit to coincide with the Foire Internationale (foire-islesurlasorgue.com) at Easter and on August 15.

If you want a break from shopping and browsing altogether, wander back to the basin where the river splits, and walk north across the bridge again. This time, head east on Avenue du Partage des Eaux as it follows the river. The little road rambles past waterfront homes and beneath shady trees all the way to Hôtel le Pescador where there's a lovely riverside cafe.

L'Isle doesn't just do bric-a-brac, antiques and other homewares. There's a book market on the last Sunday of each month, and a floating market the first Sunday in August. In July there's also the Festival de la Sorgue (music, theatre) and a parade on the canals.

MÉNERBES

THE RELUCTANT STAR

A quietly beautiful walled village enclosing quietly beautiful lanes, rising like a curious island above a sea of vineyards.

You may not have heard of the tiny remote village and commune of Ménerbes, but you've probably heard of the man who made it famous: British writer Peter Mayle.

Mayle's books about living in Provence as an expat, the most well-known of which is the bestselling *A Year in Provence* (later adapted into the 2006 film *A Good Year* starring Russell Crowe and Marion Cotillard), have leveraged this town to the top of many a traveller's 'To Do' list. Ménerbes has become something of a mecca for disillusioned souls seeking a new existence.

The story of how Mayle – and by association Ménerbes – became famous is the stuff of legend. In 1987, burned out by his years living in London as an advertising exec, Mayle decided to move to the South of France with his wife. They only had enough money to last them for six months. They found a 200-year-old farmhouse, and Mayle began writing a novel. But life intervened, and in the process of renovating his house, the wannabe author discovered reality was more interesting than fiction. So he wrote about the village and its characters instead. To the surprise of everyone, including the author, *A Year in Provence* became an international bestseller, tapping into all our desires to live a more idyllic life.

Unfortunately, neither Mayle nor Ménerbes were prepared for the onslaught of visitors, and the writer eventually packed up and moved to the Hamptons for a few years to escape the fans peering down his driveway. He has now moved back to Provence, but to a village further south, leaving Ménerbes to face the dreamers alone.

Fortunately, the village and surrounding area seem able to cope. The commune has even put on its commercial hat to take advantage of the sudden influx of tourist money. There are new boutiques selling French linen and designer clothes from the likes of Valentino, an ice-cream store that does a roaring trade, and smart new restaurants, including Le Galoubet and Café Veranda.

If you want to see what all the fuss is about, take a drive to the dramatic Luberon mountains, then approach Ménerbes from the north. You'll soon see it high on the stony cliff above the farming landscape; a walled village rising like a curious island above a sea of vineyards and orchards. The village itself is a lovely jumble of ancient medieval towers, churches and stone streets. At one end is the **Citadelle**, a miniature fortress dating from the 16th century, and at the other end is the cemetery, along with **Château du Castellet**, where the painter Nicolas de Staël once lived.

There's not much in between – the village is tiny – but the cobbled laneways and steps elegantly link each terrace. And as you step up through the levels you'll see the glorious Provence countryside spread out before you; a spectacular mix of mountains and farmland.

There are photo opportunities everywhere, but one of the best is through an arch at the top square beside the ancient *mairie* (town hall), where you can see the distant villages including Gordes. Other outlooks will allow you to glimpse the far-off ruins of the Château de Lacoste, the country residence of the notorious Marquis de Sade.

This area is also famous for its wild truffles, lavender, mushrooms and red wine, and there is a store in the Place de l'Horloge called the Maison de la Truffe et du Vin (House of Truffles and Wine), which is set inside a large and beautifully restored village home. It offers truffle and wine appreciation courses – important lessons in the art of French cuisine.

If you're a writer or an artist you may be interested in the fellowships offered at The Brown Foundation Fellows Program based at **Dora Maar**'s former home. Dora Maar was one of Picasso's much-loved models, and her beautiful home (which also has sumptuous views) now offers residences of one to three months for creative professionals to dedicate themselves to a project.

Outside Ménerbes, there is much to be inspired by. If you love lavender, make for the ancient **Abbaye Saint Hilaire**, about three kilometres south-east of the village. In the height of summer, the fields around the abbey explode with lavender, and the monks themselves go out and pick it when it's ready to be harvested: a truly memorable photo if you're there at the right time to capture it.

There are also many other villages in this region; far too many to detail in this book. However, I'll touch upon one other gorgeous place in the next section. (Peter Mayle knows a lot about this spot, too. He moved here to escape the literary fans who were following his every step around the South of France. The trouble is, many found out he'd moved here, and simply drove on down the road to see it.)

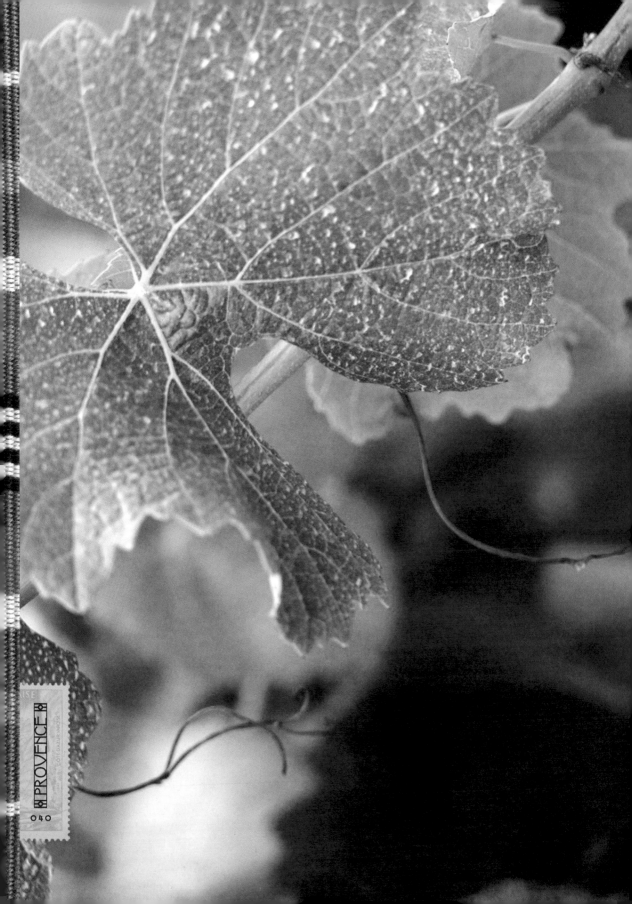

LOURMARIN

THE GOURMET LOVER

A village to lose yourself in for hours, amidst
old squares, stone walls, gorgeous stores,
and clouds of bougainvillea and jasmine.

The trick to seeing the two villages of Ménerbes and Lourmarin is to visit Ménerbes first. It's smaller, more intimate, and you can see it in a morning, with an ice-cream in one hand and a camera in the other. Larger Lourmarin is a delightful parade of shady squares, beautifully restored old houses, great shops and inviting cafes spilling out onto sunny terraces. So it really should come after, as it's perfect for a lazy, languid lunch followed by a long afternoon walk around town. Ménerbes may have the landscapes and views, but Lourmarin will entice the palate and the purse. (You can prop your partner up at one of the many cafes and tell him (or her) to wait with some good local liquid while you do a wander of the boutiques. That way, you're both happy.)

Here's a quirky fact about this village: its inhabitants are called Lourmarinois. That's a lot to get your tongue around after a few tall glasses of red. What's easier to comprehend is the layout. Lourmarin is pleasantly situated in a relatively flat landscape, surrounded by fields, vineyards and olive groves, with the forests of the Luberon to the north. Unlike the hilltop villages, it's not high on a ridge with staggering views so, in order to compete, has had to up the aesthetic factor in its urban landscape. And what a pleasing urban landscape it is.

Much of the village is set around the central bell tower, which was built on the remnants of the medieval moated castle that once defined Lourmarin. The rest of the village fans out around it – a pretty mix of old fountains, stone walls, cute houses with cuter staircases running up to the front doors, clouds of bougainvillea and jasmine drifting over terraces, and some truly captivating town squares lined with lovely cafes. There's also a handsome 16th-century castle, the **Château de Lourmarin**, part of which is open to the public. It's worth a visit to see the furnished apartments, the library of 28,000 books and the magnificent stairway

The shops here, too, have made an effort to be more than just the standard tourist deal, with stores selling lovely gardening fare, others offering fabrics and yet others specialising in toys to delight adults and children alike.

It's a quiet town off-season, but when the weather warms up in June it becomes a magnet for both the French and foreigners, who love to come here for a wander and a wine. In fact, Lourmarin is notable for its large number of great restaurants and bars. No wonder Peter Mayle moved here. On a sunny weekend you can barely get a cafe chair in any of the squares.

Outside of Lourmarin, there are yet more delightful villages, and you could happily spend a weekend driving from one to the other, becoming more and more rapturous with every passing kilometre. **Bonnieux** is particularly beautiful. Many of the scenes from *A Good Year* (based on the Mayle novel) were shot here. The crew spent nine months in and around Bonnieux in 2005 capturing the magic of Provence. It wasn't difficult: the director, Ridley Scott, lives in the nearby village of Oppède for half of the year and knows the area like the back of his wine glass.

Just outside Bonnieux is the acclaimed **Côtes du Luberon** winery. Also nearby is the village of Lacoste, better known for one of its famous – or infamous – residents, the writer and, er, sexpert, the Marquis de Sade. This village was where Sade retreated to his château to indulge his wicked ways. Sade wasn't exactly a happy man, or a well-balanced one, and his strange sexual exploits are well documented in his novels. Perched rather scarily on a hill, his former home is said to be haunted by his ghost, although I don't think it's wise to reflect on what he might be doing.

Several years ago, the Marquis de Sade's château was purchased by French fashion designer Pierre Cardin, who then proceeded to buy up much of the rest of the town and set about restoring his new properties.

Lacoste has some lovely sunny lookouts over the countryside, the prettiest of which is from the Café de France. Its terrace is a beautiful spot, and a perfect place to pause for a coffee and gaze out at the glorious vista across the valley to Bonnieux.

Gordes is another interesting and extremely scenic place. Although it's perched on a rocky cliff, it's far less intimidating than Lacoste. Indeed, it's so much like a fairytale that tourist buses stop, almost daily, on the bend on the way up to the town so that travellers can alight for the requisite photo op. The town is regularly listed among the most beautiful villages in France, and it's easy to see why: it's a picture from a distance and just as beautiful inside its walls. Tuesday morning is the best time to visit, when the town square fills with market sellers and shoppers. Look out for the Hôtel le Renaissance here, which is tucked away in the corner of a small square near the entrance to the tourist office: it was also featured in the film *A Good Year*.

If you have some time, try to fit in a visit to the **Château de Gourdon**. It features four glorious gardens, including a terrace designed by André Le Nôtre, a medicinal herb garden, an Italian terrace and a Mediterranean garden.

The **Cascade de Courmes** is also worth a stop. Located inside a gorge about four kilometres from the D2210, the 36-metre (120 foot) waterfall originates near the tiny, hidden village of Courmes, and is perfect to visit on a hot Provence day.

Lastly, there is the village of Roussillon. I've left it until last in this chapter because **Roussillon** isn't like other villages in this region. It stands out, quite literally, as it is painted in some of the boldest colours you're likely to see outside the Caribbean. Almost every house features an eye-opening, Pantone-esque splash of blood red, dusty pink or tangerine. For full effect, photograph it in late afternoon, when the place glows like a lantern on a stone terrace.

SAINT-RÉMY-DE-PROVENCE

THE AESTHETE

A shopper's delight, with charming lanes and delightful squares encircled by elegant boulevards and striking landscapes.

INT RÉMY

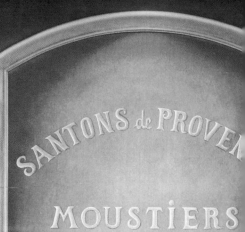

SANTONS de PROVEN

MOUSTIERS

AN

Glacier
Crêperie

TERP ASSE

PROVENCE

052

Is there a prettier town in all of Provence? Perhaps, but few are as captivating or as full of alluring pockets as the perennially delightful Saint-Rémy-de-Provence. No wonder foreigners flock here. It's what you imagine a perfect Provençal village to be.

The first clue that you're approaching a rather photogenic place is when you turn off the A7 towards Saint-Rémy and begin driving up the scenic road lined with glorious plane trees. You may also notice the hills around the town, which create a dramatic backdrop to this picture-perfect place.

Saint-Rémy-de-Provence is actually at the centre of Le Massif des Alpilles, the rugged limestone hills that dominate this region, so its setting was always going to be spectacular. Add to this the fact that it's one of the oldest towns in France (it was founded by the Celts more than 2500 years ago), and that its design has been carefully planned, with elegant boulevards and narrow streets opening onto pretty squares and fountains, and you can see why this place has attracted aesthetes and creative types for centuries.

The centre of the town itself is quite small, making it easy to wander around the circumference in less than an hour – once you find a park, that is, which can also take an hour.

Now this is a dignified settlement – it doesn't have the riffraff that blows into places like Saint-Tropez. But underneath the dignity is a friendly and occasionally cheeky personality. The locals are cheery, the bars and cafes are convivial and the weekly market is an absolute joy. Saint-Rémy-de-Provence is a thoroughly pleasing place in every respect.

The first record of Saint-Rémy-de-Provence is from the 5th century, although at that time it was a Gallo-Roman city known as Glanum. There are still some beautiful Roman remnants from this period, including a mausoleum and the oldest Roman arch in the region. The altogether prettier name of Saint-Rémy-de-Provence came about when, in order to protect it, the village was given to the monks of the abbey of Saint-Rémi-de-Reims. Remnants of 14th-century fortifications still remain in the town, and are actually used – rather enchantingly – as entrances to the town centre. You can find these at the northern edge of town near Rue Nostradamus and at the opposite end of the Old Town near the Rue de la Commune, which leads to the main square, Place Pelissier. If you enter near the Town Hall, look for the lovely dolphin fountain dating from the early 19th century.

Most people associate Saint-Rémy-de-Provence with Vincent van Gogh. The artist found great inspiration here after he admitted himself to the Saint-Paul asylum from May 1889 until May 1890. During most of his stay he was confined to the grounds of the asylum, but that didn't prevent him from painting close to 150 works inspired by the light, hills, buildings and flowers he saw.

You can still visit Van Gogh's asylum, **Saint-Paul-de-Mausole**. The route begins at the Office de Tourisme and is marked by reproductions of Van Gogh's paintings. It's a moving experience, seeing the two small rooms where the artist was interned and imagining the peace and stability he found within its walls, and then, when you emerge, seeing the irises and lilacs of the garden, and the wheat fields, vineyards, cypresses, olive trees and hills beyond that inspired him to take brush to canvas in such a prolific manner. (His legacy is still evident today in the bright sunflower-patterned plates and homewares you can buy in the town.)

Once you've seen Saint-Rémy through Van Gogh's eyes, it's time to look at it through your own. If you are here on a Wednesday, start with the market – a celebration of life and outdoor living. You won't be able to miss it: its stalls sprawl through squares and along streets, proffering produce, clothing, soaps, flowers and art.

Once you've strolled through the stalls, go for a wander through the myriad lanes of the Old Town, most lined with modern boutiques. Saint-Rémy is a shopper's town, with stores that are both interesting and upscale. There are interior design stores, linen stores and shops that sell striped French canvas fashioned into deckchairs, bags, seats and awnings. There are luxury food stores, stylish fashion stores and, of course, ceramic stores with designs as bright as Van Gogh's canvases.

The most charming part of Saint-Rémy-de-Provence is the fact that you can park your car and walk everywhere – most of the good shopping finds are tucked away down pedestrian laneways – and afterwards find a cafe in the sun for lunch. It's as if Saint-Remy has worked out the secret of a good life and designed the town around it. Certainly, the mix of beautiful Beaux-Arts buildings, medieval walls, shady tree-lined streets and elegant squares creates a charm that isn't lost on all those who visit, or those who stay for good. Princess Caroline of Monaco was so enamoured with Saint Rémy's peace and timelessness that she settled here with her family following the death of her second husband.

Nostradamus, too, was rather fond of it. The French physician/astrologer was born here in 1503, and you can still see the remains of his birthplace in Rue Hoche. Who knows whether even he would have been able to predict the popularity of this lovely place?

AIX-EN-PROVENCE

THE ELEGANT BEAUTY

Defined by a stately avenue lined with beautiful arching plane trees and dotted with grand 17th-century mansions, ancient fountains and marvellous architecture.

Dubbed 'The Paris of the South', Aix is a city with both grace and pace. The main street – the Cours Mirabeau – is lined with beautifully arching plane trees, 17th-century mansions and sidewalk cafes, but off this gentle thoroughfare are pockets of bustling activity with gorgeous stores, buzzing bars, busy squares and other delightful finds. There's a distinct energy to the place, which perhaps emanates in part from the significant student population. Whatever the reason, this city of some 143,000 inhabitants (known as Aixois or less commonly, Aquisextains after the town's original Roman name), is a wonderful place to spend a day, a week or a long summer month.

Discovering Aix and its splendour and sophistication isn't difficult: you can walk down any of the streets in the central part and be rewarded with gracious lines of sight, from the elegant architecture to the ancient fountains. The town is famous for its watery displays (there seems to be a fountain on every corner), and the sight of them on a hot day is always soothing.

The best place to begin your tour is the beautiful **Cours Mirabeau**, the city's stately avenue. Framed with double rows of the famous plane trees and embroidered with cafes, fountains and Classical-style buildings (many of which have delicious histories), the Cours is the throbbing heart of this surprising city. The boulevard is actually built along the line of the old city wall and divides the town into two sections. The new part of town extends to the south and west; the Old Town, with its irregular streets and centuries-old mansions, lies to the north.

Perch yourself on a chair in front of one of the Cours' many cafes and watch the locals go by. It's all very civilised and chic, but with a decidedly animated pace.

If you want a cafe with history and soul, head for **Café Les Deux Garçons** at the eastern end of the Cours, which was Cézanne's local. (His dad's hat shop was next door at No. 55.)

Once you're caffeinated, keep walking on the same side of the Cours until you reach **Passage Agard**. Walk through until you emerge at **Place Verdun** on the other side. This is Aix's **Old Town** and is chock-full of bars – you'll need to remember it later when you're searching for an aperitif.

The Old Town is a maze of streets and boutiques, each more intriguing than the last. Aix has as many wonderful shops as it does bars, and it doesn't matter which lane you venture down, the discoveries will be just as charming. Meander through the neighbourhood at your leisure, and if you head west again you'll soon reach Rue Maréchal Foch. Turn onto this street and head north. After a few streets you'll reach the Town Hall on the Place de l'Hôtel de Ville. Built in the Classical style of the 17th century, the building is as elegant as the square it looks onto. Nearby, almost incongruously, are the amazing thermal springs that drew the Romans to Aix in 122 BC. (They named the town Aquae Sextiae.)

Keep walking and a few streets on you'll reach the neighbourhood around Rue Gaston Saporta, which will reward you with more impressively ornate townhouses.

Once you're done admiring the architecture, you have two options. The first is to go for a bit of an urban hike (about 20 minutes) and weave your way to Avenue Paul Cézanne and the **Atelier de Cézanne** (page 205). A beautiful tribute to Monsieur Cézanne, it will seduce you with both artworks and moving personal mementoes of the artist's life. Even his beret, paint-spattered smock and still-life objects are all in place. The other option is to return to Cours Mirabeau, and cross over to Rue Mazarin, the street that runs parallel to the Cours on the southern side. This is the **Quartier Mazarin**, which contains more superb examples of 17th- and 18th-century townhouses. This neighbourhood was originally conceived as a residential area for the gentry, and features several notable *hôtels particuliers* (historical buildings) and grand residences.

When you've walked until your feet are numb, grab a baguette or some lunch fare and take a taxi to 13 Rue de la Molle. This is the site of the magnificent **Pavillon de Vendôme** (pictured on previous page), a lovely place for a casual picnic. The interior of this historic 1665 house, once home to both aristocrats and artists, isn't as gorgeous as the exterior, so don't shell out to see it. (And besides, it's often closed.) Instead, find a bench under a shady tree in the stunning walled garden and take in the peace and calm. Regarded as the best park in Aix, it's a genuine oasis in the middle of the bustling town.

One of the things you'll notice, as you're meandering around the town, is the number of fountains. Often referred to as 'The City of a Thousand Fountains' (although it has nowhere near that number), Aix is a town built on bubbling water. Some of the most beautiful are the 17th-century **Fontaine des Quatre Dauphins** (Fountain of the Four Dolphins) in the Quartier Mazarin, and three fountains in the Cours Mirabeau. The favourite for many visitors is the natural hot water fountain in the middle of Cours, where the water is around 34°C in temperature, and the fountain, dating back to the Romans, is covered in moss. It may not make you cool on a hot Aix day, but it will certainly give you an appreciation for this ancient and extraordinary place.

PROVENCE

AVIGNON

THE ARTS LOVER

Colourful, culturally rich, full of
artistic, architectural and gourmet
pleasures... a lovely place to catch
your breath and let the Provence
breezes blow the city stresses away.

Avignon is regarded as the gateway to Provence. When you drive the road from Paris to the Riviera, or hop aboard a south-bound train, Avignon is the first sign that you're finally reaching the land of sunlight, lavender, fine wine and good times. And, like the region, the city is colourful, culturally rich, full of artistic, architectural and gourmet pleasures, and worth idling in for longer than you'd anticipate. In fact, many people pause in Avignon on the trip from Paris to the coast: it's a lovely place to catch your breath and let the Provence breezes blow the city stresses away.

The city is bordered to the north and west by the mighty Rhône, a river that provides a dramatic backdrop. Rising above this grand waterway is a beguiling town comprising 39 towers, seven gates and almost five kilometres of walls. The massive ramparts that enclose Avignon give it a sense of mystery. You can't help but feel there's something worth seeing here. The UNESCO chiefs thought so too, and since 1995 the historic centre of Avignon has been classified as a World Heritage Site.

Inside the ancient city walls are broad, tree-lined streets and intriguing passageways leading to picturesque squares, shops, galleries, churches and museums. It's a town full of historical buildings, and although you can suffer from historical overload here, it's still a mighty impressive place.

To explore Avignon, begin at **Rocher des Doms**, the quiet hillside park on Montée du Moulin off Place du Palais. This park is the site of the city's first settlement and is considered the unofficial centre of the town. It's a tranquil pocket of greenery in which to shake off the travel exhaustion and take a deep breath, but more than that it's a great place to get your bearings. From here you can get a feel for the layout of the city. If you hike up to the top, there are beautiful views over the city's tiled rooftops and Provençal countryside, including the Rhône, the famous Pont d'Avignon and Villeneuve d'Avignon on the other side.

The **Pont d'Avignon**, also known as Pont Saint-Bénezet after the local shepherd boy who was told by an angel to construct the bridge here (and proved his divine inspiration by lifting a heavy stone block) is rather famous, not only in Avignon but around the world. The 12th-century bridge originally had 22 arches spanning 900 metres (2950 feet) across the Rhône and was regarded as an architectural marvel. However, the bridge collapsed frequently and had to be reconstructed multiple times. The bridge was an important strategic crossing between Lyon and the Mediterranean Sea (and between Italy and Spain) and was therefore closely guarded on both sides. (On the Avignon side, the bridge passed through a large gatehouse.) Eventually, after much of it collapsed beyond repair during floods in 1660 (several arches were already missing by this time and spanned by wooden sections instead) it was left to ruin. Today, only a few of the bridge's original 22 arches remain.

After his death, Saint-Bénezet's body was interred in a small chapel standing on one of the bridge's surviving piers on the Avignon side, as a tribute to the boy who started it all.

When you're finished taking in the lay of the land from the park, walk back down and head for the **Palais des Papes**. The Pope's Palace is the largest Gothic palace in the world, and was the seat of Western Christianity during the 14th century. It features incredible architecture and exquisite interior tile work. But be warned: it's huge, and can be rather imposing, so you may be exhausted before the hour is up.

After a tour through here you'll probably need a strong coffee, so head to nearby **Place de l'Horloge**, the town's main square. Conceived and designed in the 15th century, and named after the clock tower above the Town Hall, it has been modernised over subsequent centuries but has lost none of its charm. Pick one of the many outdoor restaurants and cafes on the square and treat yourself to a long Provençal lunch. Some travellers consider this square rather touristy; others sit back and enjoy its atmosphere, especially on a sunny day. It's also particularly lovely in the evenings.

The square is also notable for being the venue for annual events. The town has always been aware of its artistic heritage – and its creativity – and embraces this through its festivals, theatre companies, galleries, art studios and even its own opera house. The **Avignon Festival** in July (festival-avignon.com) is so popular it is now an international event, and is a great time to see this city come alive.

If you love markets, **Avignon's Flower Market** (Marché aux Fleurs) is especially charming. It's held in Place des Carmes on Saturday mornings. If you prefer bric-a-brac, there's a flea market in this same area on Sunday mornings, plus a **Petite Brocante d'Avignon** in the Place des Corps Saints on Tuesdays and the **Puces de Bonpas** outside Avignon in Montfavet (four kilometres from the Old Town) on Saturday mornings. If it's a food market you're after, there's the weekend **Marché Forain** on Remparts Saint-Michel.

ARLES
THE HISTORICAL BEAUTY

A seductive and somewhat
sultry town that teases with an
architectural wink and smile.

ARLES

0,50

079

Unlike Avignon, which can become congested in summer (particularly with frightened tourists in tiny hire cars who drive into the labyrinthine centre and can't find their way out again), Arles is rather laid-back. This is perhaps because it isn't as busy as its popular neighbours. And the reason for this is that it's often overlooked by tourists making the dash from the Cote d'Azur to Provence. 'Arles?' they say, lifting their foot off the pedal as they see the signs flashing past on the highway. 'What's there?' And then they accelerate again. This is both a good and a bad thing. It means Arles isn't overrun with people. Even during high season and festivals, it's always an easy place to navigate. The downside, of course, is that without the demand driven by the tourist dollar, there isn't a huge amount to do in terms of sightseeing

Like Avignon, Arles is a UNESCO World Heritage Site. Located on a low hill where the Rhône branches into two tributaries on its way to the sea, it's blessed with both scenery and a wonderful spirit. The bullfights are a controversial part of this spirit, but the festive atmosphere that takes over the streets is still infectious. No wonder Van Gogh loved it here. Arles' sense of joy and love of life is palpable. (Unfortunately there are no Van Gogh artworks to be found in the city, despite the fact that his time in Arles was his most productive.)

The centre of the city is still medieval in character, with narrow and winding streets weaving between ancient buildings. Every now and then a square breaks the grid, offering a splendid pause in the architectural narrative.

A seductive and somewhat sultry town, Arles teases with an architectural wink and smile. Its colourful houses flirt with the light that drifts over the landscape (Van Gogh loved painting those too), and its locals love a drink, a laugh, a dance, a bullfight and a good time. I don't advocate the killing of animals, so I won't comment on that tradition, but it's up to you to find out more about it and make up your own mind. What I will say is that it's hard to judge Arles, especially when it's so welcoming and convivial.

To discover the sweet life of this happy town, start at the **Place du Forum**, which has been the hub of Arles since Roman times. Find a cafe, order a glass of Rhône red and watch the Arlesian parade. Fortified, begin your tour with a stroll through the old laneways, where the houses are tinted with colours from an artist's palette: pink, pale blue, green, yellow and lavender. If it's a Wednesday or Saturday, head for the **market**, which stretches along the shaded Boulevard des Lices. It can be hit-and-miss here, but the food section is worth a pause, if only for the aromas of pungent cheeses, honey, lavender, mint and spices.

Grab some picnic fare (a goats' cheese salad and dessert of crème brûlée laced with lavender is fabulous) and head for the lovely park along the **Boulevard des Lices**. Find a bench in the sun or, if it's warm, under the shade of one of the great old trees (look for the gigantic cedar).

If you fancy some history with your luncheon, skip the park and head for **Les Arènes**, the enormous, two-tiered amphitheatre that dominates the town. Sitting in a sunny spot, you can dine while taking in the history of this grand place, which once seated as many as 20,000 spectators.

There's not a lot to do in Arles in terms of tourist sights. The thing to do here is immerse yourself in the lifestyle while admiring the history and beauty of the architecture, and the passion of the people.

UZÈS

THE HIDEAWAY

Lofty towers, narrow medieval streets and the heavenly Place aux Herbes.

Uzès, with its high towers and narrow medieval streets, is a place lost in time. It's almost as if it was built on the back lot of a Hollywood studio to resemble a fairytale French village. But I assure you, it's not. It's authentic Provence.

Uzès may be small (population 8300), but makes up for its size with architecture that is pure theatre. You can see the skyline long before you reach it. The town's lofty towers strike a dramatic note, while soaring buildings like La Tour Fenestrelle offer an architectural exclamation mark.

But all tours of Uzès must begin at the heart of this heavenly destination: the arcade-lined **Place aux Herbes**. (Have you ever heard of a more evocative name for a town square?) This is where most things happen in Uzès. One of the most colourful **Saturday markets** in the South of France is held here every week. It's frenetic, so if you can't abide crowds go to the smaller, Wednesday version instead. This is the place to stock up on fabulous food, including olives, cheese, olive oil, vegetables and fragrant herbs – some of the best ingredients for a great French meal.

There are also some wonderful cafes here for a leisurely brunch in the sun, such as **L'Oustal**. Once you're caffeinated, and have checked out the comestibles, make for the streets. The pretty, pedestrian-only streets of Uzès' centre offer beautiful boutiques selling gorgeous women's wear and luxury goods – much more upscale than you'd imagine from a country town miles from Paris. The side streets leading off from Place aux Herbes hide many of the more interesting and sophisticated shops. Their stylish cream and grey facades add to the experience.

When you're shopped-out and feel like grabbing a late lunch, there's **Les Terroirs** (5 Place aux Herbes) – one of Uzès' best dining spots. Check out its fine food shop for a foodie souvenir to take home. Two other excellent dining establishments are **Le Comptoir du 7** (5 Boulevard Charles Gide) and **Au Petit Jardin** (66 Boulevard Gambetta).

After you've wandered the village, you can climb one of the famous towers, or grab a photo of Uzès' own leaning tower of Pisa, **La Tour Fenestrelle**. Then, if the weather is sunny, hop back in the car and head out into the surrounding countryside for more speccy scenery.

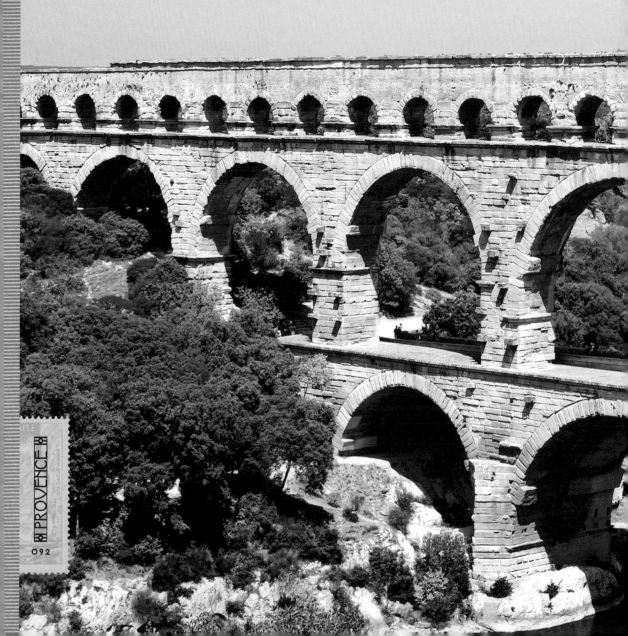

One of the landmarks of this area is the incredible form of the **Pont du Gard**, the ancient Roman aqueduct bridge that crosses the Gardon River in Vers-Pont-du-Gard near Remoulins. It is part of the Nîmes aqueduct, a structure 50 kilometres (30 miles) long that was built by the Romans to carry water from a spring at Uzès to the Roman colony of Nîmes. No visitor to this part of the region should miss it.

Lastly, if you want to finish off your visit with a small thrill (okay, a spill and a thrill), try canoeing down the Gardon River. It's one of the loveliest ways to see the landscape.

PART TWO
THE CÔTE D'AZUR

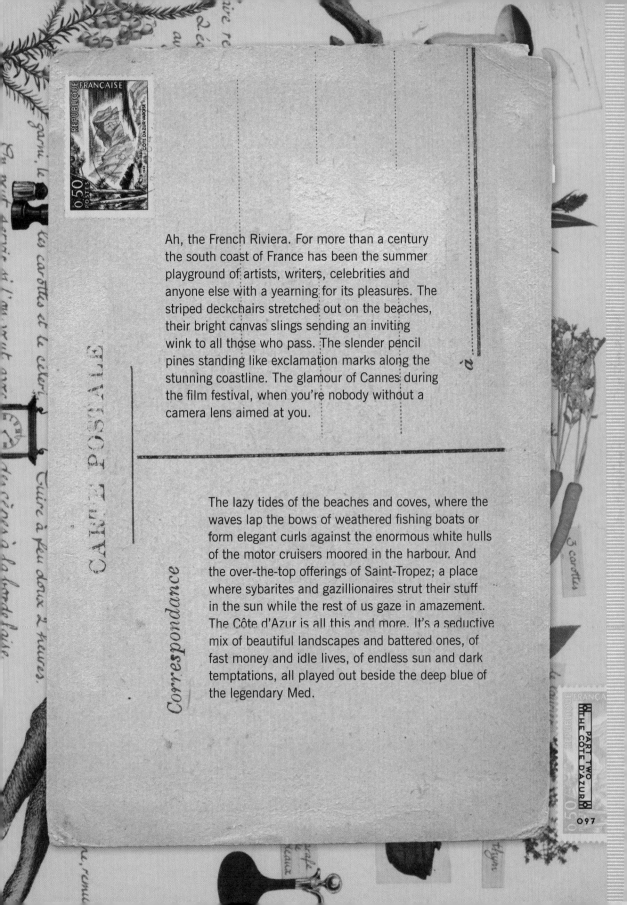

CARTE POSTALE

Ah, the French Riviera. For more than a century the south coast of France has been the summer playground of artists, writers, celebrities and anyone else with a yearning for its pleasures. The striped deckchairs stretched out on the beaches, their bright canvas slings sending an inviting wink to all those who pass. The slender pencil pines standing like exclamation marks along the stunning coastline. The glamour of Cannes during the film festival, when you're nobody without a camera lens aimed at you.

Correspondance

The lazy tides of the beaches and coves, where the waves lap the bows of weathered fishing boats or form elegant curls against the enormous white hulls of the motor cruisers moored in the harbour. And the over-the-top offerings of Saint-Tropez; a place where sybarites and gazillionaires strut their stuff in the sun while the rest of us gaze in amazement. The Côte d'Azur is all this and more. It's a seductive mix of beautiful landscapes and battered ones, of fast money and idle lives, of endless sun and dark temptations, all played out beside the deep blue of the legendary Med.

NICE

THE GRAND DAME

A grand, palm tree-lined promenade, spectacular
Belle Époque architecture, and a beach festooned
with striped parasols and canvas deckchairs.

Although this grand old town is often criticised by those who prefer the posher places down the way, Nice is actually very, very nice. For a start, it's brimming with superb Belle Époque buildings, each seemingly more beautiful than the last. Indeed, you could walk here all day and never grow tired of looking up at the ornate balconies and elegant rooflines. It's also a town of great stories that you will soon discover as you explore its excellent museums, beautiful parks, and truly lovely promenade. All in all, the city is a thoroughly entertaining place.

Nice's history is long and rather convoluted. The town was founded by the Greeks around 350 BC, although early humans had lived in the area for some 400,000 years. Over the centuries, various empires (Roman, Saracen, Ottoman) attempted to take control of the city until, in 1860, it finally came to rest in French hands for good.

Its modern popularity really began in the 18th century when aristocratic English families journeying to Italy for the winter began stopping here en route. Its location – with the sea on one side and the protective hills on the other – meant it enjoyed a perfect microclimate; something the winter-weary northerners were searching for. Many were so impressed that they didn't go any further.

Soon, so many English, including Queen Victoria, had begun trickling down that the town renamed the main seaside promenade Camin deis Anglés (the English Way) and then later the Promenade des Anglais. Suddenly, the town was a huge hit. Artists such as Marc Chagall and Henri Matisse arrived and set up their easels to try to capture the soft, gentle scenery. By the 1920s, Nice was romanticised as the perfect place to seek a more idyllic existence.

Then, during the middle of the 20th century, Nice's sheen began to rub off and the town was overlooked in favour of ritzier resorts such as Saint-Tropez and Monte Carlo, which became *the* places to be.

In the last decade or so, though, people have begun to appreciate this old Belle Époque beauty once more. The Scandinavians and northern Europeans particularly adore it, with many purchasing second homes here. The Russians have become a significant (and somewhat controversial) community, buying up a great deal of property with their new wealth. As well as the foreign investors, a new generation of entrepreneurial French people is changing the nature of the city, creating everything from offbeat exhibition spaces to unique culinary hideaways.

To explore this grand dame of a town, you really need to begin on the spectacular palm tree-lined **Promenade des Anglais,** which winds along the Baie des Anges (Bay of Angels). Curiously, for many years the seaside part of Nice was considered inferior, and the rich preferred the higher ground. (This was long before people such as Coco Chanel made sunbathing and tans popular.) Then, in the early 1800s, a clever (and rich) English businessman proposed a new waterfront walkway to replace the two-metre-wide track. The result transformed the town. The 'Prom's' beauty was finally recognised when it was inaugurated in 1931 by the Duke of Connaught (son of Queen Victoria). Today, with more than eight kilometres (five miles) of flat walkways embroidered with flower-beds, palm trees and seats all set against a magnificent view of blue, it is still one of the most beautiful places to walk on the entire Riviera. You can also hire one of the famous *chaises bleues* (loungers), but the beach is pebbly so doesn't quite have the same feeling as a sandy shore. Still, the promenade is a wonderful place for a stroll in the late afternoon, with the yachts and lines of striped umbrellas spread out before you.

As you walk along the Prom, you can picture Nice at the peak of its popularity just before the turn of the last century: the well-heeled Edwardians strolling along, their parasols in full bloom; the beach festooned with striped umbrellas and canvas deckchairs. Look out for the landmark **Hôtel Negresco** (page 187;

37 Promenade des Anglais, hotel-negresco-nice.com) – you'll recognise it from the pale pink dome and the quirky doormen in knee-breeches and plumed hats. This is one of the most extraordinary hotels in France, which is why it often plays host to visiting prime ministers, presidents and movie stars. A century old in 2013, the Negresco was built by one-time gypsy and innkeeper's son Henri Negresco in 1913 after he made his money running a casino on the Riviera. He wanted the best hotel imaginable, so hired the architect Édouard-Jean Niermans (considered the favourite of cafe society) to design the hotel and its now-famous pink dome. Negresco also picked up a discounted 16,000-crystal Baccarat chandelier after Czar Nicholas II was unable to take delivery due to the Revolution. (The chandelier's twin is found in the Kremlin.) The rest of the hotel was fitted out with a staggering glass-ceilinged rotunda and furniture that would befit a palace. Henri's hotel went into decline after the outbreak of World War I, and by the time of his death (he was 52 and bankrupt), had been converted to a hospital and then sold.

Today, however, the Negresco has returned to its former glory and if you can afford the rates, is one of the most opulent establishments to stay on the Riviera. Think mink bedspreads, a staggering art collection, and staff who are the epitome of graciousness. The dancer Isadora Duncan loved the hotel, and spent the last few months of her life there. She died tragically while driving along the coast when her silk scarf caught in the spokes of her Bugatti and broke her neck.

While you're wandering along the promenade, make time to see the beautiful **Masséna Museum of Art and History** (65 Rue de France; musee.massena@ville-nice.fr). The 19th-century Italianate villa features a sublime Empire-style hall and a beautiful garden that was the work of landscape architect Édouard André who also designed the gardens of the Monte-Carlo Casino. Inside, 20 exhibition rooms featuring more than 15,000 exhibits retrace the history of Nice through furniture, decorations and artworks. It's a beautiful building, inside and out, and well worth a visit.

Running parallel to the Promenade des Anglais is an equally lovely walking street, the pedestrian-only **Rue de France**. It's lined with cafes and restaurants, many of them with protected terraces for people-watching. Head east along here and you'll soon hit **Place Masséna**, a grand square surrounded by magnificent Italian-style yellow and chilli-red buildings reminiscent of Venice's Piazzo San Marco. (Nice was once owned by the Italians; hence the Italianate feel.) This pleasing Mediterranean plaza is considered the heart of Nice, as it's where many of the annual activities take place, including the Carnaval de Nice in February, the Bastille Day procession and Jazz Festival in July, the Christmas markets, and the general fun in the summer months. Galleries Lafayette, a branch of the famous French department store, is also situated on the north side of the plaza. And a new tramway connects Place Masséna to Nice's central train station (Gare de Nice-Ville).

Further along from the piazza is **Le Vieux-Nice** (Old Town), which is heralded by the colourful **Cours Saleya**; a wonderfully vibrant square that hosts the daily Marché aux Fleurs (flower market). It's one of the most charming surroundings for a flower and vegetable market, and the produce ranges from peonies to unusual fruits.

At the eastern end of the Cours Saleya is **Place Charles Felix**, another grand square that vies with the Place Masséna for architectural drama.

From here, you can either head a block south back to the beach and **Les Ponchettes**, a fabulous architectural folly of low white buildings tucked under the promenade that were once used by fishermen and are now galleries and eateries; or you can go north, deep into the Old Town and its labyrinthine laneways.

If you fancy a hike to burn off the gelato, head up the steep steps to Le Château, the shaded hill and park at the eastern end of Quai des États-Unis. It isn't really a château – it was named after a 12th-century château razed by Louis XIV in a fit of anger. (It should be called Ghost of a Château.) The park itself is a pleasant mix of waterfalls, pools and gardens – great on a hot day – and the views over Nice are spectacular.

On the other side of the park, the port is always photogenic, especially on a sunny day. If you really want some exercise you can walk all the way to Villefranche and Cap Ferrat and back: a three-hour hike that rewards with some of the best views on the entire coastline.

Another place worth seeking out in Old Nice is the **Opéra de Nice** (9 Rue Raoul Bosio; opera-nice.org), which provides a regular program of performances that are as grand as the building.

Back towards Cannes, there is also plenty to explore, including the **Jardin Botanique de la Ville de Nice**, the town's botanical garden (78 Avenue de la Corniche Fleurie; bgci.org/garden), and the **Musée des Beaux-Arts de Nice** (page 205; 33 Avenue des Baumettes; musee-beaux-arts-nice.org), which was created from a resplendent villa and features treasures from the Second Empire and the Belle Époque. Lastly, don't miss the **Chagall Museum** (page 205; Avenue Docteur Ménard; musees-nationaux-alpesmaritimes.fr/chagall) and the **Matisse Museum** (page 208; 164 Avenue des Arènes de Cimiez; musee-matisse-nice.org). Both are wonderful tributes to the colours, lines and joyous pleasures of this impossibly beautiful place.

There is no best time to visit Nice, as it has a mild climate year-round, however during February the town revels in the **Carnaval de Nice,** one of its favourite festivals. It features the Bataille de Fleurs, an exuberant parade of floats decorated with thousands of flowers and usually topped with equally beautiful girls. Nice loves its flowers, as the daily flower market shows, and this festival is a flamboyant celebration of colour, scent, form and style – much like Nice itself.

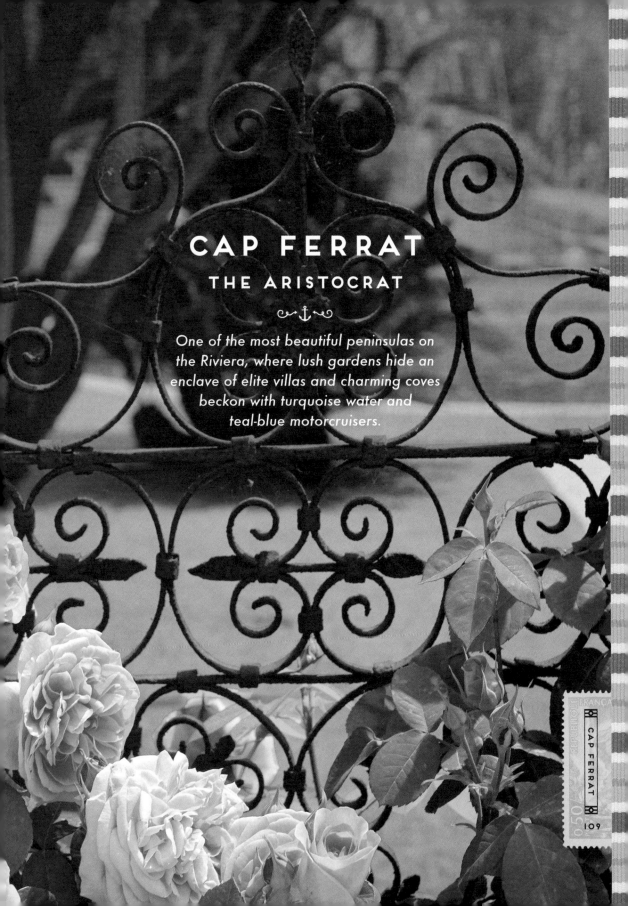

CAP FERRAT
THE ARISTOCRAT

⚓

One of the most beautiful peninsulas on the Riviera, where lush gardens hide an enclave of elite villas and charming coves beckon with turquoise water and teal-blue motorcruisers.

CAP FERRAT

0.50

109

Cap Ferrat is now the second or third most expensive real estate in the world, depending on which source you read. It's always been an exclusive piece of the Riviera, thanks to its geography and beauty, but in the last half century it's become more coveted than ever.

This idyllic part of the French Riviera was first noticed by Leopold II, King of Belgium, who came to Cap Ferrat for a visit in 1895. Back then, it was a fairly understated bit of back country used for fox hunting. There were no roads, only a few paths and some humble dwellings. The king, an astute businessman who liked buying land for his portfolio, noted the beauty of the Plage de Passable, the gentle views of the Mediterranean and, in the distance, a small villa. He decided to buy it, and then snapped up 15 plots of land around it. The locals thought he was mad. Who would want Cap Ferrat? But there was an ulterior motive. The cape was the perfect place to carry out illicit love affairs, far from the prying eyes of the palace, and the king had a mistress, Blanche Delacroix, whom he wanted to woo. The villa was to be the setting; framed by blue views of the sea and hidden in what would soon be a garden of luxuriant vegetation (which the king was also planning). He imagined it as a bucolic paradise. The king also bought a nearby villa called Les Cèdres, for his own use, and every evening, with a tiny lantern, would step between the two along a path hidden by the trees. The gardens eventually became lush and lovely, thanks to the climate, and Cap Ferrat soon grew from a wild backwater to a surprisingly spectacular oasis. You can still see the profusion of exotic plants, trees and other botanical species that the king's gardener introduced. In fact, much of Cap Ferrat is now an Eden where geraniums grow as big as hedges and hibiscus, jasmine, bougainvilleas, roses, wisteria and citrus flowers perfume the air. No wonder the intensely private celebrities love it: you can barely see the villas through the greenery.

Despite the 'Keep Out' signs on the gates, Cap Ferrat is easily explored, even without a map. In fact, one of the best walks in the world is here, the **Sentier du Littoral**, a coastal path that goes right around the cape.

The best way to do this walk is to start at the beach in front of the Hôtel Royal-Riviera (3 Avenue Jean Monnet) on the Beaulieu-sur-Mer side of Cap Ferrat. You'll see the start of the coastal path winding out to the promontory. Follow the path, known as Promenade Maurice Rouvier, as it meanders past David Niven's former home, an exquisite pink villa with its own pink harbour.

Originally called Lo Scoglietto (Little Rock), the house was built in 1880 and rented by the Duchess of Marlborough in the 1920s. It was then extended in the 1950s and bought by Charlie Chaplin, who in turn sold it to actor David Niven, who then lived here until his death. The small square in front of the villa is named Place David Niven as a tribute. (Rumour also has it that Dodi bought it as a hideaway for Diana during their courtship.)

Continue on the path, past the splendid villas and hidden gardens, and you'll shortly reach the picturesque fishing village of **Saint-Jean-Cap-Ferrat**, from which the cape takes its name. Here, you can stop for an ice-cream or lunch on the terrace of the famous La Voile D'Or hotel (page 192) overlooking the tiny harbour. (Service is slow, so go for the view.) It's also lovely just walking around the village, its quayside shops and cafes, and its little harbour – surely one of the prettiest on the Riviera. Look for the coconut ice-style Mairie (Town Hall) with its trompe l'oeil flowers painted around the door.

The artist Matisse was captivated by the purity of the light here. 'This is a place,' he wrote, 'where light plays the first part. Colour comes afterwards.' You can see the interplay of light and colour in the marina, where turquoise and teal-blue boats bob up and down in the shimmering, luminous sunlight.

Keep following Avenue Jean Mermoz, past the Hôtel Brise Marine (a great little cheapie; page 186) until you reach **Paloma Beach** (Plage de la Paloma; page 201); one of the sweetest coves on the coast and a favourite of the jet set who moor their yachts in front. Follow the steps down to the beach for lunch at the cheery cafe or (if you remembered your bathers) have a dip in the sea. Then retrace your steps back to the Brise Marine and turn down Avenue de la Puncia and then left at Chemin de la Carrière. This pretty road will eventually take you to a gate;

don't be afraid to walk around it – it's a public path. From there, you're on the track that goes around the cape, right to the base of the legendary **Grand-Hôtel du Cap-Ferrat** (page 185). There are spots for swimming at intervals, but watch the current and the waves. Eventually, near the lighthouse, you'll be able to ascend the steps back up to the residential streets. Look out for Avenue Somerset Maugham, where the writer lived at his villa La Mauresque. Maugham, who called the French Riviera 'a sunny place for shady people', spent the last 38 years of his life here (with a gap during World War II) and hosted a long list of artists, writers, politicians and royalty.

But Maugham's villa isn't the only impressive property here. The entire cape is chock-a-bloc with houses of the wealthy, including Microsoft's Paul Allen. Take photos but try not to gawp.

Find your way to the main road, **Boulevard General de Gaulle**, and follow it all the way until you reach the signs for the **Villa Ephrussi de Rothschild**; Beatrice's renowned villa and gardens (1 Avenue Ephrussi de Rothschild, page 201). This grand garden of exotic plants, glamorous fountains and beautiful pink roses offers lovely sea views over sparkling coves and is the perfect finale to a day on the Cape. The villa is decorated almost entirely in blush pink, which is more enchanting than you might think. You can also wander down to the beach, **Plage de Passable**, an idyllic cove that offers stunning views of Villefranche across the deep blue waters of the harbour. Look for King Leopold's villa, which dominates the beach's northern end.

Then, as dusk falls in the same shade of Rothschild pink, you can head for the train station at Beaulieu-sur-Mer and travel back to Nice, tired but happy. Or, if you're lucky, wander back to your hotel on Cap Ferrat to enjoy a drink as the sun sets over this truly spectacular part of the French Riviera. Oh yes, the King of Belgium certainly knew what he was doing when he invested here.

BEAULIEU-SUR-MER
THE SECRET DELIGHT

⚓

*A seaside village often missed by the masses, blessed
with fabulous beaches and gorgeous architecture.*

It may seem strange to some to devote an entire section to this tiny part of the French Riviera, but Beaulieu-sur-Mer has a history, a reputation and a landscape as impressive as any of its swankier cousins down the coast. It's just that few people are aware of its allure.

You see, Beaulieu's quaint charms have for years been eclipsed somewhat by its more dazzling neighbours: Nice, Cap Ferrat and Monaco, whom the media regard as destinations with more drama. This, however, is a good thing, because it means that Beaulieu remains a little under the radar. The last thing we want is for it to become another Saint-Tropez.

This seaside idyll has had a surprising and curious past. Having passed between Greek and Roman hands, the village was left in ruins in the 3rd century. It was eventually resettled and became the site of a monastery, which then fell to the Lombards in the 6th century, who proceeded to destroy it again. Its residents fled to the safety of surrounding hills at Montolivo, returning to live there in the 13th century. Eventually it was established as a self-standing commune in 1891, but curiously remains the smallest in the Alpes-Maritimes department (230 acres: population 4000).

It began attracting aristocratic travellers around the same time that Nice was being noticed. By the end of the 19th century the place was being touted as a potential resort. The Queen of Portugal, Kaiser Wilhelm II and Tolstoy all passed through. The village, just as the rest of the Côte d'Azur was doing, rapidly developed into a world destination for the wealthy elite.

The difference between Beaulieu and the rest of the coastline is that the former never became as built-up as some of its neighbours. Today, apart from the huge yacht harbour that takes up most of the seafront, the rest of the village remains very much as it was a century ago. It's such a quiet and seemingly understated place (apart from the luxury villas tucked among the vegetation) that the village's most distinctive landmark, **Villa Kérylos**, stands out like a beacon (Rue Gustave-Eiffel; villa-kerylos.com). Built in the early 1900s by French archaeologist Theodore Reinach and his wife Fanny Kann (a daughter of Maximilien Kann and Betty Ephrussi), the building is designed in the style of an ancient Greek villa. Perched right on the end of a rocky promontory, it took six years to complete, and no wonder: the interior combines design styles from Rome, Pompeii and Egypt, even down to the exact replicas of ancient Grecian chairs. It was bequeathed to the Institute of France in 1928 and is now a lovely museum.

Perhaps the best things to do in Beaulieu are walking and swimming. Beaulieu has some of the prettiest beaches and promenades outside Nice, shaded by low-hanging trees that are cool in summer, and the beaches themselves are sheltered and mostly sandy (unlike many others). Kids love it here. The sea also feels warmer here, perhaps because it's sandy and shallow, rather than wide and deep (as it is at Nice). Walk along the promenade and take one of the many trails that meander through the area, from which you can look back and see the wonderful views of the mountains. Try strolling from Beaulieu to Èze (about a two-hour walk; see the next section, page 125) for a view of all the walled gardens and stately Belle Époque villas peeking out from behind the pine trees. It's possible to see Bono's villa at Èze-sur-Mer; a terracotta mansion with blue shutters right on the beach.

If you go for a swim or head out on a boat, keep an eye out for a spectacular property set on a cliff with a sheer drop to the beach. This is the celebrated **Villa Leonina,** the former home of Etti and Dr Árpád Plesch (1889–1974), a Hungarian lawyer, international financier, and collector of rare botanical books and pornographic esoterica. Etti met Árpád (her sixth and last husband) through her friend Gloria Guinness, and settled down with him in their homes on the Avenue Foch in Paris and here in Beaulieu. It was at Villa Leonina that Dr Plesch indulged in his love for flora, and his botanical garden soon became world renowned. Less known is his obsession with erotica.

Beaulieu's residents can be a little whimsical if not quirky. There's **Villa Namouna,** which once belonged to Gordon Bennett, the owner of the *New York Herald,* who sent Stanley to Africa to find Livingstone. There's also the restaurant **The African Queen** (Port de Plaisance; africanqueen.fr), which offers a jungle-inspired decor (it's actually based on the famous film) and some of the best water views on the coast. The bill is presented in a video cassette case with the movie poster cover – very Hollywood. And if that's not enough Africa for you, there is a residential area called Little Africa, which is actually where Etti Plesch's Villa Leonina is set, while the longer of the town's two free public beaches is called, ironically, Petite Afrique. And if you want to rent a sun lounger, try Africa Plage, which also sells snacks and drinks.

In fact, some people have actually dubbed Beaulieu 'La Petite Afrique' (Little Africa), as much because of its mild climate as its African-inspired gardens. Like Menton further along the coast, Beaulieu is graced with lush vegetation, including palm trees, orange and lemon trees and banana palms. It is indeed a curious oasis on the Côte d'Azur.

ÈZE

THE ESCAPIST

⚓

Located high above the Riviera, with views to swoon over, gardens to enthall the senses and lovely, labyrinthine streets to enchant the cynics.

One of the most incredible places on the Riviera, Èze village is perched 500 metres (1400 feet) above the sea, and appears as if it could drop into it at any time. Yet it's been there, on the mountain, since the Middle Ages and – here's the lovely part – its location has in fact saved it. The village was fortified on top of this rugged mountaintop to protect its inhabitants from constant enemy raids. By securing the village behind dense walls and clustering the houses along narrow streets, the villagers were able to defend their settlement more easily. Today, the views are what make the village so extraordinary, although the pretty stone homes and the cobbled lanes, which have been preserved so well through the centuries and recently restored, are equally beautiful. Èze is a sheer delight for the senses, quite literally on every level.

There's a bit of irony about the name Èze. It's really not that easy to get to, you see. As a matter of fact, going to this ancient village is like ascending Jack's beanstalk to a place in the clouds. The best way to reach Èze is not by car – although if you do drive make sure you take the Grande Corniche, as it's the quietest to drive and the most glorious to look down from. (Note: The village is for pedestrians only so you need to leave all cars in the park at the base of the village.) Nor is it easy to reach by bus, although the service from Nice operated by Ligne d'Azur (route number 82) is comfortable, albeit irregular. No, the best way to reach Èze is to walk on **Le Chemin de Nietzsche** – as in the philosopher Nietzsche, who knew a thing or two about the power of landscapes on the body, mind and soul.

Firstly, you take the train to Èze-Bord-de-Mer (sometimes shortened to Èze-sur-Mer), which is Èze's sister village on the beach (don't confuse the two). The train from Nice's Gare SNCF station to Èze-sur-Mer takes 14 minutes (3 Euros one-way). Once at Èze-Bord-de-Mer, walk across the main road and follow the signs to the 'Chemin de Nietzsche'. The walk will take one to two hours (uphill). Wear good shoes (no flip flops) and bring lots of water (don't do the walk on a hot day); the views will astound. This was the path beloved by Mr Nietzsche. Some people call it 'the thinking man's hike'. (The plaque at the summit reads: 'Though the ground keeps me rooted, my mind is in the heavens.') Nietzsche was so inspired by this area that he wrote the third part of *Thus Spoke Zarathustra* here, composing much of it while hiking this trail. 'I slept well,' he said, while staying in Èze, 'I laughed a lot and I found a marvellous vigour and patience.' The Nietzsche path is a wonderful way to find some inspiration and mental strength of your own.

If you are unable to hike uphill, take the bus up to Èze village and walk back down to the beach to connect with the bus to Nice: the view will be in front of you all the way.

Once you've reached the top of the village, there are some fine things to see, including a panorama of the French Riviera, which on a clear day stretches in a magnificent arc over Cap Ferrat and on to Nice and Cap D'Antibes. You can also explore the village's ancient cobbled lanes, which are less touristy than Saint-Paul de Vence. (If you go early enough in the morning you may even have it all to yourself.) The town is a tasteful and scenic treat, with stylish shops, art galleries, restaurants and hotels. It's not a residential place as such, so some may find it slightly commercial, but it's still a charming place to wander around. Find an ice-cream, have some lunch and shop in the myriad stores that line each alley. If you want to dine somewhere special, make for **Château Eza** at the top of Rue de la Pise. The hotel is beautiful but it's the Michelin-starred restaurant that receives all the fuss. Some claim it's not as good as it once was; others say it's still superb. The food is great but expensive: you're really paying for the memorable views. Or go to **Le Nid d'Aigle** (The Eagle's Nest, 1 Rue du Château): it also has a great view out over the Riviera.

Just below the town is a Fragonard perfume outlet, which scent lovers may like. But one of the best destinations is the well signposted **Jardin Botanique d'Èze** (Place du Général de Gaulle). The garden was created after World War II on the ruins of a château and is set on a steep slope with spectacular views of the coast. The plantings of cactus and succulents are wonderful but the panoramic views over the coast are unparalleled. Consider skipping Château Eza, buying a baguette and having a picnic here instead.

MENTON
THE GARDEN LOVER

A picture of civilised gentility and understated grace; a place devoid of nightlife and noisy partygoers but blessed with blooming gardens, half a dozen gorgeous beaches, and a beautiful sweep of an Old Town.

MENTON

0.50

133

Menton is often missed by the tourist hordes, situated as it is at the far end of the Riviera near the Italian border. Some visitors to the South of France don't even realise it's there. They go as far as Monte Carlo on their daily expeditions and think they've seen it all. This is a shame, as Menton is glorious. Garden lovers will particularly adore it. It's a little piece of horticultural heaven.

Menton is known by several names: '*perle de la France*' (pearl of France), 'the garden of France', 'the lemon festival capital of the world'(!), and even Mentone (its Italian name). The town has actually changed hands several times between France and Italy, and the different names reflect the fondness people feel for it.

Much of modern Menton was, in fact, invented by the English. Queen Victoria loved it here, as did her son Bertie (later to become Edward VII). There is still a statue of Queen Victoria in the town. (She used to stay in a grand villa tucked among the hills.) They loved it because of its climate, which was so good that in the 1870s Dr James Bennet opened a clinic for consumption sufferers and became very rich. (Sadly, the climate did not heal tuberculosis, and survival rates were the same as anywhere else – more than 50 per cent of sufferers would die within five years. The antibiotic cure would not be found until 1946.)

News of Menton's mild seasons spread, and soon the British, Germans, Swedes, Russians and others flocked here and the entrepreneurs started building grand Belle Époque buildings to cater for them. Menton had become a home away from home for the British aristocracy and bourgeoisie. Katherine Mansfield, in search of a solution for her ailments, spent months in Menton before moving on and dying elsewhere. The Duke of Westminster bought a villa for his mistress Chanel near here. Many of the hotels still have Anglicised names.

To understand the appeal of Menton, you need to understand the geography as much as the climate. Picture the Golfe de la Paix (Gulf of Peace) with the Alpes-Maritimes behind it – a location that allows people to ski in the mountains in the morning and swim in the Mediterranean in the evening. In between there is nothing but clean air, bright light, picture-perfect palm trees, lovely Italian architecture and delicious French cuisine. The Old Town, the former fishing village with its narrow streets, is in the east; the tourist zone and residential neighbourhood are to the west.

To begin a tour of Menton, start at **Place des Victoires,** with the grand Edwardian Winter Palace behind you. Head south down Avenue Édouard VII and continue until you reach the beach and the Promenade du Soleil, then turn left along the esplanade. Head towards Avenue Félix Faure and turn left onto this street, then go right at the roundabout and you'll hit Rue Barel on the left. Turn right into Rue de la République and continue past the **Town Hall.** You are now in the heart of the Old Town. This is where Menton's history really reveals itself in the glamorous architecture and gracious spirit.

But Menton isn't just about grand buildings and impressive villas. The gardens here are among the most famous in France, thanks to the ideal microclimate and wealthy expats. This is where American Lawrence Johnston (who created the renowned Hidcote in England) established the **Serre de la Madone**, which has recently been restored. It's where Sir Percy Radcliffe created Val Rahmeh (named after his wife), a seriously impressive spot of horticulture that is now the **Jardin Botanique Exotique du Val Rahmeh**. And it's where the artist Ferdinand Bac conceived **Les Colombières**, a series of whimsical but pretty gardens along a picturesque promontory. There's also **Jardin Fontana Rosa**, which belonged to the Spanish writer Vicente Blasco Ibáñez and paid homage to his favourite writers: Cervantes, Dickens and Shakespeare.

A visit to any of these gardens will delight, or you can simply walk along the elegant **Boulevard de Garavan**, which overlooks many splendid pink, cream, lemon and ochre villas, with their olive and lemon groves and their terrace walls overflowing with jasmine. The boulevard has recently been redone in mosaics by Portuguese artisans, and offers superb views of the sea and villas. If you can ignore the apartment buildings (many grand old homes were sadly razed to make way for them) and focus on the views and surviving villas, you'll understand what the Riviera looked like before developers moved in.

To the west of Menton is **Roquebrune-Cap-Martin**, which is also worth a wander, and not just for the sea views and the glimpses of villas.

My favourite place in Menton is the **Musée Jean-Cocteau** (Bastion du Port, Quai Gordon Bennet; jeancocteau.net), which celebrates the life and work of the filmmaker, poet and artist. It's full of wonderful charcoals and watercolours and brightly coloured pastels and ceramics. If you don't want to pay an entry free, Cocteau's paintings can also be seen in the Town Hall's wedding room.

Menton is a picture of civilised gentility and understated grace: a place devoid of nightlife and noisy partygoers but blessed with blooming gardens, half a dozen gorgeous beaches and a beautiful sweep of an Old Town topped by the Baroque Basilique Saint-Michel. It's not for everyone, but for many, Menton is where their Riviera dreams come to fruition (if you'll forgive the horticultural pun).

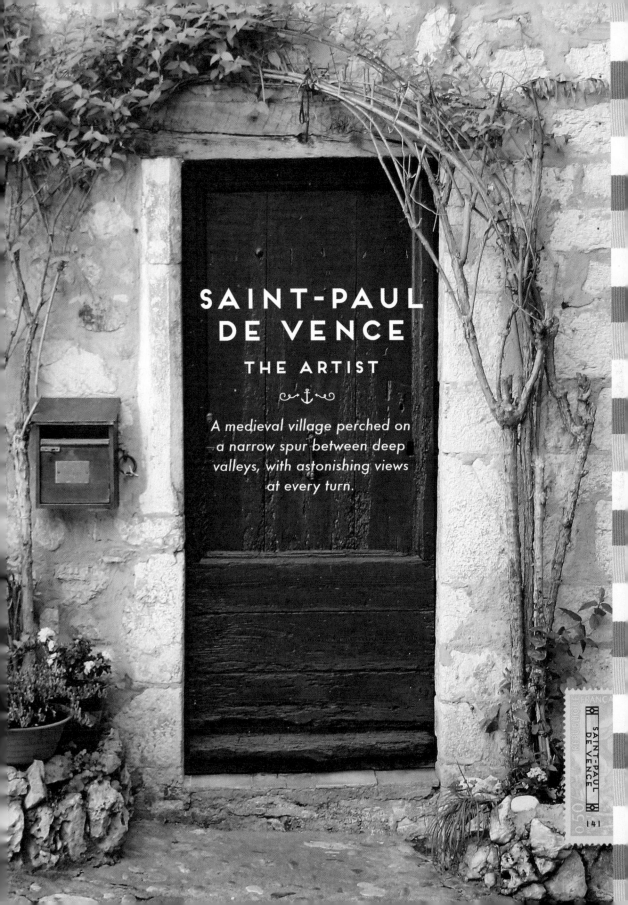

SAINT-PAUL DE VENCE

THE ARTIST

A medieval village perched on a narrow spur between deep valleys, with astonishing views at every turn.

There's no way to avoid saying this: Saint-Paul de Vence is overflowing with tourists. The problem is, unlike Nice or Cannes, this tiny town perched above the Côte d'Azur isn't really designed for them, so everyone just sort of squeezes in and then squeezes out again.

Despite this, the place is very charming – it's the archetypal idyllic medieval hilltop village. If you like art you'll love it here. Saint Paul, you see, is a celebration of the brushstroke.

There are scores of art galleries and artisanal stores selling original, authentic and sometimes not-so-authentic artwork. There is a world-famous restaurant and hotel, **La Colombe d'Or** (page 188), which displays priceless artwork from the likes of Picasso, Dufy and Modigliani, often given as gifts by the once-penniless artists in return for a meal. And there are many artists still living and working here, so you're liable to see that classic French scene of a bereted bohemian squinting before his canvas as he calculates the perspective on a landscape of dappled light.

Art seems to be the dominant commercial activity here, and when you wander around you'll soon understand why. The light is clear, and even when it's beautifully diffused in the mornings and evenings there's still a delightful quality to it. And the views are astonishing: the village's location on a narrow spur between two deep valleys guarantees that there will always be a vista to sketch. The town itself is endearing, with its old stone houses and honey-coloured stone walls – so cool on a hot Provençal afternoon. And the streets (when clear) are lovely to linger in, watching the locals play *pétanque* (boules) under the shade of the plane trees.

Saint-Paul has a timeless beauty: it could be 2013, or it could be 1913. Remove the tourist buses and the place is as it was a century ago. No wonder artists such as Renoir, Chagall, Modigliani and Matisse were seduced by the classic beauty. It's just a pity that Saint-Paul has become a victim of its own artistic success. Never mind, there are still corners you can explore without fear of being elbowed out of the way by a day pack or a digital SLR.

Not surprisingly, some of the nicest things to do here involve embracing the artistic spirit. Book in for a truly memorable lunch at **La Colombe d'Or** (1 Place du Général de Gaulle) and take in the incredible artwork lining the walls while you sip your wine. (Tip: The terrace is the best place to sit, as the views are amazing. But you'll miss out on the paintings.)

SAINT-PAUL
DE VENCE

145

Or you can visit the grave of Russian-born painter Marc Chagall in the town's pretty cemetery (Chemin de Saint-Paul), and add a small white stone as a tribute to his work. Or you can drop into some of the artists' workshops and talk aesthetics. Or you can pay a visit to the world-renowned **Fondation Maeght** (623 Chemin des Gardettes, page 205), and be rewarded with an extraordinary collection of 20th-century paintings, sculptures and ceramics, along with a museum setting that combines water, trees, shade, nature and utter tranquillity.

If you love the lively spirit of Saint-Paul, consider visiting on Saturday, which is market day. The weekly fair creates a boisterous, festival atmosphere throughout the village, filled with colour, stalls and irresistible produce.

The thing is, the tourists here may make your viewing opportunities difficult, so if you find the crowds too much then get back in the car and go further up the road to **Vence**, Saint-Paul's quieter neighbour. It's just as beautiful but has fewer people, better shops (in my opinion), more interesting art galleries and gorgeous cafes with terraces that are less cramped. There are also delicious pâtisseries, where you can buy a baguette or freshly made pastry and then find a quiet spot for a picnic.

Another village worth seeing is **Tourrettes-sur-Loup**, which is just three kilometres west of Vence, and also has lots of great art stores run by artists.

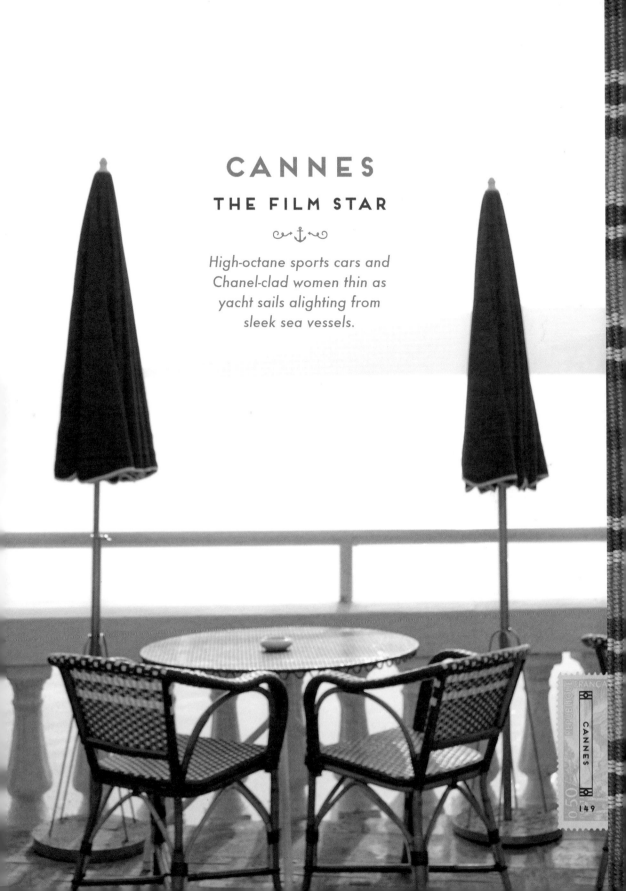

CANNES

THE FILM STAR

*High-octane sports cars and
Chanel-clad women thin as
yacht sails alighting from
sleek sea vessels.*

CANNES

0.50

149

THE CÔTE D'AZUR

150

Cannes has virtually become a star in its own right, thanks to the Cannes International Film Festival (festival-cannes.fr) held here in May each year. The festival was established in 1939 to rival Mussolini's Venice Film Festival but has long since eclipsed it to become one of the world's best. Every year it attracts a significant number of Hollywood's glamorous set, who come as much for the worldwide publicity as for the chance to get some downtime in the South of France.

But Cannes is far more than just a backdrop for a few film screenings or a place for celebs to crash afterwards. It's a lively seaside resort town with a dazzling port, an elegant seafront boulevard, and some astonishing shopping. Take away the film festival and it is still a head-turning town.

From the point of view of exploring, the best thing about Cannes is its compactness – the town is more manageable than a 10-minute art-house flick. So let's begin our tour at the dramatic **La Croisette**, the city's picture-perfect promenade. This gleaming beachfront scene features a glorious bay, soft sandy beaches, high-octane sports cars purring down the road and Chanel-clad women as thin as yacht sails alighting from sleek sea vessels.

As you walk along the western part of La Croisette, look out for the celebrity handprints and signatures in the pavement. It's cheesy to compare your own hands against them, but everyone still does. There are also wall frescoes of movie stars dotted all around Cannes. The best one is on the western side of the port and covers the whole side of a building.

Like Nice, Cannes is embroidered with the palm trees and Belle Époque architecture that gives it the essential 'Riviera look'. The town's landmark hotels are especially grandiose and proud of it. Peek inside the Intercontinental Carlton Cannes and the **Hôtel Martinez** (page 187), both favourites of Hollywood types, and you'll see why some stars need to wear sunglasses: the furniture is almost as shiny as the bling that adorns many of the fingers around here.

While you're here, ensure you take a wander down to the **Vieux Port** (Old Port). There's always a lot to look at here and not just the shiny white yachts and enormous motor cruisers juxtaposed against the humble fishing boats. Indeed, those who come and go from the yachts' gangplanks are often just as intriguing as the boats themselves, especially during festival week when, as many insiders suggest, the dozen or so girls on each craft are often C-grade actresses in various stages of dress (or undress).

If you want to swim in the sea, you're in luck: Cannes has some of the best beaches on the coast – and with sand rather than pebbles. On the main beachfront promenade there are 32 sections of beachfront bliss, each with sun loungers and umbrellas available to rent. The best choices are **Plage du Mourre Rouge** just east of Port Canto, and **Plage du Midi** along Boulevard du Midi, just west of the Vieux Port. Or you could head to **Z-Plage** opposite the Hôtel Martinez, which offers great food with your sea view.

153

Running parallel to Boulevard de la Croissette is **Rue d'Antibes**. This long, narrow thoroughfare and several streets adjacent to it constitute the main shopping area in Cannes and in the height of summer crowds fill every corner. The shops are on the pricy, designer side, but window-shopping and people-watching are just as enjoyable. A stroll here is what the French call *'un must'*. The town's movie theatres are also situated along the Rue d'Antibes.

The pedestrian **Rue Meynadier**, near the Rue d'Antibes, is also a stylish strip of stores and fashion boutiques. Roughly six blocks long, this street has markets and shops offering produce, clothes and gifts.

If food markets are more your thing, the covered **Marché Forville** (12 Rue Louis Blanc) offers a lively, colourful and sometimes noisy market experience. Treat yourself to some fresh produce – perhaps some fruit, oysters, paté and olives. On Mondays, Forville becomes a flea market (*marché brocante*).

If you fancy some respite from all the glamour and glitz, there is a lovely grassy park at the western end of La Croisette, between the Palais des Festivals and the beach, which features a wonderful carousel – ideal entertainment for littlies. There's also a park and carousel (the French love their merry-go-rounds) at the eastern end of La Croisette, just before the new Port Canto yacht harbour. And don't miss the beautiful **Jardin Alexandre III**, a lovely large park full of flowers in the spring and summer.

Once you've seen the razzle-dazzle face of Cannes, take a walk to its quieter side by wandering the winding 400-year-old streets of the old quarter. **Le Suquet** (the name means 'summit' in Provençal) is beloved by locals and is distinguished by the steep, zig-zagging cobbled lanes lined with atmospheric restaurants, and topped with a magnificent clock tower and church that faces the Bay of Cannes. This neighbourhood was originally the home of fishermen and consequently the dwellings – many with quirky tangerine and faded lime facades – are distinctly old, but the area has been beautifully preserved. Much of the old quarter is pedestrianised, so it's easy to find a great little restaurant, then sit back and enjoy a glass of red as the sun sets.

And if you want to dance like John Travolta, head for **Charly's Bar** (5 Rue Suquet; pubcharlysbar.com), where everyone from tanned beauties to hip young things dance like there's no tomorrow. Then, if you want to stretch the night (or day) out, there's **B. Pub** (22 Rue Macé), a flashy, Neoclassical-style bar featuring gilt columns and sparkler-adorned Champagne ice buckets.

Afterwards, take the posse to **Le Bâoli** nightclub, where six litres of Dom Pérignon can go for 25,000 Euros, but whose clientele (including the likes of Jude Law, Beyoncé, Snoop Dogg and Prince Albert of Monaco) isn't the kind to care. This is Cannes, after all.

ANTIBES AND CAP D'ANTIBES

THE LIT WIT

⚓

Magnificent villas and a movie-star lifestyle on one side; an ancient walled city with a traditional way of life on the other.

Before I visited Antibes, a friend told me it was an endearing place: 'a place that never fails to give you fond memories of the time you spend there'. I wondered how it could be any prettier or more memorable than the rest of the Riviera. Well, I hadn't counted on Antibes' gentle pace and easy-going nature; her architectural marvels and magnificent villas; her secret coves (especially those tucked away at Cap d'Antibes); her slinky ports (of which there are many); her fabulous festivals (antiques, jazz, teak boats), and her quiet Old Town, with its long protective port wall and exquisitely small streets.

Antibes will charm you, especially if you've just come from the manic pace of Nice and Cannes. It's the flip side of the Riviera: a promontory that seems to eschew the madness of the rest of the coast and go by its own moderate beat.

Now some people call this part of the Riviera Antibes–Juan-les-Pins. That's because Antibes and its neighbour Juan-les-Pins are so close as to be almost indistinguishable. Old Antibes and the port of Antibes are on the mainland, on the east side facing the Baie des Anges, while Juan-les-Pins is on the west side. There's also Cap d'Antibes, which is the promontory between both. Juan-les-Pins is the livelier part, with its rocking nightlife, bikini-peppered beaches and animated casino. Antibes is considered the quieter side, with its subdued ports and Old Town. And Cap d'Antibes is mostly residential – but, what residences they are! The entire area can be walked in a day or two – and walking is the best way to take it all in, as many of the best parts are tucked down side streets, at the end of narrow lanes or set around coves that are almost impossible to park beside when you want to take a photo. I'll focus on Antibes and Cap d'Antibes in this chapter, and Juan in the next.

A writer friend of mine calls Antibes one of the world's literary meccas (a position it shares with Manhattan, the Left Bank of Paris and a sprinkling of other notable places). Antibes has always been loved by writers and literary types, yet no-one seems to quite know why. Perhaps the slow pace helps the words flow? Perhaps the landscapes and endless blue skies offer inspiration for those with writer's block? Perhaps the locals are suitably eccentric fodder for novels? Or perhaps the wine is simply better here? Whatever the reason, Antibes has been, at various times, the home of Graham Greene, Guy de Maupassant, Victor Hugo, Dorothy Parker, Nikos Kazantzakis (author of *Zorba the Greek*), Jules Verne (*20,000 Leagues under the Sea*), and Gerald and Sara Murphy – patrons of people like Hemingway and F. Scott Fitzgerald, who were further fans of this part of the Riviera.

You can't walk far without stumbling over a bay, villa, hotel, street or bar that's been featured in a book or an article. Artists, too, have loved painting this region, most notably Picasso, who has a museum devoted to him here.

To begin exploring this place, so full of character and inspiration, start at the main harbour, which is divided into the old port and the newer harbour. Actually, this area has myriad ports – you'll see them scattered all around the cape – but the newest, Port Vauban, with more than 2000 moorings is the largest yachting harbour in Europe. It was designed to accommodate craft of more than 100 metres (hence the nickname 'Millionaire's Quay'). If you prefer a more traditional scene, go to **Port de l'Olivette**, a sheltered cove for sailors who enjoy the old Provençal spirit and moor their wooden fishing boats as in times past.

From Antibes' main harbour, it's a short walk south to the **Vieille Ville** (Old Town). This is where the Antibes atmosphere really begins. And you'll see it in the locals, who are strikingly individual, even eccentric. The mix of narrow streets, old buildings and interesting shops makes for a wonderful wander, especially on a sunny day when you can stop in one of the cafes for lunch and listen to the jazz that is often played. Try for a table at the **Place Nationale** or along the **Avenue Georges Clémenceau** for the best scenes.

THE CÔTE D'AZUR

In spring, the town is garlanded with jasmine, oleander and bougainvillea, and floral notes scent the laneways. Any of the streets around the covered market in **Cours Masséna** or **Rue du Safranier** are delightful, while the walk along the ramparts on the **Promenade Amiral de Grasse** offers magnificent sea views.

A lovely thing to do here is to buy some fresh produce at the markets and take it with you on your walk to Cap d'Antibes: there are lots of spots by the water to stop for a picnic. Or you can have lunch in Antibes. When the market's stallholders pack up, the area and surrounding streets fill with restaurant tables. One of the best, although it's perhaps better visited at night, is **Bar Absinthe** in the basement of an olive-oil shop just off the market. Reminiscent of an early 20th-century drinking den, it features a vaulted ceiling, wonderful vintage posters and rows of glasses backlit with the distinctive green colour.

If you don't drink too much absinthe at lunch, you may be able to find Commune Libre de Safranier (the Free Commune of Safranier), an autonomous 'village within a village' that's well hidden but worth the hunt. It has its own small Town Hall and a tiny street named after *Zorba the Greek* author Nikos Kazantzakis, who lived here.

Once you've strolled around this historic quarter, make for the waterfront esplanade and keep heading south. If you keep following the path around the coast, you'll eventually reach **Plage de la Garoupe**. This quiet and secluded beach was the favourite hangout for F. Scott Fitzgerald and his wealthy patrons Sara and Gerald Murphy. The Murphys visited one summer in the 1920s and noted the picturesque beaches and the idyllic weather. They persuaded the Hôtel du Cap-Eden-Roc to rent them a part of the hotel, which they then used for lavish parties for all their friends. Later, they bought a villa, which they called 'Villa America'. Celebrities such as Rudolph Valentino and Coco Chanel shortly followed, and soon the Riviera was the place for rich East Coast Americans to spend their summers – and their money.

The Murphy's favourite swimming inlet, Garoupe, isn't much today, thanks to seaweed and age, but it is still pretty and there's a charming cafe with red striped awnings that's a nice spot for lunch.

The real sight here is the luxury real estate, which continues all the way along the Cap d'Antibes coastline. (Note: If you want to take a short cut from Antibes to Garoupe and peek into the gardens of the glamorous villas, take Boulevard du Cap and then wind your way down Chemin de la Garoupe to the beach.)

After you've had an ice-cream or brunch at Garoupe Beach, head back up Boulevard de la Garoupe and then down Boulevard John F. Kennedy. This will lead you past Jules Verne's former villa on the right (a stunning white home with imposing black gates: look for the gold plaque), and eventually take you to the front entrance to the fabled **Hôtel du Cap-Eden-Roc** (page 187), one of the most famous hotels on the French Riviera, if not the world. This is where Karl Lagerfeld held his Resort Collection in recent years. It's where Madonna and other stars hide from the paparazzi when they've been to Cannes. And it's where some rather illustrious movie stars have stayed over the decades, as you'll see from the old black and white photos lining the restaurant's walls.

You aren't allowed in the hotel unless you're a guest, but you may lunch at the waterfront restaurant (you'll need to book), where you can peek down onto the famous cliff-side pool, the setting for so many of Slim Aarons' celebrity photographs.

It's at this end of Cap d'Antibes where it will start to feel as though you're in a film version of the French Riviera. Every bend brings a glimpse of a glamorous villa, a peek at a private plunge pool, a view of the sea or even a helicopter taking off, ferrying someone back to the airport. As you walk towards the end of the cape, the hedges grow denser and the price tags higher. There are only 2000 or so properties on the cape, and they're mostly valued in the scores of millions.

One of the best known is **Château de la Croë**, the former home of King Edward VII, the Duke of Windsor, who lived here for several years after World War II. It was also the home, for a while, of Aristotle Onassis. After being left empty for many years, it's now the Riviera escape for Russian billionaire Roman Abramovich, who is restoring it.

And then there is its palatial neighbour, **Villa Eilenroc** (Avenue Mrs Beaumont). Once regularly open to visitors, Eilenroc has since narrowed its hours to very irregular times, usually Wednesdays. The 10-acre garden is magnificent, thanks to the restoration efforts of the council, with views across the bay and plantings of pines, cypress, oaks, olive trees, lavender, rosemary, eucalyptus, roses, figs and more than two kilometres of pittosporum hedges. The villa was once owned by wealthy American businessman Louis Dudley Beaumont, and still stands as one of the most valuable pieces of real estate on the entire Riviera coast. (Its nearest equivalent, La Leopolda on Cap Ferrat, was rumoured to have been sold to a Russian for 300 million Euros.)

From the Hôtel du Cap-Eden-Roc, near the Villa Eilenroc, continue walking around Boulevard John F Kennedy, which becomes Boulevard Maréchal Juin. As you round the point, look out for the pretty cove on the left, a postcard-worthy scene of weathered fishing boats and cobalt water. There are lots of beautiful villas around here too, and a wander through any of the side streets will reward you with architectural eye candy. In fact, there are tantalising glimpses of the grand villas and gardens at almost every step: just ensure you don't get run over by an Aston Martin or a Lamborghini while you're taking a photo.

From here you can wander back to Antibes or, if you have the energy, continue exploring the other side of Antibes, the vastly different Juan-les-Pins.

165

THE CÔTE D'AZUR

JUAN-LES-PINS
THE BEACH BEAUTY

*A pontoon of brightly striped beach umbrellas,
the buzz of motor scooters and purr of convertibles,
and the chatter and chink of a constant stream
of wine glasses, toasting to good times.*

167

Juan-les-Pins is a bold and bustling stay-out-late kinda place. It's where you come if you want action. Some people love it here, particularly during summer when the streets buzz with motor scooters and convertibles and the pavements with chatter and the chink of wine glasses. Many of the globe-trotting posse adore it, because there's a casino, nightclubs and countless beaches. Other people dislike it because it's too busy and too brash. Yes, it's all that, but it's also fun. The colours are delightful (picture pontoons full of brightly striped beach umbrellas), the pine trees offer an elegant backdrop, and the palm-shaded restaurant terraces welcome guests until the early hours. And in July there's the Jazz Festival, bringing cool tunes to town. What more do you want from a summer resort?

Situated west of Antibes, Juan was originally famous for its pine trees (*pins* in French), which led to its name. It was where Antibes' locals would go for a wander along the promenade or a picnic by a bay. As its popularity increased, visitors included American billionaire Frank Jay Gould, who immediately recognised its potential as a summer resort. He joined forces with a local businessman and built the Hôtel le Provençal, a luxury Art Déco–style retreat. They also restored the casino. Soon, the town was jumping with musicians, cabaret artists and, of course, writers and painters. Juan-les-Pins had become a party town.

Dozens of luxury villas were soon erected to cater for the influx of wealthy expats. One of the most beautiful was the **Villa Aujourd'hui**, a striking, rather curvy and extremely modern-looking waterfront property built in 1938 by American architect Barry Dierks. It was owned for several years by Hollywood mogul Jack Warner, who played host to Charlie Chaplin and Marilyn Monroe, among others.

Juan-les-Pins became so well known among a certain sector of the jet set that it became a byword for a good time. The singer Peter Sarstedt even wrote about it in his 1969 song 'Where Do You Go To (My Lovely)'.

Now there are two popular sides to Juan. There is the street scene, which includes the casino plus a series of perpetually animated cafes, bars, restaurants all of which offer entertainment on every level (there are dozens of boutiques, too, although most are set up for tourists and sell resort clothes and shoes at inflated prices); and then there is the beach scene, which is where people go to sleep off their hangovers in the morning under the pretence of working on their tans.

Juan has magnificent beaches – more than thirty of them. Some you'll need to pay a fee for; others will allow you to lie down free of charge. One of the best private ones, **Les Pirates**, is just in front of the pretty park of pine trees on Boulevard Édouard Baudoin (23 Boulevard Édouard Baudoin). You can rent a sun lounger and they'll bring drinks and lunch right to your chair. There are also clean shower facilities where you can wash off the sand before heading to the cafes.

If you're looking for a free beach, there's a popular sheltered beach further up, near the harbour, on the other side of the Hôtel Belles Rives. (You can't get lunch there, however, and certainly not delivered to your chair.)

In between these two beaches is the **Hôtel Belles Rives** (page 186). You can access it from either beach via the tiny coastal path in front of the hotel. The Belles Rives is one of the highlights of the Cap d'Antibes. This, you see, is where F. Scott Fitzgerald wrote part of *The Great Gatsby*. The villa next to it claims to have been Scott's home at one stage, too, so perhaps they were part of the one estate? Yet another source claims that the Fitzgeralds only spent one summer here living off the royalties of the novel. In any case, this was Scott and Zelda's stomping ground for a little while, and it's all very Great Gatsby-ish. The Art Déco hotel has kept its original furniture and has dedicated part of its library to Scott, but the truly memorable scenes are outside on the terrace. This is real old-style Riviera glamour, with a bar outfitted in red and leopard print, a spectacular private beach and pier dotted with striped umbrellas, and a splendid terrace with navy cafe chairs set up to allow you to sip your G&T as you watch the pale Riviera light sinking over the sea. Blink and you could almost imagine you're back in the 1920s, chinking a Champagne glass with Zelda and toasting the good times.

BELLES RIVES

FRANCAISE

JUAN-LES-
PINS

0,50

173

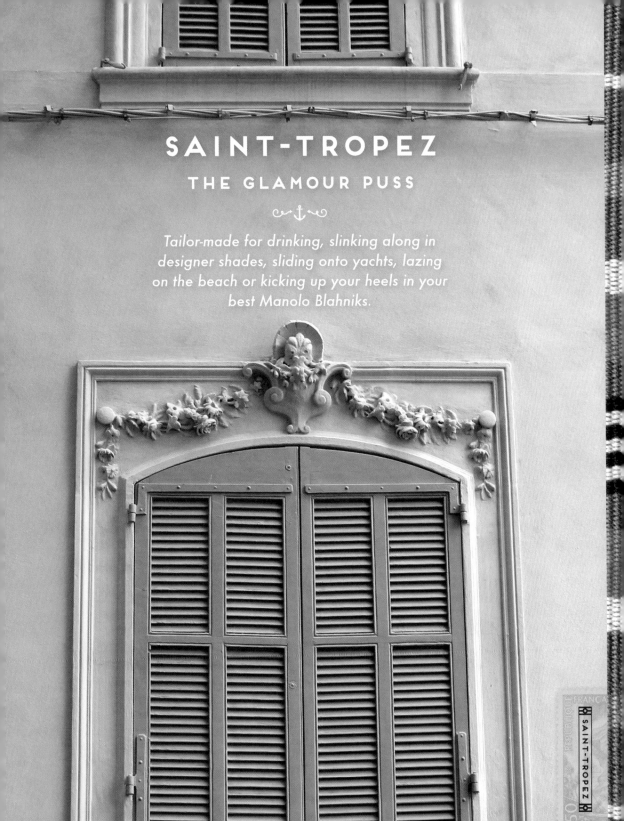

SAINT-TROPEZ
THE GLAMOUR PUSS

Tailor-made for drinking, slinking along in designer shades, sliding onto yachts, lazing on the beach or kicking up your heels in your best Manolo Blahniks.

While other resort destinations have come and gone, Saint-Tropez is still hot even after all these years. Yet its popularity is a bit of a mystery. The tiny road that leads into the one-time fishing village doesn't make for easy access; the hotels are prohibitively expensive; and to be honest, the beaches are not the best on the Riviera.

It's a wonder Saint-Tropez has survived, let alone retained its glossy status. But it has, and it is still one of the places to come if you're up for a good time on the Côte d'Azur.

Now some people debate the best time to see Saint-Tropez. There are those who think the only time to experience it is during high season (July and August) when it becomes one big catwalk. Others insist it's better out of season, when you can actually see the streets, the shops and the cute style of this celebrated village. I'm afraid I can't tell you which is better: I came in early May and although it was relatively easy to get into town, the place seemed to be devoid of character. Friends say the best time to visit is early September, when it's warm enough to swim and wear shorts or sundresses but the streets aren't choked with tourists. (The town sees up to 100,000 a day in high season.)

I guess it's a personal choice, and personally I think Saint-Tropez needs the flamboyant A-list figures (and the B and C ones) to bring it alive. It is, after all, a show-offy place. But if you do go on weekends or in the height of summer, try and get there by early morning, before 8 a.m. if possible, to avoid the snarls on the highway.

To really experience the drama of this theatrical little town, start at the harbour. You can't miss it. It's on the left as you drive in – you'll see the massive super-yachts lined up. This is the first thing that will tell you Saint-Tropez is more than a fishing village with a few fancy stores. It's a mooring spot for millionaires with more money than they know what to do with. (Although having said that, the best way is to arrive by yacht.) Wander along the promenade and count the vessels – or the money it would have taken to buy them. Everybody does. There's no shame in displaying envy here.

Running parallel to the harbour are streets lined with designer boutiques: Dior, Chanel, Louis Vuitton, Hermès et al. Ironically, the one thing you can't buy in the fishing village is bait and tackle. However, before you judge the moneyed class too harshly, take a look at the buildings.

THE CÔTE D'AZUR

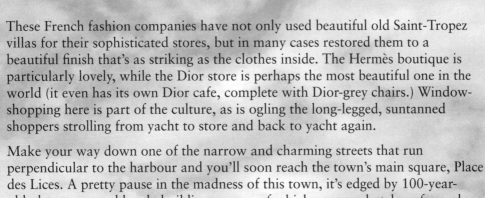

These French fashion companies have not only used beautiful old Saint-Tropez villas for their sophisticated stores, but in many cases restored them to a beautiful finish that's as striking as the clothes inside. The Hermès boutique is particularly lovely, while the Dior store is perhaps the most beautiful one in the world (it even has its own Dior cafe, complete with Dior-grey chairs.) Window-shopping here is part of the culture, as is ogling the long-legged, suntanned shoppers strolling from yacht to store and back to yacht again.

Make your way down one of the narrow and charming streets that run perpendicular to the harbour and you'll soon reach the town's main square, Place des Lices. A pretty pause in the madness of this town, it's edged by 100-year-old plane trees and lovely buildings, many of which are now hotels, cafes and stores. Perhaps the most photographed is the hotel **White 1921** (formerly Maison Blanche), which was bought by the prestigious LVMH company (of which Louis Vuitton is part) as its first venture into the hotel sector. It's a gorgeous building that looks like a mini château, and is priced accordingly (page 196).

Try to visit Saint-Tropez on either Tuesday or Sunday, when an open-air market takes over the Place des Lices from 8 a.m. until just after midday. The market traders offer all kinds of food and wares here, ranging from typical Provençal products such as lavender sachets, tablecloths and soaps to beach gear, sun hats, straw bags, towels and even bikinis. There is also a small antique section where you can find furniture, silverware, vintage bags and jewellery. However, like most things in this town, everything is quite expensive, so don't come for your weekly grocery shop: just take in the atmosphere, and perhaps one or two souvenirs. You'll have to dig to find a bargain, but the atmosphere is still free.

Once you've filled up on market sights, and perhaps grabbed a coffee from one of the cafes surrounding the square, you can wander the rest of the town, which really only takes half an hour to circumnavigate. As most of the streets are barely wide enough for two people though, you'll be going at a snail's pace, so it may take longer. Peer into real estate agents' windows to gawp at property prices, take photos of darling houses squeezed down tiny side streets, then sit at a bar with a good view of the passing crowds and toast the fact that you're here, in marvellous Saint-Tropez. That's all there really is to do here. The town is made for drinking, slinking along in designer shades, sliding onto yachts or kicking up your heels after dark at the Byblos hotel's nightclub **Les Caves du Roy**.

The real beauty of Saint-Tropez is actually outside the village. There are spectacular places high atop the wooded, rocky peninsula that offer a great vantage point to see the entire area, including across the sea to the mountains of the Massif des Maures. A great view can be had from the 16th-century **Citadelle** at the top of the village, reached via a climb up a green and wooded hill. The interior has been transformed into a museum of Saint-Tropez's maritime history.

The beaches, too, are long and wide, and worth at least one look. **Le Club 55** on Plage de Pampelonne is still one of the places to go for some serious celeb spotting, although you'll need a car to reach it as it's about six kilometres (four miles) out of town. The beaches of Saint-Tropez are not actually in Saint-Tropez but on the territory of the neighbouring commune, Ramatuelle. A few shuttle buses run there, but only from the more upmarket hotels. You can walk to the beaches from Saint-Tropez along the **Sentier du Littoral** – a good three-hour hike around the headland that takes you past some charming little beaches, such as Plage Graniers, Plage des Canebiers and Plage de la Moutte. You also start the walk at **La Ponche** in Saint-Tropez – a rather cute neighbourhood that was once the fishermen's quarter.

But the best bet is to hire a bicycle or scooter. That way you can zoom through both Saint-Tropez and the beach streets without worrying about traffic or parking. If you're looking for a quieter sandy stretch, or a cheap one, the southern end of the coastline, around **Bonne Terrasse**, is worth checking out.

However, perhaps the best way to see this flashy place is from the water. Transports Maritimes Tropéziens (Promenades-en-Mer, Vieux Port) offers one-hour boat trips that will help you truly appreciate what this place is all about.

REPUBLIQUE FRANÇAISE

CÔTE D'AZUR VAROISE

1963

0,50 POSTES

R. CAMI

FRANÇAISE

5c

ERNÉE (Mayenne). - Dolmens de la Contrie

ur Rennes

✦ DIRECTORY ✦

OF INSPIRING PLACES

Hotels and guesthouses

Provence has lured romantics, aesthetes and stressed-out city professionals to its idyllic landscapes, chic-rustique homes and sun-and-wine-filled lifestyles for decades. They dream of finding a welcoming little guesthouse where the owner pours them a fine red and tells them where to find the best beaches, restaurants, vineyards and views. Here is a selection of delightful hideaways that promise truly memorable stays.

BASTIDE ROSE

A rose by any other name

If you're seeking the perfect Provençal guesthouse, this might just be it. A former mill set in a stunning river setting, it's owned by one of the most engaging ladies to ever run a French guesthouse, Poppy Salinger. Poppy is the widow of John F. Kennedy's former media advisor Pierre Salinger, and her library is full of photo albums of JFK and Jackie in all their Camelot glory. She also has a Kennedy Museum set up in the old mill. The guesthouse is rather grand, but still has an intimate, homey feel, thanks to all the personal photos and books. The rooms are similarly splendid; a mix of spacious proportions and welcoming furnishings (including desks), with wonderfully large bathrooms, high ceilings and elegantly tall windows that open onto the courtyard. There's a pretty pool with a wisteria arbour, a stunning deck with seating beside the fast-running stream and a garden full of sculptures. But perhaps the most beautiful part is the island; the mill sits over the river that used to run its machinery, and the waterways have split into tributaries, creating a tranquil island in the garden. The gurgle of the streams and the sound of birdsong is pure bliss, especially in summer. You could check in and happily spend your week here without going anywhere else.

99 Chemin des Croupières, Le Thor; +33 4 90 02 14 33; bastiderose.com

DOMAINE DE LA BAUME

A domain

When *Condé Nast Traveler* magazine starts crowing about a place you know it must be special. This hotel, owned by the 'Martha Stewart of France' (*Condé Nast's* words, not mine), is the sister property to La Bastide de Marie, a very stylish place that attracts – and satisfies – fussy guests, so you know this place will have the same attention to detail. It's an 18th-century manor house near the pretty village of Tourtour, and sits so well in its surroundings it almost looks like a painting. (No surprise that its former owner was painter Bernard Buffet.) With an ochre facade and sky-blue shutters, it looks at one with the wide open Provence skies and fertile landscape. Like its sister property it's tricky to find, but absolutely worth the drive through the countryside.

2071 Route d'Aups, Tourtour; +33 4 57 74 74 74; domaine-delabaume.com

FIVE SEAS HOTEL

High five

Going by name alone, the Five sounds very modern, minimalist and slick, but thankfully it's not one of those cutting-edge-design places staffed with sneery hipsters in all-black Comme des Garçons. This is a hotel with substance and style. Situated just off the bustling La Croisette, close to all the action, it offers both a restaurant and a tearoom created by the pastry chef Jérôme De Oliveira. On top of this (if you'll forgive the pun) is the rooftop pool, and if you want more aquatic luxury there's also an 88-foot yacht. All this and yet rooms start from only 180 Euros.

1 Rue Notre Dame, Cannes; +33 4 63 36 05 05; five-seas-hotel-cannes.com

GRAND-HÔTEL DU CAP-FERRAT

Glamour, grandeur and grace

From its name alone, you expect the Grand-Hôtel du Cap-Ferrat to be an impressive place. Well, it's more than impressive – people struggle for superlatives here. It is the *Titanic* of hotels; a splendid illustration of what you can create with enough money, enough time and enough taste. The kind of guests who come here are the kind with a Prince in their title, or an Oscar on their mantle. You can barely imagine that the hotel started life as the dream of a coachman's son from the north. (Mr Péretmère built it in 1908 after buying almost seven hectares of land right on the end of the promontory.) The hotel is very private, but you can see glimpses of it from the public path that winds around the coast. The hotel isn't the only thing that's aged well: the cellar holds more than 140 vintage bottles of Château d'Yquem dating from 1854, and a couple of dozen bottles of Château Lafite Rothschild dating from 1799 – just the thing to open on the terrace of your majestic suite while you contemplate how good life is.

71 Boulevard du Général de Gaulle, Saint-Jean Cap-Ferrat; +33 4 93 76 50 50; grand-hotel-cap-ferrat.com

GRAND HÔTEL NORD-PINUS

Due nord

The owner of the Grand Hôtel Nord-Pinus, Anne Igou, has a penchant for art, particularly the photographic medium. It's featured strongly here, from the Peter Beard safari photos in the lobby of the hotel to Helmut Newton's portrait of Charlotte Rampling in Suite 10. But the views outside aren't too shabby either. If you stay in Suite 34, you'll be rewarded with a striking panorama over the rooftops of the Old Town. A lovely hotel for those who appreciate beauty, both inside and outside their rooms.

Place du Forum, Arles; +33 4 90 93 44 44; nord-pinus.com

HÔTEL BELLES RIVES

Bellisimo

So you like F. Scott Fitzgerald? You want to follow in the writer's footsteps? Maybe pen your own bestseller? Well, you could find inspiration here, at the villa where he wrote much of the iconic novel *The Great Gatsby*. Scott and Zelda rented this waterfront hideaway and the house next to it in order to concentrate on writing, and, okay, drinking. They'd already spent time in Saint-Raphaël, but when they arrived at this small corner of Juan-les-Pins they were immediately enchanted by the sea view, the pine trees and the peace. Thankfully, the over-development that has blighted other parts of the coast has not taken hold here. Blink and you could be back in the 1920s. The view overlooking the Med is so idyllic that people set up a sun lounger on the private beach and stare out to sea all day – usually with drink in hand. (The water is so calm and shallow that waterskiing was supposedly invented in the bay.) The interior is decorated in Fitzgerald-style glamour, including a red-and-leopard-print bar, and there is a library full of memorabilia celebrating the author. A sublime hideaway.

33 Boulevard Édouard Baudoin, Juan-les-Pins; +33 4 93 61 02 79; bellesrives.com

HÔTEL BRISE MARINE

Back to basics

Hotel recommendations can be a perilous undertaking. You can offer a suggestion, but your friends may not agree when they check in. Or the hotel may have changed. Or the owners may be grumpy that day. This is the category that the Brise Marine falls into. It's not for everybody, yet for many it's a great little find. Set deep in the lush foliage of Cap Ferrat's millionaire-filled peninsula, a mere stone's throw from the water, it's a jolly looking place that's easy to spot – look for the cheery gelato-lemon building on the hill. Tourists often walk past, look up, and think: what's that pretty place? (I know, because I did, too.) The gardens are the first hint that you may have stumbled upon something lovely, but it's the views that really woo people. Most of the balconies and terraces offer a panorama that takes in the same sights as nearby hotels that cost five times the price. Inside, the Brise Marine is a little on the simple side, but it's the kind of place my parents would love: pleasant and down-to-earth, not too expensive, but with a location that feels like a million Euros.

58 Avenue Jean Mermoz , Saint-Jean-Cap-Ferrat; +33 4 93 76 04 36; hotel-brisemarine.com

HÔTEL BYBLOS

Boogying at the Byblos

The Byblos is one of Saint-Tropez's throbbing hubs; a village-like cluster of red and yellow stucco buildings surrounded by ancient olive trees and bright bougainvillea. It includes two Mediterranean restaurants (one managed by Alain Ducasse) and the renowned Les Caves du Roy nightclub. This is where half of Hollywood has come and kicked up their Christian Louboutins, including Beyoncé and George Clooney (perhaps not together). The rooms are, as you can imagine, fairly impressive, with a smattering of antiques and big baths to sink into, but the real action is by the pool. Wear your darkest sunglasses so you can perve.

20 Avenue Paul Signac, Saint-Tropez; +33 4 94 56 68 00; byblos.com

HÔTEL DE L'IMAGE

Snap shot

I loved the idea of this when I first read about it: a hotel created from an old cinema. Then I saw it and realised the owners had done a cinematic job restoring it. Easily spotted by the grand facade, it features an equally stylish interior that continues the visual theme with walls of interesting photography. The terrace is a chic place for drinks, while the pool overlooks two acres of lush gardens and a mesmerising view of the Alpilles beyond: surprising for a hotel that's right in the centre of town.

36 Boulevard Victor Hugo, Saint-Rémy-de-Provence; +33 4 90 92 51 50; hotel-image.fr

HÔTEL DU CAP-EDEN-ROC

Hollywood on the Riviera

Travellers talk about the Hôtel du Cap in shushed tones of awe and envy. 'Did you stay there?' they ask the fortunate few who get to spend a night between these sacred sheets. This is because the hotel is like no other. Having been the favoured escape for Hollywood names for decades (the black and white photos by Slim Aarons on the walls attest to the star-studded guest list), it now sits comfortably with its celebrity status. It even looks glamorous, with its sweeping drive, iconic pool, Beverly Hills–style gardens and cliff-top restaurant overlooking the diving platforms on the Med. Visitors can peek in by booking lunch in the restaurant and then wandering around the gardens afterwards, but without a reservation, the hotel itself is strictly off-limits. Still, we can only imagine…

Boulevard JF Kennedy, Antibes; +33 4 93 61 39 01; hotel-du-cap-eden-roc.com

HÔTEL LE MAS DE PEINT

Design and style

With an interior that looks like a spread from a high-gloss, coffee-table design book, Le Mas de Peint is one for design lovers. It's not surprising that the owner's wife is an architect: good lines are evident in everything from the building to the interior design. But the most refreshing part of staying here is the kitchen garden, which supplies farm-grown produce for meals. The in-house chef loves using the garden ingredients to create new and unusual dishes. Owned by the Bon family for centuries, this lovely hotel is near Le Sambuc, south of Arles.

Le Sambuc; +33 4 90 97 20 62; masdepeint.com

HÔTEL MARTINEZ

From A to Cannes

The Hôtel Martinez is to Cannes what Château Marmont is to LA: the coolest place on the coast for celebs to crash. It's long been a favourite with the A-listers, both for its gilded interior (sweeping staircase, Art Déco finishes) and its gilded service. There's also the requisite palm-fringed pool, private beach, and spa (for when you're having those close-ups at the film festival).

73 Boulevard de la Croisette, Cannes; +33 4 93 90 12 34; cannesmartinez.grand.hyatt.com

HÔTEL NEGRESCO

Dressed to impress

An over-the-top monument to 18th-century French luxury, the Negrescro is something of a legend. Presidents in particular like to stay here, as it has the kind of opulence they've become accustomed to. Named after its founder, Henry Negresco, a Romanian who (ironically) died broke in Paris in 1920, the hotel was inspired by France's most ostentatious châteaux. There is the fancy, Belle Époque facade, a grand mansard roof, a domed tower, miles of gilt, and rooms the size of small countries. Recently renovated, many of the suites pay homage to famous names: the Napoleon III suite has swagged walls, a leopard-skin carpet, and a half-crown pink canopy. If that's not enough to satisfy your appetite for opulence, there's also an art museum within the hotel.

37 Promenade des Anglais, Nice; +33 4 93 16 64 00; hotel-negresco-nice.com

HÔTEL PRULY

Pruly cheap

If you want a cheap hotel that still comes with a measure of chic, check in here. The relatively new Pruly is a great little bargain number tucked inside a gorgeous white townhouse. Rooms are simple but bright, with lovely toile fabrics, and names like 'Agatha' (a sunny Cannes-yellow shade) and 'Hortense'. The main foyer and breakfast areas, meanwhile, are sleek modern pictures of monochrome sophistication. There's also a sunny garden with stylish seating. The rates – from 70 Euros – are unbeatable.

32 Boulevard d'Alsace, Cannes; +33 4 93 38 41 28; hotel-pruly.com

HÔTEL SAINTE VALÉRIE

Quirky charm

It's difficult to find a reasonably priced hotel on the French Riviera, especially in summer. It's even more difficult to find one that's close to the beach and has some degree of style. The Sainte Valérie is one of those secret finds that friends pass on, because it's cheap and chic! Set down a charming street behind the pine tree-lined park on the beach at Juan-les-Pins, this quaint French guesthouse is slightly Fawlty Towers, but it has charm in bucket-loads. The pool, which is set into a lush garden, is a picture of prettiness, and the rooms, especially those that overlook the pool, are a delight. Some are rather austere on the furnishing side, but they make up for it with wonderful balconies and really, you can't complain for the price.

13 Rue de l'Oratoire, Antibes; +33 4 93 61 07 15; hotel-sainte-valerie.fr

L'HÔTEL PARTICULIER

Quite particular

L'Hôtel Particulier is the epitome of a Provence hotel. The entrance: an elegantly grand black door with gilt knockers and black Versailles planters either side. The interior: all-white rooms with ornate white fireplaces and touches of gold and black. The garden: a green retreat that is both simple/minimalist and full of astonishing beauty. The ambience: delightfully overwhelming. The hotel is actually an aristocratic townhouse built in 1824 by the mayor of Arles. It was converted to a hotel in 2002 and quickly became one of the most talked-about in the area. It's still fairly much a secret, although the word is getting out. New additions include a hammam.

4 Rue de la Monnaie, Arles; +33 4 90 52 51 40; hotel-particulier.com

LA BASTIDE DE MARIE

La sanctuary

La Bastide de Marie is one of those places you really only hear about through word of mouth – or luck – and once you've been here, you feel reluctant to pass on its details in case popularity ruins it. Set deep in the heart of Provence (so deep it's a challenge to find) this splendid guesthouse makes you feel like you're staying with a very chic, very wealthy French aunt. Surrounded by vineyards and hills and a charming garden of pretty parterres and pencil pines, it's made for relaxing. There are few people, no bars or clubs and the nearest village is a drive away. Come here, open a bottle of wine and remember what the beauty of life feels like.

Route de Bonnieux, Ménerbes; +33 4 57 74 74 74; labastidedemarie.com

LA COLOMBE D'OR

La legend

La Colombe d'Or is one of the hotels that made the Riviera what it is. Many people travel to the Côte d'Azur just to dine here – and then boast about it afterwards. It's a legendary hotel that is as famous for its extraordinary private collection of art, featuring works from the likes of Picasso, Matisse and Braque, as it is for its setting and cuisine. Located in the golden hills of Saint-Paul de Vence, the hotel was a favourite place for painters. When the painters couldn't pay their bill they offered up their work instead. Decades on, La Colombe has become a mecca for people who love art as much as food – and the menus are just as amazing as the canvases. Sit out on the terrace where the light is pure Provence and take in the atmosphere, and history, of one of the most picturesque villages in France. A truly inspiring place.

Place du Général de Gaulle, Saint-Paul de Vence; + 33 4 93 32 80 02; la-colombe-dor.com

LA MIRANDE

Worthy of a palace

Some fans of La Mirande argue that it's the most beautiful hotel in Provence. Facing the famous Palace of the Popes, this sumptuous, spectacularly decorated 18th-century mansion has been restored and decorated with great care –and style – by Achim and Hannelore Stein and their son, Martin. Each room is different, but they're all decorated in exquisite antiques, sublime period tiles, and designer fabrics by the likes of Pierre Frey and Manuel Canovas.

4 Place de l'Amirande, Avignon; +33 4 90 85 93 93; la-mirande.fr

LA PAULINE

For a romantic rendezvous

A graceful allée of plane trees leads to this serene Directoire-style mansion built for Napoleon's sister, Pauline Borghese, who was famous for her romantic escapades. It is still romantic today, thanks to the care of its owners, who have created a superb guesthouse out of Pauline's old love shack. Each of the splendid rooms has a terrace, and there's also a guesthouse and a small pavilion in the gardens above the main house, should you want something really private. A perfect hideaway yet blissfully close to the charms of Aix.

Les Pinchinats, Chemin de la Fontaine des Tuiles, Aix-en-Provence; +33 4 42 17 02 60, lapauline.fr

LA PAVILLON DE GALON

A secret garden

Garden lovers will be in absolute horticultural heaven at this lovely place, which is a garden disguised as a guesthouse. And what a garden it is! Owned and restored by French photographer Guy Hervais and his wife Bibi Gex, this former 18th-century hunting pavillion (thus the name) in the dramatic Luberon region of Provence is so beautiful it was awarded a 'Remarkable Garden' status by the French Ministry of Culture and Environment.

Galon, Cucuron; +33 4 90 77 24 15; pavillondegalon.com

LA RÉSERVE

Make a reservation

People looking for seclusion love it here. The 1970s building has recently been updated for the modern generation while still retaining its original lines, but what guests really love is the privacy factor. La Réserve is a truly private retreat hidden in the hills behind Ramatuelle. This isn't to say that all you see are trees and the back of someone's parasol beside the pool. All of the villas face the sea, so you can look over the coast secure in the knowledge that it will take a very long lens to find you. Pack lots of books and check in for a good, long rest.

Chemin de la Quessine, Ramatuelle; +33 4 94 44 94 44; lareserve-ramatuelle.com

LA VOILE D'OR

A grand old soul

For a while, the Voile d'Or was the place to stay in this part of the world – if you couldn't afford the Grand-Hôtel du Cap-Ferrat, that is. With a magnificent site overlooking the gentle Saint-Jean-Cap-Ferrat harbour and its bobbing yachts, the hotel offers glorious views. The sheen has come off the glamour a little since its heyday, but it is still beloved. The day I was there, a Rolls-Royce and a brand new Bentley were parked outside: their owners having popped in for lunch. The pale-green restaurant is surprisingly stylish, in a rather nostalgic way, but the rooms could do with a refresh. Nevertheless, the views are still glorious. Sip your champers on the famous terrace and revel in being one of the lucky ones to have visited this grand old gem.

7 Avenue Jean Mermoz, Saint-Jean-Cap-Ferrat; +33 4 93 01 13 13; lavoiledor.fr

LE CAVENDISH

Bella hotel-a

This sumptuous Belle Époque beauty was built in 1897 and still hasn't lost her style. Now owned by Christine and Guy Welter, who are making a name for themselves as impressive hoteliers, it echoes the Côte d'Azur's glory days. There are charming half-moon balconies overlooking the boutiques on the boulevard below, rooms outfitted in pretty Provençal style and a lobby that winks to the glamour of the good old days. (Look for the vintage 1920s elevator.) If you want to treat yourselves, ask for the grand Rotonde room, with polished parquet floors, high ceilings and whimsical 'winter garden' bathrooms.

11 Boulevard Carnot, Cannes; +33 4 97 06 26 00; cavendish-cannes.com

LE PIGONNET

Picture perfect

Le Pigonnet has been the lodging of choice for decorators, designers and garden lovers visiting Aix-en-Provence for some years now, and it's easy to see why. It's quiet and filled with the kind of inspirational style those elegant French do so effortlessly. The rooms are the right side of sophisticated, and the grand, orangery-style restaurant offers glorious windows that look out to the beautiful garden, which is reminiscent of a country estate. The hotel's grounds are so extensive that it feels like you're out in the countryside, yet you're right in town. It's a short walk to the centre of Aix, so leave your car at the hotel (you'll never find a park anyway.) Le Pigonnet is the perfect base to explore this oh-so-gorgeous place.

5 Avenue du Pigonnet, Aix-en-Provence; +33 4 42 59 02 90; hotelpigonnet.com

PASTIS HÔTEL

More than novel

If the name sounds familiar, it might be that you've read Peter Mayle's *Hôtel Pastis*. This hotel wasn't the basis for the narrative but Mayle does love it here, and the owners are, like him, English. So, too, is the interior design. There are framed Sex Pistols and Rolling Stones album covers (very Saint-Tropez), Hockney prints, and flea-market finds that give the place a lovely sense of English whimsy. It's all very tasteful, of course, as the owners are designers, but is very entertaining just the same. The decor makes the hotel feel like a private house, and that may be why people love it so much. Even the much-photographed pool area (it's often in magazine shoots) feels like a private villa. Colourful and absolutely full of character.

75 Avenue du Général Leclerc, Saint-Tropez; +33 4 98 12 56 50; pastis-st-tropez.com

PAVILLON DE LA TORSE

Pavilion pretty

The Pavillon de la Torse looks like something you'd see in a French film; one of those sweet, pull-you-in-with-its-heavenly-scenery movies about a couple who find an abandoned house deep in the French countryside and lovingly restore it. A picture-book house with a facade the colour of egg yolks, shutters the shade of summer geranium leaves and a garden that is pure charm. It's so perfect, you half expect a director to wander in from the side and yell 'cut'. In fact, the story of the Pavillon de la Torse could be a film. Its owners bought this abandoned château and transformed it into a beautiful B&B that surely boasts the most idyllic setting in Aix. The building may look petite but the rooms are plump with comfort and quiet style. However, it's the garden that really enchants, and guests love heading outside to spend the day by the pool in a horticultural dream.

69 Cours Gambetta, Aix-en-Provence; +33 9 50 58 49 96; latorse.com

ROYAL-RIVIERA

Pure glam

The Royal-Riviera hotel is everything you imagine the French Riviera to be. Striped awnings, an elegant pool fringed by even more elegant sun loungers and umbrellas, a private sandy beach to escape the crowds, a terrace to toast the sunsets, and a perfect view of the Mediterranean. It is, quite simply, one of the most beautiful hotels on the Côte d'Azur. Of course, its allure could also have something to do with its setting. The Royal-Riviera is tucked into the crook of the bay between the pretty town of Beaulieu-sur-Mer and the tranquil village of Saint-Jean-Cap-Ferrat. (It's a delightful stroll to both.) The views are eye-wateringly gorgeous – you can ogle the villas of Cap Ferrat or simply gaze out to the yachts at sea. The staff is also entertaining – look for the YouTube clip on the hotel: it's what persuaded me to come here. Utter bliss. If I could afford to, I'd stay for a week.

3 Avenue Jean Monnet, Saint-Jean-Cap-Ferrat; +33 4 93 76 31 00; royal-riviera.com

TOILE BRANCHE

What's in a name?

It's a curious name, Toile Branche. A curious place, too. But like most curious places, it's surprising and intriguing and ultimately a satisfying discovery. *Tatler* magazine thought so, too. They called it 'one of the best bijoux hotels on the Côte d'Azur'. And bijou is the perfect word: it's a jewel of a hotel. Set out like a private home – albeit a grand manor – it's exquisitely decorated and set within a sublime garden filled with lavender. And with rooms from 190 Euro, there's money left in the budget to splurge on the French delicacies at the hotel's restaurant. Toile Blanche is famed for its cuisine, you see, which is served on the terrace overlooking the garden and pool. Why go to a Michelin-starred place when you can dine well in your own hotel?

826 Chemin de la Pounchounière, Saint-Paul de Vence; +33 4 93 32 74 21; toileblanche.com

VILLA GALLICI

Va-va (villa) voom

Unlike some of its Spanish counterparts further south, Aix is not a place that goes for over-the-top decor. This is a city that's a little more understated. It is French, after all. But the Villa Gallici has flipped Aix's traditionalism on its head. This lavish hideaway is the kind you'd ask your lover to book for a sly weekend rendezvous. Everything here is designed to be indulgent, from the discreet service to the dramatic interior design, which is a mix of Marie Antoinette-ish fabulousness and modern luxe. Think gorgeous urns, richly decorated furnishings, and silk canopies draped over beds the size of lap pools. The suites, meanwhile, are a study in boudoir beauty, with stylish wicker day beds and private gardens or terraces in which to take your room-service breakfast. The hotel also has a spectacular seven-acre oasis beside it with a stunning terrace and swimming pool. No wonder *Condé Nast Traveler* readers voted it the 7th Best Hotel in the World for 2012.

Avenue de la Violette, Aix-en-Provence; +33 4 42 23 29 23; villagallici.com

VILLA GARBO

I vant to be alone

Garbo would have loved it here. She could have holed up in this place without a worry. And it is so lovely, she may never have left. After they worked their magic on Le Cavendish, Guy and Christine Welter turned to this little gem, a former 1884 villa in the heart of Cannes. Converting it into sumptuous apartment-style suites, they mixed the Belle Époque with a little modern luxury, adding a hammam and spa, improving the delightful garden and – best of all – offering free drinks in the evening.

Villa Garbo, 62 Boulevard d'Alsace, Cannes; +33 4 93 46 66 00; villagarbo-cannes.com

VILLA MARIE

Tropezian treat

The Villa Marie is the perfect balance between high luxury, superb design and affordability. It's small, stylish, friendly, reasonably priced yet still has a lovely luxe look. Set against the backdrop of a stunning pine forest in Saint-Tropez's neighbouring village of Ramatuelle (which is where the 'in' crowd go as it's closer to the beach), this beautiful bolthole is beloved by low-key travellers looking for an endearing – and enduring – place to go each year. (*Harper's Bazaar* editors loved it.) The interior design is the kind that gets noticed in *Architectural Digest*, while the garden is a Mediterranean haven where you can laze away the day.

Route des Plages, Chemin de Val Rian, Ramatuelle; +33 4 94 97 40 22; villamarie.fr

VILLA RIVOLI

Shuttered charm

The Villa Rivoli's German owner is perhaps one of the loveliest people you'll ever meet behind a hotel reception desk. She is, quite simply, charm personified. So, too, is her hotel. Decorated in tasteful shades, it has a touch of the Gustavian (Swedish) decorating style about it (lots of muted greys and pale, painted furniture), mixed with some 19th-century French flair. The salon is a proper salon; a place to read (there are fabulous books on architecture and gardens), play the piano, have breakfast or afternoon tea (always fresh biscuits for guests), sit before the fire in winter or wander out to the pretty garden in summer. The rooms, while small, are similarly engaging. If you can't afford the largest ones, done in blue toile, opt for those on the street side. They come with the kind of faded turquoise shutters we all dream about when we stay in France, and tiny balconies that look out over the street. Best of all, it's only a block from the promenade, the beach and the just-as-delightful Masséna Museum of Art and History. The kind of place you love at first sight, staffed with people who delight.

10 Rue de Rivoli, Nice; +33 4 93 88 80 25; villa-rivoli.com

WHITE 1921

All white on the night

This dazzling white hotel had a dazzling reputation for a few years there, especially if you were the kind who liked a good time. People came for the location (on the marvellous Place des Lices), for the superb drinks in the former Maison Blanche bar (considered one of the best bars in Saint-Tropez), and for the incredible-looking building (think: mini château). It became so popular that the luxury brand conglomerate LVMH (of which Louis Vuitton is part), noticed it and thought it would be the perfect hotel to start their new portfolio of hideaways. So they bought it, and began renovations. In the process, White seems to have lost some of its personality, much like a face that's had too much plastic surgery. It's still a magnificent building, and the setting and courtyard are faultless (there are even designer boutiques at the entrance should you need new shoes for dinner) but the rooms are just a little too pared back for some people's liking. Still, have a look. If you are a minimalist, you may be someone who loves its new lines.

Place des Lices, Saint-Tropez; +33 4 94 45 50 50; white1921.com

Must-see destinations

There are hundreds of sights worth seeing in the South of France. Here are a few stand-outs.

COMMUNE LIBRE DU SAFRANIER

Community spirit

Hidden inside the Old Town of Antibes, a few blocks south of the Château Grimaldi, is a smaller village – a village within a village, if you like. It's the Commune Libre du Safranier (Free Commune of Safranier); an eccentric but utterly captivating little neighbourhood that has its own personality, and even its own mayor. Here, residents chat over their balconies, water bright flowers in window boxes and generally live the kind of life we all idolise. The stone-stepped Rue du Bas-Castelet is particularly pretty.

CORNICHE DE L'ESTÉREL

Vroom with a view

The Côte d'Azur is famous for its memorable drives, many of which are hair-raising. Most visitors know about the corniches that follow the coast near Monaco, but fewer people realise that there is an even more dramatic drive, the Corniche de l'Estérel, further along the Riviera. Also known as the N98, this road from Saint-Raphaël to La Napoule makes for a spectacular journey. On one side is the mountain; on the other the Mediterranean, and all the way along, the road clings to sheer rock faces that seem to plunge down to the tiny rocky inlets (calanques), bays and coves dotted with yacht sails and beach umbrellas. It's a drive that the passenger may enjoy more than the driver. Tip: try to leave early in the morning, as the route can become congested with afternoon traffic.

HAUT-DE-CAGNES

High-in-the-clouds

Steer clear of the congested mess of freeways and tacky beachfront eateries of Cagnes-sur-Mer, but do follow the brown signs directing you inland to 'Bourg Médiéval', for they will take you to one of the most beautiful *villages perchés* (perched villages) along the Riviera: Haut-de-Cagnes. This steeply cobbled Old Town feels like a fairytale village built in the clouds. Think tiny, cuter-than-cute piazzas, winding alleys and charming stone streets that abruptly change to stairways. You could happily lose yourself here for hours.

SENTIER DU LITTORAL

The height of hikes

Like Saint-Jean-Cap-Ferrat, Cap d'Antibes doesn't show its prestigious properties to the average person driving by. You really need to walk the cape to discover its secrets and peek down its side streets. One of the best ways to see this spectacular part of the Riviera is the *Sentier du Littoral* (a.k.a. *Sentier Tirepoil*), which is also one of the most spectacular footpaths in the world. It stretches about five kilometres (three miles) along the outermost tip of the peninsula, beginning at the pretty Plage de la Garoupe (where Cole Porter and Gerald Murphy used to hang out). Here, there are dazzling views over the Baie de la Garoupe before the route becomes a little rockier, eventually reaching 50-foot cliffs and dizzying switchbacks. (Note: the signs that read 'Attention: Mort' mean 'Beware: Death', so don't attempt the walk in windy or stormy weather.) It's a two-hour hike so wear comfy shoes. At the tip, you can continue past some truly gorgeous coves and some even more spectacular villas to reach Juan-le-Pins for an afternoon cocktail. From there, it's a short taxi ride or walk back to Antibes. Or you can pause at the tip of the cape and make your way to Boulevard Kennedy for a well-deserved lunch at the restaurant of the famous Hôtel du Cap-Eden-Roc. (There are amazing views over the ocean.) Or, if you have the energy, you can visit the extraordinary Villa Eilenroc (open Wednesdays, September to June). Designed by Charles Garnier, who created the Paris Opéra, this lavish display of wealth and style commands the tip of the peninsula from a grandly landscaped grounds featuring one of the loveliest rose gardens on the coast. The villa has been owned or rented by a string of the über-wealthy including King Leopold II of Belgium, King Farouk of Egypt, Aristotle Onassis and Greta Garbo, some of whom are said to still haunt it.

Cap d'Antibes; +33 4 93 67 74 33; antibesjuanlespins.com

LUBERON VILLAGES

More than a Sunday drive

The hilltop villages of Provence's Luberon region may not have been designed for cars, but the roads between them certainly were. The landscape between Ménerbes, Lourmarin, Bonnieux, Cucuron, Gordes and L'Isle-sur-la-Sorgue, to name just a few of the villages, is spectacularly beautiful, with its gentle vineyards, charming stone farmhouses, dramatic mountains and tranquil valleys. For one of the best views, drive the road from Cavaillon to Gordes via the D2 and D15 roads. As you approach Gordes, you'll see tour buses and cars pull over into a car park, and beyond that, the village perched high on the mountain, with a green valley spread out before it. The drive to the Sénanque Abbey is a must, too, especially in high summer when the lavender fields around the abbey are in full bloom. (If you're lucky, you might see the monks picking it.)

PLACE GARIBALDI, NICE

Cafe society

Encircled by grand vaulted arcades stuccoed in rich yellow, this grand, pentagon-shaped square is an example of just how superbly the French do architecture. (With perhaps a little Italian influence, in this case.) In the centre, the fountain sculpture of Garibaldi seems almost understated in comparison to the grandeur of its surroundings. Add in a sprinkling of cafes under the arcades, and a delightful antiques market on Saturday mornings, and you have one of the most splendid squares on the Riviera.

PLACE MASSÉNA, NICE

Simply marvellous

Place Masséna is the heart of Nice. Framed by early 17th-century, Italian-style arcaded buildings, their facades stuccoed in rich red ochre, this incredibly beautiful square is reminiscent, in a way, of the Piazza San Marco in Venice. There's always something happening here, too, which adds to the atmosphere. The high point of the year falls in mid February, when the city hosts one of the most spectacular carnival celebrations in France – it ranks among the world's top three (nicecarnaval.com).

PLAGE DE PASSABLE, PLAGE DE LA PALOMA & SAINT-JEAN-CAP-FERRAT

Luxe for very little

The lush peninsula of Saint-Jean-Cap-Ferrat is no secret, but the villas scattered around the point are, with most of them hidden behind high gates or extravagant tropical gardens. The few hotels here also seem to be exclusive to the point of no entry. However, there is a way to see this famous peninsula's beauty without paying anything for the privilege. Take the coastal walking path, the Chemin de la Carrière, and you will pass some of the richest real estate in the world. Start at the village of Saint-Jean-Cap-Ferrat, itself one of the prettiest on the Riviera, and buy a baguette or salad for a picnic lunch. Then, after you've taken in the yachts and sailboats, the pretty harbour and the view back to Beaulieu, walk the short distance to Paloma Beach (Plage de la Paloma), a stunning cove that's long been a favourite with the jet set (although they usually pull up in their yachts). There's a waterfront cafe here if you feel like a meal but the baguette-on-the-beach idea is cheaper and more fun. (Tip: Print off a Google map of the peninsula before you go. It will make navigating the area easier.) After lunch and a swim, make for Avenue des Fosses, turn right on Avenue Vignon, and follow the Chemin de la Carrière, 11 kilometres past the millionaires' villas and around the cape. When you've traced the full outline of the peninsula, you'll eventually reach Plage de Passable, where you can cool off with another swim in yet another idyllic cove that only locals know about.

QUARTIER DE LA PONCHE

The flip side of Saint-Trop

When the show-offy summer crowds of Saint-Tropez start to become too much, head for the curious-sounding Quartier de la Ponche. Here, in this maze of backstreets with buildings painted sunny shades of gold, pink, ochre, and sky blue, you'll see a different side of the glitzy village. As many of the tiny streets finish at the sea you won't get lost; and in any case, the winding, narrow alleys open to tiny squares with fountains, so you can pause and catch some spray to cool you down. The main street, Rue de la Ponche, leads into Place de l'Hôtel de Ville, which can be recognised by the pink and green Mairie (Town Hall). You'll also find the Fishermen's Port here, and the beach where Bardot did her thing in *And God Created Woman*.

VILLA EPHRUSSI DE ROTHSCHILD

Gilding the (pink) lily

Between the sparkling blue of the Med and the lush green of Saint-Jean-Cap-Ferrat is another colour: the beautifully florid pink Villa Ephrussi de Rothschild. Don't come here if you're averse to rose shades. But do come here if you love drama in gardens and architecture. The Villa Ephrussi has it in spades. Constructed in 1905 in neo-Venetian style, the flamingo-pink villa was baptised 'Île-de-France' by its owner, the Baroness Beatrice de Rothschild, in homage to her favourite ocean liner. (In keeping with the theme, her staff wore sailing costumes and her ship travel kit is on view in her bedroom.) If you can, time your visit for midday, when there's a private tour of her upstairs apartments. The most beautiful part, however, is the garden, which is landscaped with no fewer than seven gardens. There is also a fountain display set to classical music, which mirrors that of Versailles. It's all very over the top, of course, but so gorgeous you can't help but be drawn into the pink fantasy. A true example of the Belle Époque flamboyance of the South of France.

Avenue Ephrussi, Saint-Jean-Cap-Ferrat; +33 4 93 01 33 09; villa-ephrussi.com

Major museums

Provence has long been a destination for artists. They come for the quality of light, the spectacular landscapes, the mild seasons and of course the proximity to good food and wine. Many artists who drifted to this part of France in the early 20th century ended up staying, and their paintings of the area became some of the most famous – and most valuable – in the art world. Consequently, the South of France is full of museums and galleries dedicated to great names, making it a mecca for art lovers.

ATELIER DE CÉZANNE

Artful lodger

The Atelier de Cézanne is a must for art history buffs. This is where Paul Cézanne lived and painted (and immortalised) the Aix landscape. Restored in 1970, the museum is perhaps in need of another restoration, but you can still get a sense of the great artist. His painting smock, his paints, his easel and his still-life pieces are all there, but what's more evocative is the garden and surrounding landscape. Wandering around outside, you can distinctly see where he painted many of his famous canvases. (Try to find the view of Montagne Sainte-Victoire, the mountain that he painted so often.)

9 Avenue Paul Cézanne, Aix-en-Provence; +33 4 42 21 06 53; atelier-cezanne.com

FONDATION MAEGHT

Aesthetic pleasures

This is a great museum. Highly regarded by many designers, artists and creative types, it not only has superb exhibitions but the people behind the shows are also dealers, so there is an impressive archive of pieces to invest in. Plus – and this is always important – there is a very good bookshop of art and design titles. And once you're done admiring the art you can wander around the lovely garden and admire its beauty.

623 Chemin des Gardettes, Saint-Paul de Vence; +33 4 93 58 03 26; foundation-maeght.com

MUSÉE D'ART ET D'HISTOIRE DE PROVENCE

The extraordinary of the ordinary

Housed in an elegant 17th-century mansion, the Museum of the Art and History of Provence portrays everyday life in eastern Provence since prehistoric times. It's a mesmerising look at the beauty of the ordinary.

2 rue Mirabeau, Grasse; +33 4 93 36 80 20; www.museesdegrasse.com

MUSÉE DES BEAUX-ARTS DE NICE

Fine lines

The Musée des Beaux-Arts (Fine Arts Museum) in Nice, is housed in a fantastically glamorous 1878 Belle Époque villa that was the former mansion of the Ukrainian Princess, Elisabeth Vassilievna Kotschoubey. What a truly fitting place to showcase flamboyant and fabulous works by the likes of Fragonard, Monet, Sisley, Dufy and Rodin. The late Impressionist pieces by Bonnard, Monet and Sisley are dazzling, the works by Rodin are as masterful as you'd expect, but it's the room full of Raoul Dufy's works that really impress.

33 Avenue des Baumettes, Nice; +33 4 92 15 28 28; musee-beaux-arts-nice.org

MUSÉE MARC CHAGALL

Modernist marvel

The Musée Marc Chagall is dedicated to the work of painter Marc Chagall. Although not as well known as other painters who have museums dedicated to them on the French Riviera, Chagall is certainly worthy of his own tribute. The building, designed by architect André Hermant, has a modern, geometric look, as befitting a Modernist artist, and is still magnificent 40 years after it was built. It was meant to create a peaceful atmosphere in which to view Chagall's spectacular and incredibly detailed paintings that borrow from Fauvism, Expressionism, Surrealism and Cubism. The Russian artist loved this part of France for its bold colours and bright skies. Picasso once said: 'When Matisse dies, Chagall will be the only painter left who understands what colour really is.'

Avenue Docteur Ménard, Nice; +33 4 93 53 87 20; musee-chagall.fr

MUSÉE MATISSE

Master of colour

The brilliant ochre-red of the Matisse Museum is the perfect backdrop for this artist's extraordinarily vibrant paintings, sculptures, drawings, engravings, paper cut-outs and illustrated books. Much of the collection has been left to the museum by Matisse's heirs as a tribute to both Matisse and the place he loved. (Matisse lived and worked in Nice from 1918 until 1954.) It's a must-see if you're an art lover. Simply joyful.

164 Avenue Arènes de Cimiez, Nice; +33 4 93 81 08 08

MUSÉE NATIONAL FERNAND LÉGER

Striking

Léger doesn't get as much media coverage as his contemporaries and that's a shame. Come to this museum near Biot, north-west of Antibes, and you'll see what a talent he was. Housed in a splendid building marked by two of Léger's huge murals on the outside, the collection encompasses paintings, drawings, ceramics and tapestries.

Chemin du Val de Pome, Biot; + 33 4 92 91 50 20; musee-fernandleger.fr

MUSÉE PICASSO

Squared up

Set high on the Old Town overlooking the artist's beloved blue sea, the Picasso Museum is an architectural ode to the man who is arguably one of the world's most famous artists. Despite the building's grand old age (it's actually a 16th-century château that once belonged to the Grimaldis), it's a geometric, modern-looking building that perfectly suits Picasso's work. The painter lived here for six months and left behind a number of pieces as a 'thank you' when he left. The building was eventually converted to a museum as a 'thank you' to Picasso in return. Unfortunately, the collection isn't extensive – two dozen or so paintings, forty or so drawings, some oils, ceramics and sculptures– but a highlight is *La Joie De Vivre* – a painting of pure joy. Look out the window and see the view of the Med and it will elicit the same feeling. No wonder Picasso was inspired!

Place Mariejol, Antibes; +33 4 92 90 54 20; pablo-ruiz-picasso.net/museums

MUSÉE RENOIR

The light of his life

Renoir was a master of light, and the Riviera, with its open blue skies and clear bright days, was a place he loved to paint. He lived here in the last years of his life and did some of his best work at his farmhouse at Cagnes-sur-Mer. This is the same house that's now a museum dedicated to his life and work. Although closed for renovation in 2013, it features original furniture and decoration, as well as the painter's studios, almost a dozen original paintings, various sketches, lithographs, many old photographs, and of course personal possessions.

19 Chemin des Colettes, Cagnes-sur-Mer; +33 4 93 20 61 07

Art galleries, decorating stores and other design destinations

During the 18th century, which was the high tide of French furniture design, much of the best Provençal furniture came from the wealthy environs of Arles and Avignon. Two centuries later, antique dealers flocked here to satisfy a growing international market for fine Provençal pieces. The region is still home to some of the best antique dealers in France, and also some of the best flea markets, however, as authentic Provençal furniture from the 18th and early 19th century is harder to find, reproductions are now common. Even high-end dealers sell reproductions alongside the rare antiques. But the area is also known for many other kinds of design, from architecture to homewares, and linen to landscape photography. Here are a few destinations for lovers of design.

ANTIQUITÉS MAURIN

Antiques in Arles

Antiquités Maurin is an old family business with an impressive pedigree and an even more impressive reputation. The Maurins manage a business comprising three shops that carry an extraordinary collection of antiques and vintage collectibles, including armoires, tables, commodes, 18th-century mirrors, and even collectible paintings by Provençal masters. Don't come here if you're on a budget. But do come if you're on the hunt for something very fine.

4 Rue de Grille, Arles; +33 4 90 96 51 57; antiquites-maurin.com

CAROLYN QUARTERMAINE

Well scripted

If you're a fan of textile and interior designer Carolyn Quartermaine's spectacular, hand-printed fabrics, including the famous silk taffetas with swirly script designs, you can now shop from her collection in the intimacy of her own home. An exquisite getaway that's been featured in *Vogue Living*, Carolyn's holiday cottage is worth seeing as much for the architecture as for the goodies displayed inside. The building was originally a 17th-century woodworker's house and then became a modern art gallery (associated with artists such as Matisse and Picasso) thanks to the French designer Jacqueline Morabito. Carolyn spent four years renovating it, adding a light-filled studio where she designs the fabrics that are for sale from her London studio and other stockists. Visit by appointment only, as she divides her time between London and the Riviera.

La Colle-sur-Loup; +44 20 73 73 44 92 (London); carolynquartermaine.com

DIOR

J'adore Dior

You may think all Dior stores have the same sophisticated finishes and sleek facades. Well, the Saint-Tropez Dior does all that, but it's also a little different. It's one of the prettiest designer stores in the world. Dior's designers have taken their cues from the distinctive architecture of the Côte d'Azur and fashioned a store that looks more like a chic private villa on the coast than a generic boutique. Created out of the grand shell of the 18th-century Jardins de L'Ambassade, it combines classic 18th-century French style with contemporary elements, all of it dressed in a sophisticated palette of Dior grey. There's also a café in the front garden, where Dior-grey chairs nestle among the greenery and grey gravel backdrop, and food is served on Lily of the Valley Dior crockery. From the chic shutters to the stylish front gate, it's a store that entices as much for its clever design as for what's inside. Oh – and Dior loves the town so much it's called one of its nail lacquers 'Saint-Tropez'.

13 Rue François Sibilli, Saint-Tropez; +33 4 98 12 67 63

EBENE

French decorating

Ebene is one of the many home-decorating stores in Saint-Rémy-de-Provence. Who knows why this village is a shrine to design boutiques? Perhaps it's a sign of the stylish locals? Whatever the reason, there are streets full of them, and Ebène is up there with the best. The showroom features sofas, chairs, lamps, homewares, beds, headboards, screens, lanterns and other French-style pieces, but the prettiest are the drapes and curtains: guaranteed to make your living room at home look as charming as a Provençal B&B. You'll have to search to find it – it's tucked away at the end of a courtyard off Boulevard Victor Hugo – but it's worth the meander through the town to discover its decorating riches.

38 Boulevard Victor Hugo, Saint-Rémy-de-Provence; +33 4 90 92 36 10; ebene-deco.net

EDITH MÉZARD

Linen loveliness

Many linen lovers are aware of Edith Mézard's store tucked inside her home, the Château de l'Ange, in the lovely village of Goult. It's only open for a few hours every day, but it's so popular that those wishing to buy fabrics usually re-arrange their travel schedules to suit. Edith sells all sorts of linen, and can make to order, but is most famous for her delicate hand-stitched embroidery. She and her staff embroider beautiful script (including elegant monograms) onto the equally beautiful French linen fabrics that they stock. You can't imagine how popular they are. There are exquisite tea towels with the names of herbs embroidered onto them, bed linen with beautiful phrases, and even blue linen coat dresses. It's all very French. And all very coveted.

Château de l'Ange, Lumières Goult; +33 4 90 72 36 41; edithmezard.fr

ESPACE BÉCHARD

Antique heaven

Virtually an antiques warehouse, Espace Béchard houses 11 different dealers, each offering staggering (and sometimes staggeringly big) antiques and other pieces. Be warned: it's a highly seductive source of gorgeous French foods. You may not be able to carry these things home on the plane, but you'll certainly consider it.

1 Avenue Jean-Charmasson, L'Isle-sur-la-Sorgue; +33 4 90 20 81 40

FABRIQUE DES FLEURS

Scented pleasures

The Fabrique des Fleurs grows the aromatic plants it uses for its perfumes and other products in the superb gardens that surround the modern factory building.

Les 4 chemins, Route de Cannes, Grasse; +33 4 93 77 94 30

GALERIE BRAUNSTEIN

Déco delight

Art Déco is making a huge comeback, thanks in part to Baz Luhrmann's film *The Great Gatsby*. Lovers of this glamorous age will adore visiting this gallery, managed by Alain Braunstein, whose remarkably good eye makes for a remarkably good collection. The window displays are particularly beautiful and look more like a stylish apartment than a storefront. There are always exceptional pieces inside, including many from Lalique.

26 Rue de la Liberté, Nice; +33 4 93 87 96 28

GALERIE DU CHÂTEAU ESPACE GRAPHIQUE

Line and light

A local favourite for modern art and design, this great gallery is tucked away in Nice's Old Town, where there are many fantastic places to buy art. Château Espace Graphique has a fine collection of graphic works and photography, and often exhibits the work of talented newbies – a welcome chance for them to show their illustration and photography skills to a larger audience.

9 Rue Droite, Nice; +33 4 93 85 94 36

GALERIE JACQUELINE PERRIN

Remembering the eras

Just a short walk from the Museum of Modern and Contemporary Art (Musée d'Art Moderne et d'Art Contemporain, known as MAMAC), Galerie Jacqueline Perrin showcases magnificent work, mostly from the 20th century but also some from the 19th century. Both French and international artists are shown, and the exhibitions are always a stand-out.

14 Avenue Saint-Jean-Baptiste, Nice; +33 4 93 92 57 47; galerie-perrin.com

JACQUELINE MORABITO

Pièce de résistance

Ms Morabito's showroom is full of fine pieces. The interior designer whose homes and projects have appeared in *Vogue Living* has an astute eye when it comes to decorating. You're liable to pick up some beautiful things here, in her store, but you're also liable to walk away with a couple of new ideas. And she doesn't just deal in furniture – there's also ceramics, china and a few unusual pieces. Eclectic, yet still elegant.

65 Rue Yves Klein, La Colle-sur-Loup; +33 4 93 32 64 92

JEAN-LOUIS MARTINETTI

Impressive imagery

Tucked in amongst all the art galleries that make Nice such an art lover's city, this small gallery is dedicated to a different medium: photography. It displays the artistic legacy of Jean-Louis Martinetti, a renowned photographer who loved Nice as much as he did photography, and delighted in trying to capture his favourite town through his lenses. His work is beautiful, and captures well-known landmarks such as the Promenade des Anglais, as well as rare moments such as the Mediterranean during a storm. The gallery also has a little shop with great gift ideas, from photo albums to postcards and diaries.

17 Rue de la Préfecture, Nice; +33 4 93 85 61 30; martinetti.fr

JEAN CHABAUD LES MATÉRIAUX ANCIENS

A treasure trove of château-esque pieces

With design lovers seeking more and more unusual pieces with which to decorate their newly restored holiday cottages – or their own houses back home – Jean Chabaud has become the go-to man for great statement pieces. Think grand fireplaces and Louis XV limestone mantels. There are also impressive château gates, huge stone fountains and other items that wouldn't look out of place in Versailles. Just incredible.

20 Route de Gargas, Apt; +33 4 90 74 07 61; chabaud-materiaux-anciens.com

L'ÎLE AUX BROCANTES

Brocante bliss

There are dozens of antiques shops in L'Isle, but this place concentrates forty or so dealers into one convenient location. It's a great source of different items, too, from unusual garden pieces to rare homewares.

7 Avenue des Quatre Otages, L'Isle-sur-la-Sorgue; +33 4 90 20 69 93; www.lileauxbrocantes.com

LA COLLINE

Sweet as sweet

Is this the prettiest store in Provence? It's certainly one of the most photographed. With an endearingly aged facade that's topped – in picturesque style – with wisteria vines, and a welcome sign that says simply 'Jardin des Chats', you have to go in to see what such a store could sell. Well, the interior is just as sweet as the outside, with cute garden ornaments, delightful homewares and things you'd never expect. It's slightly different from the usual linen-and-lavender fare, and the kind of store that's popping up a lot in Provence. Wander in and be enchanted. (Lourmarin is lovely to visit anyway.)

6 Rue Henri de Savournin, Lourmarin; +33 4 90 09 95 21

LA MAISON BIEHN

Fabulous fabrics

Michel Biehn is the gentleman many designers go to when they want the real deal – authentic vintage French fabrics to upholster their clients' pieces. He's also renowned for his traditional Provençal quilts, which can date from the 18th century and be priced accordingly. These are heirloom pieces; fabrics you keep forever. Biehn also offers some faded, rustic-style, contemporary linens and household accessories, but it's the antique fabrics people really love. The shop is housed in a stunning home with a walled garden. One or two people have mentioned that he closes regularly, so do check before you go.

7 Avenue des Quatre Otages, Isle-sur-la-Sorgue; +33 4 90 20 89 04

LA MAISON DES LICES

De-licious

Saint-Tropez may not be the place to shop for bargains, but it is the place to shop for goods with a wow factor. This store has a gorgeous selection of merchandise, from an impressive range of furniture (in case you want to furnish your new villa), to tabletop pieces, bedware, flatware, dinnerware, pretty summer clothing (lots of linen) and household trinkets. A fab one-stop-shop if you're in need of a chaise and a casual summer frock – all at once.

18 Boulevard Louis Blanc, Saint-Tropez; +33 04 94 97 11 34

LE VILLAGE DES ANTIQUAIRES DE LA GARE

A mini village of antiques

There are numerous antique dealers in L'Isle-sur-la-Sorgue, and wandering through them all (or even contemplating it) can be exhausting. This place makes it easier by clustering more than a hundred small dealers in a warehouse, so you can see them all at once. It's a good source of great pieces, including gilt-framed mirrors, zinc-top tables, crystal liqueur-glass sets, grand old lamps and fine heirloom silver.

L'Isle-sur-la-Sorgue

FRANCE
RÉPUBLIQUE
ART GALLERIES
AND DESIGN
0,50
215

LES OLIVADES FACTORY OUTLET

Fabric from the source

Many people know and love Les Olivades. And there are many copies around. Indeed, go to any French market and you'll see fabrics in bright Provençal designs that are cheap imports rather than the authentic thing. Olivades, which is reportedly the only company still manufacturing traditional fabrics in Provence, has shops in Aix, Avignon, Carpentras, Nîmes, Saint-Rémy and Vaison, but this factory outlet is the best source for these famous fabrics at cheap prices. As well as fabrics by the metre, there are napkins, table runners, tablecloths and other items. There are also guided morning tours of the fabric printing workshop (in English) – although call first to arrange an appointment.

Chemin des Indienneurs, Saint-Étienne-du-Grès; +33 4 90 49 18 04; olivades.fr

SACHA DÉCORATION

Slick interiors

You know those sleek, Flamant-style interiors you often find in luxurious homes? The ones with linen slipcovers in that perfect French grey-beige shade? Where the furniture is distressed timber but still looks modern? And where everything is perfect, from the topiary trees to the coffee-table displays? Well, Sacha Décoration excels in such perfection. The aesthete of this fiercely stylish store is one of understated luxury. It's a surprise to come across a store like this in the tiny village of Ménerbes; you'd usually see this 'look' in boutiques off Saint-Germain or on the Upper East Side. But it shows how far Ménerbes has come since Peter Mayle put it on the map.

Place Albert Roure, Ménerbes; +33 4 90 72 41 28; sachadecoration-designers.com

SAVONNERIE DE BORMES

Soap star

Traditional soap-making is still practised in Provence, and foreigners adore it. They come here and they buy soap in bucket-loads. (The scent reminds them of their time in the South of France.) Savonnerie de Bormes still makes soap the old-fashioned way, however the soaps themselves are far from boring. The range of scents includes almond, fig, lavender, jasmine and seaweed. There's also a huge range of bath and body products. Stocked at various places or phone the factory in Bormes-les-Mimosas for a visit.

Bormes-les-Mimosas; +33 4 94 01 03 00; savonnerie-bormes.com

SAVONNERIE MARIUS FABRE

Soapie drama

This company has been producing blocks of traditional all-purpose soaps by hand for more than a century. Visiting here is a complete sensory experience: sight, smell and touch. There is also a shop and a little soap museum, which is oddly interesting.

148 Avenue Paul-Bourret, Salon-de-Provence; +33 4 90 53 24 77; marius-fabre.com

SYLVIE T.

Putting art into architecture

Sylvie T.'s drawings are just delightful. They're the kind of drawings we all wish we could do, had we the time, the skill and the patience to sit in a spot for an hour. With her love of architecture, she naturally gravitates towards the gracious lines of the French Riviera's most famous cities, but she's also adept at capturing the scenery of the coast – old fishing boats, ancient winding streets, even the markets. Her work makes for a great memento; she's also illustrated a book about the cultural heritage of Vieux Nice (Old Nice).

14 Rue Droite, Nice; +33 4 93 62 59 15; sylvie-t.com

THÉATRE DE LA PHOTOGRAPHIE ET DE L'IMAGE – CHARLES NÈGRE

History in print

Charles Nègre is well known in Nice, certainly among the artistic community. The photographer spent the main part of his life here, and his legacy is an enormous portfolio of photographs that depict the beauty and history of this celebrated seaside town. This venue shows the depth of his talent, and the incredible images he took. Apart from the large selection of Nègre's photos, the museum also displays the works of famous 20th-century masters of photography from all over the world.

27 Boulevard Dubouchage, Nice; +33 4 97 13 42 20; tpi-nice.org

TRUFFAUX

Hats off to you

Ever wondered why all the locals in Saint-Tropez always look so stylish, even in the sweltering, high-summer heat? They buy their hats at Truffaux. Milliners Oska and Imogen Truffaux were originally from Ecuador, but have brought their award-winning, hand-woven hats to Saint-Tropez, sensing (quite rightly) that there would be a market here for them. Panama hats, fedoras and trilbies are fitted to your head in the shop with the help of the on-site steamer. The result? A hat that looks like it was tailor-made for you. Just see if you can resist.

44 Rue de la Citadelle, Saint-Tropez; +33 6 69 55 86 54; truffaux.com

VAN HALEWYCK

Channelling the masters

Van Halewyck is a tiny shop crammed with Old-Master-style paintings. It's the kind of place you go to when you want some of those gilt-framed pieces that have become fashionable again, the ones that make your home's interior look more handsome – and high brow. The only problem is getting them home in the luggage. Some people have been known to carry them in their totes, all the way from Provence to New York City.

15 Quai de Rouget de L'Isle, L'Isle-sur-la-Sorgue; +33 4 90 38 65 25

VILLA NOAILLES

Villa aristocrat

Anyone with an interest in 20th-century design will be fascinated by the avant-garde 1920s home of art patrons and aristocrats Marie-Laure and Charles de Noailles. It's an early Modernist house built by architect Robert Mallet-Stevens between 1923 and 1933 in the hills above Hyères. Throughout the 1920s and 1930s, the two were important patrons of Modern art, particularly Surrealism. They supported Man Ray, Salvador Dalí, Luis Buñuel; and commissioned paintings, photographs and sculptures by many others. They were also friends with Pablo Picasso and Jean Cocteau. Many of their friends, including Buñuel, Man Ray all came to stay, and many left something behind. The result is a villa brimming with beauty and history.

Parc Saint-Bernard, Hyères; +33 4 98 08 01 98; villanoailles-hyeres.com

XAVIER NICOD

Xanadu

Xavier Nicod's extraordinary boutique is like walking into a L. Frank Baum book. You almost expect the Wizard to greet you from behind the front counter. Think grand trees lining the entrance, gravel on the floor instead of carpet, and almost cinematic flower displays in a huge copper bath. It's retail, but not as you know it. Another worth seeing when you're popping in to experience Xavier's Xanadu is Gérard Nicod. Both stock beautiful designs but with a twist.

9 Avenue des 4 Otages, L'Isle-sur-la-Sorgue; +33 4 90 38 35 50/07 20; xavier-nicod.com

Markets and flea markets (a selection)

Some people travel to Provence for one reason: the markets and shopping. The area has become famous for its antiques, fabrics, vintage furniture and markets. Unfortunately, the influx of tourists has meant that in the last few years those places that had the best antiques, such as L'Isle-sur-la-Sorgue, have become increasingly overrun with old bric-a-brac (brocante). Nevertheless it's still fun to fossick, so don't discount a place just because you see a stand with 'I Partied Hard in Saint-Tropez' T-shirts.

AIX-EN-PROVENCE

Aix is so fond of markets that it has scheduled three different markets on three different days: Tuesday, Thursday and Saturday. The first is a very large general market that spreads across Place des Prêcheurs, Place de la Madeleine, the Quartiers d'Encagnane and Jas de Bouffan. The second is a flower market on the Place Hôtel de Ville. The third is a flea market on the Place Verdun near the Palais de Justice. There's also a daily farm market in Aix, on the Place Richelme near the City Hall. If you're after high-end antique pieces, time your visit for high summer in July and August, when antique dealers and artisans gather on the Place Jeanne d'Arc and Cours Sextius. Or you can shop the antiques stores that are permanently open in Aix: there is a cluster on Rue Manuel and Rue Emeric David, just to the west of Boulevard Carnot in the centre.

ANTIBES

The daily covered market in Antibes' Cours Masséna is an ebb and flow of produce and promise. Sometimes it's great; other days not so good. But the atmosphere on a good day can't be beaten. Just try to resist the olives and tapenade, and the stall holders' persuasive charm. A better market in Antibes is the Brocante market, held from 8 a.m. to 7 p.m. at Place Jacques Audiberti and Boulevard d'Aguillon in Old Antibes on Thursdays and Saturdays.

ARLES

Arles has a weekly market on Saturday and a flea market on the first Wednesday of every month, both on the Boulevard des Lices. As these are some of the largest markets in Provence, they can get congested, so watch your belongings. But they're still great occasions that celebrate markets in true grand style.

AVIGNON

Avignon hosts a flea market on Sunday mornings in Place des Carmes. It starts at 6.30 a.m. and it's worth getting there early. There's also a market across the river in Villeneuve-les-Avignon, held every Saturday morning in Place du Marché and Avenue de Verdun (similar goods, better value). For a really colourful – and scented – experience, try the Avignon Flower Market, held on Place des Carmes on Saturdays.

L'ISLE-SUR-LA-SORGUE

One of the most concentrated sources of vintage bits and bobs is L'Isle-sur-la-Sorgue's market, held every Sunday from 8 a.m. until 1 p.m. or so. (There's also a smaller one on Thursday, if you can't make Sunday.) Most of the stalls are set up on the series of canals that run through town, creating a picturesque walk. It has become very touristy, but it's still a great experience on a warm sunny day. If it's more 'serious' goods you're after, then hit the antique arcades and stores that are scattered throughout L'Isle, most of which are open during the week as well. They offer a more high-end selection of goods, with prices to match.

NICE

Many regard Nice's market as one of the best on the French Riviera. It's certainly one of the most atmospheric. Held in the stunning Cours Saleya square daily (except Mondays), it's a riot of colourful awnings surrounded by even more colourful buildings. Unlike many other markets that are held only once or twice a week, this is a morning festival of food, flowers, scents, colour, conversation, laughter and the joy of life. The flower stalls are as marvellous as the food ones, especially in spring/summer when the peonies overflow from every bucket. The market is held from Tuesday through Sunday, 6 a.m. to 1 p.m. On Mondays, when the food and flowers are packed away, the Cours Saleya becomes one big beautiful outdoor antiques market, with an endless array of period furniture, vintage jewellery and collectible porcelain.

SAINT-RÉMY-DE-PROVENCE

The attractive town of Saint-Rémy-de-Provence holds its weekly market on Wednesday mornings, when the streets of the Old Town become crammed with scores of stalls. There's both food and other fare here, so you can nibble on some cheese while you're looking for souvenirs of Provence. One of the most popular markets in Provence.

SAINT-TROPEZ

Saint-Tropez isn't known for its bargains, and the town's market is no exception. However, it's still great for a browse because the range is so interesting. There's everything from bikinis to straw bags for sale here under the canvas awnings. Saint-Tropez's outdoor market has clothes, food and brocante (second-hand goods), and takes place on Tuesday and Saturday mornings on Place des Lices from 8 a.m. until noon.

UZÈS

Uzès' market is held in the impossibly romantic setting of the medieval square, known as Place aux Herbes, in the heart of town. The square comes to life every Saturday morning with stalls selling local produce and crafts, although there are yet more stalls that fill the narrow side streets. From 8 a.m. until midday.

VILLENEUVE-LÈS-AVIGNON

The convivial Marché à la Brocante in Villeneuve-lès-Avignon takes place every Saturday morning on the Place du Marché. There is always a tempting assortment of merchandise, from lovely vintage quilts to monogrammed linens and printed fabrics and also Art Déco jewellery – very fashionable after the success of *The Great Gatsby*.

Pages 4–5

A quiet cove at Cap d'Antibes,
which has barely changed for
a century.

Pages 6–7

The mountain-top village of
Gordes.

Pages 8–9

One of the many charming roads
that wind through Provence.

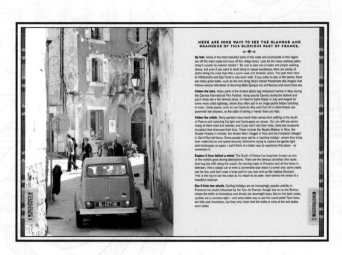

....

Page 20

L'Isle-sur-la-Sorgue's weekly markets have become world famous.

....

....

Pages 24–5

One of the splendid bridges in L'Isle-sur-la-Sorgue.

....

....

Page 27

L'Isle's markets offer everything from vintage conservatories to chateau shutters.

....

....

Page 30

The ancient, narrow lanes of
Ménerbes make for a delightful
wander on a spring day.

....

....

Pages 38–9

Left: the views from the village of
Ménerbes are as photogenic as the
town itself.

Right: a quiet stone backstreet of
Provence offers the perfect place for
artists to find inspiration.

....

....

Page 44

An old stone fountain is
a welcoming sight on a hot
summer day.

....

....

Page 47

One of the many intriguing
and whimsical stores in
Lourmarin.

....

....

Pages 48–9

The pale ochre buildings of
Provence sit quietly in the
landscape.

....

....

Page 50

Tomato-red shutters strike a
bold note against the pale
stone and ochre façades of
Saint-Rémy-de-Provence.

....

With colours this bright, it's
not surprising that Saint-Rémy
inspired Van Gogh to paint again.

....

....

Page 60

Aix's architecture is some
of the most elegant in
the South of France.

....

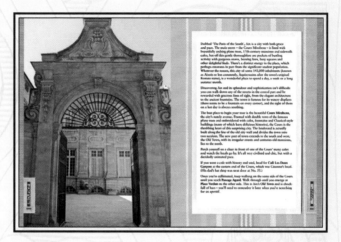

....

Pages 62–3

The garden of the Pavillon de
Vendôme is a lovely place for a
picnic lunch on a warm day.

....

....

Page 65

The grand fountains of Aix are famous for their beauty.

....

....

Pages 66–7

A view over Avignon.

....

....

Pages 72–3

The Pont d'Avignon.

....

....

Page 86

Beautiful deckchair canvas in
bright stripes is just one of the
kinds of fabrics created in the South
of France.

....

Page 88

A typical example of the intricate ironwork on gates throughout Provence.

Pages 90–1

A quiet river in the countryside near Uzès.

Page 96

A glimpse of the garden at the Villa Ephrussi de Rothschild.

PROVENCE
AND THE CÔTE D'AZUR

....

Page 106

A salon in the Villa Ephrussi de Rothschild, located just down the road from Nice at Cap Ferrat.

....

....

Page 108

The Royal-Riviera at Cap Ferrat, one of the most beautiful hotels on the French Riviera.

....

....

Page 110

Paloma Beach, where the rich and famous moor their yachts and stop in for lunch and a swim.

....

....

Pages 118–9

Classic French timber shutters –
seen on many buildings on the
French Riviera – screen the harsh
summer sun while still allowing
the breezes to flow through.

....

....

Pages 122–3

The sheltered beach at
Beaulieu-sur-Mer, popular
with families.

....

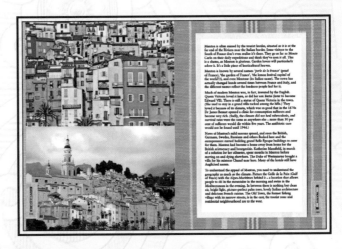

....

Page 134

Menton's architecture is a
riot of colours, a legacy of the
Italians, who heavily influenced
the shape of this city.

....

....

Page 140

A tiny window boasts a splendid
horticultural display.

....

....

Pages 144–5

The views of Saint-Paul de Vence
are so beautiful it's no wonder
artists flock here.

....

....

Page 148

Some of the best views
in Cannes come through
looking up at the architecture.

....

....

Page 150

The harbours of Cannes are always filled with impressive yachts and amazing motor cruisers, while the esplanade is just as eye-catching.

....

....

Page 156

Antibes's ancient fortifications offer a stunning way to wander the city.

....

....

Page 162

One of the many luxurious villas of Cap d'Antibes.

....

....

Pages 164–5

The famous pool of the
Hôtel du Cap-Eden-Roc.

....

....

Page 166

The waterfront terrace
of Hôtel Belles Rives
in Juan-les-Pins.

....

....

Pages 170–1

The grand façade of Hôtel Belles
Rives, which was once
F. Scott Fitzgerald's villa.

....

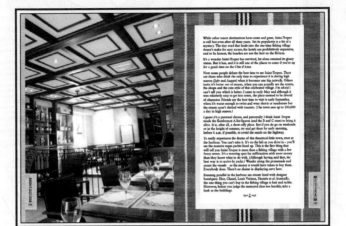

....

Page 195

The lovely pool of the
Bastide Rose guesthouse
in Provence.

....

....

Page 198

Turquoise beach
umbrellas shade the pier at
Juan-les-Pins.

....

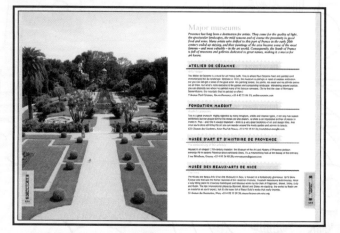

....

Page 204

The spectacular gardens
of the Villa Ephrussi
de Rothschild.

....

INDEX

MERCI

Heartfelt thanks to the following people for their gracious assistance:

Mary Small, Ellie Smith, Jane Winning, Michelle Mackintosh, Miriam Cannell, Margaret Barca, Jo Rudd and Splitting Image Colour Studio. Thanks also to the kind management and staff of the Royal-Riviera Hotel at Cap Ferrat, Bastide Rose B&B in Provence and the Hotel Villa Rivoli in Nice.

PROVENCE
AND THE CÔTE D'AZUR

254

A PLUM BOOK
First published in 2013 by
Pan Macmillan Australia Pty Limited
Level 25, 1 Market Street,
Sydney, NSW 2000, Australia

Level 1, 15–19 Claremont Street,
South Yarra, Victoria 3141, Australia

Design by Michelle Mackintosh
Edited by Miriam Cannell
Proofread by Margaret Barca
Index by Jo Rudd
Colour reproduction by Splitting Image Colour Studio
Printed and bound in China by 1010 Printing International
Limited

A CIP catalogue record for this book is available
from the National Library of Australia.

10 9 8 7 6 5 4 3 2 1

PASCAL, PINXT

RÉPUBLIQUE FRANÇAISE

CÔTE D'AZUR VAROISE

1963

R. CAMI

0,50 POSTES

JRN

FRANÇAISE

5c

POSTES

ERNÉE (Mayenne). - Dolmens de la Contrie